FIRES
of
CHANGE

ALSO BY SARAH LARK

The Fire Blossom Saga

The Fire Blossom

In the Land of the Long White Cloud Saga

In the Land of the Long White Cloud
Song of the Spirits
Call of the Kiwi

The Caribbean Islands Saga

Island of a Thousand Springs
Island of the Red Mangroves

The Sea of Freedom Trilogy

Toward the Sea of Freedom
Beneath the Kauri Tree
Flight of a Maori Goddess

Other Titles

A Hope at the End of the World

TRANSLATED BY
KATE NORTHROP

SARAH LARK

Author of *The Fire Blossom*

Previously published as *Der Klang des Muschelhorns* by Bastei Lübbe in Germany in 2016. Translated from German by Kate Northrop. First published in English by Amazon Crossing in 2020.

Published by Amazon Crossing, Seattle

www.apub.com

ISBN-13: 9781542092425
ISBN-10: 1542092426

Cover design by Faceout Studio, Amanda Hudson

Printed in the United States of America

First edition

E rere kau mai te awa nui nei
Mai i te kahui maunga ki Tangaroa.
Ko au te awa
Ko te awa ko au.

The river flows
From the mountains to the sea
I am the river
The river is me

Song of the Whanganui Maori tribe
(freely translated)

Part 1

MISSION

Russell, New Zealand (the North Island)

Adelaide, Australia

1863

Chapter 1

"Are we there yet?"

Mara Jensch was in a bad mood, and she was bored. The journey to the Ngati Hine village seemed to be taking forever, and even though the landscape was beautiful and the weather was good, Mara had seen enough manuka, rimu, and koromiko trees. She'd had enough of rain forests and fern jungles. She wanted to go home, back to the South Island, back to Rata Station.

"Just a few more miles," Father O'Toole replied. He was a Catholic priest and missionary who spoke good Maori and was taking part in the expedition as an interpreter.

"Don't whine," Mara's mother, Ida, reprimanded. She glanced disapprovingly at her daughter as she guided her small brown mare next to Mara's gray one. "You sound like a spoiled child."

Mara began to pout. She knew she was annoying her parents. She'd been in a bad mood for weeks. She hadn't enjoyed the journey to the North Island at all. She shared neither her mother's enthusiasm for wide beaches and warm climates nor her father's interest in mediation between Maori tribes and English settlers. Mara saw no need for mediation. After all, she was in love with a chieftain's son.

For a while the girl drifted off into daydreams, wandering over the endless grasslands of the Canterbury Plains with her beau, Eru. Mara held his hand and smiled at him. Before her departure, they'd even exchanged tentative kisses. Suddenly, a cry of surprise shook Mara out of her fantasy.

"What was that?" Kennard Johnson, the representative of the governor who'd hired Mara's father for this mission, listened fearfully, his eyes on the woods. "Could they be spying on us?"

Mr. Johnson, a short, rotund man who seemed to be having difficulties with the many hours of riding, turned nervously to his two English soldiers. Mara and her father, Karl, had privately laughed at the man for bringing bodyguards. If the Maori tribe they were going to visit was inclined to kill Mr. Johnson, it'd take an entire regiment of redcoats to keep them from doing so.

Father O'Toole shook his head. "Must have been an animal," he said reassuringly. "You would neither see nor hear a Maori warrior. But we're quite close to their village now. Of course we are being observed."

Mr. Johnson turned white as a sheet, and Mara's parents exchanged knowing looks. For Ida and Karl Jensch, visiting Maori tribes was nothing unusual. If the two of them were afraid of anything, it was the possibility that the English settlers would panic. The Maori called them *pakeha*. Mara's parents knew that violence between the Maori and the *pakeha* was seldom initiated by the tribes. It was much more likely for the Englishmen's fear of the tattooed "savages" to result in a foolishly fired shot that would have terrible consequences.

"Above all, stay calm," Karl Jensch advised.

Aside from Johnson and his soldiers, they were accompanied by the two farmers who had made complaints against the Ngati Hine in the first place. Mara regarded them with all the resentful eyes of a young woman whose romantic plans had been thwarted. Without these two idiots, she would have been home long ago. Her father had wanted to be back at Rata Station for the shearing, and he'd already booked the sea crossing. But at the last moment, the governor's request had arrived, asking Karl to help resolve the conflict between the two farmers and the Ngati Hine as quickly as possible. It should simply be a matter of comparing a few maps. Karl had done the surveying himself when Chieftain Maihi Paraone Kawiti had sold the land several years ago.

"The Ngati Hine mean us no harm," Karl told the men. "Remember, they invited us to come. The chieftain is just as interested as we are in a peaceful solution. There's no reason to be afraid—"

"I'm not afraid of them!" declared one of the farmers. "They should be afraid of us!"

"They probably have fifty armed men," Mara's mother remarked dryly. "Perhaps armed only with spears or clubs, but they know how to use them. You would be wise not to provoke them, Mr. Simson."

Mara sighed. During the five-hour ride, she'd had to listen to three or four similar exchanges. At first, the two farmers had been noticeably more aggressive. They seemed to think that this expedition had more to do with punishing the natives than finding a solution. Now, drawing near to the village, the farmers seemed tenser, more subdued. That didn't change as the *marae* came into view.

For Mara, the colorful totem poles framing the village gate were familiar. But seeing them for the first time could be intimidating. Kennard Johnson and his men had certainly never been in a *marae* before.

"They mean us no harm?" the government official repeated nervously. "They look anything but friendly." He pointed agitatedly at the warlike welcoming committee that was now approaching the riders.

Mara was surprised, and her parents looked alarmed. In a Maori *marae*, one would usually see children playing and men and women calmly going about their daily work. But here, they were greeted by the chieftain himself, flanked by a proud phalanx of warriors. His bare chest and his face were tattooed, and the richly decorated loincloth made of dried flax leaves made his muscular body look even more imposing. A war club hung on his belt, and he held a spear in his hand.

"They won't attack us, will they?" asked one of the English militiamen.

"Don't worry," Father O'Toole replied. The priest, a gaunt, aging man, calmly got off his horse. "It's simply a show of strength."

As the white men came closer, Maihi Paraone Kawiti, *ariki* of the Ngati Hine, raised his spear. His warriors began to stamp rhythmically with their feet planted wide, moving back and forth and swinging their weapons. Then they raised their voices in a powerful chant that grew stronger and louder the faster they danced.

Johnson and the farmers ducked behind the bodyguards, who reached for their weapons.

Mara's father guided his horse between the soldiers and the warriors. "For goodness' sake, don't draw your weapons!" he ordered the Englishmen. "Just wait."

One warrior after another stepped forward, pounding spears on the ground, grimacing and shouting at the "enemies."

Mara, the only member of the expedition who understood every bit of the war dance and songs, rolled her eyes. These North Island Maori were so old-fashioned! The Ngai Tahu tribe she'd grown up near had long since given up such displays at every confrontation. Since Eru's *pakeha* mother, Jane, had married the chieftain, the Ngai Tahu greeted their guests with a simple handshake. This greatly simplified their dealings with visitors and trading partners. Eru's mother and his father, Te Haitara, had founded a successful sheep-breeding business, which had helped make the tribe wealthy.

"According to the ritual, we should now, hmm, sing something," Father O'Toole said quietly, as the warriors completed their dance. "That's part of the exchange, as it were. Of course, the people here know that *pakeha* don't usually do such things. These tribal rituals look very savage, but actually the people are quite civilized. Heavens, I baptized the chieftain myself."

His words were intended to be comforting, but it sounded as though O'Toole was surprised, and not a little worried about Paraone Kawiti's backslide to the old tribal rituals.

Mara perked up. If the ritual could be finished quickly, perhaps she could ride back to Russell that evening and take a ship to the South Island the next morning. But if there was an argument, and if the men had to discuss the next steps at length, she could be stuck here for ages.

Mara dismounted her horse, handed the reins to Karl, and pushed back her hip-length dark hair. She had worn it loose, the way the Maori women traditionally did. She stepped forward confidently.

"I can sing something," she offered, and pulled her favorite musical instrument, a little *koauau*, out of a bag.

The *pakeha* looked just as startled as the warriors, who had been snarling and baring their teeth. Mara raised the flute to her nose in the traditional way and played a short melody. Then she began to sing. It was a lovely and strikingly simple song, nothing like the warriors' dramatic cries, about the Canterbury Plains on the South Island. She described the endless swathes of swaying grass, the rivers bordered with thickets of raupo, and the snow-covered mountains that hid glass-clear lakes full of fish. The song was intended for a *powhiri*, the formal greeting ritual in which an arriving tribe would introduce themselves to their hosts by describing their home, and served to join the hosts and their guests into one group. Mara sang with calm self-assurance. She had a pure, alto voice, and both Ngai Tahu musicians and her English tutor back home had been pleased with her performances.

On this day, too, her listeners were impressed. Not only did the chieftain and his men lower their weapons, but a stirring came from the decoratively carved wooden houses ringing the meeting ground. An old woman stepped out of the *wharenui*, the communal house, followed by a group of girls Mara's age. They purposefully led their sheep past the warriors and returned her song with their own. The girls sang of the beauty of the North Island, the endless white beaches, the thousand colors of the sea, and the spirits of the holy kauri trees that protected the open expanses of green hills.

Mara smiled and hoped that the Ngati Hine wouldn't take it as an invitation to begin an entire *powhiri*. That could last for hours. But the old woman, obviously the tribal elder, kept the greeting brief. She approached the two *pakeha* women. Ida tipped her face to offer *hongi*, the traditional greeting. The farmers, Johnson, and the soldiers looked on mistrustfully as the women touched noses and foreheads.

Karl and Father O'Toole looked relieved. Mara, too, breathed a sigh of relief. Finally, they were getting somewhere.

"I brought gifts," Ida said. "My daughter and I would like to visit with the tribe while these men clear up a misunderstanding. Of course, only if that's all right with you. We don't know how serious the disagreement about the land is."

Mara interpreted happily, and the woman nodded and welcomed them.

Then Karl spoke with the chieftain as O'Toole interpreted. Maihi scowled at the farmers but seemed open to Karl's suggestion to examine the maps to determine ownership of the disputed piece of land.

The elder who had initiated the temporary truce quickly returned to one of the houses. She came back immediately with a copy of the contract and the maps that the tribe had received when they sold the land. The documents had obviously been well taken care of, preserved as though they were sacred.

Mara watched with moderate interest as Karl carefully unfolded the papers and laid his own documents next to theirs.

"May I ask which parcels are being contested, Mr. Simson, Mr. Carter?" he said, turning to the farmers. "That would save us some time. Then we won't have to ride the entire perimeter."

Peter Carter indicated an area directly on the border of the Maori land. "I bought this here for my sheep to graze on. Then I discovered that the Maori women had planted a field there. When I drove my sheep over anyway, warriors with spears and muskets appeared, defending 'their' land."

"Fine," Karl said. "We'll go there. *Ariki*, will you accompany us? And what about your land, Mr. Simson?"

The square-built, red-faced farmer pushed to the front of the group but couldn't make heads or tails of the map.

The old Maori woman pointed to the paper. "Here. Land belong not him, not us," she explained in English. "Belongs gods. Spirits live there. He not destroy."

"There, you heard it!" Simson shouted. "She said herself that the land doesn't belong to them. That means—"

"It's documented as Maori land," Karl said sharply. "See the little mark on the map? She means that place. We'll have to go look at that too. Please come, *ariki*. The sooner we go, the sooner we'll have this sorted out. Mr. Johnson, please inform Mr. Simson and Mr. Carter that they'll have to accept our decision, whatever it may be." He shot them an annoyed look.

Karl walked back to his horse, and Ida and Mara followed to get their gifts for the Maori women out of their saddlebags. They were just small things—colorful scarves, costume jewelry, and a few sacks of seeds. They hadn't been able to transport more practical gifts like blankets or pots and pans. But Mara could tell that it wasn't necessary. The women and children were already wearing mostly *pakeha* clothing, which provided more protection against the cool climate than the traditional flax garments of the Maori. Many of them also wore little wooden crosses on leather bands around their necks, in place of the traditional god figurines carved from pounamu jade. Several of the women approached Father O'Toole trustfully, spoke with him, and allowed themselves to be blessed.

"We all Christians," a young woman declared to Ida, and proudly touched her cross. "Baptized. Mission Kororareka."

"Our mission in Russell was founded in 1838," Father O'Toole added. "It was started by French Dominican priests and Marist priests and nuns."

"Are they . . . Catholic?" Ida asked. She herself had grown up in a strict community of Lutherans where Papists had been viewed as the enemy rather than as brothers and sisters in Christ.

For her part, Mara had never differentiated very much between different types of Christianity. There was no church near Rata Station, so attending regular services was impossible. Ida led the family in prayer when she was home, but if she was accompanying her husband on his travels as a surveyor, Mara and her sisters were left in the care of Cat Rata. Ida's best friend and the girls' second mother didn't pray to the Christian god. She had grown up with a Maori tribe and was more interested in teaching the girls about native gods and spirits. Their religious education was further complicated by a touch of Anglicanism from their tutor, Miss Foggerty. She had taught Sunday school lessons with great fervor, but without much success. The children hadn't been able to stand the strict, humorless woman. Mara would much rather commune with Maori spirits than Miss Foggerty's god. In fact, Mara and Eru had tried asking them to send Miss Foggerty back to England. It hadn't been a successful experiment, though. Mara couldn't remember one prayer that had ever been answered, by any god.

Father O'Toole smiled. "I don't think it matters how the Maori find their way to God. The important thing is that we manage to get them to stop praying to heathen idols."

"The important thing is that everyone is peaceful," Karl grumbled.

Mara knew he was also anxious to be home, not wanting to leave Cat and his friend Chris Fenroy alone with the shearing. "Come now, Father, you can count your flock later."

The men set off, and Ida and Mara followed the young woman who had shown them her cross. She invited them to help prepare a big evening meal. The women of the tribe chatted excitedly, and some brought sweet potatoes and raupo roots to the meeting ground to peel and chop. Others brought birds and fish to roast over open fires.

Ida automatically reached for a knife and began to peel vegetables. Mara noted how naturally her mother fit in. Ida Jensch had smooth, dark hair, which she wore pinned up in a style that was becoming more popular among Maori women as well. The North Island sunshine had tanned Ida's skin; she was no longer as pale as she had once been. But her porcelain-blue eyes made her immediately identifiable as an outsider—as did her difficulties with the language.

"Do I understand correctly, Mara, that they are planning a feast?" she asked her daughter. "I mean . . . of course that's very nice. But it's a little strange, isn't it? They greeted us with a war dance. Does the chieftain really wish to honor those farmers?"

Mara had already asked a few girls her own age about it, and their answer had been a relief. A feast would have meant they'd have to spend the night with the Ngati Hine.

"The feast isn't for us, Mama," she replied. "They've been planning it for a while. Kawa, the chieftain's wife, is very excited about it. They are expecting a missionary to arrive tonight, a preacher. Te Ua Haumene is Maori, from a tribe in the Taranaki region. He was raised in a mission there and studied the Bible. Then he served in other missions, and now he will probably be ordained as a priest. Apparently, he's seen as a kind of prophet. Some of their gods told him something important. He wants to give a sermon about it today."

"But there are no new prophets," Ida said sternly. "If there were, then . . . the Bible would have to be rewritten."

Mara shrugged. "I guess we'll find out soon, assuming Mr. Johnson doesn't get into a fight with the chieftain. The women have already invited us to the sermon. And Father O'Toole will surely want to stay for it. Even if Te Ua Haumene is Anglican or whatever."

"Oh yes, Father O'Toole is great man, good Christian," said a Maori woman who'd been peeling vegetables next to Ida. She seemed very proud to show off her English. "We read stories from Bible in our language. And now even better! Now Te Ua Haumene own prophet for Maori. Write own Bible for own people."

Chapter 2

The men returned just two hours after they'd left. The chieftain and the tribal elder, who were walking next to the *pakeha* on their horses, smiled broadly, and Kennard Johnson and his men looked relaxed. Even Carter seemed to be satisfied. Only Simson was brooding.

"I won't let them get away with it," he grumbled to Karl and Father O'Toole. "I'll involve the governor, and even the Crown. England has to protect a man's rights!"

"You can't go out and cut down your neighbor's trees in England either," Kennard Johnson said bluntly. "Though maybe they wouldn't immediately threaten to kill you for trying. The chieftain did rather overreact."

"That tree is holy for the tribe," Karl said. "And you saw it yourself. It's a splendid kauri tree, hundreds if not thousands of years old."

"Worth hundreds if not thousands of dollars!" Simson cried. "It's the best wood. They're drooling over it in Wellington. And the old lady said herself that they didn't even want the land."

He pointed rudely at the tribal elder, who was walking calmly next to the chieftain, not dignifying Simson with a glance.

"She didn't say that," Karl replied. "I keep telling you: they have a claim to that land, which they made clear when the rest was sold. I drew the map for them. All she means is that the land is not for their use but for the spirits who own the tree. That must be respected."

"I thought they were baptized!" Simson persisted.

The men got off their horses and tied them to a post.

Mara moved closer. If her father didn't unsaddle his horse, there was a good chance that they would soon be on their way. Perhaps they would get around the sermon somehow. But Karl patted his horse on the neck and took the saddle off.

"Don't you think it's wrong, Reverend?" Simson asked.

"Father," O'Toole said, correcting him. He looked as though he'd just bitten a lemon. "To be honest, I'm a little torn. My beliefs tell me to chop down a tree like this, in the tradition of St. Boniface. The Lord says we should not bow down to false idols. On the other hand, it's a beautiful tree, and a glorious example of the wonder of his creation."

"Mr. Simson, it doesn't matter what Father O'Toole says about it," Karl said, interrupting the priest's sermon. "It doesn't matter if it's a special tree either, or a southern beech like all the others. The only thing that matters is if the tree is standing on your land or the neighbors' land. In this case, the land clearly belongs to the Ngati Hine. The tree belongs to them, too, so do what's right and leave it alone."

"And don't go thinking you'll get away with it somehow if you just chop it down anyway," Kennard Johnson added. "The Crown doesn't want to start a war if Maihi massacres you for it. There are precedents. Remember Wairau!"

In Wairau, many Europeans had lost their lives after a *pakeha* man shot a chieftain's wife. The governor later accepted responsibility for the colonists and apologized to the Maori instead of avenging his people.

Simson finally rode away in annoyance, and the chieftain invited the remaining men to the party and to the prophet's sermon. Carter accepted. For him, the decision had been positive. Carter took a bottle of whiskey out of his saddlebag, sent it around the circle to celebrate the peaceful resolution, and then took a few deep swallows. Afterward, he sat by the fire with the English soldiers, surrounded by giggling Maori girls.

Mara saw her hopes of a quick departure melting away.

"Does that mean we're staying the night?" she said, turning to her father as he looked around for Ida.

Karl shrugged. "Father O'Toole is determined to hear the prophet's sermon, and Mr. Johnson is moving as though he's in pain. It's not likely that he'll want to get back on a horse tonight."

Mara frowned. "I thought—"

"I can't change it, Mara," Karl replied. "You know I'm just as keen to get to Rata Station as you are. And for more important reasons, my dear. You just want to see Eru as soon as possible, and that will present its own set of difficulties. Jane will defend her son with tooth and claw."

Mara glared at her father. "I can be tough too, if I want."

Karl laughed. "When you and Eru are grown, Mara, you can fight his mother for him. Or you can just let him choose for himself. But now you're only fifteen, and he's fourteen, if I remember correctly. You'll just have to comply with Jane's wishes. Your mother and I are of the same opinion, by the way. Eru is a nice boy, and perhaps someday you'll be a couple. But at the moment, you're both much too young." His eyes lit up. "Oh, there's your mother."

Knowing her parents would pay no attention, Mara bit back a few tart words about her father's opinion of her relationship with Eru. She listened grudgingly as he reported the day's events to Ida.

"Simson can be glad that he survived his misdeed," Karl said. "A priestess caught him red-handed as he was about to swing the ax to cut down her holy kauri tree. She made a huge scene, and a few warriors caught wind of it and stopped him. I don't want to think about what might have happened if he had managed to do it."

Ida nodded. "What about the other farmer?" she asked. "Why was there trouble with Mr. Carter?"

Karl smiled. "In his case, the mistake was the tribe's. You know how they think. For them, the land belongs to whoever uses it. Since Carter had neither sown the field nor used it for grazing his sheep, one of the women decided she wanted to expand her *kumara* garden. She didn't understand why he was so upset. But he shouldn't destroy her garden either! Now we have clarified matters, and they all reached an agreement. This year, the woman can harvest her sweet potatoes and give half of them to Mr. Carter. Next year, she won't plant in the field again. It was only a misunderstanding. The farmer wasn't even particularly concerned about the half acre she used. He was just afraid that the tribe would continue that way."

"Then at least in that case everything worked out for the best."

Karl took Ida's arm, and the two of them walked between the cheerfully glowing fires. Mara followed. The women had begun their cooking and roasting.

Delicious aromas were spreading through the village, and they made Mara hungry. But before they could eat, they'd have to listen to the sermon.

As twilight fell, a little boy announced that three warriors were approaching the village. "Te Ua Haumene is coming!"

Ida furrowed her brow. "What is the man, anyway? A warrior, a priest, or a prophet?"

Father O'Toole, who was sitting at a nearby fire, shrugged. "I don't know. But I hope he's an asset to Christianity in this country. The issue with the tree today that the Maori were praying to . . . they probably wouldn't understand, but for me, it's like a slap in the face. It's as though my life's work was for nothing. I've known this tribe for decades. I've taught their children, baptized their people . . . and now this! Perhaps I should go back to Ireland."

The missionary looked depressed. Karl handed him the whiskey bottle.

"Come now, Father," he said. "They just can't give up their gods and spirits so fast. After thousands of years of Christianity, don't the Irish still have 'lepichans'? Isn't that what they call the little spirits they build huts in their gardens for?"

A smile stole over the priest's face. "You mean leprechauns. And those huts . . . I suspect they are used by my countrymen to hide the extra whiskey from their wives. But yes, I suppose the old beliefs sometimes survive alongside the new ones."

"That's exactly how you have to look at it," Karl said. "So don't be upset with the Maori. Personally, I think Simson's behavior was far more scandalous. He actually believed he could do whatever he wanted to the tribe and still be protected by the English Crown."

O'Toole sighed. "Yes. Our white countrymen aren't all good Christians. Sometimes—oh, don't listen to me, sometimes I think too much. There are also Maori who are baptized and then still do whatever they want. There have been senseless battles in recent years because one stubborn, probably drunken chieftain cut down a flagpole, and the public authorities took it as a personal attack on the Crown. And the natives are understandably defending themselves against their land being seized by people like Simson. If a Maori Christ has appeared and wants to be a teacher, I will accept him as a shining light in the darkness. I only hope I won't be disappointed."

Te Ua Haumene was a stately man of middle age. The prophet had a wide face and no tattoos. He had sideburns, and heavy brows over his sleepy-looking dark eyes. His garments were neither the cassock of a Catholic priest nor the traditional black suit of an Anglican missionary. His was the attire of a well-to-do Maori: a finely woven top over a skirtlike loincloth made of flax, and an elaborate cape worthy of a chieftain. His companions were more simply dressed in traditional warrior garb.

Father O'Toole watched, his face impassive. The women of the tribe approached Te Ua Haumene just as enthusiastically as they had the priest, and devoutly asked for his blessing.

The Maori men mostly hung back. Two of the village elders exchanged *hongi* with the prophet, as did a relative of the chieftain, but not Maihi himself. North Island chieftains often kept a symbolic distance from their subjects.

The chieftain's wife offered Te Ua Haumene and his men a place by the central fire, which they accepted. They were obviously hungry after their journey. The prophet came from Taranaki, but he preached to a different tribe every few days, accepting each one's hospitality. The Ngati Hine obviously enjoyed providing it to their guest. The tribe honored their visitor with a delicious meal and a complex greeting ceremony. Every now and then, the chieftain's wife would gesture to Father O'Toole, and several villagers showed Te Ua their crosses. But the prophet made only a vague gesture of greeting in O'Toole's direction.

"Perhaps he has something against Papists—I mean, Catholics," Ida said, trying to comfort the slighted clergyman. "He was trained by Anglicans, after all."

Father O'Toole shrugged sadly. Karl handed him the whiskey bottle, and he accepted it gratefully.

Mara wished she could take a swallow too. In the meantime, she had eaten her fill, and she was bored again.

When Te Ua Haumene finally stood to speak, it was already dark. The moon was shining, and its light, together with that of the flickering fires, lent the scene an almost ghostly atmosphere. The wind blew the prophet's long hair back from his face.

"I welcome you, wind!" Te Ua Haumene said. He didn't look at his audience as he spoke; his eyes were fixed on the sky. "Your messenger greets you!"

Father O'Toole translated for Karl and Ida.

"Messenger?" Ida asked.

"*Haumene* means 'man of the wind,'" Mara remarked and then stood up to get some water, disturbing the reverent silence. The prophet looked at her sharply.

"Hear through my mouth the words of God. The wind blows to us his spirit, the good news, the new gospel. I bring it to believers!"

"Pai marire," chanted the two warriors who accompanied the prophet.

"Pai marire!" Te Ua cried, and his listeners repeated it in chorus.

"That means 'peace,' doesn't it?" Karl asked his daughter and the priest.

They both nodded. "Goodness and peace, to be exact," O'Toole said. "That's what they call their religious movement. Or sometimes Hauhau."

"But what does he mean by 'the new gospel'?" Ida asked doubtfully.

A morose expression came over the priest's face.

"I greet you, my people, my chosen people . . ." Te Ua Haumene paused for a moment to allow his words to take effect.

O'Toole sighed quietly.

"I am here to bring you together in his name," Te Ua continued. "I call you, as I was called myself by the greatest of all chieftains—by Te Ariki Mikaera, commander of the forces of heaven."

Karl looked confused. "Huh?"

"He means the archangel Michael," O'Toole said in annoyance.

"See, I am one of you. I am Maori, born in Taranaki, but the *pakeha* took my mother and me to Kawhia. I served them like a slave, but I am not angry at them, because it was God's will that I learned their language and their writing. I studied the Bible, God's word, and I allowed myself to be baptized, because I was sure that the *pakeha* could lead me to a better life. But then Te Ariki Mikaera appeared to me and told me I should not be one of the sheep but the shepherd. As Moses once led his people out of servitude, so have I been chosen. I have been chosen to tell you about God's son, Tama-Rura, whom the *pakeha* call Jesus. I tell you this, even though I have been told that Tama-Rura is another name for the archangel Gabriel."

"The man is out of his mind," Ida murmured.

"The man is dangerous," Karl hissed.

"And they are all waiting with spear and sword in their hands, to lead their chosen people to freedom."

"Pai marire!" the men cried, and the villagers repeated it loudly.

"Goodness and peace—with swords?" Ida asked.

Mara raised a sarcastic eyebrow—a gesture that she had recently adopted to communicate to adults what she thought about their ideas.

"For you are not free, my chosen people!" Te Ua thundered to the crowd. "You share your land with the *pakeha*, and often enough, you have believed they were your friends because they gave you money and things you could buy with it. But truly, I say to you: they give nothing for free! They take your land, they take your language, and they will also take your children!"

The women reacted with shocked cries, and some of the men with shouts of protest.

"You did not invite these people here. They only came to take your land!"

Karl was about to speak, but Father O'Toole had already leaped to his feet.

"We also brought you God, whom you are currently blaspheming!" the priest shouted.

Te Ua Haumene glared at him. "You may be the canoe that brought the true God to Aotearoa," he spat at the missionary, "but sometimes one must burn the canoe in order to truly feel at home. God will still be here long after we have driven the *pakeha* out of our country. Long after they have been blown away by the wind! *Pai marire, hau hau!*"

Father O'Toole sank back to the ground in stunned disbelief. He rubbed his brow painfully as more and more of the people he had converted and baptized evoked the Holy Spirit in the wind.

Next, Te Ua Haumene set the gathering in motion. He had his followers erect a pole that he called a *niu*, which was supposed to represent the good news he'd brought. His men danced around the pole almost in the manner of a war dance, and encouraged the crowd to join them. Te Ua Haumene chanted as they did so, and continued to proclaim other fundamentals of his new religion. More and more young villagers sprang up and joined the warriors as they danced around the *niu*.

"We should leave as quickly as possible," Karl told his wife and daughter, "before the prophet decides to start freeing this village of *pakeha*. Mara, go get Mr. Johnson and the redcoats, and I'll pry Mr. Carter away from those girls.

Ida, take Father O'Toole straight to the horses. We don't want him trying to challenge that madman."

Mara didn't have to be told twice. The ghostly atmosphere, the dark words of the prophet, and the men's mad dance around the *niu* scared her. She saw the Maori as her people. If she married Eru, she would be a member of the Ngai Tahu tribe. But she had never seen her countrymen this way before. It seemed as though all of their common sense and wisdom had been blown away by a bewitching wind.

Father O'Toole looked to be in a trance as Ida led him between the fires, fortunately without incident. A few of the villagers noticed the *pakeha* leaving. The chieftain, who was sitting off to the side, was certainly aware. But Maihi Paraone Kawiti didn't stop them. Nor did he seem particularly impressed by the prophet currently entrancing his tribe. Perhaps he could sense the danger radiating from Te Ua, or perhaps he was afraid of losing his own power over his people. He nodded to Karl and regarded Father O'Toole with an expression somewhere between disdain and regret.

"Keep moving," Ida urged the missionary.

After helping Carter and the alarmed soldiers saddle their horses, Mara handed Father O'Toole the reins of his gaunt bay mare. He stared at them in his hand as if rooted to the spot.

"I want to go now," Mara said.

"As do I," Father O'Toole whispered. "This is the end. Irrevocably. I'm going back to Galway. God save this country."

Chapter 3

"God called, and you answered!"

The voice of Reverend William Woodcock filled the little church at St. Peter's College. The archdeacon of Adelaide looked appraisingly at the young men lined up in front of the altar. They gazed up at him expectantly.

"'Go ye therefore, and teach all nations, baptizing them in the name of the Father, and of the Son, and of the Holy Ghost: Teaching them to observe all things whatsoever I have commanded you: and, lo, I am with you always, even unto the end of the world.'"

"Amen," said the eight freshly ordained missionaries and their family and friends who had gathered for the celebratory service.

The Australian Church Missionary Society ran a seminary that sent a handful of enthusiastic, pious young men into the world every year to convert the "heathens." Most of them stayed in the country—the huge continent of Australia offered plenty of opportunities. But every now and then, a new missionary was sent to New Zealand, India, Africa, or another destination.

William Woodcock had been given the task of assigning the new missionaries to their future posts. He raised his arms as the last "amen" resonated off the church walls. The eight young men lined up for a formal exit from the church while the organ played and the college's choir sang. Most of the congregation joined in the singing. Almost all of the missionary-school students came from strict religious families and knew the words and melodies of the popular hymns quite well.

Franz Lange strode third in line through the church, his head lowered reverently. But when he heard German coming from the final pew, he glanced up and saw his father. Jakob Lange stood stiffly between Franz's younger half brothers and sang defiantly in his native language. His deep, sonorous voice drowned out those surrounding him, who eyed him with annoyance that he neither noticed nor cared about. Franz knew his father thought it crucial that the Gospel be spread in the language of Martin Luther and regarded foreign languages as a nuisance. Twenty years after his emigration from Mecklenburg, Germany, Jakob could still barely speak a word of English. As a result, he hadn't understood very much of his son's ordination ceremony.

In truth, Franz hadn't even dared to hope that his father would be there at all. The Australian Church Missionary Society might have Lutheran roots, but it was now part of the Anglican Church, and they didn't adhere to the Gospel nearly as strictly as Jakob Lange would have liked. But for Franz, there had been no alternative. The Lutheran community near Adelaide that Lange's family belonged to had no seminary. If Franz wanted to follow God's call, then his only option was St. Peter's College.

At the sight of his father and his brothers and the thought of God's call, Franz was briefly racked with guilt. More than any true yearning to be a priest, Franz had simply had enough of the unrelenting, monotonous, and difficult farm work that was only relieved by church services and prayer circles. The young man had been weak and fragile since childhood, when he'd repeatedly suffered from terrible colds and shortness of breath. Neither the climate in Mecklenburg nor that of the South Island of New Zealand, where the Lange family had formerly lived, was suitable to his constitution. The heat in Australia was better for Franz, but the remorseless drudgery of making new land arable hadn't improved his health. Jakob Lange had demanded that the youngest son of his first marriage put all his energy into the family farm. When they had arrived in Australia, Jakob had sent the ten-year-old to the German school, but in the afternoons, Franz was forced to work to exhaustion.

"It'll keep you from getting any foolish ideas," his father had said.

Franz had heard that sentiment countless times while growing up. It always came with complaints about his siblings, who had escaped their father's influence. Franz's brother Anton and his sister Elsbeth had actually run away. Franz assumed they must be somewhere in New Zealand, but their father had never shown any interest in finding them. What was more, Jakob and his second wife, Anna, exchanged only occasional and superficial letters with his eldest daughter, Ida. Ida had gotten married to a member of the Lutheran community shortly after their arrival in New Zealand, and had later become a widow under dubious circumstances. She had then gotten remarried to a man whom, as Franz understood it, Jakob didn't approve of.

Franz and the other young missionaries passed through the church doors and waited outside for their families. The Langes were the first to step outside into the bright winter sunlight. Franz smiled tentatively and reached out a hand to his father and stepmother. Though men and women were forbidden to sit together inside the church, Anna was standing with her husband now, as were their three daughters and two sons. Anna, at least, returned her stepson's friendly greeting. With her eyes slightly lowered in humility, she smiled at him from under her bonnet.

Franz gathered his courage and broke the silence. "Father! Stepmother! You can't imagine how pleased I am that you've come."

Franz hoped that his father would embrace him, but Jakob stood stiffly.

"In the winter, there's not as much to do on the farm," he grumbled.

Anna shook her head indulgently. Then she took her stepson's outstretched hand. "Your father is proud of you," she said.

Anna also spoke German, but she'd learned to at least understand English. The school in Hahndorf taught the local language, even though many settlers didn't think it important for their children to learn, as most never left the village.

But the lessons had been important to Franz, who thought constantly about the example his sisters had set. No matter how angry he was at Ida and Elsbeth for deserting him, he knew that his sisters' ambitious efforts to learn English quickly after their arrival in New Zealand were what had set them free. Franz, too, would have to embrace the language of his new country if he ever wanted to escape the drudgery in Hahndorf. So he'd studied English with a fiery enthusiasm, even though he was far more talented with numbers and would have made a better bookkeeper or bank clerk than a preacher. Sometimes he even dreamed of higher education in mathematics. But that was unthinkable. If Jakob Lange ever let his son go, it would have to be in the name of the Lord.

The older man stroked his full white beard, frowning at his wife's warm words. "I feel pride for sons who know their places and humbly stay where they belong—sons who support their parents in the hard fight for daily existence," he replied. "You, Franz, are rather a disappointment. But very well, I accept that God has called you. The ways of the Lord are unfathomable. And who knows, perhaps you are atoning for the sins of your father when you go out into enemy territory to tame the savages. I don't want to argue with my Creator. I just don't want to lose the last of my sons."

"You still have two wonderful sons," Anna reminded him.

The small woman in traditional Lutheran garb was barely older than Ida. After the wedding, she had given birth to seven children in quick succession. Two boys and three girls had survived, and all of them were strong and healthy. Young Fritz and Herbert were already a big help on the farm, and the girls seemed to be just as domestic and proper as Anna.

Jakob Lange nodded. "I told you, I don't want to disparage the Creator. He has been generous with me, after all. But Franz, don't forget the homeland! Don't give up your language and your past. No matter where you go, always remember that you are a boy from Raben Steinfeld."

"Are you coming, Franz?" Marcus Dunn, who had been Franz's roommate during their studies, interrupted Jakob's sermon. "The archdeacon already invited John and Gerald into his study. He is telling everyone where we'll be sent! You're surely next."

Franz seized the opportunity to excuse himself. "You're welcome to stay," he told his family. "There's food and drink for celebrating our commencement."

Jakob Lange snorted. "I see nothing worth celebrating here. And we must get home; there are ten cows to milk. So, go with God, Franz. I hope he guides you on your path."

Franz bit his lip. His father had already turned to leave. Anna shrugged helplessly. She was a gentle, accommodating person. When Jakob had married her, she had lovingly accepted Franz as her son and made his life easier in many respects. But she was unconditionally devoted to her husband. She never contradicted him or stood in his way. Franz wondered if he would have a similar kind of wife one day. But if he were honest with himself, he would much rather have a partner with whom he could have a real conversation. A wife who didn't always comply with his wishes. A wife who sometimes said no. Franz wanted to be able to ask questions and share secrets.

But now he had no time to dwell on such things. This day had been a whirlwind of emotions: his brief joy over the successful commencement, his pride at being able to call himself reverend, his renewed feelings of guilt toward his father, and his fear about the future. There was something that Franz had never told anyone, that he didn't even want to admit to himself: no matter how quickly he learned, how intensely he prayed, or how enthusiastically he proclaimed God's word, the thought of standing face-to-face with the heathens he was supposed to convert made him rigid with fear. Franz had never had any real contact with the Australian Aborigines. The previous owners of the land on which Hahndorf stood had long since been relocated to distant places. That was also true for the tribe that had occupied the area around Adelaide. One could still see some natives on the streets as beggars or drunken vagrants—unpleasant but harmless.

During Franz's education as a missionary, guest lecturers had occasionally brought baptized tribesmen as examples. These men weren't scary; they were calm and quiet. They wore European clothing and kept their eyes humbly lowered. But Franz clearly remembered his family's arrival in New Zealand, when their town of Nelson had ended up in the middle of the Wairau conflict. The Langes had never seen a Maori in person, but for a fearful child like Franz, the horror stories had been enough. And the Australian Aborigines were supposed to be much more aggressive than the Maori. Every settler knew about massacres of immigrants, perilous expeditions, and bloody battles. Sketches of savages with war paint, armed with spears and boomerangs, had been passed around. What was more, the outback was full of dangerous animals. When Franz had helped his father plow, he'd often barely missed being bitten by a deadly snake or attacked by a dingo. The thought of being sent once more into virgin territory to found a mission gave him panic attacks.

As he waited outside the archdeacon's study, Franz's heart pounded and he began to sweat. He swallowed with a dry throat when William Woodcock finally called him in. What would he do if he was sent on an expedition into the wilderness? Could he give up and leave? Would God punish him? Or worse yet, would God punish him right now through the hand of the archdeacon, banishing him to a far worse place than the one he was fleeing?

The archdeacon's bright eyes bored into Franz's own. He seemed to be able to look directly into the young man's soul. "Sit down, Reverend Lange. You're terribly pale. Was it the reunion with your family, or are you already feeling the burden of duty?"

Franz murmured something unintelligible. But then he pulled himself together. "I haven't broken my fast yet," he admitted.

The future missionaries had spent the day before their ordination fasting and praying, and Franz had almost collapsed with hunger during the ceremony. But then the encounter with his family had taken away his appetite, while his classmates were already enjoying the refreshments the school had provided.

The archdeacon nodded. He covertly appraised the wispy young man. Franz Lange was of medium height, was very thin, and had slightly hunched shoulders, as though he were constantly ducking the stroke of a whip. The traditional black missionary suit fit him loosely. William Woodcock briefly scanned the evaluations from Lange's teachers: *reliable, pious, patient, extraordinarily well versed in the Bible, but unfortunately not a good speaker.* The young man also seemed to have difficulties looking someone in the eye. Woodcock persisted with his steady gaze anyway, staring into the childish round face with big blue eyes—fearful eyes. Woodcock didn't want to torture the boy. He spoke to him kindly.

"I won't keep you long. After all, you'll have to fortify yourself for the duties that lie ahead. Tell me, Reverend Lange . . . If you could choose a posting, where would you go? Which country, what kind of work?"

Franz rubbed his temples. Was there really a chance that the archdeacon was going to include him in the decision? But this could just as easily be a trick question. His father, at least, would have taken a direct answer to reveal a lack of humility and then would have given him a task that was particularly contrary to his wishes.

"I—I will take the place that God has ordained for me. I—"

The archdeacon dismissed his words with a wave. "Of course you will. I'm assuming that. But there must be some duties that attract you more than others."

Franz bit his lip again. He desperately searched for a noncommittal answer. "I like to teach," he said. "I like to work with children."

Truthfully, the only children Franz had ever worked with were his younger half-siblings, and they often seemed rather slow-witted. But he'd never minded when Anna had asked him to help them with their school work. To the contrary, it had been a pleasure because then at least his father didn't send him to work in the fields. And Franz thought that perhaps if the natives were civilized enough to send their children to school, then they couldn't be all that dangerous.

The archdeacon nodded and made a note on the documents in front of him. "So, you are a born teacher," he said kindly. "Good to know. Unfortunately, at the moment none of our missionary stations have requested teachers. On the other hand, there is surely a need in the larger stations where the work with the heathens is in a more advanced phase. Would the summons to such a station attract you, Brother Franz? I have a request from New Zealand. One of our long-serving missionaries, Reverend Voelkner, requires assistance. Didn't you come from New Zealand with your family, Reverend Lange?"

Franz felt a seed of hope germinating inside of him. His memories of New Zealand were fraught, the settlement that his father had founded having fallen victim to a catastrophic flood. But he'd liked the town of Nelson. And the countryside there harbored no snakes, scorpions, or dangerous animals.

"I came from Mecklenburg," he replied. "Raben Steinfeld."

"But you've lived in New Zealand. Would you like to be sent there, Franz? Please, speak openly. I can't grant every wish, but if it's possible, I would like to allow the preferences of the young missionaries to influence my decisions. For example, the first three brothers let me know they were interested in founding a new mission in China. We could use a fourth man there. So, if you would prefer—"

"No!" Franz's objection was a little too quick and too loud. If the archdeacon did mean to test him, he might be on his way to China in a few days. "I—I mean, of course I'd follow the call to distant lands, but I—"

The archdeacon smiled. "Very well, Reverend Lange. Then it's official. I will send you to Opotiki. That's on the North Island of New Zealand. The mission has been there for several years. Good luck, Brother Franz. Go with God."

Staggering out into the sunshine, Franz felt dizzy but also indescribably relieved. Now he just had to make his way to the long tables of food to satisfy his hunger and to congratulate his brothers for their posting in China, and perhaps endure their friendly teasing that he "only" got to go to New Zealand. But instead, he walked back into the little church. There, he thanked God fervently for answering his prayers.

Part 2

RETURN

Canterbury Plains, Christchurch, and Lyttelton, New Zealand (the South Island)

1863

Chapter 4

"You'll see, Carol, this time we'll win. Last year, with Jeffrey, we were just paddling around. Joe is teaching me a completely different technique now. After all, he's from Oxford. His team won the boat race, you know, that famous regatta on the Thames."

Linda suppressed a sigh of boredom. Mrs. Butler had left the garden to fetch the tea, and her son, Oliver, was already back on his favorite subject, the upcoming regatta being organized by the Christchurch Rowing Club. Linda found it difficult to feign interest. Her half sister, Carol, on the other hand, was making an assiduous effort to listen and smile encouragingly at her fiancé's descriptions. Linda and Carol were looking forward to the regatta, which included colorfully decorated boats and a cheerful picnic on the bank of the river. The entire population of Christchurch would gather by the Avon, and the boat races were a welcome distraction from the particularly grueling work on the sheep farms in spring. But Oliver's constant talk about his rowing technique and his fabulous new rowing partner, Joe Fitzpatrick, and above all, his endless analysis of their chances to win would have tested the most patient of listeners. At least Carol's fiancé showed strength of purpose, enthusiasm, and ambition when he talked about the event, all qualities that seemed to be missing when he worked on his parents' sheep farm—or so Captain Butler complained. But Oliver's mother thought it perfectly acceptable for him to be a gentleman rather than a farmer.

"The trick is not rowing completely simultaneously," Oliver continued. "The strokesman should row a little bit before the bowman. That way you eliminate the yawing that would otherwise come from . . ."

Carol nodded enthusiastically, concentrating less on Oliver's words than on his pleasant, sonorous tenor. She loved his voice, as well as his slender figure, curly black hair, aristocratic features, and heavy-lidded, soulful brown eyes. At the moment, they were flashing with eagerness, but Carol also liked it when they were gently shadowed and full of dreams, which was more often the case. Linda, on the other hand, found Oliver lethargic and pale.

Carol's fiancé looked very much like his mother, an extraordinary beauty who had come from the upper echelons of English society, and Carol and Linda's parents had always wondered how Captain Butler had convinced her to emigrate to his sheep farm. Lady Deborah had probably had a completely different vision of her life as a "sheep baroness" in the empty Canterbury Plains. She must have imagined fox hunting, picnics, and garden parties rather than playing hostess only to the drovers who traveled between the distant farms to shear sheep.

In New Zealand, an invitation to tea was a rarity. People usually drank coffee in their simple farm kitchens, and the conversations had more to do with training sheepdogs or Merino-Romney crossbreeds than with caring for rosebushes. In fact, these were frequent subjects of conversation between Deborah's husband, Captain Butler, and Linda's mother, Catherine Rata. Catherine, who, to Deborah's dismay, was called Cat, had declined the tea and headed straight to the shearing shed, leaving Carol and Linda in the garden with their hostess.

"Perhaps before we leave," she'd said. "But first I really must speak with your husband about the young ram, Mrs. Butler. And pretty soon we'll have to go. We'll take Georgie with us. There isn't much time."

Georgie was the boatman who delivered mail and packages to the farms along the Waimakariri River. He had brought Cat and the two young women with him that morning. The river was the only way to travel between Rata Station and Butler Station in one day. With horses, the journey took at least two days, even though the path along the river was well maintained. It connected Rata Station with the Redwood brothers' farm, as well as a more recently founded settlement to the north. Usually, Cat didn't mind being on the road for a couple of days and would have been happy to sit and chat. Right now, though, the shearing was fully underway, and the last pregnant ewes were lambing. Everyone had their hands full. In October, the only person who had time for a leisurely tea party in a well-kept garden was Deborah Butler, and that was because it had never even occurred to her to get near a sheep.

Linda wondered how Captain Butler could stand Deborah's idleness. Before he'd invested in sheep, the old salty dog had made his fortune as the captain of a whaling ship. But even after twenty years of marriage, he still seemed to be madly in love with his gorgeous wife. Everything at Butler Station pointed toward his blind obsession with her. The house wasn't simple and practical like those at Rata Station or Redwood Station—it resembled a castle more than anything else. An English specialist had been hired to tend to the gardens, and the stable was full of thoroughbreds instead of solid crossbreeds. Captain Butler obviously viewed his wife as a rare kind of luxury, like the horses. But that indulgence didn't extend to his son. If it had been up to his father, Oliver would be making himself useful in the shearing shed instead of taking tea with his fiancée and chatting about regattas.

"Don't bore the young ladies, Oliver," Deborah Butler said as she crossed the perfectly trimmed lawn.

She was trailed by a Maori girl in a maid's uniform who carried a tray with a teapot and English biscuits. Deborah wore an elegant sky-blue day dress with a fitted bodice, bolero jacket, and hoopskirt. Cream-colored lace adorned the hem of the skirt, neckline, sleeves, and jacket. Deborah's full dark hair was combed back and coiled tidily into a matching bonnet.

Both Linda and Carol felt awkward in their simple blouses and skirts, in spite of the fact that Carol had made an extra effort to look pretty that day. She had decorated her white muslin blouse with blue trim but had had to take off the matching cape; it had gotten warm in the spring sun. Her shiny blonde hair was pinned up in a complicated style. Linda had helped her braid it and had woven in dark blue ribbons to match the trim on the blouse and skirt. The result should have been enough to satisfy Deborah, but of course the long boat trip in the stiff breeze had been enough to set free a number of unruly strands that danced around Carol's pretty face. Oliver thought it terribly fetching, but his mother regarded her rather skeptically.

And for Linda, Deborah Butler's stern gaze held no mercy. After Linda had helped her excited sister with her outfit and hair, she'd had no time to worry about her own. She wore a pale blouse and a gray skirt, her hair in a simple ponytail. It had been more susceptible to the wind than Carol's braided style, and even more stray blonde strands surrounded Linda's face.

The girls, who had both turned eighteen in May, passed easily as twins. They both had big blue eyes, although Carol's were a little darker and more expressive, and Linda's were a lighter blue and gentle. Her eyes were also a bit too close together and, like her full lips, had been inherited from the girls' father, Ottfried Brandmann. Most men couldn't keep their eyes off Carol's or Linda's sensual lips. Carol's face was narrower, and Linda's was rather oval. But all that was only evident when one studied them closely. At first glance, the impression of sisterly similarity won out.

"How is your needlepoint going, Miss Carol?" Deborah Butler asked. Following English tradition, she poured their tea herself. The Maori girl stood aside to wait for further instructions. "Are you satisfied with the pattern?"

Carol nodded uncomfortably. Her future mother-in-law had initiated her in the art of petit point embroidery several weeks ago. The border that she was working on at the moment was intended to be a decoration for her wedding gown. Unfortunately, Carol had neither enthusiasm nor talent for fine needlework. And no matter how carefully she scrubbed her hands after a day of handling reins and leashes, wrestling with sheep, and petting horses, there was always enough grime caught under her nails to turn the border gray instead of the intended shades of cream. Fortunately, Linda helped her every now and then. She was more domestic than her half sister, and above all much more patient—when she didn't have to listen to endless chatter about regattas.

"I'm afraid I don't have much time for embroidery," Carol explained. "I work on the farm, and in the evenings I'm tired. Besides, you need daylight for such fine work."

Deborah Butler made a face. "Doubtlessly," she agreed. "Although I don't understand why a young lady has to work with sheep and sheepdogs. I mean, I have nothing against riding sometimes or owning a little dog. I had a kitten when I was a girl—they can be terribly charming. But my husband says you won the herding-dog competition in Christchurch?"

Carol nodded delightedly and turned to look for her dog. The tricolor border collie she called Fancy was a purebred from the Wardens' kennel at Kiward Station, and her pride and joy. Her adoptive father Chris Fenroy liked to say that Fancy had cost him a fortune, but she was worth every penny, and in the coming years, she would be the dam for their own breeding stock at Rata Station.

"When you live here with us, it will be more necessary for you to pursue . . . ladylike activities," Deborah Butler said before Carol could reply. "I certainly won't allow my husband to involve Oliver's wife in the farm work. As a member of the Butler family, you will have social obligations!"

Linda and Carol exchanged glances and almost giggled out loud. The social duties of a sheep baroness in the Canterbury Plains were limited to accompanying her husband to the annual meeting of the Sheep Breeders' Association in Christchurch. Afterward, Carol would have to be careful not to drink herself into a stupor at the complimentary dinner at the White Hart Hotel. Many of the sheep barons had started out as whalers and seal hunters. The ladies didn't like it when they got drunk and talked about their past experiences at the formal dinner that followed the meeting.

"I enjoy working with the dogs," Carol began, then fell silent as her mother approached.

"Could I please have that cup of tea, Mrs. Butler?" Cat asked with a smile, gazing out over the lawns.

Almost five acres of the original grassland had been landscaped into a formal garden, and aside from the occasional southern beech that Deborah Butler tolerated for shade, none of the plants were native to New Zealand. Deborah and her gardener had hacked out all the pervasive rata bushes that had lent their name not only to Cat's farm but to Cat herself.

Cat Rata had grown up without a family. Her mother, Suzanne, was a mentally feeble prostitute who didn't even remember her last name or bother to give her baby a first one. The neglected child had just been referred to as "Kitten."

But Cat had given up being upset about all that a long time ago. She had escaped the whaling-station brothel at the age of thirteen and lived for several years with a Maori tribe, where she had been called Poti, which meant "cat." She'd been adopted by Te Ronga, the chieftain's wife and tribe's healer, and Cat mourned the woman whose murder had set off the Wairau incident.

"This is a very beautiful garden," she remarked politely. "Even if it is a little strange. England looks like this, right?"

Deborah gave a small nod, eyeing Cat just as critically as Cat had eyed the garden. If she hadn't been so properly raised, she would have chosen the same words to describe Cat: very beautiful, but a little strange. Deborah took in Cat's brown cotton dress, simply cut and absolutely unsuitable. She wasn't wearing a hoopskirt under it either, and Deborah suspected that she didn't even own such a garment.

Of course a hoopskirt was impractical for farm work and for the boat trip, and Deborah could almost understand the lack of one. But Cat had also elected not to wear a corset, and that really was unacceptable! However, her appearance was another matter. Cat Rata was quite slender, and her finely formed oval face was dominated by expressive brown eyes filled with awareness and intelligence, and at the moment, a little sarcasm. Her hip-length blonde hair was bound into a thick braid at the back of her neck, which made her seem younger than her almost forty years. It was an improper hairstyle for a grown woman, Deborah thought, but she had also seen Cat wearing her hair loose, held back with a broad Maori headband.

"I modeled our garden after the park at Preston Manor," Deborah said primly. "Of course, the original was much larger. It even had space for bridle paths—and long walks."

She gave her son a short, meaningful glance, which caused him to spring to his feet. Oliver had been longing to take Carol for "a little walk"—it was the only chance for intimacy that Deborah's strict rules would allow.

"May I show you the yellow roses, Miss Carol?" he inquired formally. "My mother is very proud of them; they don't usually survive here. You are welcome to join us too, of course, Miss Linda."

"Don't worry, I'm not interested in roses," Linda lied.

In fact, Linda enjoyed accompanying Cat and the local Maori tribe's medicine woman when they searched for medicinal herbs. Having read an English book about herbal medicine in the Old World, she knew the effects of rose oil on infections, insect bites, and minor heart difficulties, and had even planted a rosebush in the kitchen garden at Rata Station. Linda experimented not only with rose oil and rose water but also with rose hip tea and mashed rose hips for menstrual difficulties and stomach pain. However, she didn't care about the color of the blossoms or Deborah's valuable cultures. She was happy for her sister, who would enjoy the short time alone with her fiancé.

"Just don't be gone too long," Cat said. "Georgie will be here in half an hour or less, and we don't want to keep him waiting."

They certainly wouldn't miss the arrival of the boatman. Deborah's garden bordered the Waimakariri River, which enabled promenades on the riverbanks and summer picnics by the water.

Oliver gallantly offered Carol his arm as they hurried away on the gravel path that led around the garden. To Cat, it seemed almost like an escape. But they wouldn't be able to avoid Deborah's sharp eyes. The imported English shrubbery wasn't nearly dense enough to hide a stolen kiss.

"The two children really don't get to see each other very often," Deborah remarked as she poured tea for Cat.

"In bad weather, the journey from one farm to another is very difficult," Cat replied. But she was personally of the opinion that a young man carried on the wings of love should ride through the rain and mud much more often than Oliver did. Carol would have liked to visit Oliver by herself, but Chris and Cat had forbidden it. They could well imagine what Deborah would have thought of a young girl who rode a horse two days alone through the wilderness. "But in a few days, there will be another opportunity for the young couple to see each other," Cat added casually. "Your husband is selling us a breeding ram, and of course Oliver won't want to miss the chance to bring the animal to Rata Station himself."

Deborah Butler raised her eyebrows. "My son is no drover."

Cat smiled. "It's not that hard," she replied. "I'm sure he'll manage."

Linda suppressed a giggle.

"It was his father's idea," Cat continued, and took a sip of tea. "He thought Oliver would be thrilled at the chance to combine business with pleasure."

"I hope he doesn't lose the ram on the way," Linda joked later, as Cat shooed the two girls toward the pier.

Cat had comforted Carol with the hope of a swift reunion with Oliver. At Rata Station, she would see much more of him than she did under Deborah's strict supervision. Neither Chris Fenroy nor Cat herself had any interest in playing chaperone. They approved entirely of the relationship between their adopted daughter and the Butlers' only son and heir. Carol would bring a large herd of sheep into the marriage as a dowry and would be able to run her own farm. Linda and her potential husband, who still had to be found, would one day run Rata Station.

"That way, we'll be neighbors and can do everything together!" Carol had said happily when she'd told her sister about her engagement to Oliver Butler.

The two young women couldn't imagine ever being separated. They had been raised as twins, although they knew that they only had their biological father in common—a secret that the neighbors didn't know. Of course there were rumors. The situation at Rata Station seemed rather strange even to the relatively open-minded settlers in the Canterbury Plains. When Linda and Carol were younger, the neighbors had been scandalized at their two sets of mothers and fathers: they'd been raised by Carol's mother, Ida; Linda's mother, Cat; and their respective partners, Karl Jensch and Chris Fenroy. It was particularly hard for Deborah Butler to accept the unusual family structure. She complained constantly about Ida having left Linda and Carol in Cat's care while she traveled the North Island with Karl, and would doubtlessly be shocked if she found out the truth about Linda and Carol's parentage. Because of reactions such as hers, Cat and Chris, like Ida and Karl, had concluded that it would be better to raise the two girls as twins from Ida's previous marriage to Ottfried Brandmann—and to talk as little as possible about how Ida had become a widow.

Chapter 5

"Are you going to join the regatta?" Cat asked Georgie.

He was a short, strong man with tousled red hair. He rowed his flat-bottomed riverboat with powerful strokes to the middle of the Waimakariri. There, the current would speed their progress.

The boatman shook his head. "No, Miss Cat. I paddle around enough. I don't need to do it on Sundays too."

"A few of the boatmen on the Avon are joining in anyway," Carol remarked.

Several of those men had easily beaten Oliver and his friend Jeffrey the previous year, and the pair had wound up in fifth place.

Georgie shrugged. "Sure. Some of them just can't wait to show the young 'gentlemen' from the rowing club how it's done. But it doesn't matter to me. I don't want to spend the time practicing either. It's actually not that easy to row in teams of two or four or eight. The trick is not to row all at once, but—"

"Oh, really?" Linda asked, her voice saccharine. "That's so interesting! You'll have to tell us more about it." She repeated Carol's honeyed words to Oliver while Georgie blinked in confusion.

"Let's talk about something else," Carol grumbled. "And if you ask me how far along I am with my needlepoint, Lindy, I'll throw you overboard!"

Cat listened to the half sisters' friendly bickering. She lounged on a bench at the bow and watched the grass- and reed-covered banks of the Waimakariri slide past. The landscape seemed wild and untouched, though most of it had briefly been farmland. But the settlers in the Canterbury Plains had given up planting fields long ago. The towns were too distant for effective deliveries, and the pervasive tussock grass was much too tenacious, quickly overwhelming any crops. Instead, the plains had proved ideal for raising livestock. Sheep grazed by the thousands in the wide grasslands, and in summer they were driven high into the mountains. The majestic, snow-covered peaks of the Southern Alps rose behind the plains. In the clear air of the South Island, they seemed close enough to touch, but the yearly journeys there and back with the sheep could take days.

Cat knew it would soon be time to make the trip again, and she was glad of it. For years, she'd accompanied Chris and the drovers on their trek to the mountains. She loved making camp in the wilderness, hearing the cries of the night birds, and gazing at the stars while the campfire slowly burned to embers. The men would pass around a whiskey bottle and tell stories about their adventures, and would sometimes take a harmonica or fiddle out of their saddlebags and play a few tunes. It reminded Cat of nights in the Ngati Toa village where she'd spent her youth. She could almost still hear the lyrical melodies of *putorino* and *koauau* flutes and Te Ronga's gentle voice as she told stories about her peoples' gods. And Cat loved nestling against Chris, feeling safe and at home by his side.

The boat sped along the river, and Cat and the girls waved as they passed the Redwood house. Cat had been friends with Laura Redwood for years, but there was no sign of her now, or of her husband and his brothers. Still, Cat wanted to be polite in case anyone was standing at the window. Laura had just given birth to her fourth child and would hopefully be taking it easy at home. Usually, she worked as tirelessly on her farm as Cat did at Rata Station. Although Laura preferred handling sheep and horses to housework, she was quite a good cook, and certainly more domestic than Cat was. Laura was very proud of the stone house that her husband, Joseph, had finally built for her after years of wooden ones. Her living room was filled with her handwoven rugs and throws and embroidered pillows, whereas Cat felt uncomfortable surrounded by abundant furnishings. She preferred the minimalist, practical interiors of Maori homes.

Cat gazed ahead expectantly. Somewhere here was the border between Redwood and Rata Station. She looked beyond the wild flax and raupo reeds that grew thickly on the banks and tried to catch a glimpse of her sheep. She was able to make out a few ewes much closer than she had expected, sitting in the shade of manuka and cabbage trees, chewing their cuds. One animal was perched atop one of the large rocks that jutted out of the grasslands. In Cat's opinion, the stones gave the plains character, and she knew the Maori considered them the dwelling places of gods and spirits that protected the land.

"What are the sheep doing here?" she asked Linda and Carol. "Did you drive them over for grazing? They're supposed to be going to the highlands with the drovers next week."

Carol shrugged. "They probably escaped from Chris. The fresh grass is tempting. I can ride out tomorrow morning and bring them back. Fancy will be delighted."

The dog let out a bark of acknowledgment. The three women laughed.

"Speaking of escaping," Georgie said, "I found another letter for you. It had somehow escaped from the stack." He dug in one of his heavy bags and pulled out an envelope. "So sorry."

"It happens," Cat said unworriedly. "Oh, look, girls, this is from Karl and Ida."

Linda and Carol turned, curious. Karl and Ida had been away for several months. Karl had surveying jobs all over the North Island, and Ida and their younger daughter, Margaret—who went by Mara—were accompanying him. Now they were expected to be back soon. Cat smiled as she read.

"They're in Lyttelton already! They arrived yesterday with the ship, direct from Wellington. Ida says they want to recover there overnight. Apparently, the crossing was quite stormy, and her horse is still seasick. That means they must be setting out about now, and they'll be here in a few days! Karl will be able to help with the droving. Ida thinks he feels guilty because their trip took so long. And she has exciting news."

Carol giggled. "Maybe Mara is betrothed."

Linda rolled her eyes. "Mara only has eyes for Eru. And it would break his heart if she got engaged to a *pakeha*—"

"Girls, Mara is only fifteen!" Cat scolded. "We're not even thinking about her getting engaged yet. And whatever you do, don't let Jane hear you talking about Mara and Eru! She wouldn't take kindly to her golden boy being interested in a local girl. She wants to send him to college."

"And he'll have to marry a Maori princess, at the very least, who will bring half of the North Island into the marriage," Linda said with a laugh.

"No, a sheep baroness would be even better!" Carol countered. "Let's see: aristocratic lineage is a must—"

"After all, he's a chieftain's son!" Linda said, imitating Jane's haughty voice.

Jane Te Rohi to te Ingarihi—formerly Jane Beit—was English. The Maori name her beloved husband had given her meant "English rose." Before she had fallen in love with Te Haitara, the local Maori chieftain, she had been married to Chris. Their marriage had never been a love match, and the tribal elder had granted them a divorce, to the relief of all.

"And of course she'd have to be the sole heir of at least ten thousand sheep," Carol went on, describing Jane's dream daughter-in-law. "As well as being a vision of beauty, and able to intelligently quote Adam Smith between kisses."

Linda giggled. The Scottish economist was one of Jane's guiding lights. "In the evenings, she'd entertain Eru by reciting logarithm tables by heart."

"And instead of carving hearts on trees," Carol continued, "they'd carve formulas for maximizing profits."

"Stop it, you're both terrible!" Cat scolded.

Georgie grinned. Jane's head for business was well known. She had made her husband's tribe rich first by setting up trade for traditional medicines and good-luck charms, and then with sheep breeding. However, her salesmanship had also put her in constant conflict with the Maori tribe's traditional spirituality and placidity. Additionally, her cold, self-assured manner put a strain on the relationship between her husband and his people.

But Jane's son, Te Eriatara, whom she called Eric and everyone else called Eru, was considered a very agreeable boy. He was six months younger than Ida's daughter Mara, and it had been practical to educate the children together. Jane had hired Miss Foggerty, a middle-aged Englishwoman who devoted herself wholeheartedly to giving the children of the local settlers and Maori a strict, classical education. Mara and Eru hated her, a fact that brought the childhood friends closer than ever. Before anything could happen, though, the Jensches had taken their daughter with them to the North Island.

The boat now drifted past the outbuildings of Rata Station, and Cat smiled with satisfaction at the stable fences, the roomy shearing shed, and above all, the multitudes of sheep crowded together in their pens. The shearing was in full swing, and hundreds of beautiful, valuable fleeces sat stacked on the bed of a wagon. Cat, Chris, and Karl had started their farm years ago with three herds of Merino-Romney crosses and French Rambouillets. They were among the first to bring sheep to the Canterbury Plains, after the Deanses and the

Redwoods, and their farm was now one of the leading businesses on the South Island. In large part, they had Cat to thank for that. Catherine Rata of Rata Station was very well known, far past Christchurch, the city at the mouth of the Avon.

Chris Fenroy didn't mind not being as famous as his partner. He loved his work, and he loved Cat. Linda and Carol were like daughters to him. Neither did he mind that, in the last few years, Rata Station's third associate, Karl, had been traveling more than he was on the farm. Karl's earnings as a surveyor had contributed to the early advancement of their breeding business, and now further investment was hardly necessary at all. Rata Station was self-sustaining, and it was flourishing. Chris was a happy man.

And it showed. When Chris saw Georgie rowing the boat toward the pier, he dropped everything and ran over, smiling and waving. Strands of his unruly brown hair had escaped from the leather tie that bound it in a ponytail. His warm hazel eyes glowed with anticipation. He put his hands around Cat's waist and lifted her effortlessly to dry land. Then he helped Linda and Carol, and laughingly defended himself from Fancy's jubilant greeting.

"Here you all are!" he said happily. "I missed you!"

"All of us, or just the dog?" Cat teased.

Chris patted Fancy. "Well, she does most of the work," he teased back. "But of course, I prefer the company of cats." He took Cat's hand in his own and kissed it. "How did it go with the Butlers?" he asked, after everyone had thanked Georgie and the boatman had been paid and sent on his way. "Are they going to sell us the ram?"

Cat nodded.

"And what about your future mother-in-law?" Chris said, turning to Carol.

She winced. "I don't think I quite meet her standards. I don't make enough effort with ladylike activities, and I might not be able to keep up with my 'social obligations.'"

"Mrs. Butler would obviously prefer a proper young lady," Linda added archly. "One with a talent for landscaping formal gardens modeled after the park at Preston Manor."

Linda captured Deborah's tone of voice so precisely that Chris and Cat had to laugh, though they knew they should scold her for being disrespectful.

"If that's what the lady wants, we can surely give Carol a few cuttings to take over." Cat toyed with a blossom from the rata bush at the end of the pier. "Then her garden would bloom like Rata Station."

"And we can work out the aristocratic part too," Chris joked. "I just have to adopt Carol. Or would it be better if I had an honest talk with Deborah about what happens if one marries for name alone?"

Chris's brief marriage to Jane had been arranged on the strength of his noble lineage. It hadn't made either of them happy.

"I'm going to marry Oliver!" Carol declared. "Not his mother or his farm or his name or anything else! Oliver loves me, and I love him. He would marry me even if I—if I—"

"'She was a lass of the low country, and he was a lord of high degree,'" Chris sang, horribly out of tune.

Cat remained silent. She wasn't convinced that Oliver didn't share his mother's prejudices a little. It was doubtlessly better that the Butlers didn't know how Carol and Linda had been conceived—even if Oliver had unwittingly chosen the "twin" born in wedlock.

Oliver Butler actually did accompany his father's ram to Rata Station, and Carol rode out to meet him. But she didn't get the romantic tryst she'd hoped for. Captain Butler had sent two experienced drovers with his son, and at a time when every hand was needed on the farm! Carol suspected Deborah had intervened, and she felt sorry for Oliver. She herself would have been mortified if Chris and Cat hadn't trusted her with such a simple task. But for his part, Oliver was quite pleased with the men's company. If he'd been alone, he told Carol cheerfully, he would have had to return home immediately. Captain Butler had traded the young ram for three ewes from Rata Station and wanted to integrate the creatures into the herd before they were taken to the highlands for the summer.

"But the drovers are going to work here for a couple of days, so now I can stay with you and then ride down to Christchurch for the final training for the regatta. Joe will be happy. We'll be unbeatable!"

Chris Fenroy furrowed his brow when the young man made his plans known at dinner. "Can your father do without you for so long?" he asked in surprise. "Doesn't he need every man for the shearing?"

Oliver shrugged. "Oh, Father sees it from an athletic point of view. It's an honor if we win the gold medal for Butler Station! And if I were in college in England now, I wouldn't be able to help either."

Deborah Butler would have liked to send her son to Oxford or Cambridge. As far as Chris and Cat knew, that was the only wish her husband hadn't capitulated to. He wanted Oliver to stay in the plains and learn how to run a sheep farm from the bottom up. For that, he didn't need any higher education. Perhaps allowing Oliver to train for the regatta was part of Butler's compromise with his wife.

In the next two days, Oliver made himself useful at Rata Station—mostly because Carol didn't give him the option of drinking tea or taking strolls. Instead, she asked him to accompany her when she rode the perimeter to check the fences and when she herded the sheep in and out of various pastures. In that way, Carol finally got her romantic time alone with Oliver. She held his hand as the horses walked across the wide fields, and she got dizzy when the knee-high tussock grass moved like waves in the wind. It felt as though they were riding through a spring-green ocean, from which bizarrely formed stones occasionally stuck out like islands.

And of course they found time to let the horses graze while they spread out a blanket in the inviting shade of a manuka tree. Carol wasn't an enthusiastic cook; she didn't have time to prepare the kind of delicacies that Deborah Butler liked to spoil her son with. But she had packed some cold roast lamb and fresh bread from the kitchen, and told him she'd felt very baroness-like when she'd added a bottle of wine to her basket.

"Cat will kill me," she said with a giggle.

Her adoptive mother enjoyed wine, but it was expensive and complicated to order from Christchurch. For that reason, Cat seldom allowed herself the pleasure. She wouldn't be pleased to find out that a bottle was missing.

Oliver didn't really care what he ate or drank as long as Carol was with him and didn't resist when he put his arms around her. Now out of his mother's sight, she returned his affections enthusiastically, and even allowed him to undo a few buttons of her blouse and kiss the tops of her breasts.

For her own part, Carol allowed her hands to roam under Oliver's shirt and stroke his smooth skin and muscular body. Finally, she encouraged him to take off his shirt and regarded him with obvious pleasure.

"I finally understand why men row," she murmured, and traced his biceps with the tip of her finger. "You look like one of those marble statues. You know, the Greek ones in the foyer of the White Hart."

In England it was fashionable to decorate noble homes with antique Greek or Roman art, and the owner of the hotel in Christchurch had embraced the trend. Since then, there had been dissent in the provincial religious community about whether the exhibition of naked male bodies should be allowed in the name of culture, or if it was corrupting the innocence of the youth.

"Michelangelo's *David*," Oliver said, smiling as he pushed Carol's blouse a little farther over her shoulders to get a look at her breasts. "Did you know my mother's seen it? The real one, in Florence. Oh, Europe must be fascinating. Perhaps I should have gone there to study. Or maybe we'll go together someday. Would you like that? Of course, we would only stay at the best hotels."

Carol and Oliver had a certain glow about them when they returned to Rata Station that evening. Cat regarded Ida's daughter thoughtfully, and Linda looked at her sister in annoyance. But there was no excuse to scold her. Carol had checked the fences as she had been told to, and Fancy danced happily around the five escaped sheep that Carol had found and brought back. Cat trusted both girls when it came to the temptation of physical pleasure. They knew very well what happened in bed between men and women. After all, they'd grown up in close proximity to a Maori tribe, and most of their friends had already had experiences with boys. The Maori didn't share the Europeans' prudery. They allowed their teenagers to experiment before they finally chose a partner. Some of the Maori boys had made attempts with Linda and Carol, and they had been allowed a few stolen caresses in the shelter of rata thickets. But nothing more had come of it. The girls listened to Cat, who dissuaded them from going too far.

"The problem is that rumors would go around with the *pakeha*. Believe me, all it would take would be for some boy to brag a little in front of the drovers, and your good reputation would be gone, stupid as that is."

Cat knew all too well how the European community felt about girls' sexuality. When she'd had to leave the Maori and move to Nelson, the white citizens of the town had made up such wild stories about her that her safety was threatened. In the end, she'd had to flee.

Of course, Linda and Carol were not in that kind of danger; they had the protection of their families. At the same time, they hadn't shown signs of serious interest in any Maori boys, and Cat suspected they would seek their future husbands among the *pakeha*. For that reason, Cat thought it better if they conformed to *pakeha* customs.

That night, Oliver attempted to convince Carol to ride out into the night with him, but she declined. Still, she was delighted about the idea of going with him the following year when they were married to drive the sheep to the mountains, like Cat did with Chris.

"Then we'll make love under the stars," she whispered, after they'd kissed an acceptable distance from Cat and Chris's Maori-style wooden house. The land stretched down to the river, like Deborah Butler's garden. The Waimakariri twisted through the open plains like a band of liquid silver in the moonlight. The silhouette of a cabbage tree threw strange, magical-looking shadows on the riverbank. "It'll be like a dream, Oliver. Much, much more beautiful even than Florence."

Oliver nodded, but he didn't look particularly convinced. He wanted Carol and longed to explore her body in moonlight or sunlight, under the stars or under the canopies of the luxurious English beds at Butler Station. If he were honest, he'd prefer a comfortable bedroom to a tent on the plains. But it was better if he didn't admit that to Carol. She would be more reasonable when they were married. And if his mother managed to talk his father into letting her send them to Europe as a wedding present, he knew Carol wouldn't object.

He kissed her again, leaning her against the trunk of a tree and pressing his body against hers. Perhaps she'd give in and let him open her bodice. As Oliver felt for the buttons, voices and hoofbeats broke through the darkness of the early night.

Carol freed herself from his arms. "Horses are coming!" she cried. "And I think—" She dashed along the riverbank toward the three riders who were approaching. "Mamida! Kapa!"

Oliver followed his fiancé slowly. He knew that Mamida was the twins' name for Ida, to differentiate her from their other mother, Cat, whom they called Mamaca. It surely wouldn't be appropriate to disturb their reunion, even if Carol wasn't acting ladylike when she jubilantly threw her arms around Ida. Just as unabashed, she returned Karl Jensch's embrace, although the man was definitely not her biological father. Oliver thought that relationships in general were treated far too casually at Rata Station. Just the way the girls referred to their parents! Mamida, Mamaca, Kapa . . . it all sounded far too exotic—and childish. Oliver had been stopped at ten years old from calling his parents Mummy and Daddy, and instructed to address them as Mother and Father instead.

"What are you doing alone here in the dark?" Ida asked. She was a slender woman, who now, in the coolness of the evening, was wrapped in a shapeless riding coat. "Oh, you're not alone!"

Ida's voice hardened at the sight of Oliver. At Rata Station, things were definitely less formal than they were at the Butlers', but Oliver knew that Ida came from a very devoutly Christian German family. She must not be pleased to find her daughter alone with a man on a moonlit riverbank.

Oliver bowed formally. "Mrs. Jensch, Mr. Jensch, please rest assured that in no way did I come too close to your daughter."

"You didn't?" Karl Jensch asked with a smile.

He was a tall, thin, but strong-looking man with curly blond hair, which he wore longer than usual, like his friend Chris Fenroy did. It poked untidily from under his broad-brimmed hat and gave him a rakish air.

"Then something must be wrong with you, young man. With a girl as pretty as Carol, and the moonlight—" He smiled. "The two of you have been engaged for a couple of months, haven't you? So, what exactly were you doing out here without getting too close to her? Counting sheep?"

Oliver squirmed under Karl's teasing look. But Carol leaned against him with a smile.

"Of course he got too close to me, Kapa!" she said. "But not *too* too close. It was just right."

Oliver could hear the grin in her voice, and Ida and Karl returned it.

"Can we go home already?" The bright soprano voice came from above. A third rider hadn't gotten off her horse. "I mean, can we ride into the yard, put the horses in the barn, and go in the house? I'm dying of hunger."

“Mara! My goodness, you’ve grown so much!” Carol greeted the girl just as enthusiastically as she had her parents. “You’ve met my sister before, haven’t you, Oliver?”

Oliver looked up at Margaret Jensch, his breath catching in his throat. Of course he’d met Mara, and she had always been a pretty little child. But now . . . The foyer of the White Hart Hotel also had beautiful goddess statues, but none of them compared to the girl perched on her horse in the moonlight like an apparition. And a white horse, at that. The sight made Oliver think of fairies.

“I—I’m enchanted,” he said, unable to tear his eyes away from Mara’s delicate face with its Madonna-like features, long black hair, and huge eyes with dark, arched brows.

Karl rolled his eyes. He had obviously noticed the effect his daughter had recently begun to have on men.

“Then you can take my horse,” Mara instructed Oliver casually.

She dismounted and handed Oliver her reins as though he were a groom. She wasn’t very tall, but she held herself straight and smiled with self-assurance. The girl also seemed to be aware of her effect on men and obviously knew how to use it.

Chapter 6

The reunion at Rata Station was so cheerful and noisy that Oliver felt uncomfortable. His mother surely would have been appalled at all the hugs and kisses, laughter and teasing. Ladies and gentlemen should act more distinguished. It made Mara's aloofness seem even more attractive. She didn't rebuff her family's embraces, but seemed to be wishing she were somewhere else. Oliver offered to carry her bags into the house, but she declined.

"They can stay outside," she said. "We're sleeping in the stone house."

That was another thing that Oliver found strange about Rata Station. There were two houses on the farm, one of which almost met Deborah Butler's standards. It was made out of stone, at least, the local gray sandstone. It had two stories, and was built on a low hill that offered a lovely view of the river, meadows, and garden—if one could call it that. At Rata Station, no one bothered with decorative gardening. There were only a few beds of vegetables and medicinal herbs. After Chris Fenroy had started the farm, he'd had the house built to please his wife, Jane. But when Jane had left Chris for the Maori chieftain—an event that had actually caused Deborah Butler to faint in shock—Chris and Cat had moved into a much smaller wooden house on the edge of the river. They'd left the stone manor house to Ida and Karl, and Carol and Linda had their rooms there as well. It would have been easy for Oliver to sneak into his fiancé's room if she'd wanted him to. The young man felt a quick stab of regret, but then turned to Mara again.

"I'd be glad to carry your things over later," he said.

For now, everyone had convened in Cat and Chris's cheerfully lit house. Carol and Linda were helping Cat quickly prepare an improvised meal. As there wasn't enough seating for all, Mara sat down with natural grace on one of the colorful, handwoven rugs. Oliver took a chair opposite her. Now he could see the girl in good light—which only served to magnify her charm. Mara Jensch looked much more like her mother than Carol did. She had dark hair and a widow's peak, which made her face look heart-shaped like Ida's. But Mara's cheekbones were more defined, like her father's. Her fine features made the gauntness look exotic and almost ethereal, especially next to her strong, sweeping eyebrows and thick dark eyelashes. Her eyes were a captivating shade of sea green, but not like the sea lit by sun. They were more the color of the shadows that clouds cast on the water. The girl had cherry-red, finely formed lips; while not as sensual as Carol's or Linda's, they were just as attractive.

Oliver felt almost irritated when Carol sat down by his feet and carefully leaned her head against his knee. Resigned, he tore his gaze from the beautiful girl who was much too young for him, and played inconspicuously with Carol's blonde hair. The others seemed not to notice, or at least pretended not to. Linda smiled to herself.

Mara paid just as little attention to Oliver as she did the rest of the family. At the moment, she only had eyes for the plate of sandwiches that Linda had just put on the floor. She'd obviously never heard the rule that a lady should eat like a sparrow in public. Mara ate heartily and drank three glasses of cold tea. Cat had brought out a bottle of wine for the adults. She gave Carol a look.

"We will talk later, young lady!" she whispered, but seemed to forget about the stolen wine when Ida smiled mysteriously and opened her saddlebag.

Ida herself almost never drank. Where she had grown up, alcohol had been frowned upon. But she knew Cat's weakness for a good drop. She delightedly pulled out two bottles, and even accepted a glass when Karl filled one and handed it to her.

"Let's drink this one; they recommended it at the White Hart," he said. "Actually, we wanted to bring a bottle of champagne, but I was afraid it wouldn't survive the pounding in the saddlebags." Karl raised his glass, looked around at everyone, and then allowed his eyes to rest lovingly on Ida's. "To Korora Manor!"

Ida smiled back. "To Korora Manor!"

"To what?" Cat inquired. "Does this have something to do with the news that you wrote about, Ida?"

Ida nodded. "You shouldn't give it all away at once," she said, scolding her husband. "I thought we could discuss it in a quiet moment. We don't even know how Cat and Chris feel, and—"

Karl shrugged. "Don't worry so much, Ida. Cat and Chris will be happy for us. They—"

"What will we be happy about?" Chris asked, taking a sip of the wine.

Ida and Karl exchanged a look, as though each wanting the other to break the news.

Mara sighed. "Mamida and Kapa are buying a house."

"Mara!" Ida scolded.

Mara shrugged. "Mamida, if we wait until you come out with it, I'll never get to bed tonight, and I'm already falling asleep. So please just tell them all about your dream house in Whangarei, and the beach and garden, and everything that makes you so happy about it." She yawned demonstratively. "Kapa and Mamida are moving away," she announced. "But I'm staying here. I don't want to live on the North Island. You promised I don't have to, right, Mamida?"

Ida sighed. "Yes, we really are buying a house. But first we have to discuss it with Chris and Cat before we know if you can actually stay here."

Cat smiled at her friend, who was obviously frustrated with her teenage daughter. She remembered only too well how Carol and Linda had gotten on her nerves at that age. But this conflict was very easy to solve.

"How could we have anything against Mara staying?" she asked kindly. "This is her home!"

Karl bit his lip. "I hope you'll still see it that way when . . . Well, we should really talk in private among the four of us."

Cat and Chris looked at each other. If the house in Whangarei was really Ida's dream house, then it probably wasn't cheap. That meant Karl would need money, and most of his fortune was invested in the farm.

Cat stretched. "Whatever you've got planned," she said warmly as she reached for Ida's hand, "you won't have to worry about Mara, or Carol and Linda either. The children all belong here. Now tell us, Ida! You really plan to leave us? For a beach house on the North Island? The Whangarei area is the northernmost tip of Aotearoa, isn't it?"

Cat used the Maori name for New Zealand, just as she preferred to use the original names for the rivers, mountains, and villages of the country. She felt the European settlers' desire to rename everything showed a deep lack of respect for the Maori.

Karl shook his head, obviously glad to move on to a less volatile topic. "No, the house is a good bit farther south, between Cape Reinga and Whangarei." Cape Reinga was the northernmost village in New Zealand, and Cat knew about it from the Maori myths. According to the legends, the souls of the dead started there on their journey to paradise, to Hawaiki. "But it's in Northland, on the east coast. Our house is in Russell—you would know it as Kororareka, Cat."

Cat nodded. Kororareka was one of the original *pakeha* settlements in New Zealand, but it hadn't always had the best reputation. At first, it had been a port of call for sailors, whalers, and escaped prisoners, and later a focal point for Maori revolts. More recently, it had been renamed after Lord John Russell and become a peaceful, pretty town in the midst of the breathtakingly beautiful landscape of the Bay of Islands.

"It's a dream," Ida said as her youngest yawned again. "It's a cottage on a small bay, with a view of the sea and a little beach." Ida's clear, porcelain-blue eyes glowed. "The sunset over the sea is—is just—"

Karl smiled. "Almost as beautiful as it was in Bahia."

Both Karl and Ida had come to New Zealand on a brig called the *Sankt Pauli*, and on a stopover in Brazil, Ida had fallen hopelessly in love with the climate and beaches of Bahia. Back then, Karl had asked her to run away with him and stay there, but she hadn't dared to defy her father and abandon her arranged engagement. Ever since, through all these years on the rainy South Island, Ida dreamed of sun-drenched beaches. Then she'd accompanied Karl on surveying trips to the North Island and discovered its subtropical climate.

"It's a stone house, the kind I'm told they build in Ireland. The seller is Irish, too, a Catholic priest. He was one of the first missionaries in the area. Now he's old and longing to go home, he says, back to his roots. He wants to die in Galway."

"Perhaps he doesn't remember what the weather's like there," Chris said doubtfully.

Chris had been born in Australia, where he'd worked as an interpreter for the governor, and he'd often had contact with Irishmen who told tales of their island's wet climate.

Karl shrugged. "He's quite bitter. The Maori mission didn't work out as he'd hoped. And the local *pakeha* are not exactly behaving like good Christians. In any case, he wants to go back to Europe. He was very happy to be able to sell his house. And it's in wonderful condition."

"The yard is fantastic," Ida said enthusiastically. "Father O'Toole had a vegetable garden, an herb garden, and a lot of flowers. Of course, I would change a few things."

"But at least the hard work has already been done," Karl said. "Ida wouldn't have to strain herself to take care of it, and the housework won't be a problem either. The cottage is just the right size for us. There's a parlor, a large kitchen, two bedrooms, and a guest room. Enough space if all of you should ever manage to come together for a visit." He smiled invitingly, although it would be quite unusual for all members of a farming family to leave their farm at the same time. "There's even a barn that could easily be converted into a sheep stall and cheese dairy."

"You want to make cheese again?" Cat asked Ida. "I thought we'd figured out that it wasn't profitable."

Originally, Ida had run a cheese dairy at Rata Station. Only after it became clear that the economy of the Canterbury Plains would be based on wool had the women finally given up.

Ida smiled. "I always enjoyed making cheese," she said simply. "More than any other work. Of course, it won't be a large business. I thought perhaps I'd have fifteen to twenty sheep I can take care of by myself. And distribution won't be a problem because the house is close to the town. I could sell my cheese to the grocer there, or sell it myself at the farmers' market. I would love that!"

Oliver furrowed his brow at Ida's happy glow. His fiancée's mother a cheese maker and market woman? He could well imagine what his mother would have to say about that.

But Cat was happy for her friend. She knew that Ida had felt superfluous after the dairy sheep were gone. But Rata Station had only become truly lucrative when it focused fully on sheep bred for their wool.

"But you'll be back for my wedding, won't you?" Carol asked. She was a little surprised and annoyed that her mother had decided to move to the other end of the country without discussing it with her first.

Ida nodded. "Of course! I wouldn't miss it for the world. And as I said, we have plenty of space. For you and Linda, and for Mara. From now on, you'll have two homes. You're welcome at Korora Manor anytime."

"Well then, let's drink to Ida and Karl, their new house, and their new business," Chris said cheerfully, and filled the wine glasses again.

Mara let out another yawn. "Does anyone mind if I go to bed?" she asked. "We were riding all day, and I'm bone-tired."

"We are too, actually," Linda said, and cast Carol a meaningful glance.

Oliver had stopped playing with his fiancée's hair, and his hands had begun to work their way down her neck. In an unobserved moment, they had even drifted below the neckline of her blouse. She was pink with excitement. At any minute, Cat, Chris, Ida, or Karl might notice what was going on. Mara was smirking at her sister, but Linda thought Oliver was going too far. It would be best to put an end to it for the evening.

Ida and Cat nodded.

"Go on over, then," Cat said. "Your bed is made up, Mara. And your room is ready too, Ida." She smiled tenderly at her partner. "It's not as though Chris used the house very much while you were gone."

The agreement between Cat and Chris was that they would live separately, and just "visit" each other often. For that reason, Chris's bedroom was in the main house, but he'd been sleeping in Cat's home for years.

Oliver stood politely when the girls got up. Clearly disappointed, but also very properly, he wished his fiancée and her sisters a good night.

"I thought you were going to carry over my things," Mara said.

She looked meaningfully from Oliver to Carol, and her eyes flashed conspiratorially. Mara was paving the way for more stolen moments for the couple.

However, Karl saw through her ploy and shook his head. "It would be better not to tempt the young man," he said calmly. "No disrespect intended, but I'm not going to send you into a house with three girls, unchaperoned." His teasing smile took the sting out of his words. "I'll bring over your things, Mara," he told his daughter.

Everyone laughed, but Oliver felt as though he were being reprimanded. He had secretly hoped that he'd be offered a proper guest room in the main house after the Jensches' return. So far, he'd been on a Maori sleeping mat in a kind of wooden shed next to Cat's house. The accommodation was barely more than a storage space, and entirely unacceptable as guest lodgings. Oliver knew there were plenty of properly furnished rooms in the main house that met even his mother's high standards. His own family had sometimes spent the night there when they traveled to Christchurch for the sheep breeders' meetings. But leaving Oliver without a chaperone in a house with his fiancée was out of the question, even for liberal Cat. Oliver excused himself with clipped words and moved to go. His hostesses didn't notice his disconcertedness, and wished him a good night. Cat and Ida had much to discuss; Carol's fiancée would have only been a distraction.

Chris Fenroy winked at Karl Jensch as Oliver left the room. "Once you've got the girls settled, come out to the barn to check on the horses."

Karl nodded and returned his wink. Oliver thought this was all very strange. Over the course of a sociable evening with friends and business partners, his father also liked to retreat with the men to drink whiskey and smoke cigars. But that's what a study was for! Chris and Karl seemed to prefer to meet in the barn, and would probably pass a bottle back and forth like the drovers. Perhaps his mother was right: Chris Fenroy might have noble blood, and the others were clearly sheep barons, but his fiancée's family didn't take their social standing seriously. It was good that Carol would soon be under his mother's wing.

To overcome his annoyance, Oliver tried to think about Carol's passionate kisses, the soft fullness of her breasts under his hands, and the flowery scent of her hair. But he had to fight against the image of her impertinent little sister, who kept sneaking her way into his head.

Chapter 7

Chris was waiting in the barn with a flask of whiskey, but Karl grinned at him as he pulled a bottle of amber-colored liquid from his own saddlebag.

"Here, this is single malt. To celebrate. Unlike champagne, shaking doesn't ruin it."

Chris laughed, put down his flask, and willingly uncorked the bottle. "Can you still afford that after buying the house?" he said with a grin.

Karl sighed. "Actually, I wanted to talk to you and Cat about that."

Chris nodded. "Do you need an advance against your share of Rata Station?"

Karl rubbed his temples. "Not really," he said. "We were thinking more of . . . Chris, this is a little difficult for me to say. I love Rata Station; we built it together. But our decision to move to the North Island is final."

Chris raised his eyebrows. "So, you're totally serious? You want to settle down so Ida can milk twenty sheep? Or do you intend to keep traveling as a surveyor? You surely have many years of work ahead of you, and Ida probably wouldn't like staying alone in Russell."

Karl took a sip from the whiskey bottle. It was part of the men's tradition that they didn't bother to bring glasses to the barn. After all, the origin of their secret meetings was Chris's fear of his ex-wife's unkindness. Before Jane had left him, he'd endeavored to escape from her almost every evening.

"I wouldn't like that either," Karl said. "Of course I'll be helping Ida, especially while the cheese dairy is getting established. Afterward, I will be traveling sometimes, but not for months on end as a surveyor. Recently I've been doing more, hmm, mediating. The situation between the *pakeha* and the Maori on the North Island is heating up again, Chris."

"I thought there was peace in Taranaki now," Chris said in surprise.

Three years before, in the Taranaki region, there had been an actual war prompted by the sale of land at Waitara. Both sides had been furious, but most sensible New Zealanders now agreed that the British government had taken things way too far when it had sent 3,500 heavily armed soldiers from Australia to fight around 1,500 primitively armed Maori warriors. Afterward, an uneasy truce had been negotiated, both sides concluding that the war was not really winnable for anyone. For the *pakeha*, the economic damage caused by the fighting outweighed the benefits. Compromises had been made, and the fighting had stopped. But no one knew for how long.

"First of all," Karl replied, "the land disputes are ongoing. As before, the government confiscated land as a 'punishment' for the fighting in recent years. That gave the impression that the owners of the best land were the most rebellious—but I think it was basically an excuse to redistribute the land to their own advantage. And now this Maori preacher is traveling around and encouraging the villagers to throw the *pakeha* off their land. War could flare up again at any time, no matter how much the government is trying to avoid it. That's why there's a very large demand for mediators. I've been asked by both the Maori and the *pakeha* to accept the role. I have a good reputation with both sides, and it helps that I can also speak a little Maori."

Karl smiled at his friend. After all, it was mostly Chris he had to thank for his skill. Fenroy spoke the language fluently.

"Isn't it dangerous when you wind up on the front lines?" Chris wanted to know.

Karl shook his head. "So far, it's always been very civilized, even though of course they are all rattling their sabers. I think it was more dangerous for me as a surveyor. Don't forget Cotterell."

Cotterell, a surveyor with whom Chris had worked as an interpreter, had lost his life in the Wairau conflict.

"Of course, I'll be able to decide for myself where I do and don't want to go," Karl continued. "It's common knowledge which chieftains tend to be hotheaded." He laughed grimly. "And also which *pakeha* officials. As you know, some of them are much worse."

Chris nodded knowingly, and the men fell deep into discussion about their memories of volatile military strategies, ignorant government officials, and the hotheaded settlers they had encountered during their work for the land claims agency.

Karl told him about his recent adventure with the Ngati Hine.

"How well do you get paid for that kind of work?" Chris asked.

Karl shrugged. "It doesn't pay as well as sheep farming," he admitted. "But together with Ida's income, we should have enough. We don't need very much, and you know Ida. She'll feed us with her labor in the garden and fields. She's already getting excited about what can be made into jams and chutneys, and is asking for an oven to bake bread in. This house will make her happy, Chris. She'll finally have everything she's dreamed of: a home she can care for, like she had in Raben Steinfeld, a community she can join—not Lutheran, of course, but Russell has a pretty Anglican church with a kind priest and an enthusiastic women's group. They exchange more recipes than Bible verses, if you ask me. They're good people, and very tolerant. Ida will love them. And most of all, the climate, the sea, the beach—"

"And you," Chris finished for him. "I hope it makes you just as happy. That brings me back to the financial question. What about Rata Station?"

Karl took another swallow of whiskey. "We want to offer to sell you our share," he confessed. "If that's possible. Of course we don't want to drive you to ruin, we—"

Chris silenced his friend with a wave. "Karl, we're sheep barons!" he said, laughing. "The wool business is booming, and the English can't get enough. Our profits are increasing every year, and most of our investments have been amortized. Everything is in good shape here, from the barns to the shearing shed. Of course, we don't have a lot of savings—but you know that yourself." Cat, Chris, and the Jensches had reinvested most of their earnings in further development of the farm. "But we can take out a mortgage at any time. The banks—" Chris paused, looking around. "What was that? I thought I saw someone pass by the window."

Chris stood up and took the flickering lantern from its hook, then stepped outside the barn door. He peered over toward the stone house, where the lights were already out, and at Cat's house, where they were still lit for Ida and Cat's own discussion.

Chris sat down again, but still listened suspiciously.

"Maybe you're just a bit jumpy?" Karl said, teasing. "Or perhaps you haven't spent a night outside in a long time? Some night bird, surely, an animal. I didn't see anything."

"Your back's to the window," Chris grumbled. "But back to the banks. It's no problem at all."

Mara Jensch held her breath. She knew very well how to move silently. After all, she had spent half of her life with Maori children playing at being warriors and hunters. Supple and slender as she was, she had outdone even Eru at stalking. However, she'd assumed her father and Chris would no longer be in the barn. How long could it take to make a last check on the horses? Mara thought she'd waited long enough before sneaking out of her room, tiptoeing down the stairs, and closing the front door so quietly behind her that not even Fancy reacted. Once outside, she'd stopped being so careful. That had been a mistake.

From behind a rata bush, Mara watched Chris peer into the darkness before finally walking back into the barn. She let out a quiet sigh of relief. Now, more carefully, she slipped between the outbuildings, keeping an eye out for other unpleasant surprises. Like Carol, for example. She seemed to be determined to keep her good-looking fiancé in suspense, but perhaps that was just a masterful diversion and the two of them were actually meeting somewhere in the moonlight.

Mara didn't like the moonlight. It would have been easier to slip out on a dark night. Actually, there wasn't any reason for her to sneak away. The Maori village would still be there the next morning. But Mara wasn't the least bit tired. She was wide awake, and she couldn't and wouldn't wait any longer!

Finally, she left the buildings of Rata Station behind and ran as quickly as her skirts allowed. She had taken the path so many times she could have walked it in her sleep. Mara had been away with her parents for five months. She knew that she'd grown, and to a certain extent had become an adult. But here, everything was still the way it had always been. Mara didn't know if she found it annoying or comforting.

She finally saw the tikis guarding the gate. The red-painted wooden statues of gods could look frightening in the darkness, but they had been familiar to her since childhood. Mara walked between them and entered the *marae*. It was completely dark, and the last fires had long since died. Unsure of herself, she glanced hesitantly between the kitchen and storage houses and the communal sleeping house, and finally to the chieftain's dwelling. It was a beautiful building decorated with intricate carvings, almost as large as the *wharenui*, the tribe's meeting and sleeping house. Te Haitara lived much more luxuriously than was normal for the Ngai Tahu.

Usually, Maori chieftains lived alone in relatively small houses. Their wives visited them occasionally, and often within the contexts of ceremonies that were centuries old. However, Jane had done away with those traditions when she had married Te Haitara. In her mind, it was important that he make a few concessions to her *pakeha* origin. Among other things, she had insisted that she and her husband live under the same roof, and raise their child there together. She never would have tolerated sleeping in the meetinghouse with all the other members of the tribe.

But where would Mara find Eru that night? At almost fifteen years old, he counted as a young warrior, and he should be living with his friends and not still under his mother's roof. On the other hand, there were at least ten unmarried girls who slept in the meetinghouse, all of whom were eager to have their first experiences with love and, Jane suspected, "to nab the chieftain's son for themselves."

Mara had once heard Cat say that Jane was still thinking like a *pakeha*, with fairy-tale notions of sought-after princes. But Eru's status as the chieftain's son didn't necessarily make him any more attractive to the Maori girls. Tribal leaders were traditionally no richer than any of the other villagers, and the role of chieftain wasn't exclusively heritable. Te Haitara had many nephews and other relatives. The likelihood that the villagers would pick his half-*pakeha* son to be his successor wasn't very high. And as a chieftain's wife, Jane didn't have any special privileges. The opposite was true, and even more so on the North Island, where traditions were followed much more strictly. There, the chieftains' families were completely *tapu*, and were subjected to major limitations. In those tribes, aristocratic marriages were still arranged, just as they were in European noble families. So, if a girl was interested in Eru, it would only be because he was a kind person, a good hunter, and very affectionate. Although Mara hoped that he hadn't let other girls know that yet. She was extremely jealous. And Eru's mother was irritatingly stubborn.

Mara decided not to search for Eru in the meetinghouse, but instead to focus on his parents' house. It stood a bit apart in the shadow of a southern beech grove and was surrounded by a fence made from raupo reeds. The fence wasn't necessary, however, as Jane had neither planted a vegetable garden nor kept any animals. Mara leaned against one of the trees and pulled a little flute out of her pocket. She raised the small, beautifully decorated *koauau* to her nose. A soft, delicate melody came out, not unlike the call of a night bird.

Actually, the *koauau* was played to attract birds, and to welcome newborn children. It was said that the sound of the flute was supposed to awaken faded memories. Mara smiled as she thought about it. Eru's memories wouldn't be all that faded after just five months. She herself remembered every detail of the last time they'd been together.

As she repeated the melody for the third time, something stirred in the house. Mara recognized the husky young man's shadow. She had been sure that his thick black hair would be loose and falling below his shoulders. He'd been so proud that he was finally allowed to let it grow so he could make a warrior's knot. But either he hadn't taken out the knot before going to bed, or he'd cut his hair again. Eru had a blanket wrapped around him, and was otherwise only wearing a loincloth. Mara's heart beat faster as she took in his supple gait and tall silhouette.

She played the melody one more time to let him know where she was, and then he finally appeared in front of her. She grinned, enjoying her successful surprise. Te Eriatara stared at her in disbelief.

"Ma—Mara!" he stammered. "Marama, the moonlight! Am I dreaming?"

Mara reached out her arms to Eru, and he took her hands. Carefully, and ready to let her go at any second, he pulled her close and rested his forehead against hers tenderly, his nose touching her nose. It was the *hongi*, the traditional greeting. Mara breathed in his familiar scent, a strange mixture of the earthy-smelling sweat of a young warrior and the flowery soap that his mother insisted on. Mara felt as though she were coming home.

Eru, on the other hand, noticed many new things. The scent of salt and the sea were caught in her hair from the journey. Her skin smelled of exotic flowers and spices; and somehow, her own body scent had changed. The girl he'd said goodbye to, who was somewhere between a trusted sister and a lover, had become a woman. Mara smelled divine, and she glowed like a goddess in the moonlight.

Eru was reminded of a traditional love story in which Hinemoa guided her lover to the island with the sound of a *koauau*. Hinemoa and Tutanekai, a couple that had the whole world against them . . . He sighed.

"You just got back?" he asked as they released each other, and the magic subsided a little. "And you walked here?" He smiled at her. "You're mad."

Mara shrugged. "I know. I could have waited until tomorrow, but I wanted to see *you*, and not the whole village at once. And I wanted to know if everything is still . . . the way it was before. If we can still—"

Eru took Mara's hand and led her deeper into the little glade. "So you didn't practice with any other boys?" he asked her seriously. "With *pakeha* boys?"

Mara shook her head, feeling a little insulted. "Of course not. I promised. And you didn't either? I know other girls in the tribe don't kiss, but you could have done other things with them . . ."

Eru shook his head determinedly. "I promised too! And I kept my word. I dreamed only of you. I—I practiced in my dream, again and again."

Mara smiled. "Me too," she admitted. "So, shall we try it?"

She gazed up at Eru and offered him her lips. He was taller than she, which wasn't true with every boy her age. But both Eru's father and mother were tall and stocky. He would soon be taller than all the other Ngai Tahu men, and he was already stronger than most of them. Now he bent down to Mara, wrapped his arms around her, and pressed his lips against hers. They remained that way for the space of a heartbeat, unsure about who was meant to initiate this *pakeha* custom. Then they both parted their lips almost simultaneously and allowed their tongues to explore each other's mouths. Mara's delicate hands wandered over Eru's naked back, while his caressed her through the fabric of her riding habit. The buttons stopped him, and he tugged a little—and Mara stepped back abruptly.

"Don't ruin my dress!" she scolded, but then gave him her most radiant smile. "That was good, wasn't it?"

"That was—" He paused to search for the right words. "That was unbelievable. Much nicer than in my dreams."

"So, we can both still do it," Mara said happily.

They kissed again and again, walked arm in arm through the glade, and finally found a side gate in the fence around the *marae* and followed the path that led along the banks of the river. Their next kiss was bathed in moonlight.

"I will never do this with anyone but you," Mara promised.

Eru nodded. "I won't either!" he assured her. "So we'll have to get married."

Mara laughed. "That was the plan. Unless you changed your mind."

She looked at him appraisingly. Only now in the shimmering moonlight could she see Eru clearly. His childish face had become more sculpted and defined. Eru looked like his father, but had slightly lighter skin. The only other thing he had inherited from his mother was her green eyes, which gave him an exotic look. His dark hair wasn't in a warrior's knot.

"What happened to your hair?" she asked. "I thought you were letting it grow."

Eru sighed heavily. "My mother," he murmured. "She was fussing at me every day about it. 'Eric, a young man shouldn't walk around looking like a girl! Everyone will laugh at you!'" He captured her tone of voice perfectly, but it wasn't funny. He sounded bitter.

"Who would laugh at you?" Mara said in surprise. "All the other boys are letting their hair grow too. Well, almost all of them. A few are determined to become *pakeha*."

The tribes of the South Island were increasingly influenced by the customs of the white settlers. Unless they were taking part in an important ceremony, most of the Ngai Tahu wore Western clothing, mainly because the garments offered more warmth in the cool plains. In addition, most of Te Haitara's tribe now also declined to get *moko*, the tribal tattoos that had been obligatory two decades ago. Many of the girls braided their hair, and the boys were starting to cut theirs short. But it certainly hadn't gone so far that the traditional hairstyles would be a reason for ridicule. Young warriors were proud of their traditional knots.

"There's a kind of war going on here right now, Mara," Eru said. "My father and mother are fighting about whether I should be *pakeha* or Maori. Or both, if that's even possible. At least they agree that I should follow in my father's footsteps as a leader one day. But for my father, being chieftain is most important, while my mother sees me more as the chairman of the Sheep Breeders' Association. 'A mediator between cultures,' she says. They're all pulling me in different directions, Mara! My father's people are teaching me how to make spears and use war clubs. My mother thinks that's totally useless, since guns are more effective. Of course, she's not wrong there. The English have conquered half the world without ever having danced a *haka* before a battle."

Mara had noticed a strong British military presence on the North Island, even though many of the soldiers who had fought in the Taranaki war had been sent back to Australia. The thought of the redcoats doing any kind of dance before battle made her laugh.

"This is serious!" Eru said. "My mother thinks war is old-fashioned, anyway. She says in the end economics will rule the world, and instead of learning how to beat people up, I should go to college and study economic theory. Then I could improve the sheep-breeding business, and the tribe would have more money and prestige. And, well, anyone who has money and prestige doesn't need to fight a war. She's probably not wrong about that either. It's just that I—"

"What do you want, Eru?" Mara asked gently. "Do you want to go to college?"

The two of them had sat down on a sand spit and were gazing out over the glistening water of the Waimakariri. Mara nestled against her beau, and he put his bare arms around her in the cool night air.

He sighed again. "Not really. But at the same time, I do want to be taken seriously. And I see how the Sheep Breeders' Association treats my father."

Te Haitara hated the meetings in Christchurch, but Jane insisted that their tribal breeding business be represented there. Behind Jane's back, the breeders sarcastically referred to the village as Iron Janey's Station.

"If I had a college degree, they'd be more likely to accept me," Eru said. "I don't want to go to England, but the only college in New Zealand is a medical school."

Mara squeezed Eru's hand and played with his fingers. "How much economics do you really need in the Canterbury Plains?" she asked. "I don't know of one sheep baron who's read your mother's beloved Adam Smith."

Eru shrugged. "I think it's more important to learn as much as possible about sheep."

Mara nodded. "Then work for the Deanses for a year, or for the Redwoods," she suggested. "Or for the Wardens at Kiward Station. That's the gigantic farm Carol got her dog from. And afterward, maybe you can go to high school in Christchurch or Dunedin for a year. There must be some kind of private school there."

Eru shrugged. "Maybe. My mother was also talking about one in Wellington."

"Wellington." Mara hesitated for a moment. "We were just there. It's a very modern city, and it surely has a high school. And probably a school for girls too! Eru, if I ask my parents, then maybe we could both go to high school! We could go to Wellington together. Would you like that?"

Eru straightened his shoulders. "I'd go anywhere with you," he said, but didn't sound completely convinced.

Mara, however, was on fire. The more she thought about it, the more ingenious the plan seemed. She was determined to marry Eru. It was what she had always wanted, and any lingering doubt had disappeared with their first kiss. However, it was clear to Mara that they were still both too young for marriage. So, she and Eru would have to figure out how to keep themselves busy for the next couple of years doing something they enjoyed.

For Eru, that wasn't a problem. Mara had assumed he'd stay in the village and be educated as a warrior. But she hadn't been able to come up with anything for herself. Unlike Carol and Linda, she had never been interested in special duties at Rata Station. She could neither train dogs nor help bring newborn lambs into the world. She'd always done routine tasks like checking the fences, herding the sheep, or helping in the shearing shed, but she hadn't really enjoyed any of it. Fortunately, her parents were preoccupied enough not to question why their daughter wanted to stay on the farm instead of moving to Russell with them. And if she told her family that she wanted to go to school, Karl and Ida would be thrilled. They'd always regretted the fact that grouchy Miss Foggerty had never managed to motivate the children. They themselves had adored their village school in Mecklenburg, but had been forced to leave at the age of thirteen. Later, they had educated themselves as best they could in the undeveloped new country while doing farm work. And of course, they had happily shared the cost of the tutor that Jane had hired. If that now bore delayed fruit and additionally helped attract their daughter to the North Island where they wanted to settle, Mara's persuasive skills wouldn't be put to a difficult test.

For Eru, it would be different. Te Haitara wouldn't be very happy about sending his son to the North Island. Most of the tribes there were enemies of the Ngai Tahu, which meant Eru wouldn't be able to keep in contact with other Maori. He would have to concentrate entirely on his *pakeha* schoolmates. Of course, that would be fine with Jane—and Mara.

"Then that's what we'll do!" she declared after they had both thought quietly for a few moments. "You just have to be smart about it. Your mother can't know that I'm going to be in Wellington too. It would be better if you try first, and I wait until my parents have moved. Then I'll write and tell them how bored I am at Rata Station, and how I suddenly got the idea about Wellington." She smiled mischievously.

But Eru looked at her in shock. "You want me to go to the North Island alone? Should we separate again now, for months?"

Mara shrugged. "We can't start in the middle of a semester. That means it will be at least three months before you can go to Wellington, Eru!"

She smiled when she thought about the long, hot summer when she'd sneak away from Rata Station as much as possible to be with him.

Eru rubbed his forehead. "Let's keep practicing the kissing, anyway," he said as Mara moved to stand. "Who knows when we'll get another chance?"

Mara offered her lips willingly again. He found her mouth, and they joined in a long, tender kiss that made everything shiver inside of her.

"Well," she said breathlessly, "I don't think we really need practice anymore. If there was a degree in kissing, we'd already have it."

Chapter 8

Jane had been born with the surname Beit, had married and divorced as Fenroy, and was now harnessed with a Maori name that no one but her loving husband could take seriously. She had heard the birdcall that lured her son out of the house, but hadn't paid attention to it. Jane didn't care about birds, and she wasn't interested in the sounds that talented Maori musicians conjured from their *koauaus* either. The only thing she managed to get excited about was running the tribe's sheep-breeding business. But she didn't even like sheep. In fact, Jane had preferred the previous venture she'd arranged for the Ngai Tahu: the manufacture of herbal medicines and good-luck charms, which offered a predictable profit, a negligible investment, and guaranteed growth. Settlers had been streaming into New Zealand for decades, but there were very few doctors among them. Therefore, the people at farms, whaling stations, and seal-hunting outposts had eagerly purchased everything from the traveling merchant who had sold the items for Jane, and had ordered more. As news of the medicines' effectiveness spread, the tribe could have hugely increased production. But the *tohunga*, tribal elders, and wise women hadn't wanted to do it. For them, the tinctures for coughs or stomachaches weren't just concoctions. They contained the spirits of the plants, who had to be invoked in complicated ceremonies. That was all very time consuming, and apparently the spirits didn't always want to be conjured. In any case, Jane's efforts to expand the business had failed. Finally, she had invested the profit they had earned in sheep, which had been imported to New Zealand by the *pakeha* and thus had no close relationship to the local spirits.

The *tohunga* kept her distance from the sheep business, and the Ngai Tahu seemed to have a natural talent for working with the animals, so the tribe had achieved prosperity. That made her husband happy. Te Haitara had eventually made his peace with the "spirits of money," whose successful conjuring had been demanded of him by his people since they had discovered the amenities of the *pakeha* lifestyle.

Te Haitara's position as chieftain had been questioned, but he had made it possible for every member of his tribe to fulfill their material wishes. Since those wishes were mostly limited to things like cooking pots, fabric, bird-hunting weapons, and fishing gear, there was always enough left over for the necessary investments in the sheep farm. Jane, too, could have been content. But she wasn't. That night, she tossed restlessly while her husband slept peacefully next to her.

It simply wasn't enough for Jane to have a smoothly working farm that turned a good profit. She wanted to have the best animals, the most valuable fleeces, and the largest herd. Of course, that would lead to the highest income, which then could be used for other investments. Jane was flirting with the idea of investing in mining or railway construction. Coal had been found on the west coast, and train tracks were planned on the North Island. There were many opportunities to become rich by making intelligent investments in New Zealand. Her father had known that but hadn't handled it well. Jane was determined to trump John Nicholas Beit in every respect. She would prove what his underestimated daughter was capable of!

The problem was that Te Haitara and his tribe had no interest in Jane's goals. They showed no understanding for her efforts to increase the size of the herd, to improve the breeding stock, or to reduce costs by learning to shear sheep themselves.

"But we're rich already, Raupo," Te Haitara said affectionately. Raupo was his pet name for Jane. He thought she was as flexible, multifaceted, and clever as the spirit that made its home in the cattail reeds. "We can buy anything we want."

But the chieftain didn't understand how much fun making money was for Jane, and how much she enjoyed the challenge. And for that reason, he didn't understand why Jane was constantly in competition with Cat Rata and Chris Fenroy. He thought of their neighbors as friends, and didn't care that their farm was larger and more profitable. And he certainly didn't try to keep up with them, which made Jane absolutely furious.

"Haitara, we have twenty young men who do nothing all day but swing their spears around and conjure war spirits, even though we don't have any enemies here! And then there are all the women and old men. We could get at least fifty people involved with the farming. Cat and Chris have twice as many sheep as we do, and they only have five hired hands. Can't you encourage the people to work every day, and not just when they feel like it?"

Te Haitara could only shake his head at such outbursts. He didn't see his tribe as lazy in the least. They were always available when there was important work to be done, and the women and girls who had chosen to make caring for the sheep their main occupation responsibly drove them out to pasture and back to the sheds. However, they never went to the trouble of separating the rams and the ewes. They were delighted about every lamb that was born, whether it was sired by a slaughter animal or a prize-winning ram. They thought intact fences were overrated. The men only maintained the fence around the *marae* in order to keep the sheep out. What was more, Te Haitara's tribe thought the shearing shed, a long, hall-like structure that enabled the shearers to work in bad weather, was horrible. They refused to bless it with the usual ceremonies, insisting that the spirits weren't comfortable there. When Jane finally gritted her teeth and asked Cat for advice, she just shrugged.

"The sheep don't feel comfortable there either," she said. "From a spiritual point of view, it's not a good place. On the other hand, we want to sell the wool, and the sheep can't walk around all summer in their thick fleeces. You'll just have to try to convince the tribal elder of that. Perhaps she knows an incantation to ask the spirits of the sheep for forgiveness. They do that for hunting and fishing."

Appalled, Jane had declined the suggestion. Delaying the shearing with hours of ceremonial singing was the last thing she wanted. She would rather try to work it out with her husband.

Cat and Chris owned the better breeding animals and had better connections for selling their wool. They had just purchased an excellent Romney ram from the Butlers. It was exactly the breeding stock Jane needed for her herd. It was also what was keeping Jane from sleeping that night. The next day, she wanted to ask Chris and Cat if they would allow her to bring over a few ewes to join their breeding group. She was sure they wouldn't refuse. To the contrary, Cat and Chris were the most accommodating neighbors imaginable. They were always ready to coordinate with Jane when it came to herding, breeding schedules, shearing, and shipping the fleeces. Te Haitara was very grateful, but Jane felt they were being patronizing. When she went to talk to them the next day, Cat would surely ask again about Eru's plans for the future. Te Haitara assumed she was just being polite, but Jane interpreted it as covert criticism. Cat, too, had grown up caught between the two cultures. She had been maligned from both sides, seen as either a white Maori or a traitorous *pakeha*. Perhaps she had honest interest and understanding for Eric—but perhaps she just wanted to see Jane's ambitious plans for him fail.

Jane was still pondering the ram and Eru's further education when she thought she heard someone open and close the front door very softly, and then footsteps. For the space of a heartbeat, she was afraid, but her common sense won out. She was safe in the middle of the *marae*. No one broke into a chieftain's house. So it could only be . . .

Jane got up, lit a candle, and walked out of her bedroom. Her son was just making himself comfortable on his sleeping mat.

"Where were you?" she asked sternly. "You scared me half to death!"

"I didn't mean to," he said sheepishly, although he was secretly convinced that nothing in the world could scare his mother. "It's just—I couldn't sleep. It's a full moon."

"So?" she said. "Since when has that bothered you? What's going on, Eric, some kind of secret meeting? Is it one of the initiation rituals or warrior games, or something else I should know about?"

Eric shook his head, annoyed. It was true, sometimes the *tohunga* called young warriors out. Jane always made it difficult for Eric when he was called. So far, Te Haitara had always stood up for him, but he hated having to fight for everything that his friends took for granted.

"Nothing's going on. I just needed a little fresh air." He smiled. "I wanted to talk to the spirits."

Jane rolled her eyes. If there had been a missionary school in the area, she would have rather sent him there than expose him to the influences of Maori superstition. On the other hand, it hadn't hurt Te Haitara to conjure a few spirits every now and then. As long as Eric didn't overdo it.

"What did they say?" she asked grumpily.

"Um, I think I might want to go to college after all," Eru murmured.

Jane's expression transformed completely. "Seriously, Eric? You're thinking about it? Then there must finally be some sensible spirits around here! That's wonderful, my son. You won't regret it! But now you have to sleep. Tomorrow you have to select a few sheep to breed with Butler's ram. And I need sleep now too. You're not wrong about the full moon. It makes it hard to wind down."

Jane repressed the impulse to pull the covers up over her nearly full-grown son. She was indescribably relieved when she lay down next to her husband again. At least the problem with Eric was solved. Jane fell asleep peacefully as soon as her head touched the pillow.

Eru lay awake longer. He was exhausted, too, but excited from the encounter with Mara—and distressed by the shock of nearly having been caught by his mother. Finally, he fell asleep and dreamed of kisses in the moonlight, there in the village and maybe soon in Wellington . . .

Mara could have slapped herself. She made the same mistake returning to Rata Station that she had when she'd left. She rushed passed the horse barn without caution, and this time she wasn't as lucky. She ran directly into Chris, who was staggering a little. He had walked Karl to the stone house and then returned to the barn to pick up the bottle and put the lantern back on its hook. When the farmhands arrived in the morning, they would see no signs that anyone had been celebrating there. Chris was usually the first person in the barn, but after his overindulgence that night, it was better not to make any ambitious plans for the morning. But when he bumped into Mara, he seemed to sober up instantly.

"Mara! What are you doing here? You were so tired you could barely keep your eyes open. I thought you were asleep a long time ago."

Mara bit her lip. "I—I was," she said. "And then I woke up again and wanted to get a little fresh air. A moonlit night like this is so beautiful."

Chris regarded her skeptically. "You put on your riding habit and boots just to walk around the yard a little? And since when have you been interested in moonlit nights? Out with it, Mara! Where have you been?"

Mara thought feverishly but came up empty. Chris was right, this was her home. If she had really wanted to step outside for some fresh air, she would have just wrapped a shawl over her nightgown.

Chris took in her windblown hair and the wakeful expression on her face. Mara surely hadn't been to bed. And as for her sudden appreciation of moonlit nights . . . Chris sighed. He had suspected something of the sort six months ago, before she'd left.

"Were you in the village, Mara?" he asked. "Were you with Eru?"

Mara shook her head defiantly, but her cheeks burned. "I was just—"

"Mara, you know very well what kind of trouble that can get you into!" Chris said. "Not to mention the kind of trouble it will get your beau into. And you're much too young! Your parents won't be happy at all. What were you doing, anyway? Do Karl and Ida have to plan for grandchildren already?"

Mara shook her head again, offended. "We only kissed."

Chris sighed. "Well, that's not so bad," he admitted. "Didn't he want more? There are so many girls in the village, I wouldn't be surprised. Or does Jane lock him in her broom closet every night?"

Mara had to laugh in spite of herself, and Chris grinned.

"Eru doesn't do anything with other girls," Mara declared with conviction. "We promised each other. Someday we'll get married."

Chris slapped his forehead. "You're only fifteen, Mara, and he's fourteen. A lot of water will flow down the Waimakariri before you're allowed to marry. And if Jane catches you . . . Mara, the boy has it hard enough already! Don't make things worse."

"What's so bad about me?" Mara asked, annoyed. "Why wouldn't Jane be happy? Sure, I'm no Maori princess, but I'm still a kind of sheep baroness. And for the dowry, I'd surely be able to take a few sheep with me, wouldn't I?"

Chris smiled. "You can have just as many sheep as Carol, if you want them," he said kindly. "You are a very beautiful girl from a good household, as desirable as any princess. Men are already falling all over themselves when they see you. Just wait, in two years, every marriageable young man between Christchurch and Australia will be knocking on your door."

Mara's brow furrowed. "But why shouldn't I marry Eru? I don't mean now, but in two or three years? What do Jane and Te Haitara want?"

Chris sighed. "That's exactly the problem; they don't know what they want. And until they figure it out, Eru won't be able to do anything. And you won't be able to either, Mara, so don't get ahead of yourself!"

Chapter 9

The next day, Jane dressed carefully before she went to Rata Station. In the village, she usually dressed similarly to the native women. In spring, she combined a simple brown skirt with a woven top in the tribal colors. And to Te Haitara's delight, she joined the Maori women in eschewing any form of brassiere. Jane had even stopped wearing corsets when she went to Christchurch to have suits and dresses fitted in the current English fashions. She ordered clothes occasionally when she visited the city, and Te Haitara gave her money for it just as readily as he did any member of his tribe. Jane sometimes wondered if he somehow still couldn't do arithmetic after all these years of living with her. Otherwise, he would have realized long ago that her visits to the seamstress cost much more than all the fabric purchased by all the other women combined. Jane kept a few good excuses ready about why the investment was necessary; after all, she had business meetings with wool buyers and breeders. But Te Haitara never asked any questions.

Jane put on her newest dress, a stylish creation in dark green with a flared skirt. However, she didn't have a crinoline to go with it. She found them too impractical. The skirt and bodice were detailed with a black cord trim, which made the dress even more elegant. The loose tailoring of the bolero jacket made the outfit a little less formal.

She had given up fighting her figure long ago. Jane enjoyed eating, and it was easy to see. That had always decreased her chances with *pakeha* men, but she embodied the Maori beauty ideal in almost every respect. In daily life, Jane didn't bother to pin up her thick brown hair, but instead wore it down, only held back by a wide, woven headband. But for her visit today, she'd styled it carefully. Her hair was up in a high bun, which made her look even taller.

Te Haitara gave her a sidelong look when she set out in her elegant ensemble. Jane, who'd already been nervous all morning, was just waiting for him to ask whether she'd dressed up for Chris Fenroy. Te Haitara and Chris were old friends, but the chieftain still couldn't understand why he'd divorced Jane so willingly. To Te Haitara, the idea that anyone wouldn't find her loveable was incomprehensible, so he was still a little jealous. On the other hand, the chieftain knew his Jane all too well. In her present mood, it was better not to give her any excuse to fly off the handle.

So Te Haitara kept his mouth shut, just as Eru had. The young man was wearing his traditional warrior garb. He would use his mother's absence to join the other apprentice warriors and their mentor. They wanted to visit a few places in the area that had been *tapu* for centuries, places where blood had been drawn. The men would meditate and consult the spirits there, and ask them for strength.

Jane wasn't particularly enthusiastic about the plan, and when she finally arrived in Rata Station, she was in a bad mood in spite of her new dress. Even though she knew Chris and Cat lived in the wooden house, she walked toward the stone one out of habit. There, she ran into Ida Jensch, who was hanging skirts, riding clothes, and shirts to dry on long lines.

"Jane! How nice to see you," Ida said, smiling politely, even though she was surprised by the sight of Chris's former wife.

"The pleasure is mine," Jane said stiffly, eyeing Ida's bedraggled housedress critically. Ida had been wearing that thing for years, and she never seemed to get any older or fatter.

The truth was that neither of the women were very pleased. Even when they'd both lived at Rata Station, they'd had little interest in each other.

Then a rather unpleasant thought occurred to Jane. If Ida was back, then her daughter Mara must be too. That could throw a very different light on Eru's little excursion the night before.

"When did you arrive?" Jane asked.

Ida took the empty laundry basket under her arm.

"Yesterday evening," she replied. "Would you like to come in for coffee? Oh, but you prefer tea, don't you?"

But Jane felt a sudden urge to get home. "I won't take either, thank you. I just wanted to talk to Cat for a moment. Where is she?"

Ida shrugged. "I assume she's in the shearing shed. They're finishing up today. Aren't the shearers coming to you next? In any case, Cat and the others are getting ready to drive the herds to the highlands. Just go on over! Oh, and if you're going anyway, perhaps you could bring something for me. I just baked."

Before Jane could think up an excuse, Ida had disappeared into the house. She returned a few seconds later with a large tin pot of coffee and a huge bowl full of delicious-smelling muffins.

"This is a snack for the shearers," Ida explained. "Can you carry all of this? Wait, I'll get you a basket . . ."

Jane seethed at being demoted to the role of errand boy. What was more, the basket wasn't exactly light. When Ida was out of sight, she put it down on a tree stump and helped herself to a muffin. She had to admit that Ida was an exceptionally good baker. If she happened to pass that skill on to her impertinent little daughter, there would be at least one point in Mara's favor. Jane frowned grimly, vowing to talk to Eric as soon as she got home.

Jane struggled under the load on her way to the shearing shed, and was greeted there with enthusiasm. Chris, who knew her well enough to read her mind, grinned sarcastically. But no one else seemed to feel she had sacrificed any authority by appearing with coffee and muffins. As usual, Cat greeted her with an open smile. She was wearing a dirty riding habit and a sou'wester to protect her from the sun. Her hair was plaited into a thick braid, and she looked young too. Jane sometimes wondered if she herself was the only one around here who aged—or who had even grown up.

"Wonderful! A picnic," Cat said happily, and slipped between two fence slats from the paddock where she'd been tending to a group of freshly shorn ewes. She took the basket of muffins from Jane with obvious pleasure. "Sorry about my appearance." She looked down at herself with an impish grin, feigning a guilty look. Then she reached hungrily for one of the muffins. "Did you make these?"

She couldn't possibly believe that. After all, there wasn't even a proper oven in the Maori village. Of course Jane could have gotten one if she'd wanted it, but she didn't bake. She left Cat's question unanswered and instead skipped immediately to the reason for her visit.

"I wanted to talk to you about the new ram."

As expected, it wasn't difficult to reach an agreement with Cat and Chris. Jane started the negotiations quickly and proceeded in a businesslike manner. If she felt any emotion, the only way to tell was that she ate another muffin after each sentence. Karl finally made a deft grab for the bowl to save at least some of the treats for the shearers in the shed. Otherwise, he didn't offer any input, which Jane thought was little strange. After all, a third of Rata Station belonged to him.

"First thing tomorrow, we'll have the twenty ewes sheared, and then we'll bring them here," Jane said in conclusion. "Thank you, Cat, Chris . . . Butler's ram offers a welcome addition of new blood for our herd."

Cat nodded. "For ours too," she said kindly, which Jane once again interpreted as being patronizing.

After all, Rata Station had enough valuable rams of its own. For Cat, it was really just about new blood, not urgent improvements in her herd. And then Cat was even rude enough to ask if Jane needed more help.

"Shall we send Carol over with Fancy? She could pick up the ewes for breeding, and also help you corral the other sheep that need to be sheared. The dog needs constant practice, and there's nothing else for her to do here before we drive the herd to the highlands."

Jane clenched her jaw. "We have our own dogs," she said defensively.

Her people worked with collie mixes that had good herding instincts. Unfortunately, no one had made an effort at training them properly. If they helped, it was good. If they didn't, the Maori children herded the sheep themselves.

Cat shrugged. "I should get back to work. The shearers are starting up again." A few sheep that had just been freed from their wool sprang out of the shed with obvious relief.

Jane turned to go, and she normally would have felt a sense of relief, too, when she headed for home. But today she had more serious things on her mind than just a few ewes and a ram. She still had to confront Eric about sneaking out the night before. And now he was out walking around on his own again! Jane would have liked to know the whereabouts of Ida's daughter Mara.

Mara had been restless all morning. She didn't want to help her mother with the baking, or the others with the shearing. She would have preferred to work with the horses, breaking in the three yearlings currently grazing in the pasture.

That was usually Carol's job, but aside from her work with the dog, she also had wedding preparations to deal with.

That morning, Mara listened with vague interest as Carol bid her fiancé farewell. Oliver was heading to Christchurch, but not without cornering Mara for a chat. He was obviously trying to keep up a gentlemanly, noncommittal tone, but the look in his eyes gave him away. Mara replied to his questions politely, but listened to his enthusiastic musings about rowing technique without the slightest indication of interest.

"He's really serious about all that paddling around," Mara said to Linda as Carol quickly kissed her fiancé before he departed. Cat, Chris, Ida, and Karl had already said goodbye at breakfast and were now going about their business on the farm. "I mean, the regatta is a lot of fun, but does it really matter who wins?"

Linda shrugged. "Oliver thinks it will officially make him into a gentleman," she said flippantly. "Don't ask me what Carol sees in him either. I think the marriage is just practical because he's a neighbor."

Mara grinned. "Then it would be even more practical if she married a Redwood! Too bad Edward and James are too old for her, and Timmy is too young."

Timmy was Joseph and Laura Redwood's older son, and he was just twelve. Aside from him, Joseph and Laura had two more boys—and a little girl who'd just been born. It had taken some time for Laura to get pregnant at first, but then the children had come quickly. Joseph's brothers, Edward and James, were still unmarried.

Linda laughed. "Timmy wants to marry *me*. He gave me flowers last time I was over there with Mamaca. He's a sweet boy. Maybe he'd be right for you." She winked at Mara. "In a few years, the age difference won't matter. And isn't Eru a little younger than you too?"

Linda gazed inquiringly at Mara, who attempted to look innocent. She had been waiting all morning for her parents to bring up the subject of Eru and her tryst with him, but it looked like Chris Fenroy had decided to keep her secret. She certainly wasn't about to give it away to Linda.

"A man from the Maori village would also be a possibility for Carol," she deflected. "Actually, I'd much rather imagine Carol with a warrior than with this, um, gentleman."

Linda giggled. "Ollie is really kind of a dud, isn't he? Carol will soon be bored to death of him and his aristocratic mother. Good thing she has Fancy. Actually, the people at the farm Fancy came from also put on airs. Gwyneria Warden's husband is like Oliver. But she's a great talent with dogs and sheep. That's how I imagine it working with Carol and Ollie. Do you have plans for today? Otherwise, maybe you can ride my horse. I've been busy in the shearing shed the last few days, and Brianna hasn't even gotten out of the stall."

Kiward Brianna, a strong Welsh cob, had come from the Warden farm like Fancy. Linda had fallen in love with the mare during a visit, and had assailed Cat and Chris so long with her pleas that they'd finally bought it for her. Cat had thought it only fair to give one of the sisters the dog, and the other the horse.

Mara shrugged. "I can do that."

As she said it, another plan flashed through her head. Eru would be out with the other young warriors today. With a little luck, she'd be able to find them.

A little while later, she was sitting on the elegant brown mare, riding astraddle like all the women from Rata Station. Every time Ida sewed a riding habit, she made it with a divided skirt. It would have been terribly uncomfortable to ride Brianna sidesaddle, because she moved so powerfully. Mara happily urged her into a trot. She could understand Linda's passion for the horse when the animal broke into a smooth canter and then fluidly began to gallop. Fast as the wind, Brianna sped toward the mountains. Mara stood in the stirrups and sensed the concentrated energy of the horse moving underneath her, feeling at one with the green land and the blue sky. Sometimes she understood what the *tohunga*s meant when they encouraged their students to melt into trees or bushes and connect their spirits to those of other living beings. That was easiest for her with Eru.

Once Mara had left Rata Station and the Maori village so far behind that she could see the first of the tribe's sacred sites, she slowed Brianna and attempted to concentrate on the presence of the chieftain's son. She wasn't always able to do it, but sometimes she thought she could hear Eru's thoughts, even at a great distance.

Eru was sitting with the other young warriors on a rock that stuck out of the wide plains like the tip of an arrow. The *rangatira*, the experienced warrior who was leading the group, had told the story of this place. Two gods had been fighting over a goddess, and some mortal had died . . . But Eru hadn't been listening very carefully. In any case, he thought he could feel the vibrations in the rock. Or was he sensing something else?

While the others closed their eyes and concentrated on the *karakia*, the prayer they used to gather their strength, Eru looked up and thought he saw a horse in the distance, the image flickering in the sunlight like a mirage. The horse carried a rider. It wasn't Mara's white steed, but he couldn't help thinking it was her—which wasn't really surprising, given that he thought of Mara constantly. The melody she'd played on the *koauau* the night before still rang in his head.

The horse's hooves seemed to be gliding above the ground. Eru saw long dark hair blowing in the wind. He closed his eyes and opened them again. It was definitely Mara! Eru made up his mind.

"May I stay here?" he asked the old warrior who'd indicated to the younger ones that they should follow him and move on.

The old *tohunga* didn't talk very much; actually, he spoke with the spirits more often than he spoke to his students. Now he looked at Eru questioningly, and his gaze seemed to hypnotize the younger man.

"I—that is—I think this is a special place for me, full of power. I—" Eru stopped.

A slightly sarcastic smile spread over the old warrior's face. "The place where a boy becomes a man is always a special one, Te Eriatara," he remarked. "Just don't offend the spirits with a lie."

With that, he turned and led the other warriors toward the mountain. Eru expected to hear his friends laughing, but the boys didn't dare. He touched the rock and felt nothing more than the sun-warmed stone. But then he saw Mara riding toward him. Her silhouette gradually gained dimension and clarity in the piercing sunlight.

"I was looking for you," she said as the brown mare stopped in front of him.

Eru nodded. "You found me."

She slid down from the horse and nestled in his arms.

This morning they would do more than kiss, and Eru knew that whatever happened would have the blessings of the spirits.

Chapter 10

Though Jane could barely contain her anger and worry, there was nothing to do but wait. As expected, Eru was still away when she returned from Rata Station. Jane wanted to send someone to look for him, but Te Haitara stopped her.

"Jane, the boy is out with his *taua*." The *taua* was a group of warriors, technically the crew of a war canoe. "He would lose face with his friends and the *rangatira* if his mother checked up on him. Just wait until he returns. Nothing will happen to him. There's no war going on, Raupo. They're just visiting a few sacred sites to talk to the spirits."

But Jane grew even more agitated when Te Ropata, the *rangatira*, finally returned with the other warriors and Eru was not among them.

When she furiously confronted Te Ropata, he ignored her. But at least he spoke to the chieftain after Jane badgered him into approaching the old man.

"No, nothing happened to him," Te Haitara reported to his wife. "It's completely normal for the group to go separate ways. The spirits lead the warriors to the places where they can gather strength. Then they're allowed to stay away overnight and speak to the stars. Enough worrying, Raupo! He will come back—if not today, then tomorrow. He's a man!"

Jane heard the pride in his last words. It sounded almost as though Eru had made the leap from boy to man precisely on this day.

Jane snorted and turned away—and stormed out of the village. She wasn't likely to find Eru in the boundless plains, but she had to try. Still furious, she made her way down to the river. One Maori sacred site was as good as another, so why not start with the rock surrounded by raupo reeds that was Te Haitara's special place? There, he prayed to the river spirits, and was still convinced that it was they who had guided Jane to him. She had to smile at the thought of their first meeting, and it calmed her when she laid a hand on the stone and felt its warmth. But then she stiffened. She heard voices coming from what had once been her favorite bathing spot.

"It's much too cold! No, Eru, don't push me in!"

Splashing, rustling, giggling . . . Jane made her way through the ferns and raupo reeds as inconspicuously as she could. Here, a stream joined the Waimakariri, forming a little waterfall, and the water flowed into a natural pool. Jane could stand up in the water there, which was important, as she'd never learned to swim. But that wasn't a problem for the two young people. Mara Jensch glided through the water like a slender fish, followed by Eru's powerful form. He looked more like a whale, but he moved just as sinuously as she did. Jane stopped bothering to conceal herself. The young people were relaxed, totally unworried about being discovered.

Jane looked on in disbelief as her son pulled the girl close and kissed her. As they kissed, they kept slipping into the water, diving down and resurfacing, shrieking and giggling all the while. They baited and chased each other—and they were totally naked.

"Let me out, Eru! I'm freezing!"

Mara tried to get past her beau to the riverbank, but Eru caught her again and put his mouth on hers. Jane could see the goose bumps on their young bodies. The water must still be ice cold at this time of year. If the two of them were swimming anyway, it must be to wash off the telltale scent of love so it wouldn't give them away.

Jane stepped out from the shade of the trees. "Let her out of the water immediately, Eric. And you come out now, too, and get dressed. We have some things to discuss. With your parents too, Mara. This is over!"

"Calm down, Jane. We can't just send her away. And certainly not immediately!"

Cat was trying to be diplomatic, but it seemed no one would be able to appease Jane that evening. She had burst into a cheerful gathering around Ida's big kitchen table half an hour before. Cat, Chris, Karl, and Ida, as well as Carol and Linda and Joseph Redwood, who had stopped by on his way from Christchurch, were all there. He'd hoped to reach Redwood Station that evening, but he was traveling with a herd of twenty sheep that he'd bought from the

Deanses in Lyttelton, and the creatures had slowed him down. Now they were grazing on the hill above the stone house, guarded by the Redwoods' clever collies and the enthusiastic Fancy, while Joseph exchanged news with his neighbors. One look at Jane's face was enough to tell them that something was wrong. And she was dragging Mara behind her like a prisoner.

The girl looked distressed and angry. She had certainly been crying, but now seemed determined to defy Jane. Mara gazed at the others grimly as Eru's furious mother listed her offenses.

"I demand that she be sent away! I don't want her anywhere near Eric. I—"

"Then send your son away," Joseph Redwood said.

He was obviously amused by the situation, while Karl and Ida looked paralyzed with fear.

"It's usually boys who start such things," Joseph continued.

Jane glared at him, but it was Mara who answered.

"Neither of us started it!" she declared proudly. "It just happened. Eru thinks the spirits—I mean, we believe it was fate! We are destined for each other, and we will marry."

Cat rolled her eyes. "Can we leave the spirits out of it, please?"

"You're too young," Ida said quietly, and cast Karl a helpless glance.

It would have been hypocritical to brush off Mara's devotion as childish nonsense. Ida herself had always known that she loved Karl Jensch, and Karl had gone so far as to follow Ida to the other end of the world. She had no idea whether that had anything to do with God or the spirits. She also wasn't sure if Mara and Eru felt the same way. But she couldn't tell them not to care for each other.

Jane turned to Joseph Redwood, her eyes cold. "I also intend to send the boy away. There's a missionary school in Christchurch that accepts Maori boys and prepares them for college, provided they're good students. That wouldn't be my first choice, but my husband refuses to send him to England, and the private school in Wellington that I wanted to send him to doesn't start until autumn. The missionaries would take him right away. They don't send their students home for vacation because they don't want them to revert to their roots. They work on the fields in the summer. Eric can do that too; it will be good for him."

"But he's a warrior!" Cat cried. Only she, who had grown up with the Maori, could fully understand how Jane's decision would affect Eru and his father. "What does the chieftain have to say about this?"

Jane's gaze became even colder. "Te Haitara has agreed that Eric will have to comply with my wishes. My husband doesn't want him to be bound to an unsuitable girl either, especially not at his age."

Ida's eyes flashed angrily. "I'd like to know why you think my daughter is unsuitable."

Jane snorted. "Because she's only fifteen, Ida, and she's already not a virgin. That says everything! Eric is a chieftain's son—"

Cat took a deep breath. "Jane, you won't find a fifteen-year-old in your entire village who is still a virgin. And no one thinks that's bad, including Te Haitara. Maori girls have experiences just as early as Maori boys."

Jane's voice rose. "That isn't true for chieftains' children. I heard that chieftains' daughters are kept like—goddesses—"

"Yes," Cat said in agreement. "But that's only in certain warlike tribes on the North Island. Of course, a girl like that would never be wed to the son of a chieftain from an insignificant little Ngai Tahu *iwi.* Honestly, I don't know if those girls ever get married. They—"

"You wouldn't want that for your son, anyway," Chris interjected. "Te Haitara was only able to marry you because he's not so strongly bound by tradition. Believe me, you would not appreciate the customs of the North Island tribes."

"We're still too young to marry anyway!" Mara said, her voice ringing clearly through the room. "We'll wait for a while. But Eru certainly isn't going to marry anyone else, and neither will I!"

"The idea of waiting separately isn't so bad," Karl remarked. "Perhaps you're really destined for each other. I'm the last person who can deny that things like that can happen. But until you know for sure, you shouldn't be together, at least not in the way you were today. You—were together, weren't you?"

Mara nodded hesitantly and lowered her eyes. "We didn't actually mean to," she murmured.

"However it happened," Jane snapped, "it's not going to happen again. I repeat: send the girl away! Better today than tomorrow."

"We'll take her with us to the North Island," Ida said. "Don't try to fight me on this, Mara—you're coming with us to Russell. But we can't leave right away; there are too many things we have to sort out here. You'll have to be patient, Jane. And I can't promise that I'll lock Mara in the house either."

"Well, you can't just—" Jane's voice rose to begin a new tirade, but she went silent when Joseph Redwood held up his hand.

"Peace!" he said with a smile. "And a suggestion for the good of all: What if Mara came to visit us for a few weeks? Laura would be more than grateful for a little help around the house, especially since the sheep are being herded to the highlands soon and she'll be alone with the children. You could help her take care of the baby. Then you'll get some practice, since you're planning to be married." He winked at Mara. "Maybe you'll even decide you don't want to do that anymore. When a baby cries all night, you don't feel like doing anything." He grinned. "That should calm troubled waters a little."

Ida turned to her daughter. "That sounds like a good idea to me." Ida would have trusted Laura Redwood with her life. She couldn't think of a better influence on her daughter. "What do you think, Mara?"

Mara shrugged. For the space of a few heartbeats, she seemed to be resigned to her fate. But then she straightened her shoulders and looked Jane directly in the eyes.

"Great," she said defiantly. "I love babies!"

Chapter 11

Jakob Lange would have preferred his son to spend the last few weeks before his departure working on the farm in Hahndorf, plowing, planting, shearing sheep, and helping with the calving. Franz felt guilty about leaving, but he wouldn't have stayed even if Anna hadn't slipped a piece of paper into his hand with Ida's address on it.

"Here. Perhaps you'll have an opportunity to visit her. I know your father is angry at your older sister for some reason. But she's still your sister."

Franz knew that Rata Station couldn't possibly be anywhere near Opotiki. His posting was on the North Island, and Ida and her husband lived on the South Island. And anyway, he was still angry at Ida. She had been almost like a mother to him. How could she have left? Rationally, Franz knew Ida hadn't had a choice. She'd had to obey her husband, and Ottfried Brandmann had refused to emigrate to Australia. Neither Ottfried's father nor Jakob Lange had approved of his decision, especially since Ottfried hadn't planned to settle in a God-fearing community. He wanted to take Ida to an undeveloped area to buy and sell land. And Jakob Lange certainly never would have agreed if they had offered to take Franz with them. Perhaps Ida had even suggested it.

Franz hoped and believed that Ida still loved him. Now, God and the kind archdeacon had led him back to the country where she lived. So why shouldn't he use the remaining three weeks before his posting began to visit Rata Station? If he could only get there.

Franz's sea voyage, which had been paid for by the mission, took him only as far as Wellington, and he didn't have the money for an additional journey. But then luck seemed to be on his side. There turned out to be a ship going from Wellington to Lyttelton, which he'd heard was the closest harbor to the

Canterbury Plains. The captain was willing to take the young missionary with him if he could make himself useful, which Franz diligently attempted to do. He scrubbed the deck, helped hoist the sails, and tried all kinds of other work, but his efforts were constantly stymied by seasickness. It had plagued him on the voyage from Australia to New Zealand, and the waters of the Cook Strait were notoriously rough. Soon the sailors were joking that all he had to offer were prayers. Franz was embarrassed, and felt as though he wasn't earning his passage. Fortunately, the captain was patient, and the young missionary tried to compensate by helping as much as he could with unloading the ship at Lyttelton. Afterward, he was extremely glad to finally be on his way. He had been warned that the footpath that led from the harbor town and over the mountain to Christchurch was difficult, but there wasn't an easier alternative. Under no circumstances did Franz want to spend money for a place to sleep in Lyttelton if he could stay for free at the missionary school in Christchurch. He also didn't want to spend it on a mule ride or a boat trip to Christchurch. So, he decided to take the Bridle Path, so named because it was so difficult and dangerous that one had to lead horses and mules by the bridle to keep them from falling into canyons and over ledges.

It was still morning when Franz set out. His ship had docked at dawn, and the unloading had been completed in four hours. If the hike took five hours, he'd arrive in Christchurch in time for the evening service, and perhaps even in the afternoon. However, the first few hours of the walk seemed to take forever. Franz wondered dejectedly if God had decided not to bless his decision to visit his sister after all. The steep, narrow path went unrelentingly upward. Franz, already tired from the heavy unloading, had to stop every few steps to catch his breath. The landscape was barren and gray, and the path was lined with craggy rocks. It had been washed out in many places by rain, and was partly blocked by fallen stone that he had to scramble over. He struggled not to stumble on the slippery path, and fought back nausea all over again when it was necessary to creep along the rim of a crater. If he fell there, he wouldn't survive.

Now the sun was high in the sky. Franz was sweating in his formal black suit with the high collar. He said a prayer and asked God for help but got no answer. He worried for Ida, living in such an oppressive place. But then he reminded himself that the Canterbury Plains were known as a sheep-breeding area. That meant it couldn't be a volcanic landscape like this. Franz thought back to his family's time on the South Island, remembering green fields and meadows. Sankt Pauli Village, founded by the immigrants from Raben Steinfeld, had been beautiful—at least when the river wasn't overflowing its banks. Franz's father was still angry about how the settlers had been sold land in a floodplain, how they'd been swindled out of their dream.

Franz wiped the sweat off his forehead and walked on determinedly. He just had to get over the pass, and everything would be fine.

And then, after two more endless hours, he finally reached a plateau that was marked by a small sign as the highest point of the pass. There was a little hut there, and as Franz swayed toward it, an old man stepped outside.

"Oh, look! A customer!" He smiled broadly, showing his few remaining teeth. "I was just about to walk down to Christchurch. The regatta is going to start soon. But since you're here, can I get you a ginger beer and a sandwich?"

"Just some water, please," Franz replied.

The man raised his eyebrows. "Not the best business of the year," he grumbled, but brought a cup and pitcher and poured some fresh, cold water. Franz thought he'd never tasted anything so good.

"You run, um, an inn here?" he asked as he put the glass down, and the man refilled it. "Is it worth your while?"

The man grinned. "Well, the pub definitely isn't. I can hardly imagine that anyone would come up here just to drink a few beers. But most people who walk over the pass treat themselves to a tankard of ginger beer or a sandwich, and thank the Lord for it. So, God doesn't have anything against what I'm doing here, Reverend. Even if the beer has a little alcohol in it." He laughed.

"But I'm the only one crossing over the pass today," Franz said. "You surely can't make enough to live from."

"No, I can't live from serving you two cups of water out of charity," the innkeeper confirmed. "That's why I don't usually even open the place on Sundays, but walk down to Christchurch myself—to a proper pub! There's more traffic here on weekdays. And once or twice a month, a ship arrives with settlers from England, and then I really do good business. They're usually all dried out by their long voyages."

"So, it's worth it?" Franz asked again. "I don't mean your business; I mean the long voyages. Is it worth it for the settlers to come here?"

The innkeeper nodded. "I think so. It's a beautiful country. Look around!"

The old man gestured to the other side of the plateau. From this peak, hundreds of settlers got a look at their new home every year. Tired though he was, Franz walked around the hut to admire the view. He gazed down at a sunlit landscape, enchanted. He saw wide plains, sometimes relieved by copses of trees or large boulders. The grasslands stretched all the way to the mountains, which seemed close even though they were surely miles away. A river wound its way through the green plains. Franz had vague memories of the Moutere River where Sankt Pauli Village had been. But this river wasn't bordered by farmland. Instead, it flowed through a growing city. He could see church steeples, town squares, colorfully painted wooden houses, and a huge building made of sandstone that was still under construction. He remembered that he'd heard a cathedral was planned.

"That's Christchurch, right?" he asked.

The innkeeper nodded proudly.

"Is that where you're headed, Reverend? To the Maori school? It's a little ways out of town. The settlers don't want savages so close to them, even if they've been tamed by missionaries."

Franz shook his head. "I'm going to serve at a mission on the North Island," he explained. "I'm just visiting here. I mean, I want to visit my sister."

The man nodded kindly. "Where does she live, then? Right in town? Perhaps I know her. I know almost everyone in Christchurch." He grinned. "After all, they all had to come through this way."

Franz silently handed him the paper with the address. The innkeeper studied it for a moment.

"Oh, you have quite a journey ahead of you," he informed Franz. "Rata Station is one of the farms on the Waimakariri River. The estuary is north of Christchurch. If you're walking, it will take you a few days. It would be better to find a boatman who's going upriver and will take you with him. But today they aren't paddling for money, just for fun. It's a regatta, like they have in England." The man took Franz's empty cup and began to close up the hut. "I'll walk down with you, Reverend. Probably half of Lyttelton is already in Christchurch today, whether they're taking part in the race or just want to watch. The first regatta was two years ago in Lyttelton Harbor, y'know. Now they prefer to paddle on the Avon—the gentlemen think it has more style. Like in England. Are you from England, Reverend?"

The innkeeper, who'd introduced himself as Benny, led Franz down the pass with shocking agility for his age. The way down was almost as difficult as the way up had been. Here, too, the path was steep, and one had to be terribly careful. But every step brought Franz closer to his goal. Benny, who was often lonely up on the mountain, entertained his companion with ceaseless chattering. Everything he said seemed strange and foreign to Franz. He had never heard of rowing races, and aside from a few members of the Church Missionary Society, he didn't know any English people either—certainly not gentlemen—who took part in sporting events. Physical effort for its own sake struck him as absurd.

"It's quite possible that folks from Rata Station could be at the picnic," Benny remarked, as the steep mountain trail finally gave way to a more even footpath. "Best if you ask around a bit."

"The people come so far just for a—a regatta?"

Benny grinned. "Why not? The shearing is done, and many of the sheep are already in the highlands. Why shouldn't they enjoy a little distraction?"

Franz didn't respond. For the members of his community, rest and a change of scenery were achieved by reading the Bible or going to church. But of course they all celebrated together sometimes. There were weddings, feast days, and christenings. But nothing could have prepared Franz for the noisy, colorful festival that had taken over Christchurch that day. The entire town seemed to be on the move. Men, women, and children all wore their Sunday best, which was in no way limited to dark suits and dresses, white aprons, and tidy bonnets. Many local businessmen and their families wore their wealth on their sleeves. The women paraded in brightly colored dresses under matching parasols. Their hoopskirts rustled alluringly, and their corsets were laced tightly, creating wasp waists. The men wore elegant three-piece suits, and heavy gold watch chains poked out of their pockets. Franz noticed with surprise that most of the pubs were open, even though it was Sunday. The pub owners were serving ginger beer and punch on the street, and the people were standing in groups, drinking and laughing.

Benny was greeted cheerfully from all sides. As they walked, he was offered a beer and a few glasses of schnapps, which he happily consumed as he led Franz toward the river. There, in a parklike area surrounded by lush green lawns, was the center of the festival. Blankets were spread out on the grass everywhere, and happy people ate food from picnic baskets. Little stands had been set up to sell refreshments or to offer games of chance. Franz was shocked when a man from one booth challenged him to a hand of blackjack, and a woman at the next offered to tell his fortune.

And now something was happening on the river. Accompanied by the sounds of a marching band playing "God Save the Queen," all the boats that were taking part in the race rowed past together. They were colorfully decorated with flowers and garlands, and the audience greeted them with shouts of glee. Friends and family of the participants cheered for their favorites. Franz stared at the multicolored flotilla with fascination. There were boats of all sizes. The smallest carried only two oarsmen, and the largest carried eight. The band changed to an Irish folk song, and some of the audience joined in.

"Look, there he is! Hey, could you please step aside? You're blocking our view."

Franz started in surprise at the clear, high voice. Confused, he turned and saw two young women lounging in an unladylike manner on their blanket. They were gazing out at the boats, not caring whether their skirts covered their ankles. One of them was craning her neck to look past Franz, while the other lay on her stomach to peer between his legs. That was the girl who had spoken to him, and who didn't seem to have the least trouble reprimanding a strange man.

"Move already! Look, Linda, rata blossoms! He decorated the entire boat with them. How sweet!"

Franz stepped aside while the girl sat up and began to wave urgently.

"He doesn't see me! And I even told him where we would be sitting."

In all the excitement, her blonde hair was escaping from her pretty braids, and her blue eyes were flashing in a way that suddenly reminded him of Ida. A tricolor dog bounced happily by her feet.

"He has to row, Carol," the girl named Linda said, and then arranged her skirts more properly over her ankle boots. She took the barking dog by the collar to keep it from rushing to the river and following the boats. "As he told you many times, it's not easy to keep the boats on course. Don't worry, he'll find us afterward. Just let him win first! We don't want him to say afterward that we distracted him."

Now teams of four were passing on the river, which seemed to interest the girls less. The blonde with the braids sank back onto the blanket, resigned. To Franz's surprise, the other one, also blonde, turned to look at him.

"You're welcome to join us on the blanket, Reverend," Linda said in a melodic voice. "Then you won't be in anyone's way, and we'll all be able to see well."

Franz looked more closely at the girl, and couldn't stop the blush that crept into his cheeks. He felt impolite looking so directly, but the young lady's light blue eyes seemed to draw him in. They looked kind and gentle, and the sun flashed on golden flecks. She had an evenly formed face with strawberry-red lips. Her hair was combed cleanly back from her face and fastened in a loose bun, covered by a blue net that matched the color of her summer dress. The charming hat that the net was attached to was also sky blue and decorated with flowers. Franz had never seen such a pretty girl.

"That—that wouldn't be, um, appropriate," he murmured. "I mean, no one has introduced us."

The girl smiled. "I'm Linda Brandmann," she said. "This is Carol." Linda pointed to the girl next to her. "My sister. She's not usually so rude, but today she's a little nervous. She has to cheer for her fiancé."

Franz caught himself wondering if Linda had a fiancé too. She seemed young but remarkably self-possessed. Franz had often thought about a future wife. He'd had to. Missionaries were expected to marry, and most of his classmates from the missionary school had done so right after their ordination. They'd often chosen cousins or other distant relatives who wouldn't distract them with lustful thoughts. Franz, too, had so far only regarded women in terms of their appropriateness as preacher's wives. But looking at Linda, he suddenly began to daydream about a warm, comfortable home; laughing children; and—God save him—holding his wife in his arms and kissing her. He had to force himself to look away.

"I'm—" Franz began, but at that moment Benny appeared.

"There you are, Reverend! I see you're already getting to know some of the ladies here!" He grinned, and Franz blushed deeply. "I found someone who might know your sister. Come, I'll introduce you."

Franz stuttered a polite goodbye, which was returned cheerfully by Linda and disinterestedly by Carol, who only had eyes for the boats. Linda smiled apologetically, and Franz would have liked to return her smile but was afraid it might be inappropriate. He followed Benny without another word. The old man led him to a hay wagon that was outfitted with pillows and blankets. A large family was spread out on top of, under, and next to it. A pleasant woman with brown hair and a plump face was passing out muffins to a horde of children. Boys of various ages were playing happily. In Hahndorf, the oldest of them would already be working the fields. Here, they were chasing each other and fighting for sweets, and playing with the three or four dogs that frolicked around the wagon. A girl with long dark hair and an angelically beautiful face watched the start of the first boat race as she bounced a baby on her knee.

"Do you have a moment, Mrs. Redwood?" Benny said to the woman on the wagon, who smiled.

"Benny O'Rourke! I haven't seen you in ages. Are you still guarding the Bridle Path? And would you like a muffin?" Mrs. Redwood held out the treats.

"You know I would, but first, I'd like to introduce you to someone," Benny said. "This is Reverend—what was it again? In any case, he's looking for someone you know. Reverend, this is Laura Redwood."

Franz bowed formally. "My name is Lange," he said. The woman on the wagon showed no recognition, but the dark-haired girl turned sharply to appraise him. Franz thought he recognized something in her face. Yes, there was a certain similarity to Ida, wasn't there? He rubbed his eyes in confusion.

"I'm looking for my sister Ida," he said decisively. "Ida Jensch."

Laura Redwood beamed at him. "My goodness! You must be Franz! Ida has spoken so often of you, and worried about you. God, she'll be delighted to see you again! What a pity that she's not here right now. But I was just talking to her about—"

"Ida's here?" Franz asked, confused. He was reeling to hear that Ida hadn't forgotten him, that she'd talked about him and even worried about him.

Laura Redwood smiled indulgently. The young man seemed to be a little slow-witted. "No, she's not here," she repeated. "She's just returned from a long trip, and decided to spend more time with her friend Cat while the young people are watching the rowing. But her husband and daughter are here." Laura turned to the dark-haired girl.

"Mara," she said, "give me little Julie. And then take your uncle to your father. Reverend Lange, may I introduce you? This is your niece Margaret. We call her Mara."

Chapter 12

Mara Jensch stopped for a moment to orient herself, and then caught sight of the refreshment stand by the river. She set off toward it as elegantly as a dancer, moving so quickly that Franz could hardly keep up.

Finally, Franz spoke to her. "Your name is Margaret, child?" he asked. "Margarethe was my mother's name."

Mara nodded vaguely. "I know. Mamida told me. It's the name of a flower that doesn't grow here. I prefer Mara. Or Marama." Her voice sounded yearning. "That's a Maori word, and it means 'moon.' You, um, you're a reverend? Are you going to take a parish here?"

Franz shook his head. "No, I'm a missionary. I'm going to—"

"That's what I thought!" A triumphant smile spread over Mara's pretty face. "You're going to teach at the missionary school in Tuahiwi, aren't you?"

"I'm going to teach at the school in Opotiki," Franz said, correcting her. "On the North Island."

"Oh."

The girl seemed to be disappointed but pulled herself together again quickly. At the refreshment stand, Mara pointed to a group of men who were sipping from beer glasses and conversing comfortably. One of them, a lanky blond man, looked familiar to Franz.

"Kapa," Mara said, tapping the man on the shoulder, "this reverend says he's Mamida's brother."

Karl turned and stared at Franz Lange in disbelief. Then he smiled. "Franz! The last time I saw you, you were eight years old and horribly seasick! And now—my God, how happy Ida will be!"

Thou shalt not take the name of the Lord thy God in vain. Franz heard his father's voice in his head.

"I still get seasick easily," he replied instead, and shrank back a little when Karl kindly put an arm around his shoulders and seemed to be about to embrace him. "But since following God's path led me back to New Zealand, I saw fit to call on my sister and also to—greet her for our father."

Jakob Lange hadn't asked him to do any such thing, but after all, he hadn't known about Franz's plans to visit the South Island. Ida would expect a greeting from her father, and with this careful wording, it wasn't really a lie.

"That's a lot better than not letting her know you're in the country," Karl said. "Chris, did you hear? This is Ida's little brother! Franz, this is my friend and business partner, Christopher Fenroy."

Franz greeted Chris and the other men Karl introduced him to, including Joseph Redwood. Joseph had just ordered another round of beer, and generously pushed a tankard toward Franz.

"Let's drink to the return of the prodigal son!" Joseph said, laughing. "Or rather, the prodigal brother. Cheers, Reverend!"

Franz swallowed, but his throat was still dry. He didn't want to drink beer. Fortunately, the men quickly lost interest in him. Only Karl continued to ask questions.

"So, you intend to do missionary work with the Maori? That's a challenging task. I always get the impression that they're completely happy with their own gods. Do you speak their language?"

Franz frowned. "It has nothing to do with whether they're satisfied with their heathen beliefs. It has to do with sparing them from eternal damnation," he replied stiffly. "And as for the language, the savages should learn the language of Martin Luther, instead of us learning theirs."

Karl raised his eyebrows. "You want to teach them to speak German? I don't think that's very likely to be successful. But if you say so." He certainly didn't want to get into a theological discussion with someone from Raben Steinfeld—and somehow there seemed to be one here in front of him, twenty years after the devastation of Sankt Pauli Village. It was surreal. "Let me introduce you to the girls," he said, changing the subject. "And if you just came over the Bridle Path, you must be hungry. Come, we'll watch a few boat races and plunder the picnic basket. That is, if your older niece is in her right mind again." He turned to Mara. "Has Oliver raced yet?"

Karl smiled at his daughter, and she glanced toward the river.

"The first heats are over," Mara said. "I think they started with six- and four-man sculls. There weren't so many of them. But there are twenty of the doubles. There will be quite a few heats before it gets very exciting."

Karl sighed. "It doesn't matter. I'm hungry now. And we should make sure we get at least a few of Ida's delicious tidbits before the champion arrives and expects everything to be fed to him by his fiancée's fair hand."

Mara giggled. "Can I come with you?" she asked. "One doesn't get to meet a long-lost uncle very often!"

Her voice sounded mischievous, and Franz was surprised. Before the talk had turned to his duties at the mission, she hadn't seemed terribly interested in him.

Karl nodded. "Yes, if Laura can spare you. You haven't even told us yet if you like working for her. Do you really like babies?"

Ah, Franz thought. Ida and Karl had hired out the girl to the Redwoods. Their sheep farm must not be all that profitable.

Mara shrugged. "Julie is sweet," she said, "and I like Laura too. Have you—have you heard anything from Jane?"

Karl grinned. "You mean, have we heard anything about Eru? No, not a word. Jane must have come down hard. Oh, there are the girls!"

The commentator was just beginning to announce the final round, and four small boats were practically neck and neck. The audience cheered as soon as one pulled a little bit ahead, and shouted loud encouragement when one fell back.

As the trio made their way across the lawn, Franz's eyes sought Linda of their own volition. Carol couldn't be missed. The young woman was hopping up and down with excitement and shouting encouragement at the rowers. The energetic dog circled her, barking enthusiastically.

Linda, too, was on her feet, but she showed a little more restraint. Then she shouted for joy as well and fell into her sister's arms as a blue-and-red-striped, two-man rowing scull shot forward, just a few yards before the finish line.

"The winners of the coxless double category are Oliver Butler and Joe Fitzpatrick!" cried the rowing club representative through a gigantic megaphone.

"Yayyyy!" Carol cheered, and the dog howled along with her.

Franz realized with amazement that Karl was leading him straight toward the two young women.

"We won!" Carol threw her arms around Mara. "Did you see it, Kapa? Did you see Oliver?"

Karl grimaced. "We're not blind," he said dryly. "But at the risk of sounding like your future mother-in-law, a lady should keep her composure. Please stop leaping around like a jack-in-the-box, Carol. You too, Fancy."

The dog stopped barking and let her tail hang. Carol attempted to school her features into a more serious expression.

"Anyway, we have much more important news," Karl added. "We have a visitor from Australia." Smiling, he turned to Franz and gestured proudly at the girls. "May I introduce Reverend Franz Lange, your mother's brother. This is Carol and Linda, Franz. Our two older daughters."

Franz couldn't begin to define the feeling that overcame him when he realized Linda was his niece. It was as though he were looking at the sunny day through a dark veil. Franz only hoped that the others wouldn't notice his distress, and attempted in his mind to justify the strange attraction he'd felt for Linda by some similarity to Ida. Of course, Ida had a kind, gentle voice and a beautiful, evenly formed face as well. And his sister Elsbeth was also blonde. He thought he could see her reflected in Linda somehow too.

Still, something inside of Franz refused to acknowledge the kinship.

"But—didn't you say your name was Linda Brander?" he stammered.

"Brandmann," Linda said, correcting him.

Franz felt as though the sound of her voice not only touched his soul but his body as well. Horrified, he fought back the feeling. But now he understood. Karl had introduced the girls as his and Ida's, but they were actually from Ida's first marriage to Ottfried Brandmann.

"Now that the races are over, maybe we can open the picnic basket," said Karl, and Franz was grateful his brother-in-law's eyes were on the food and not his own burning face.

"Yes, of course!" Carol cried. "We have to lay out the picnic. Oliver will be here any minute. I invited Fitz too." Fitz was what Joe Fitzpatrick's friends called him, and she had picked up the nickname from Oliver.

While Fancy lay down politely on the grass and watched her mistress's every move, Carol got out porcelain plates, silverware, water glasses, and wine glasses, which she laid out artistically on a white tablecloth.

"It's time for the first award ceremony," Linda said.

Carol put aside her domestic endeavors for the moment and looked back to the river. The winners' boats had tied up at the pier where Christchurch's dignitaries and the board of the rowing club had been watching the regatta. To renewed strains of "God Save the Queen," the winners lined up. Mrs. Tribe, the wife of one of the rowing club's founding members, congratulated them and passed out medals.

Oliver Butler was standing in the middle of the group of athletes, and next to him was a significantly shorter, wiry man—his partner, Fitz. He shook hands with Mrs. Tribe and her husband, George Henry Tribe, as though he never wanted to stop. The Tribes seemed uncomfortable, and Mrs. Tribe pulled her hand back quickly and focused all her attention on chatting with Oliver. Carol and Linda spotted Captain Butler and his wife. They were celebrating with their son, in the midst of the most important figures of local society.

"How did the Butlers get onto the dignitaries' stand?" Linda asked.

Carol was wondering the same thing about her future in-laws, and also why they hadn't invited her to join them.

"Perhaps they joined the rowing club and donated the cost of one of the trophies," someone behind her remarked. Franz recognized Chris Fenroy, whom Karl had previously introduced. "That's how it works in aristocratic circles. You don't get the honor for nothing. But personally, I wouldn't want to be over there. There's no beer, only affected conversation with Mrs. Tribe, who is about as clever as a sheep." Chris set down the pitcher of beer he'd brought and scratched Fancy. "I prefer the company of this nice young collie. But if your happiness depends on it, girls, I'd be glad to apply for membership in the rowing club."

"You don't even row!" Carol objected.

Mara laughed. She had just opened the picnic basket, and was pulling out a bowl of grilled chicken legs. She unabashedly served herself before offering any to her father, Chris, or Franz.

Chris raised his eyebrows and took a piece of chicken. "Captain Butler probably hasn't rowed since he worked his way up from whaler to captain. God knows how he did it. Help yourself to the beer; it's for everyone."

Franz took a sharp breath as Karl picked up one of Carol's carefully polished crystal glasses and filled it with Chris's contribution to the picnic.

"That Fitz fellow rows like the devil," Chris continued, as Franz covertly crossed himself at the reference to the prince of hell. "But I hear he's still not allowed to join the club. Apparently, he's not aristocratic enough for the fine gentlemen of Christchurch."

Karl laughed. "And Butler is?" He took a chicken leg too, and watched the men on the pier silently for a moment as he chewed. "What about Weaver? Isn't he supposed to have won the money for his farm at poker?"

Chris shook his head, grinning. "No, that was Warden from Kiward Station. Apparently, Weaver found gold in Australia. He claims he wasn't sent there as a convict; bless the man who believes it."

Franz crossed himself again. Aside from Mara, who regarded him with slight astonishment, no one else seemed to notice.

"Whatever. Now they're all sheep barons, and Fitz is just the caretaker for the rowing club's boats. Oh well. Perhaps this win will help the poor devil."

Franz made a strangled sound. "And what makes you assume that there would be nothing against your own acceptance into the club?" he asked. "As a, um, gentleman so quick to blasphemy?"

Chris looked down at his chicken leg irritably. "My name," he replied casually. "And my money. The Fenroys are old English nobility, and Rata Station is a kind of sheep barony, if you will. Of course, one never knows for sure. The club votes on new members by secret ballot. Everyone gets a black and a white marble. White means yes, and black means no. If there are three black marbles in the urn—bad luck! But as Mara already said, I don't row anyway."

"And Carol will get to go to the dignitaries' stand next year anyway," Linda said, smiling consolingly at her sister. "As Oliver's wife."

In the meantime, the award ceremony had ended. The winners got in their boats and rowed back to the clubhouse. Now the teams of eight were in formation for the final heat of the regatta. The long rowing sculls were an impressive sight, and even Chris and Karl let themselves get carried away by the enthusiasm and cheered loudly with the others as the boats raced toward the finish line.

Chris recognized one of the previous farmhands of Rata Station among the oarsmen, and the men began to cheer on his boat with shouts and whistles, until it finally got a slight lead over the other.

Franz thought indignantly that his sister's husband and his friend were behaving like schoolboys, probably due to the alcohol they had consumed. His gloomy mood only lifted again when Linda caught his eye and winked conspiratorially. She, too, seemed to have notice the men's childish behavior, though she obviously didn't judge them as sternly. Her lighthearted smile seemed to lift the dark veil from Franz's eyes a little.

Carol turned back to the meal preparations, and scolded Mara for her attack on the picnic basket. "We don't eat with our hands!" she said as the girl licked the fat off her fingers. She still somehow managed to look graceful, like a Persian cat cleaning itself.

"How else is she supposed to eat?" Karl said with a smile, coming to Mara's defense. "This is a picnic, Carol. Do your mother and Cat bring porcelain plates when we drive the sheep to the highlands?" In fact, neither Ida nor Cat even owned such fancy dishes. Carol had found these in the back of a cupboard in the stone house. They had surely been part of Jane's dowry. "Relax! Oliver will be so hungry after the race that he won't be thinking about table manners, anyway."

Before Carol could express any doubts, they heard more applause and shouts from the audience at the edge of the water. They were cheering for Oliver Butler. The young man was walking along the riverbank, happily greeting his fans on all sides.

Carol waved him over exuberantly.

Franz was embarrassed, but the others applauded as Oliver took his fiancée in his arms and kissed her.

"We won!" he cried. "Didn't I tell you we would?" He triumphantly took the medal from around his neck and put it on Carol. The young woman nestled proudly into his arms. "And it's all thanks to Fitz. Where did he go, anyway?"

Chapter 13

During Oliver's march of triumph through the crowd, Joe Fitzpatrick had been standing in the shade nearby. It was no wonder that everyone knew Oliver Butler. Butler Station was one of the oldest and best-known sheep farms in the region. But Joe had only been in the Canterbury Plains for a few months. His curious gaze took in the residents of Rata Station. Then he focused on Linda, who was standing slightly apart from the group, like him.

Their eyes met, and Linda openly returned Joe's gaze. Unlike Oliver, who was almost a head taller than Carol, Linda thought Fitz must be only slightly taller than herself. His legs seemed a little short in relation to his strong, muscular body and arms—it was easy to see he was an accomplished oarsman. His face wasn't classically handsome like Oliver's, but quite interesting. He was square-jawed and tanned. His full lips seemed perpetually poised in a mischievous smile. His nose was straight and distinctly formed, and his eyebrows and hair were lush and dark. His hair was short but nonetheless unruly, as though it didn't want to capitulate to being cut. His blue eyes offered an unusual contrast to his otherwise Mediterranean looks. Linda also thought she'd never seen such astute eyes. Fitz's eyes seemed to flash, but without making his gaze seem piercing or unsettling. He simply showed a steady, mindful interest in everything that was happening around him. The man was doubtlessly a good observer, and he managed to make whomever he was with feel important. Without a doubt, it was ungentlemanly to stare at anyone as intensely as he currently stared at Linda. Yet she didn't feel bothered, but rather flattered and blessed by a sense of warmth for being the center of his attention. Without breaking eye contact once, he sidled over.

"Are you the other twin, then?" he finally asked, and winked at her. "I'm the second oarsman, at least from the audience's point of view. They only have eyes for Ollie. How is it for you? Were you the first or the second?"

Linda looked bewildered. "First or second at what?" she asked.

"At birth," Fitz said. "Which of you has the—birthright, as the Bible puts it? And who is the coxswain who steers the boat?" He grinned.

Linda had to laugh, though she knew she should really have been offended.

"Carol was the first," she replied. "She's a few hours older." Actually, it had been a few days, but the girls had introduced themselves as twins so often that the small deviation from the truth had almost become reality for them. "She's the one who usually calls the shots," Linda admitted. "People pay more attention to Carol."

A second later, she could have slapped herself for making it sound as though she were jealous of her sister. It's just she'd never thought about things that way before. And now this man would assume she felt inferior. Which would mean that he'd pity her.

But Fitz just shrugged. "We're two of a kind, then," he said simply, and immediately changed the subject. "Is that fantastic-looking feast for us?" He pointed to the picnic cloth, the bowls, platters, and baskets of bread and cheese, ham and cold meats, eggs, and various preserves from Ida's kitchen.

Linda nodded.

"Then may I accompany you to the table?"

Fitz bowed formally to Linda, as though they were at a society ball. Smiling, he offered her his arm. Before she could take it with an equally theatrical gesture, Oliver caught sight of his friend.

"Fitz, there you are! Carol, this is Fitz. Linda—"

"Joe Fitzpatrick," he said politely. "I'm pleased to make your acquaintance."

He directed his words at Carol, but somehow managed to make Linda think he wasn't speaking to anyone in the world but her.

The rest of the afternoon was as relaxed and wonderful as Carol had hoped. The picnic was fabulous, even if it began awkwardly when Reverend Lange pointed out that no one had said grace. Of course Karl and Chris offered politely to let him say it himself, whereupon everyone had to listen for a quarter of an hour as

Franz thanked God. After that, it took several jokes from Fitz to loosen things up again. Linda opened the two bottles of wine they'd brought, and Karl and Chris refilled the beer glasses as well before they began to eat.

Carol realized that no one was saying "please" or "thank you" the way people did at the Butlers' garden parties. She hoped Oliver wouldn't take it too badly. But then she relaxed a little when she saw how much everyone was enjoying the food.

Oliver and Fitz were both famished from their efforts and ate with gusto. Oliver at least pulled the chicken from the bone using his fingers instead of his teeth, while Fitz gnawed just as shamelessly as Mara, Chris, and Karl. And just like Mara, he somehow managed to look graceful while he did it. While Carol served the wine with a flourish and Oliver formally tasted it before she filled his glass, Fitz helped himself to some beer.

Fitz was quite entertaining company, and seemed to relish making the girls laugh. He interrupted Oliver's third long-winded description of the race, and instead told stories about the legendary boat races between Oxford and Cambridge.

"You went to school in Oxford?" Linda asked in surprise.

Fitz nodded. "You could say that. Student life was very appealing."

"What did you study?" Carol asked.

He shrugged. "This and that. Rowing. How to drink and fight like a man. How to handle horses and write poems. How to court a girl—" He winked at Carol.

"But above all, *whaikorero*, the art of talking nonsense," Mara remarked, unimpressed. "Did you also happen to study something useful?"

"You sound just like Jane," Linda scolded.

Mara giggled. "Perhaps I'm more like her than she thinks. So, tell us now, Mr. Fitzpatrick! What were you intending to do with your life? Were you planning to become a doctor, lawyer, teacher? And why didn't you?"

"Mara!" Linda cried. She thought she'd sink into the ground with embarrassment. Of course it had also occurred to her that Fitz must not have completed his studies, but she never would have dared to ask why.

Fitz grinned at the girls, totally unruffled. "At some point I figured out that I didn't *have* to become anything else," he replied. "I'm already something. I'm

Joe Fitzpatrick. And anyone who doesn't like what I am doesn't have to spend time with me."

Karl had been listening to the young people's conversation. He himself was bored to death with Franz. The reverend wasn't an enthusiastic conversationalist, and any detail about his studies or his family had to be pried out of him. Now he noticed the glow in Linda's eyes.

"You still have to make a living somehow, young man," he remarked. "It wouldn't hurt to earn some money, especially if you're planning to court a girl."

Fitz shrugged. "Money comes and goes," he said. "I'm happy when I have it, but I'm also satisfied when I don't. It's like the Bible says: 'Behold the fowls of the air: for they sow not, neither do they reap, nor gather into barns; yet your heavenly Father feedeth them.' Or something like that."

"Faith is the only true wealth," Franz added, without having really caught what the conversation was about. "True happiness is only found by following Jesus Christ."

Fitz's expression sobered. "Our Lord, too, was poor. That's exactly what I mean, Reverend. We shouldn't cling to material things!"

Franz nodded enthusiastically.

Chris reached for the empty beer pitcher and got up. "Blessed are the poor," he remarked, and crossed himself. There had been tension between him and Ida's brother from the beginning. Karl hardly seemed to notice, but it annoyed Chris that Franz seemed to resent every sip of beer the men took. Now he'd had enough of the young missionary's judgment. "I'm going to continue praying at the beer stand. Would you like to join me, Karl?"

Karl wavered. He did want to follow his friend, but he didn't want to be impolite. After all, he'd have to deal with Franz as a guest for a while.

"What are your plans, Franz?" he said, turning to the missionary. "For today, I mean. We're sleeping at the Deanses' farm in Riccarton, along with the Redwoods. I could ask if they have an extra bed for you. And of course, tomorrow you'll come with us to Rata Station."

Karl knew that putting up the Redwood family was already a huge demand on the Deanses' hospitality. They had offered guest rooms for Linda, Carol, and Mara. Karl and Chris were prepared to sleep in the barn. Of course, there would be space in the barn for Franz, too, but Karl rather thought that the reverend wouldn't feel comfortable with the company of cows and horses. What was more, Karl and Chris had brought a bottle of whiskey to help them fall asleep, and they didn't need Franz's disapproving looks.

"I will be staying with the brothers at the mission in Tuahiwi," Franz Lange said stiffly. "They answered my letter very kindly, and are pleased to be able to show me their school and will allow me to stay as long as I wish."

Mara listened closely. Would her uncle be useful to her after all?

"That means you still have a good distance to travel. It's quite far from here to Tuahiwi. If you really intend to walk there, you'll have to be on your way soon," Karl replied.

Franz swallowed. He'd assumed that the missionary school was in the town of Christchurch, and wasn't ready for another long hike. But he accepted his fate with humility. A long walk would still be better than watching Linda exchange compliments with Joe Fitzpatrick. At least the young rower seemed to be a good Christian in some way. But every smile that Linda bestowed on Joe was painful for Franz. Although he told himself that, as her uncle, he had no right to be interested, and in general must never stare at young women, he couldn't tear his eyes off Linda.

Over the course of the picnic, Franz's feelings had swung between irritation and envy of Fitz and Oliver. He was reluctant to approve of Karl, because his brother-in-law acted as though he didn't even see Carol and Oliver's kissing or Fitzpatrick's shameless flirting with Linda. And Mara sat there casually and kept making sarcastic remarks instead of taking care of her employers' children, as was seemly for a girl of her station. Incomprehension and resentment were building up in Franz. The walk to Tuahiwi was probably God's way to punish him for it.

"Then perhaps I should take your advice and be on my way," he replied. "And who knows, perhaps I'll find a generous soul headed that way in a wagon. Could you please just point out the way, Karl, and tell me where to meet you tomorrow morning for the journey to Rata Station?"

Mara leaped to her feet. "I'll show you where to go, Reverend—I mean, Uncle Franz." She smiled. "I have to get back to the Redwoods, anyway. I'll see you all later at the Deanses'!" She waved innocently at her sisters, Chris, and her father before they had a chance to think up a reason why she shouldn't go. "Come, Uncle."

Franz Lange said goodbye and followed the girl through the festivities and then to a well-maintained road that led north, parallel to the coast. "You just follow this road until you reach the Waimakariri River. You'll have to find a ferryman to take you across. Afterward, you go north again. I've never been that way, but it's such a well-used path, you'll find it for sure."

Franz nodded. "And where shall I meet everyone tomorrow?"

Mara thought a moment. "We'll be going upstream by boat, but you don't have to worry about that. I'll pick you up at the school early tomorrow morning."

Chapter 14

Mara slipped out of the Deanses' house before dawn. She didn't know if the reverend could ride, but she expected it from a man who planned to bring God's word to an undeveloped area. If the Church Missionary Society wanted the new messengers of the Lord to get anywhere, they must surely teach them about horses.

Mara took her white horse and one of the Redwoods' horses—the residents of Rata Station had come by boat—and made her way north. The strong brown gelding that walked politely next to her own steed belonged to Joseph Redwood, and of course he would wonder where it had gone. Mara briefly considered leaving a note for him, but she'd already written one for Laura. She'd stuck it on Julie's bassinet so they would know where she was and that she would meet the others at the river. She hoped that she wouldn't get in too much trouble when she arrived with the reverend. His sudden appearance was a gift from heaven—or from the spirits. She would have ridden to Tuahiwi anyway, but Franz Lange offered a perfect excuse.

In spite of the darkness, the well-traveled road to the Waimakariri was easy to follow. Mara quickly put the first few miles behind her. The river crossing was more difficult. She didn't find the ford immediately and got wet when her steed unexpectedly sank up to the edge of the saddle. Then she noticed a rowboat that was tied to a pier, and backtracked. Without a moment's thought, Mara took the boat and let the horses swim next to her. She tied it up on the other side, intending to be back with the reverend before the ferryman appeared to start his work.

On the north side of the Waimakariri, the path was considerably narrower. Mara had thought she'd be passing a few farms here, but apparently the missionary school was really quite far from any *pakeha* settlement. Now the girl was happy that she was on horseback and hadn't brought a wagon. There must be a track that was obvious during the day because the school had to get supplies from Christchurch somehow. But now in the darkness, it was almost impossible to see anything. The path wound through dark thickets of raupo and southern beech woods. Every now and then, Mara recognized the silhouettes of nikau palms or ironwood trees, which were related to the "fire blossoms" that grew all over Rata Station.

Mara felt almost sorry for the reverend, who'd had to hike through this dismal area alone the day before. He had almost certainly not been offered a ride as he had been hoping.

But then, finally, a building came into view. The sign read "Tuahiwi Missionary School."

In front stood a large double gate of solid wood, and of course it was closed. A gigantic bell hung next to it, but Mara decided to ride around the high fence instead. There would surely be other, less well-protected entry points. Aside from its height, the woven fence looked like the kind that would surround a *marae*. If Maori workers had built it, the missionaries seemed to have requested something more appropriate to enclose a *pa*, a fort, than a village or a school. The fence was solidly made and almost impossible to see through. Pointed, sharpened stalks at the top discouraged climbing. Mara was shocked. Where had Eru been sent? This wasn't a school; it was a prison!

Peering through as best she could, she thought she could make out some kind of sleeping house, and pulled the *koauau* out of her pocket. But no matter how many secret calls she played, nothing stirred inside the compound. Disappointed, Mara continued along the fence. That, too, proved unsuccessful. At least she knew now how huge the school grounds were. It took her quite a while to ride around them, even though she was moving quickly. Outside, the school was surrounded by fields and orchards. These were probably cared for by the students, an idea that made Mara feel a little better. Eru must at least be let out sometimes under supervision, which meant escape was possible.

Now dawn was beginning to break, and she could hear voices, orders, and whispers. Finally, she heard a kind of church bell ringing, which must be the call to morning prayer. There would probably be breakfast soon after that.

Mara had reached the main gate again, and felt a twist of hunger alongside a little burst of nerves as she pulled the bell rope.

She waited with a pounding heart until she thought she heard a bolt being moved from inside. But the heavy gate didn't open. Instead, a small shutter was folded back, and a man in a priest's cassock peered out from between bars, looking irritated.

"What do you want at this hour?"

Mara put on her friendliest face. "Good morning," she said politely, and hoped the man didn't expect to hear something like "God's greetings." "I'm sorry to bother you so early. My name is Margaret Jensch, and I'm here to pick up my uncle, Reverend Fritz Lange."

A few moments later, Mara was sitting in a surprisingly large room, which had space not only for the missionaries and their staff but approximately fifty students as well. The church was a longhouse, similar to the Maori meetinghouses. And like a *wharenui*, it was decorated with carvings. Of course, no tikis guarded the entry, and Bible scenes replaced the traditional fernlike designs. A missionary was giving a sermon at a simple altar in front of a wooden cross.

Mara sat down in one of the first pews, next to her uncle. She couldn't see Eru but thought she could sense his surprised and confused gaze on her back. He must be far in the back with the oldest students. The younger ones were sitting up front.

Mara had only gotten a fleeting look at the children, and had quickly determined that they were exclusively mixed children of Maori and *pakeha*. Their school uniforms looked to her like prison clothes. The boys wore wide linen trousers and shirts, and the girls wore unornamented linen blouses and skirts. The boys' hair was chopped short as matchsticks, and the girls' was tightly braided. Aside from two or three students who were being strictly reprimanded by the missionaries, the children were perfectly behaved.

The silence before the first prayer was eerie in comparison to the usual noisy, happy chaos of normal tribal children. Maori children grew up free. They were loved by the entire tribe, and never beaten or scolded. When Mara tried to imagine what must have been done to the six- and seven-year-olds to make them sit in the pews quietly with their heads lowered and dispassionately sing hymns, she felt sick to her stomach. Mara herself didn't even know half of the prayers that were said in the next hour, but she did know most of the songs. Miss Foggerty had insisted that, if she was to teach in a Maori village, she wanted to bring the children closer to Jesus. Te Haitara had agreed, and Jane didn't care as long as the usual lessons didn't suffer for it. Chris Fenroy had joked that he didn't care if she taught the children to multiply the twelve apostles by the seven plagues, as long as they were taught math.

Miss Foggerty had quickly realized that the children weren't particularly interested in Bible stories, but they did like the hymns. Therefore, there had been plenty of singing in her Sunday school classes, and Mara made use of that now. Her unusually beautiful voice rang out effortlessly over the subdued, listless voices of the students. At the end, she was singing "Amazing Grace" as a solo, the others having reverted to awestruck silence. She put all her longing for Eru into the song, winning the hearts of the missionaries and their devout Maori staff. When it was over, the cook wept, and the gardener reverently labeled the girl a *tohunga*. Mara politely declined the honorific.

To Mara's astonishment, the only person not pleased with her singing was Franz Lange. "God gave you a beautiful voice, Margaret," he said sourly, "but every talent conceals the risk of falling prey to the sins of pride and arrogance."

Before Mara could reply, the headmaster invited her to breakfast. Mara and her uncle were to take their morning meal in the missionaries' private dining room, not with the students. Mara was pleased. They would probably be served better food, and what was more, it would give her the chance to slip out and look for Eru.

As soon as she'd devoured two slices of buttered toast with cheese and English marmalade, Mara excused herself and left the mission house. She had seen where the children had gone after the morning service—the compound was made up of various buildings with specific purposes, again very much like a Maori village. She could hear the clanking of dishes from the long, low wooden dining hall, and would have expected to hear chitchat and laughter as well. After all, fifty children and teenagers were eating there. But apparently the decree of silence extended to meals. It made Mara feel sorry for the children, but it was also to her advantage. In the shadow of a southern beech, she took out her flute.

Eru appeared quickly. He must have been waiting for her and had an excuse ready. Now he silently put a finger to his lips and gestured for her to follow. They sought cover behind houses, bushes, and trees, until Eru led the girl to a shed and closed the door behind them with a sigh of relief. The room was full of rakes, spades, and other gardening tools.

"We can be alone here for a moment," he whispered, "but not very long, unfortunately. Right after breakfast they send the children to the fields, and before that they have to pass out the tools."

"I thought this was a school!" Mara said, shocked.

Eru snorted. "We get a 'day off' for the planting. And it's not so long until the summer vacation begins. Didn't you tell me about the wonderful three months before we start school in Wellington?"

Mara shrugged. "It seemed like a good idea," she said.

Eru nodded. "We should have been more careful. But let's not talk about this place, or our shattered plans. How did you get here? I thought I was dreaming when I saw you next to the old ravens."

Mara laughed. It was a good name for the dark-robed, serious-faced leaders of the Church Missionary Society.

"I wanted to see you," she said. "And I thought maybe you'd kiss me again."

Eru's tense face became softer. "Of course," he said softly, and pulled her close.

Mara tilted her face toward him, and gave herself up to joyful abandonment as she finally felt her beau's body against hers again. His tongue in her mouth, his rough skin on her cheek, his warmth as she nestled against him . . . Only his smell was different. The mission students washed with curd soap, nothing like Jane's lavender. He didn't have the earthy sweat smell of a warrior anymore either.

"You're so beautiful," Eru whispered. "Marama, however did you manage to get here?"

"Can anyone stop the moon from shining on you? Can anyone stop the stars from lighting the path that leads to you?" she asked in Maori. "You're beautiful too, Eru. I had to see you again."

Eru kissed her again. "You're a poet," he whispered. "And it's good to hear my language again. It's strictly forbidden to speak it here, you know."

Mara's jaw dropped. "So that's why the children are so quiet! They probably can't all speak English yet."

Eru nodded. "That's true for a few of the younger ones," he said. "But the older ones—we talk, but only when the ravens aren't listening. We speak

English, mostly. The students who have been here a long time have forgotten a lot of their Maori. After all, the missionaries are working hard to turn us all into brown-skinned, black-haired *pakeha*. As if no one who looked at us would be able to tell the difference!"

"That's horrible!" Mara said. "To forget your own language—how are the children supposed to speak to their parents and the rest of their tribe when they go home?"

Eru snorted. "They don't. At least, they're not meant to. That's why the school is open during holidays. Then the children learn agriculture, gardening, and animal husbandry, as well as kitchen and housework. The way the *pakeha* do it, of course. Don't go thinking the kids here dare to sing a *karakia* when they dig up sweet potatoes. As soon as they're old enough, they're given jobs. The settlers in Christchurch are constantly looking for staff. Apparently, they tried importing orphans from England, but it didn't work out very well. The children arrive here hungry and terrified if they don't die during the voyage, and they aren't particularly useful either. This school, on the other hand, produces ten powerful young Maori workers a year, well mannered and God-fearing, and accustomed to hard work. And the mission takes half of their pay as compensation for all the 'charity' they've shown." His hands clenched into fists.

Mara stared at him. "Are these all orphans?" she asked. "They must belong to a tribe."

He shook his head. "Only a few are orphans. Most of them come from converted tribes. Their parents have been talked into believing that they should be grateful for being accepted to the school. The tribes have been cheated in land sales and every other kind of deal with the *pakeha*. They want to avoid that in the future, and they think sending their children to a *pakeha*-type school is a good way to do it. If they only knew what it's like, and what's happening to their children . . ."

Mara nodded in agreement. The tribal elders would doubtlessly be appalled at how the children were being treated. "When they leave here, they aren't Maori anymore, but they aren't *pakeha* either," Mara said softly.

"Exactly," Eru said bitterly. "They'll all be turned into compliant slaves if no one does anything about it! But believe me, the Maori won't put up with this for very long. In Taranaki—"

"In Taranaki there was a revolt," she said, furrowing her brow. "But now there's peace. We were just there. Of course, there's still some disagreement—"

"Disagreement?" Eru laughed. "Things are coming to a head, Mara. My people are banding together, even in the missions! There's a man on the North Island called Te Ua Haumene. At first, he was just a well-behaved sheep like these children, but now he has visions. He foresees the Maori rising up and expelling the invaders from our country! We have to accept our birthright and fight for Aotearoa like the Israelites once fought for their holy land!"

Mara considered telling her beau about her encounter with the prophet. "Where did you hear all that?" she asked instead. "I mean, the missionaries surely aren't telling you about revolts on the North Island. And your tribe—"

"My tribe isn't interested in politics," Eru agreed. "My mother only thinks about money, and my father about how to keep his people calm. Bread and games, just like the old Romans."

"Bread and games?"

Mara vaguely remembered her history lessons with Miss Foggerty. She struggled to see the connection between Te Haitara's attempts to conjure the spirits of money so he could fulfill the wishes of everyone in his tribe and the decadence of the Roman gladiator games.

"It all comes down to the same thing," Eru said. "They're trying to keep the people from thinking too much, and they are starting to forget their traditions. Te Ua Haumene will lead us back to honor."

Mara bit her lip. "Eru, you're scaring me a little. Your people, my people—I always thought Aotearoa belonged to all of us. Who's telling you all this?"

"There's a boy here from the North Island," Eru explained. "He was at a missionary school there, but then he heard Te Ua Haumene's words and figured out what was what. He started to preach to the other students, so the old ravens sent him away."

"And now he's preaching here," Mara said. She marveled at the missionaries' shortsightedness. How could they have thought that sending the boy to the South Island would silence him? Of course he'd found new followers. After Te Ua Haumene's speech to the Ngati Hine, Mara hadn't given the preacher another thought. To her, his words and airs had just seemed crazy. Her father, however, had said the man was quite dangerous.

Eru himself didn't seem to want to expound further. Perhaps he was thinking of how Mara would be affected if the *pakeha* were indeed driven out.

"You still haven't told me how you got here," he said.

Mara told him briefly about her strange uncle. "That means I have to go soon," she said unhappily. "They'll be looking for you as well."

Eru sighed. "It was wonderful to see you again," he said after he'd kissed Mara once more. "I thought I would never—"

"Never see me again? What do you mean? Eru, are you planning something?"

Eru nodded uncertainly. "I'm planning to run away. If there's fighting on the North Island, if we make a stand against the English, then I want to do my part!"

Mara stared at him, horrified. "Eru, you're half-*pakeha* yourself! You—"

"First and foremost, I am Maori," Eru said gravely. "Otherwise, I wouldn't be in this awful place! And I will do what I must."

"I'll get you out of here!" Mara said desperately. "I don't know how I'm going to do it, but I'll manage somehow. You're getting out of here and you're coming home. I swear! You just have to promise me that you won't do anything stupid. Stay here, Eru; don't go to the North Island! Don't leave me, Eru!" She reached for his hands.

Eru took her hand. "I would never leave you," he said. "But—"

"No buts, Eru! Promise me that you'll stay here until your parents bring you home."

"They'll never do that," he replied.

"Swear it!" Mara wouldn't be deterred.

Eru rubbed his brow. Then he conceded. *"Ki taurangi,"* he murmured. "I swear it. Could we seal that with a kiss?"

Mara took a deep breath for courage as she finally turned back toward the mission house, while Eru returned to the other students. She hoped the missionaries would believe her flimsy excuse that she'd gone to check on the horses and gotten lost. And above all, she hoped that Eru would keep his promise until she found some way to free him.

Chapter 15

"We thank thee, Lord, our Father, for blessing us with food and drink . . ."

Ida Jensch kept her eyes lowered, mostly just grateful for having survived another dinner with her brother. In a few more days, Franz would finally leave for the North Island. No matter how ashamed it made her, Ida could hardly wait. Of course she'd been overjoyed to see her brother again. She had embraced him, laughing and crying. But when she asked if her father, Anna, and the children were happy in Australia, she was met with a stony silence. Franz first gazed at her uncomprehendingly, and then replied with a sermon. A Christian should be happy anywhere he can hear God's word and serve him with his hands and prayers, he'd said. Australia's soil was fertile, and they had filled the earth and subdued it, as the Bible instructed. Decent people shouldn't expect anything more.

When Ida despondently told Karl about the conversation, her husband replied sarcastically.

"If Franz wanted nothing more than to grub in the earth while Jakob Lange cracked his whip, then why did he go to seminary?" Karl didn't buy it, no matter how often the young missionary insisted that he had merely submitted to the Lord's call.

"The man lacks everything that makes a good preacher," Chris Fenroy said in agreement. "Sure, he seems to know the whole Bible by heart." Franz often surprised them with extended recitations. "But he doesn't have any presence or charisma. Could you imagine him describing the kingdom of God colorfully enough to the Maori that they would want to give up all their spirits and eternal paradise under the Hawaiki sun?"

The Maori afterlife was set on a gorgeous South Sea island. Ida, who was always longing for sun and wide beaches, found it far more attractive than the Christian version of heaven—something she'd always felt a little guilty about.

"I don't know what they taught him at missionary school," Karl said, "but to deliver God's word to the wilderness, he has to be able to get there first. The man doesn't even know how to ride."

It was true. Franz had driven Mara crazy on the trip from Tuahiwi to the mouth of the Waimakariri. The young reverend had insisted he could ride, but had actually slipped helplessly back and forth in the saddle. Joseph Redwood's bay had carried him faithfully, but as soon as Mara had made any attempt to pick up speed, Franz had almost fallen off.

Finally, he admitted to only having ridden his father's draught horse to the watering hole occasionally, and Mara had to adjust her tempo for his weakness. As a result, uncle and niece only arrived at the river by late afternoon, which got Mara in trouble with her father and Joseph Redwood. Their irritation was also aimed at Franz. After all, if he'd admitted his limitations, they could have left earlier. What was more, Karl was angry at himself for allowing fifteen-year-old Mara to pick up her uncle. That had meant a long ride alone through the dark for the girl.

"Franz just doesn't think about things like that," Ida said, defending her brother, as she felt she must at every opportunity. "He's too excited about bringing the Maori closer to God."

"Oh, really?" Karl said after she'd used that excuse several times. "I get the feeling he's scared of them. Even of Te Haitara. Franz behaved quite strangely when he was here."

Ida had been watching her brother and knew Karl was right. Franz couldn't manage a conversation with any of the Maori who worked on the farm or came to visit. He seemed to be offended by their tattooed faces, and made no attempt to learn even a few words of their language, even though Cat had offered to help him several times.

Chris refused to support the missionary in any way, and Mara's shocked report about the conditions in Tuahiwi had only hardened his anti-proselytizing stance. He liked to say that the Maori already had enough gods, and it was pointless to try to convert them.

He tactlessly informed the young missionary of his opinion during a Maori-style dinner that Cat had prepared, prompting heated discussion. Cat had served fish with sweet potatoes and taro, seasoned with berries and herbs from the plains. It was Mara's favorite meal, and she had come to join them for a weekend after working with the Redwoods. She had told her employers she needed a break from the hubbub with the children. Now she ate enthusiastically and entertained the group with anecdotes about the Redwoods' family life, until she and all the others noticed that Franz was poking skeptically at the unfamiliar food. He announced that, at the missionary school in Tuahiwi, he had been served shepherd's pie, and the students had been given porridge and stews, as they would eat at similar institutions in England.

Mara objected immediately. She was no longer trying to impress her uncle. Since her visit to Tuahiwi, she categorically rejected everything that had to do with missionaries.

"Eru says it tastes terrible. At the beginning, most of the children refuse to eat it," she said, interrupting the reverend.

Franz gave her an angry look. Having learned about her motivation for meeting him in Tuahiwi, he could only see the girl as a sinner.

"We must all thank God for everything he gives us to eat, and that's especially true for the heathen children we educate in our school—" Franz began.

But Chris wasn't having it. "You aren't doing the Maori any favors by repressing their beliefs and culture, Reverend. Besides, in the end, they'll just add the Father, the Son, and the Holy Ghost to their own contingent of spirits. I highly doubt that what Te Ua Haumene is preaching on the North Island is still Christianity."

A few days before, Chris had received a letter that made him deeply uncomfortable. It was from the chieftain of a nomadic tribe and had actually been sent to Te Haitara, who'd shown it to Chris. The northern chieftain reported that a preacher had stopped at his *iwi*, wanting to found a new church called Hauhau, after Te Hau, the spirit of the wind. He'd included in his letter a booklet of sorts, a piece of scripture written by Te Ua Haumene. The prophet had been born as Tuwhakaro, but changed his name after an epiphany in which the Christian God and angels had appeared to him.

Cat, who was even better at Maori, had read the booklet, titled *Ua Rongo Pai*, and discovered a hodgepodge of Christian scripture and Maori legend.

Essentially, Haumene applied everything that had happened to the Israelites to the Maori. Suddenly, the Maori were the chosen people, and Canaan was replaced by New Zealand. The text was also full of many new terms derived from English, like *niu* for "news."

"Such a corruption of the Holy Scripture will not be tolerated!" declared Franz Lange when Chris showed him Haumene's words.

Chris shrugged. "How do you propose to stop it? This nonsense has already spread like wildfire."

"You could also say the bush is burning," Karl added. For Ida's sake, he had been trying to mediate between Franz and Chris, but now he had also received an unsettling letter. The governor and the head surveyor wanted to know how quickly he could get back to the North Island. "There's more and more unrest. There just aren't enough preachers who can reassure their flocks that God is always with them."

"The Church Missionary Society preaches only peace," Franz intoned, but Chris just laughed.

"During the Musket Wars, missionaries sold weapons to the Maori!" he said. "Even though they like to deny it. That has nothing to do with love."

"I would never sell weapons to anyone!" Franz insisted. But it was hopeless; the discussion was obviously over his head. He knew as little about the Maori as he did about the history of his own church. "I became a missionary because I wanted to bring people light, and teach them to read and write—"

Chris raised his eyebrows. "They already know about gas lanterns," he joked, "but they usually don't have the money to buy them. Of course, reading and writing can be useful in order to earn some. But, Reverend, it isn't your main goal to turn the Maori into faithful servants of the Lord?"

"No, it isn't," Karl said, abandoning any attempts at neutrality. "To the contrary. The goal of the missionaries is to put people in their place. And in the case of the Maori, that place is very low on the ladder. The *pakeha* can read and write, but they require the natives to give up their gods in order to be allowed to learn. And then the missionaries only teach them enough to be able to read the scriptures that establish their inferiority as a rule. I recognize all that from Raben Steinfeld. I had to flee my home in the dead of night because I refused to acknowledge 'the life that God has ordained' for me. So, I can understand it very well if the Maori have loftier ambitions than servitude."

"You understand Te Ua Haumene?" Mara asked. To Chris and Cat's surprise, she had asked to read the little booklet and had practically devoured it. "I thought you said he was dangerous."

Karl shook his head. "What I mean is, I understand his anger and I understand his strategy, which is basically the same one the missionaries use. It's no wonder, considering that's where he learned it. Haumene has just turned the tables. Now he wants the Maori to feel superior to the *pakeha*. In the end, two armies will be facing each other who both think God is on their side. You can't bring anyone light that way," he told his brother-in-law. "All you're doing is feeding the fire."

Ida sighed with relief when Linda shyly changed the subject and told a story about something funny that had happened in the Maori village. Since Miss Foggerty had quit, surprising them all by marrying a gold prospector and moving to Australia with him, Linda had been teaching the village children three times a week.

They finished the meal, and Franz said a short prayer of thanks. Then he retreated to the guest room where he was staying in the stone house.

Ida wasn't sorry to say good night. She was tired of the arguments and ready for Franz to finally leave for the North Island. She wasn't worried about him, in spite the volatile political climate. The mission at Opotiki had been established for a long time; Ida and Karl had even stopped there during their travels. The head missionary, a German named Voelkner, seemed to be a peaceable, simple man. He would never provoke a Maori tribe intentionally.

At Rata Station, Franz's departure would restore the peace—not only within the family, but also Ida's personal peace. After all, Franz wasn't the only one who'd given hesitant and unsatisfying answers about his life. Ida didn't feel able to speak freely with her brother either, even though she would have liked to pour out her heart to him. She wished she could tell him about her ex-husband's responsibility for the Wairau conflict and his crimes against herself and Cat.

But Franz was so physically fragile and so removed from reality that sometimes Ida had the feeling she was talking to her father. Of course she never would have told Jakob Lange about both women becoming pregnant after being raped by Ottfried, or about the lie of necessity that Carol and Linda were twins. So, Ida kept the secret from her brother as well. Ida also lied to him about the events surrounding Ottfried's death. She said that her first husband was caught stealing sheep and had been killed during his attempt to avoid arrest—which was true. But what Ida left out was that she herself had fired the deadly shot.

Ida suffered for her silence. She hated lies and secrecy, and wished she could relax and enjoy the reunion with her brother. Additionally, Cat made an observation that unsettled her even more. Her friend actually didn't care whether Franz learned the truth about the girls' parentage, but left it to Ida's discretion. At the beginning of the second week, though, Linda had taken Franz out to teach him how to ride.

"Ida, are you sure Franz believes that Linda is his niece?" Cat watched the two of them ride away with her brow creased in puzzlement. "I'm only asking because—I've seen the two of them together quite a few times now, and the way he looks at her—well, it's not the way a reverend should look at a young relative. Ida, forgive me, but he looks at her with desire."

At first, Ida had laughed at the idea. Surely the young missionary, whom Mara had aptly nicknamed "the raven" because of his slightly hunched shoulders and black suit, had control over all of his mortal desires. Of course, she'd also noticed that he spent more time with Linda than any of the other residents of Rata Station. But that didn't surprise her. Linda had always had a heart for the lost and rejected. Her interest in healing often brought her together with the Maori priestesses and wise women, and she had absorbed much of their spirituality. It was possible she recognized the unhappy, injured child in Franz. Or perhaps she felt sorry for his helplessness in the face of Chris and Karl's criticism.

Linda listened to him patiently when he talked about his schooling with the Church Missionary Society. She accompanied him on walks around the farm and even took him with her one day into the Maori village, although that required all her powers of persuasion. Then she broke the ice by asking her students to sing a few hymns and recite some English poetry. When Franz began to relax, she offered him the opportunity to teach the class. Surprisingly, he managed quite well. His stiff formality left him as soon as he was with the children. All the children in Jane and Te Haitara's village spoke at least a little English, and Franz quickly won their trust when he told the story of Jonah and the whale in simple terms. He didn't even lose patience when one of the little boys remarked that whales don't eat people.

"Perhaps it was another kind of big fish," he said.

"Like the one that Maui caught," a little girl explained.

Then the girl told the missionary how the demigod Maui's gigantic catch had created the North Island of New Zealand, which was shaped like a fish. Linda preserved the peace by leaving the word "demigod" out of her translation and just presenting Maui as a legendary hero. Afterward, Franz taught the children math for an hour, and Jane immediately offered him a job in the village school. He declined, but returned to Rata Station proudly after his first teaching experience.

Ida happily observed the good relationship between her brother and his niece. It wasn't until Cat pointed it out that she noticed the way Franz's eyes lit up when he looked at Linda. She also noticed his efforts to please the girl, and the shadow that flitted across his features when Linda offered her smile just as freely to the farmhands and Maori workers. The latter made Ida's heart a little lighter. At least the family secret wasn't destroying any budding young love here. Linda was friendly to Franz, but nothing more. Perhaps the young missionary had fallen in love with her and was wrestling with feelings of guilt, but Linda didn't reciprocate his feelings. She wouldn't be sorry when he left for the North Island.

Chapter 16

Franz Lange had already put off his departure several times, in spite of his discomfort at Rata Station. His sister was no longer the pious, subdued woman he remembered. And his father had been right about Karl Jensch. Ida's second husband couldn't accept the Lord's will, and always thought he knew better—and that Chris Fenroy was a total heathen!

It was Linda whom Franz couldn't bear to leave. She was so kind and understanding, and she seemed so self-assured, especially when she interacted with the natives. Franz still couldn't get comfortable with them. It was difficult for him to look the large, tattooed men in the eye. None of them seemed particularly interested in the word of God, as he had been promised at seminary. Actually, Te Haitara and his people seemed to be quite happy with their gods and spirits, and weren't the slightest bit worried about eternal damnation. The chieftain's English wife had surprisingly little influence on them in that respect. When Franz asked her about it during a visit to Maori Station, as they had started calling the Maori sheep farm, she just laughed.

"Reverend, I've never seen Te Haitara's spirits, and I've never seen God either. So, one or the other might exist—or both, or neither. I suppose I'll find out when I die. Until then, I have a sheep farm to run, and when it comes to that, I'm glad that my people aren't constantly praying. If you want, you're welcome to stay here and teach the children. I really don't care if they count the Ten Commandments or ten sweet potatoes. But please don't pester the adults. Our tribe is content, and my husband and I wish for them to stay that way."

After that discussion, Franz was ready to end his sojourn in the godless place immediately. But again, it was Linda who changed his mind.

"We're going on a family outing to Christchurch," she said cheerfully. "Chris and Kapa have to visit the notary, and Oliver and Carol want to choose a church for their wedding. Carol likes St. Luke's, but Lady Butler thinks St. Michael & All Angels is more stylish. We'll have to meet with the reverends. Do you want to come with us? We're also going to the rowing club. They have a very fine restaurant, and Oliver can finally row Carol across the river the way gentlemen in England do with their sweethearts." She laughed, and her eyes flashed. "Maybe I'll find someone to row me across too."

Franz wondered if her last words were a subtle challenge. For the space of a heartbeat, he allowed himself to daydream about Linda sitting across from him in a boat, wearing a light-colored summer dress and holding a parasol coquettishly against her shoulder, her golden-blonde hair glowing in the sunlight. But then he fought back the thought. He wasn't allowed to think of Linda as his future wife. What was more, it was disrespectful to his niece to imagine her lightly dressed and indulging in useless pleasure. A reverend's wife had to be dignified, in a dark dress with a high neckline, her hair hidden under a respectable bonnet. Besides, Franz didn't know how to row.

He was attracted by the idea of the outing anyway, especially since the alternative was staying with Cat at Rata Station. Cat Rata scared him almost as much as the self-assured Maori men did. The woman had a tight grip on the reins of the farm. She told the Maori workers what to do, and even wore trousers! Of course, it was a trouser-skirt that didn't show any more of her legs than a normal dress would, but Franz had already been shocked that the women here rode astride, as Mara had. Additionally, Cat also had a strange kind of marriage with Chris Fenroy, while his previous wife lived with the heathen chieftain. Perhaps they'd all burn in hell. The worst part was that Cat refused to attend the prayer meetings Franz led every morning. Karl and Ida attended on Sundays, at least. Chris came once for the sake of keeping the peace, as did Jane and Te Haitara. The Redwoods brought the entire family. Laura said it would do her children good to attend a Sunday service every now and then. But Cat claimed to believe in Maori spirits, even though she didn't seem to pay them much attention in daily life. When Franz had scolded her for her godlessness, she had informed him that she'd had two foster mothers: one a Christian, and the other a *tohunga* and priestess. No god had stood by either woman when they'd needed help, nor had any stood by Cat herself. She told Franz if he was so worried about her soul, he was welcome to pray for her.

"How about it, Uncle Franz?" Linda asked enthusiastically. "Are you coming to Christchurch?"

Franz nodded stiffly. "It would be a pleasure to meet the reverends from St. Luke's and St. Michael's," he said. "I will use the opportunity to ask about a ship to the North Island. I have to start thinking about how to get there."

Linda nodded. Of course, Georgie, the boatman, could easily tell him when ships bound for the North Island were leaving Lyttelton. But Franz clearly couldn't allow himself a pleasurable experience without finding a dutiful pretext.

"We'll be leaving tomorrow around noon," Linda said. "Georgie will be going up the river then, and he'll be able to take us with him on the way back as well."

The next day at noon, Franz's breath caught in his throat when Linda came to the pier. That morning she had been wearing an old riding habit to work in the barn, but for the outing, the girls had dressed up. Franz blushed when he realized how similar Linda looked to the way she had in his daydream. She was wearing a light cotton dress that even had a hoopskirt. Her hair was braided just as prettily as Carol's had been for the regatta. It was crowned with a little hat decorated with flowers, and Linda beamed so cheerfully that even Karl noticed.

"You look pretty today, Lindy," he teased. "Do you have a secret admirer in Christchurch?"

Karl laughed, but Ida looked at her daughter shrewdly. Did she disapprove of her appearance? Franz wondered. As a good Raben Steinfeld Christian, she certainly should. Anna Lange would have never bought such clothes for her daughters! Then Franz found himself caught in Ida's doubtful gaze. Was she afraid of his disapproval? Was there enough Lutheran piousness left in her to at least be ashamed of her daughter's appearance in front of her brother? Franz wanted to believe it, and above all he wanted to feel disapproval of her himself. But he couldn't. All that mattered to him was Linda. She was simply breathtaking, and he just couldn't manage to see her as the embodiment of sin that all women represented.

Carol, who greeted her fiancé just as enthusiastically as she had at the regatta, had dressed more modestly that morning, perhaps in anticipation of visiting the churches. Her dress was simple and had a high neckline, and the hat covered all but a little of her pinned and braided hair.

Ida, too, was dressed conservatively, if not on par with the women of Hahndorf. She wore a cream-colored blouse with an elegant, dark blue ensemble, and a matching hat instead of a bonnet. After his initial doubts, Franz had learned that Rata Station had indeed made its owners rich.

"I don't want to rush anyone, but we have to leave soon. Perhaps you could catch up on the sweet nothings later," Georgie said, grinning at Carol and Oliver, who let go of each other reluctantly. "You'll be married soon anyway, won't ya?"

Carol nodded, but a shadow flitted across her face at the mention of the wedding. She wanted a reception on Christmas Day in the middle of summer so they could celebrate outdoors. However, Deborah Butler said she wouldn't be able to complete the preparations by then. She had ordered various things from England for the young couple, and the ship full of furniture, rugs, curtain fabric, and dress material wouldn't arrive before January. For that reason, they'd set a date in February, and the party would take place in Christchurch instead of at Rata Station.

"We want to pick a church today," Carol declared, and proceeded to bore the boatman with the details of the preparations for the next half hour.

Franz Lange wasn't listening. During the river journey two weeks earlier, he'd been too gloomy to enjoy the landscape on either side of the Waimakariri. Now, cheered by Linda's presence, he made up for it. He gazed in amazement at the endless openness of the plains, and at the mountains, which rose in the distance, fresh and white as clean laundry. Behind the stands of cattail reeds on the riverbanks, nikau palms gave the landscape an exotic flair.

"The Lord created a paradise here," Franz said at last. "But has he really put it in human hands without any further requirements? Sankt Pauli Village looked similar, didn't it? Especially when the river wasn't flooding—" Franz looked mistrustfully at the water of the Waimakariri.

"The Moutere Valley was marshland," Karl said patiently. He'd had to ease Franz's mind whenever it rained and the level of the river rose. "It always had been. In order to settle there, it would have been necessary to build dikes, like on the Elbe in Mecklenburg. Just trusting in God wasn't enough."

Franz crossed himself. "But if you don't trust in God—"

"Franz, certain characteristics of a landscape determine whether a river tends to flood or not. That has absolutely nothing to do with God!"

Franz was about to respond, but Linda put a hand on his arm and her adoptive father's at the same time. "The Maori would see that completely differently," she said. "They'd say you can trust the river gods, that they made the river the way they did for a reason. If they've allowed it to flood since the dawn of time, you can be sure it will do so again after the next big rain. And we can be just as sure that the Waimakariri won't flood no matter how hard it rains. That's very comforting, Franz! God isn't inconsistent. He always makes it rain so the grass grows. A spring follows every winter. Just imagine what would happen if God kept changing his mind and you never knew when it was time for the lambing or to harvest the sweet potatoes!"

Franz looked confused, but Ida smiled at her adopted daughter.

"Wise words," Chris said. "And we could add how smart it is of the gods not to answer every prayer. Just imagine if Jane could influence how fast her sheep's wool grew. She would bring the village's wool to market early, and then all the other breeders would have to be satisfied with whatever business was left!"

Franz pursed his lips as everyone laughed in agreement.

"This is the Deanses' farm," Linda said, pointing to the riverbank, changing the subject.

Karl and Chris talked about the quality of the sheep grazing near the water, and Oliver talked about the rowing club; Fitz had applied for membership again, but he'd been turned down. Ida and Linda talked about the wedding. It would soon be time to get dresses made. The two of them wondered if they would have time to visit the seamstress in Christchurch.

"You used to make your own dresses," Franz remarked unmercifully.

Ida nodded. "Yes, but I never really enjoyed it."

Franz prepared a cutting remark about humility, but then he glanced at Linda's pretty face and fetching hat, and the words got stuck in his throat. No, he didn't want to imagine her in the dark, traditional dress of Hahndorf. So he held his peace, returned Linda's smile, and allowed his thoughts to roam freely for a moment.

Chris, Karl, and Ida had an appointment at the notary; Franz had caught wind of that. Karl wanted to sell his share of Rata Station and move with Ida to the North Island. Ida had kindly invited her brother to visit them there, but Opotiki was still three hundred and fifty miles away from Russell. He certainly wouldn't be coming very soon. But Ida had insisted that she didn't want to wait another twenty years to see him again, and it had warmed Franz's heart. Ida wasn't the woman he remembered, but she was still his sister, and she still loved him in spite of everything that had changed.

"Tell them it's time to chill the champagne!" Oliver cried as Georgie steered toward to the rowing club's pier. "We're here to eat, and we have something to celebrate!"

Franz shot him an indignant look. While Chris, Ida, and Karl went to the notary, Oliver had brought the girls to the rowing club. But were they really planning to drink alcohol before visiting prospective churches? Oliver led them into the boathouse, where, to their surprise, a table was already waiting, complete with a bottle of champagne.

Joe Fitzpatrick appeared from behind an eight-man rowing scull that was hanging from one of the roof beams. He had been painting the bottom of it with tar. He beamed at the new arrivals. His white shirt and canvas trousers showed no signs of tar stains, and Franz had the impression he'd just been pretending to work.

"Welcome!" he said to the girls. "I thought I'd repay you for the last picnic. Miss Linda . . ."

Fitz bowed formally, and Linda blushed, grateful for the dim light.

"Miss Carol, Reverend—and I finally get to see you again, Ollie! I've missed you since the regatta. Has your old man been keeping you busy working on the farm, or was your winning a medal enough for him?"

Oliver reassured him that of course he wanted to continue rowing practice, but it seemed to Linda, at least, that Fitz wasn't even listening to his excuses. His eyes twinkled whenever he looked at her. As he handed her a champagne glass, she allowed herself to be captured by his gaze completely.

"Do you have a boat for me, Fitz?" Oliver asked after the young people had toasted to their reunion.

Of course, Franz declined the alcohol. He stood to the side, totally ignored by Fitz and Oliver. Oliver had no objection to Franz's presence. Indeed, without her uncle there to chaperone, his fiancée wouldn't have been allowed into the boathouse with him. But no one was talking to Franz anymore. Even Linda seemed to have forgotten all about him.

"I have to row Carol across the Avon." Oliver winked at his fiancée and his friend.

Fitz grinned. "But of course, old boy! And there's no one around to notice if you row into the reeds by the riverbank. You can take that one." He pointed out the doors to a little rowboat bobbing in the water, which had obviously been made ready. There was another one next to it.

"And perhaps the reverend would like to accompany Miss Linda?" Fitz asked politely.

Franz's temperature shot up. "I—I've never rowed before," he stammered.

Fitz seemed to have expected this. "Well, then the pleasure is mine!"

His smile was self-assured and irresistible. Franz knew he should object, but he was dumbstruck.

"Miss Linda . . ." Fitz sprang into the boat and held out his hand to her.

Linda tried to climb in gracefully, but it didn't work very well. The little boat rocked far more than Georgie's vessel, and she staggered. Fitz caught her without getting inappropriately close, but then smiled at her as though he knew how much both of them would have enjoyed it if she had fallen into his arms. Linda shyly pulled her hand out of his. Fitz acted as though he hadn't noticed the electricity between them. He waited until Linda was sitting securely on the bench across from him, and then he took the oars.

"Wait! You can't just—"

Franz had remembered his duties as a chaperone far too late. Fitz was already rowing onto the river when Franz cried out. He made no effort to turn the boat around.

"You can follow us on the riverbank," he called to Franz, and winked at Linda. "Like a proper chaperone," he whispered, making her laugh.

She felt wonderfully lighthearted with Fitz. He continued to joke with her and waved periodically at Franz, who really was following them on the riverbank, and he rowed with powerful strokes. They made much quicker progress than Oliver and Carol. But those two disappeared in the other direction, downstream.

"Do you actually have permission to do this?" Linda asked as Fitz rowed her past the clubhouse without hesitation. "I mean, to just take the boat and row out here with me. Aren't you supposed to be working?"

Fitz grinned. "My dear Miss Linda, this rowing club needs me much more than I need them. If only the old windbags—excuse me—if only the old gentlemen of the steering committee would finally admit that! That's probably why they still haven't accepted me as a member. A real gentleman could never handle all the maintenance that has to be done on the boats."

"Hmm," Linda said. In truth, she thought that sounded quite plausible. She had never heard of a gentleman who painted boats. Only staff was responsible for maintenance work—at least, in the English books she read. "You could look for a different job. What else would you like to do?"

Fitz laughed. "At the moment, nothing more in the world than to be here with you in this boat, watching the world go by." His disturbingly bright eyes caught her gaze and easily held it captive. "Have I told you yet how enchanting you look today? That hat makes your face look even more fetching than usual. Is it intentional, Miss Linda? Did you have plans to catch someone's eye?"

Linda blushed immediately. "I—no, I—"

Fitz winked at her again. "Come now, you can admit it! Actually, you already have. After all, you're here in this boat with a strange man. Or would you prefer to be doing something else, Miss Linda?"

Linda shook her head, marveling at how easily he seemed to read her thoughts. "Right now," she admitted, "I want nothing more in the world than to sit here in this boat."

Fitz smiled contentedly. "Then let's forget about the rowing club and enjoy the moment. Carpe diem, as they say in Latin, Miss Linda. Seize the day!"

Linda didn't have much practice with flirting, but Fitz's flattery and her confession that she enjoyed his company just as much as he did hers had made things plain. What surprised her most was that Fitz didn't take advantage of the situation. He didn't try to take her hand or kiss her. If his gaze felt like a caress, she thought it must be purely her own interpretation. Fitz remained a perfect gentleman, polite and obliging—and he was a wonderful listener.

After an enchanting hour, Fitz rowed the little rowboat back to the boathouse where Franz was waiting, sweating and annoyed, and Linda still knew almost nothing about Joe Fitzpatrick. But he knew Linda Brandmann better than anyone besides her family. He knew that she hoped to be a doctor but was a little scared about the examinations in medical school, especially because she'd probably be the only girl there—if they even accepted her. He knew her true opinion of Oliver and the story of Mara and Eru, and she'd even told him that she would probably inherit Rata Station one day. To her relief, Fitz hadn't reacted in any way to that revelation. He seemed not to care if she were rich or poor. Linda felt light and happy.

Carol seemed no less joyful, although she was considerably more disheveled than her sister. Oliver hadn't stayed decorously in full sight, but instead rowed the boat to a spot along the riverbank where the trees and ferns hung heavy, hiding them in a dense thicket. He'd kissed her there, and in her romantic mood she'd allowed him to touch places and do things that she had previously denied him. It was so much more beautiful to give him her love on this sunny day instead of waiting for a dark wedding night. Now she was overjoyed and jittery, and whispered to her sister that she couldn't wait to tell her everything.

The girls were oblivious to Franz's stony silence during the lunch at the rowing club that followed. At least Linda was polite enough to apologize to him. On the river with Fitz, she hadn't spared a thought for Franz, but in retrospect, she felt bad for leaving him alone, and ashamed at having laughed at Fitz's jokes about him.

The young missionary listened to her apology with an impassive face and didn't say a word. What could he have said, anyway? That it wasn't just Joe Fitzpatrick's impertinence making him seethe, but also jealousy?

Linda, who had no notion about the man's feelings, figured he probably wouldn't tell her parents about the little boat ride. Even if he did, Ida, Chris, and Karl probably wouldn't scold them very much, but they'd doubtlessly take an interest in Joe Fitzpatrick. Karl would probably use all of his connections to find out as much as he could about the young man, and Linda didn't want that—but why not? Fitz surely didn't have anything to hide, and if their relationship became more serious, her parents would need to ask him a lot of questions. Still, Linda wanted to keep Fitz to herself, at least for a little while. The only person she would tell was Carol.

Ida, Karl, and Chris didn't notice Franz's bad mood during the lunch either. They were so used to his disapproval that they assumed his sourness had to do with their consumption of good food and champagne in the afternoon.

However, Ida was a little more restrained than usual, and scolded her husband when he poured himself a second glass.

"Karl, we can't be tipsy when we speak to the reverends. If we make a bad impression, Deborah won't get the church of her choice for the wedding, and then she'll put the whole thing off again."

After that, Oliver and Carol didn't touch their champagne. The last thing they wanted was another delay.

Ida was a little surprised when Franz didn't join them for their church visits. She'd assumed that meeting his colleagues was the main reason he'd joined them. But she refrained from mentioning it. In truth, she was happy not to have to deal with the uptight missionary. After all, the priest from St. Luke's had a reputation for being very modern and open.

While the others went to the church, Chris accompanied Franz to Lyttelton to help him arrange a crossing to Wellington. Franz was worried about the cost. He didn't want to have to work on a ship again, sick as sailing made him. But Chris dismissed his worries.

"It's on Rata Station. Ida was so happy to see you again. We certainly aren't going to let you work for your crossing."

Chris also paid for the boat that took them from Christchurch to Lyttelton, despite Franz's protests. They would have never managed it on foot over the Bridle Path in an afternoon, but the boat got them there in no time. At the mouth of the Avon, the water was calm, and Franz was able to make the short trip without getting sick.

"Next Friday I'm leaving with the *Princess Helena*, a direct crossing to Wellington," he announced formally when they finally all met for tea in the White Hart Hotel.

Ida was ashamed of the relief that washed over her.

"And we're getting married at St. Michael's!" Carol chimed in so she didn't have to feign regret over Franz's departure. "I thought St. Luke's was prettier, but Oliver's mother is right; that church is too small."

"Only if she plans to invite half of the South Island," Karl grumbled.

He, too, had preferred the homey little chapel with its rather liberal priest. The reverend of St. Michael's hadn't made any secret about wanting to be appointed bishop if Christchurch soon built a cathedral.

Ida elbowed her husband, smiling. "That's your duty as a sheep baron," she joked. "The squire of Raben Steinfeld didn't let his daughters get married in the village church either."

"I'm terribly afraid the queen won't be able to come to the wedding, even though I'm sure Deborah is going to invite her," Chris said with a wink.

Franz was surprised and touched when Ida insisted on seeing him to the ship. Karl didn't have time. He wanted to use every moment before he left to help Chris with farm work. He was struggling with regret about the decision to move; he and Ida had been so happy at Rata Station.

However, Linda joined Franz and Ida, which warmed the young missionary's heart. He'd been avoiding his niece all week. Now he regarded his feelings of humiliation in Christchurch as a punishment from God for his infatuation with a relative, and prayed every evening for forgiveness.

But when Linda arrived at the pier wearing a flowing summer dress, Franz was overwhelmed with sinful feelings all over again. This time, her hair was hidden under a straw hat, and her eyes shone. The way they sparkled with excitement almost hurt Franz physically. He didn't know what had made Linda want to come along to Lyttelton, but it was clear that she wasn't particularly sad about bidding him farewell. At least Ida seemed moved. When it was finally time for him to board the ship, his sister embraced him with tears in her eyes.

"I wish you well, Franz. Write to me! Write often, please. I want to know how you're doing. And please, take this. I know you'll think it's pretentious, but please keep it. Don't give it away . . ."

Ida pulled a necklace out of the front of her dress, which surprised Franz. She didn't normally wear jewelry. But now she opened the clasp of a valuable-looking, heavy gold chain, which was attached to a cross decorated with precious stones. She pressed it into his hand.

"I can't accept this!" he cried. "This is a cross for a bishop. It would be pure arrogance for a simple missionary to wear such a thing."

"Then hide it away," Ida said. "Please, I want you to keep it. To remember me by. I got it from a very dear friend, and I'd planned for Carol to inherit it one day, but I can leave other jewelry to her. This is for you!"

Franz wondered why she wanted Carol to have the cross and not Linda, who was listening without the least sign of envy. Apparently, she didn't mind that Ida intended to put her twin sister first.

He reached reluctantly for the piece of jewelry. "I will cherish it," he said formally.

With relief, Ida kissed him on the cheek. "We'll see each other again soon! Karl and I will stop in Opotiki on our way to Russell. Then we'll be able to see where you work. Herr Voelkner is a nice man. He—"

"Ida, you don't have to worry about me," Franz said with dignity. "God will protect me. I will do his work. Even if there's an uprising on the North Island, the Lord will protect his own."

Ida wished she could believe that. But since Sankt Pauli Village had been washed away, she couldn't trust in the Lord's help blindly anymore. But she nodded anyway, and willingly said a prayer of farewell. Then she waved to her brother as the ship cast off.

Linda cheerfully joined in. She was wearing a colorful shawl with her dress, and now she took it off and waved it back and forth in wide arcs. Franz was still watching her as the ship left the harbor, and his heart was heavy. But then he made up his mind to forget the young woman. He had important tasks ahead of him.

"Finally!" Linda said with a sigh of relief, after the ship had disappeared beyond the horizon. "I really do like him. When he's not endlessly praying or trying to atone for imaginary sins, he's a very nice fellow. In the end, it seemed like he found it hard to say goodbye. Now stop crying, Mamida; he hasn't disappeared from the face of the earth. As you said, you'll see him again soon."

"I hope he'll actually keep the cross," Ida said, snuffling. The jeweled cross was one of two valuable pieces that Cat had kept out of the inheritance she'd received from her motherly friend, Linda Hempleman. Cat had kept a medallion-shaped one for herself, which she wanted to leave to her daughter, Linda, one day. "I'm worried he might sell it and donate the money. Missionaries aren't supposed to have any worldly possessions."

"You'll just have to bug him about it every time you visit," Linda said brightly. "And now I'm hungry! What do you think? Shall we treat ourselves to a lovely lunch?"

They were approaching the rowing club in the boat Ida had chartered for the return from Lyttelton. At Linda's behest, the oarsman steered toward the boathouse pier instead of the one closer to the restaurant. Too distracted to notice, Ida disembarked and paid the oarsman while Linda looked around for Joe Fitzpatrick. She wanted to feel the strength of his hand again as he helped her onto dry land. But Fitz was nowhere to be seen. Instead, a young blond man was lowering an eight-man scull into the water.

Linda climbed out by herself and approached him. "Where is Mr. Fitzpatrick?" It would be a pity if Fitz just happened to have the day off!

The young man shrugged. "Gone."

"Gone how?" Linda asked.

"Just gone. Apparently, he got too cheeky. Talked too much."

The same thing couldn't be said for his successor.

"Do you mean he was fired?" Linda inquired unhappily.

The man nodded.

"Do you happen to know where he is now, or what he's doing?"

Another shrug. "No, miss. He made a big scene when they threw him out. Ranted and made threats, things like that. And now he's gone."

"So, he isn't training rowers anymore either?" Linda said, grasping at straws.

He shook his head again. "No, he's forbidden to come back, after everything he said to the management. Cheeky, as I said." The young man turned back to his work.

Linda followed her adoptive mother to the restaurant with a heavy heart. She had lost her appetite. It looked like her romance with Fitz had ended before it began.

Part 3

LOSS

Canterbury Plains, Lyttelton, and Christchurch, New Zealand (the North Island)

Campbelltown, New Zealand (the South Island)

1863–1865

Chapter 17

"Of course you're coming!" Cat turned determinedly to Carol. "And I don't want to hear another word about it. There's no way we're going to leave you alone here for three weeks. And it'll do you good to see a bit more of the world, especially with the wedding coming up. You and Linda have hardly been anywhere."

The argument was about a trip they'd planned to Southland, the southernmost tip of the South Island, which was known for its exceptionally beautiful fjords and mountains. A sheep breeder who'd visited Rata Station last year had invited them all to his oldest son's wedding.

"It's not just about seeing Southland," Carol said cheekily. "Halliday wants us to meet his younger sons."

Cat shrugged. "Nothing wrong with that. Yes, I know you have Oliver and you never want to even look at another man again. But Linda is still unattached. If Frank and Mainard Halliday look like wetas and behave like keas, she can just have one dance and forget about them. But if they turn out to be just as nice and well mannered as their father, then it's entirely possible that Linda could fall in love with one of them."

"Then just take Linda!" Carol insisted. "I'll stay here and keep an eye on the farm. If we all go, Rata Station will be abandoned."

Karl and Ida had departed for the North Island several days before. Mara was still living with the Redwoods. In spite of the assurances her parents had made to Jane, the girl had vehemently refused to accompany her parents. She was obviously not interested in having the entire Cook Strait between her and Eru, even if there was no chance of seeing him in the near future.

Cat smiled sarcastically. "I appreciate your concern. But the farmhands will manage just fine for a little while without us. In case of an emergency, they can always turn to Jane and Te Haitara. Then maybe Jane will sell our breeding ram to the highest bidder and we'll be millionaires when we get back! Really, though, nothing will go wrong. Most of the sheep are in the highlands, anyway. And Oliver will survive a few weeks without you. If you stayed here alone, he wouldn't be allowed to visit, anyway. That would only ruin your reputation. Seriously, Carrie, I'd be much happier if you weren't constantly glued together."

Now that it was summer, Oliver didn't have any trouble making the ride to Rata Station. Plus, he didn't have to go to Christchurch to practice rowing anymore. He didn't know where Joe Fitzpatrick was either, but didn't seem very sad about his missing friend. Oliver didn't make plans very far in advance, and it would be at least nine months until the next regatta. Carol, on the other hand, wanted him immediately. Once the couple had celebrated their wedding night early, he had gone to great lengths to repeat the experience. He had spent almost all of the previous week at Rata Station, constantly badgering Carol and keeping her from her work with the horses and dogs.

That bothered Cat, even though she knew it didn't make much sense. In two months, Carol would be married and training sheepdogs at Butler Station. Deborah Butler wouldn't like that, but they had made it clear a long time ago that Carol would bring Fancy to her new home. The dog's entire first litter would be returned to Rata Station afterward, fully trained.

Cat didn't entirely know why she didn't like to see Carol and Oliver together. Even if they were sleeping together, the wedding was in just two months, so the child would be born in wedlock. But the better Cat got to know Oliver and his family, the less sure she was that he and Carol actually fit together. Of course, everything related to the farm and the inheritance fit, and they had known for some time that Oliver wasn't particularly smart or industrious. But she was worried about the young man's obvious self-absorption, his indifference to the disappearance of his friend Fitz, his unreliability, and his complete disinterest in the farm and his father's work. She was also deeply bothered by Deborah Butler's behavior. The woman's aristocratic airs got on Cat's nerves, and her tendency to wasteful extravagance was terrifying. Perhaps, Cat told herself, Captain Butler still had unlimited reserves from his time as a whaling captain.

But she had difficulty believing that. Butler Station was flourishing just like Rata Station and all the other halfway well-run sheep farms. They provided their owners with a high standard of living, but was it enough to keep up a gigantic manor house like the Butlers', with its huge staff? Was it enough to maintain the park and pay the English gardener?

The furnishings for Carol and Oliver's future "suite" had just arrived from England. Carol had been allowed to briefly admire their grandeur, and had admitted afterward that she'd felt suffocated by the sumptuous, heavy furniture. There were sideboards, tables, and bookcases of mahogany; thickly upholstered armchairs and chaise lounges; and richly ornamented grandfather clocks. Not to mention a porcelain dinner service, and sheets and tablecloths made of the finest satin, damask, and linen.

"If Fancy jumps on the bed, it'll probably be ruined immediately," Carol said worriedly.

Cat was more concerned about the price. The Butlers had already spent a fortune, and now they wanted to pay for part of the expensive wedding reception in Christchurch as well. But Ida and Karl had drawn the line there. They could live with St. Michael's and the White Hart Hotel. But more than a hundred guests, a five-course menu, and limitless French champagne? Karl had said bluntly that he couldn't and didn't want to pay for it all. But he didn't want the Butlers to pay for it either; it was a matter of not only pride but also common sense for him. And now Oliver was talking constantly about a honeymoon in Europe, and Deborah Butler seemed to be encouraging the idea. If Captain Butler didn't stop them soon, in the end Carol wouldn't inherit a sheep barony but a mountain of debt, with Oliver as its inept manager. Would he allow Carol to take over the responsibility for it then? Cat got the impression he was just as narrow-minded and old-fashioned as his mother when it came to the division of labor between men and women.

But Carol didn't want to think about any of that. She was blindly in love with Oliver, and of course it would be almost impossible to cancel the wedding now, even if she'd wanted to. Still, Cat clung to the vague hope that the trip to Southland would work wonders. It was possible that Carol would spontaneously fall for Frank or Mainard Halliday—perhaps both sisters would discover that the brothers were the loves of their lives!

"Start packing, Carol," Cat told her adopted daughter determinedly. "You and your sister certainly have plenty of options to choose from. The dresses Deborah had made for the wedding should suffice for all the festivities in the next ten years."

Deborah had taken the girls into town and outfitted Linda, the maid of honor, no less elegantly than Carol. However, the bills for all of Linda's party dresses, tea gowns, travel outfits, and hats had been sent to Rata Station. Chris and Cat had financed them reluctantly. After all, it was nothing compared to the cost of the trousseau that Deborah Butler had paid for.

Cat had also bought herself new clothes to wear at Carol's wedding, and was glad to have them for Ralph Halliday's festivities. Just the journey by ship to Campbelltown would offer opportunities to dress up. Chris had booked them passage on a very modern sailing vessel. The *General Lee* offered every imaginable comfort, from three-course menus to evening balls.

"You didn't have to book first class," Cat said as she entered the luxurious cabin, feeling torn. "Really, Chris, this is too expensive!"

Chris laughed. "I think we should indulge in something like this at least once," he said. "We've never traveled together, aside from driving the sheep to the highlands. And I know how much you love soft beds and champagne. Just think of it as our honeymoon."

Cat furrowed her brow. "Is that some kind of proposal?" Years ago, Cat had sworn that she'd never give up her freedom.

Chris shrugged. "I'd need a formal divorce from Jane. But it's possible, Cat. Perhaps we should think about it."

Cat smiled and shook her head. "I'm very satisfied with what I have. And don't forget, a proper wedding for sheep barons would mean a celebration in Christchurch with hundreds of guests. We would drive Rata Station into eternal debt."

Chris sighed theatrically. "I knew you'd say that. But we're still traveling today as Mr. and Mrs. Fenroy. The shipping company doesn't rent first-class cabins to unmarried couples."

Linda and Carol had also settled into their cabin, which was no less luxurious. An hour later, they met Cat and Chris on deck as the *General Lee* got underway. During the trip to Lyttelton, Carol had been sullen and hadn't spoken much, but now she seemed to have come to terms with the situation. She looked very pretty in her travel ensemble. The girls had decided on blue outfits for the occasion. Carol's was sky blue with dark blue buttons and trim, and Linda's had yellow trim. They played happily with their matching parasols, which were currently very fashionable. For their work on the farm, Linda and Carol mostly wore wide-brimmed hats, which served as protection from both sun and rain. The girls' skin was always lightly tanned in summer, and made a fetching contrast to their blonde hair. And it looked as though they had already found a male admirer. A young man in an officer's uniform was hovering close by.

"Truly, ladies, you will not be disappointed," he said enthusiastically. "Fiordland is exceptionally beautiful. When the mountains are reflected in the water, it looks like the clouds are drifting across the bottom of the sea. It's like a fairy tale. One wouldn't be surprised to see elves and dwarves dancing in the sunlight and basking in the moonlight."

"You're a poet, Lieutenant Paxton!" Carol said cheerfully.

The young man smiled. "I'm just a man who loves his home. Perhaps it's been too long since I've seen it."

"Are you from Campbelltown?" Chris asked. "I'm Chris Fenroy. I'm a sort of father to these two young ladies."

The young man immediately turned to greet Chris and Cat. "William Paxton," he said. "But you can call me Bill. Lieutenant Bill Paxton. I do have family in Campbelltown, though I wasn't born there. My parents live on Milford Sound. It's the most beautiful part of New Zealand, sir, and I know what I'm talking about."

The young officer met their gaze openly. He was of medium stature, slender, and muscular. The uniform clung perfectly to his well-toned physique. Paxton had smooth dark hair, an oval face, and brown eyes that seemed almost too kind and gentle for a soldier. Perhaps it was because they still glowed with memories of home.

"Lieutenant Paxton was stationed on the North Island," Linda explained. "He was telling us about Taranaki and the battles with the Maori."

"Taranaki is supposed to be at peace again," Cat said. It made her very uncomfortable to hear about fights between the Maori and the *pakeha*. She felt loyal to both parties, and enjoyed helping them communicate with each other.

"Indeed, Mrs. Fenroy," Paxton replied, sounding less than convinced. "Even if there is still occasional dissonance. But I didn't want to bore the young ladies with unpleasant details. Actually, I was just telling them about the loveliness of Milford Sound. Have you ever seen seals, Miss . . . ?"

"Linda and Carol Brandmann," Carol said, introducing her sister and herself. "No, we've never seen seals before. We live on a sheep farm."

As she spoke, the young woman gazed back toward Lyttelton. The *General Lee* was leaving the harbor surrounded by green hills, and turning south. The sailors were hoisting more sails, which filled with wind immediately. It looked as though the ship would make good progress.

"Perhaps we can continue our discussion over dinner," Cat suggested.

Lieutenant Paxton nodded. "It would be my pleasure to accompany the two young ladies to the table," he replied, and offered an arm each to Linda and Carol. "I've heard the cook is a genius. But I'm also biased, because he's my cousin."

Paxton led the sisters to the ship's dining hall, which was richly decorated with crystal chandeliers, carved wooden paneling, and furniture that looked like it belonged in the ballroom of an English manor house. As he walked, he confided with a smile that he had his cousin to thank for his first-class ticket.

"The British Army only pays for the cheapest tickets. But when Tommy heard that I was on board, he arranged a better cabin for me. In truth, I don't care much about the soft bed, but I'm very much looking forward to Tommy's cooking."

"Why is the army sending you to Southland, anyway?" Chris asked, gallantly pushing in Cat's chair for her. Paxton did the same for Linda and Carol, no less elegantly. "The South Island is almost all Ngai Tahu tribes, and they're quite peaceful."

Paxton nodded and sat down between Linda and Carol. "Of course." He smiled bitterly. "And if there were a real problem, Wellington would send an entire army, not me. Two years ago, General Pratt led two thousand soldiers against the tribes from Waikato. We were constantly stepping on each other's feet. Whereas the Maori only had about fifteen hundred warriors. But they know their way around. We bombarded their fort for an entire night. What do they call it?"

"A *pa*," Cat said.

Paxton nodded. "Exactly, a *pa*. And the next day, we discovered that the place had been given up as soon as the first few cannonballs were fired. No one knows how the people snuck out. There were no fatalities, thank God. I'm not supposed to say that, but it seemed terribly unfair to me to attack with cannons when the natives could only defend themselves with spears and clubs."

"The Maori didn't have muskets?" Carol asked in surprise.

"They did." Paxton picked up the menu, clearly uncomfortable. "But they were hopelessly outgunned. Besides, I don't think they like to fight."

"Some of the chieftains are very warlike," Cat explained. "They just approach battles differently than the English do. They don't launch huge campaigns with thousands of soldiers; instead, they attack in short skirmishes. And when it's time to sow the fields, they postpone the war until after the first harvest."

"All the saber-rattling is important too," Chris added. "They often make a great show of intimidation so they don't have to attack at all. Or they disappear, as you experienced at that *pa*. The chieftains may not have written or read books about the art of war, but they're very inventive."

"One chieftain is supposed to have flown away over a cliff, hanging from a kite, after he had been captured and was being held prisoner somewhere," Linda said.

Paxton smiled. "You seem very well acquainted with Maori traditions."

Chris explained about his work as a translator for the New Zealand Company, and Cat talked about her childhood with the Ngati Toa.

A uniformed waiter served aperitifs and a shrimp cocktail as an appetizer.

"You still haven't told us why you're going to the South Island now," Carol said. "What are you doing there for the army? Spying, perhaps?" She grinned mischievously.

Paxton laughed. "Your parents would make much better spies, Miss Carol. I personally don't speak a word of the Maori language. In Taranaki, I was just a liaison officer between the volunteer native troops and the army from Australia. Sometimes it was worse than a real war. The Maori troops weren't interested in following orders, but they understood what was happening locally. And the Australians didn't understand why they were there in the first place. Thank goodness they've been sent home now."

"Will they be brought back if the conflict flares up again?" Chris said.

"No," Paxton said, and took a sip of champagne. "Instead, new troops will be recruited in New Zealand. The unit even has a name: the Taranaki Military Settlers. And that's why a few other officers and I are being sent to the South Island, Miss Carol—we're recruiting. At whaling stations and in places like

Lyttelton where settlers arrive. We're going to the gold prospectors' camps next. Anywhere young men are trying their luck."

"And you promise them that luck?" Chris sounded skeptical.

Paxton shrugged, looking depressed. "I promise them land. And they won't be disappointed. In Taranaki, there are thousands of acres of excellent farmland that the government is prepared to give the settlers for free."

"What does that mean?" Cat asked. "Settlers who want the land have to fight the Maori for it first?"

"Something like that," Paxton admitted. "The land is being taken away from rebellious Maori tribes under the New Zealand Settlements Act. Unfortunately, the Maori aren't always aware of the law—"

Cat laughed cynically. "That's an interesting way of putting it. According to what my surveyor friend Karl tells me, the government's not actually bothering to differentiate between rebellious tribes and nonrebellious ones. They just confiscate what they want. It's understandable that it makes the people angry."

Paxton pressed his lips together. "The conflict with the tribes can be solved peaceably in most cases," he replied. "There's enough land for everyone. And if you go about it a little diplomatically, most tribes are willing to sell. Unfortunately, not all of the government officials keep their word. And now there's the Hauhau movement to deal with as well. I don't know if you've heard about it?"

Chris and Cat nodded.

"A preacher with strange visions," Cat said. "Is he that big a concern?"

Paxton snorted. "You must not have heard the latest news. But it's no subject for a formal dinner with ladies. I'll just say this much: Haumene must be stopped. We don't need bloodthirsty fanatics and cannibals running around. There were certainly mistakes made in the land-claiming process. But after they hear Haumene's ravings, the Maori see themselves as victims. They're forming bands of marauders." He rubbed his brow. "The governor wants to protect the settlers from their attacks. That's why we're planning fortifications around new settlements, and recruiting settlers who know how to use weapons. The members of the new regiment will be trained and given battle experience—and each will be granted twenty acres to start a farm on."

"It'll work. Your recruits will fight bitterly to keep what they think is theirs much harder than they would if they were just soldiers," Cat said, shaking her head. She remembered the settlers in Sankt Pauli Village battling the elements to save their farms. "The Maori won't stand a chance."

Paxton turned up his palms helplessly. "I can't do anything about it, Mrs. Fenroy. The tribes are allowing Te Ua Haumene to preach in their villages, and aren't stopping their sons from slaughtering settlers in the name of peace and love. And now we really must change the subject. What brings you to the south, Miss Linda, Miss Carol? A wedding, you said? But not your own?"

The rest of the evening passed pleasantly. Paxton chatted enthusiastically about the wonders of his home, and accompanied Linda and Carol for a stroll around the deck. Cat and Chris followed at an appropriate distance and were delighted by the silver shimmering of the waves in the moonlight. They gazed at the stars and the distant coastline.

"Some of the beaches are supposed to be breathtakingly beautiful," Chris said when the travelers finally returned to their cabins. "If the weather is nice tomorrow, we can spend the entire day on deck if you want."

Cat smiled. "Sounds nice," she said. "Now come get in bed. We've made love under the stars many times, but never with the sound of water lapping on a ship's hull. I'm going to feel like that girl in the ballad from the Orkney Islands. You know, the mortal who falls in love with a selkie."

Cat loved romantic stories. During the sheep drive, she loved it when the Scottish and Irish farmhands sang old songs by the fire.

Chris kissed her. "As long as you don't insist I turn into a seal, or sing . . ."

Chapter 18

Cat and Chris spent several wonderful days aboard the *General Lee.* During that time, Cat really did feel as though she were on her honeymoon. The weather was perfect, and the coastal scenery—a mixture of pastoral beauty and craggy cliffs—was breathtaking. Bill Paxton hadn't exaggerated about his cousin's cooking talent either. Tommy Paxton spoiled his guests, and in the evening, a band played.

Linda and Carol also enjoyed the trip far more than they had expected to. Linda was still sad about Joe Fitzpatrick. Who knew what would have come of their flirtation if he hadn't disappeared from Christchurch? It had also been difficult for Carol to part from Oliver. But now she was enjoying Bill Paxton's attention. When he was free from duty, George Wallis also joined them. The second officer of the *General Lee* turned out to be an excellent dancer. He was much more coordinated than Oliver, whom Carol had to beg at least three times before he took her on the dance floor at the Sheep Breeders' Ball. Now, she happily allowed George to twirl her around in time with the band. She laughed when the sea was a little rough and seemed to be trying to throw her out of rhythm. Bill Paxton danced with Linda, but it was obvious that he would have preferred to dance with Carol. He had reserved the last dance of the evening with her right from the start, and Carol didn't turn him down. She felt flattered by his attention, at least as long as Linda didn't mind.

"You're not in love with him or Mr. Wallis, are you?" Carol asked Linda on the second evening as they fell into their beds, tired and happy.

"No. They're both very nice. But there's no spark. Sometimes I think I don't have the right receptors for it. You seem to flirt easily, and all the men are crazy about you. But me, sometimes I think I'm not interested in men. At least, not most of them." Linda couldn't shake off the thought that, so far, Joe Fitzpatrick was the only man who had managed to "capture her heart." Linda knew that expression from the penny dreadfuls, and she thought it silly and clichéd. Yet somehow it described exactly the way Fitz had made her feel. Fitz's gaze, his smile, just his presence . . . He hadn't even put a hand on her except to help her out of the boat, but Linda could still remember the feelings of closeness and trust that touch had evoked. When she was with Fitz, just a word or even a thought had been enough to make her laugh or cry. She didn't know if that was love. She certainly didn't feel anything like it when she thought about Bill Paxton or George Wallis.

Of course, both Paxton and Wallis were gentlemen, and certainly weren't about to neglect Linda. It was also clear that George Wallis wasn't hung up on either of the young ladies. He was equally polite and kind to both. Toward the end of the trip, he asked Linda to accompany him to the last ball of their voyage. It was to take place on their last evening, following a gala dinner. The afternoon of the next day, the ship would arrive in Campbelltown. Paxton had already asked Carol. He wanted to have her to himself.

There was a dress code for the ball. Carol and Linda excitedly helped each other into the gowns that they'd packed for the Halliday wedding. Cat, too, got out her ball gown, and Chris thought she was more beautiful than any other woman on the ship.

Cat's dress was made of shiny silver silk. She wore her pearl jewelry, and the low-cut bodice showed the tops of her breasts. Her waist was as slender as a girl's, as—making a rare exception—she had worn a corset. Cat had pinned up her honey-blonde hair, and pulled down several fetching strands on either side of her face. Her brown eyes glowed, and she was followed by the eyes of all the men in the dining hall. Chris proudly led her to the table. He couldn't stop admiring his wife's beauty.

"Enjoy it while it lasts," she warned him. "This corset is killing me. I don't understand how women can stand to wear these things every day! And I can hardly eat anything. It's a terrible pity with such a fantastic meal, but I can't get down more than a few bites. I will certainly be leaving early this evening."

Chris smiled. "*We* will leave early," he said, correcting her. "I'm also eager to get you out of that dress . . ."

Cat made it through dinner, but after just one dance with Chris, she surrendered.

"Let's go, darling. We can bring a bottle of champagne to the cabin and celebrate there. The voyage was wonderful, Chris, indescribable! Booking first class was the best idea you've ever had. But I have to get out of this whalebone cage or I'll scream."

"I just feel sorry for the girls," Chris said as one of the waiters brought them a champagne cooler with two bottles on ice. "I'm sure they'd like to stay longer."

Cat looked over to where Carol and Linda were dancing with their admirers. Their gowns had hoopskirts and corsets, too, but the restrictive garments didn't seem to bother them. Linda wore a powder-blue gown and Cat's necklace set with blue stones. Carol's dress shimmered in dusty rose, and she wore a necklace made of coral. Both sisters' hair cascaded in loose ringlets down their backs; they must have spent hours curling it. All that work just for a few dances! Chris was right, they would be disappointed. Cat briefly considered just leaving them alone at the ball, but that would go against every rule of etiquette. Sighing, she called them over and steeled herself for their protests.

"It's only nine o'clock!" Carol cried. "We've only had two dances. You can't do that, Mamaca! Come, sit down and have another drink. You have to give us at least another hour."

"Longer!" Linda demanded. "In an hour, it will only be ten. The fireworks are at eleven. We have to stay at least until then. Please, Mamaca, Chris, we promise not to do anything foolish!"

"We'll take good care of your daughters," Bill Paxton assured them. "And we would never take advantage in any way, you may rest assured."

Cat and Chris looked at each other regretfully. They hated to spoil the evening for the girls, and they trusted that everyone would behave. But there were acquaintances from Christchurch aboard, and Cat and Chris didn't need their lax parenting to be the talk of the town.

"It's not possible, girls, as sorry as I am," Cat said finally. "I knew I shouldn't have bought this dress. I take full responsibility, but I can't change it. So, say goodbye for now. You'll dance at many more balls."

But of course, Bill Paxton and George Wallis didn't pass up the opportunity to walk the family across the deck.

"Such a pity there are no stars tonight," Linda said.

"It's also getting cold," Carol added, pulling her shawl tight around her shoulders. "And choppy."

Wallis nodded and offered Linda his arm as the ship began to sway. "Yes, it looks like a storm is brewing. I might have had to leave the festivities early tonight anyway. The captain may call the officers to the bridge."

"It's not going to be dangerous, is it?" Cat asked, holding on to Chris tightly.

Wallis shook his head. "No, Mrs. Fenroy, don't worry about that. We're very close to the coast. However, it could become quite turbulent. I hope you don't get seasick."

He politely said good night to Cat and Chris, and gallantly took his leave from Linda and Carol. Carol was still whispering with Bill Paxton, and they exchanged a conspiratorial smile before the sisters descended to their cabin, observed by Cat and Chris.

"You aren't going to be unfaithful to Oliver, are you?" Linda said, teasing. "All those long looks with Mr. Paxton. Come, help me out of this corset." She reached for the buttons on her dress.

Carol shook her head. "Keep your dress on. Mr. Paxton is waiting on deck for both of us. We just want a few more dances. I would never betray Oliver!"

She glanced in the mirror and checked her appearance, and then nearly staggered. The ship was beginning to pitch unpredictably.

"You want to go back to the ball? Without Cat and Chris?" Linda asked in disbelief.

"Of course!" Carol tidied her hair. "Lindy, the ball only just started. We aren't going to let them spoil our fun, are we?"

"But what about the Hestons and the Wesserlys? Cat's right. They would gossip terribly about us in Christchurch." Linda didn't mention Mrs. Butler and how she'd react to rumors about her future daughter-in-law.

"If you ask me, they probably didn't even notice that Cat and Chris left," Carol said unworriedly. "And with the rough seas, they'll probably be back in their cabin already. Mr. Heston was seasick the day before yesterday even with the tiny waves, and Mrs. Wesserly has been complaining since the beginning of the voyage. They're guaranteed to be gone soon. Anyway, we have to wait here for half an hour to be sure that Chris and Cat are asleep . . . or too busy otherwise to hear us in the corridor."

The girls giggled.

"So, what do you think? I can't go alone." Carol gave her sister a challenging look.

Linda nodded. "All right. I really want to see the fireworks. I've only seen them once, and it was so beautiful. Let me use the mirror. I need to check my hair."

Linda and Carol spent the next half hour impatiently combing their hair and adjusting their gowns. Carol was right: the seas were getting rougher, and there was regular traffic in the corridor as the older passengers of the *General Lee* opted to ride out the storm in their cabins.

"We just have to catch a moment when no one is rushing to the privies," Carol whispered as the girls finally opened the door and peered out. "Some of them have surely been sick already. The ship is bucking like a horse! Do you have your shawl?"

Linda shook her head, and then took two wide, hooded cloaks out of the closet.

"We'll take these instead," she said. "It must be pouring out there. Come now!"

She threw a cloak around her sister's shoulders and stepped into the corridor. The ship was rolling so wildly that they were thrown from one wall to the other. As they climbed onto deck, they were almost tossed back down the stairs, and were immediately met with a deluge of ice-cold rain. But Bill Paxton had kept his word, and was waiting under an awning.

"I was afraid you wouldn't come back in this storm," he said with a grin. "I see you've got tenacity!"

Carol laughed. "A little wind isn't going to keep us from dancing. I'm just sad it's too wet for fireworks."

Wearing heavy slickers against the weather, the sailors who would have been responsible for the spectacle were busy taking down sails and stowing anything that the wind could blow overboard.

In the ballroom, few passengers remained—mostly young people who thought the rough seas were exciting, and enjoyed staggering into each other's arms while dancing. But the barman and the wine steward remained on duty, and the band, which consisted of three young men, continued to play. But they could barely be heard above the sounds of the raging wind and pouring rain that was whipping against the windows of the raised hall. After a time, dancing became impossible, so the young people amused themselves by trying to carry full champagne glasses across the room without spilling them.

Then suddenly the music stopped. A sailor staggered in, soaked and out of breath.

"No one is allowed back on deck. Captain's orders. I'm sorry, but you'll have to spend the night here. The danger of being washed overboard is too great. We're also battening all the hatches so no water gets into the cabins."

"Washed overboard?" Linda was immediately sober. "We were told it wasn't so bad."

"No one has fallen overboard yet," the man explained, in a voice that was supposed to sound comforting. "But you're staying." His gaze swept enviously over the bar. "At least you won't go thirsty."

Carol laughed uneasily. But several of the others were taking the situation with less humor.

"What impertinence!" said a young man, the son of a sheep baron from Queenstown. "Not only are we forced to spend the night in this hall, but the captain doesn't even have enough decency to send an officer to inform us."

"The officers are surely busy," Bill Paxton said. His worried look reflected Carol's own fears. So far, the captain had shown the greatest gentility. If he was now dispensing with etiquette, the situation must be serious.

The cries and fearful remarks began to grow louder. Married women took shelter in their husbands' arms. Bill reached for his jacket and went to the door.

"Stay here," he told Carol and Linda. "I'm going out to see if I can find George. I want to know what's really going on."

"What if it's too dangerous?" Carol asked.

Bill smiled at her. "I'll be careful."

The wind slammed the door shut behind him as he left the hall. Inside, the waiters and barkeeper attempted to tie down tables and chairs, which were sliding across the room as the boat pitched. Several guests, including Carol and Linda, tried to help. But they struggled even to stay on their feet. Soon, Bill returned. He was soaking wet, but seemed less worried.

"George is in the wheelhouse, watching the gauges. He says it's a stronger storm than the captain was expecting. Otherwise, he would have canceled the ball."

The girls' eyes went wide.

"No, don't be scared. The *General Lee* is a good ship. Just because the wind is tossing it around a little doesn't mean it's going to sink. That's what George said. However, we are being blown off course. That means the trip will take longer. We're going to need at least one more day."

Linda managed a smile. "Well, if it's nothing worse than that, maybe we can see the fireworks tomorrow."

Paxton picked up a wayward tablecloth and used it to dry himself off. "As I said, you two are a couple of tough young ladies. Would you like another glass of champagne? I could do with a whiskey about now."

On the way back from the bar, he staggered, and the tray of drinks flew across the room. The expensive crystal glasses shattered on the floor. The young people laughed, but it sounded forced. The band was playing again, but no one could dance. Over the next few hours, some of them began to feel seasick. A few moaned and threw up into ice buckets. Someone started to scream when not only rain whipped against the windows, but waves as well. The deck was pounded by the roiling sea. More and more, the cheerful party transformed into a nightmare. Several guests had spread coats and cloaks on the floor in a corner and were lying down, but sleep was impossible.

"Well, tough or not, I would really rather be somewhere else right now," Linda murmured when the musicians finally gave up and put their instruments away. "I hope Chris and Cat won't go into our cabin to check on us. They'll worry if they see we're gone."

Carol shook her head. "They'll find out tomorrow either way. But I'll bet that the Hestons and Wesserlys stay in bed until noon. At least if they're seasick." She glanced at a young man who was emptying his stomach for the third time.

"How long do storms like this usually last?" Linda asked Bill.

He shrugged. "I have no idea. A night? Several days? How long was it in the Bible before they threw Jonah into the sea?" His joke sounded tired.

"I wish it were at least bright again. The helmsman surely can't see anything in this weather. Who knows where we'll end—"

Carol hadn't even finished speaking when the ship was suddenly shaken by a powerful blow. For a moment, everything was motionless, until they were swept forward and tossed by waves again.

"Did we just hit rocks?" Linda asked.

There were loud cries from the deck. They could see the outlines of sailors through the window as they fought against the storm to open the hatches to the cabins below deck.

Alarmed, Bill Paxton ran to the door and snatched Linda and Carol's cloaks from the coatrack. "Put these on in case we have to leave quickly. That didn't sound good. Do you feel like the ship is listing to one side?"

The girls threw on their cloaks, watching through the window as the sailors let the lifeboats down from their mounts.

"They're lowering the boats!"

"We're sinking!" someone cried.

The other guests, too, had noticed the frantic activity outside and were rushing to the exit.

Bill waved them back. "Stay calm!" he ordered. "We'd just be in the way out there. Let the sailors do their work."

Then the captain appeared on deck, shouting orders. The first passengers appeared from the cabins below and were led to a lifeboat, which elicited another outbreak of terrified cries from the ballroom. The captain looked over, then pointed them out to some of his crew. To Linda and Carol's relief, it was George Wallis who came to the door, wearing an oilskin coat and carrying a wooden box under his arm.

"Listen up!" he shouted. "You are all to come with me. We can get you all into boat number two. We're going out now together, so please hold on to each other. Men, please support the women and make sure no one falls. There is no reason for haste or panic. We went aground against some rocks, but the ship is sinking very slowly, and there are enough lifeboats for everyone. So, please, stay calm!"

George Wallis held the door open, and Bill Paxton and the girls were among the first out.

"What—what about Chris and Mamaca?" Linda cried as they staggered into the storm. "Will they—"

The wind blew the words from her lips.

Chris and Cat had enjoyed the evening and fallen asleep full of champagne. But soon the bucking and rolling of the ship shook them from their slumber.

"Is this normal?" Cat asked worriedly as she lit a gas lamp in their cabin.

Chris, who'd experienced many stormy passages to the North Island, comforted her.

"This is definitely a strong storm, but ships don't sink that easily. Think of Ida and Karl, and what they told us about their voyage on the *Sankt Pauli*. And they were in the middle of the Atlantic Ocean, not a few hundred yards from land."

"I'm going to check on the girls," Cat said.

She threw on a dressing gown and stepped into the corridor. When she returned, she had other things on her mind than the weather.

"The little beasts!" she cried. "The cabin is empty. They snuck back to the ball!"

Chris laughed. "In their position, I would have done the same thing," he admitted. "The only question is why they aren't back yet."

He reached for the pocket watch he'd left on the nightstand, but it wasn't there. Cat found it on the floor.

"Three o'clock," she said. "You're right, they should have been back a long time ago. Come, get up. We have to find them."

Cat quickly threw on a comfortable dress, and Chris dressed with a sigh.

"You'll have to come up with some terrible punishment when we catch them," he said. "The last thing I want now is a stroll around the deck."

The two of them hurried along the corridor, where they had to edge around puddles of vomit. A few passengers were sitting against the walls, groaning.

Cat wasn't surprised that the companionway was closed, but began to panic when she realized it wasn't possible to open it from the inside.

"Chris, what's going on? We're locked in, we—" She hammered against the wood.

Chris reached for her hand. "Stop that, no one will hear you," he said. "They'll only hear us in here, and then everyone will start to panic. In a storm, the sailors seal them to stop water from getting in. Besides, they have to keep passengers from walking around on deck and being washed overboard. If it really gets bad, they'll open them again."

He'd barely finished speaking when a shock went through the hull of the ship, as though someone were pounding on it with a gigantic hammer. They heard the sound of wood cracking, and then of rushing water.

"The ship is leaking!" Cat cried.

There were shouts from behind them and also on deck. Cat took a breath of relief as she heard someone opening the companionway from outside.

"Keep calm. Please stay here until the lifeboats are ready."

Cat and Chris were looking into the serious but controlled face of the first officer. Other passengers were coming up behind them.

"You'll be out of here quickly. There is space for all of you."

"Come now!" Bill Paxton reached out a hand to Carol.

A sailor was guiding the passengers over the side of the ship on a rope ladder that stretched down to lifeboat number two. Some boats were loaded before being lowered, but others already bobbed in the water, and reaching those was quite a bit more difficult. George had chosen the young revelers for the latter.

"But what about Mamaca and Chris? Mamaca won't go without us!"

"The girls!" Cat balked in front of the boat the first officer was trying to help her into. "My daughters! I don't know where they are!"

"They'll be along," the young man said calmly. "There are boats for everyone; no one will be forgotten. Now you must get in, quickly!"

"Can't we wait? I want to be in a boat with my children!" Cat looked around frantically.

Chris scanned the deck. Everywhere, members of the crew were guiding passengers into boats. Of course they kept hearing shouts, and some women were crying, but everything was progressing in a fairly orderly manner. Finally, he spotted Linda and Carol on the other side of the ship.

"There they are, Cat," he said. "Look, over there!"

"Can't we please wait for our parents?" Carol asked. "It doesn't matter which boat we're in—"

"Of course it matters. If everyone starts walking back and forth to choose a boat, there will be pure chaos," George Wallis said sternly. "Get in now, Miss Carol. That's an order!"

"But Mamaca—"

"There's Chris!" Linda spotted her adoptive father and waved to him excitedly. "And Mamaca! We're here!" She shouted into the storm, though there wasn't a ghost of a chance her parents would hear.

"Get in!" Wallis shouted. "Bill, do something! Throw them over your shoulder if you have to."

"You will get in this boat right now," the first officer said, and took Cat's arm.

Though relieved at having seen the girls getting into a boat, Cat didn't like the thought of letting them out of her sight again.

"Will the boats stay together?" she asked worriedly as she finally climbed in and sat down on one of the benches.

"We'll do everything we can, madam," the first officer replied.

"No matter what, we'll see the girls when we're back on land," Chris said and took Cat's hand. "Don't worry."

As the boat was lowered over the rail of the ship by the winches, Cat saw her daughters climbing down the rope ladder and breathed a sigh of relief. At least the two of them had gotten safely off the sinking vessel. So close to the coast, the lifeboats shouldn't run into problems. They probably wouldn't even have to row for more than a few minutes.

Cat clung tightly to the bench as the boat hit the water. It landed safely in the sea, though it was immediately tossed by the waves, and the people shrieked as ice-cold water sloshed in. Cat steeled herself against the cold. It would only be a short ride.

Chapter 19

"Bail!" George Wallis shouted. "There are buckets under the seats!"

Now that they were drifting away from the *General Lee*, the small lifeboat was quickly filling with water. The rain was contributing just as much as the waves.

"Will we reach land soon?" Linda asked breathlessly as she scooped water as fast as she could. "We were so close to the coast."

Wallis shook his head, as did the five other sailors who had been assigned to lifeboat two. They rowed with all their strength to get away from the whirlpool created by the sinking ship.

"I don't know where we are, miss," he shouted against the noise of the wind. "The *General Lee* drifted, and we couldn't figure out our location. That's also why we ran aground. On the normal route, there are no shallows, no rocks for the ship to hit."

"Where are we rowing to, then?" Carol asked, her teeth chattering. She couldn't remember having been so cold in her entire life. The freezing water had long since soaked through her cloak and ball gown, and waves kept swamping the boat. So far, she had been able to comfort herself with the thought that it would soon be over.

"For now, we just have to get away from the ship. Otherwise, we'll get sucked down with it," Wallis said. "Then we'll pull in the oars and wait until dawn, until the storm dies down."

"Are there any signs of that yet?" asked Edward Dunbar, the arrogant young man from Queenstown.

"Of course, sir," Wallis replied. "It's already let up significantly. At the peak of it, we would have never been able to get the lifeboats into the water."

"And dawn always comes," Bill added encouragingly. He, too, rowed powerfully. "It can't be much longer. Shall we pull in the oars now, George?"

The men stowed the oars and then helped the women to bail. As they did so, they watched the ghostly silhouette of the *General Lee* as it sank. They could hear cries of dismay from the other lifeboats.

"I hope everyone got off safely," Linda said. In their boat, too, some people were crying. A few women prayed aloud.

Wallis attempted a comforting smile. "I don't think anyone was lost yet."

"Yet?" Carol demanded shrilly.

The young officer rubbed his forehead. "We haven't reached land."

As morning broke, the sky finally grew brighter, but the gray storm continued to rage. The lifeboat was tossed mercilessly by the waves, and there was no sign of the coast. The occupants took turns bailing. Linda and Carol nestled close together, and fell into a short, exhausted, restless sleep. The waves and cold soon woke them.

"We shouldn't sleep," Linda insisted through her chattering teeth. "If you fall asleep, you can die of hypothermia."

It only stopped raining toward noon, and the wildly breaking waves finally gave way to less extreme swells. The boat still rocked, but no more water came over the sides. It was finally possible to row again. The question was in which direction.

The passengers gazed despondently at the gray, seemingly endless water around them. There was no land to be seen, and no sign of the other lifeboats either.

"They—they couldn't have all sunk, could they?" Linda asked fearfully.

Wallis shook his head. "No, that's very unlikely. We've just all drifted in different directions. Don't worry. We—"

"Don't worry?" Edward's young wife shrieked. "You must be joking! We're drifting without food or water, half-dead with cold on the open sea. No one knows where we are. But we shouldn't worry?"

Wallis pressed his lips together. They were cracked from the saltwater and cold. "That's not what I meant, Mrs. Dunbar. Our situation is doubtlessly serious. But I can't tell you how serious until I have determined our position." He reached for the wooden box he'd stowed under the seat. "As soon as the sea is calm enough to use the sextant, we can find out how far off course we are, if land is anywhere near, or if we can hope for aid from passing ships. Until then, you'll have to be patient."

At the last light of day, George Wallis was finally able to take the readings. He focused on the cusp of the setting sun and murmured numbers to himself. For the anxious passengers, it seemed to take hours.

"Ladies and gentlemen, unfortunately I must tell you that we are very far from our original course. To the best of my knowledge, we are approximately one hundred and fifty miles to the southeast of Campbelltown. We are on the open sea, and quite far from most of the usual shipping routes."

"What does that mean?" Dunbar asked apprehensively.

"We're going to die!" a woman cried.

Linda and Carol felt paralyzed with fear. A hundred and fifty miles of sea between them and the South Island. The cold alone . . .

Wallis shook his head determinedly. "We're going to row," he said, "and pray that the currents and wind are on our side. If we can manage five miles per hour, we can reach land in two days."

"We could make a sail too," Bill said. "We have enough fabric on board." He pointed at the women's ball gowns. "Anyone have a needle and thread?"

He'd said it in jest, but to everyone's surprise, one of the women produced a tiny sewing kit from her little evening bag.

"A lady should be prepared for every possible inconvenience," she said, and was rewarded with tense laughter.

"Then I would suggest that the men row and the women start constructing a sail," Wallis said.

"And please don't worry about propriety," Paxton added. "It's probably best if you sacrifice your petticoats, ladies."

The following days were a long nightmare of cold, hunger, and thirst. The first night, it rained, soaking them all over again. The women huddled together for warmth, while the men rowed so hard they sweated in spite of the cold. But George Wallis was lucky with the occupants of the rowboat entrusted to him by the captain. The passengers were young and strong, and mostly optimistic. Only two young sisters from Auckland didn't stop crying and praying, and the spoiled heir, Dunbar, refused to exert himself beyond making pointless complaints. The other young men committed themselves to the adventure and took turns rowing with the sailors. There were two accomplished seamstresses among the women, and thanks to his upbringing on Milford Sound, Bill turned out to be a skilled sailor of small boats. With his help, the women constructed an irregular, stiff sail made from hoopskirts and linen petticoats, which they put into service the next day when it stopped raining. When the wind was neither too strong nor too weak, it worked quite well. The main problem was that the board serving as a mast wasn't strong enough to stand up against the wind. Two men had to brace heavily against it to keep it upright, which was almost as hard as rowing.

On the third day, the weather stayed dry and the sun came out. The women freed themselves from their clammy gowns, and Linda and Carol sat there in just their bodices and remaining layers, long past worrying about propriety. As the garments slowly dried on their bodies, they were finally able to warm up a little. But they still suffered from hunger and thirst. The latter would have been life-threatening if the castaways hadn't been clever enough to collect rainwater in their bailing buckets the day before. At least the rowing men were saved from dehydration that way. There were only a few swallows left for the women, whose primary task was not to move very much and to save their strength.

Linda and Carol would have preferred to change places with the men. Being condemned to idleness only caused them more worry. Besides, the men needed help. By this point, the hands of even the most weathered sailors and farmers were cracked and bleeding. Nonetheless, the men still put their full strength into the oars, laughing off Linda and Carol's offer.

At the end of the third day, everyone was exhausted. Linda and Carol dozed listlessly, and even the Auckland sisters' crying and praying had given way to weak whimpers. In spite of it all, Bill Paxton goaded the men to keep rowing, and kept readjusting the sail to catch as much wind as possible. George Wallis's most recent measurements were the only thing that gave the passengers hope.

"Only thirty miles now. If we can hold out for another night and perhaps a day, we'll have done it."

The men oriented themselves by the position of the sun during the day and by the stars at night. They made a great effort to guide the boat farther northwest, hour by hour.

Then, at dawn on the fifth day, Linda was startled out of a restless, feverish sleep and thought she must be hallucinating. In the early morning mist, she saw the silhouette of a mast and sails. It was still far away, perhaps only a dream. She shook Carol.

"A ship," she whispered. "I think—I think I see a ship."

Half an hour later, the women were wrapped in blankets with big cups of hot tea in their hands, aboard the *Prince Albert*. George Wallis had informed the captain of the brig about the sinking of the *General Lee*.

"We heard that the ship didn't arrive," the captain said. "We sailed from Campbelltown yesterday, and they'd been expecting you for days."

"Didn't—didn't any other lifeboats arrive?" Carol stammered.

The captain shook his head. He was a kind older man who had organized the rescue operation quickly and efficiently, and had immediately turned his ship around to take the castaways back to Campbelltown.

"No, miss. The way it looks, you may be the only survivors."

"That doesn't mean anything yet," Bill told the women. "The others could just as easily have been rescued as we were. Wait until we get to Campbelltown."

"Were the others even able to find out where they were?" Carol asked. "Did they have a sextant, like Mr. Wallis?"

Bill looked questioningly at Wallis.

"The captain had the only other sextant," he admitted. "But there are other ways to navigate. Not as precisely, of course. But you can still use the sun and stars."

"Mamaca knows how to read the stars," Linda said to Carol comfortingly. "The Maori were sea travelers a long time ago. And Chris—"

"Chris is a farmer, Lindy. He's never been at sea." Carol saw things more realistically. "And of course Mamaca knows the constellations, but would Te Ronga have taught her how to navigate by them? The Ngati Toa lived on a river. It's been centuries since they traveled by sea."

"Don't be so pessimistic, Miss Carol," Wallis said. "The captain didn't assign an officer to every lifeboat for nothing. The sailors know what to do. Let's take courage from that, and for now we should be happy about our own rescue. Once we're in Campbelltown, we'll find out about everything else."

Bill Paxton reached for a bowl of the hot soup that the *Prince Albert*'s cook had made them. In spite of all their worries about Cat and Chris, Linda and Carol ate it just as hungrily as all the others. Shortly afterward, they fell asleep, finally safe and warm.

They awoke as the *Prince Albert* was entering the natural harbor of Campbelltown. The little city was located on the southern tip of a peninsula, surrounded by hills.

"This is the southernmost point of New Zealand," Bill Paxton said.

The young officer looked much better than he had the night before. Like George Wallis, he had used the short trip not only to recover but also to bathe and shave. The sailors had provided the men among the castaways with clean clothes. Bill wore a wide-cut shirt and loose linen trousers. Instead of the grizzled adventurer of the last few days, Carol and Linda were seeing the man with the friendly, clean-shaven face again. The effect was just as comforting as his kind words. It was almost as though the disaster hadn't happened.

"Perhaps the other lifeboats have already arrived," Linda murmured.

That hope was not fulfilled. The residents of Campbelltown were shocked to discover that the *General Lee* had sunk. No other survivors had been found.

Chapter 20

The citizens of Campbelltown showed the castaways great kindness and sympathy. They provided them with clothing and room and board without reservation. Not much more was necessary. Aside from Carol and Linda and one young couple who had been traveling with the woman's parents, none of the castaways were missing family members. Most could simply continue on their journeys as soon as they had replaced the personal items lost in the wreck. While waiting for friends or relatives to transfer money to the Campbelltown bank, the castaways stayed in guesthouses or private homes.

Things were different for Carol and Linda. The young couple, too, didn't plan to leave before making every effort to find their missing relatives. The couple moved into a guesthouse, but Bill insisted that the sisters stay with his aunt. She was an elderly lady who was grateful for the company and who took care of the girls with great kindness. The girls spent the first few days in a kind of trance. Linda developed a fever, and Carol was so exhausted she could barely do more than eat and sleep. They asked constantly for news, and Bill contacted all the public authorities for them. He was staying with other relatives and had put off his recruiting duties for the time being. As before, there was no sign of the other lifeboats. However, there was no bad news either.

"Neither wreckage nor bodies were found," Bill told the sisters. "No trace of the *General Lee* at all."

"How could there be?" Carol asked tiredly. "Just think how far off course the *General Lee* had gotten. No one even knows where it sank."

The young couple, who were very rich sheep breeders from the North Island, initiated a search. They chartered a sailboat and had it follow the original route of the *General Lee*. But they had no success in finding the survivors.

"I should have insisted on joining Mamaca and Chris's lifeboat," Carol lamented. "We saw them. If they drowned—"

"No, Carrie," said Linda. "I know she's alive. If Mamaca were dead, I would feel it. She's my mother—"

"She's my mother too!" Carol said, offended.

Linda nodded. "Yes. But she gave birth to me. You know how the Maori see it. The entire tribe is your family, but there is a special tie to your blood relatives."

In a Maori tribe, it was normal to call all men and women of the right age *papa*; *mama*; *poua*, meaning "grandfather"; or *karani*, meaning "grandmother." The unusual kinship ties at Rata Station had made perfect sense to Te Haitara's tribe.

"There's *aka* between Mamaca and me," Linda insisted. "I don't know where Mamaca is, but she's not dead!"

Aka was the Maori word for a spiritual connection between two people. The bond could stretch endlessly, but it couldn't break as long as they were both alive. Carol nodded, and was comforted by the thought. After all, she felt such a bond between herself and her sister.

Linda's confidence gave Carol new courage. They spent hours at the harbor every day, talking to sailors about the possibility of a rescue operation. They were constantly accompanied by the loyal Bill Paxton, who was just as plagued by guilt as Carol was. Carol talked to the harbormaster, the captains of ships anchored in Campbelltown, and finally an old whaler who was a bubbling spring of information.

The man spent most of his days in the local pubs, and was delighted by the company of a pretty young woman. "Stewart Island is just off Campbelltown. If they'd fetched up there, they would already have been found," he said as he stuffed his pipe.

"In our lifeboat, we discovered we'd drifted a hundred and fifty miles southeast," Carol told him. "Are there any other islands in that area that they might have gotten stranded on?"

The old man considered. "There's nothing but open sea in that direction. But the Auckland Islands are about two hundred and fifty miles from here."

"Are they populated?" Carol asked excitedly.

The old whaler shook his head. "No. There was a seal-hunting station until all the seals were gone. Then some Maori and a few white settlers came, but they couldn't grow anything. It's a cold, windy place. Not much thrives there but grass, scrub bush, and rata."

"Are there any animals?" Carol asked, determined to stay positive.

"Goats, sheep, and pigs. Depends which island, and what survived. The animals were purposely left so they could be hunted later, as provisions for passing ships. And also for castaways. It's happened before that people washed up there."

"Really?" Carol asked excitedly. "Then shouldn't we send a boat to search for survivors?"

The man shrugged. "The islands are very far away. No telling if the lifeboats could have drifted so far. And there are a lot of islands. Five or six are of a reasonable size, with lots of bays and inlets, and there are countless little ones. You'd be searching for years, little lady."

"Then why do castaways keep being found there?" Carol asked stubbornly.

The old man shrugged again. "Coincidence, lass. Currents. The mercy of God. Take your pick. But sorry as I am, I believe you'll have to accept facts. Your parents are no longer alive."

Afterward, Carol waylaid the harbormaster and the captains of several departing ships. However, the Auckland Islands were far from all of their routes. Why would anyone be sailing toward the Antarctic? She also approached the young couple, and tried to encourage them to launch another search, but they'd given up. The Auckland Islands seemed too far away, and success was too improbable.

"My wife has to come to terms with it now," the young husband said. "It's senseless to cling to hope. We just found out that she's pregnant. We will name the child after her father or mother, and keep their memory alive—but we won't keep searching."

Chapter 21

Eventually, Carol and Linda had exhausted every possibility, and no longer had a reason to stay in Campbelltown hoping for a miracle.

After receiving the girls' letters, which they'd sent immediately after their rescue, Ida had advised them to go home. The sisters had also contacted the Hallidays, who had offered to finance their return trip.

If Cat and Chris do manage to find their way to Campbelltown, you will find out within a few days once you're at Rata Station, Ida wrote.

In truth, she was inconsolable and wanted to rush to the South Island herself. Aside from her daughters and husband, Cat and Chris were the most important people in her life. Ida had a desperate urge to be as close to them as possible, and wished she could have seen what had happened with her own eyes. But some time ago, Karl had left with a government delegation to Taranaki. The government wanted to purchase new land from the tribes, and Karl hoped to make it a peaceful process. Ida was alone at Korora Manor and had no way of contacting her husband. A trip to the South Island was impossible.

> *Please understand: I share your hope of finding Cat and Chris safe and whole. I wish with all my heart that they are still alive. But they would never want Rata Station to be left to ruin. Someone has to take care of the farm, and at the moment that's the best thing you can do for them. Stay strong. I love you, and my heart is with you. Mamida.*

In the meantime, the new year had begun. Carol and Linda had stoically endured Christmas and New Year's Eve, and Bill's aunt had made a great effort to distract them with good food and gifts. Now January was drawing to a close, and Carol was supposed to be getting married in less than two weeks. But she couldn't bear to think about celebrating, and was wondering if she should ask Deborah Butler to reschedule the wedding—but Lady Butler wrote to her first.

The Fenroys were only your adoptive parents, but it would be improper to proceed with the celebration so soon after your painful loss, Deborah wrote. *We'll postpone indefinitely. I've also told Oliver that, although he misses you terribly and is very unhappy about my decision.*

"*Her* decision?" Carol cried in annoyance. "How can she think it's suitable for her to make decisions for Oliver and me?"

"She's probably thinking about the cost of the reception," Linda said. "Our family is supposed to pay for at least part of it, aren't we?"

"So what?" Carol said angrily.

Linda shrugged. "Someone has to transfer the money. Someone has to take over the business for Cat and Chris. Mrs. Butler is just worried. And I know you're anxious to marry Oliver, but Carrie, you can't leave me all alone with the farm! I can't possibly handle everything myself—" Linda's voice broke. For the first time since Cat and Chris's disappearance, she wept bitterly.

Carol took her sister in her arms. "I certainly won't leave you alone until everything has been sorted out," Carol promised. "I was just angry at Mrs. Butler. Mamida is right. We have to go back to Rata Station before summer is over. We have to organize the return of the sheep from the highlands, the winter feeding . . ."

Linda gazed at her fearfully, her eyes still wet with tears. "Will we be able to do all that alone?"

Carol nodded encouragingly. "Of course! You and me, and Fancy! And maybe Oliver too. After all, he doesn't have very many responsibilities at Butler Station. He could come over more often and help us out."

Bill Paxton was heartbroken that it wasn't possible for him to accompany Carol and Linda on their journey back to the Canterbury Plains. But he'd neglected his recruiting work for too long. Still, he helped wherever he could. Since the sisters had no desire to get back on a ship, he organized a journey by land with a traveling merchant. Bert Grisham and his family supplied isolated farms along the coast with groceries and luxury goods. They traveled with two covered wagons and purchased their wares in Dunedin, Oamaru, and Timaru. The Grishams had been traveling the coast road for years and were pleasant, honest people.

Unfortunately, the journey seemed endless to the girls. The Grishams never covered more than five to ten miles a day. They spent more time in farmers' large kitchens exchanging the latest gossip than out on the badly maintained roads. After three days, it was too much for Carol. At the next stop, she asked to buy two horses.

The farmer's family and the Grishams looked at her aghast.

"Two young ladies alone on the road! That won't do. It's dangerous and absolutely inappropriate," the farmer said.

"Lieutenant Paxton entrusted us with your care," Mr. Grisham added.

"What's so dangerous about it?" Carol asked. "Besides, Lieutenant Paxton has no say in it; he's neither a relative nor engaged to either of us. We appreciate your help, but now we'd like to take our fate into our own hands. So, will you sell us two horses, Mr. Baker, or shall we ask somewhere else? We could find a horse trader in Dunedin, but that would cost us valuable time."

Finally, the farmer gave up two young geldings for a small fortune. It was all the money Linda and Carol had. But that didn't worry them too much. There was a telegraph station in Dunedin, where they could contact Ida and ask for travel funds. In the meantime, they took Linda's necklace to a pawnshop. The chain had held through the entire ordeal, which meant a lot to Linda. The necklace made her feel connected to her mother.

"We'll be coming back for it in a day or two," she told the pawnbroker as he handed her a receipt. "I certainly don't want to lose it."

The valuable necklace gave them a substantial sum of money, which made their stay in Dunedin easier. Most of guesthouses refused to take in two women traveling on their own. But the best and most expensive hotel in town rented them a room without any moral judgment. The sisters discovered that, provided they had enough money, women could be accepted as independent.

Once Ida's funds had arrived and Linda retrieved her necklace, the girls rode north quickly and mostly in silence. Neither Carol nor Linda had eyes for the beauty of the landscape. The green hills of Otago, the plains surrounding the mouth of the Waitaki where Captain Cook had originally landed, the beaches and caves around Timaru . . . for Carol and Linda, everything was covered with a gray veil. All they wanted was to return to Rata Station as quickly as possible.

After a difficult three-week journey, the sisters finally arrived home. But they had no time to give themselves up to grief. Summer on sheep farms was quiet, but after more than two months without proper management, Rata Station had several problems that needed to be solved. Most urgently, Carol had to stand up to the head shepherd, Patrick Colderell, who'd decided to rearrange the business to his own liking after he'd received the news that Cat and Chris were missing. Carol quickly dismissed the man, in spite of his strident objections. Of course, that caused even more trouble. He argued that no one was allowed to fire him but Chris Fenroy, and what was more, he was indispensable to the farm.

"No one here is indispensable, Mr. Colderell," Carol told him. She had become tougher and less eager to please over the last several weeks. "As you know, we have to get by without Chris and Cat for a while. If you would still like to work at Rata Station, no one is going to stop you. However, no one will take orders from you, and I'm not going to pay you. So, it would be in your best interest to seek other employment."

In the end, two other shepherds quit in solidarity. The rest, who had all worked there for many years, remained.

It was Linda's job to deal with Jane. That, too, was unpleasant. When the sisters returned to the farm, they immediately discovered Jane's sheep grazing on the lawn. Te Haitara apologized profusely. Colderell and his men hadn't driven the creatures away, so Jane had continued to use the pasture.

"It didn't occur to you to question Mr. Colderell's neglect of his duty?" Linda scolded. "I'm disappointed, *ariki*. Chris would have wished for more loyal friends and neighbors."

Te Haitara made amends by sending over three of his best shepherds as replacements for the ones who had quit—despite knowing it would prompt a tantrum from his wife. The three Maori shepherds were delighted to escape Jane's iron discipline for a while, and they were unbothered by taking orders from Carol and Linda. For the Maori, female tribal elders, *tohunga*s, and sometimes even chieftains were not an unusual sight. Only Rata Station's white neighbors were shocked that Linda and Carol had taken over its management.

"Of course, someone has to make the decisions," Deborah Butler said mincingly. She had actually lowered herself to visiting Rata Station, and was taking up Carol and Linda's precious time by drinking large amounts of tea. She justified her presence as a kind of condolence visit, but it was clear her true motive was to find out what her future daughter-in-law was up to. "I completely understand that you and your sister must take over these cumbersome tasks for now. But, my dear Carol, I've heard that you aren't behaving in a very ladylike manner. And sorry as I am, I now see that it's true! Just the way you're dressed, child . . ."

She glanced at Carol's old riding habit disapprovingly. Lady Butler had arrived on Georgie's boat, unannounced, and the sisters hadn't had time to prepare for her visit. However, Carol wouldn't have made any great effort, anyway. She and Linda no longer cared very much about anything that didn't have an immediate effect on the farm's business. The work took all their strength and concentration. They had no time to think or allow themselves grief, let alone to curl their hair or choose outfits more "appropriate to the situation," as Deborah had remarked in annoyance. It was her opinion that the sisters should be dressed for mourning.

But Linda was strictly against it. "Cat and Chris are alive!" she informed Carol's future mother-in-law. Usually, Linda wanted harmony. She'd always hated disagreements. But now, her gentle voice had turned tart. "We have no proof that they're dead, and so there will be no mourning. And now I must go, Mrs. Butler. I have a sheep drive to organize. I'm going to check the covered wagon, Carol. I think it needs some repairs. You'll entertain Mrs. Butler, of course." She gave Deborah a disapproving look.

Carol watched her sister go, her eyes shining with respect. Linda was getting more assertive every day, in anticipation of running Rata Station alone in the not-so-distant future. After all, Carol hadn't given up her plans for marriage. The first sight of Oliver had been enough to make her forget Bill. Of course, she'd never been in love with the young lieutenant, but his restrained and persistent courtship, his tireless dedication to their cause, and his kindness had made an impression on her. She had thought he might actually have a chance. When they had said their goodbyes, Carol had even allowed him to kiss her on the cheek, and of course he was permitted to write letters.

But when Oliver kissed her again for the first time, the image of Bill faded completely, and Carol's deep feelings for her fiancé were the only thing that pulled her from an otherwise dismal mood. Oliver kissed and caressed her with all the old passion. But her hope that he could help on the farm was in vain. Deborah forbade him to spend the night at a farm that was managed by two unmarried women without guidance from legal guardians.

"I'm my own guardian," Carol told Oliver bitterly. "You can tell your mother that my good reputation is just as important to me as it is to her. You could spend the night in the shepherd's quarters, or in the Maori village. You wouldn't be alone. There would be plenty of witnesses to say that you don't sneak into my room at night."

Oliver made a face that said how much he'd rather spend the night in her room than work for her during the day. Carol ignored it, and tried not to show her disappointment when he argued.

"I can't help you, Carol; you have to see that. How would it look if I slept in servants' quarters? Besides, this isn't my farm. The shepherds would refuse to follow my orders."

"I'm the one who gives the orders," Carol said.

Oliver gave her an indignant look. "You think that I, your future husband, should obey you? Impossible, Carol. I'd be the laughingstock of the Canterbury Plains. No one would take me seriously anymore, not even on my own farm."

"No one takes him seriously anyway," Linda remarked later.

Before the ship sank, her criticism of Carol's fiancé and his family had been very circumspect. Now her tone was sharper. As opposed to the Deanses and the Redwoods, who had kindly offered their help and tactful sympathy for the sisters' loss, all that came from the Butlers was nagging. Captain Butler had even complained that his ram hadn't been returned yet, though Carol and Linda were under the impression that Cat had paid for the creature, not just borrowed it to serve her sheep.

Infuriated by Oliver's unpleasant talk with Carol, Linda had given him the animal to take home. It would surely take him hours, and the ram would probably escape before he'd crossed the Redwoods' land. In the eyes of sheep breeders, that was far more demeaning than a few nights in the shepherds' quarters would have been.

Chapter 22

Linda and Carol had often helped their parents drive the sheep back from the highlands in autumn. Linda, Cat, and Ida cooked for the shepherds and kept track of the animals that had already been collected, while Carol, Chris, and Karl set about finding the herds that had wandered farther away. Now, the girls had to lead the expedition on their own. Fortunately, Jane and Te Haitara had sent more help from the Maori village. Traditionally, Rata Station and Maori Station organized the drive together and only separated their flocks once they'd reached the valley. The sisters were grateful when several women arrived. Linda and Carol couldn't figure out if Jane had showed some sensitivity for once, or if Te Haitara had applied his knowledge of *pakeha* customs. They were just relieved not to be the only women involved in the undertaking.

At night, Carol and Linda shared a covered wagon with two Maori girls, while two married couples set up their tents nearby. Not even Deborah Butler would be able to insinuate that anything improper was going on. Besides, the sisters were far too tired each night to do anything but sleep. The herding of the sheep and the search for strays in less accessible parts of the mountains were difficult and often dangerous tasks.

But the drive was also a special time. They rode through craggy, enchanted-looking landscapes. They discovered hidden valleys, fairy-tale lakes that reflected snow-covered peaks, and streams as clear as glass that were full of fish. Linda, Carol, and Mara had always enjoyed the journey. Cat had shown them sacred Maori sites, often ones that were dedicated exclusively to women. She had told them the stories that her foster mother, Te Ronga, had told her, and had taught them to sing *karakia* and how to sense the presence of spirits. Linda would never forget how her skin had prickled when Mara's ethereally beautiful voice echoed off the rocks. In the evenings by the fire, Cat had told them the legends of the mountains. For the Maori, every peak had a personality, and had a friendly or adverse relationship to the other mountains and their gods or spirits. The Scottish and Irish shepherds had often told stories and sung songs from their own homes. On clear nights, the sisters had stayed up late and tried to name all the constellations that shone incomparably bright in the dome of the sky.

But this year, the memories only made Carol and Linda feel bitter. With Mara still at the Redwoods' farm, Ida and Karl on the North Island, and Cat and Chris missing, the sisters felt deeply alone. Each night, they retired to their wagon early, while the shepherds were still passing whiskey around the fire. Sometimes they slept nestled tightly together, the way they had as children.

During the day, though, they let none of their insecurities show. Linda, the future head of Rata Station, gave the orders. Carol demonstratively followed her lead, even when she had a different opinion. And so, the men came to accept the young woman as their leader. They saw how hard Linda was working, and how smoothly everything functioned with her guidance.

Linda and Carol were very satisfied when they returned to the farm after ten days in the mountains. The sheep had survived the summer well. The ewes and lambs were well nourished, and their fleeces looked excellent. They'd hardly lost any animals.

But the sisters couldn't relax. The creatures still had to be sorted, divided into separate herds, and then pastured and fed for the entire winter. If Carol and Linda used their fields cleverly, they could keep hay consumption to a minimum. The flocks needed to be driven between various pastures, and in rainy weather, they were kept near the house to prevent them from turning the pastures into seas of mud. There was plenty of work for the shepherds and sheepdogs. Carol was busy with Fancy most days, and was also training the first of her ten puppies sired by one of the Redwoods' dogs. The adorable black-and-white balls of fluff had herding in their blood. As soon as they could walk, they ran barking toward the sheep. Linda, who had taken care of them in the first few weeks, constantly had to keep them from getting under the hooves of an irritated ram.

In June, Ida and Karl finally managed to visit Rata Station. They were impressed by how the farm was flourishing. Linda cried in Ida's arms, but continued to insist that Cat and Chris were alive. Karl told them about worrying developments between the Maori and *pakeha* on the North Island. The Hauhau movement was gaining momentum, and as much as Te Ua Haumene also preached peace and love, there were occasional riots.

"They've developed a special ritual," Karl said. "We got the first taste of it back then with the Ngati Hine, but now they've gotten even wilder. They set up a pole that they call a *niu* and dance around it for hours, chanting nonsense and conjuring the Holy Ghost. They think the trance will make them invulnerable, so then they fight like berserkers. Of course, bullets can still hit them, if the English can get off a shot. But that's not always the case. The Hauhau prefer to attack isolated farms, plunder the houses, and kill the residents. They practically butcher them. Your friend was right about that."

Carol and Linda had told them about Bill Paxton and his work recruiting for the Taranaki Military Settlers. The girls were worried about the young lieutenant. In his last letter, Bill had said he might soon be reassigned to the North Island.

"He was talking about war," Carol said apprehensively.

Karl shrugged. "Soon you'll be able to call it that."

Karl and Ida visited the Butlers and set a new wedding date for Carol and Oliver. Oliver wanted to marry right way, but Carol insisted on waiting until after the shearing and the spring drive to the highlands.

"It's much nicer in summer," she said when Oliver began to protest.

It seemed he couldn't bear waiting another half year or longer. But his parents agreed with Carol.

"Perhaps by then Rata Station will be sorted out," Captain Butler said.

"What do you mean, sorted out?" Linda asked in annoyance.

Butler shrugged. "Well, once it's been a full year since Christopher Fenroy and Catherine Rata disappeared, they can be declared dead."

"They aren't dead!" Linda cried.

Deborah Butler pursed her lips in disapproval. "Child, even if you don't want to admit it—"

"It has nothing to do with admitting it," Linda said. "I know that they're alive. There's no reason to declare anything."

"Well, we are of different opinions about that," Butler said. "There are inheritance matters to settle."

"Carol will get her dowry, as planned," Karl assured him, his voice hard. "You don't have to worry about that. As for everything else—" He broke off in anger. Everything else about Rata Station was none of the Butlers' business.

"I can't stand that woman!" Ida exclaimed on the way back. "And the captain is circling the farm like a vulture. He's probably planning to sue Linda in your name, Carol. Do you really want to marry his son?"

Carol nodded. "I love Oliver, Mamida! And like I said, I'm marrying him, not his parents. Oliver would never sue Linda. And certainly not in my name!"

"We'll have to work out an appropriate marriage contract," Karl said. "Don't be mad at me, Linda; I also don't want to believe that Chris and Cat are dead. But Butler isn't wrong. The legal situation is unclear, and that could cause trouble."

Karl and Ida said their reluctant goodbyes, and the winter passed without any incident. Linda and Carol worked hard. Above all, Linda did everything she could to consolidate herself as manager of the farm. She preferred working in the house and barn to herding sheep or training horses and sheepdogs. Now she was trying to be everywhere at once. She was training one of Fancy's puppies so she would have the perfect sheepdog by her side. She was out in all weather with the pup, whom she'd named Amy. When spring finally arrived, the young woman had reached the end of her strength, but an excited Maori boy came by to announce the approach of the shearers.

Linda groaned. "I can hardly even think about cooking and baking for the shearers for days on end to keep them in a good mood, let alone having to be in the shearing shed as much as possible too." She shook her head. "It's sure to be a record year. The fleeces look fantastic. I only wish we already had the shearing over with."

"Things will be calmer again in summer," Carol said comfortingly.

What she didn't say was that they also would have to survive the anniversary of Chris and Cat's disappearance. Not to mention her wedding in March. The date had been set. Then Linda would be alone with the farm.

But there was no time for lamenting. They heard hoofbeats and cheerful shouts. Men swung down from their horses, and covered wagons rolled up. The shearer brigade—twelve strong young men, self-assured and proud to be able to free hundreds of sheep of their wool in one day—had arrived.

Carol and Linda stepped outside to welcome them. The men complimented both their beauty and their skill with Fancy and her promising puppies. Linda was pouring whiskey and attempting to smile when she suddenly saw a familiar face. At first, she thought her eyes were playing tricks on her. The confident grin, the smile lines around the wide mouth, the snow-white teeth, and the dark curls . . . they could all belong to someone else. But the unsettlingly bright blue eyes were unmistakably Joe Fitzpatrick's.

"Fitz?" Linda asked, startled into informality.

Fitz grinned at her. "Miss Linda! I hope the surprise is a pleasant one. Or are you angry that I disappeared so suddenly?"

He immediately sought eye contact, but Linda didn't think it right to sink into his gaze. "No. Of course not, Mr. Fitzpatrick. It wasn't your fault."

Fitz shrugged, and then grinned again. "Some people have different opinions about that. The snobs at the rowing club thought I shouldn't have used a club boat to take the most beautiful girl in the world on a little excursion."

Linda blushed. "Oh no! Then it was my fault—"

"Nonsense!" Fitz waved off her concern. "I wasn't happy there anyway. Those arrogant people had no appreciation for my efforts. I wanted to train their oarsmen, not paint their boats. I didn't care about that job. I only stayed a little longer because of you, Miss Linda, hoping you'd come by again. The following week perhaps, with the excuse of bringing your Bible-thumping uncle to his ship."

Linda blushed more deeply. Back then, she'd had the feeling he could read her mind, and now she was sure of it.

"What makes you say that?" she murmured, but his triumphant expression made her blush. "It's true, I was with my mother in Christchurch. But I—"

Fitz's grin gave way to a warm smile. "Let's not talk about that, Miss Linda. It's all in the past. Yesterday's news, one could say. Let's talk about now."

Linda knew he would bring up Chris and Cat and, as he had done before, would approach the most sensitive subjects without any warning. But she couldn't be angry at him. To the contrary. She would tell him everything—probably more than she had even told Ida and Karl. Linda longed to talk about it, to feel Fitz's undivided interest, sympathy, and understanding.

But there was no time for that now. She had to take care of the shearers. Confused, she tried to break Fitz's spell on her.

"What brings you here, Mr. Fitzpatrick?" she asked. "Are you part of the shearing brigade? Did you learn that at Oxford too?"

Fitz laughed. "No, you could say I learned it at mother's knee. I went to college, but I was born on a farm. Horses, sheep . . . I know my way around them all."

"Then you'll have to join in our little contest," Linda said. "We honor the fastest shearer every year, and we throw a party—" Her forced smile faded as Fitz furrowed his brow.

"Can't imagine you feel like celebrating. I heard about the shipwreck, Miss Linda. But take heart. Sometimes survivors are found after months, or even years."

Linda felt as though a stone had been lifted off her heart. No one, not a single other person who'd heard about their loss, had been so optimistic or hopeful. Linda felt her walls crumbling, just as she'd feared they would.

"I want to believe that," she whispered. "It's just so hard sometimes." She lowered her eyes.

Joe Fitzpatrick reached out and gently lifted her chin with one finger. "Things are only as difficult as we make them," he said kindly. "Look around you! We're in a beautiful country on a beautiful day, and the sun is shining."

Linda stared at him, and suddenly the shadows that had been dimming her view of the world since the shipwreck became softer. She noticed the brilliant red blossoms of the rata bushes again, the blue sky, and the snow on the peaks of the distant mountains. She noticed her mare, Brianna, who was standing in the pasture looking at her curiously, and saw her little dog jump up on Joe Fitzpatrick delightedly. Fitz bent down and picked up the puppy. He laughed as Amy licked his face.

Linda felt the corners of her mouth tilting upward and her eyes begin to glow. It was the first honest smile she'd allowed herself since Chris and Cat had disappeared.

"You're right," she said in amazement.

"I'm always right," he said.

Chapter 23

Linda was convinced that Joe Fitzpatrick had been sent to her by the angels. There was no problem that he didn't find a simple, quick solution for.

It began on the first day. While Carol rounded up the sheep with Fancy and helped drive them into the pens, the shearing brigade had distributed themselves around the shed, and Linda again had the feeling that there had to be at least two of her. Traditionally, it was her duty to supervise the shearing; at the same time, though, the ingredients for the stew for the men's evening meal were sitting in the kitchen. She thought the sheep were more important, so she spent the day with the creatures. In the evening, Linda almost broke into tears when she came back to the house, completely exhausted from her efforts. In front of her still lay the monumental task of turning a huge pile of vegetables and meat into a stew. Quickly. The men only took a short time to wash after work, and then expected to be served their meal. Joe Fitzpatrick found Linda in the kitchen, just as she had unhappily begun to peel the first potato.

"Miss Linda! I wondered where you'd gone. I thought we could sit around the fire and talk about old times." He smiled at her mischievously. "Already working again. Can I help somehow?"

Linda looked up at him with tired eyes. "If you can peel potatoes . . . ," she said dejectedly. "Carol will be here in a moment, but she's still in the sheep pen."

"My pleasure!" Fitz replied cheerfully, reaching for his pocketknife. He picked up a *kumara* and peeled it in no time at all. "But don't you still have to wash all the vegetables, Miss Linda? Then it will be hours until everything is on the table. And you'll fall asleep while you're working, tired as you must be. No, there must be a better way. Do you have palm trees in the garden?"

Within minutes, Fitz had packed meat, potatoes, and sweet potatoes into a large basket. He carried it outside to the shearers and shepherds, who had already started campfires in the meadow in front of the house. The men always slept under the open sky if it didn't rain. After heavy work in the shearing shed, a little whiskey was all it took to put them to sleep.

"Listen up, lads!" Fitz jumped up onto a bale of hay. "Miss Linda is treating us all to a Maori barbecue! We call it *hangi.* Come here, you can all help. We need big palm leaves, and raupo leaves will work too. We need four volunteers to cook at each fire."

Linda gave Fitz a baffled look. In the Canterbury Plains, there was none of the volcanic activity to heat the traditional ovens made of hot stones buried in the earth. What was more, digging and using earth ovens would take far more work than preparing a stew. But Fitz beamed at the shearers, as though inviting them to join the fun. As the men collected the leaves, he poked and banked the campfires until there were enough coals. Then he separated the meat into portions and dexterously wrapped them in palm and raupo leaves, confidently adding spices and herbs that Linda couldn't have mixed better herself, and instructed the men to cover the little packages well with coals. He did the same thing with the vegetables. All the while he offered fanciful explanations of what he was doing. He waxed lyrical about the exotic spices from the kitchen of Catherine Rata, who was known to have lived with the Maori for many years.

Linda watched him, speechless. Fitz's method had nothing in common with Maori cooking. The children of Rata Station knew this technique as a "potato fire." Every autumn during the potato harvest, Karl had lit a fire to burn the old potato leaves, and he'd roast the fresh roots in the coals. On those evenings, Karl and Ida had reminisced about their childhoods in Raben Steinfeld and had laughed a lot because the autumn potato fires were among their few happy early memories.

She was sure that some of the shearers knew the tradition, but no one objected. After all, the Maori could have also had the idea to roast root vegetables that way. The idea of meat wrapped in leaves was new to her, and she could only hope that it was successful. But Fitz seemed to have no doubts. For every bundle of meat, he came up with a different combination of spices. Sometimes he soaked the pieces of mutton with beer and whiskey, and said that it made the spirits of the fire happy.

"The spirits will make the food delicious. To celebrate the *hangi*, we should also sing special songs. They're called *karakia*, aren't they, Miss Linda?"

The men, who'd already begun to drink on empty stomachs, were soon bellowing English and Irish drinking songs. Linda was worried that they would all be totally drunk by the time the food was ready. But the mood was festive, and when the meat was finally unpacked, everyone thought it tasted good. Some of the meat and vegetables were burned on the outside and half-raw on the inside, but the men didn't seem to mind, after Fitz told them that was how it was supposed to be.

"The Indians over in America burn very specific woods to give food flavor, and stir ashes into maple syrup. It's supposed to be very good for your health."

The men pulled the peels off the half-roasted potatoes and laughed about their sooty hands. When Fitz playfully touched Linda's nose with a blackened finger and left a cute spot, the shearers began to paint Maori-style "tattoos" on each other's faces. The evening turned out to be great fun, and Linda finally began to relax and enjoy it, with great feelings of relief. Carol didn't refuse when the men passed the whiskey bottle her way as it went around the fire. But Linda declined each time.

Fitz looked at her worriedly. "You should feel free to have a drink, Miss Linda, ease your nerves. Of course you're worried about Miss Cat and Mr. Chris, but Miss Cat wouldn't want to see you so unhappy."

Linda smiled sadly. "Whiskey makes me sick to my stomach. But I do like a little wine every now and then."

Fitz grinned. "That's more ladylike, anyway," he said. "But should we beg, borrow, or steal? Or do you have a secret stash?"

Linda bit her lip. "Stealing would work," she said uneasily.

Fitz furrowed his brow as she told him about Cat's personal reserve. "That's not stealing, Miss Linda!" he said. "You don't call it stealing when you harvest Miss Cat's sweet potatoes or eat her chickens' eggs. No, you don't need to feel guilty about that. We should get a bottle of wine now and drink to Miss Cat's health!"

Linda felt bad as she fetched the bottle from the pantry. But when Fitz opened it in the style of the smug wine steward at the White Hart, tasting it delicately and declaring that it had a "marvelous bouquet" and "the sweetness of burnt cherries," she had to laugh. After the first sip, her heart immediately felt lighter, and when she fell into her bed later, tired but relaxed, she slept without nightmares, and without being woken at dawn by dismal thoughts.

The next morning, Fitz helped fry eggs and bacon for the shearers. He took over the kitchen in the stone house like a professional.

"I've been a cook before," he confided as Linda realized with embarrassment that half of the work had already been done before she'd even gotten dressed. "I had a café in Oxford."

"I thought you rowed in Oxford," Carol said with grudging admiration.

She had found Joe's "Maori barbecue" cavalier and showy, and she'd been truly annoyed when he'd talked Linda into opening a bottle of wine. Cat's stash had been holy to her. Linda should have at least asked Carol if she thought it was all right to take a bottle. But now Fitz was undoubtedly making himself useful. And, Carol reflected, perhaps the barbecue hadn't been so bad. The sisters hadn't had to wash any dishes.

"Weren't you studying?" Linda asked.

Fitz shrugged. "It's not mutually exclusive with working," he replied, and shot her another winning smile. "Just sit down now, both of you, and eat some eggs. You'll soon be back in the shearing shed. Don't worry about the cooking! I have everything under control."

Linda and Carol ate with the men, but Carol's enthusiasm for Fitz's help waned quickly when she had to spend an entire hour cleaning up after him before she could go back to her duties in the shearing shed. When she finally came out of the kitchen, she watched Fitz as he sheared a sheep. He was quite skilled, she had to admit. He wasn't the fastest, but his jokes and optimistic outlook put the men in a good mood. The head shearer obviously wasn't terribly impressed, and rebuked him regularly. Fitz let the criticism roll off his back.

Toward noon, he proved to be useful again. Linda's mare threw a shoe, and she cursed in an unladylike manner when she realized what had happened. The only farrier at Rata Station was also a shepherd who happened to be busy herding sheep in the farthest pastures. Linda either had to go get him and lose a lot of time or put Brianna in her stall and saddle another horse. But then Fitz stepped in.

"If I can find a hammer and some nails here, I'll have that shoe back on in a jiffy," he offered.

Fitz calmed Brianna with a few kind words, astounding Linda. The horse wasn't always easy to deal with, especially if something like a thrown shoe had made her nervous. Fitz got her to stand still while he took her hoof between his knees and reattached the horseshoe with quick, sure strokes.

"Here, as good as new!" He smiled and passed Linda the mare's bridle. "It's not perfect, but it should hold for a day or two."

"You learned how to do that in Oxford too?" Linda asked in surprise.

"No, Ireland. My uncle was a blacksmith," Fitz replied. "Happy to be able to help!" Then he went back to the sheep.

Linda could hardly contain herself when she told Carol about it that evening. "The man is the answer to my prayers!"

Carol was less impressed. "So what? I could have put a horseshoe back on that way too," she said. "Robby will have to fix it. And the mess he left in the kitchen this morning! I might as well have fried the eggs myself."

"At least he's doing something," Linda said pointedly.

She was referring to the reason that her sister was in such a bad mood. Oliver Butler had stopped by that afternoon to see Carol and ask when the shearers would be ready to move on to Butler Station. Of course, Carol had no time to spend with him, unless he wanted to work at her side. But the thought didn't seem to occur to him. So he just rode home in a bad mood.

Over the next few days, Linda's increasing enthusiasm for Fitz made Carol more curious about the young man—and piqued her own vexation. She observed Fitz carefully and finally asked the foreman of the shearing brigade about him. Linda became annoyed when her sister told her what she'd learned.

"His boss isn't at all satisfied with him," she told her sister, who had just been praising the man for repairing a saddle when he was supposed to be in the shearing shed. "Fitz is not exactly an efficient worker. He talks more than he shears, and keeps the others from their work."

"Not efficient?" Linda said, scoffing. "He won third place in the contest yesterday!"

The breeders awarded a little prize almost every day for the fastest shearer, or held a friendly competition between shearers from different brigades. That sped up the shearing and kept the men in a good mood.

Carol rolled her eyes. "Of course he can do it if he wants to. Competition excites him. He also rowed like a devil when it mattered. The man is a gambler."

It was true, Fitz enjoyed card games. In the evenings, the shearers played poker with the shepherds. On the third day of shearing, Fitz relieved two Maori shepherds of an entire month's pay. The two complained to Te Haitara, who then turned to Linda. She reluctantly brought up the subject with Fitz.

"The Maori don't understand how it works. We don't allow gambling here. The men were shocked when they suddenly owed you ten pounds."

"I won that money fair and square!" Fitz crowed triumphantly, but then backpedaled. "Excuse me, Miss Lindy . . ."

Fitz had recently started to use the familiar form of Linda's name, and she wasn't sure if she liked it. Only family members called her Lindy. And "Miss Lindy" somehow felt much more intimate to her than if he'd just called her "Linda." She didn't want to complain; she had called him by his nickname as well. Of course, in front of Carol and the others, they were both quite formal.

"I didn't want to cause any trouble. Of course I'll give the money back."

Linda nodded, relieved. "That's very kind of you. I hope you understand, we have a good relationship with the Maori, and I don't want to endanger that in any way—"

Fitz looked her in the eye. "Miss Lindy, I would never purposely do anything that would make your life more difficult. To the contrary. I only want to help. Just tell me what I can do for you."

"I want him to stay."

In the farmyard, it smelled deliciously of roasting meat, and Linda and Carol had brought out bowls of vegetables and a basket of bread to where the shearers were eating outside at long tables. The shearing at Rata Station was complete. The shearers were celebrating their traditional farewell before they left to work in the Maori village and then continued to the Redwoods and the Butlers. Linda couldn't wait any longer to tell Carol about the decision she'd made.

"I offered Joe Fitzpatrick a job as foreman of Rata Station."

Carol set a bowl of rice on the table. "Linda, do we have to talk here in the middle of everyone? It would be better to discuss this in private."

"It's my job to hire people," Linda said.

Carol nodded. "Of course," she said as the sisters walked back toward the kitchen. They stepped in and closed the door. "I'm not trying to tell you what to do. I know you'll have to run the farm on your own soon. But as foreman? You'll be stepping on the toes of people who have been working for us for years."

"But as you say," Linda said as she filled a bowl with sauce, "*I* have to run the farm alone. I need someone at my side I can trust."

"You don't trust Robby, David, Tane, or Hemi?" Carol asked.

Linda turned to face her. "Yes, of course I do. It's just that I need someone I can talk to. Someone who thinks like me, who understands me. A—a friend."

Carol pressed her lips together. "You can't hire someone as a friend, Linda. Stop pretending. You're head over heels in love with the man. That's why you want to keep him here. And let me guess: Mr. Fitz refuses to stay as a normal farmhand."

"That's ridiculous!" Linda's face turned bright red. "We're not in love. We just understand each other very well. And if he were just a farmhand, Fitz would get much lower pay than he does as a member of the shearing brigade."

Carol gave her sister a long look. "That wouldn't have bothered a friend," she said softly.

"My sister is afraid that the other workers might not respect you," Linda told Fitz the next day.

She had led him around the farm again and introduced him to the shepherds and farmhands in his new role as foreman. As Carol had feared, they had reacted with perplexed silence.

Fitz shrugged. He strolled across the pastures with Linda, gazing at the thick grass, the freshly shorn sheep, and the shearing shed in the distance. He radiated a great sense of calm. As usual in the young man's presence, Linda felt more relaxed, self-assured, and less vulnerable.

"Don't worry," he said. "I'll win them over." Fitz stopped, turned to her, and sought her eyes. "All I care about is that you respect me, Miss Lindy."

Linda looked away. "I—of course I respect you. I gave you this job—"

The familiar mischievous grin spread over Fitz's face. "More's the pity, Miss Lindy," he said, "if there's nothing between us but respect. Because I'm a little bit afraid to do something like this with a woman I respect so much . . ."

At that, he pulled Linda into his arms and kissed her. It was a long, tender kiss, which became wild and passionate as the young woman responded to it. Fitz pulled her tightly against his chest until it hurt, as though he wanted to be sure that nothing could ever come between them. Linda was out of breath when he finally released her.

"So?" he asked gently. "Still nothing but respect?"

"No," Linda admitted. "I—I think I love you."

Chapter 24

Over the next few months, slowly and patiently, Joe Fitzpatrick helped Linda discover what it meant to be in love. He anticipated her every wish, and was gentle, caring, and passionate. And he never went any further physically than Linda wanted to. He kissed and caressed her, and enjoyed unbuttoning her dress and pleasuring her body with his hands. If she hesitated or stiffened, he stopped immediately. Linda felt safe in Fitz's arms, and she felt that he took her seriously. When they weren't kissing and touching, they were talking for hours. In addition to sharing her confusion and grief over the shipwreck, Linda told him about her entire life, about Chris, Cat, Karl, and Ida, and about Rata Station and Sankt Pauli Village. Fitz listened attentively and made her feel that she was the center of the universe.

Fitz didn't talk much about himself, but Linda never felt as though he were keeping secrets. After all, he answered all of her questions willingly. She thought she knew the story of his life, but every time Carol asked Linda how he'd learned to do something, she was annoyed and ashamed that she didn't know the answers. But those were just tiny drops of bitterness in the sea of love that Linda was losing herself in.

At the same time, Rata Station was flourishing. The wool harvest was even better than it had been the previous year, the lambing had gone quickly and smoothly, and Linda had an entire herd of top-quality yearlings for sale. The most famous breeder on the South Island was interested in buying them. Not even Carol's grim predictions about Joe Fitzpatrick's promotion to foreman had come true.

Of course the men were displeased at first that their boss's lover had been promoted over them. But Fitz managed to impress them with his knowledge of sheep breeding and the management of farm businesses. No one knew for sure how much he'd already known and how much he was learning from Chris's books, which he studied at a blistering pace. Additionally, he was friendly, genuine, and understanding with the farmhands. Fitz bantered with them, but at the same time displayed authority when he needed to. Even the skeptical Carol wondered if she'd been mistaken about him. Perhaps he really was the right person to manage the farm with Linda.

Only the Maori didn't warm up to the new foreman. Te Haitara still felt that Fitz had taken advantage of his men in poker. He didn't talk to Linda about it, but there had been more dissent when Fitz had given back the money. And Jane had a basic mistrust of anyone with such a relaxed attitude toward life, even though the young man also impressed her. He could do figures just as quickly as she could, and was adept at dealmaking. He bargained down the price for transporting the fleeces from Rata Station and Maori Station to Christchurch so much that it actually embarrassed Te Haitara. But amazingly, he managed not to annoy the contractor when he did it. To the contrary, the man and Fitz parted as friends.

"He's a born salesman!" Joseph, the elder of the Redwood brothers, said with a laugh. "That man will convince you in three minutes flat that every ewe from Rata Station can be shorn three times a year and bear five lambs. Where did you dig him up, Linda? He's certainly useful. Though perhaps a little, uh, slick."

Joseph chose his words carefully. News of Linda's relationship with her new foreman had gotten around. Now Joseph sat in Rata Station's large kitchen to negotiate a price for the flock. Fitz had wanted to join them, but Joseph insisted on speaking with Linda and Carol alone. The young man wasn't happy about it, and neither was Linda. Still, she didn't want to contradict her fatherly friend.

Now she blushed. "He arrived with the shearing brigade," she replied vaguely. "And he's not slick, just friendly."

Joseph Redwood furrowed his brow. "Friendly? You hire people because they're friendly? Good, that's your business. I—"

"Are you interested in the lambs?" Linda asked coolly. "We wanted to offer them to you first. They're all from Butler's ram."

Joseph Redwood chewed on his cigar and gazed thoughtfully out the window. The recently weaned lambs were standing in a pen in the farmyard. Fitz moved toward the gate as though he were ready to open it and drive them back out to the pasture.

"The lambs are excellent," Joseph said. "That's not the problem." He put out his cigar and toyed with a coffee cup.

Linda was confused. "Is something stopping you from buying them, Mr. Redwood?" she asked. "Is it the price? I thought it was appropriate."

"No, lass. The price is completely in order. It's just that I don't know if we can do business with you—or with the two of you, rather." He rubbed his forehead, looking a little embarrassed when he saw Linda's injured look and the flash of anger in Carol's eyes. "That is, I have nothing against you girls. You have everything under control. Chris and Cat would be proud. It's just—the conditions at Rata Station—good Lord, you're making this difficult for me!"

"What about the conditions at Rata Station?" Carol asked with annoyance.

Joseph Redwood pulled himself up straighter. "You aren't officially cleared as owners, Carol. You and Linda are operating a business here, but with Chris and Cat still legally missing, no one knows if everything is in order or not. Another heir could nullify everything."

"Another heir?" Linda asked in amazement. "Aside from Carol and Mara and me, there are no heirs. And Carol will be married soon. Of course she's receiving sheep as a dowry, as planned. Chris promised the same number of sheep to Mara, and we're sticking to his decision. We're in total agreement."

Carol nodded.

"You and Linda may be in agreement," Redwood said, "but the Butlers definitely want more. If I know old Butler, he'll demand half of Rata Station once Carol marries Oliver. And what about when Mara marries? Not to mention, we're afraid that Chris could have relatives in England who might suddenly want their share. That's unlikely, but it must be cleared up. Do yourself a favor, girls, and have Chris and Cat declared dead. The shipwreck was a year ago now."

"But they still could be alive," Linda said. "Castaways have been found after much longer. And they could have survived on some island easily. Cat used to live with the Maori, and Chris had to make his own way everywhere." When Captain Butler had expressed the same misgivings months before, Linda had been furious. But now there were tears in her eyes. "If we give up on them, it would be a betrayal."

Joseph Redwood shook his head. "Nonsense! Nothing that you do here has any kind of influence on whether Chris and Cat are alive. If they are really found, which God knows I wish from my deepest heart, then the declaration of death will be nullified. But now you need transparency at Rata Station. Is there a will, by the way?"

Linda and Carol had to admit that they didn't know.

Joseph raised his eyebrows. "You should find out as soon as possible," he advised the sisters. "Until you do, I'm afraid I'll have to pass on the lambs. You'll find that the other breeders will see things the same way."

At first, the sisters ignored Joseph's concerns, and continued to offer the lambs to other breeders. But their old friend turned out to be right. Other neighbors, too, advised the sisters in more or less diplomatic words to clarify the situation at Rata Station. Linda finally discussed it with Fitz, and Carol talked to Oliver. Carol finally had a little more time to spend with her fiancé.

"Darling, that's something you'll have to figure out for yourself," he remarked between kisses. The two of them had ridden out for a picnic and had taken another bottle of Cat's wine with them. But Oliver was hungrier for love than for the cold roast lamb. He couldn't keep his hands or lips off Carol. "My father thinks you should declare Cat and Chris dead, and that the line should finally be drawn. Personally, I would leave things as they are. All that hassle with the notary and municipal authorities . . ." He reached out to unbutton Carol's dress.

"It has nothing to do with the notary or any of that," Carol replied. "It's more about what Chris and Cat would have done. Linda has the feeling we'd be betraying them if we act as though they're dead."

She sighed when she saw Oliver's uncomprehending face.

Fitz reacted to Linda much more considerately. "Mr. Redwood is right," he said when she told him about the conversation. "The death declaration would be instantly nullified if your mother and Mr. Fenroy returned. And it's not as though you want to change anything here. You don't want to sell the farm or separate it, rename it, or do anything else that Miss Cat and Mr. Chris wouldn't have done themselves."

"But we'll have to file the document. When—when we sign it, we'll be saying that they're dead," Linda said, and began to cry.

Fitz kissed her tears away. "Nonsense! You'll just be putting your name on a sheet of paper. That has no sway with the universe or the spirits or fate, or whatever it is you're afraid of. Light it on fire and let the wind take the ashes. Lindy, darling, there are thousands of people in this world who can't even read a form like that! It would be different if you set up a gravestone for Cat and Chris, or had a funeral for them. You don't have to do that, do you?"

Linda wiped the tears off her cheeks. "People are acting as though they expect us to," she murmured.

"Forget those people!" Fitz made a dismissive gesture. "Forget the document too. Once it's signed, no one will ask you about it anymore. If you want, we can go to the closest Maori sacred site by night and burn it, and conjure Chris's and Cat's spirits. Maybe you'll reach them. Don't the Maori believe in telepathy?"

Linda smiled through her tears. "No. They say the Aborigines in Australia do. But my mother's brother Franz says it's nonsense."

"As a reverend, he's not allowed to believe in any spirit but the Holy Ghost," Fitz said unworriedly. "Just think about it, Linda. And don't believe you're doing anything to hurt Chris and Cat. Think about what would be best for you, and how you can get by in life most easily. Cat and Chris always wanted the best for you, didn't they?"

Fitz's argument finally gave Linda the strength to make a decision. It was also he who comforted her before she made her way with a heavy heart to the notary and public officials in Christchurch. Deborah Butler had suggested that she wear mourning clothes. Fitz thought it wasn't necessary.

"You don't have to look like a black crow just because you're signing some sheet of paper. And you don't have to be all morose in Christchurch. Enjoy your day, and go out for a good meal!"

Fitz didn't accompany Linda and Carol to Christchurch himself. Deborah Butler sent her son to support the girls "in their time of need." And Oliver was certainly successful at cheering Carol up. In fact, half of Christchurch was gossiping about them afterward. They complained that the Fenroys' heirs had been celebrating in the rowing club after they had filed papers to declare Chris and Cat dead.

"We still don't want a funeral," Linda told Laura Redwood, who had hesitantly mentioned the gossip to her, and had suggested ways to minimize the damage. "Chris and Cat are alive! I'm sure of it."

The judge in Christchurch saw things differently. It only took a few days to verify Linda's and Carol's statements, and to verify the shipwreck with the shipping company. No further survivors had been found, and the *General Lee* had not sunk in the immediate vicinity of an island where anyone could have been stranded. The disaster had occurred 250 miles from the closest of the Auckland Islands, and the area was seldom traveled by ship, as Carol and Linda had found out in Campbelltown. The captains of the few ships to pass the islands had been asked, however, and they hadn't seen any signs of life.

Based on this information, the judge officially declared Catherine Rata and Christopher Fenroy dead on January 10, 1865. All the other missing passengers and crew members of the *General Lee* had been given up on much earlier.

"The will, if there was one, could now be opened," said Mr. Whitaker, a lawyer from Christchurch who had been helping Linda and Carol. "Unfortunately, neither Mr. Fenroy nor Miss Rata left one."

"But we know what they would have wanted," Carol said. "Can't we just do it that way?"

The lawyer frowned. "It's a little more complicated than that, even though we're hoping for some compassion from the judge. Chris Fenroy was fairly well known, as was your relationship to him. And over the last few weeks, you haven't exactly, well, behaved like ladies. There's been loose talk about you both. Neither of you displayed any mourning when you declared their deaths, and you have planned no funeral."

"That's because we don't believe they're dead!" Linda exclaimed.

The lawyer made a conciliatory gesture. "I know that, Miss Linda," he said. "And I can understand your position. But that doesn't change the fact that, legally, we must search for other potential heirs. If we don't find any, the justice of the peace and the governor will settle the issue out of court. Perhaps after questioning friends and acquaintances. There must be other people who know about Mr. Fenroy and Miss Rata's intentions for the inheritance of the farm."

Carol nodded enthusiastically. "Of course. The Redwoods, the Deanses, the Butlers, and Karl and Ida Jensch."

"Jane and Te Haitara as well," Linda added. "Basically, anyone Chris and Cat knew well."

The lawyer nodded with satisfaction. "Good. Then it shouldn't be a problem. We won't have to go to great lengths with the search for other heirs, provided these acquaintances support your claim. For example, I find it unnecessary to advertise in England. Chris Fenroy has been living in New Zealand for decades, and Catherine has no relatives, anyway. We'll put advertisements in the *Timaru Herald* and the *Otago Daily Times*, and also in newspapers in Auckland and Wellington. Then we'll wait for four weeks at the most."

"That's very kind of you," Linda said. "And as far as the gossip goes, my, uh, our foreman had a good idea. We could have a kind of party at Rata Station for Cat and Chris. Invite a few people to celebrate them, but not to mourn. Do you know what I mean?"

The lawyer suppressed a smirk, obviously having heard the gossip about Linda and Joe Fitzpatrick. "Your foreman," he said slowly, "is very clever."

A week later, Linda and Carol invited their friends and neighbors over to "keep the memory of Chris and Cat alive," as Fitz put it. The celebration was very touching. The Redwoods, the Deanses, and Te Haitara told stories about Chris and Cat's life together without using the word "death" even once. Makuto, the Ngai Tahu priestess, conjured the spirits and sent greetings from everyone present to Chris and Cat, wherever they happened to be. Then she focused on Linda, sensing her connection to Cat. She sang a *karakia* and helped Linda send thoughts and good wishes along the *aka* bond between daughter and mother. Linda wept with deep emotion. She had almost stopped believing in the bond. The fact that Makuto could also "see" Cat strengthened her conviction that she would see her mother again someday.

Mara played the *koauau* and sang Cat's favorite songs, accompanied by Maori musicians and Irish farmhands. Most of the women had tears in their eyes, and even the men were sniffling. Laura Redwood said a prayer. Only Deborah Butler observed the events without emotion. This was clearly not what she felt a funeral ceremony should be.

Captain Butler, on the other hand, seemed satisfied after asking the girls about plans for the inheritance. "Of course, we'll have to talk more about the details later," he remarked.

Oliver devoured Carol with his eyes. She was too much at the center of attention for him to touch her or kiss her. But he still whispered incessantly in her ear.

"Just a few more weeks until the wedding," he said softly. "I can hardly wait."

Carol, who wasn't really feeling the urge for physical affection on that emotional day, wished that he would just hold her hand the way Fitz held Linda's. It was clearly intended to be comforting, and not at all clandestine. Fitz somehow managed to do it in such a way that no one saw the gesture as inappropriate or possessive, but rather an expression of fondness and sympathy.

Two days after the party, Georgie brought a letter from the lawyer. The sisters opened it right at the dock after he'd rowed away. Mr. Whitaker had invited Linda and Carol to a meeting in Christchurch.

"'It is with regret that I must inform you that someone has made a claim to Christopher Fenroy's legacy,'" Carol read aloud.

Linda gave her a startled look. "Who?" she whispered.

Carol looked up, her eyes dark with anger. "Jane Fenroy-Beit," she said. "His wife. In the name of his son, Eric Fenroy!"

Chapter 25

"Mrs. Fenroy is in possession of a valid marriage contract," the lawyer said. Linda and Carol had gone to see him the day after receiving his letter. "She also has a birth certificate for her son, which was prepared by the magistrate here in Christchurch. That's incontestable."

"But she divorced Chris!" Linda cried. "It was years ago. She's married to Te Haitara now."

"Are there any documents?" Mr. Whitaker asked, his brow furrowed. "To my knowledge, divorces have to be made by way of England. That's very complicated and very expensive. There must be a record of it in Chris Fenroy's papers."

Carol cleared her throat. "They, uh, were divorced in a Maori ritual called *karakia toko*. The divorce is official in the eyes of tribal law. Jane married again immediately afterward, also in the Maori tradition."

The lawyer rubbed his temples. "Well, the divorce and the new marriage may be binding for the Maori, but they certainly aren't for the Crown. Mrs. Fenroy is appealing to that fact now, and demands the inheritance for her son, Eric."

"Eru isn't even Chris's son!" Linda said. "He's—"

"Officially, he was born into marriage. Mrs. Fenroy had a birth certificate issued for him. And you, Miss Linda and Miss Carol, as far as I know, aren't even related to Mr. Fenroy." Mr. Whitaker shuffled his papers, looking slightly embarrassed.

"We're Catherine Rata's daughters," Carol shot back.

The lawyer sighed. "Your surname is Brandmann. According to your birth certificates, you are the daughters of Ida Brandmann, né Lange, who was remarried to Karl Jensch. And that doesn't help you, because your father or stepfather, whatever you prefer to call him, sold his share of Rata Station to Christopher Fenroy.

Catherine Rata doesn't appear in the documents at all. According to the deed of ownership, she owns only one piece of land between the local Maori village and Rata Station. It was signed over to her by Ida Brandmann many years ago, after her deceased husband, Ottfried, made a deal with the Maori for it. Apparently, he cheated them, and Mrs. Fenroy is arguing in retrospect that the Ngai Tahu would like to have the land back. Officially, Catherine Rata has no heirs."

"That witch!" Carol hissed. "Jane knows very well to whom Chris wanted to leave his land, and that half the farm was Cat's. She knows that they were a couple."

The lawyer shrugged. "The term for it is 'informal marriage.' Everyone accepted Miss Catherine's position. But unfortunately, it was never officially confirmed. Mr. Fenroy should have at least made a will. But like this . . . I'm sorry, ladies. A lawsuit would be pointless. You'll have to leave the farm."

"A week's notice?" Linda stared at the document in her hand in disbelief. The sisters were now standing outside the lawyer's office. "Where are we supposed to go?"

"Jane obviously doesn't give a damn!" Carol exclaimed. "'With this very short notice, Mrs. Fenroy isn't doing you any favors, but her demand is completely legitimate in the eyes of the law,'" she said, quoting Mr. Whitaker's letter. "Is he our lawyer or Jane's?"

"He can't do anything about it," Linda said. "You heard him. Jane has been planning this for years now. She even got a *pakeha* birth certificate made for Eru."

"I'd be very interested to hear what Te Haitara has to say about it." Carol still sounded as though she were prepared to fight. "And what do you mean, she's been planning this? It almost sounds as though you think she had something to do with the shipwreck."

Linda shook her head. "No, of course not. But she had obviously taken it into account that Chris might die before she did. And then she coldly calculated how to make Rata Station her own. Cat wouldn't have stood a chance against her! And Karl and Ida would have had to just deal with the fact that she was a business partner."

"She must have been thrilled when she found out that the farm would belong to her alone. She probably didn't even know that Karl sold his share." Carol wiped her eyes. "I'll speak to her and Te Haitara today. I can't imagine that he's supporting her decision."

"How could you do this?"

Carol dispensed with any words of greeting when the sisters found Jane Fenroy-Beit at Rata Station, just as they were getting out of their boat. The new "owner" was leisurely inspecting the barns and shearing shed. Fitz was following her. He looked like an angry pit bull on a strong leash. He had probably tried to stop Jane, but capitulated when she'd shown the papers that legitimatized her claim.

Jane was wearing a comfortable, frayed tea gown. She had not dressed formally for this occasion, and her hair was pinned up loosely. Had she known that the sisters had gone out? Or did she just want to demonstrate how easily she could lay claim to her inheritance?

"I'm only taking what I have a right to," she replied calmly. "There's no reason for you to be so disagreeable, Carol."

"I shouldn't be disagreeable?" Carol shouted. "When you're cheating us of our inheritance? You haven't been married to Chris for decades! And Te Eriatara isn't his son—"

"Just like you and Linda aren't Chris's daughters. But Eru is his heir by English law; he was born into marriage without a doubt. It's immaterial who the father is. So you'll just have to accept it. The lawyer probably already told you everything. You have a week to leave the farm. You, Carol, will almost be married by then, anyway. And Linda, perhaps you should take little Margaret to the Jensches on the North Island. Under the circumstances, the girl won't want to stay with the Redwoods for much longer."

Linda pursed her lips. So Jane had an additional motive for claiming Rata Station. She was trying to finally get rid of Mara. Then she could get Eru back under her thumb and turn him into a sheep baron. When Te Haitara's tribal lands were combined with Rata Station, it would be the largest breeding business in the country, and all in the Fenroy name. No one on the South Island would be able to surpass Jane's son and heir.

"What does your real husband have to say about all this?" Linda asked, less provokingly than unhappily. "Te Haitara was Chris's friend."

Jane shrugged. "You're welcome to ask him," she replied. "But please don't distract me from my work now. I have to make a few lists, of the living and material inventory of Rata Station. I'm sure you understand. Not that anything might disappear."

Linda would have liked to give up and crawl under a bush to lick her wounds. But Carol dragged her toward the Maori village. "Who does that woman think she is?" she said, raging. "'Not that anything might disappear'—as though we would be stealing something from *her*!"

Linda sighed. "We'll have to go through all the papers carefully. In any case, I have Brianna. Mrs. Warden wrote my name on the sales contract. Chris didn't think it was very important, but Mrs. Warden told me she wouldn't have come to New Zealand as a girl if she hadn't been able to take her horse with her. And that was only possible if she was the sole owner of Igraine. Just like Cleo, her dog. You'll have to look at Fancy's papers, Carol. She's certainly yours too."

"And Amy and the other puppies. At least that's something. We could start a dog- and horse-breeding business."

"Without land?" Linda asked bitterly.

"At Butler Station," Carol replied. The sisters had reached the Maori village, and they began to look for Te Haitara. "You'll come with me when I get married. Butler Station is huge; there's plenty of space for you."

Linda didn't answer. She had spotted the chieftain. He was deep in conversation with the tribal elder. As Carol and Linda approached, Makuto, the *tohunga*, remained seated. She sat at a slight remove, but not so far that she couldn't listen to the conversation between the chieftain and the sisters.

Linda nodded to the older woman respectfully. Makuto wore traditional garb. The sisters had never seen her in *pakeha* clothing, although other women in the tribe often wore it. Her woven skirt came to her knees, and her upper body was naked. She'd wrapped a blanket around her shoulders to ward off the evening chill.

Te Haitara watched Carol and Linda sorrowfully as they approached. "I'm so sorry," he said.

"Is that all? Do you have nothing else to say?" Linda said sharply in Maori. For the first time, she didn't address him formally. "Can you do nothing? Jane is your wife. She can't be married to two men."

"That's what I told her," Te Haitara said. "And the *tohunga* told her too. But Jane thinks it's all *pakeha* business, just a matter of papers. She says it has no meaning for us."

"It has no meaning that Eru isn't considered your son?" Linda demanded.

The chieftain rubbed the tattoo that covered his wide face. "Anyone can see whose son Eru is," he replied evasively.

"Even if his name is Eric Fenroy? *Ariki*, after his birth Jane registered him in Christchurch as Chris's child!"

It was difficult to find the right word to say "registered." There was nothing comparable in Maori.

"She had it written down that Eru was Chris's son," Carol said helpfully when Te Haitara looked at Linda blankly.

"Had it written down," the chieftain repeated. "I don't really understand."

His injured expression said more than any words could. Te Haitara knew very well what kind of game Jane was playing with him and Chris.

"Chris's legacy is not intended for Eru, *ariki*," Linda said. "You have to see that."

The chieftain touched his tattoo again. "Eru is not inheriting immediately," he said. "Jane is. And I can't stop her from claiming it. Not even if I go to Christchurch and say she's married to me."

"*Pakeha* judges don't recognize Maori marriages, do they?" Linda asked.

Carol snorted. "Not unless both partners were single before. But Jane and Chris weren't divorced yet. Of course they were divorced through the *karakia toko*; I know, *ariki*. But a marriage formed in the *pakeha* way has to be ended that way too. Without a divorce, which is also just a piece of paper, there can be no new marriage."

The chieftain ran a hand over his hair, which was bound in a warrior's knot, and then put the hand to his nose. It was a ritual gesture. According to the Maori beliefs, the god Raupo lived in a chieftain's hair, and his spirit had to be breathed in again after the chieftain touched his head.

"Chris warned me about Jane," he murmured. "Back then, I thought he just didn't want to give her to me. I even got angry. But I just didn't understand. I will never understand the *pakeha*, even though I've been with Jane for so long . . ." He looked away.

The sisters waited.

"In any case, I can't help you," the chieftain said after he'd pulled himself together. "According to our laws, I have no rights to Jane's land. She can do whatever she wants with it."

As opposed to in England, where a woman's property automatically belonged to her husband after marriage, a Maori woman could inherit and manage her own land. That cultural difference also created problems with the *pakeha* settlers. It sometimes happened that Maori men sold their wives' or sisters' land without permission. When the women complained, the *pakeha* buyers didn't understand that they'd been party to a deception, and of course they refused to give the land back.

"Jane follows every law that is to her advantage," Linda said bitterly.

Te Haitara shrugged. "At least I can offer you some sheep from our stock, as *utu*."

Utu was the Maori concept for a compensation payment with which it was possible to right a wrong.

"Don't bother, *ariki*," Carol said angrily. "Who knows what would happen if you tried to give us the animals. Your sheep probably all belong to Jane too—of course, only on paper. We'll manage somehow."

"You're welcome to stay here," the chieftain offered. "Chris and Cat, Karl and Ida, her children . . . We've had our *powhiri*, and you've learned and danced with our children. We're part of the same tribe."

Linda shook her head. "We can't stay here and play shepherd to Jane's sheep," she said bitterly. "And we're not part of the tribe either. I used to believe that, but now everything is different. Te Ua Haumene said it loud and clear: you are Maori, and we are *pakeha*. The land can only belong to one of us. The only question is, who?"

Makuto, the old priestess, had remained silent so far. Linda was important to her; she had initiated the young woman in many of the secrets of her people. She'd taught the girl everything about healing that Linda hadn't been able to learn from Cat. Now she got up and faced the chieftain. She was majestic, even though she was significantly shorter than Te Haitara. In the light of the rising moon, her body cast ghostly shadows.

"She's right, *ariki*," the priestess said softly. "They must leave. Poti's daughter must find her own way in the world, and your Jane must go as well. When all is said and done, Linda will know who she is. Jane will never know that unless she allows herself to be shown. You must find out, *ariki*. Show Jane who she really is, before she destroys you as well."

Chapter 26

"Perhaps you should have accepted Te Haitara's offer," Linda said as the sisters walked back to Rata Station, exhausted and discouraged. "A few sheep as *utu*, in case the Butlers insist on your dowry."

Carol shook her head. "No, Linda, Oliver will have to take me as I am. He loves me. He doesn't care if I bring a few hundred sheep into the marriage or not."

Linda wondered if that also applied to Fitz. They'd never talked about marriage. But would Fitz really not care if she was a rich heiress or a pauper?

Fitz was waiting for the sisters in the farmyard. He already seemed to be distant when they arrived. Linda wondered if he was just being tactful or if he was already preparing for a retreat. Jane had doubtlessly made it clear to him how much had changed in Carol's and Linda's lives that day.

"Are you hungry?" Carol asked.

The sisters walked into Cat's old longhouse. Though they lived in the stone house, they felt close to Cat and Chis in the wooden structure. This kitchen was cozier than the other. And since they hadn't changed anything there since Cat's disappearance, it gave them the feeling that she and Chris could walk through the door at any moment.

Linda shook her head. "Not really. But we should still eat something." She tried to smile. "And we should leave as little for Jane as possible."

Carol searched the cupboards and came up with some bread and cheese. "That means starting tomorrow, we should eat a sheep every day," she joked.

Then her face fell. "Oh, Lindy, we never should have let ourselves be talked into declaring Mamaca and Chris dead."

Linda shrugged. "It would have occurred to Jane sooner or later that she could do that herself," she replied. "Don't beat yourself up about it. Instead, check Fancy's papers and make sure she really belongs to you. It would be a big relief if we didn't have to give her up. Wait, where are the dogs? I'm going to go check the barn."

As soon as Linda opened the barn door, the collies leaped up so enthusiastically that she felt as though she'd been gone for weeks instead of just one day.

"How'd you get in here?" Linda asked, smiling through her tears.

Fitz stepped out of the shadows. "I put them out of the way so that horrible witch wouldn't get any ideas. She made a list of every horse, dog, cow, and chicken that was walking around. She probably knew the exact number of sheep by heart already, considering the envious way she always eyes the herd. So I brought Brianna and Shawny and the dogs to this wing of the barn. She hasn't searched it yet." Shawny was Carol's horse.

Linda leaned into Fitz's embrace. "That was kind of you. And very smart. But Brianna belongs to me officially, and the dogs belong to Carol, we hope. Shawny isn't worth much, so Jane won't insist on keeping her."

"I wouldn't be so sure about that," Fitz said, and pulled Linda close. "She's a greedy beast. My poor darling . . ."

Linda nestled against him, grateful that he was looking out for her and the animals.

"I don't know what to do," she whispered against his chest, weeping while he kissed her hair. "There was always only Rata Station for me. I wanted to stay here until the end of my days. I was happy here."

Fitz leaned back and pushed her hair from her face. "Lindy, don't cry," he said gently. "You can be happy anywhere. If you can't have the farm anymore, then you'll do something else."

Linda gazed at him in confusion. "But I can't do anything else . . ."

"Nonsense!" Fitz made a dismissive gesture. "You can do anything you want. For example, you could come with me. Obviously, I'm not going to stay here and work for that witch. They found gold on the west coast, Lindy! We could stake a claim and get rich! And then we'll return and buy the farm back. You will laugh again, my darling!" He gave her an irresistible smile.

Linda furrowed her brow. "Are you serious?"

Fitz put his arms around her again, stroked her back, and kissed her. "Of course I'm serious. I'd do anything for you. You know that."

Linda felt her fear and tension dissolve. With Fitz, everything seemed easy. He seemed so self-assured, invincible . . . even if he was talking nonsense. She certainly wasn't about to go off chasing after gold. But perhaps Fitz could find employment at Butler Station. After all, he and Oliver were friends. Then Linda could still be with him.

The sales contract for Fancy really was made out to Carol Brandmann, and of course that meant the puppies belonged to her as well. Most of the litter had already been sold, but three puppies were left, two male and one female. They had been carefully trained, and would bring several hundred pounds.

"So I'm not coming to you as a total pauper," Carol teased Oliver when he arrived at Rata Station the next day.

It touched her that he'd set out as soon as he'd gotten the news. She had wondered if she should write him a letter, but of course Georgie had already heard everything and had spread the word. Now Carol sought comfort in her fiancé's arms.

"That is, *we* aren't coming as total paupers," she added. "Because of course I have to bring Linda. At least for now. Perhaps in the long run she'd prefer to go live with Mamida and Kapa on the North Island. The two of them are coming to our wedding, so we can discuss it then. Right now there's so much to think about, I—"

"I have something to discuss with you too," Oliver said. He gently freed himself from her embrace and pushed her away from him. "You know I'm really sorry about this."

Carol nodded. "Of course you are, I know, I—"

"No—no, you don't understand." Oliver sounded tortured. "Carol, after what happened with Rata Station, it turns out that you—you aren't Chris Fenroy's heir."

Carol frowned. "You already knew that," she said. "I'm Ida Jensch's daughter from her first marriage. That's no secret."

"Of course not." Oliver began to squirm. "It's just that it always looked as though you were the heiress of Rata Station. So, the heir of Butler Station would marry the heiress of Rata Station—"

"What are you trying to say?" Carol asked. Her voice broke.

"Well—please, Carol, don't be angry. But my mother thinks—my parents—the thing about the dowry—"

"Oliver!" Carol was trying to stay calm. This couldn't be true. She needed confirmation, and he'd have to say it. "Oliver, are you trying to say that you don't want to marry me anymore?"

Olive nodded, relieved. "Yes. Yes, exactly. I knew you'd understand. And I'm really terribly sorry. I—honestly, I love you, I—"

Carol's hands clenched into fists, but she stopped herself right before she lost her temper. Perhaps not all was lost. "Oliver, we're already engaged. We celebrated our wedding night early, don't you remember? If you love me, then marry me. It doesn't matter if your mother thinks I'm not good enough for you, or how important the dowry is for your father. Butler Station is a large, rich farm. A few hundred sheep more or less won't matter!"

"But I can't. The party in Christchurch—" Oliver bit his lip.

"We don't need a party in Christchurch!" Carol cried. "All we need is a justice of the peace. Stay here tonight, and we'll ride into town tomorrow or take the boat. By the way, we have our own boat; you could even row us there if you want. Then we'll officially be man and wife, the day after tomorrow at the latest."

"My parents would disinherit me," Oliver said.

Carol shook her head. "That's nonsense, Oliver! You're their only son. They probably couldn't disinherit you even if they wanted to. They would come to terms with it quickly, believe me."

Oliver shook his head. "No. No, I can't. And it would be unfair to Jennifer Halliday."

"Jennifer Halliday?" Carol asked in confusion. The Hallidays in Southland had not only three sons but also a daughter.

"Mr. Halliday discussed it with my parents when he was here last year. He said he was looking for a husband for—for Jennifer. And my mother just wrote to him."

Carol stared at the man she loved in disbelief. "They immediately looked for a replacement for me? And you agreed? You feel responsible for her, a girl that you don't even know?"

"She's supposed to be pretty," Oliver murmured.

Carol's hand rose of its own volition and landed hard on his cheek. The blow left a mark. Oliver touched his face and gazed at her in complete confusion.

"You're crazy!" he said. "I never wanted to believe it, but my mother thinks—well, she always said that here at Rata Station things were somehow deranged. And now—I'm sorry, Carol."

Oliver turned to go. Only then did Carol realize that Georgie's boat was still tied up at the pier. Oliver had actually asked him to wait. The boatman was staring at Carol. She had doubtlessly just given him plenty of fuel for the gossip-hungry settlers in Christchurch. When Carol's gaze met his, he lowered his eyes sheepishly.

Carol considered shouting something after Oliver, perhaps threatening him. She could pretend that she was pregnant, which fortunately, she wasn't. But then she decided to remain silent. He wasn't worth the effort, not even the effort of a lie. None of the Butlers were worth anything.

Carol kept control of herself with an iron hand until she reached Linda in the kitchen. Then she broke into a flood of tears.

"We'll have to go to Mamida and Kapa in Russell, after all," Carol said once she'd finally calmed down. She had cried for almost an hour.

Linda had held her sister tight, all the while fighting back her own tears. It wasn't just Carol's world that had crumbled. Another hope had also been destroyed for Linda. Now there was no chance Fitz could join them at the Butlers', and it was unlikely that he'd want to go to her parents on the North Island. Fitz would go on his way, wherever the wind carried him, and she would lose him. Unless . . .

"I'm going with Fitz to the gold rush," Linda said.

It was rare for Carol and Linda to fight, but now a dam broke.

"You can't go gallivanting around with a man you've only known for a few months!" Carol shouted. "And Fitz is undependable, Lindy. He's a con man!"

"Half of Christchurch believes he's a marriage swindler, after me for my money," Linda shot back. "And what happened yesterday? He proposed to me, just when I'd lost everything. He's not only dependable, Carol; he's my rock!"

Carol slapped her forehead. "You call that a proposal? Did he fall on his knees and beg you to spend the rest of your life with him? No, Linda, he asked if you happened to want to accompany him on his next adventure. The man's had three jobs just since we've known him! He tries anything, talks his way out of trouble, he lies—"

"The Maori call that *whaikorero*," Linda said.

"Do they?" Carol said, scoffing. "The art of beautiful words? Our Maori workers were calling him *ngutu pi* . . ."

Ngutu pi meant a braggart, someone who talked nonsense to make himself look impressive.

"Fitz is a decent man!" Linda insisted. "I just know it."

Carol took a deep breath. A sharp retort was on the tip of her tongue, but she bit it back. "That's what I thought about Oliver too," she said, and rubbed her temples. "You have to make up your own mind, Linda. But you can't just go to the gold rush as a single woman. You know what people say about those places. Thousands of men, grubbing in the dirt. A paradise for tricksters and hell for the desperate. The only women there are—" Carol blushed.

"Couples and families went to Otago, too, after gold was found," Linda argued. "Just think of Miss Foggerty and the Chatterleys."

Carol twisted her tearstained handkerchief and bit her bottom lip. "Families and couples. That's what I mean. Linda, I'm sorry to say this, but I don't like Fitz. But if you really want to go run off with him, then he'll have to marry you first."

Chapter 27

Linda had no idea how to get a real marriage proposal out of Joe Fitzpatrick. She finally decided to try a picnic. There was no reason for her or Carol to work on the farm anymore, so she gave the foreman the day off and invited him for an excursion.

"That's the way to do it!" Fitz said. "Enjoy your last days on the farm. We'll celebrate the future, Lindy!"

Linda nodded. She didn't feel the slightest inclination to celebrate, but perhaps things were about to change. In any case, the day started well. Linda led her friend to a clear lake in the foothills of the highlands. The sun drenched the Southern Alps in golden light, mirroring their image in the still water and warming the two lovers as they stretched out on the blanket after their meal.

It made Linda feel sordid and calculating, but she allowed Fitz to touch her more than she ever had before. At first, she was afraid of losing control when she allowed him to stroke and kiss her breasts. But Fitz kept himself in check and charmed her again with creative, amorous play. With great ceremony, he removed one of Cat's last bottles of wine from one of his saddlebags.

"Don't be angry, darling. I filched it. Or did you want to leave it for Jane?"

Fitz filled two glasses, but didn't drink from his immediately. Instead, he dipped a finger in, drew wet lines across Linda's breasts, and then kissed them away. At first, Linda was shocked, but then she laughed. She felt set afire as he licked the wine out of her navel and gently stroked her mound. Finally, something exploded inside of her, and Linda felt this was how it must feel to give yourself up completely to your beloved.

Afterward, Linda gathered her courage. As Fitz lay next to her, leaning on his elbows and tickling her with a piece of grass, she finally broached the subject.

"I've been considering if perhaps I really should come with you to the gold rush."

Fitz stopped his game and sat up. Before Linda could continue, he pulled her up into his arms.

"That's my Lindy!" he cheered. "No more moping around, no more complaints. You're coming with me, and we're going to make you rich! I will bury you in gold, Linda Brandmann!"

He kissed her again and played with her hair.

Linda took a deep breath. "Carol thinks that I can't go to Otago as Linda Brandmann."

Fitz let her go, looking puzzled. "What do you mean? Do you have another name?" But then the old familiar grin overtook his features. "Hell, you want to marry me? Your sister railroaded you into proposing?"

Linda nodded, embarrassed. She was blushing all over her body.

Fitz laughed loudly. "And I always thought Miss Carol couldn't stand me!"

Linda lowered her eyes. "If you don't want to . . ."

She wasn't prepared when Fitz grabbed her by the waist and then rolled with her over the grass, laughing.

"You better believe I do! I've never really thought about getting married before, but it's something that should be given a try, isn't it?"

Linda swallowed, torn between elation and trepidation. "Marriage is forever, Fitz."

Fitz kissed her. "Until death do us part," he quoted. "I know, sweetheart. I was just having a little fun. Good, when shall we do it? I should take the next boat to Christchurch and arrange the ceremony, don't you think? So we can tie the knot before we have to leave Rata Station." He grinned. "We'll take to the road in a few days, and we don't want to be traveling together in sin."

Linda attempted to sound triumphant when she told Carol about her engagement. But she couldn't disguise the bitter aftertaste that Fitz's initial reaction had left her with. Of course she was happy. He had never wanted her for her money. Instead, he was marrying her now that she was poor, and doing so enthusiastically. Linda just wondered if there shouldn't have been a little more talk about love. Had Fitz ever really told her he loved her? She pushed the thought aside. He didn't have to say it. He showed it.

Carol congratulated her sister. "We'll have to telegraph Mamida," she said. "And we have to tell her about Rata Station. We have to tell Mara, too, if the Redwoods haven't already. I hope she won't make a fuss about having to go to the North Island after all."

Linda nodded. "There's nothing else left for her to do; she has to see that. In any case, Jane won't let her come within bowshot of Eru. Pity that he's still so young. Otherwise, he could disobey Jane and marry Mara. Then Rata Station wouldn't be completely lost."

Ida telegraphed back immediately, horrified by Jane's behavior. But her lawyer in Russell couldn't tell her anything different than Carol and Linda's attorney in Christchurch had told them. Karl selling his share of the farm had been an unlucky coincidence. With the Jensches as partners, Jane wouldn't have been able to throw the sisters out. But now, Ida had no influence. She could only comfort Carol and Linda, and urge them to come to Russell as soon as possible.

I'm so incredibly sorry, she wrote, knowing full well she'd have to pay the telegraph station a small fortune to send such a long message. *We were all so happy at Rata Station, and you were all our children. No one could have imagined that selling our share of the farm could endanger your inheritance. We thought it was clear that Rata Station would belong to the three of you in the end. Now, through Jane's unforgivable scheming, your inheritance has been reduced to our little house in Russell. But we can all live here too. You are welcome at Korora Manor. This is your home, and once you've arrived, we'll make plans for a new start. I love you, and in spite of all the adversity, I am thrilled about having you here. Looking forward to seeing you soon. Mamida.*

Karl was traveling again, so the sisters couldn't get his point of view. After his return, he and Ida had planned to come to Carol's wedding. Of course, they wouldn't be able to come to Linda's. Fitz had managed to get the prescribed waiting period shortened from two weeks to three days.

Ida also sent a telegram to the Redwoods and instructed them to send her daughter to the North Island immediately.

Two days later, Mara appeared at Rata Station, accompanied by Laura Redwood. She was moody and sullen, but had her belongings packed and was obviously ready to obey her mother. There was nothing else she could do. Laura and Joseph wouldn't have allowed her to stay against Ida's will.

Laura, as spirited as she was, got into a fierce argument with Jane. In the name of the Redwoods, she revoked all future collaboration for sheep breeding. It didn't bother Jane very much. Her new, combined sheep farm would be one of the biggest in the country, and largely self-sufficient. And if it wasn't, Jane would have her choice of sheep barons to work with.

"She's still going to need her neighbors," Laura told the sisters, her eyes still aflame.

Then she bid them a tearful farewell. Linda hadn't invited the Redwoods to her wedding, too embarrassed that there would be no reception. The young couple simply couldn't afford it, even though Linda wasn't completely penniless. Carol had sold Fancy's last puppies and had shared the money with her. What was more, Ida sent another telegram to say that the money she'd paid in advance for Carol's reception at the White Hart could of course now be used for Linda's. Fitz immediately began planning a celebration, but Linda could only shake her head.

"Fitz, we'll need that money for household supplies! We can't just squander it on luxury and then set off without even a blanket and cooking pot. You can't rely on finding gold our first day in Otago!"

The two of them finally agreed on a small family dinner at the White Hart. Fitz undertook negotiations with the hotel keeper in his usual winning manner, and somehow convinced the man to give back the full balance of Ida's down payment. It was enough to buy a covered wagon that Brianna could pull, and the most essential supplies.

The evening before Jane's deadline and one day before the wedding in Christchurch, they were all ready to leave. Carol, Linda, and Mara were startled when Fitz brought out the last two bottles of wine from Cat's stash.

"I'd like to keep one of them," Linda said. "For the day when—if—they come back."

"If they come back, we'll be drinking champagne!" Fitz declared as he filled the glasses. "You can't carry a wine bottle with you to Otago. And you certainly don't want to leave it here for Jane."

So the sisters drank, though without being able to enjoy it much. They were sitting for the last time in Cat's once-cozy kitchen, which now looked as though it had been plundered. Linda and Carol had taken all of Cat's and Chris's little keepsakes. There were a few Maori rugs, some little statues made of jade and soapstone, and a few pieces of jewelry. Linda still had Cat's medallion necklace, having scarcely taken it off since the shipwreck. She also loaded the pots and pans into their covered wagon. It wasn't much of a dowry. Cat had never liked to cook very much, and had left most of the meal preparation for the family and farmhands to Ida.

After the first glasses had been emptied and Fitz and Mara had proclaimed their hunger, Carol and Linda put bread, cheese, and cold meat on the table. Just then, they heard a knock on the door.

Linda sighed. "I hope it's not more neighbors wanting to tell us how sorry they are. I know they mean well, but today it would just make me cry."

Over the past few days, all their friends and neighbors had come to Rata Station to proclaim their outrage and solidarity. Jane had never been popular, but now no one had anything good to say about her. Linda sometimes felt real pity for Eru. If the young man hadn't inherited Jane's smugness and ignorance, it wasn't going to be easy for him with the Sheep Breeders' Association.

Fitz got up to open the door, and Linda noticed his startled reaction. Then she heard a deep voice outside, and Fitz let in a tall young man in the uniform of a British soldier.

"Lieutenant Bill Paxton is here to see Carol," Fitz said.

Carol stared at Bill with her mouth open.

Bill Paxton bowed formally. "Of course, I am also here to visit Miss Linda," he said, correcting Fitz. "I'm on the way back from Campbelltown, and I have a few days' leave before I rejoin my regiment in Taranaki. I thought I'd pay a call and see how you're doing."

Fitz raised an eyebrow. "Not exactly a direct route."

Bill smiled boyishly. "Caught me, Mr.—what was your name? I admit, I went a bit out of my way."

"Lieutenant Paxton helped us a great deal after—after we lost Chris and Cat," Linda explained. "Mr. Bill, this is Mr. Joe Fitzpatrick, my fiancé. We're getting married tomorrow."

Now it was Bill who looked confused. "You're getting married, Miss Linda? Wasn't it Miss Carol who was engaged?" He smiled. "To the most envied man on the South Island, by the way, of course followed quickly by you, Mr. Fitzpatrick."

Fitz made a gesture of self-depreciation. "Call me Fitz," he said cheerfully.

"My engagement was broken," Carol said, blushing.

A look of amazed joy crossed Bill's face, which he immediately suppressed.

"I'm sorry to hear that," he said. "The wedding was meant to take place in a few weeks, wasn't it? Isn't that what you wrote in your letter? I hoped I could be here to offer my congratulations."

"You're cordially invited to *my* wedding," Linda said. "But there won't be a very big celebration. A lot of things have changed here. Do you want to tell him, Carol, or shall I?"

Carol and Linda briefly told him about Jane's takeover of Rata Station, revealing more about their family history than they had previously. Bill didn't react with shock, but with honest sympathy.

"So you're going to the North Island?" Bill asked. "If you don't mind, I'd be delighted to accompany you. The journey to the North Island isn't completely safe at the moment. Even if you will, of course, be under the protection of Mr. Fitz."

"Fitz and I aren't going to the North Island," Linda said. "We're headed for the gold rush."

Bill looked from her to Fitz in surprise. "You're taking your young wife to the west coast?"

"To Otago first," Fitz replied. "It's closer. Gabriel's Gully, you know."

Gabriel's Gully, about fifty miles west of Dunedin, had been named after its discoverer, Gabriel Read.

"Gabriel's Gully has been stripped bare," Paxton said. "Thousands of adventurers have picked it clean. The prospectors are all leaving now. There have been new finds on the west coast, but no one knows yet how promising they are. It's hard to say if the journey over the mountains is worthwhile. In that inhospitable area—"

Fitz waved his hand. "That's why I want to go to Otago and take a look around. Who knows, maybe we'll discover new goldfields, right, Lindy?"

Paxton laughed. "Others have tried that already," he said. "If you don't happen to be a geologist, Mr. Fitz, there's not much chance. Read was one, and he says there's no more gold."

"He probably didn't look carefully enough. He was already rich," Fitz replied casually.

Linda glanced from one to the other doubtfully.

"If you say so." Paxton shrugged. "And in that case, Miss Carol and Miss Margaret, my offer to you is even more serious."

"Call me Mara, please," Mara said.

She was a bit annoyed that this good-looking young man only had eyes for Carol. At the same time, though, Mara was happy for her sister. She liked the lieutenant much better than Oliver Butler. And even if she enjoyed the effect she usually had on men, Mara didn't really want to flirt. She took her promise to Eru seriously.

"Miss Mara. Please allow me to escort you to the North Island. The army could offer you protection," Paxton said.

"We don't need protection," Mara said defensively. "We speak Maori very well and know the customs of the tribes. I went with my parents to visit the Ngati Hine and the Ngai Takoto. We'll be fine."

Bill Paxton regarded her skeptically. "From what I hear, Miss Mara, the situation on the North Island has changed considerably. It's not about single tribes anymore; they've joined forces. And the Hauhau movement—"

"Are they actually attacking people?" Mara asked in alarm. She hadn't forgotten Eru's plans, and she was deeply worried about him and his friends. After all, it had been over a year ago that he had promised to be patient. Now, perhaps Jane and Te Haitara would bring him home, and he could more than just dream about war.

"They've become a serious threat," Bill said. "Believe me, it's in your best interest to travel under protection of the army."

Carol nodded. "We certainly will," she said. "Thank you for your offer, Mr. Bill. Perhaps you'll find space for two more on your ship, even though the thought of another sea voyage terrifies me."

Bill smiled at her encouragingly. "As you know, Miss Carol, nothing can happen to you when you're with me. I'd row you back from the edge of the world if I had to."

In order to travel from Rata Station to Christchurch with the horses and wagon in one day, it was necessary to get up long before dawn. Linda and Carol left their farm in darkness, and they couldn't look back at the beloved barns and pastures, houses, and shearing shed. Linda wanted to believe that she might see it again one day under happier circumstances, but she couldn't. She had to admit to herself that Cat and Chris were gone, irrevocably—no matter how often she dreamed of them and thought she felt a connection to her mother. It was extremely likely that they were dead.

The young woman fought back tears and tried to be happy about her impending marriage. It was comforting to feel Fitz next to her on the seat of the covered wagon. It was pulled by Brianna, while Fitz's horse walked tied behind. All the others were riding. Linda would have been nearly content if Bill's talk the previous evening hadn't scared her. What would they do if there really wasn't any more gold in Otago?

"What if we try the west coast, after all?" she said to Fitz.

He shook his head. "Nonsense, sweetheart. The journey is much more difficult. Our fortune is waiting in Otago! You can count on me."

Linda leaned her head on his shoulder. There was nothing she would rather do.

They finally arrived in Christchurch in the afternoon, and Linda just barely had time to change from her damp, wrinkled travel dress into her Sunday best. It wasn't particularly beautiful. All of Carol's and Linda's fancy clothes had gone down with the *General Lee*, and in the year of mourning that followed, they hadn't bought anything new. Now, of course, they didn't have the funds. Linda's rather worn-out dress, which was also now too large, since she'd lost quite a bit of weight over the last few months, didn't make a much better impression than the travel dress did. During their trip, it had rained constantly, and even the things in their baskets and cases were damp.

Still, Carol did her best to deck her sister out with something borrowed, blue, old, and new, and also tucked a sixpence into her shoe. She put a blue shawl over her shoulders, lent her a barrette, and insisted that she wear the special gold medallion. The most difficult part was something new. Finally, Mara helped with a pair of stockings she'd never worn before. The sisters did their best to laugh about it all and tried not to worry that they didn't even have a mirror for the bride to see herself in.

At least they had wedding rings. While Linda was changing, Fitz had run off and bought some. They had an unnatural shine to them, and were made of fool's gold.

"I'll have a new one made for you from the first nugget we find," Fitz assured her.

Linda wanted to believe him.

It was a rather damp and weary group that gathered in front of the altar. Mara and Carol hadn't had the chance to change their clothes. Fitz had no suit, only a leather jacket, which was at least in passable condition. Bill made the best impression in his uniform, and at first, the priest thought he was the groom. The priest combined the ceremony with a late afternoon church service, so at least a few members of his little congregation were present.

Linda carried a bouquet and a wreath of rata flowers that Carol had surprised her with before they entered the church. The flowers were drooping a little because of the rain, but Linda was deeply touched and thanked her sister through her tears.

As the bridal procession made their way to the altar, Mara sang a Maori wedding song, trying to create a celebratory atmosphere in the gloomy church. The sun should have been pouring through the colorful stained-glass windows, but on this rainy day, the house of the Lord was lit exclusively by candles. It came as a relief to Linda. That way, maybe no one would notice how worn out her dress was.

As the priest performed the ceremony in a clear voice, the church doors opened for a few latecomers. The man paused and looked up with a warm smile before turning to Fitz.

"You may now kiss the bride," he said.

Fitz pulled Linda close, and the wedding party joyfully applauded. They all were expecting a closing prayer to end the ceremony, but the priest turned to his congregation again instead.

"You're late, but you're still in time for the blessing," he told the newly arrived members of his flock. "My dear ones, please welcome John Baden from the missionary school of Tuahiwi. His school, which works tirelessly to make good Christians of the children of our Maori citizens, is the beneficiary of our offerings today. Reverend Baden, would you like to come up and tell the congregation a little about your work?"

Mara spun around in disgust. The last thing she needed now was to hear a sermon from one of the black ravens holding Eru prisoner. But then her eyes widened in surprise. Next to the small, plump man who had just stood to speak were two Maori boys. One of them was perhaps twelve years old, wearing a black suit that was far too large for him. The clergyman took him by the hand and dragged him toward the pulpit. The boy followed with a resigned expression.

The other boy was Eru.

Chapter 28

Mara and Eru were paralyzed for a moment. They broke into ecstatic smiles. Eru stood up, walked quickly along the pew, and gave Mara a sign to follow him.

The missionary, who had brought the younger boy with him as a successful example of the detribalization of the natives through his fabulous school, glanced at Eru skeptically but made no move to stop the young man. Mara noticed that Eru was wearing neither his school uniform nor a suit like the boy at the altar. He wore a simple, clean outfit, like the clothing of a farmer's son visiting the town.

Whispering, Mara excused herself to Carol, who hadn't noticed Eru's presence. Neither had the joyfully smiling Linda. Linda only had eyes for her groom, who himself looked rather restless. The missionary's speech was holding Fitz up. He wanted to register the marriage with the magistrate as soon as possible.

Carol nodded, and Mara slipped out of the church as inconspicuously as possible. Once outside, she heard Eru whistle her flute melody. He was tucked between a sheltering southern beech and the hedge that surrounded the cemetery. Eru smiled at her in delight and spread his arms invitingly, and Mara rushed into them. As much as she burned to talk to him, it was more important to feel him first, to kiss him, and to finally be close to him again after such a long time. As their mouths melted together, Mara's hands ran over Eru's body and through his short dark hair. He was there. He was real! For the first time since she'd left Tuahiwi, Mara was truly happy.

Eru seemed to feel the same. He only let her go reluctantly, and held both her hands tightly as they stood facing each other.

"How did you do it?" he asked her, his green eyes shining with admiration.

Mara furrowed her brow. "How did I do what?"

He spun her around. "This, here! You promised me. You said I'd have to be patient. It was hard, and sometimes I could barely stand it. You said you'd somehow arrange for my parents to get me out of there. And now it's happening. A letter arrived yesterday that said I should come home to the *iwi*, immediately. Old Baden brought me here, and of course he couldn't resist showing off at the church."

"Won't you get in trouble for walking out?" Mara asked worriedly.

Eru shook his head. "No, the old raven can't do anything to me anymore! I told you, I'm free. One of the boatmen is taking me up the Waimakariri tomorrow to Rata Station, and we can be together again. Now tell me, which spirits did you conjure in order to change my mother's mind?"

Mara let his hands go. "Jane didn't tell you anything else?" she asked carefully. "Only that you should come home?"

"Not much more," Eru said. "She wrote that she needed me on the farm. That was a bit strange, since it's still summer and there's not very much to do."

Mara pushed her hair out of her face. It had finally stopped raining. The wind was gusting from the river and blowing the first autumn leaves off the trees.

"I didn't do anything at all," she said. "And we won't be together again either. Your mother—your mother is driving us away. We had to leave Rata Station."

Mara told him the story in short, broken sentences. She brushed past the news of Cat and Chris's disappearance, her feelings about it still too raw. And the farm wasn't as important to her as it was to Carol and Linda. For Mara, the most important thing about Rata Station was Eru. Growing up, she had spent most of her time in the Ngai Tahu village and genuinely felt like a part of Te Haitara's tribe. She had danced and sung with girls her age, had learned to play the flute, and had conjured the spirits without even thinking about it while planting a field or harvesting vegetables. Over the last year, she had missed Eru terribly. She had wanted to write to him, but in the end, after having seen what the school in Tuahiwi was like, she had decided that her letters might make more trouble for him with the old ravens. At least she had been able to see the separation as temporary. And Jane couldn't really keep Mara away from her other Ngai Tahu friends. Whenever Mara had visited Rata Station during her time with the Redwoods, she had snuck over to the village.

Of course Te Haitara had known about it. Nothing that happened in the tribe was a secret from the chieftain. But he hadn't given Mara away. To the contrary, the girl had the feeling that Te Haitara liked her and would someday welcome her as a daughter-in-law. But now that Jane's takeover of Rata Station had forced the sisters to go to the North Island, her separation from the Ngai Tahu would be complete. The sadness and anger colored Mara's voice as she described Jane's foul play.

Eru was horrified. "How could she? And how could there be a birth certificate that my father doesn't know about? I can't pretend I'm Chris Fenroy's son! I couldn't even if I wanted to. I'm Maori. I look like my father. This is insane!"

Mara shrugged. "Yes, but it's also true. You'll see for yourself when you get home tomorrow. You, my dear, are the official heir of Rata Station."

"I won't go along with it," Eru promised. "I'll give the farm back to you. I—"

"Jane won't sign it over to you now," Mara said. "She's not stupid, and you're still too young to own it."

"I'm always too young for everything!" Eru said bitterly.

Mara nestled into his arms again. "Not for *everything* . . ." She smiled meaningfully and kissed him again.

Eru kissed her but then pulled away. "Mara, it still counts, doesn't it?" he asked. "You're still going to wait for me, aren't you? You won't kiss any other man, you—"

"That counts forever," Mara assured him. "At least, as long as you're just as true to me. If Jane tries to marry you off to a sheep baroness as soon as you're old enough—"

"My mother won't be marrying me off," Eru said sharply. "I will go back now and find out what she's up to. And of course I will speak to my father about it. If I can't change things, maybe I'll stay there and just try to survive the next few years. When I'm old enough, I'll come for you, I promise. Just like you promised that you'd come for me."

Mara sighed. "Well, let's hope it doesn't take another catastrophe. The last thing I would have planned to get you home would have been the loss of Cat and Chris and Rata Station."

"I'm so terribly sorry," Eru whispered.

Mara glanced back at the church doors just as they were opening. A few friendly members of the congregation had taken their places on either side of the stairs and were tossing rice at Linda and Fitz. The bridal couple walked between them, smiling. Fancy and Amy, who had been waiting outside, leaped up delightedly, leaving muddy paw prints on Linda's dress.

"I have to go," Mara said. "You do too, Eru. It would be better if the old raven doesn't see us together. I'll be thinking of you!"

They kissed once more in farewell just before the missionary emerged from the church. John Baden looked around in irritation, seeking Eru.

"See you soon," Eru said as they parted.

The dinner at the White Hart Hotel that Linda had agreed to with such a guilty conscience turned out to be a very pleasant end to the rainy wedding day. After the strenuous journey and prolonged ceremony, they were all ravenous. Mara indulged in second servings of everything, and Carol was delighted to finally be warm. She also enjoyed the special attention that Bill Paxton was paying to her. The young woman had almost forgotten how gentlemanly and obliging the young officer had been on their sea voyage. And she found it immeasurably relaxing that he chatted with her as though it were just another nice evening, and not the beginning of a completely new life for her after the old one had been shattered.

Only Linda was hesitant about the good food and wine. She kept slipping bits of meat to Amy and Fancy under the table. Her wedding night still lay in front of her, and although she knew what to expect, she was nervous. She would spend her first night with Fitz in the covered wagon. Carol could only shake her head about the decision.

"Mamida and Kapa sent us money for lodging," she said, trying once more to convince her sister. "There's still a room available at the inn where we're staying, and it's quite affordable." Carol, Mara, and Bill would go on to Lyttelton the next day. "You don't have to spend the night in that damp wagon."

"Carrie, we'll be sleeping in the wagon every night for the next few weeks," Linda said. "Why should we waste the money for a single night in an inn?"

Linda didn't like to talk about her poverty, especially since Fitz was so carefree. But she was terrified of winding up on the street and fiercely guarded the little money that she had.

"Don't worry, I'll keep my wife warm," Fitz said. "Getting a room isn't worth it. We want to leave very early tomorrow morning."

The entire day, Fitz had been bursting with energy. He couldn't wait to set out for the goldfields. He seemed to have absolutely no doubt about the success of their venture. He enjoyed the evening and even ordered a third bottle of wine. That was another thing that made Linda nervous. She didn't want her husband to be drunk on their wedding night.

Fitz laughed off her concerns as he later ordered a fourth bottle. "Sweetheart, I'm not really drunk until I've had at least four bottles of whiskey," he bragged, putting his arm around Linda, who blushed uncomfortably. "Don't worry, Lindy, darlin'! You're my wife! That has to make you happy!"

When they finally left the restaurant around midnight, Fitz lifted Linda in his arms and carried her jokingly over the threshold of the White Hart Hotel.

"The wagon doesn't have a threshold, so we have to improvise," he said happily.

Linda tried to laugh with him.

Bill gave Carol a skeptical look. "Aren't you supposed to carry the wife in, instead of out?" he said quietly.

Carol nodded. "Exactly," she said, tight-lipped. "Into a safe life. Not the other way around."

In spite of their rather uncomfortable encampment in the covered wagon, among the damp quilts and pillows, Fitz made his young wife happy on her wedding night. Nothing that Linda had heard from other *pakeha* girls about pain and humiliation and slime and blood turned out to apply.

Linda asked Fitz to wait outside until she'd put on her nightclothes. He did so patiently, only to take them off her immediately with practiced hands. She felt burned by his touches. Fitz's fingers searched the most secret places of her body. He made her breathless by stroking the smooth skin of her neck and breasts, and then her wrists and the crooks of her arms and the backs of her knees. He felt the blood pulsing through her veins, bluish through her pale skin, tracing them with kisses and massaging her breasts to the rhythm of her heartbeat. Finally, he penetrated her with a finger and brought her to climax by stimulating her with small, circular motions. And then his head was between her legs. He kissed her thighs and entered her with his tongue. For a moment Linda was confused, but quickly gave herself up to the sensation and writhed with lust. At some point she began to wonder when the part with his swelling organ was going to come. The Maori girls had always whispered about size and length and had compared their experiences, giggling. Linda attempted to return Fitz's caresses, and carefully took hold of his penis. It vibrated in her hand when she rubbed it gently, becoming slightly stiff—and then soft again.

"Maybe I really did have too much wine," Fitz said with a smile.

Linda didn't understand the correlation, but was also far from complaining. It would have hardly been possible to make a woman more lustful than Fitz had done that night. Finally, she nestled against him, warm and satisfied, and fell into a deep sleep with his arms around her.

The next morning, Linda would have liked to repeat the experience immediately, but Fitz awakened her before the first light of dawn. He harnessed Brianna while Linda was groggily unwrapping herself from the quilts. Amy, who had slept under the covered wagon, danced excitedly around it.

"Can't we have breakfast somewhere first?" Linda asked with a yawn. "I'm still not properly awake."

Fitz pulled the blankets away with a laugh. "We can stop on the road somewhere and make coffee," he promised, although it had already begun to rain again. To light a fire in such weather would take much longer and be much more difficult than looking around Christchurch for a café. "This is the beginning. Can't you feel it, Lindy, sweetheart? Can't you hear the gold calling our names?"

Part 4

SIGNS

Canterbury Plains and Otago, New Zealand (the South Island)

Wellington, Taranaki, Whanganui, Opotiki, and Maketu, New Zealand (the North Island)

1865

Chapter 29

Eru became more and more incensed the closer he got to Rata Station. Georgie, who was bringing him up the Waimakariri, had confirmed Mara's story.

"Your mother was very unkind. The other sheep breeders are quite angry," the boatman said. "But the lawyers say nothing can be done. Iron Janey is within her rights. It's good luck for you, Eru—or do I call you Eric now? You're going to inherit a huge farm one day."

Georgie's assumption that Eru could somehow be happy about Linda and Carol's eviction was the last straw for the young man. As soon as they'd pulled up to Rata Station's pier, Eru set off for the Ngai Tahu village, burning with rage.

The village was humming with the usual bustle of activity. Children were playing, and the women were weaving and peeling sweet potatoes and raupo roots. Te Ropata, the old *rangatira*, was coaching the young warriors as they practiced swinging their clubs. The sight made Eru a little wistful. But he would surely be part of the group again soon. He waved to the old man respectfully, and Te Ropata nodded back.

At one fire a little ways from the others, Te Haitara sat with Makuto. The old woman was burning ritual herbs, and Eru knew he should wait until she finished. But he was too upset.

"*Ariki* . . . *Matua* . . . Chieftain . . . Father . . ." Eru approached the fire.

Te Haitara leaped to his feet. "Eru!"

A smile spread over his tattooed face when he saw his son. He reached him with one step, put his hands on Eru's shoulders, and greeted him with the *hongi*. Te Haitara squeezed him so tightly that it hurt.

"May I still call you Father, or do you have doubts about my parentage?" Eru asked stiffly. "Or have you already agreed that I'm Chris Fenroy's son? A little lie in exchange for a few thousand sheep? Let me guess, Mother told you that a birth certificate is just a piece of paper."

"In this case, it is just that," the chieftain said. "Eru, that is no way to speak to your father—which I am. There isn't the slightest doubt. If you want, we can take that cursed birth certificate and burn it."

Eru laughed bitterly. "Mother would hardly leave it around for us to find. And besides, the magistrate in Christchurch will certainly have a copy. The *pakeha* are very careful about such things. I'm sorry for speaking so disrespectfully, but why haven't you done anything to stop what's happening here? You can't possibly approve."

Te Haitara lowered his eyes. "There's nothing I can do. Jane's soul is poisoned, and Makuto is trying to purify it." He gestured to the fire and the herbs. "But the spirits of money are strong."

"Where is Mother now?" Eru asked defiantly. "I'd like to see if *I* could drive away a few of those spirits."

"She's at Rata Station. She's—preparing the stone house."

"She's doing what?" Eru cried. "Father, maybe you can't force her to give up the inheritance, but you certainly can't allow her to leave you and live in Chris's house."

The chieftain shook his head. "No, she lives with me. She comes home every evening. She says she has to get the house ready for—I don't know, some *pakeha* ceremony."

"She's probably planning a ball or something like that to celebrate her takeover. Fine, I'll go back and talk to her. And I'll tell her very clearly what I think about all this!"

Snorting with anger, Eru left the village. He found Jane in the barn at Rata Station, where she was busy giving orders to some of the shepherds. She wore a practical but attractive linen dress, with her hair up in a nice bun.

Eru was surprised when his mother sent the men away and greeted him with an open smile.

"Eru, my boy! How wonderful to see you," Jane cried. She even kept smiling as he responded with an avalanche of accusations.

"I don't understand why everyone is so hung up on that birth certificate," she said, shaking her head. "Sure, it helped the lawyer take the wind out of the Brandmann sisters' sails. But I wouldn't have used it. It's enough that I'm still married to Chris on paper, and you were officially born into that marriage, Eric. I only had the certificate made back then so you could study in England someday. Oxford or Cambridge would be far more likely to accept a Fenroy than a Te Haitara. And maybe we should apply to those universities soon. After all, the farm doesn't need another shepherd as much as it needs a veterinarian or a lawyer. You could be much more useful here after getting a degree like that."

"So you can cheat more friends and neighbors?" Eru asked, incensed.

Jane stared at her son uncomprehendingly. "Eric, my dear, I did this all for you. You should be grateful. The world is at your feet . . . Come, have a look around!"

Eru shook his head. "I know Rata Station."

Jane rolled her eyes. "Of course you know the outside. I meant the stone house. As far as that goes, Chris really outdid himself trying to please me." She grinned. "He was terrified of me. In any case, it's a proper little manor house. Good enough for social events!"

"You really want to dance on Cat's and Chris's graves?" Eru couldn't believe his ears. "I can assure you, none of our neighbors will come. You've made yourself a pariah, Mother—and Father and me with you. No one will talk to you anymore, and they certainly won't do business with you."

Jane laughed. "Don't be so melodramatic. Of course everyone is upset now, even though I didn't do anything but claim what was mine. Eru, this farm was once my dowry."

"There are different versions of that story, Mother," Eru shot back.

He knew the story of the farm. Jane's father, John Nicholas Beit, had cheated the Maori out of this land in order to use it as Jane's dowry for her marriage to Christopher Fenroy. He had traded a few pots and blankets for hundreds of acres. The trade had never been confirmed by the governor, and the Maori didn't honor it either once they realized they'd been taken advantage of.

Of course Chris had quickly realized what had happened. In order to keep the peace, he had given up ownership of the land and paid Te Haitara a yearly rent. When the chieftain had married Jane, he had given Chris the land as *utu*—compensation for taking his wife away.

"The farm belongs to me," Jane repeated. "The other farmers on the Waimakariri are going to have to accept that. What could they do about it, anyway? Hire their own shearing brigades because they don't want to work with the same people I do? Sell to different distributors? That would be ridiculous, Eric. And as far as the house goes, I'm not planning any festivities there for the time being, but it will be very useful not to have to make deals with wool distributors and agricultural machinery makers in a *marae*. Try to see the house as a kind of office for now. Later, when you have a wife—"

"I'm not going to marry some silly sheep baroness just because you like her father's breeding animals!" he said, enraged.

Jane smiled again. "You won't have to, boy. Just wait. After you've been in England for a few years, maybe you'll find yourself a real baroness. After all, you're a chieftain's son."

Eru slunk back to the village. He was still determined not to go to England or to help Jane with Rata Station. But once again, he hadn't succeeded in making his mother listen. She was so convinced by her own righteousness that Eru didn't have a chance. Nor did Te Haitara. The chieftain was a warrior, a man of deeds. Rhetorically, both of them were hopelessly outgunned.

But Eru was at least happy to be back in the village. The next morning, when Te Ropata called the young warriors, Eru rejoined his *taua*. The *rangatira* welcomed him by singing a *karakia* of joy: "Our tribe is stronger. The warrior who was far away has returned. Thank the gods and the ancestors! Our enemies will know fear again."

Eru blushed with pleasure and self-consciousness as the other young men accepted him as part of their community again. He'd missed out on parts of his training, but his natural strength would help. In the mock fights that followed, he beat two opponents, and the *rangatira* praised him.

Eru felt happier than he had in a long time. This was where he belonged. He would stay here until he was grown, and then he'd bring Mara here and marry her. It didn't matter what his mother had to say about it.

His elation only lasted until Jane saw the young warriors returning to the village, laughing and singing.

"I can't understand it, Eric! You're the manager of a huge sheep farm, and soon you'll be playing an important role in the Christchurch Sheep Breeders' Association. Everyone will respect you. Good Lord, I've even got papers for you that will be accepted in every *pakeha* court. And what do you do? You run around half-naked in a grass skirt like a dancing girl, singing silly songs and swinging ridiculous weapons."

Eru held her gaze steadily. "I am a warrior, Mother."

Jane snorted. "You don't have any enemies here, Eric! And thank goodness, because even Ida Jensch could put an end to your ridiculous band of warriors with a few shots from her pistol. We aren't in the Stone Age anymore, using spears and clubs. Now, get dressed properly; we need to check on some of the sheep. Besides, it would be a good idea for you to choose a horse. There are a few at Rata Station, and you can ride, can't you? It would make things much easier if we had a few shepherds on horseback."

Eru pressed his lips together, torn between anger and shame. "I'm not a very good rider."

Mara had occasionally put him on a well-trained horse and had taken him with her into the plains, but he'd never really enjoyed it. Maori warriors always walked.

Jane frowned. "Time to learn. At least that would be one useful skill. Come now."

Eru left his *taua* with his eyes lowered. At least the others didn't make fun of him the way his fellow students back in Tuahiwi surely would have. Jane was known as a woman with much *mana*—courage and strength—and also as an adviser to the chieftain. The tribe knew they had her to thank for their prosperity, and every one of the young warriors was as deferential to her as Eru was. But the tone in which she spoke to him was not appropriate. The young man could only hope that the others hadn't understood everything she'd said. But Eru had no illusions. Miss Foggerty hadn't held her classes in Maori, and even though Mara or one of her sisters had almost always translated, every boy and girl in the tribe knew some English.

Eru followed his mother sullenly, and spent an awful day inspecting the sheep pens and shearing shed. He was tired and depressed when he finally returned to the village that evening. But suddenly he felt himself coming back to life. Behind the trees between the chieftain's house and the boundary fence of the *marae*, exactly where he had met Mara that one night, he saw a shadow.

Te Ropata, the *rangatira*, was waiting silently. His form blended seamlessly into the landscape and plants that surrounded him. Eru was proud of being able to spot him. After Jane disappeared into the house, he snuck over.

"Rangatira," Eru said, "are you waiting for my father?"

"No, I'm waiting for you, Te Eriatara. I want you to follow me."

Eru bit his lip. "Do I—do I need to be appropriately dressed?"

The old teacher usually insisted that his students wear traditional warrior garb when they practiced fighting or meditation. Like Makuto, he never wore *pakeha* clothing himself. Even in winter, he stood before his students with his chest bare. A warrior, he explained, could drive away the wind's chill with the heat of battle.

Now Te Ropata shook his head. "You can come as you are, so you will remember who you are," he said calmly.

Te Ropata left the *marae* and headed for a pond that the tribe considered to be a place of power. Eru could barely keep up with him. Te Ropata wasn't young anymore, but he was wiry and muscular, and his body glided through the grass and thickets. His tattoos, which covered not only his face but his entire body, seemed to dance with his movements, making the warrior look both fascinating and dangerous. Eru tried to adapt his steps to the man's rhythm.

They arrived at the pond and kneeled at the edge. Te Ropata was quiet, seeking connection between his spirit and the gods.

It was Eru who finally broke the silence. "*Rangatira*, I'm sorry about what happened this morning. If my mother offended you—"

Te Ropata shook his head. "I'm not offended by a woman. But I would kill a man for what she did. This is not about me, Te Eriatara, it's about you. Who are you?"

Eru blinked in confusion. "You know that, *rangatira*," he replied. "I am Te Eriatara, the son of Te Haitara of the Ngai Tahu tribe that lives between the river and mountains and—"

"I don't need to hear the *pepeha*. I know who your parents are, and I know which canoe brought your ancestors to Aotearoa." The *rangatira* looked out over the pond, where the shadows of twilight were now falling. "Te Eriatara, you have the blood of both *pakeha* and Maori inside you. Your body comes from both; your spirit is touched by both. But what makes up your soul?"

"I am Maori!" Eru cried without hesitation. If he'd had any remaining doubt, it had been driven out of him by the missionary school. "I want to be a warrior. Please don't turn me away, Te Ropata. Let me be part of my *taua*. Even if there are no enemies."

The old man gazed at Eru intently for a long moment. "There are always enemies, my son. The first enemy a warrior has to conquer is the enemy inside himself."

Eru considered his teacher's words. "That means he has to learn courage?"

Te Ropata nodded. "In the old days, he had to prove his courage. Long before he had to stand before an enemy for the first time." He ran his fingers over the tattoos on his face.

Eru stared at the old warrior, and his eyes went wide.

Chapter 30

In Te Haitara's village, there wasn't a real *tohunga-ta-oko* anymore. Te Ropata had said that one of the tribal elders understood the art, but when Eru asked the man, he declined.

"Te Eriatara, you are the chieftain's son. You should entrust your *moko* only to a master—not an old man who hasn't tattooed a face for twenty years."

Such a master lived in another Ngai Tahu village, not far to the northwest in the foothills near Lake Whakamatua, which the *pakeha* called Lake Coleridge.

"We will visit that *iwi* when we fetch the sheep from the mountains at the end of summer," Te Ropata said. "I will join the herding with my young warriors. That should please Jane Te Rohi."

Jane didn't know whether she should be happy about the unexpected help or not. She thought it was very strange that an old warrior *tohunga* suddenly wanted to lower himself to such a practical chore. At least, that's what she told Eru, who remained stoically silent. But Jane couldn't refuse Te Ropata's offer. After all, she had always complained to the chieftain how little support she had from the tribe when it came to the farming business. The fifteen strong young men would be extremely helpful. They could practice their tracking and help find escaped animals in the mountains.

And in light of Te Ropata's decision to take his warriors on the sheep drive, half of the village decided to join them. Te Haitara finally admitted to Jane that they wanted to combine the drive with a visit to a friendly *iwi*.

"We could go along too," he suggested. "You've never gone before."

"I don't intend to now either," Jane retorted sourly. "It's a sheep drive, not a family outing. I have to get the farm ready for the animals and then sort them into the barns, pens, and pastures. I'll need help for that. It will take more than just the three *pakeha* shepherds I have."

All of Rata Station's staff had quit when Linda and Carol were driven out. Then Patrick Colderell had returned and gotten his job as head shepherd back. He had also hired two other *pakeha* men. Both of them had rather bad reputations among the local sheep breeders, but no one else was willing to work for Jane.

"There will be plenty of men returning with the sheep," Te Haitara said.

The trip would have been good for Jane. That's what Makuto had said when she joined the group headed for the mountains.

Patrick Colderell uttered a few profanities when he saw all the warriors, women, children, and tribal elders that he was supposed to lead to the mountains for the sheep drive. "These people will only slow us down!"

Jane shook her head. "They walk faster than you do," she said. "And even if you need a day longer than usual to reach the highlands, it won't matter. Just keep an eye on my son."

At Jane's order, Eru mounted a horse. It was the same gentle black pony he'd ridden to accompany Mara. The animal reminded him of her, which made it a little easier to have to ride with the *pakeha* instead of walking with his *taua*.

But Eru's honorable plan had been made known to the young warriors. Even among the Ngai Tahu, there was talk about Te Ua Haumene and the men fighting for freedom on the North Island. They were all tattooed. Now the rest of Eru's *tuau* was eager for that test of courage.

First, though, the young warriors would help with the sheep drive, which was easy for them. They'd grown up with shepherding duties and were quite good at working with the animals. For that reason, the *pakeha* foreman didn't even notice when Te Ropata and Eru disappeared on the first day of the drive. Jane may have instructed him to keep an eye on her son, but to Colderell, all the Maori looked the same. He had plenty of help and didn't really care what "Eric Fenroy" was doing.

Eru could have waited until the drive was over to have his *moko* ceremony with the other young warriors. But Eru had a much more ambitious plan than his friends, who only wanted small tattoos. He wanted to prove to his *rangatira* and his father that he was as strong and worthy as the best of his people.

That's what he told the *tohunga-ta-oko*, a small, plump man whose own body had few tattoos on it. The artist had brought Eru and Te Ropata to his favorite place, set slightly apart from the village at the edge of Lake Whakamatua. There was black gravel at the water's edge. The lake was an iridescent blue and smooth as a mirror, ringed by mountains with snowcapped peaks. The men breathed in the clear, ice-cold air. The winter came earlier here than it did in the plains.

"You want everything in one day?" the *tohunga* asked in disbelief.

Since Eru had approached him, he'd observed the young man's face with the concentrated attention of an artist. Eru was careful to hold his gaze, looking into his clear, dark eyes. The man was known as a craftsman far beyond the borders of his tribal lands. The warriors of his *iwi* all had extremely intricate, expertly made *moko* in unusual designs.

"Your entire face? That's impossible, boy. No one can stand that."

"I can!" Eru said proudly. "I can withstand any pain."

The *tohunga* regarded him skeptically. "It takes me several years to tattoo an entire face," he said. "And not just because of the pain. It's also because the warrior changes as he gets older. I carve an image of your life and soul into your face."

Eru nodded. "But I don't have that much time. I've been told you can look into the soul of a man when you tattoo him. My soul won't change over the years, and I can stand the pain. Please try, at least."

The *tohunga* pressed his lips together. "I can try to do it over a few days," he suggested. "Three or four days . . ."

Eru nodded. "As long as it's finished when the others from our tribe arrive. I want to surprise them all."

The master nodded. "You're at a crossroads. When I looked into your face for the first time, I saw crossed lines on your forehead. Now it looks as though they've opened up, like *koru* ferns."

The fern leaf was a symbol of hope and renewal.

"I want to show the world that I am a man and a warrior!" Eru announced.

The artist laughed. "I also see *toki* and *mere*. We'll see which ones you keep. First the eyes and nose, the *uirere*. I will begin with the symbols of your rank, the *taitoto*. You are highborn."

The *tohunga* took a piece of charcoal and began to draw lines on Eru's face.

"I don't care about my birth rank," Eru said, protesting. "I want an original, very special *moko*."

"I will design the area under your nose to be just as headstrong as your entire face. You will be unmistakable."

Te Ropata nodded as the *tohunga* began to work on Eru's chin. "A young warrior with much *mana*," he said, looking at the symbol that the master had drawn.

Eru suppressed a smile of pride, and when the master fetched a hollowed-out half pumpkin filled with lake water and told him to look at his reflection, he didn't recognize himself.

"Is that what you imagined?" the *tohunga* asked.

Eru nodded ecstatically. "It's beautiful! Can you start now?"

The artist shook his head. "You must be prepared. You must meditate and commune with the spirits. Let the symbols work on your soul for a time. Perhaps you will want to change something after all. We will start tomorrow."

As the *tohunga* had advised, Eru spent the night praying and singing. He didn't eat or drink, and the *moko* master fasted as well. In the morning, Eru followed the man to the lake again. Te Ropata accompanied them, along with three of the *tohunga*'s apprentices. One lit a fire at the edge of the lake and burned shells and the sap of kauri trees in it. The sharp odor penetrated Eru's nose and throat, and almost made him cough. But he was determined to show no weakness.

"Light and power are strong in this place," the *tohunga-ta-oko* explained.

When the fire had burned down, the master mixed the ashes with oil to form a paste. Eru swallowed. That was the ink.

"Are you ready?" the *tohunga* asked. He reached for a very fine, sharp chisel made of whalebone. In his other hand, he held a small hammer. Eru nodded.

Nothing and no one could have prepared Eru for the pain that tore through him as the *tohunga* applied the chisel beneath his right eye. *Moko* should be not only visible but also tangible, such that a blind person could trace it. As the master cut the skin off his face, Eru wanted to howl with pain. Before he could open his mouth to do so, Te Ropata and the *tohunga*'s apprentices started singing. Their song called on the young warrior's courage and asked the spirits to help him. Eru bit his tongue and controlled himself. He wouldn't make a single sound.

After a short time, his face was dripping with blood. It ran down his neck and dripped onto the ground. In some corner of his pain-filled mind, he thought how fortunate it was that he was naked. As soon as the *tohunga* had cut a line, he wiped away the blood, dipped the chisel in the ink paste, and filled the wound with it. A new sensation seared through Eru's body. Then the artist began again, around the eyes where the skin was particularly sensitive. Eru clung to consciousness. He mustn't pass out. He was a warrior. He was strong!

The men's songs bolstered his strength. The *tohunga* himself sang a *karakia* of power. Eru felt nauseated, and suddenly his fast made sense. There was nothing for him to throw up. His mouth was dry, and he longed for water. Again and again, the hammer struck the sharp chisel, and the master carved his face. Eru felt as though there wasn't one whole piece of skin left around his eyes. His flesh was beginning to swell.

"I can't see anything," he said with a gasp.

"That's the way of it. You will be blind for a few days," the *tohunga* said calmly. "The *uirere* is finished. Do you really want me to go on?"

Eru nodded, although his head felt like it was already swollen to twice its size, and everything inside of him screamed.

"You are strong," the master said, and put the chisel to Eru's chin. The pain flared, and the men sang. Eru clenched his teeth.

"Is it finished?" he asked when the *tohunga* stopped after what felt like an eternity.

"For today." The master tilted Eru's head to inspect his work. "Tomorrow I will do the cheeks and forehead. I'm going to reconsider the pattern, if that's all right with you. You are stronger and more courageous than I believed."

In spite of the praise, Eru didn't smile as Te Ropata and the master's apprentices led him away. He couldn't move a single muscle in his swollen face. The thought of continuing the next day was unbearable.

"Can I drink?" he asked.

The noise told him that they had reached the village again. Eru heard men's and women's voices, and admiring words. Most people here were tattooed. They understood what the young man had suffered that day. Te Ropata brought him into one of the houses and advised him to lie down on a mat.

"Water is allowed," Te Ropata said, and turned to one of the master's apprentices. "Only from the horn," he said.

Eru felt something hard being held to his lips. The wooden or bone vessel was traditionally used only for an *ariki*, who was considered to be on equal standing with a god. It was *tapu* for the chieftain to touch food with his hands, so the vessel was used as a kind of aid. Its smaller opening was placed in the chieftain's mouth, and the food or drink was placed in the larger end. Eru knew about the tradition, even though it had not been practiced for generations on the South Island. The horn was still occasionally used in ceremonies—or at least it had been until Jane had banned it. It was unthinkable to her that one of their *pakeha* business partners might watch while she fed her husband like a baby.

Now water flowed through the horn into Eru's dry mouth. Until the wounds healed, he was *tapu*, just like a North Island *ariki*. And until the tattooing was finished, Eru would have to continue fasting. So far, he didn't mind that at all. Nothing seemed less desirable at the moment than food.

When the men left, he tried to relax. He clung to the hope that he would feel better the next day, and finally fell into a restless sleep.

The next day, his wounds pulsed with pain, and his face was even more swollen. When the master resumed his work, Eru no longer wanted to scream, but to whimper and cry. At one point he passed out, but Eru survived the second and third days of his self-imposed torture without once losing control of his voice.

At last, the *moko* master chiseled the last line in the sensitive area beneath Eru's nose. It was the *raurau*, the signature. The filigree spirals were the final step in making something extremely special. When it was complete, the man bowed to Eru. Te Ropata had to tell him about the *tohunga*'s magnanimous gesture. His eyes were still swollen shut.

"The *moko* is healing quickly," Te Ropata said as he helped Eru back to his bed. "You'll soon be able to see again. And the next time you see your reflection, you will see a man!"

Eru had hoped for so much more. When he was finally able to look into the water-filled pumpkin that Te Ropata brought to his bedside, he didn't see a courageous warrior, but gazed instead into a face that was completely misshapen from swelling. The young man had been burning with fever for several days, and was barely able to stand up. The village healer sang *karakia*s day and night in front of the hut, but the *tohunga-ta-oko* wouldn't allow her to go to him.

"If she uses her salves on you, they will ease the pain and lower the fever," he said, "but they will also erase the lines. They will make the designs fade and smooth the *uhi* that were cut into your face."

Eru nodded and endured the pain stoically. The master only allowed him to have a tea made from manuka leaves against the fever.

"It won't stay like this, will it?" he asked.

The *moko* master shook his head. "Of course not. It's a terrible sight right now, but it's healing well. It will look very beautiful."

Eru attempted a dark smile. "I'm afraid my mother won't share that opinion."

He had been at Lake Whakamatua for almost ten days. The sheep drive must be over by now, and Eru waited for the other young men from his *taua*. He had imagined greeting them triumphantly with his new face, but now it was unthinkable. When they arrived, he actually didn't show himself at all, but watched the *powhiri*, the ceremony for greeting guests, from the hut where he'd been recovering. It had been built especially for him. As long as he was *tapu*, he would not be tolerated in any of the communal buildings.

On the next day, he had some company. All of the other men from his *taua* had also tried their courage under the *tohunga-ta-oko*'s chisel, but they had only gotten small *moko*s. After they had passed their own tests, they regarded Eru with awe.

"You will be their new chieftain," Te Ropata prophesied when they had finally bid farewell to the tribe and the *moko* master. "When it's time to choose, they will remember this time. They will remember your courage and your words. And your spirit, too, is strong."

The words he was referring to weren't just Eru's, but Te Ua Haumene's. The young man had passed the time during recovery by reading aloud from the prophet's gospel, *Ua Rongo Pai*. Additionally, Eru had told his *taua* about his time in the missionary school in Tuahiwi, and about the boy from the North Island who had heard the prophet speak. The young warriors and their teacher had listened enthusiastically. Te Ropata found many of his own convictions reflected in Haumene's words, even though he couldn't follow the allusions to archangels and Israelites. But he shared the opinion that the *pakeha* should be banished from Aotearoa—as quickly as possible!

Eru glowed with pride. Before now, he had never been able to imagine that he could be his father's successor. He'd thought his *pakeha* ancestry and Jane's disapproval meant the tribe would never choose him. Te Haitara had cousins and nephews who could take the chieftain's place when it was time. But now his own son had proven that he had *mana*. From the *rangatira*'s point of view, Te Eriatara had also proven that he had the right kind of soul. From now on, he would be one of the most revered men of the tribe.

And yet, there was angst in the young warrior's heart when he thought about the confrontation with his mother. His wounds were healed now, and the symbols shone in a clean, deep blue. In a ceremony of purification, the *tapu* was lifted from him and the other freshly tattooed warriors, and the tribe celebrated with a great feast in their honor.

But the healing process had taken three weeks. He knew his mother would be seething with anger.

Chapter 31

“This is about a girl! Admit it!”

Jane had turned on her husband in annoyance again. It had been two weeks since the shepherds had returned from the highlands with the sheep, and a week later, the first women and children had arrived from the village on Lake Whakamatua. But so far, there was no trace of Eru and his *taua*. The only possible reason Jane could imagine was that he’d met a girl in the highlands.

“I don’t know,” Te Haitara answered patiently. “Ask Makuto. I wasn’t there, as you know.”

The old *tohunga* sat at her weaving while Jane studied the ledgers from Rata Station and argued with the chieftain. Makuto looked up when she heard her name but didn’t say anything.

“She won’t tell me anything!” Jane said, complaining loudly in Maori so that the *tohunga* would hear her. “But I saw you two talking. You were conjuring some kind of spirits. Stop lying to me!”

Jane’s eyes flickered between her husband and the tribal elder. Of course she had asked her *pakeha* foreman all the same questions, and Colderell had assured her several times that there had been no accidents or fights. He only knew that Eru had gone somewhere with some other Maori, and nothing more.

“Makuto told me the same thing she told you,” the chieftain said calmly. “She said Eru is on his way to becoming a man, and there is a *tapu* on him at the moment. He will return as soon as it is lifted. You’ll have to content yourself with that, Jane, as will I.”

“But you must suspect something!” Jane said triumphantly, switching back to English. “You can’t tell me that you have no idea. After all, you went through those strange rites.”

The concept of initiation rituals was new to Jane. Ever since she'd begun to have serious worries that Eru could break away from her, she had secretly been reading books from Chris's house about the customs of indigenous tribes all over the world. They sent shivers down her spine.

Te Haitara shrugged. "Those were different times. These days, many traditions are being broken. I don't know how important they are to Te Ropata, but he is a good *rangatira*. He wouldn't do anything that would hurt the young warriors, and Eru isn't the only one who hasn't returned. Te Ropata will bring them all back safely. Try not to worry so much."

"I still think it's a girl!" Jane said stubbornly. "That could be a huge risk for him. If he gets one of those crafty little things pregnant—"

"Then we would welcome our grandchild with joy," Te Haitara said, cutting her off. "Calm down, Jane. That isn't part of a warrior's testing. Lying with a woman doesn't make a boy into a man."

"On the contrary, it can make a man into a slave," Makuto remarked.

Jane gave her a withering look, and then she looked up in alarm. From the village square, she could hear shouts as someone blew a conch horn. The call of the conch. It was traditionally a signal for attack, but the Ngai Tahu had no enemies. These days, Te Ropata used it to call his students, and to announce their coming and going from the village.

Now the conch's rich tones were mixed with the voices of singers:

"Thank the spirits, thank the ancestors! Our warriors have returned, victorious. The women's fires are no longer abandoned, and no one must fear approaching enemies anymore. Our tribe is strong! Joy fills hearts and homes."

Te Haitara straightened his shoulders. "There you have it, Jane," he said. "Our son has returned."

Jane followed her husband to welcome Te Ropata and his *taua*. She walked with deliberate steps, determined to keep control of herself. It would be an affront to Te Haitara if she pounced on Eru during the welcoming ceremony. If the tribe was going to celebrate her son's return, she would have to wait and confront him later.

Te Ropata had the young men lined up in the square, and the villagers were beside themselves with excitement. That was no surprise. The Ngai Tahu were always happy about the return of their friends and relatives, and expressed their feelings loudly. But this time the joyful greetings were mixed with cries of admiration. Women and girls complimented the beauty of the warriors, and the men their courage. At first glance, nothing seemed to have changed. As expected, they were shirtless, carrying spears in their hands and war clubs on their belts, and their long hair was wound into warriors' knots. Only when Jane caught sight of their faces did her eyes go wide.

There were blue spirals around the chin of young Tane, one of the chieftain's nephews. A third eyebrow seemed to have grown above Arama's eyes, and Hemi had a kind of fan pattern on his forehead.

"Te Haitara . . ." Jane's fingers tightened around her husband's arm. "Thank God they didn't do that to Eru. Where is he, anyway? He—"

"Here I am, Mother." Eru stepped forward.

Jane lost her grip on reality for a moment. The face that spoke to her was completely covered with blue spirals, circles, and wavy lines. The tattoos reached from nose to chin, and the forehead was covered with artistic designs. The eyes were surrounded by delicate lines. Eru's mouth stretched into a smile. He was enjoying Jane's horror. This was the end of her dream of college in England, of the role she had imagined for him with the Sheep Breeders' Association.

Te Haitara gently freed himself from Jane's grip, went to his son, and looked him up and down approvingly.

"A child left my house," he declared, "and a man has returned. You have shown courage, my son. More courage and strength than I have ever seen in a warrior. Welcome back to your tribe, Te Eriatara."

In the meantime, the older women, led by Makuto, had gathered in the square. Makuto took stock of the warriors, first with respect. But when she saw Eru, worry and anger flashed across her features.

"An entire face, created in a few days? The images of a lifetime, chiseled into a young man's forehead?" Makuto ran her fingers over her own *moko*. Like most women, she was only ornamented around the mouth with blue spirals. It was a sign that she breathed the breath of life. Makuto turned to Te Haitara. "It's good when a warrior shows courage," she told him. "But a child cannot become a man overnight. It's foolish to force maturity. Your *rangatira* should have known better, Te Eriatara." She gave Te Ropata a disapproving look. "I would have expected more wisdom from the *tohunga-ta-oko* as well! You will now have to live with a face that may no longer be your own in ten years, Te Eriatara. You believe it reflects your courage, but in truth, it only reflects your wish for revenge. I hope your soul can transcend that wish and triumph over your face." She turned and walked away.

Eru stood there, dumbfounded. Before he could react, he was attacked by his mother. Jane's shock had given way to blazing anger.

"There you have it!" she crowed. "I never thought Makuto and I would agree about anything, but this time even *she* said it. You're no warrior, Eric! You're just a spoiled, rebellious little boy."

Eru thought he could feel the *moko*'s power strengthening him. "I'll prove to you that I'm a warrior, Mother," he said in an unwavering voice. "I will prove it to all of you."

Very slowly, he pulled a tattered booklet out of his bag. It was the *Ua Rongo Pai*, the Gospel according to Te Ua.

"On the North Island there is war now, a war that Te Ua Haumene says we must win. That's what he prophesied, and it shall be so. The prophet says we will feel the call within us. And today, I, Te Eriatara the warrior, hear him! I will leave today to follow him!"

Jane saw her husband go pale under his own tattoos.

"Eru, my boy, all of this honors you. Your intention honors you. But you don't really want to go through with this, do you? That isn't our fight, Eru! It is not a war of the Ngai Tahu." The chieftain took a faltering step toward his son, as though he wanted to embrace him and keep him from leaving.

"A war?" Jane asked. She had briefly read Te Ua Haumene's diatribe, and had written it off as the product of a sick mind.

"This fight belongs to all of us!" Eru said, looking intently at the faces surrounding him. Part of his *taua* watched him with their eyes flashing, while the others lowered their heads in shame. "It's a fight for every Maori!"

Jane looked at her husband. "He doesn't really want to go to the North Island and join some insane mob, does he?"

Te Haitara covered his face with his hands. His silence was answer enough for Jane.

"You must forbid him!" she shrieked.

The chieftain took his hands down and lowered his eyes. "I can't," he said. "He has made his transformation, with more courage and strength than even I showed in mine. He is a warrior. He is a man."

"And you are his chieftain!" Jane cried.

Te Haitara looked at her sadly. "I am only his father," he replied. "I taught him what he needed to know. I raised him to be a warrior. It's you he is striving against. Perhaps it's good that he's leaving."

Jane turned furiously back to her son and scrutinized his face, scowling with disgust. Malice flashed in her eyes.

Her voice was cold as she wound up for the blow. "Well, at least that clears up the problem with the Jensch girl." She forced a cruel smile. "No *pakeha* woman will ever look at you again."

Eru stared defiantly back at her. Then he made a gesture of farewell to the village elders, exchanged *hongi* with his father and his *rangatira*, and picked up his spear. He turned to leave, marching past the rows of villagers. The people let him go, staring with both fascination and sympathy. Eru took a deep breath of relief when two other young warriors spontaneously ran to follow him. One began to dance a war *haka* as they left the village. Eru sang along, but his mind was elsewhere. His mother's bullet had found its target. Would Mara recognize him? Would she like his new face?

Deep in his heart, he knew the answer. Mara loved him no matter what he looked like. But if he slaughtered her people the way a Hauhau warrior was supposed to, how could she do anything but hate him?

Chapter 32

Carol endured the sea voyage from Lyttelton to the North Island stoically. After the difficult days before the journey, she was too depressed to be afraid. The loss of Rata Station was still painful, as was her separation from Linda. And now, for the first time, it became clear how permanent her separation from Oliver was. Up until a few days before, she had been a bride, her life secure. But now Linda was married instead, and she herself was single with an unforeseeable future ahead. If it had been up to Carol, she would have crawled under a blanket with Fancy and shut out the world.

But Bill Paxton did everything he could to distract her and keep her entertained. He insisted on leaning against the ship's rail with her so they could feel the wind in their hair and the salty spray on their faces. In the evening, he escorted her formally to the first-class dining hall and treated her like a princess. He'd had to bribe the steward to get them in, as Carol and Mara didn't have enough money for first class. The lieutenant didn't urge Carol to react to his jokes and stories as cheerfully as she had before. His face simply radiated his joy to be with her again, and his wish for her approval.

To Carol's surprise, Mara also turned out to be a pleasant travel companion. The girl was in an unexpectedly good mood. She talked about earlier trips across the Cook Strait and allayed Carol's fears when it became stormy.

"It's always like this here, Carrie; it doesn't mean anything. And we'll be there in just a few hours."

In Wellington, so many new impressions overtook Carol that she didn't have time to remember her grief. The city was much larger than anything the young woman had ever seen. She gazed in amazement at the shops, restaurants, hotels, government buildings, and churches. And Mara was surprised by the military presence, which was much stronger than during her previous visits. Even redcoats were stationed in Wellington, along with the local troops. But there were no Maori to be seen.

"There's a war going on, Miss Mara," Bill Paxton said. "There were uprisings in Taranaki and Waikato, and the governor reacted very strongly to them. General Cameron drove the Maori warriors back into a small area."

"Then it's over now?" Carol asked worriedly. "They aren't fighting anymore?"

In order to get to Russell, they'd have to traverse the entire length of the North Island from south to north. Carol shivered to realize that Bill Paxton's insistence on accompanying them was not mere kindness or gallantry.

"Why do they need all the soldiers if there's peace now?" Mara asked.

Bill shrugged. "There have been aggressive land seizures in the offenders' area, but it seems like the government views the uprisings as an excuse to claim the land unfairly. Governor Grey is using his proclamation of 1863."

"What's that?" Mara asked.

"In 1863, Grey gave the chieftain in Waikato an ultimatum. Whoever remained peaceably in the village or went willingly to where the government was resettling the tribe would not be harmed. But any Maori who attacked settlers, protected troublemakers, or dared to roam freely would lose the rights granted to them by the Treaty of Waitangi. I can't say how that went over with the chieftains at the time. In any case, it didn't have an effect on the outcome of the war."

"But they're still using it anyway?" Carol asked incredulously. "Two years later? Do they even know which chieftains or tribes were involved? The English think all the Maori look the same."

"I agree that the governor's tactics are concerning," Bill admitted. "General Cameron is complaining too. He's not gathering troops between Whanganui and the Patea River for nothing. That's where I'm going now, to work as a liaison officer. It's another mixed bag of English, New Zealanders, and Australians, though Cameron's pulling out the English. Grey is replacing them with the military settlers and other volunteers."

Looking into the sisters' alarmed faces, Bill smiled. "May I accompany you to the inn now, Miss Carol and Miss Mara? I have to check in at headquarters. Later, I would be delighted to treat you to dinner in a good restaurant, if you'll allow me. We will start on our journey north tomorrow."

Carol hesitated for a moment. She'd of course noticed how enthusiastically the young lieutenant was courting her, and didn't want to encourage his attention. After so much grief and upheaval, fresh off Oliver's betrayal and uneasy about Linda's new husband, Carol didn't have space in her heart for a new love. On the other hand, they would only be traveling for a few days before Bill left them in Waikato. Couldn't they be friends?

"We would be delighted if you would accompany us to dinner," she replied. "But please, don't take us to such an expensive restaurant again! It makes me uncomfortable."

Bill Paxton laughed. "Starting tomorrow, I won't have to spend a thing for months. So please allow me to enjoy a little luxury with you today. There are some excellent seafood restaurants here."

The next day, the travel was quite difficult but not as hard as Carol had feared. Bill had been assigned to a troop of soldiers that had been detached from Cameron's camp. The sisters rode with a group of twenty men and were followed by a cook wagon that Fancy immediately joined. The cook seemed to like dogs and enjoyed slipping her treats. The group traveled north from Wellington on a well-maintained road that Governor Grey had constructed for the transport of troops. It couldn't have been easy to build. The landscape was mountainous, and occasionally Carol held her breath as they thundered along steep abysses or over precarious bridges.

None of it bothered Mara. She'd traveled this road with her parents while it was still under construction, when the journey was much more challenging.

"There were just Maori roads here before," she said. "And, of course, those were hardly more than footpaths through the jungle."

"Ideal for ambushes and attacks," said one of the soldiers, an experienced captain. "That was the first thing we cleaned up. Governor Grey was quite right to build this road, even though it was expensive and the troops didn't want to do it. Only later did they come to understand. If you have to face those tattooed, spear-swinging fellows in the depths of the jungle, you learn to appreciate civilization. That was the problem in the first war in Taranaki. We played too much by their rules. This time, Grey and Cameron did it differently. We fought by our own rules, and won!"

"This land used to be beautiful," Mara remarked.

The hills and wooded valleys, the craggy mountainous landscape, and the grass-covered plains had been disfigured by the construction. The soldiers hadn't even carried away the trees they'd chopped down. Thousands of passing soldiers had added to the mess.

The captain shrugged. "Now it's safe."

On the way north, they saw numerous military bases along the new road. Some were Maori forts that had been taken over by the English, and some were unembellished, thrown-together new buildings. On the first day of the journey, the group stayed the night at a base near Paekakariki, and Carol and Mara stared at the structure in surprise.

"This wasn't a *pa*," Mara said, "though there's a *pa* on an island nearby. I found out by chance because Te Rauparaha died there. You know, Carrie, the father of Mamaca's foster mother."

Te Rauparaha and his tribe had originally lived on the South Island. After the Wairau conflict, the chieftain had escaped to the North Island.

"You're right," Carol said. "This was once a *marae*. A village. Families used to live here." She pointed to the meetinghouse, sleeping house, and kitchen that had been converted into soldiers' quarters. "Where did they go?"

The captain shrugged.

The next morning, Bill asked the commander of the base what had happened to the Maori who had once lived in the *marae*.

"They were moved," he told Carol and Mara later, as their caravan continued north through farmland. Sheep were grazing on both sides. "They were sent somewhere in Taranaki."

"Taranaki?" Mara said in surprise. "Are there tribes there that belong to the Ngati Raukawa? I thought just Nga Rauru and the Nga Ruahine live in Taranaki. Most of the North Island tribes are enemies!"

"We didn't notice anything like that," the captain replied. "When it comes to the English, the Maori forget their differences quickly."

"That isn't true," Bill said with a frown. He'd been trying not to contradict the captain, but he couldn't just let that go. "There are plenty of Maori warriors who have fought on our side, and some are still doing so—between fifteen hundred and two thousand of them."

"I've never trusted them," the captain said.

Bill rubbed his temples.

On the second day, the travelers passed Otaki and spent the night in a missionary station. It was there that Carol and Mara saw Maori for the first time since they'd been on the North Island. Shy, fearful-looking women and children stood by the side of the road and sold drinks. Most of them wore crosses around their necks and addressed the soldiers "in the name of Jesus." When Mara asked, they told her that they were Ngati Raukawa. The mission was close to their *marae*, and "of course" they were all Christians now.

"They would probably be more spirited if Te Rauparaha was still alive," Mara said to her sister. "Look at that old man. According to his *moko*, he was once a warrior. Now he's selling crosses made of pounamu jade."

"With the soldiers, he'd probably make more money with *hei tiki*s," Carol replied, referring to the carved figurines of Maori gods. "At least if he called them good-luck charms. The whalers loved those back when Jane started trading."

"Of course, he'd have to be able to tell the right stories," Mara said, laughing. "Which reminds me of Linda's new husband. I wonder what yarns he's spinning."

That night, the soldiers put up their tents in the fields. The area had been settled for a long time, and the local farmers were mostly growing flax. There were more military bases to the north, where the fields and meadows of Manawatu gave way to the Whanganui hills. All the mountains and valleys, the curves of the Whanganui River, and the lakes and waterfalls between which the road led north were extremely beautiful, but they'd posed enormous challenges to road construction. The Maori hadn't settled there.

"But they wandered here," Carol said. "And they had their sacred sites in the forests."

"And there are many settlements around the town of Whanganui," Mara said. "My father surveyed that land a few years ago, and always had to keep coming back to resolve disputes. We once spent the night there with the Ngati Hauiti. They were furious with the New Zealand Company. My father agreed with them completely. We had such a nice time with them."

"Nice?" the captain said. "Are you insane? They're cannibals and rebels!"

"The Ngati Hauiti live very peacefully with the settlers in Whanganui," Mara shot back. "They have no particular connection to Te Ua Haumene. I don't think you realize that there are six or seven totally different tribes in this region. The Ngati Rahiri, the Ngati Paki—I can't remember them all."

"The similar name is a coincidence, Captain," Carol explained. "*Hau* just means 'wind.'"

At the moment, the town of Whanganui was above all a military base. Mara remembered it being surrounded by thick woods, but now they rode through large, completely deforested areas.

"Is someone planning to build here?" Carol asked, saddened by the sight of the indiscriminate clear-cutting. "And over there—was there a fire?"

Mara gazed uncomprehendingly at the ash-covered fields and blackened tree stumps. The atmosphere was eerie and alien.

"There were villages here," she whispered. "This is where the tribes had their *maraes*."

"And they posed a constant threat to the settlers," the captain said with a huff. "Absurd to claim they had nothing to do with the Hauhau! We had plenty of trouble from them. This here"—he gestured at the obliterated fields—"was a punitive strike."

"Where are the people now?" Carol asked. She realized she'd asked the same question in Paekakariki. She got the same answer.

"They were moved," the captain replied. He didn't elaborate.

Carol's eyes stung. She couldn't even bear to look at Bill Paxton anymore.

In stark contrast to the desolate area along the road, Whanganui itself was teeming with life. The town had originally been founded and settled by the English. Most were honest, deeply religious people who'd scrimped and saved to buy their land. But over the last few years of war, the town had been transformed into a military hub, with all the positive and negative effects that entailed. The local shopkeepers were doing good business, but so were the pubs and brothels. Carol was grateful for Bill Paxton's help finding them an appropriate inn. Many places that called themselves by that name rented rooms only by the hour.

When the sisters had finally settled into a clean, simple room, Carol's fears caught up with her. The North Island had changed considerably since Mara had last traveled here. Carol's little sister, who was currently gazing out the window at laughing soldiers and whores with brightly painted faces, had been completely sure several days ago that they could travel alone from Wellington to Russell. Karl and Ida had been hospitably received everywhere, as easily in Maori *marae*s as they were on settlers' farms. Now, the farmers were fearful and suspicious. And the Maori had hardly any place at all to call their own. How would they keep traveling after Bill had arrived at his post? Carol slept restlessly and felt even more exhausted and depressed the next morning than she had the night before. Bill Paxton appeared at the inn as they were having breakfast.

"Please forgive my early intrusion," he said. "It's urgent. I must ask you for help. Yesterday, a Maori tribe who were removed from their land on the Patea River came here. General Cameron ordered them to leave their village when he passed through it. If I understood correctly, the people were told where they were supposed to resettle, but instead they came here and are refusing to leave. The situation is strained, and the missionary who was supposed to translate yesterday didn't know the language nearly well enough. But you do."

Carol nodded. "Though I don't know the dialect here as well," she said. "Mara can certainly do better. Where are the villagers now?"

Bill grimaced. "The military police have literally got them penned in, at a sheep farm. They say it's an aggressive tribe."

Carol frowned. "When people are driven from their homes, they don't usually feel very kindly toward those responsible." She stood up. "Come, Mara. Let's find out what's going on."

A phalanx of guards had surrounded the shearing shed and pens, but there were no Maori to be seen. It was raining, and the people had fled into the sheds to stay dry—and hide from the heavily armed soldiers. Carol and Mara nervously followed Bill Paxton and a military officer between the columns of guards. Even Fancy hung her head and whined.

When the sisters entered the shed, they were surrounded by not only the familiar scent of lanolin but also the sweat and fear of the humans being kept there against their will. There were almost only women and children. The few men among them were very old or looked ill. The space was far too small for all of them.

"This is one tribe?" Carol asked in surprise. "Are there such big *iwi*s on the North Island?"

Mara shrugged, and so did the officer. He hadn't bothered to ask the people who they were.

"Who is their leader, or their speaker?" Carol asked. "I don't see an *ariki*."

A chieftain on the North Island wouldn't have mingled with his people, but instead would have been standing somewhat apart. And, of course, he would have immediately stepped forward.

The officer looked around. "There were two old people here yesterday; they're the ones in charge. Unfortunately, they barely speak a word of English." He turned to the crowd. "Hey, you," he shouted so loudly that the women and children started in fear. "We have an interpreter here. Anyone who has something to say should come forward. Do you understand? An in-ter-pret-er!"

"Kaiwhakamaori," Mara explained.

Three people in a dark corner stood up. They were elderly and needed a moment to get to their feet. Then they walked toward the officer and the young women with slow dignity. They were all wearing traditional garb, the women in woven tops and long skirts. The only man among them wore a cape over his shoulders with feathers woven into the fabric. He must have been a person of high rank, perhaps a former chieftain.

Mara made a deferential gesture. She showed she was ready to exchange *hongi* with the women, and waited to give them the chance to initiate, but none did. They remained at a distance from the *pakeha* girl.

"Is this child to determine our fate?" asked the oldest woman.

Her hair was gray, and she stood straight-shouldered. She had no tattoos, and Mara realized that it meant she was a priestess, the woman with the highest spiritual rank in the tribe. She was of such a high rank that even the *tohunga-ta-oko* was forbidden to touch her and draw her blood.

"Of course not. I am only translating the words of the *pakeha ariki* into your language," Mara replied.

"What did she say?" the officer asked impatiently.

Carol told him.

"I will tell him in his own language what you have to say," Mara continued.

"You are *tohunga*?" the elderly man asked. "The gods have given you the gift of speaking in different languages?"

Mara shook her head. "No. I'm just the *makau* of a Maori warrior," she said proudly, using the word that could mean either lover or spouse.

Carol shot her a look, and didn't translate for the soldiers. But Mara's explanation seemed to satisfy the Maori.

"Which tribe does your *taua* belong to?" asked the priestess.

"I come from the South Island," Mara said. "We belong to the Ngai Tahu tribe."

"The Ngai Tahu are not our friends," the old man with the feather cape said uncertainly.

"Perhaps they were once our enemies, but that was long ago," the younger woman said. "We should speak to the girl. At least she understands our words, even if she doesn't fully comprehend their significance. That's more than the man who accompanied the *pakeha ariki* yesterday could do."

Carol spoke up. "I, too, understand your words, *karani*," she told the old woman, respectfully addressing her as "grandmother." "I also believe I can understand a little bit of your pain. I was driven away from my own land recently."

"What did she say?" The officer turned impatiently to Mara, who ignored him.

"Please," Mara said to the old *tohunga*, "tell my sister and me what happened to you."

The old woman looked from Mara to Carol, and then began to speak. "I am Omaka Te Pura, and I belong to the Ngati Tamakopiri. This is Aka te Amiri of the Ngati Whitikaupeka, and Huatare te Kanuba of the Ngai Te Ohuake. These are all *iwis* of the Mokai Patea. We all once came with one canoe, the *Aotea*, to Aotearoa."

Carol turned to the officer. "It's not one tribe, it's three. Their ancestors came to New Zealand in the same canoe."

"So?" the officer replied disdainfully.

"We have lived in Patea since our ancestors arrived in this land. We live from fish and mussels that the river gives to us."

"Ko au te awa. Ko te awa ko au!" the two others chanted together.

"I am the river. The river is me," Carol said, translating for the impatient officer.

The priestess continued. "A few days ago, the *pakeha* came to us and told us we had to leave our land."

Mara relayed this to the officer.

"Yes! It has been confiscated under the stipulations of the New Zealand Settlements Act," the officer declared. "You'll have to go somewhere else. Do you hear? Some! Where! Else!" Some of the children began to whimper in distress.

The priestess nodded to Mara. "We understood that. We were told to move to Mount Tongariro. But we can't do that."

"Why not?" the officer bellowed. "I warn you, if you refuse—"

"Let her explain," Bill said, stepping toward the furious officer.

The priestess gazed at the man fearlessly. "If we move to Tongariro, we will all die. We are river folk."

"Ko au te awa. Ko te awa ko au!" the others repeated, and the Maori around them joined the chant.

"We are fisher folk. Tongariro is a land of volcanoes. We won't be able to find anything to eat there," the priestess said.

The officer snorted. "There are plenty of tribes living there. Just ask them what to plant."

"That's the second problem," Carol said, translating after the old chieftain had replied with a stream of rhetoric. "The Ngati Tuwharetoa live in Tongariro, and they have been enemies with the Nga Rauru Kiitahi for centuries. If these people enter their territory without a reason that is acceptable to the other tribe, and without the protection of their warriors, it's very likely that they will all be slaughtered."

"What?" The officer laughed. "They're fighting among themselves too?" He turned to the uncomprehending group and waved his arms. "You're all Maori! All one people!"

"Just like the English and French?" Mara remarked. "Like the English and Irish and Scottish? They're all *pakeha*, and they would never fight among themselves."

The officer glared at her. "That's different."

"Stop it, Mara," Carol said. "Sarcasm won't help right now. Officer, isn't there another place these people can go?"

The man shrugged. "Lake Taupo? They could fish there."

Carol repeated the man's suggestion to the tribal elder, then shook her head again.

"They're also enemies with the Ngati Toa at Lake Taupo," Carol said, translating. "Without the protection of their warriors—"

"Why are they here without the protection of their warriors, anyway?" the officer asked with a snarl, and continued immediately before Mara could translate. "I can tell you! Because their warriors have gone to the fort at Weraroa to join the rebels. *Rire rire, hau hau*, isn't that what they say, old woman?"

He waved a scolding finger in front of the *tohunga*'s face as he imitated the Hauhau warriors' battle cry. The priestess shrank back in disgust.

"That's why your land was confiscated. You brought this on yourselves. And instead of locking you up like I should, I will provide you people with an escort to Lake Taupo. We'll even make it clear to the Gati-whatevers that they should refrain from eating their fellow countrymen," the officer said. He looked at Carol and Mara. "Thank you, ladies, for your interpreting services."

With that, he turned to leave. Bill Paxton followed, trying to appease the man's temper.

Carol and Mara broke the news of the officer's decision as gently as possible. "He says you will be under the protection of the Crown," Carol said, trying to comfort them. "The Ngati Toa won't dare to attack you."

"Not as long as the *pakeha* are pointing guns at them," the priestess said bitterly.

"And not afterward either."

A boy who had been sitting nearby with his mother and siblings straightened his back.

"The *pakeha* man is right about one thing," he declared. The chieftain glanced down at him indignantly, but the boy didn't let the disapproval bother him. "We are one people! The chosen people! We will go to the land of the Ngati Toa, and we will carry Te Ua Haumene's message with us! There will be Hauhau warriors among the Ngati Toa as well, and they will be our warriors. *Pai marire, hau hau!*"

A few other young men took up the chant. Carol thanked the Lord that the officer had already left.

"We should get out of here," Mara said.

They found Bill outside.

"I tried to make the man understand," he said unhappily. "If these people must settle at Lake Taupo, then they will have to be guarded for a long time. But he just doesn't care."

Mara shrugged. "It looks like the villagers have already found a solution."

Bill furrowed his brow. "What kind of solution?"

Carol sighed. "A biblical one," she said. "The officer invoked the wind, but he will be confronted with a hurricane."

Chapter 33

After Whanganui, Lieutenant Paxton was supposed to head for the Patea River with his recruits. There he would meet General Cameron's troops. Bill was assuming that the women would be joining him, but Carol had doubts.

"You'll be going too far west. If we want to get to Russell, it'd be better to split off and travel inland to Auckland."

"You want to go directly through Waikato?" Bill asked, horrified. "That's impossible, Miss Carol. The area is only theoretically at peace. In truth, it's full of marauding Hauhau hordes. No, please believe me; it would be best to come with me and then continue northward under the protection of Cameron's offensive."

"'Offensive'?" Carol asked suspiciously.

"The general is supposed to enforce the Settlements Act, and that means he has to send the Maori away from the Patea River. That land is supposed to be made available for white settlers. It works very well when the Maori abdicate. But when they don't—I don't know exactly what will happen, Miss Carol. I'll find out more when we're there. And perhaps we could take it as a stroke of fate! Cameron would certainly be grateful for skilled interpreters."

"Carol, let's just ride back to Wellington and take a ship," Mara urged. "The journey so far hasn't been dangerous. We can ride on these roads alone."

Carol rubbed her temples. "A ship? Halfway around the island? I'm sorry, Mara, but I'm not ready for that yet."

Mara groaned. "Well, I'm certainly not going to interpret for General Cameron!" she declared. "If he wants to throw people out of their villages, he'll have to tell them himself."

Carol shrugged. "No one will force you," she said. "All right then, Mr. Paxton. Let's ride to the Patea River."

The landscape around the Patea River reminded Carol painfully of her home on the South Island. Beech trees, pukatea trees, raupo, and rata grew there, as well as the resilient, ever-present ferns. The lower reaches of the river flowed through broad plains, and then into a wide estuary to the sea. However, the Patea didn't flow through grasslands like the Waimakariri did, but through dense forests. Carol had heard that the South Island had once looked this way before the Maori cleared the land. Once the forests had been cleared, they didn't grow back. Instead, the tussock grass spread. Currently, land around the mouth of the Patea was being cleared for settlers—and for General Cameron, who needed both space and wood for his military bases.

The general and his English troops had reached the mouth of the Patea several weeks earlier. They had set up an encampment for two hundred men, which had later been converted into headquarters. The camp was on a hilltop facing the sea, not far from the settlement of Patea. It offered an excellent view of the river and boasted accommodations for six hundred men. They were a mix of professional soldiers from Australia and volunteers from New Zealand. Many of the latter were either Maori warriors or members of the new military settlers regiment. The officials responsible for the new recruits sought out liaison officer Bill Paxton immediately after his arrival.

"What kind of men did you send us?" an Australian officer complained. "They're a bunch of milksops who climb the nearest tree if I say 'boo'! Pitting them against Hauhau warriors would be unimaginable. And right next to them, we have the complete opposite: ruffians and crooks, directly from the goldfields—or from Van Diemen's Land. I swear some of them must have escaped from chain gangs."

"What do you want me to do about it?" Bill asked.

"Make them get their heads on straight!" the English official ordered. "They're here in service of the Crown, even if all they want is land. They'd better pull themselves together and make themselves useful in exchange for what they're receiving!"

"They also have to learn to obey orders," the Australian added. "In my regiment, they just do whatever they want."

Bill called a meeting. He did his best to explain the strict English regulations to the cocky, self-assured "Kiwis," as the English liked to call New Zealanders.

"The seal hunters and the whalers feel powerful because they almost never lose in barroom brawls," he told General Cameron two days later. The general had invited his new liaison officer and the two ladies in his company to dinner. "The idea that one person gives orders and all the others obey simply doesn't fit with their view of the world."

Cameron laughed. He was a tall, slim man in his fifties with thinning hair and graying sideburns. He was exceedingly experienced in battle, but he wasn't enjoying his current job. In his opinion, Governor Grey had provoked the recent conflicts. He suspected the military settlers of the same transgression.

"Perhaps they're exactly the sort of people the governor needs," Cameron said. "I'll carry out Grey's plans and expel the Maori from that land, but then my men and I will leave. Permanently. The military settlers will have to have an abundance of self-assurance if they're going to hold their ground. And now we should stop boring the young ladies with administrative problems," he said. "Miss Brandmann and Miss Jensch, are you satisfied with your quarters? I'm terribly sorry that you can't continue on your journey directly."

Carol and Mara assured him that they couldn't have wished for more comfortable accommodations. They had been given a clean, spacious room in the officers' area, which consisted of a collection of log cabins. The cabins were new and smelled of fresh wood, and the interiors were simple and practical. The women were welcome to take meals in the mess hall, which was set up in another large cabin.

"You aren't boring us at all, General," Carol replied. "To the contrary. Since we are now stuck here, we are quite interested in everything that's happening at the base."

"What are all those Maori doing here, for example?" Mara asked.

She found it strange to see so many dark, tattooed faces in New Zealand Army uniforms. Some of the warriors combined the blue wool uniform jackets with their traditional skirts of dried hemp.

"They are all volunteers," the general said, and signaled to a uniformed steward to refill the wine glasses. "They join in order to fight rival tribes."

"Do they do a good job?" Bill asked.

The general toyed with his wine glass. "There's an Arabic proverb: 'The enemy of my enemy is my friend.' If you pit those men against the right opponents, they will fight like berserkers. It's strange with these people. If their ancestors came here eight hundred years ago in the same canoe, they still see each other as brothers and they'll do anything to protect one another. But woe to anyone who paddled here in a different boat! To be honest, I don't really like to use them in direct combat. They are too, hmm, barbarous for my liking. But that is certainly not a subject to discuss in front of young ladies."

"I've heard the Hauhau cut their enemies' heads off," Mara remarked casually while her plate was being refilled. After the sparse rations on their journey, Carol and Mara were delighted with the seafood cocktail and stuffed kiwi breast with kumara. "The food is delicious, by the way. Please convey my compliments to the cook, General."

Cameron stared at her indignantly. "Yes, some of the Maori do such things," he admitted. "They have a method to preserve the heads by smoking them. Then they carry them around and show them off." The subject was visibly uncomfortable for the Englishman. "Of course we don't allow them to do that in the army. After all, we're civilized men. I mostly employ the Maori volunteers as scouts and trail finders here in the woods."

"Then they probably aren't doing much interpreting," Bill said thoughtfully.

Mara repressed a giggle. Carol kicked her shin under the table.

The general shook his head. "So far we haven't had any need for interpreters."

Bill told him about the Maori tribes in Whanganui, and about Carol and Mara's roles in negotiating with them.

The general rubbed his temples. "I didn't know about that, and I'm sorry to hear it. I didn't intend to send those people into enemy territory. You could help us, Miss Brandmann, Miss Jensch. Of course you would be properly compensated. And we wouldn't put you in any danger. You'd only be asked to work after the battles are won."

"If they negotiated from the start, perhaps they wouldn't have to fight in the first place," Carol said later to her sister, whose stilted silence was getting on Carol's nerves. "Mara, I don't know if it's right to take part in this, but the general seems to be a reasonable man with good intentions. He's much more decent than that officer in Whanganui. I'm going to help him. It's not as though we could make it any worse for the people being displaced. And if we're lucky, we can help."

General Cameron had the task of commandeering the land on both sides of the Patea River. Every Maori tribe there had to be removed. According to Governor Grey, all of those *iwis* had fought against the *pakeha* during the war.

"How can he possibly know that?" Mara asked.

She had finally agreed to at least accompany Carol during her interpreting duties. They were getting bored after two weeks in Cameron's camp. There was nothing for the sisters to do there, and they didn't want to explore the area alone. It wasn't particularly dangerous, but the sight of the young women distracted the men who were clearing trees and building roads. Cameron took his troops up the river and ousted the Maori who were living there. He secured the area with cannons and forts, which kept the advancing troops safe and hindered the return of the Maori. All this building required a constant supply of wood, and the path along the river had to be made passable for supply wagons. After all, the troops still required ammunition and provisions. The military settlers' new commanders preferred to employ the recruits less suited to combat as builders. In Bill's mind, that didn't align with the intentions of the Settlements Act. "They're precisely the ones who should be getting used to the scent of gunpowder," he said. "And they couldn't go too far wrong with the general's offensive."

At first, the *pakeha* troops met with almost no resistance. The *marae*s they came across were wealthy fishing villages. The people had large houses with colorful roofs and elaborate carvings on the gables and walls, watched over by majestic statues of gods. In most of those *marae*s, they found only women and children. The men had disappeared.

"They spot us long before we find them," said one of the *pakeha* scouts, a member of the special Forest Rangers unit that Cameron had put together. The man had been born on the North Island, and was very experienced at navigating through the woods. However, his abilities didn't compare to those of a Maori warrior. "Then the fellows leave, and probably go to some kind of Hauhau *pa*. I don't know if it's the right strategy to let them run away—they're much less controllable that way. If we used the Maori scouts more often, we'd catch some for sure. But the general has reservations about that."

The women and children usually waited for the *pakeha* stoically. They had often already packed their belongings. If they hadn't, the soldiers would rudely demand that they do so before they set about burning down the houses and destroying the crops. The older women wailed and lamented, but the young women, girls, and little boys took up clubs and attempted to defend their homes.

"Why don't you at least wait until they've left?" Carol asked disgustedly, after it had almost ended in bloodshed again.

"That's part of the punishment," the young colonel replied, unimpressed. "They're supposed to watch and tell the others what happens when they support the rabble-rousers."

"Are you sure that these tribes really fought in the war?" Bill asked doubtfully.

The *marae*s seemed so peaceful. There weren't any protection measures in place at all, not even a fence.

"If they didn't have anything to hide, then the men wouldn't run away," the colonel insisted.

As it turned out, it made no difference to the *pakeha* forces whether the men remained in the villages. The warriors of the next tribe that Cameron's scouts found were obviously not guilty of anything. The chieftain greeted the army in festive traditional garb, followed by his warriors—it was the peaceful prelude to a *powhiri*.

Carol was horrified when the soldiers attacked anyway, disarming the warriors and herding them together like animals. Of course, a few tried to fight, but they had no chance against the superior weaponry. Cameron went so far as to fire one of his cannons. Finally, the villagers were captured and held as prisoners at the military base. The next morning, Carol was red with shame as she approached their pen to deliver a message. She was greeted by a chorus of *"Pai marire, hau hau!"* Several warriors had managed to escape during the night.

"Now we've created even more enemies," Mara remarked. "Carol, can't you see what you're doing? You aren't helping the Maori; you're only making yourself into one of the *pakeha* henchmen."

After that, Carol withdrew for a while, but soon began to obey the general's orders again. Later, everyone would claim to have known nothing about the ruthless "cleansing," and Carol thought it was important that someone bear witness. Grey's policies weren't universally accepted. In Auckland, several newspapers were said to be very interested in what was happening in Taranaki.

"Sure, back in Auckland," Mara said, scoffing, when Carol shared her thoughts. "We're very far from there now, and the roads aren't getting any safer."

Chapter 34

Eru and his two friends planned to make their way to Blenheim and take the ferry to Wellington from there. Jane had always felt it was important for her son to learn to manage his finances, and he'd taken all his savings with him to Lake Whakamatua. He'd given most of it to the *moko* master, and now he needed to spend the rest in Christchurch on new clothes.

"Fifty years ago," Eru complained, "it would have been normal to travel from one *marae* to another dressed as a warrior. But now? It is truly as Te Ua Haumene says: our land has become their land. We're ashamed of our own traditional dress."

Tamati, one of his friends, nodded. "You're right. Unfortunately, there aren't any canoes that travel regularly between the South and North Islands. We'll have to take the ferry, and the *pakeha* won't let us on board that way."

So Eru reluctantly bought a pair of canvas trousers and a plaid shirt, and the three men earned the money for the trip with odd jobs. Eru's *moko* proved to be an impediment. The *pakeha* farmers viewed him mistrustfully, and sometimes fearfully. Even his perfect English and feigned submissiveness weren't enough to change their minds. That made Eru angry; he interpreted it as a lack of understanding of his people's traditions. However, the resentment of the people of the South Island was still minimal. Very few of the *pakeha* there had had bad experiences with the natives. But on the ferry to the North Island, a woman and a little girl were terrified of Eru's face, and the captain of the vessel asked the three Maori to stay below deck during the crossing.

"I can't order you to stay away, but listen: The little one and her mother are survivors of a Hauhau attack. The father died. They just spent six months with relatives on the South Island to recover. But as you can see, the girl is still scared to death. So, if you would be so kind . . ."

Eru complied, gritting his teeth. On one hand, he wanted to be proud of his *moko*, and on the other, he didn't want to terrify children. The old Eru felt sorry for the child who cried hysterically at the sight of him and hid behind her trembling mother's skirts. But the new Eru should be happy about the *pakeha*'s fear. It meant they would leave Aotearoa sooner.

In Wellington, people reacted to the young warriors with more aggression than fear. They spat on Eru and his friends and insulted them. As a result, the young men had to give up their plan of trying to earn some money there before making their way into the wilderness. Just one day after their arrival, they set off for Taranaki, avoiding the newly improved roads. They relished the adventure of it. Like their ancestors, they were finally living from only what they could hunt, fish, and gather. There were no more sheep farms, no luxuries like blankets and cooking pots, soap, or warm clothing. Kepa only had a bottle of whiskey that he'd bought in Blenheim. The three of them drank it around the campfire on their first evening, delighted to be all on their own. No parents, no *rangatira*s, no *tohunga*s who wanted to share their wisdom.

Kepa laughed and imitated Makuto, and Tamati imitated the chieftain. With his heart racing a little, Eru attempted Jane's voice.

"You are a chieftain's son!" he quacked, reproducing her accent with uncanny accuracy.

"And you will marry a sheep baroness!" Tamati added.

"He's more likely to marry a sheep," Kepa said with a grin.

All three of them collapsed in gales of laughter. They were dressed as warriors again, and proud of themselves for being able to traverse the woods without being noticed by the *pakeha*. In truth, they were just lucky. The area around Wellington had long since been "cleansed" of all Maori settlements. No one bothered to patrol the unsettled areas here.

That didn't change as they passed Porirua and Paraparaumu, always staying deep in the woods. The rimu trees, miro trees, and matai trees were often so close together that their tops blocked the view of Mount Taranaki. That made it difficult for the companions to find their way toward the snow-covered volcano.

"Te Ropata called it a sacred mountain," Kepa said, remembering the *rangatira*'s words. "He said its soul once lived on the South Island, together with Tongariro and Ruapehu and the other volcanoes. But then Tongariro and Taranaki fought over the goddess Pihanga, and Tongariro destroyed the peak of Taranaki. When he escaped, he made a crack in the North Island. That's how the Whanganui River was formed."

"The peak is still missing!" Tamati exclaimed.

Eru grinned. "That's because it's a volcano. That's where the lava comes out when it erupts." The young man spun around. "Did you see that? It looked like a dragon!"

The friends gawked at lizards and gold-striped geckos. On the South Island, there were no reptiles. Eru managed to capture a tuatara, but released it after studying it carefully. No one wanted to try to eat the lizard with scaly, leathery skin and a spiky ridge on its back. They preferred to set traps for birds and roast them over their campfire.

It wasn't until the three companions reached the area of Otaki that they saw people again. Some haggard-looking Maori in *pakeha* clothes were digging for edible roots in the woods. Only one older warrior dared to speak to the strangers.

"Stay away from the town," he warned. "The missionaries report every Maori who's seen in the area. They're terrified of being attacked, even though there haven't been any *marae*s here for a long time. The Te Ati Awa were resettled somewhere. Now there are only a few dispersed members of other tribes. They aren't doing very well. Where are you planning to go?"

"We are looking for Te Ua Haumene," said Eru, daring for the first time to share what had brought them to Taranaki. He glanced at his friends. *"Pai marire."*

"Hau hau!" Kepa and Tamati replied enthusiastically. They were careful to keep their expressions serious, but their eyes betrayed their lust for adventure.

The elder nodded solemnly. "The prophet is in Weraroa. That's the large *pa* near Waitotara, to the north. It's a few days' journey from here. Be careful. If you make as much noise as you did last night, scouts will find you. We won't give you away, but there are tribes that are enemies of the Ngati Taahinga and work for the *pakeha*. Good luck."

The companions stayed where they were for a while, their pride hurt. They had overestimated their stealthy progress through the forest.

"Who are the Ngati Taahinga?" Kepa asked in a small voice after the old man was gone. Previously, none of them had wanted to admit their ignorance about the North Island.

"They're probably the tribe that owns the *pa* in Weraroa," Eru said. "There are many tribes on the North Island. Many are enemies with each other. That's why my father didn't really want to send me to the school in Wellington. Most of the tribes there don't like the Ngai Tahu."

"Then, would it be better not to tell anyone where we're from?" Tamati asked uneasily.

Eru shook his head. "Our accents would give us away. No, the easiest solution is just not to let ourselves be seen until we reach the *pa*. To the prophet, there are no tribes. He says we are all one people."

After that, the companions took to heart the lessons that Te Ropata had drilled into them. They moved silently, peered carefully down every path, and in that way arrived unharmed on the outskirts of Whanganui. The town was an important *pakeha* army base. Every offensive for the Taranaki War started there, and the three warriors were very proud when they managed to skirt around the settlement at a healthy distance. They felt safe again. The forest here was much too large for the *pakeha* to control all of.

"They'll never find the prophet," Tamati said as he sat with his friends around the campfire, roasting a kiwi he'd hunted with his spear at twilight. "They'd have to bring thousands of settlers."

"And they'd have to be able to shoot very accurately!" Kepa said with a laugh. "No, this is Maori land, and it will stay that way. No matter what the governor says."

The next day, the trio encountered a patrol of Maori warriors, and were lucky that the tribe was sympathetic to Te Ua Haumene.

"We aren't fighting for him, but we won't betray him either," the elder told them, echoing the old man in Otaki. But he kept a stern eye fixed on his own young warriors, who seemed to be itching to joining in the adventure. "His gods are not our own, even though our goal might be the same. We would also like the *pakeha* to leave Aotearoa. But we've seen what their muskets and cannons can do."

"Pai Marire will make us invulnerable," Kepa replied.

The elder shook his head. "Not even Maui could conquer death," he said calmly.

According to legend, the demigod had attempted to lead the goddess of death astray, but his friends betrayed him with their laughter. Despite feeling invincible, it was finally he who fell victim to death.

"But Maui was no Hauhau," Eru said thoughtfully.

The elder didn't reply. He just raised his eyebrows, making his *moko* dance. His entire face was tattooed like Eru's, but an entire lifetime of wisdom was written beneath the designs. He had doubtlessly looked death in the eye more than once. The old warrior didn't believe in invulnerability.

The young men of his tribe had enough reverence not to follow Eru and his companions. But they did tell them how to get to the *pa*.

"It's in Waitotara, you can't miss it," they explained.

The adventurers thanked them and continued northward.

Two mornings later, tantalizingly close to their destination, the young men woke up to find their camp surrounded by grim-faced warriors.

"Who are you, and what do you want?" the leader asked sternly. He wore the garb of a warrior and carried the traditional weapons, but he also had a pistol in his belt.

Eru's head spun. They had spent so much time selecting their hidden camp and making it secure.

"We, um, we are Hauhau warriors!" Kepa announced, and was met with howls of laughter.

"He means that's what we want to become," Eru said, and cast his friend a reprimanding glance. "We are going to the *pa* at Weraroa to join the prophet's troops." He met his companions' eyes. *"Pai marire,"* he chanted.

"Hau hau!" the two answered obediently.

The men laughed even louder.

"We've been waiting for you," the leader said sarcastically.

"Let it be, Aketu. It was certainly they who scared old Cameron so much that he avoided coming anywhere near Weraroa," another joked.

In his summer offensive, General Cameron had attacked ordinary *marae*s instead of actually advancing on Te Ua Haumene's stronghold. The attacks on previously peaceful people had swelled the rebels' ranks. The local tribes were impressed. If even the English feared the prophet, there must be something to his teachings.

"Are you from Weraroa?" Eru asked hopefully.

The leader smiled. "I am Aketu Te Komara, and this is Ahia Te Roa." He gestured at the other men who were surrounding the campsite. "This is our *taua*."

Eru introduced himself and his friends.

"You're from the Ngai Tahu on the South Island? Te Ua will be pleased—there's still too little support coming from the south." Aketu finally lowered his spear.

"Does that mean you'll take us with you?" Kepa asked.

Aketu rolled his eyes. "If we leave you here, you'll attract the *pakeha* scouts in no time, the way you're staggering through the woods. We've been observing you since yesterday afternoon, and we thought it must be something like this. After all, you're not the first milksops who've come looking for us. But you"—he turned to Eru—"are wearing the face of a warrior. Even if your eyes are a little strange."

Since he'd been tattooed, Eru was no longer recognizable as half-*pakeha*. Only his green eyes set him apart.

Eru took a deep breath. "I have the face and the soul of a warrior. Perhaps I don't have all the skills yet. It's possible that we are really staggering through your land like lost children. Our land is completely different, and our tribe has never been at war. But that doesn't mean we lack courage. So don't insult us. We are here to learn and to fight. We will drive the *pakeha* out of Aotearoa."

Aketu's gaze became respectful. "Is that what you see with your pale eyes?"

Eru shook his head. "I'm not a prophet," he said cautiously. "But doesn't Te Ua see it?"

"Te Ua says it depends on us," Ahia explained. "It depends if we believe, how we fight, and how many we kill."

Eru fixed his gaze on the two warriors. "Then I see it with my pale eyes," he said formally. "There's no one who could believe more strongly, fight more bravely, or kill more mindlessly than you." He pointed to Ahia, and then, motioning toward Aketu, said, "Or you, or any of you." He raised his arms in an encompassing gesture that included all the warriors.

"Yes, and us too!" Kepa added enthusiastically.

"Rire rire!" Tamati cried in excitement.

This time, all the warriors answered. *"Hau hau!"*

Chapter 35

Weraroa was a gigantic fortress. The *pa* was on a hilltop above the river and was currently home to more than two thousand men. It was surrounded by high wooden palisades that were sunk deeply into the ground and bound together with cords of flax. Behind the fence were houses similar to those in a *marae*: meetinghouses, cookhouses, and a prayerhouse. They were all connected by a network of ditches through which the warriors could move without being seen from the outside, and where they were protected from cannon fire. At first glance, the fort looked unoccupied, almost ghostly.

The Hauhau warriors had been trained to move silently whenever they weren't rallying men or shouting war cries. Much of the space in the *pa* was taken up by a drill ground with a gigantic *niu* in the middle. The warriors surrounded the pole, singing and praying before and after each exercise. Spiritual strength seemed every bit as important to them as physical strength.

Eru and his friends witnessed such a ceremony immediately after arriving. Hundreds of warriors moved in formation, lined up in rows in front of the *niu*, and stamped their feet and spears in rhythm with their cries.

Kira, wana, tu, tiri, wha—Teihana!
Rewa, piki rewa, rongo rewa—Teihana!

Kill, one, two, three, four—Attention!
River, large river, long river—Attention!

Eru interpreted this to mean that the men were evoking the rivers, mountains, bushes, and trees of their homeland. But then he stopped thinking about it and let himself be swept along by the noise. Kepa was the first of the three companions to join the ring of warriors. Tamati followed, and finally all three were shouting and dancing with the others. By the time the ritual ended at sunset, they were smiling and feeling strong.

Aketu and Ahia seemed to be satisfied with them, and now other warriors wanted to exchange *hongi* with the newcomers. There was no further mention of their belonging to a tribe that had not long ago been at odds with many of the North Island tribes. Now they all stood as one behind their prophet.

"Will we—will we get to see Te Ua soon?" Kepa asked excitedly as they followed Aketu to their quarters.

The *rangatira* seemed to have taken them on as his own. He nodded. "He speaks to his warriors every morning. Perhaps he'll even ask you to step forward. As I said, we have few men from the South Island, and very few who look like you." He turned to Eru, who blushed.

"I don't want to be anything special," Eru said.

Aketu gave him a stern look. "It doesn't matter what you want."

The young men were shown to a sleeping house just like the ones at home. The only differences between this part of the *pa* and a typical *marae* were the ditches and the undecorated houses. No one had made the effort to elaborately carve the roof tree and support beams of the military quarters or to place tikis in front of the buildings. There was a simple meal offered before they went to bed—just a quickly made stew that consisted mostly of *kumara*. No one sat around the fire afterward either. To the contrary, the *pa* was cloaked in darkness in order not to attract scouts.

At first, Eru was too excited to sleep. He wasn't used to sharing a sleeping house with so many other men. So he thought of Mara, for the first time in many days. *Someday soon,* he thought in half sleep, *when the battle has been won, I will go to Russell and get her. Just in time before the prophet banishes the* pakeha.

He fell asleep thinking about how joyfully she would welcome him when he saved her from exile.

A *rangatira*'s cries awoke the warriors at dawn. Everyone else jumped up, but Eru and his companions needed a few moments to orient themselves. Then they rushed outside and breathed the fresh air hungrily. In the sleeping house, the stuffy air smelled of gun oil and unwashed bodies.

"Is there something to eat?" Tamati murmured hopefully as all the men moved together silently in one direction.

A warrior shook his head. "Morning song," he whispered, pointing to the drill ground.

Eru was reminded painfully of his time at the missionary school. There, too, the children had been called to prayer when they were still half-asleep, and there, too, he would have preferred to be in a cozy breakfast room instead of in a church. He immediately scolded himself for having such thoughts. This was completely different than the dreaded morning church services in Tuahiwi. Here, the spirit of the prophet ruled. If Aketu was right, Te Ua Haumene would soon be speaking to them personally.

Next, they all gathered around a *niu*. There were several such poles in the *pa*, arranged in the various drill grounds. An impressive number of men stood around every pole, between three hundred and five hundred warriors. As the prayers began, they all raised their right hands.

"My glorious *niu*, *mai merire*!" a prayer leader cried.

"My holy *niu*, have mercy upon us!" the men replied.

"God, the Father, have mercy upon us!"

"Mercy, mercy!"

"God, the Son, have mercy upon us!"

Eru, Kepa, and Tamati glanced at each other in surprise. They'd had to repeat similar prayers in Miss Foggerty's lessons, and of course Eru was reminded again of his time at Tuahiwi. The young men had hoped that the prophet would offer different kinds of prayers.

But the invocations at the *pa* differed only in their ending. Instead of "amen," the warriors concluded, *"Rire rire, hau hau!"*

Now the companions were very hungry indeed. But everyone streamed toward the main drill ground. A podium had been erected there so everyone could see the speaker. In front of the *niu*, Te Ua Haumene was waiting calmly, his head lowered in humility.

"The archangel is speaking to him," whispered a young man next to Eru.

The men gathered quickly around the podium. There was complete stillness, which seemed almost eerie after the deafening morning prayers. Then Te Ua Haumene looked up.

Eru gazed at the man's wide face and short hair. The prophet wore no warrior's knot. He wasn't tattooed either. Eru remembered hearing that he'd been captured by an enemy tribe as a small child and had been kept as a slave. Slaves were never given *moko*. Later, he'd been raised in a Christian mission. Of course there hadn't been a *moko* master there. But Te Ua Haumene was dressed as a chieftain. Under an elaborate cape luxuriously ornamented with kiwi feathers, he wore a white robe. As he began to speak, he raised a hand and spread his first two fingers. Eru remembered seeing images of Jesus Christ in the same pose.

"Pai marire, hau hau!" the large, heavy man with the resonant voice called in greeting.

His warriors replied, and once more the fort seemed to quake with the power of their voices.

"I greet you on a new day in our land! The Promised Land, the land that God and the angels intended to be ours. Ours, and ours alone!"

The men cheered.

"A land where our people shall live in peace, as Archangel Gabriel told me. In earlier times, our people killed one another in fratricidal war. That weakened us. It angered God and his angels. But now that the Last Days are upon us, they are once more by our sides! Gabriel, Tama-Rura, and Michael, Te Ariki Mikaera!"

"Riki," the warriors chanted. Archangel Michael, defender of heaven, was obviously their favorite among God's servants.

"God and his angels will help us create the peaceful, loving, and fair society that Tama-Rura spoke to me of. Milk and honey will flow in the Promised Land—Aotearoa, our land!"

"Rire rire, hau hau!" the crowd cheered.

"But first, my friends, there is work to be done," the prophet said. "Because we, God's chosen people, are chafing in slavery. Our land is in the hands of enemies who do not respect it. Our people are being hunted and killed, just as the people of Israel were once chained in Egypt." The prophet's face darkened. "But God is with us!" he announced. "With his help, we will once again reclaim our land and our inheritance. Jehovah himself will fight by our sides as we drive the *pakeha* into the sea from whence they came."

The prophet paused for a moment and gazed out over his crowd of followers. Then he resumed with a stern voice. "Now, you say the *pakeha* are strong. The *pakeha* are many. The *pakeha* have weapons that spit fire. We cannot conquer them. But I say unto you: Rura is strong, Riki is strong. Both of them lend us their strength. The angels are our legion. God's weapons are lightning and thunder, and the words of the prophet make every one of us invulnerable when we stand against the *pakeha*'s weapons of fire. Your faith will deflect bullets, your belief will make the cannons melt into useless clumps of iron. Not only *can* we defeat them, we *will* defeat them! So take up your arms. Pray! Fight! Conquer!"

"Kira!" Kill!

The warriors took up the cry, repeating it again and again until they had worked themselves into a frenzy.

"Rire rire, hau hau, rire rire, hau hau!"

Stamping and shouting, the men celebrated their prophet as he stepped down and relinquished his warriors to their day.

Eru, Kepa, and Tamati were swept away by the excitement, longing to practice their fighting skills in order to combat the fatal bullets of their enemies. But even with divine assistance, warriors couldn't go into battle on empty stomachs. For breakfast, there was flatbread and dried fish, but the three young men's hunger soon returned. They devoured their meal to the last crumbs, then saw Ahia was standing next to them.

"When you're done, go to the chieftain's house," he said. "Te Ua Haumene wishes to speak with you."

The prophet sat on a stone in front of one of the houses in which the chieftain and commanders lived. This was an exclusive area of the fort, separated from the warriors' quarters. On the North Island, *ariki*s and their families had always been constrained by many *tapu*s. Eru and his friends only knew the stories they'd heard from their elders. The Ngai Tahu had never been so strict about such things. Before the *pakeha* had come to Aotearoa and given the South Island a new appearance with their grazing animals and seeds for crops, the tribes had often suffered from bad harvests, hunger, and cold. One needed strength simply to survive. There wasn't time for complicated battles and ceremonies that made everyday tasks more difficult. And in Eru's *iwi*, Te Haitara and Jane had done away with most of the last remaining rituals that set the chieftain apart. Te Haitara was affable with the *pakeha* and his own people alike. No one worried much which purification ceremonies should be used when his shadow accidentally fell on one of the members of his tribe.

Here it was different. The three adventurers approached the prophet, shy and unsure of what rites they were supposed to observe. As they approached, he was listening to a group of about twenty warriors who looked exhausted and terrified.

"We walked all night," the leader said. "No, no, don't worry, the *pakeha* didn't follow us, we—"

"I am not worried," Te Ua said, "for my faith is strong. The *pakeha* know who I am, but they fear my power. They fear *our* power. *Pai marire, hau hau!*"

"But the men in the fortress weren't afraid," a warrior said. "They were vigilant, and when we attacked, they shot at us."

"They couldn't hurt you," the prophet replied calmly.

"That's what we thought too!" one of the warriors burst out. His arm was wrapped with a dirty, blood-soaked bandage. "We prayed and conjured the wind and Jehovah and the angels. We gave our battle cries and stormed them with the holy words on our lips." His voice broke.

"Hapa, hapa!" one of the others added. "Fly past! That's what we are supposed to say to deflect the bullets. But it didn't work."

"Didn't work?" Te Ua said sternly. "Aren't you here, almost uninjured?"

"We are," the leader said. "But there were fifty of us when we attacked the fort. The others—"

"The others are dead," one of his comrades said.

Te Ua snorted. "If they're dead, it's their own fault. Their faith wasn't strong enough. They didn't trust in the power of the *karakia*."

"But *ariki*—"

"Go now. And look deep within yourselves! Especially those of you who didn't fully manage to deflect the enemy's bullets." He gazed intently at the young man with the bandage. "Go and pray for the strength of the *niu*. Pray for mercy, for you have disappointed Rura and Riki today. It was your duty to hinder the building of that fort. You weren't able to do it. You did not bring me the heads of our enemies. Go and repent."

He dismissed the men with a wave of his hand. Heads lowered, they slipped away unhappily.

The prophet took a few moments to pull himself together, and then he called Eru, Kepa, and Tamati.

"You are the warriors from the South Island?" he asked. His gaze wandered over their face, and stopped on Eru. "You!" he cried. "You have the eyes of a *pakeha*!"

Eru gasped, but then gathered his wits. "I have the heart of a Maori, and the courage of a warrior."

"You have the face of a warrior," Te Ua remarked. "The face of an old warrior, but you are young. Have you ever killed, Te Eriatara?"

Eru straightened his shoulders, amazed and flattered that the prophet knew his name. "I am prepared to kill for my people," he said.

"And you know what I preach?" Te Ua asked. "I have not yet sent a prophet to the south."

"I have read your gospel," Eru replied.

The eyes of the prophet flashed. "You can read?"

Eru nodded. "I read it to the men in my *taua*," he declared. "We all know what you preach, and we all believe." He fought to keep his voice steady. The conversation he'd just overheard had shaken his belief in the invulnerability of the Hauhau warriors.

The prophet narrowed his eyes. "Tell me your story. Tell me what brings you here."

Eru began hesitantly, but then his anger overtook him. He told about Jane and Te Haitara's devotion to the god of money. He spoke of the pressure Jane had put on him, and finally about his decision to become a whole Maori, and a whole warrior.

Te Ua stopped him only once, when he nervously admitted having a *pakeha* mother.

"You speak language of *pakeha* without have to seek words?" he asked in broken English.

Eru nodded. "Of course," he replied in English. "It's my mother's language. I speak it fluently, without an accent."

"And the rest of you?" Te Ua asked. His eyes held something dangerous.

"We speak English well," Kepa answered slowly, being careful not to make any mistakes. "Not as well as Eru, but well. We learned it at school."

The prophet nodded and then asked Eru to continue with his story.

"We are here to do battle for our people," Eru concluded. "We will throw the *pakeha* into the sea. We—"

The prophet silenced him with a gesture. "Your intention honors you. But I don't need you as warriors."

"What?" the trio replied in chorus, shocked and disappointed, and prepared to argue. But then Eru lowered his head. He remembered Aketu's words. *It doesn't matter what you want.* And then there was that quote from the Bible . . . Eru took a deep breath.

"Te Ua, our prophet and our father. Your will be done."

The prophet grinned. *"Rire rire, hau hau,"* he replied in acknowledgment. "I don't need you as warriors, but only because you are too valuable for that. I need you as ambassadors. You will help me spread my teachings across our land."

Chapter 36

Six hundred miles away, Linda stared into the decimated valley called Gabriel's Gully. She was just as stunned as Carol and Mara had been to witness the scorched earth where Maori villages had stood on the North Island. There were no trees or bushes as far as the eye could see. Not a single blade of grass reached for the sunlight, even on the abandoned claims. The famous goldfield was the most depressing sight Linda had ever seen. Five years prior, when the Australian Gabriel Read had found gold there, it must have looked just as beautiful and idyllic as the rest of Otago.

For several days, Fitz and Carol had been guiding their covered wagon through the mountainous region, which alternated between grassland, scrubland, and sparse forest. Linda liked Otago, and she had easily been able to imagine having a small farm there. She had gazed covetously at the farmhouses they passed along their way, but she never had a chance to chat with their owners. Even when Fitz and Linda stopped to buy food, the people greeted them with weapons in hand and demanded to see the money up front.

"Nothing personal," one of the farmers' wives drawled as she allowed them to take water from her well with a rifle trained on them. "Over the last few years, so many scalawags have come through that we've had to learn how to protect ourselves. But now the goldfields are used up, and most of the rogues are gone. Do you actually believe they left a few nuggets behind for you?" she asked sarcastically.

"Especially for us, milady," Fitz confirmed, offering her a charming smile. "But for now we're a little short on funds. Is there any work we could do for you, perhaps?"

Actually, the young couple hadn't spent any of their money on the journey. In spite of all of the locals' mistrust, Fitz somehow managed to find little jobs along the way. Linda was pleased about that, even though she grew worried and ashamed whenever he disappeared after dark and returned a few hours later with a chicken or a few eggs.

"I've been hunting," he would say with a mischievous grin. "I got a kiwi hen and a few eggs. Very easy to catch. You dig them out, you know."

Linda, who had spent half of her childhood in a Maori village, knew much more about it than he did. Kiwis did dig burrows, but during the day. The birds were nocturnal.

"This one here preferred daylight," Fitz said with a grin when Linda called him out. "It was the odd one out. And you can see what became of it."

Laughing, he held out the freshly plucked bird. Linda roasted it without asking any more questions.

Aside from such feelings of suspicion, the young woman was happy with her marriage. Fitz was almost always cheerful. He joked with Linda and never tired of describing their future wealth to her. He satisfied her in bed every night, even if it was in a different way than her friends had described. Fitz was skilled with his tongue. He played with her body, caressed and excited her with his dexterous fingers. But his manhood rarely rose to the occasion, and when it did, it never remained hard long enough to penetrate her. Still, Linda bled once. Fitz must have torn the thin area of skin that Cat had told her about.

Linda was pleased not to be a virgin anymore. But she still wondered what was happening with Fitz, and finally worked up the courage to ask again.

He brushed aside her worry. "I'm thinking more of you than I am of me, sweetheart," he said. "It's a fine art. You're satisfied, are you not?"

Linda tried to be satisfied with this answer, but lovemaking with Fitz left her with a slightly bitter feeling. He knew how to excite her, but why couldn't she do the same for him? Wasn't she beautiful or interesting enough? Was she missing something that other women had? Linda began to doubt herself, and worked all the harder during the day to be a perfect wife. She managed well during their journey, but it became more difficult when they finally arrived at Gabriel's Gully.

"This is terrible," Linda said, looking out over the sweeping fields. In order to turn over the top layer of ground so thoroughly, thousands and thousands of prospectors must have toiled here. Now, just a small smattering were working on their claims. The desperate figures looked as gray and lost as the landscape. Linda could see men and women armed with sieves and shovels. It had rained the day before, and some of them were up to their knees in mud. Gabriel Read had discovered the glimmer of pure gold the first time he had been here, but the ones seeking it now were searching in vain.

"Fitz, there isn't any gold left here," Linda said quietly. "The farmer's wife and Bill Paxton were right. It's all gone."

Fitz laughed. "Don't be silly. Smile, Lindy! We're here, we made it! Gabriel's Gully is right in front of us!"

Linda stared at him in disbelief. "Made it, Fitz? You want to stay? You want to try scratching something out of the ground down there?"

Shuddering, she watched a young woman who had just laid her sieve aside, exhausted, to sit down and take a baby down from her back to nurse.

Fitz nodded enthusiastically. "Of course, sweetheart. But first we have to find somewhere to stay. We can't live in the wagon forever. What was that backwater they changed the name of three times? We'll go there. And we can find out how to make our claim right away. Sounds good, doesn't it? Our claim!"

If Linda were honest, she found the prospect of hammering more poles into the marred ground of Gabriel's Gully neither appealing nor promising. But it was impossible to communicate that to Fitz; he was too euphoric. Linda only hoped the license to dig here wouldn't cost them anything.

The road between Gabriel's Gully and the village of Tuapeka had been overused, and sometimes the covered wagon got stuck in deep ruts. But at least the ground was packed so hard that it didn't soften in the rain; the water just collected in puddles. The vegetation here wasn't as destroyed as in the goldfields themselves, but it was meager. The grass was yellowed and flattened, the bushes had been cut, and the trees chopped down, and there were traces of campfires everywhere. At the high point of the rush, the prospectors' camps had stretched all the way from Tuapeka to the goldfields. Now there was hardly anything left of them aside from rubbish, an occasional decaying tent, and a few improvised huts about half a mile from the village. Linda shuddered when she saw the rough constructions of canvas sheets and wood scraps that people were living in. A few women were cooking over open fires, and children played in the dirt.

Fitz seemed not to register any of it. He was looking for a gold bullion dealer's, hoping for information about staking a claim. But in this slum, they found nothing, and the woman that Fitz finally asked only pointed in the direction of the town.

"There's a dealer's office next to the bank," she said curtly. "The man it belongs to is called Oppenheimer."

Tuapeka's bank wasn't hard to find. The tiny town barely consisted of more than a bank, post office, and general store. The only remarkable features were three pubs with brightly painted façades. These clearly catered to prospectors, not the few citizens of the town. As two garishly made-up young women left one of the establishments, a primly dressed lady demonstratively moved to the other side of the road. Linda greeted her politely as the wagon rolled past, but the woman ignored her. Apparently, she had the same opinion of gold seekers as she did of whores.

The bullion dealer's office was between the bank and the post office. Inside, an old man was tinkering with a delicate scale. He didn't look up when Fitz and Linda entered. Another man in dirty, worn-out clothes stood across from him. He stared as though entranced at the scale, a tiny pile of shimmering flakes upon it. The bullion dealer began to put weights on the opposite tray, but couldn't find one small enough. Finally, he looked up and peered at the man through a monocle.

"I'm sorry, Bob, but I can't give you more than ten pounds for this," he said.

The prospector's face turned red. "Ten pounds, Oppenheimer? That's a week's work! I used to get a hundred pounds for that!"

The dealer shrugged. "I don't pay by the hour, Bob. I pay by the ounce. And this isn't even a gram. The scale barely registers it. If you used to earn more, that's 'cause you used to find more gold."

"You used to have more competition," the prospector retorted. "When there were ten or twenty dealers in town, you had to pay better prices!"

The dealer shook his head. "No, not really. We all based our rates on the gold price in London."

The prospector snorted. "Then I'd get more in London, wouldn't I?" he said acerbically. "You Jews always put half of it in your pockets, you—"

The old man carefully brushed the contents of the scale onto a sheet of white paper. He folded it up carefully and handed it to the prospector. "Here, Bob, take this to London. You might get thirteen or fourteen pounds for it there, if they'd buy such a small amount."

The prospector's face fell. "I, uh, didn't mean it that way—"

The bullion dealer shrugged. "You want the money after all? I don't care either way. But if you want to do business with me, then we'll have to agree that we won't try to trick each other, and that you won't insult me."

The prospector grumbled to himself as Oppenheimer counted out the money, and then stalked out.

"And what can I do for you?" the old dealer asked kindly as Fitz and Linda stepped forward. His brow creased as Fitz spoke about his plans. "You want to stake a claim? You don't need to. Just take one that's abandoned. I must have the map somewhere." Oppenheimer stood up with difficulty and began to search the room without success. "Hmm. Let's try the post office."

The young couple followed him into the next building.

"Hello, Jeff," he said, greeting the postmaster. "Do you still keep a record of who has a claim in the gully?"

Linda and Fitz peered over his shoulder and saw the postmaster point outside, telling Oppenheimer to look there. On the back of the door, they found a sun-bleached, tattered piece of paper with a roughly drawn map. Parcels were marked on it in faded ink. Oppenheimer carelessly tore the paper down and began to examine it.

He thought for a moment and then pointed to one of the parcels. "Here. Roberts made good money right at the beginning, and then he took it and went off to Dunedin. Afterward, Bernard had the claim. He also found something, but he gave it up pretty quickly. Now he's on the west coast. The claim is free. And this one here was Peterson's. At first, it looked promising, but unfortunately it was used up quickly. Peterson tried and tried. Last winter he killed himself. No one wanted his claim after that. Here's another: Wenders. He also didn't do badly at first, but it just didn't go fast enough for him. He gave the claim to Feathers, and he struck it rich. Today he has a sheep farm somewhere near Queenstown. Afterward, three or four others sifted through it. If you ask me, there's nothing left there."

"Is there gold left anywhere at all?" Linda asked.

Oppenheimer raised his eyebrows. Then he ran a hand thoughtfully over the edge of his bald head, as though there were hair there to smooth down. "Missus, when Read first came here, Gabriel's Gully was twenty inches higher than it is now. Then they carried away all the topsoil, and one after another they dug everything up again and sifted through it. It could be that a few flakes weren't found. And you can pan for gold in almost any stream in the area. It's the local boys' favorite game. Afterward, they come here proudly and trade it to me for a few pence of pocket money. But you can't get rich here anymore. I'd bet my life on it." He turned to Fitz. "If you're smart, mister, you'll look for a different job. Or go to the west coast, where fortunes are still being made. Of course, it's a tough place. With your missus—" He frowned. "You're married, aren't you?"

Linda nodded proudly and showed him her ring.

But Oppenheimer frowned. "You can't take an honorable woman out there."

"I want to try here first, anyway," Fitz said warmly. "Perhaps on the edges of the gully. Maybe no one's looked there yet."

The bullion dealer laughed. "I can't stop you. If you turn up something shiny, you know where to find me. Is there anything else I can do for you?"

"Do you know a place we can stay?" Linda asked. "Does anyone here have homes for rent?"

Oppenheimer pointed toward the prospectors' camps on the outskirts of town. "Just take one of the ones that have been abandoned. But they aren't castles. None of the prospectors wanted to lose time building anything more stable."

As the man limped back to his office, Linda realized that he hadn't even bothered to lock the door. There couldn't be much money lying around there, or much gold. They both thanked him politely.

"Looking forward to doing business with you!" Fitz called cheerfully.

Fitz steered the horses and wagon back toward the shacks. It was raining again, and Linda stayed in the wagon with Amy, feeling depressed, while Fitz went to look around. He returned quickly, in a good mood.

"I found us a house!" Fitz announced. "It's nothing special, but at least it's free. Well, almost free. I promised the owner a couple of pence per week."

That made Linda a little more optimistic. If the house was for rent, at least it must have a roof.

Fitz guided the wagon into the encampment, with Brianna straining to pull it through the mud. When Fitz finally stopped, the sight of the ramshackle hut in front them immediately dampened Linda's spirits again.

"This is the house?" she asked.

There was barely enough covered space for two people to sleep next to each other. Inside, a stained mattress was on the floor, accompanied by a small rickety table and one chair. The walls had been roughly nailed together, and it was easy to see where the wind would whistle through the cracks during a storm. But at least the roof didn't seem to be leaking. Someone must have repaired it many times.

"Can I help you with anything?" Linda heard someone inquire. "Is there anything I can carry in, or something?"

Linda recognized the young woman who had been nursing her baby on the goldfield. She was still carrying the child on her back.

Linda shook her head. "No, thank you, we can manage. You should take your little one home; otherwise, he'll get wet. Or is it a she?" She tried to smile.

The woman was thin and haggard, her lips cracked and her eyes dull. She didn't return the smile.

"A he. At least he was lucky that way. He's not a girl."

Linda felt a flash of annoyance. She approached the little boy and tried to make him smile by pulling the necklace out of the front of her dress and dangling the shiny medallion in front of his face. "What's his name?"

"Paddy," the woman replied. "After his father. I knew him, in case you were wondering. Even if no one believes me. And as for that," she said, pointing to Linda's necklace, "I would keep it hidden. Everyone is desperate for gold here, no matter where they find it."

Linda nodded nervously. "I won't wear it anymore, or at least I'll keep it under my dress," she said. "My name is Linda Fitzpatrick. Are you a neighbor?"

The woman laughed. "You could say that, but I'm also your landlady. This hut belongs to me, and the one next to it as well. Of course nothing really belongs to anyone here. We just built here because no one chased us away."

As they spoke, Amy trotted in and threw herself onto the mattress. Linda scolded her half-heartedly.

"Nice dog," their visitor said. "But don't let it walk around alone. Otherwise, it'll end up on a spit. The fellows here eat anything."

Linda gasped. "People here eat dogs?"

The young woman shrugged. "Dogs, cats, rats . . . The gold they find isn't enough to buy both food and whiskey. Guess which they choose? And if there's enough whiskey, anything will taste good."

"That's dreadful!" Linda eyed the door, wondering how to leave immediately. She took a breath to steady herself. "The dog's name is Amy. She's a trained sheepdog, a border collie."

Amy heard her name and came over, her tail wagging.

"I'm Irene," the woman said. "Irene Sullivan. Or Miller. I don't know for sure if the fellow who performed my wedding was actually a priest."

Before she could continue, Fitz stormed into the tiny hut and set down all their worldly belongings. Then he swept Linda into his arms. "I'm all done, sweetheart! Welcome to your new home! As I always say, a light load makes light work." With a grin, he uncorked a bottle of whiskey. "Let's drink to a good start!" He took a long swallow and passed the bottle to Irene.

Linda repressed her disgust and put the bottle to her lips. Perhaps the alcohol would give her courage to face this new life. Fitz looked on cheerfully as Linda and Irene passed the bottle between them.

"Do we have anything left to eat?" he asked his wife.

A little unwillingly, Linda shared their provisions with Irene and Paddy, who hungrily stuffed pieces of soaked, softened bread into his still-toothless mouth. Irene devoured bread and jerky just as ravenously.

"Does your husband have a claim here, Mrs. Miller?" Fitz asked as he doled out the last scraps of food with unbroken optimism.

Linda watched with mixed feelings. She didn't begrudge it to Irene and Paddy to eat their fill for once, but she'd have to buy more tomorrow, and her savings wouldn't last long.

"My husband is gone," Irene said curtly. "I dig wherever I want to, or pan in one of the streams. But it's starting to get too cold for me. With bare feet in the water so long . . ."

"Do you find enough for you and the child to get by?" Linda asked cautiously.

Irene glared at her. "Yes, madam, thank you for inquiring!" she said sarcastically. "I won't pretend I say no to other opportunities. A person has to live. But I don't sell myself on the street! The child shouldn't have to hear folks damning me as a whore!"

Linda raised her hands conciliatorily. "I was only asking," she said quietly.

Actually, the thought that Irene might be a prostitute had never crossed her mind. The young woman was the opposite of the painted, buxom barmaids

Linda had seen in Tuapeka. Irene was pale and sickly, her blonde hair thin and stringy, and her watery, light blue eyes seemed to have no lashes.

"I have to go," Irene said with an unhappy glance at the remaining whiskey. "If I drink any more, I won't be able to get anything done tomorrow. Would you like to come with me then to look for gold? Alone, you'll hardly be able to find enough for the two of you."

Chapter 37

Te Ua Haumene assigned Eru, Kepa, and Tamati to accompany a group of warriors whose job it was to preach his gospel on the east side of the North Island. It would be a long journey, and the three young men's duty was to mediate if they met *pakeha*. The warriors were to act assimilated and friendly, and perhaps to pretend they were members of the Maori auxiliary forces. The prophet ordered them to dress in *pakeha* clothing.

"I don't want to do anything like the *pakeha*!" raged Kereopa Te Rau, who was supposed to lead the expedition with Patara Raukatauri.

These two men had been Hauhau warriors from the very beginning, and had often been called prophets themselves. Kereopa, in particular, was a compelling speaker, and he burned with hatred for the *pakeha*. In the previous year, his wife, children, and sister had died in battle with General Cameron's troops. Their deaths had added to his rage.

"You can't order me to crawl on my hands and knees in front of them," he cried.

Alarmed, Eru tried to edge away from Kereopa. He had spent the past few days close to the prophet and had quickly realized how much the prophet disliked it when anyone contradicted him or even asked questions. That shocked the young Ngai Tahu man. The elders in his tribe had always encouraged young people's thirst for knowledge. Every question was permitted and welcomed, and if the elders couldn't provide answers, they turned to the gods and spirits. After all, not even a *tohunga* could know all of the gods' plans. That was no shame to the priests and priestesses.

By contrast, Te Ua Haumene's behavior reminded Eru of the missionaries in Tuahiwi. They, too, had reacted harshly when he had asked questions, and they valued blind faith above knowledge. Fortunately, the prophet did not lash out at Kereopa Te Rau. Perhaps he saw the old warrior more as a peer than as a student.

"Then you should use the power of your faith and make yourself invisible," Te Ua replied. "Don't forget, Kereopa, the most important thing is to reach the tribes in the east. Many of them have never heard about us, or at least have never been part of our movement. It's your task to win them over. If you have to adapt to the situation or conceal yourself in the process, it's for the good of our cause. Only together as one people can we effectively fight against the *pakeha*."

Kereopa snorted. He had thick dark hair, a wild beard, large eyes, and elaborate tattoos around his nose and on his forehead.

"If we meet any *pakeha* along the way, they will meet the same end as these here!" he declared and reached for a sack that his friend Patara had been carrying.

Eru and his companions started with shock as he pulled out the head of a *pakeha* soldier. They'd heard that the Hauhau had revived the old tradition of cutting off enemies' heads and keeping them as trophies. So far, he'd only seen one such horrible souvenir, and now he shuddered at the sight of the shrunken, smoke-tanned face. Kereopa held the head aloft by its blond hair. There seemed to be more in the bag.

"These men were trying to destroy our fields at Ahuahu," he said, grinning at the young men who had gone pale beneath their tattoos. "One year ago. We stopped them and took seven heads."

Eru fought back a wave of nausea. He thanked all the gods when his leader put the head back into the sack.

The prophet watched without any indication of disgust, but his eyes were stern. "Kereopa, you know this is a peaceful assignment. We are bringing the good news to our people. They must hear the words of Tama-Rura and Riki. They must believe in the Promised Land full of peace and love that we intend to turn Aotearoa into as soon as the *pakeha* are gone. Waging war is our duty, not our wish. We kill without mercy, but also without joy."

Kereopa shrugged. "Dead is dead, Te Ua." It was clear that the old warrior wasn't afraid of his prophet. "The more *pakeha* we can kill, the better. Killing them is our most important task, and that's what I will tell people. We can talk about peace and love later. Or as far as I care, you can let your precious little missionary students handle that."

He nodded to Eru, Tamati, and Kepa. Ever since hearing about Eru's experience in Tuahiwi, Kereopa had regarded the trio with mistrust. He also disapproved of their role as translators. In his opinion, no mediation was necessary. In spite of the long and dangerous journey during which they were supposed to be as inconspicuous as possible, he was determined to rely on his fighting skills instead of camouflage.

The prophet didn't join in with his hard laughter, but instead looked at Eru and his friends earnestly. "You heard," he said. "Kereopa has given you a task. He will preach war, and you will preach peace. Here—" Te Ua got up and fetched a beautiful, leather-bound volume of his gospel. "Read it again during your journey, learn it by heart, and preach it to the people."

"Will they listen?" Kepa asked.

Te Ua glared at him. "If you believe in the power of the archangel's words, then you will be able to convey them to others as well. It's your belief alone that counts. He will make you invulnerable. He will make your voice as loud as thunder and your words as sweet as manuka honey. But if you doubt—"

"I—I have no doubt!" Kepa said, reassuring him.

The prophet nodded. "Then you will leave tomorrow."

The next day the three young men learned to appreciate Kereopa Te Rau and his warriors. The missionary group crossed the *pakeha*-occupied Whanganui district and entered the volcanic landscape surrounding Tongariro without seeing one white face. In spite of his lust to kill, Kereopa did obey the prophet's orders. He turned himself invisible even without the help of the Hauhau incantations. His warriors simply slipped noiselessly through the forests, seemed more to sense the *pakeha* patrols than to see them, and melted into the bushes and trees as soon as the whites were at all close.

Eru and his companions still had much to learn, but Kereopa and Patara turned out to be good teachers and skilled leaders. After the rocky start to their relationship, Eru had feared that they would be dogged with insults and sarcasm throughout the journey. But Kereopa restrained himself. It seemed not to bother him that Te Ua had entrusted the young men with the missionary duties that had originally been intended for him. Apparently, he wasn't particularly interested in preaching. He also left them in peace when they practiced their speeches along the way, learning Te Ua Haumene's gospel almost by heart. But it proved impossible to read the book at night around the fire, as Eru had planned. As long as they were in *pakeha* territory, no fire was lit. The warriors didn't hunt either, but instead ate the provisions they'd brought with them—smoked fish and meat and flatbread. But Eru had problems with the fish. Whenever he tried to soften a piece of the smoked meat in his mouth, he couldn't help but think of the smoked heads in Patara's sack.

Kereopa only began to relax a little once the forests lay behind them. The volcanic landscape surrounding Tongariro had very sparse vegetation. One could see far even when heavy clouds built up on the horizon and broke into torrential rain, as happened almost every day. Eru, Kepa, and Tamati were happy about their leader's decision to travel wearing traditional warrior garb instead of disguising themselves with *pakeha* clothing. With bare upper bodies, they were cold during the downpours, but dried again quickly when it stopped. The skirts made of raupo fiber didn't absorb the water at all.

The first Maori tribe the men met was living on the shore of Lake Taupo, and was still largely unmolested by the *pakeha*. A beautiful, hilly, forested landscape opened out behind the *marae*. In front of it were the waters of the largest lake on Aotearoa, a rich source of fish for the Ngati Tuwharetoa. The residents of the *marae* regarded the strange warriors skeptically at first, but then welcomed them and served fresh fish as well as sweet potatoes and grain from the surrounding fields. The land here was fertile. It was only a question of time before the *pakeha* would attempt to steal it.

That was the crux of Kereopa's message when he began to tell the curious people about the Hauhau movement. In his sermon, the archangels played a lesser role, and he spoke more about invulnerability, combat strength, courage, and the will for victory.

"And now Te Eriatara will tell you more about our prophet's visions," he said finally.

The tribe's young men were already won over. They stared at the smoked *pakeha* heads with equal amounts of disgust and fascination. Patara had arranged them around the fire after the sun had set. The light danced eerily around the sunken eye sockets and the twisted mouths of the dead.

"Jehovah, Tama-Rura, and Riki have banished their spirits," the people whispered.

It was clear to Eru that he could not preach only peace and love in this setting, so he began his speech with a warlike quote from the Bible: "'For they have sown the wind, and they shall reap the whirlwind.'"

He spoke of the wind that Te Ua Haumene had conjured, the prophet's visions of a free Aotearoa, and the chosen people. He encouraged his listeners to join in with chants of *hau hau* and *mai merire*, and was rewarded with a nod of acknowledgment from Kereopa. Only at the end did he speak briefly about peace and love among the tribes.

"Tama-Rura and Riki and Jehovah and his Son all want Aotearoa to be unified. Now in war, and later in peace. We can only win together. And only together can we realize the prophet's greatest vision: eternal life in a land where milk and honey flow! *Rire rire, hau hau!*"

"You added in the part about eternal life, didn't you?" Tamati whispered to Eru after he'd sat down with his friends again.

Eru shrugged. "Well, if we're already invulnerable, then how would we die?"

Kereopa and Patara hadn't noticed the deviation from Te Ua Haumene's vision, and the Ngati Tuwharetoa accepted it all. The next morning, they erected a *niu* to the delight of everyone. Only a female tribal elder and a few *tohunga* were unconvinced. Patara won the approval of the men of the council of elders by showing them the *pakeha* heads. Eru finally understood the trophies' full purpose. The head-hunting reminded some of the old men of the glory days of their youths when the tribes of the North Island had still fought bitterly with each other. Back then, they had often taken the heads of their enemies and put them on display.

By bringing the old traditions back to life, the Hauhau warriors presented themselves as defenders of the old ways. Their new gods and strange prayers would be more easily forgiven if they could encourage the young people to be enthusiastic about battle again. It was difficult for many of the old warriors to see the younger generation preferring to trade with the settlers instead of honoring the spirits. They didn't like to see a young man learning English instead of proving himself in battle, or a girl primping in *pakeha* clothing. Most of the young people no longer saw their neighboring tribes as enemies, but as friends with whom they could discuss land prices or gossip about the strange traditions of the *pakeha*.

But now the young warriors were dancing excitedly around the *niu*. They listened with their eyes gleaming to Kereopa's and Patara's stories of triumphant battles, and began to arm themselves to join the Hauhau. Eru and his companions realized quickly that their mission would succeed in mustering troops for Te Ua Haumene.

As with the first tribe, in every other *iwi* that Kereopa and his people visited, numerous young warriors decided to join the cause. Some chieftains weren't happy about it, and many women spoke out against it. But their arguments were ignored or invalidated in strange ways.

"Yes, your young warriors will go west," Patara had said. "But they will return as men, as soon as we conquer the *pakeha*."

"And what shall we do until then?" a woman asked pointedly. "Who will defend our tribe until then? Who will marry our girls? Who will father our children?"

Patara laughed. "Daughter, you don't need a man for each one of you. Te Ua sees not only the future in his visions, but also Aotearoa's past. In the golden days, when we were still Moas and could remember hunting on the beaches of Hawaiki, there was more than one wife for every warrior. They lived in happiness and peace together. So be humble and remember a time long past that will surely come again. *Rire rire, hau hau!*"

The startled woman fell silent while the men rejoiced at the prospect of polygamy in the Promised Land. But Eru felt only embarrassment. Mara wouldn't want to share him with another woman, and he couldn't imagine loving more than one either.

Some of the young women wanted to accompany their men westward, and Kereopa didn't try to stop them. Eru wondered if he remembered the old days of female warriors, or if he just wanted to leave the decision up to the prophet. In any case, the missionaries wasted no further thoughts on the future of the troops they had recruited. The next day, they simply continued to the next tribe. Before Aotearoa could be unified, many *niu*s had to be raised.

When they arrived in Rotorua, where boiling hot springs shot geysers into the sky, Kereopa convened the group.

"We have arrived at our goal," he announced. "From now on, we will not only seek out the tribes we meet along the way, but proselytize to the entire coastal area. To do that, we will split up. Patara, young Eru, and I will go to Whakatane and then continue to Opotiki along the coast. The others will stay inland and go to Ruatahuna and the Wairoa valley."

The men, and above all Kepa and Tamati, looked shocked. Kepa began to object, but Kereopa continued.

"I will hear no complaints. This was already organized with Te Ua. So far, Patara, Eru, and I have given sermons, but the rest of you can do it just as well." Aside from Kepa and Tamati, the second group included two older warriors who were more sedate, but no less experienced and determined than Kereopa. "Of course, we will share the heads. You get four, we'll take three. Use them. You know they are an important tool for convincing people. Prove to them that the *pakeha* aren't invincible. When we have completed our mission successfully, we will all meet again. *Pai marire, hau hau!*"

The men answered hesitantly. Only Eru echoed the chant with full enthusiasm. After all, he'd been chosen to travel in the leader's group to the most difficult areas. Opotiki was home to one of the biggest Christian missions in the country, and tribes in the area were supposed to have been converted to Christianity long ago. Their men were unarmed, and their children had been corralled into schools like the one at Tuahiwi. But now Te Ua Haumene's apostles were coming. They were ready to bring war to the mission, determined to replace the cross with the *niu*.

Eru could hardly wait.

Chapter 38

The next morning, Fitz seemed almost offended by the idea of sending Linda out with Irene.

"Darling, of course I'll find enough for both of us! My little sheep baroness doesn't need to wade around in the mud."

"What do you expect me to do here all day?" Linda asked. "Clean the house and polish the silver?"

Irene laughed. She had come to the hut with Paddy to warm up by the fire Fitz had built. There was nothing left to eat, but at least Linda had made fresh, strong coffee. They invited Irene to join them again. Linda couldn't watch the young woman shivering while she and Fitz helped themselves. The rain had dissipated in the night, but not the cold. In Otago, winter came earlier than it did in the Canterbury Plains. With a shudder, Linda thought about how cold it would get over the next two or three months. Would she still be living in this ruin then, cooking over an open fire?

"People always work together to find gold," Irene said, coming to Linda's aid. "Men, women, children . . . It used to be all about speed. You had to dig out as much as possible before someone else came along. Now it's about survival."

Linda finally got her way. Armed with a spade and a gold pan and followed by the cheerful Amy, she walked toward Gabriel's Gully with Irene. Fitz saddled a horse instead. He wanted to try the parts of the goldfield that were farther away from town. He explained to Linda that fewer people would have dug there.

"Plenty have tried that," Irene remarked when Linda told her about her husband's plans. "But there's nothing to find there. I don't know why, but the goldfields somehow have clear boundaries. And this one here has been used up, believe me. Your Fitz would have to sell his soul to the devil to find some corner that got missed by the twenty thousand men who already passed through."

Linda sighed and followed Irene north to a stream. On the way, they passed a number of men and women working their claims. Mostly, the men would dig deep holes in the ground, and the women would sift through the soil.

"You can't find anything that way," Irene said with a sideward glance at the diggers. "There's no gold that deep here. Yes, I know in gold mines they dig long tunnels in the earth. They tried that here too. One or two died when the things collapsed. Here it's in the upper layers. Probably washed down from the mountains. It's still coming down in the streams. You can always find a little bit in them."

Irene clamored nimbly over the steep, muddy ground. Linda stumbled along behind her.

"Have you been here for a long time?" she asked, out of breath.

Irene showed no signs of fatigue herself, despite carrying Paddy in a sling on her back. She nodded.

"I came with the very first group of prospectors. My daddy owned a pub in Ireland. He always had one foot in prison, and was up to his eyeballs in debt." Bitterly, Irene shifted her heavy spade from one shoulder to the other. "When he heard about the gold, we snuck out of Galway in the dead of night. The entire family: Father, Mother, and four daughters. We traveled on credit. Back then, they filled entire ships with prospectors, and the ship owner would advance the men the money for the voyage. The prospectors were supposed to pay it back with their earnings from the goldfields. Of course, that didn't apply to us children; our father had to pay for us. But my sisters brought in at least two or three times their costs during the journey."

"Brought in?" Linda asked uncertainly. "They worked?"

Irene laughed. "You're just a babe in arms, aren't you? Haven't been with your Fitz for long, huh? How did you find him, anyway? Doesn't fit, an innocent little thing from the countryside like you with—"

Linda tried to object, but Irene waved her off and continued.

"Yes, my sisters worked. My father sold them to the men who were traveling alone. Three months at sea and they get randy. Plus they're all excited, convinced they're going to get rich here in three days. No problem for them to spend their last few pence on board ship for a whore."

"What about you?" Linda asked, shocked.

"I was only twelve," Irene said.

Linda's eyes widened. That meant Irene could hardly be more than sixteen now. She had thought the young woman was at least in her midtwenties.

"My ma looked out for me. Unfortunately, she died of typhoid when we were still on the ship. But I still got a reprieve. And when we got to Dunedin, the fellows realized that the streets of Otago weren't paved with gold. They needed at least a minimum of equipment to get started. Spades, gold pans, tents . . . They didn't have anything left to spend on whores.

"And at first, there was really gold here. Da sent us to the fields. Believe me, each one of us girls worked the claim like two men. We knew what would happen to us if we didn't."

The women had reached the stream. Linda was surprised. The streams she knew flowed through green, grassy landscapes and often had raupo reeds along their banks. This one wound through a desolate landscape, its banks just as gray and muddy as everything else. Irene was right. Every bit of Gabriel's Gully had been dug up.

Irene hiked her skirts above her knees, heedless of who might see. Linda did the same and thought uneasily of Deborah Butler, who had always scolded the sisters for riding astraddle, even though their stockinged ankles had hardly been visible at all. If Mrs. Butler could see her now . . .

Like Irene, Linda took off her shoes and socks. Afterward, her new friend showed her how to use the pan to scoop sand out of the streambed, and then separate dirt and gold with careful circular motions. She carefully shook more and more sand and water out of the pan until only gold dust remained.

Linda didn't need long to grasp the technique. Once she actually found her first few specks of gold, she threw herself into the work with a fiery ardor. Amy dug on the bank of the stream with just as much enthusiasm.

"Well, she's a quick study," Irene said with a smile. "I wonder if you can teach dogs to smell gold?"

"You'd need a tracking dog for that," Linda said, trying to keep her tone light. "Amy is a sheepdog. She'd be more likely to try and herd the gold together."

Irene sighed. "My da could have used a dog like that. Gold just seemed to slip between his fingers. When there was less, we girls had to take up the slack. Me too, later. But I fell in love . . ." For a moment, the girl looked smitten.

"Paddy was Australian. He was like your Fitz. Always cheerful, promised to fetch me all the stars in the sky. Not that I believed him. Even when he offered to buy me from my father. 'Course, he never got enough money together for that."

"Your father wanted to sell you to Paddy?" Linda asked in disbelief.

Irene shrugged. "A young whore is worth her weight in gold on the goldfields," she said with resignation, and then smiled sadly. "But I foiled his plans. I got pregnant. And I wasn't about to get rid of little Paddy here so quickly either. Believe me, my father tried. He beat me to a pudding. But I didn't lose the baby." Her voice rang with pride.

"Did you marry your Paddy?"

Linda glanced with disappointment at her empty gold pan, and immediately refilled it from the streambed.

"Yes," Irene replied. "At the beginning, it was wonderful. He even built a hut for me. That's where you're living now, and I'm in the one where my father and sisters lived. Then little Paddy was born, and it was a difficult birth. I'm so small, and the midwife was too expensive. The baby cried a lot at the beginning. I didn't want another child immediately, so Paddy decided to lie with my sister, and got in a fight with Da. Finally, Da took my sisters and moved on to the west coast. There was hardly any gold left here. A few days later, Paddy left too. Now there's only me and the little one."

With practiced ease, she swirled her gold pan. Sighing, she put the specks of gold dust in a small leather pouch.

"Now it's your turn!" she said to Linda. "Are you really from a sheep farm?"

By the end of the day, the women had found a little gold, and had become firm friends. Irene had listened to Linda's story with great empathy, but Linda felt privileged when she compared her own bad luck with young Irene's. At least she still had Fitz, who took care of her. When the women returned to the hut, tired and shivering, he had already lit a fire and was chopping vegetables for a stew. A little ham was cooking over the fire. Linda felt deeply grateful, and didn't want to ask any probing questions about what her husband had been doing all day. But Irene had no such reservations.

"So," she said, "did you find any gold?"

Fitz grinned and began to tell the story in his usual lively manner. Of course he hadn't found gold, but he'd made plenty of new contacts. All kinds of prospectors had expounded on theories about how it might still be possible to find gold in Gabriel's Gully. He'd made an appointment to dig with one of them the next day.

"It's a sure thing," he declared.

Fitz spent the next day at the edge of Gabriel's Gully, digging under a boulder and then lighting a fire under it. The goal was to make the rock crumble, and then to hammer it apart. Fitz's new partner, Sandy, was certain there would be gold underneath. As usual, when Fitz attacked any new project, he worked as though possessed. On the fourth day, the boulder finally cracked. Underneath it they found black earth, but nothing more.

When Linda got home that night, no one was there. There was no fire, nothing to eat, and the last of her money was gone.

"Where could he be?"

"The pub," Irene said.

She was carrying two buckets of water from the Tuapeka River. Once, there had been an improvised water system leading to the camp, but no one had bothered to maintain it.

"I saw Bobby and Freddy at the river. They're all laughing about Sandy and Fitz's boulder. They actually managed to crack it apart today, but they didn't find a vein of gold underneath. No doubt they're drowning their sorrows in beer right this minute. Don't you worry, now, he'll be fine!"

Linda was less worried about Fitz than she was about their savings. Besides, she was hungry. She finally mounted Brianna bareback and helped Irene and Paddy up behind her. Together, they rode to Tuapeka to sell the gold dust they'd collected.

Fortunately, Oppenheimer's office was still open, and he treated the ladies, as he called them, in a gentlemanly manner. He even slipped a bit of candy out of his desk for Paddy, which surprised Linda. After all, not many children came by. But his offer for the gold dust was disappointing. For five days of hard work, the two women hadn't earned more than four pounds. And that was after he'd rounded up. Oppenheimer obviously liked Irene, and he seemed to feel sorry for Linda.

"It might work better if you try the upper reaches of the stream," he said encouragingly. "You have the horse now; you can ride there. You'll have to build up a little reserve. Can't stand in cold water all day in the winter."

"He's right about the horse," Linda said after they'd thanked him and left. "We should have thought of it ourselves. We're surely more likely to find something farther away. But build up a reserve? It doesn't seem likely."

Irene nodded darkly. She, too, was worried about the coming winter. At least Linda still had boots and warm clothes. Irene and Paddy hardly had anything more than what they were wearing.

The women couldn't save anything from their four pounds. It was barely enough for a little food. If they wanted to have enough for the coming weeks, they'd have to go right back to work the next day.

Nonetheless, Linda's stomach was full by the time she rolled herself up in blankets, without Fitz for the first time since her wedding. Instead, Amy leaped onto the mattress, the way she had in Linda's room at Rata Station. Linda cuddled her and was warm and comfortable, but she couldn't sleep. Her mind was occupied with too many dark thoughts. So far, their stay at the goldfields had been a misadventure, and Fitz would figure that out soon enough for himself. But what could they do next? She slowly began to worry about his absence. Irene's question nagged at her as well. How could such different people be together? Linda thought about Fitz's lust for adventure and her own caution; his idiosyncratic relationship with the truth, and her cultivated honesty. His tendency toward improvisation, and hers toward responsibility. Did those qualities complement or contradict each other?

As Linda brooded, she heard footsteps in front of the hut, and then someone fumbling at the door. So, Fitz had drunk the last of their money. Anger rose inside her.

She had no doubt that it was Fitz who entered the darkened room in a draft of cold air, reeking of beer and pipe smoke. Amy would have barked at a stranger. Linda was wondering if she should complain to her husband or if she should pretend to be asleep, but then she saw him lean over her and begin to scatter fistfuls of paper money over her and Amy's heads. The dog left the mattress indignantly.

"Wake up, Lindy! Lookie here, your husband found a vein of gold!"

Linda looked around in confusion and sat up. She smelled the beer on Fitz's breath as he kissed her, but he didn't actually seem very drunk. He told her all about his futile search for gold as though it had been a great joke.

"You should have seen old Sandy's face when the boulder cracked into a thousand pieces, and nothing was under it but a few grubs!"

"Then how did you get this?" Linda said, collecting the bills. "It's at least ten pounds."

Fitz grinned at her. "Blackjack. They were playing in the pub. And, well, I'm very good at cards." He puffed out his chest proudly.

Linda raised an eyebrow. As far as she knew, blackjack was largely a game of chance.

"That's good," she said. "We need the money. But, Fitz, it can't go on like this. You've seen for yourself that there's no gold to be found here."

Fitz laughed and took her in his arms. "We haven't found any gold *yet*! Sweetheart, that's how life is. One day you win, one day you lose. The trick is to be able to deal with both. To be happy, Lindy, with money or without it. It always works out somehow. And so far, you haven't had to go hungry, have you?"

Linda bit her lip. She didn't like the "so far" part. Besides, didn't one need a little more than a full stomach to be happy?

As though he'd read her mind, Fitz began to kiss and fondle her. "You worry too much," he murmured. "You ask too many questions."

Linda gave herself up to his caresses, feeling guilty. As before, he skillfully brought her to climax, but his member barely hardened. Was she doing something wrong? Didn't he love her? Or was she just being ungrateful? Perhaps he was holding back because he knew a child was the last thing they needed at the moment. Linda tried to convince herself of that as she lay next to him after their lovemaking.

Perhaps she really did worry too much. Maybe she just had to be more lighthearted. Linda tried to push all of her dark thoughts aside. Starting tomorrow, she would be more like Fitz. She would try to be happy with what she had.

Chapter 39

At the beginning, Franz had been happy at the missionary station in Opotiki. Carl Voelkner, the station's director, had welcomed him with open arms and brotherly love. Voelkner and his wife, Emma, were extraordinarily friendly, warmhearted people, and dramatically different from the hard, God-fearing folk Franz had grown up with. Actually, Franz wondered how such a gentle man had managed to create such a flourishing mission. The Te Whakatohea tribe seemed to idolize the ordained missionary, and had joyfully built a church and a school with his encouragement. Almost all their children were baptized and learning English. Money always came from somewhere, although Voelkner wasn't particularly skilled in economic matters. Franz, who had immediately taken over his bookkeeping, was appalled at the state of it. But the man had more experience when it came to saving souls. He had been a missionary in New Zealand for over fifteen years, and director of the station in Opotiki for four.

The conditions here were ideal for Franz to use his talents to serve God without having to face his fears. The Te Whakatohea were not at all dangerous, but obedient and eager to learn. The church services were led by Voelkner, so Franz didn't need to give sermons. Instead, Voelkner happily turned over the management of the missionary school to his new colleague, and Franz realized that he truly enjoyed teaching. He did everything he could to awaken the students' interest and inspire them to perform well. He would never have admitted it, but teaching soon became more important to him than his faith.

Franz thought about his sister Ida's warm memories of their old schoolmaster in Raben Steinfeld, and decided to search for some of the stories that Master Brakel had captivated his students with back then. For the first time, Franz read books other than the Bible. He lost himself in Homer's *Odyssey* and *The Life and Adventures of Robinson Crusoe*, and followed along with Captain Cook on his *Voyages*. Later, he read aloud to his students from the books and was pleased when the children could hardly wait for the next chapter, zealously trying to read it themselves. He'd never been able to inspire them that way with biblical stories. The Maori had originally been a nomadic, seafaring people. Sagas set on the ocean interested his students far more than stories about Israelites wandering the desert.

But mathematics was even closer to Franz's heart. Numbers had always fascinated him. He had been better at it than all of his classmates. Unfortunately, that had been just as undesirable at the seminary as it had been in Hahndorf. Finally, the young man had found a book about the economic management of church offerings and taught himself some financial skills.

For Franz, the subject was not only interesting but also extremely useful, and he yearned to pass on his knowledge to his students. The young missionary tried to acquaint them with arithmetic, but had to fight against a lack of interest. The Whakatohea tribe wasn't very wealthy, and no one in the mission had tried to teach them the art of doing business. They lived traditionally, from basic farming, fishing, and hunting. Anything they desired beyond that, such as Western clothing, seeds, or livestock, they received in the form of charity. This ensured that they'd always be grateful to the mission and to Voelkner.

Since Franz's students had never had a single penny in their pockets, they found arithmetic abstract, and for a time, the young man couldn't think of any way to motivate them to learn. But then he caught several of the older students attempting to play blackjack. Of course Franz confiscated the cards immediately and talked to the children about the dangers of gambling, but then he realized that each card showed numbers.

Reluctantly, he asked an old prospector who had found refuge at the mission how much arithmetic was necessary to play cards. Finally, he spent a night praying, begged God for forgiveness in advance, and then took the cards to the next lesson. It was a complete success. The children were suddenly enthusiastic about sums, and turned themselves inside out laughing when someone carelessly took a card that brought their total over twenty-one. Voelkner, who had no idea what was happening, scolded the young teacher. There was so much laughter in Franz's classroom that he assumed the students weren't learning.

Teaching also helped Franz understand Cat and Chris and Karl and Ida a little better. He had become mellower through the work with the children and

Carl Voelkner's gentle guidance. He was no longer thoughtless about boring listeners with endless prayers, knowing how important it was not to lose his students' attention first thing in the morning.

Raben Steinfeld and Hahndorf slowly fell away from Franz. But he kept in contact with Ida via letters, and of course he thought of Linda. His young niece haunted his dreams night after night. He remembered her laugh all too well, her bright voice, and her understanding and patience, even when all the others at Rata Station had grown irritated with him. His memories of Linda inspired him to answer Ida's letters diligently, even when he didn't really have anything new to say. Ida kept him informed about the girls, and he heard about the loss of Cat and Chris. Of course he prayed dutifully for them. He also heard about Jane's treacherous behavior. He even wrote a reprimanding letter to her, but didn't receive an answer.

In her last letter, Ida had told him about Linda's marriage, which sent Franz spiraling into a whirlwind of conflicting feelings. He should be happy for her and actually for himself as well, because now hopefully thoughts of her would no longer tempt him. He must never awaken from a dream about her with an erection again! On the other hand, he grieved his loss, and worried terribly about her safety in the goldfields of Otago.

Franz didn't have great trust in Joe Fitzpatrick. He remembered very well how the young man had made a fool of him in Christchurch. He would have wished for a more reliable, stable partner for Linda, especially since Ida herself seemed uneasy about the match. Franz prayed for his beloved niece whenever he had the time and the inspiration. Unfortunately, that was ever more rarely the case, since one catastrophe after another had cast a shadow over the peaceful world of the missionary station.

Franz's peaceful life, his studies, and the laughter in his lessons came to an end with the war that raged through Taranaki and Waikato. At first, nothing was noticeable at the station. As before, everyone went about their daily work. The fields were tilled, and the Maori christened their children. But then things began to bubble beneath the calm surface. In the *iwi*s on the east coast, people were arguing about whether it was their duty to support other friendly tribes in the war zone.

A few weeks previously, a troop of inexperienced, adventure-hungry warriors from Opotiki had made their way to Waikato to join the Hauhau rebels. They were led by Te Aporotanga, a young, aggressive chieftain of the Te Whakatohea tribe who had never been interested in adapting to the ways of the missionaries. Voelkner was happy to be rid of the man, no matter how much he had preached against rebellion in his church.

The warriors first tried to reach Waikato directly by traveling inland. But they soon met an enemy tribe that blocked their way. Te Aporotanga retreated and took the coastal route. There, they had no luck either. At Maketu, two days' walk from Opotiki, Te Aporotanga got into a skirmish with British troops. He was taken prisoner and, through a series of unfortunate events, ended up in the hands of enemies. Finally, the wife of a chieftain of the Te Arawa tribe had him killed. The exact reasons for his execution could only be speculated on.

"We will pray for him," Voelkner had said when he was informed about the tragedy. Carl Voelkner had never said a bad word about anyone who'd died, but Franz could tell by his tone what the missionary must be thinking: the young chieftain had probably had a hand in his own death. He had been known as a womanizer. Perhaps he'd overstepped the boundaries with a chieftain's wife or daughter.

But for the Te Whakatohea, prayer was not enough. They were outraged at the death of their chieftain. They believed that the governor should have prevented his murder.

What was more, the warriors' excursion had brought the war to Opotiki. It didn't come in the form of battles, but the English employed the same strategy they had used in Taranaki: rebellious tribes were punished by having their land confiscated. Of course, the missionary station was untouchable, and the *marae*s immediately surrounding it were largely spared. Only a few fields were appropriated and some others destroyed before the missionaries could halt the reprisal. But the episode served to fuel Maori anger against the *pakeha*.

And then typhoid broke out.

"He'll feel better soon," Franz Lange said kindly to a Maori woman who was sitting on her three-year-old son's bed, crying. He hoped he wasn't lying to her. In truth, Franz had no idea if the child would survive or not. He didn't even know if the mother could understand his comforting words. His linguistic abilities were still woefully insufficient, even though he had finally been trying to learn Maori.

"We should pray together."

The woman nodded, and Franz recited the Lord's Prayer in Maori. However, he no longer spoke it with the same enthusiasm he'd had a year ago at Rata Station. Since then, he'd prayed far too often at the beds of the afflicted without getting an answer. Even now, he had the sneaking suspicion that his prayers would have little influence on whether little Hanu survived. What might make the difference was whether Voelkner returned from Auckland with the new medicine in time. *If* he returned . . .

Franz sighed and moved on to his next patient. It was another child, a little girl. Kaewa had a high fever, and he didn't know if she also had typhoid, or perhaps measles. Both illnesses had been rampant for months. Reluctantly, Franz undressed the child and washed her. He did his duty, but it required all of his humility. Ever since the beginning of the epidemic, it had been clear that he wasn't cut out to be a doctor or nurse.

So far, neither Carl Voelkner nor Franz Lange had been able to determine who had brought the epidemics to Opotiki. Voelkner traveled to Auckland regularly, but assumed he was not guilty because not one single white person at the station had come down with either illness. It affected the Maori alone. In a short time, the school and the tribal meetinghouses had been converted to provisory hospital wards. Franz had long since put aside his lessons, and had to watch one student after another die. Almost a third of the Maori population in Opotiki had been buried in the last three months, and the end still wasn't in sight.

In the face of such suffering, Franz Lange was slowly losing his faith in the power of prayer, and the Maori were losing their faith in the missionaries. After the people had humbly begged God for help and sought out the mission doctor with no results, rumors began to circulate. Was it possible that the whites were trying to poison them? Had the Christians made the old gods angry? What was Voelkner doing in Auckland so often? Was he really collecting donations in order to fight the illness more effectively, or was he hiding there to avoid contagion?

The people had become so restive that, on his previous trip to Auckland, Voelkner even decided to leave his wife there.

"She's safer," he'd told Franz, "though I'm sure it'll be fine. I've always gotten along well with the people here. With God's help, we will withstand this trial together and be the stronger for it."

Franz was less convinced. Voelkner's friends in Auckland had advised him to stay there as well until the epidemic had run its course. But Voelkner hadn't listened then, and Franz hoped that the missionary would come back to Opotiki after this trip as well. Under no circumstances did Franz want to be alone with all the suffering people. After only two weeks he was feeling out of his depth with the temporary management of the mission. The Sunday sermons were particularly difficult for him. What could he say to people who had to bury one relative after another, no matter how fervently they prayed?

Franz covered the little girl again and looked up as one of his favorite students, a clever boy of about thirteen, approached respectfully.

"Reverend Lange," Paora said, and helpfully took the bowl of water that he'd been cooling the child's forehead with. "I thought I should be the one to tell you. People have come from Taranaki. The tribe has welcomed them hospitably."

Paora himself was not one of the Te Whakatohea. He was a foundling who had been living in the mission since a whaler had brought him there years ago. The boy looked Maori, but Voelkner believed he must be half-*pakeha*, with a Maori mother who'd lived alone with a white man. Otherwise, a tribe never would have allowed the child to be abandoned.

Lange nodded. "That is well and good, my son, if at the moment perhaps not wise. The last thing we need is for this epidemic to spread past the borders of Opotiki."

The boy shook his head. "That would be terrible, Reverend, but that's not why I'm here. It's because—I believe these men are missionaries for Te Ua Haumene."

Chapter 40

"Voelkner is a spy!" Kereopa proclaimed. "It's obvious. Look how his mission is flourishing. What it must have cost to build the church and this school . . ."

Kereopa, Patara, and Eru had arrived that afternoon at the *marae* of the Te Whakatohea and had been welcomed kindly. Now, over a rather meager meal, the villagers were pouring out their hearts to them. The primary subject was Carl Voelkner. What was he doing in Auckland? Had he turned against the Maori? And how much responsibility did he have for all the deaths? And now, thanks to Kereopa, what if he was reporting to the governor?

"We built the church and the school ourselves," an old man said. "Not much money was needed. And even if Voelkner had been a spy from the very beginning, what sense would it have made for him to spend his earnings for the good of those he was spying on? What would he have gotten out of it?"

"Your souls," Patara said darkly. "Look at yourselves. You're all wearing *pakeha* clothing. You're learning their language. You're reading their books. You're attending their church. Voelkner made sure that you'd always have to be grateful to the English."

"We aren't grateful to the English," a woman said indignantly. "They burned our fields! We hardly have anything to eat. If Voelkner hadn't—"

"There you have it!" Kereopa declared. "You're beholden to Voelkner again. He made you poor and helpless. He only gives you enough to survive. He's *pakeha*, people! He's one of them, doing their dirty work! He has the same goals, except he's trickier about it. So far not a single shot has been fired in this region, but half of your people are dead, while not a single *pakeha* has died. Doesn't that make you suspicious?"

The people looked at one another.

"You think he brought us typhoid and measles?" one of the tribal elders asked, toying with the cross that hung around his neck. "A curse?"

"That's entirely possible," Patara said. "Just like our belief can make us invulnerable, a wicked thought can be poison." The idea seemed to inspire him. "And now we're here to break the curse!"

"Rire rire!" Kereopa said encouragingly.

"Hau hau!" Eru added.

"Listen to the prophet's words. Accept that you took the wrong path when you followed Voelkner on the road through the darkness!" Kereopa stood up, and the people thronged around him by the fire. He spoke of the whites' evil deeds in Taranaki and Waikato, and also about the power of the Hauhau and their prophet. "General Cameron has destroyed every *marae* with his murderers and thieves—but none of his men even dare to come close to Weraroa! Just the presence of the prophet makes his fortress invisible and invincible. The power of the belief of thousands of men has created a ring of fire around the *pa*."

Eru smiled at the contradiction between invisibility and a glowing ring of fire. He'd long since stopped taking Kereopa's speeches literally. He had great respect for his leader, but the man was certainly not a prophet himself, even though he called himself one. Kereopa wasn't saying what the archangels told him to, but rather what he thought his listeners wanted to hear.

Eru had perceived very quickly that these people were not warlike. Their minds were occupied by fear and grief. They were looking for someone to blame for the epidemics, and Kereopa and Patara were giving them Voelkner.

Eru decided to ease their fears. "You are all baptized in the name of the God that the *pakeha* brought with them to Aotearoa," he said. "That isn't wrong. He is a powerful God, and Te Ua Haumene himself served him for many years. And you've heard the stories that they tell about his Son. All the healings in the Bible." Eru paused for a moment.

"We prayed to Jesus!" a woman cried. "We begged him to heal our children, but he did nothing."

"You sent your prayers in the wrong direction," Eru explained. "God the Father sent Jesus to the Israelites. To us, he sent the archangel Gabriel, Tama-Rura, who spoke to Te Ua Haumene. And, of course, you've heard of the healings that Te Ua performed in his name."

As expected, the Maori on the east coast had not heard this confusing story. In fact, Eru hadn't yet told it in any of the *marae*s they'd visited. Supposedly, the archangel had ordered the prophet to take a child in his arms and cut off its leg. There had even been rumors that it had been Haumene's own son. Of course the prophet had done it, and that's where the stories diverged. Some said that the child prayed to be healed, and others said that the tribal elders or even the *pakeha* authorities had jumped in, only to find the child healed, happy, and healthy in his parents' house. Eru didn't believe a single word, and to Haumene's credit, he had never bragged about it. But now Eru was using the story for his own ends, although he told it a little less dramatically. In his version, Te Ua had healed a broken leg, and not one that he himself had chopped off.

"Couldn't he come here to heal our children?" a mother asked hopefully.

"You can heal them yourselves," Kereopa declared, and Eru nodded. "You can heal them by receiving the faith of the prophet, planting peace and love in the hearts of your people, and sowing hatred against your enemies. You must destroy these enemies, my friends! You must use their blood to wash away your children's sickness. We will set up a *niu* for you! Today! Learn the magic words! Learn the words of healing!" Kereopa began to chant. *"Rire rire, hau hau. Pai marire, hau hau."*

Eru and Patara joined in, and most of the Te Whakatohea followed suit. A group of men hurriedly got up to find a pole. Finally, they took wood from the frame of a new house. The people cheered as the *niu* was erected.

"God the Father, *mai merire*! Tama-Rura, *mai merire*!"

"Te Ariki Mikaera!" Patara bellowed. "Guide our hands when we kill! *Kira, wana, tu, tiri, wha!*"

"Kill, one, two, three, four . . ."

Paora, Franz's student, translated Patara's words in a low murmur. They had been sitting in the shadows on the edge of the *marae* for hours, listening with increasing distress to the speeches of the Hauhau recruiters.

"Let's leave now," Franz whispered to the boy, as the people of the village began to dance ecstatically around the *niu*.

"Holy, wonderous *niu*, fill us with your power! *Rire rire, hau hau!*"

Their voices cut terrifyingly through the night.

Paora regarded Franz with a serious expression. "Isn't that idolatry, Reverend?"

Franz nodded. "Yes," he said. "The most evil, darkest kind of idolatry. They are dancing around a pole as once the Israelites danced around the golden calf."

The boy swallowed. "Then don't we have to—I mean—like Moses—"

Franz Lange quickly withdrew beyond the protection of the fence, Paora close on his heels. He felt a burning sense of shame. The boy was right. Of course he should throw a flaming sword between the villagers and the Hauhau recruiters. His father certainly would have. Jakob Lange's people had feared his authority. But Franz had never managed to scare anyone in his life.

The young missionary still didn't know if God had truly called him to do his work. But one thing was painfully clear to him as he scrambled and crawled through the bushes, trembling with fear: he was no Moses, and no martyr either.

"Trying to stop them now would be suicide," he said honestly, when they finally reached the safety of the woods between the *marae* and the mission and could stand up again. "The only thing we can do is warn Voelkner. We have to head toward Auckland as quickly as possible and intercept him. If he returns here, he'll be killed."

Franz would have preferred to start for Auckland that night, but he was hindered by not only his fear of riding through the darkness but also his sense of responsibility. There were eighty sick people depending on his care, many of them children. He couldn't leave them to the Hauhau mob, at least not without warning the doctor and the other caregivers. The doctor was also *pakeha* and might decide to flee as well. But the caregivers were Maori. If he explained the situation to them properly, they could manage their tasks and the everyday running of the mission until help arrived. It was clear to Franz that the army had to be alerted. It was the only way to stop the Hauhau recruiters.

Franz spent a restless night on his narrow cot in the schoolhouse. He had been sleeping there since the beginning of the epidemic so he could always be available for the sick. At dawn, he rose to pray and awakened the other caregivers. Then he looked for Paora. The boy usually slept in the mission house, but now he was nowhere to be seen.

Franz washed his face and went over to the church. He would have expected complete silence so early in the morning, but he could hear voices as he approached. Franz could hardly believe his ears. Carl Voelkner was loudly chanting a song about God's love!

Confused, the young missionary threw open the church door and saw the old missionary kneeling in front of the altar with a younger man in a dark suit and priest's collar. Voelkner glanced up, then smiled.

"Reverend Lange! Awake so early? How nice! You can join us in our next devotion and then help us unload. We have an entire wagon full of medicine and food for the children. Oh yes, this is Reverend Thomas Gallant. He's here to help us."

"Reverend Voelkner," Franz exclaimed, "we must leave! The people have gone completely mad. I wanted to ride out to stop you. You're no longer safe here!"

Voelkner laughed. "My life, Brother Franz, is in God's hands. Wherever I am and whatever I do, I am not afraid, for he is with me. He guided us safely through the days and nights of our journey. Whenever possible, we traveled by night, to get the medicine here as quickly as possible."

Franz rubbed his temples. "Brother Voelkner, you don't understand." As quickly and clearly as he could, he told the missionary about the ceremony he had witnessed the night before. "The people are no longer their own masters," he said in closing. "They know not what they do."

Voelkner put a comforting hand on Franz's shoulder. "My poor brother, that was surely too much for you. Especially since you probably didn't understand everything they were saying."

Franz shook him off. "Paora translated for me. And it wasn't so hard to understand, anyway. Brother Voelkner, they want your head! In the truest sense!" He shuddered at the thought of the smoked heads that Patara had put on display.

"It's rumored that the Hauhau warriors really will decapitate people," Reverend Gallant said. "If our brother here thinks—"

"How narrow-minded you are, and how weak your faith is!" Voelkner's eyes filled with reprimand. "If our flock's senses have been dimmed, then we must shine a light on them again. If they direct their anger at us, then we must counter it with love. If they threaten us, we must stand before them without fear, because the power of the Lord is within us!"

Franz's eyes widened. Those were almost the same words that had come out of the mouths of the Hauhau warriors the day before. Everyone here thought themselves invulnerable—aside from himself and Thomas Gallant, who now lowered his head in prayer.

"Come, let us sing God's praise once more and then go about our work. We'll go to the *marae* later and talk to the people."

Voelkner turned to the altar and began his song again. He had a beautiful, deep voice, but beneath it, Franz heard the chant that suddenly sliced through the morning, with the strength of many voices.

"Glorious *niu*, *mai merire*! By the mountains, by the rivers, by the lakes, kill!"

The warriors arrived as Franz was carrying a sack full of flour on his back. Voelkner and Gallant were also unloading the wagon full of supplies, with the assistance of the Maori helpers.

"The good people of Auckland have donated much," Voelkner told them.

Franz noticed that the helpers were quieter than usual. They hadn't joined in with the ceremony in the village, but they doubtlessly knew what kind of danger the mission was in.

And then the Te Whakatohea men strode through the gate into the mission, led by Kereopa and Patara, all heavily armed and dressed in traditional garb. Silently, they formed a circle around the missionaries. Franz's heart raced. Voelkner remained calm, and even smiled.

"What a welcome!" he said. "This looks like a *powhiri*. But haven't we been one tribe for a long time?"

"We will never be one tribe!" Kereopa declared, and spat at the missionary's feet. "Why should we join forces with thieves and traitors?"

He spoke in Maori, but it was translated in accent-free English by the young warrior by his side with the entirely tattooed face.

Voelkner stepped toward Kereopa and his men. "Those are strong words, my friend. But I don't know you, and you know nothing about me. Shouldn't we talk to each other first, and perhaps pray together? I've heard that you are ambassadors of Pai Marire. And doesn't Te Ua Haumene preach love and peace, just like my brothers and I?"

The missionary tilted his face toward Kereopa in an offer to exchange *hongi*. Franz didn't know if the gesture was brave or simply crazy. Kereopa reacted unambiguously, at lightning speed. He struck Voelkner to the ground.

"Rire rire, hau hau!" Patara cried.

The warriors took up the words and chanted them rhythmically. For the first time, the look of calm and blind trust left Voelkner's features.

"What have I done to you?" he asked them.

A young man stepped forward. "I am Pokeno, a son of Te Aporotanga."

Franz's breath caught in his throat. Te Aporotanga was the chieftain who'd been killed by the Te Arawa. The tribe blamed the government for his death.

"I know, Pokeno," Voelkner said in a gentle voice. "I christened you."

The young man ignored this. "I accuse you of my father's murder! You sent him to the *pakeha* troops, where he met with their knives. You were spying for the governor. You told the army about our plans."

"What plans, Pokeno?" Voelkner asked kindly.

"Shut up!" Pokeno shouted. "You have betrayed my people, and poisoned them! And sold them! There are surely settlers waiting to steal this land . . ."

"Rire rire, hau hau, rire rire, hau hau!"

When the boy didn't know what else to say, Kereopa prompted the warriors to chant again.

Voelkner shook his head uncomprehendingly. The accusations made no sense. He'd worked so hard to protect the tribe's land.

"Take him prisoner," Kereopa demanded. "Take them all prisoner!"

The ring of warriors closed more tightly around the missionaries, then pushed them toward the church.

"What will happen to us?" Franz asked, his voice breaking. He was too panicked to remember the words in Maori, so he spoke English to the young interpreter.

To his surprise, the man answered. "You will be tried. And you will probably be killed."

The day passed in a nightmare of prayer and song, both inside and outside the church. Voelkner wouldn't let the threats discourage him. He prayed and sang in front of the cross, while outside in the churchyard, a *niu* was set up. All the old and new Hauhau devotees gathered around it. Kereopa and Patara spoke to the villagers. The warriors danced around the pole and shouted invocations while worried mothers brought their children out of the hospital ward and lay them on the ground in front of the *niu*. The mission doctor and his helpers were nowhere to be seen. Perhaps they, at least, had been able to escape in time.

"Can the prayers heal the children?" a woman asked fearfully. Her little daughter whimpered.

Kereopa shook his head. "No, *wahine*. The only thing that will heal her is the blood from the heart of the traitor."

"Kill!"

Again and again, the prisoners heard the word ringing through the air.

While Voelkner prayed, seeming as sanguine as ever, Franz cowered in a corner of the church and surrendered to his terror. He was convinced that he would die the next day.

Chapter 41

Eru watched with fascination as the Te Whakatohea tribe was transformed from a herd of obedient sheep to a pack of bloodthirsty wolves. He was more than a little proud of his role. After all, Te Ua had told them that this *iwi* in particular would be difficult to sway, because the people there were in thrall to the Christian missionaries. He'd wanted to cheer when the missionaries were locked away the day before.

After a night full of enthusiasm and invocations of the archangels, though, Eru began to fear the wrath of heaven. When the last notes of the morning hymn had faded, the villagers brought out wood and tools. Several others had had the same idea as Eru: a trial. They had been amused by the idea of parodying a *pakeha* court. Laughing, they appointed witnesses, lawyers, and judges, who passed whiskey bottles among themselves. The missionaries didn't keep alcohol, but it turned out that the mission doctor had hidden a supply in his own quarters. In hopes of finding something valuable, the warriors had ransacked everything. But the only truly valuable thing was the bejeweled cross that Mara's young uncle wore around his neck. Eru had seen it first but hadn't told the others. He recognized the necklace as Ida's. Mara wouldn't approve if Eru took it.

During the trial, Voelkner had been sentenced to death by hanging. He was sentenced in absentia; no one felt it necessary to bring him out of the church to face the "judge." Eru himself had joined in celebrating the sentence with cheers, but he hadn't believed it would truly be carried out.

Now his body grew cold as he watched the Whakatohea build a kind of platform under the willow tree that shaded the churchyard. A noose already dangled from its branches. The women were carrying out their children so they could be healed with Voelkner's blood. Eru was shocked. Of course, he and the other Hauhau warriors had promised the people something like this. But they couldn't take it literally!

"Kill, one, two, three!" Kereopa sent the warriors to march around the *niu* again, swinging their spears.

"Now go get him!" Patara cried, raising his arms.

The new recruits stormed the church and dragged Voelkner outside.

"Kereopa, what's happening?" Eru turned to his leader in shock. "What are they going to do to him?"

The warrior laughed, his face twisting. "What do you think, great warrior?" he said sarcastically. "They will kill him now. We will kill him! *Rire rire, hau hau! Rire rire, hau hau!*"

The words stuck in Eru's throat. Of course they would kill him. That was the point of war. Voelkner was the enemy, and now he would pay with his life.

Eru attempted to sing and dance with the others as Voelkner was led to the gallows with calm dignity. But he couldn't do it. So far, everything had seemed like a game, an adventure. Sure, there were the heads in Patara's sack, but even they seemed like props in the play they were performing to recruit followers for Haumene. But now blood would flow. Kereopa wasn't playing a game. And the enemies weren't English soldiers, as Eru had always imagined when he'd thought about defending himself in battle. They were all united against one aging man with an oval face, sparse hair, sideburns, and gentle eyes. A black raven, true. Eru had often cursed the missionaries in Tuahiwi. But you couldn't just kill someone like this!

Frozen with terror, Eru watched as young Pokeno followed the missionary onto the platform with Kereopa and Patara. Voelkner ascended with his head held high, and apparently without fear. He kneeled and prayed in front of the dangling rope.

"I forgive you," he said, his voice sonorous, and then turned to Pokeno. "I'm ready."

Eru managed to watch as Pokeno put the noose around Voelkner's neck, but then he turned away. He staggered behind one of the mission houses and vomited as the Te Whakatohea cheered at Voelkner's death. When he returned, torn by stomach cramps and shame, the corpse was swinging from the gallows.

The recruits surrounded the *niu* again, singing and howling, and the women brought out food.

Eru hoped Kereopa and Patara wouldn't look for him. He remained at the edge of the celebration and thought, appalled, of Mara. Her uncle would surely be the next victim of this deadly mob—a mob that he, Eru, had helped create. How could he? And how could he ever look Ida Jensch in the eye again?

But soon, after more fanatical celebration, singing, and drinking, things got worse. Eru watched in disbelief as Kereopa and a few other men took down the dead body of the missionary. To the shrill cries of the Hauhau warriors, Patara cut the head off and splashed blood onto the sick.

"This will heal you, this will heal you!" he cried, as the children cried and squeezed their eyes shut.

Kereopa, intoxicated with dance, conjuring—and, of course, whiskey—laughed as he cut the dead man's eyes out. Eru almost vomited again as the warrior swallowed them.

"Watch me eat the English Parliament!" he shouted through his blood-smeared lips. "And the queen, and English law!"

Eru staggered away. Trembling, he rolled himself into a ball in the shadow of the mission house and waited for the nightmare to end. Perhaps he'd wake up later and everything would be the way it had been before.

Hours later, his stomach had finally settled and his head still hurt, but Eru could finally think clearly. Only then did he remember Franz Lange. He couldn't allow Mara's uncle to die the same horrible death.

No one noticed Eru slipping into the dark church. The men were still in the side chapel where Eru had helped lock them the day before. Now he tore off the boards nailed over the chapel door. His fear and desperation seemed to give him superhuman powers, but he was bathed in sweat when he finally revealed Franz Lange and the other missionary. Both were pale with terror. Thomas Gallant held up his crucifix in front of him.

"God protect us from the devil," he whispered.

Gallant was trying to speak as calmly and clearly as Voelkner had sounded hours before, but it came out in a whimper. Franz only stared at Eru. It was the terrified gaze of a trapped animal.

It suddenly struck Eru how unworthy it was for a true warrior to direct his anger against the weak. No matter what Te Ua Haumene said, killing people like Lange and Gallant surely wasn't righteous.

Eru made a placatory gesture. "Be quiet," he said harshly, before he finally stepped through the door. "Come with me. I'm helping you escape."

Franz Lange didn't understand what was happening when the tattooed young man, whose speech the day before had fired the bloodlust of the mob, suddenly led him to freedom. Franz had already come to terms with dying. His knees shook. No courageous last words came to him; he could remember no prayers. He only felt emptiness and fear. Now, he straightened his shoulders and followed the Hauhau warrior into the church. The young man looked around anxiously.

"Is there a back way out of here?" he asked in that crisp English accent.

Thomas Gallant shrugged helplessly. Franz would have to take the initiative.

"Yes," he replied hoarsely. "Through the vestry." He pointed to an inconspicuous wooden door nearly covered by a folding screen. "It leads out to the barn."

The warrior nodded, relieved. "Go out that way, and don't let yourselves be caught. Take horses from the barn and run. Good luck!"

Franz hesitated. He wanted to ask why the warrior was freeing them, and what had made him change his mind. He wondered if perhaps the whole thing was a trap. But Gallant ran ahead. Franz followed without saying a word to the young man who spoke English. He had a vague feeling of shame. Fleeing felt undignified. Perhaps they should say something, words of forgiveness, as Voelkner had. But if Franz were honest, he didn't feel forgiveness. The only thing he felt was relief, mixed with fresh fear.

The way from the vestry to the horse barn was clear. Gallant hastily threw a saddle on the closest animal, and Franz did the same.

"I can't ride very well," he admitted.

Gallant shrugged. "I can't either. God will guide the horses. Just the way he enlightened the young savage and guided him to us." He looked at Franz, his eyes wild. "We—we should pray."

Franz shook his head. This day had permanently shaken his faith. No one could have more faith in God than Voelkner. And how had the Creator rewarded him?

"We should ride," he said.

The barn door was open, and Franz shuddered with fear at the thought of what lay beyond. To leave the mission, they didn't have to cross the churchyard, but they did have to pass close by.

Franz thought for a moment, and then lifted the saddle off the back of the peaceful gelding he'd sometimes ridden for a leisurely visit to Maketu. Instead, he saddled an elegant little bay stallion that Paora had said ran like the wind. The words that Franz had scolded Chris Fenroy for a lifetime ago popped into his head.

"We should ride like the devil."

As soon as Franz was on its back, the little stallion shot out of the barn. The animal bucked and shied as it galloped past the gallows, saw the dancing people, and picked up the scent of blood. Franz kept himself in the saddle with a strength born of desperation. He clung to the horse's mane as cries rang out behind him, and Gallant's large black gelding flew past him. His brother in the Lord was hanging onto the saddle just as desperately. Falling would have meant certain death.

The horses raced between the mission buildings, villagers diving out of their way in surprise. The howls faded as they passed through the gates of the mission and the *marae*.

"Where to?" Gallant shouted.

"Maketu! The coast!" Franz called back.

There was a military base in Maketu. However, it was more than fifty miles away, and Franz was already exhausted. The horse had slowed to a fast trot, which was shaking him up even more. If he could stay on at all, it was only thanks to the few riding lessons that Linda had given him at Rata Station. Arrogant as he'd been back then, he hadn't even thanked her properly.

It was already twilight, and soon it would be dark. The path they were on ran parallel to the coast, but it was quite craggy and led through dense woodland. The riders could hardly see their hands in front of their faces. But Franz's little stallion led the way unflinchingly.

"Maketu's still too far. What about Whakatane?" Gallant asked. After an hour of riding, he was sitting crookedly in his saddle with a pained expression on his face.

Whakatane was the closest town to Opotiki, and had originally been a Ngati Awa settlement. A mission had been there for a long time, too, led by Catholic priests, and the town had flourished. There were fields, farms with livestock, a mill, and a school. The local Maori were known to be friendly to the *pakeha*. But now? What if other Hauhau recruiters were rampaging there? Would they just be putting themselves in danger again?

The decision was finally made for them by the little bay stallion. On the Whakatane River, there were not only the mission and a well-known Maori *pa* but also several *pakeha* farms. At the first one they passed, several mares were grazing in the meadow. Franz had neither the strength nor the riding ability to stop his horse from heading toward them. He barely managed to fall out of the saddle before the whinnying bay pushed his way through the wooden fence, knocking out the crossbars.

Four excitedly barking dogs roused the farmer, who came out of the house with his sons to find out what all the noise was about. After he'd caught the stallion and handed the reins to one of his boys, the man looked up. His torch illuminated the missionaries' pale, exhausted faces.

"Where the devil did you come from?"

A little later, Franz Lange and Thomas Gallant, still trembling with exhaustion and tension, were sitting by a crackling fireplace in the Thompson family home. They gratefully sipped hot tea while the farmer and his sons saddled horses. They, too, were ready to ride like the devil, and they could do it. They reached the military base at Maketu that night. At dawn, a regiment of the English cavalry sped toward Opotiki.

Eru awoke late the next morning in the Te Whakatohea's community house. Kereopa and Patara slept by his side, both still smeared with blood. When Eru got up and looked around, he found a few quiet women making fires and baking flatbread. Others were weeping and preparing graves. Many of the children had died during the night. The blood of the slain missionary hadn't healed them, nor had the belief of their fathers in Te Ua Haumene's cause. To the contrary, the trauma and cold of the night had worsened their condition. They had been better off in their beds in the hospital ward than on the ground around the *niu*.

Eru realized then that no one was attempting to sing the morning hymns. The few warriors who were awake seemed more afraid than invulnerable. Eru briefly wondered if he should speak to them, but then gave up the idea. Kereopa could figure out for himself how to rally his followers again. Instead, Eru approached a fire to ask an old woman for some flatbread. She gave him herbal tea, some bread, and *kumara*, and sat down across from him. Eru recognized her as one of the village elders. Like some of the other old people, she had withdrawn when Kereopa began preaching to the tribe.

"What will happen now?" she asked quietly as Eru ate and drank.

Eru looked down. "I don't know. I—I've never done anything like this before, or seen such a thing. To cut off a man's head and eat his eyes—"

The old woman laughed without humor. "No," she said. "You're still too young for that. When I was your age, it happened more often. It's *tikanga*, you know. Part of war. The strength of the enemy enters the warrior who kills him and eats parts of his body. That's what they said, anyway. Later, we learned from the *pakeha* that it was a sin."

"What do *you* believe, *karani*?" Eru asked.

"I believe it is better not to wage war," the woman replied. "Then you don't need the strength of your dead enemy. And above all, it's better not to wage war with a tribe whose warriors have more warriors and sharper spears."

"You mean the *pakeha*?" Eru asked. "But we have to protect ourselves! We can't allow them to take our land away. We—"

The old woman made a gesture to silence him. "The whites gave us seeds; they brought the sheep whose meat we eat and whose wool keeps us warm. Of course they wanted part of our land, but they gave us blankets and pots and pans for it. And then the missionaries came and told us it was too little, that we'd been tricked. They taught our children what land is worth in the eyes of the *pakeha*. They taught us their language and reading and writing so that no one can fool us anymore."

Eru started with surprise. "But for that we had to give up our gods, our customs—"

The woman laughed bitterly. "You gave up your gods for that prophet. We'll see if he gives you anything better than sheep and seeds. And you don't like his customs either."

She glanced pointedly at Kereopa, who was staggering out of the sleeping house and looking for water to wash the blood off his face. Then the old woman stared into the fire for a long time before she spoke again.

"Of course we can ask ourselves if we wouldn't have been better off if we'd never met the whites, as your prophet says. But we liked the blankets and pots and pans . . ." She smiled weakly. "My beliefs are very different from those of the *pakeha*. I don't know if their gods are as strong as ours, or how strong those of your prophet are. But I do know that a god has never come down from heaven to protect warriors in battle. And that will not happen now, no matter what lies your prophet tells you."

"What do you mean, 'now'?" Eru asked helplessly.

The woman gave a snort of disapproval. "Do you believe the *pakeha* will just sit back and accept what you've done to Voelkner? You have brought war to our village, son!"

"Us?" Eru heard the scathing voice of Patara behind him. "Oh no, *karani*, it was your people who put the noose around the priest's neck! We didn't have anything to do with it!"

Eru spun around and stared at Patara, appalled and uncomprehending.

The old woman remained calm. "So you will leave, and we will die."

"No!" Eru cried. "Of course we'll help you, we—" He broke off as he saw the chain of events unfold. Even if he hadn't freed Lange and Gallant, Voelkner's death wouldn't have been a secret for long. There were probably soldiers on their way already. "We should gather around the *niu* immediately. The warriors—"

"The warriors who want to join us will travel westward today to meet Te Ua Haumene," Kereopa declared, and sat down beside them. The old woman got up and left the fire. "We'll accompany them a ways and then continue southward to Turanganui, to bring the message of the prophet to the tribes on the river there. Just as planned."

"But the English will come here!" Eru cried in disbelief. "They'll want revenge!"

Kereopa shrugged. "Then they will awaken even more anger in our people, and even more warriors will join us."

Eru couldn't stand to listen anymore. He jumped up and walked away, wanting to follow the old woman and apologize. But he couldn't bring himself to do it. Filled with shame and rage and fear, he slipped into his hiding place behind the church. He didn't know where he belonged. Should he stay here and fight a battle that couldn't be won, accept the responsibility for Voelkner's death, and die himself? Should he run away? Should he try to get back to the South Island and herd his mother's sheep like a good boy, a boy with the face of a warrior that wasn't real?

In the meantime, Kereopa had gathered his followers and sworn them in to their new beliefs again. Eru heard them singing the morning hymn and stamping around the *niu*. But only when Kereopa had blown the conch to signal that it was time to move on did he leave his hiding place. Then he was witness to one last terrible scene. Kereopa and Patara were refusing to let young Pokeno join them.

"How old are you? Twelve? I'm sorry, boy. We don't need any children in the *pa*. In a few years you'll be old enough to fight, but now . . ." Kereopa shook his head.

"I was old enough to hang the priest!" Pokeno cried in protest. He was a tall boy, gawky, but just as overbold as his father had been. Now his voice was shrill with indignation and fear. "If you don't take me with you now—"

"Then the English will hold him responsible for the crime," Eru said.

Patara shrugged. "Just hide for a few days," he advised. "It won't be that bad."

"They will kill him," said the village elder who'd spoken with Eru that morning. "He's not safe here, or anywhere on the east coast."

Kereopa shook his head. "Then he should go find some friendly tribe. In any case, he can't go with us. We only take warriors. Adult warriors."

Eru saw Pokeno's tears spill over. He, too, felt a fresh wave of helpless outrage. Pokeno's life was ruined. He would have to pay for what Kereopa, Patara—and Eru—had done.

Eru ran a hand over his face. Makuto had been right. The *moko* hadn't made him into a man. If he was a man, he would stay and fight and die with Pokeno. He tried to gather all his courage, but he couldn't do it. He wanted to live.

With his head lowered, he followed Kereopa, Patara, and their recruits. The men turned toward Gisborne.

Barely two hours after the warriors had left, the cavaliers arrived in Opotiki. The soldiers found a destroyed mission, a *niu* in the churchyard, and the remains of Carl Voelkner. Someone had left his head on the altar of the church, his empty eye sockets staring out at his devastated realm. The anger of the English was boundless. The Maori who had not yet fled, the women, children, and old people who had hidden in terror, had to watch as their fields were destroyed, their orchards were chopped down, and their houses were set on fire. Finally, soldiers herded the villagers into the churchyard, forced a few young boys to make confessions, and arrested Pokeno. The boy listened with a stony expression as his friends and relatives pinned the sole blame for Voelkner's execution on him.

Only the tribal elder spoke for him. "He's just a child," she said. "Not even the Hauhau warriors wanted him. They said he was too young."

The leader of the cavalry unit laughed. "Too young? You don't even believe that yourself, old woman. Those villains are just washing their hands in innocence. When we catch them, they won't admit to having anything to do with all this. Of course the boy was misled. But that won't help him. In Auckland, he will hang."

The soldiers took not only Pokeno but also a few other boys and two old men who had attempted to stop their houses from being burned. The tribe's land was confiscated, and the missionary station suspended. After all, there was no one left there to missionize. The Te Whakatohea were thrown to the winds.

Part 5

DESTRUCTION

Otago and Campbelltown, New Zealand
(the South Island)

Waikato and Otaki, New Zealand
(the North Island)

1865

Chapter 42

"Where is your husband, Mrs. Fitzpatrick?"

Linda had been checking if the laundry was ready to be taken down from the line, but it was too damp. She turned around and recognized Tom Lester, the farrier and horse trader from Tuapeka. The stocky, red-haired man looked annoyed. She put on an innocent smile.

"I thought Fitz was with you, Mr. Lester."

Lester snorted. "If he was, I wouldn't be looking for him," he retorted. "Apparently, he didn't turn up yesterday because his horse was lame. He obviously can't walk because that would be beneath his dignity. The barn has to be ready before it snows, Mrs. Fitzpatrick. And I can only finish building it if your husband happens to be in the mood to work."

Linda sighed. They'd been in Tuapeka for more than three months, and as hard as she'd tried, she was a long way from being happy. Fitz's excitement for prospecting had dwindled significantly. During the first few weeks, he had started one project after another, all of which Irene had promptly declared to be insane. He had dug deep shafts in the ground to try his hand at mining. Then he'd gone to the mountains to chip away at boulders with hammers and chisels. After all, there were other parts of the world that had veins of gold in solid rock, so why not here? Linda had shaken her head and let him go. But just as Fitz was about to get to work, he'd been surprised by two armed Maori warriors. It turned out that the boulders were a sacred site to the tribe, and he would have paid for their desecration with his life. Fortunately, he hadn't laid a hand on them yet, and as usual, he charmed his way out of the predicament.

When it came down to it, Linda's husband hadn't managed to scrape together a single ounce of gold, and he was slowly losing his enthusiasm for the undertaking. He was hiring himself out to the local businessmen as a handyman more and more often. Skilled as he was, he enjoyed a good reputation at first, but he became more and more lackadaisical. Linda could understand Tom Lester's annoyance. Fitz had agreed to help him build a livery stable, and now . . .

"I'm sure that something—important came up," Linda stammered.

It was much more likely that Fitz had let himself be distracted by something frivolous—a card game or a conversation with an Australian prospector who'd promised him insider information, maybe shoptalk about betting on horses. Linda had stopped worrying about such things. At first, she hadn't believed it, but Fitz really did win at cards more often than he lost. Without his passion for gambling, they would have often had to go hungry in the last few weeks. So far, he'd always kept his promise that his wife would never want for something to eat.

But for the most part, they lived from the money that Linda found with her humble gold panning. It was work that became more and more difficult the closer that winter came. It hadn't snowed or gone below freezing yet, which was a small miracle in Otago, where it was often bitterly cold in late autumn. Instead, it rained almost without pause, and the streams became raging rivers. So Irene and Linda wound their way through the deserted claims and sifted through the soil and mud. When they got home, they were soaked to the skin, and Irene didn't even have anything dry to change into. She had been sniffling and coughing for weeks, as had little Paddy. Linda shared her food with the two of them, and with her heart bleeding, parted with one of her dresses and a shawl that Irene could wrap the child in. With the increasingly bad weather, it became more and more difficult to light an open fire to cook over or to get warm by. Even when it didn't rain, the wood was damp and produced more smoke than heat.

Tom Lester cast a half-angry, half-pitying glance over Linda's dilapidated hut, the smoking fire, and the damp laundry. Then he turned to leave.

"I'm sorry, Mrs. Fitzpatrick, but when you see your husband, please tell him I'm looking for a new helper. I can't work with Fitz. As for his credit—" Tom had shoed both Brianna and Fitz's horse recently, and Fitz had promised to work off the debt. "He can bring me the two shillings whenever he has the chance."

Linda pressed her lips together grimly. Fitz surely wouldn't give him the coins. Recently she had been questioned by multiple people her husband owed money to. It was never very much. No bank would have given Fitz a loan. But the barman in the pub allowed him to start a tab, the general store keeper gave him credit for groceries, and every now and then another prospector would loan him a few shillings for some other reason. Fitz treated these small amounts as unimportant, but all together they came to a handsome sum. Linda had no idea how Fitz intended to pay all the money back. She was often sleepless with worry while he snored contentedly next to her. If he was home at all. The worse it got with their finances, the more time he spent at the card table. That might also have to do with the bad weather—Fitz preferred the warm pub to drafty building sites.

This evening, too, Linda prepared herself for a lonely night warmed only by Amy. As she tried to keep the fire going at least long enough to cook her dinner and dry the damp laundry, Irene appeared. The young woman seemed excited, and Linda noticed that she was wearing new boots. Paddy was wrapped in a warm jacket. Linda was about to ask what was going on when she heard hoofbeats. Fitz was racing toward the hut, the horse's hooves spraying mud in the air.

"Lindy!" For once he wasn't smiling as he jumped down. "Lindy, I'm sorry, but we have to pack. I changed my mind—we're going to the west coast."

"Wh—what?" she stammered. "We're leaving? Now?"

Fitz nodded and moved toward Brianna, who was tied to a tree, to harness her for the covered wagon.

"Come on, Lindy. Maybe we can still get going while there's light."

"Do you think that's a good idea, Fitz?" Irene asked sarcastically. "Maybe it would be better for you to escape when it's dark. Or doesn't your sudden change of heart have anything to do with the fellows who were firing shots in the pub?"

Linda took a closer look at her husband. Fitz had a fat lip, and one of his eyes was almost swollen shut.

"Fitz, you're hurt! Someone—someone shot at you?"

Worriedly, she scanned his body. Neither his ripped canvas pants nor his old leather jacket showed any traces of blood.

"It was nothing," he said. "Just a little difference of opinion. You were right, Lindy, this place isn't for us."

Linda glanced at Irene, seeking help. She shrugged.

"I don't know any of the details," she replied. "Oppenheimer and I heard shots in the pub. There was some kind of brawl. The postmaster fetched the police officer, but the fellows were gone by the time he arrived. He didn't come particularly quickly, not wanting to be shot. The barman was as white as the wall, and said something about poker and cheating. The shots were just a warning, right, Fitz? Otherwise, you'd surely be dead. It's hard to miss your target in such a small room."

While Irene spoke, Fitz had harnessed the horses and was starting to throw Linda's damp laundry into the covered wagon. He certainly wasn't packing. It looked more like fleeing.

"I should have never taken up with those chaps from Queenstown," Fitz said, trying to explain. "I should have realized they were crooks. But it's just hard for me to resist a good round of poker."

"You had a job," Linda said. "The farrier was here."

Fitz furrowed his brow. "I was challenged," he insisted, as though it would have been dishonorable for him to turn down the game. "I said I'm sorry. It was a mistake. But the chaps were playing with marked cards, I swear. Lindy, it wasn't just a stroke of bad luck for me, it was—"

"So you lost," Linda said. "And then you accused them of cheating."

"I was angry, Lindy. That's no reason for them to start a brawl and pull a gun."

Fitz strode into the hut and took more of their possessions, hurling them all under the wagon cover. Amy sprang nervously onto the seat. She was afraid of being left behind.

"Then why do you have to leave so quickly?" Linda asked. "I mean, they gave you a beating. That should be enough for them."

Fitz rubbed his forehead. "It's just that—they want a thousand pounds by early tomorrow morning."

Linda's heart began to bang against her ribs. "We can't pay that much," she whispered. "Not even if we sold the horses."

"I would never sell Brianna!" Fitz declared. "I know how much you love her."

"Is that why you gambled everything?" Linda spat back. She'd carefully avoided fighting with her husband, but now she was in the grip of naked panic. "Fitz, people like that are dangerous. Who knows, they might even follow us!"

"Oh, fiddlesticks," Irene said. "Those fools aren't ice-cold killers, just some down-and-out ruffians who somehow found their way here. I don't think they're big on making plans. But it would be a good idea to leave town. Just put as many miles as you can between yourselves and that pack. And tomorrow, it would be better for Fitz to hide in the wagon—you drive, Linda. Then, if they happen to spot you, the only risk would be them recognizing Fitz's horse."

Linda made a quick decision. "Fitz's horse stays here," she said. "I trust you, Irene. Sell it, pay off all our debts, and if there's anything left over, keep it." She smiled crookedly. "For the rent."

Irene had never asked for the agreed-upon rent for the use of her hut.

Irene smiled. "I could also send it to you somewhere, if you ever settle down," she suggested. "Because—I don't need it anymore."

"You don't need money anymore?" In her confusion, Linda forgot momentarily about the disaster. "What happened? I wanted to ask you before." She cast a glance at Irene's new boots. "Irene, you aren't selling your body, are you?"

Irene shrugged. "Sort of. I'm getting married." She smiled shyly.

"You're doing what? Who are you marrying so suddenly? You didn't even have a boyfriend, you—"

"Oppenheimer," Irene said softly. "I'm marrying Ely Oppenheimer. He asked me today. He's closing his office. There's no gold to buy here anymore. What little business he has left will be taken over by the banker. Ely made good money over the last few years, and saved it too. He can retire now. He has a nice house in Queenstown, and he says it's a pretty city. And he likes me, and Paddy."

She jogged the little boy in her arms. Paddy didn't react; he was unnaturally quiet.

Linda sighed. "Irene, you—you're so young. How old is Oppenheimer? Sixty?"

"I didn't ask him," Irene replied sharply. "And I don't care if he's a hundred. Yes, I'm young, and I'd like to live to be a little older and see Paddy grow up. If we go on like this, he may die this winter. Look how thin he is, and how tired and weak! As for me, I'm practically coughing my soul out of my body every night. Who would take care of him? With Oppenheimer, I'll have a warm house and enough to eat, and Paddy can go to school later. Ely says he'll adopt him. I'd have to be crazy to say no, Linda."

"It's still not right, it—maybe he could adopt both of you."

Linda watched Fitz throw the table and chair onto the wagon, even though the furniture actually belonged to Irene. She began to feel angry.

Irene smiled sadly. "He loves me, Linda, but not that much. A man is a man, whether he's twenty or sixty. He wants to get something for his money. So he gets me, body and all, by day and by night. He won't want it that often. And he's clean, Linda. He smells nice."

Linda didn't know what else to say. Irene had made the only intelligent decision.

"I'll miss you," Linda said softly.

Irene hugged her. "I'll miss you too. It's such a pity that you won't be able to come to my wedding. It will be a proper wedding, you know? In the church. Paddy and I were only married quickly by some fellow in the prospectors' camp, between two shifts on the goldfield. That doesn't count."

Linda wondered if she'd even told Oppenheimer about that marriage. Perhaps the old bullion dealer had decided for himself how little it mattered.

"I'm going to have a wedding gown. And everyone is coming, the postmaster and the banker and their wives. I'm becoming a proper lady, Linda. The postmaster and the banker congratulated us. Can you imagine that?"

Irene's voice became more animated. She had surely always dreamed of such a wedding. Linda tried to smile and be happy for her. She didn't know much about Jewish people, but if the bullion dealer was getting married in a Christian ceremony to make Irene happy, he must think a lot of the girl. And in Queenstown, the only thing that might be gossiped about would be her age. No one would know anything about her less-than-ladylike past.

"In any case, I wish you luck," Linda said and hugged her friend tightly. "I would have loved to come to your wedding."

Fitz passed Irene the bay's reins. "It's a pity that I didn't think of visiting Lester on the way here. Perhaps I could have exchanged him for another horse."

Linda put her head in her hands. Fitz was giving up his horse only because he was afraid of the ruffians from Queenstown, who would probably also head for the west coast. He somehow didn't understand the necessity of paying his debts.

He patted the bay on its neck regretfully. "Come on, Lindy, let's get out of here."

Linda was still in shock when Fitz urged Brianna into a trot and turned onto the road to Christchurch. They would leave the same way they had come, and then after Christchurch, they would turn west and travel over the mountains. Linda was terrified about the journey over Arthur's Pass. During the sheep drives, she'd had to travel in the foothills of the Southern Alps, and it had often been difficult and dangerous. Now, in the snow and ice, they would have to go much higher.

"Can't we spend the winter in Christchurch?" she asked unhappily.

She leaned against Fitz, seeking warmth. They'd driven through the first night, and had only stopped the following day for Brianna to rest briefly. Linda was chilled to the bone and exhausted. Amy nestled around her feet. It had started to snow. Winter was here, and up in the Alps, it would rage with all of its ferocity.

Fitz shrugged. "I don't know, sweetheart. I was very glad to get away from there."

Linda sat up abruptly. "Fitz, do you owe money to people in Christchurch too?"

Fitz kept his eyes forward. "It must be too long ago to count now."

Linda groaned. "The people you owe probably see things very differently. What's going to happen to us, Fitz?"

Fitz took her by the shoulders. "Are you going to start that again?" he asked, but his voice sounded different, tense and annoyed. "I've told you so many times, it doesn't help at all to moan about things. Life goes on. And hey, Lindy, the west coast is full of gold! Nice, fresh gold."

Linda turned away. According to everything she'd heard, the west coast was more full of thieves than anything else. She didn't want to go there. But she didn't know what else they could do. She wondered if she should try to convince Fitz to go to the North Island. She missed Ida and Karl so much, and above all Carol. How was her sister faring?

Chapter 43

"Aside from my pleasure in your enchanting company, I've asked you to come because a possibility for you to continue your journey has finally arisen."

General Cameron raised his wine glass in a toast before telling Carol and Mara the details. He had invited the two of them to dinner again, along with Bill Paxton, whose work he obviously valued. As for Carol and Mara, the general's feelings were mixed. Carol had been criticizing him persistently since she'd witnessed the eviction of the Maori along the Patea River. She thought his politics concerning the native people were a complete debacle. Bill Paxton tried to reassure the sisters that Cameron basically shared their opinion. They'd discussed it just the day before.

"The general doesn't at all enjoy violently appropriating land for the governor," Bill said. "He's told Grey several times that it's not his job."

"What *is* his job, then?" Mara asked.

Bill shrugged. "He's a soldier. A commanding officer. This was presented to him as a war, and his job is to win."

"By destroying peaceful tribes and not touching Haumene's fort?" Carol said indignantly.

"The tribes are being removed at the governor's orders," Bill said. "Cameron himself would prefer not to go about it so—directly. As for the fort, he's depending on starvation and isolation. Attacking it has proven to be inefficient. Cameron has suffered countless defeats over the last few years. Siege wars aren't his strength; they cost time and are ineffective. And experience has shown that Maori warriors won't wait indefinitely for the battle to come to them. At some point, the Hauhau will come looking for a fight. If it's possible then to lure them onto open ground, Cameron will be at an advantage. But he could shoot at the palisades of their *pa* for months without having much effect."

"The way he's treating people is still horrible," Carol insisted. "And a strategic disaster." Ever since Patea, she'd regarded the general quite coldly.

But this evening, he'd awakened her curiosity. "What possibility to continue our journey? Are you going to provide us with an escort to Auckland?"

"In a way," Cameron replied. "I can't spare any of my people, as I explained when you arrived. However, we've recently captured some new Hauhau recruits from the east coast. We want to take them to Auckland—get them out of the area, scare them so they'll go back to their tribes and give up the Hauhau ideas. I'm assigning twenty men to the convoy. That should be enough security for you as well. If you want to continue your journey, you may ride with them."

Carol beamed. "Of course we will! Thank you, we—"

"Excuse me, but perhaps you shouldn't make up your mind so hastily, Miss Carol," Bill Paxton interjected. He looked more than worried. "I mean, without contradicting you, General, the route is in no way safe! Of course the land along the river is currently at peace, and even if the tribes are still hiding in the woods, they would hardly dare to attack. But the convoy will have to go right past Haumene's stronghold in Weraroa."

"Which is constantly losing strategic value," the general said, his eyes flashing. He was very content with the way things had developed. Weraroa was now almost completely isolated from the land controlled by the English.

"Haumene is still mustering his warriors there," Bill retorted. "Please don't get me wrong, General. I completely support your decision to send the prisoners to Auckland—"

"That is a great joy and honor to me," the general said sarcastically. "How pleasing, Lieutenant Paxton, that you approve of my decision."

Bill's face turned red, but he continued anyway. "Still, I think it would be extraordinarily dangerous for Miss Carol and Miss Margaret to join that convoy. And unnecessary, as you say yourself. Weraroa is isolated. Before long, we will either take over the fort, or the Maori will give it up. You should stay here until then, Miss Carol. Please, don't put yourselves in danger."

Mara raised her eyebrows. "I'm not in danger on Maori land," she said haughtily. "I'm much more likely to hear a warrior sneaking up on me than your troops are."

"And then what?" Bill asked. "Will you make the prisoners and all twenty soldiers disappear? Miss Mara—"

"We don't have to decide immediately," Carol said. "I think for now we should thank the general for his offer and apply ourselves to the delicacies that the cook has conjured for us. This, at least, I will miss." She gave a charming smile. "When do you need an answer, General?"

Cameron signaled a steward to refill his guests' glasses. "The convoy will depart tomorrow morning."

"It's extremely dangerous, Carol! I don't care what the general says. You can't go!"

After dinner, Bill had accompanied the sisters back to their quarters. Now the two of them were walking Fancy, and Mara had retired to her room. She had said she was going to pack.

Carol sighed. "Bill, we can't stay here forever." In recent weeks, the two had begun to use each other's first names when they were alone, and talking about more personal matters. "If the general thinks the journey is safe—"

"It takes you past the fort where two thousand bloodthirsty warriors are so crowded together that they're stepping on each other's toes! Of course Haumene is keeping quiet for now because our troops keep passing by. But if he gets wind of the prisoner convoy to Auckland, that will change. If he doesn't make a show of force, his followers will lose faith. It's a huge risk, Carol. Please don't go!"

Carol toyed with the fringe of her shawl, feeling undecided. In spite of the generally mild temperatures of the North Island, the winter air was quite chilly.

"Mara would be disappointed," she murmured.

"Mara is still a child," Bill argued. "And besides, Carol—" He took off his uniform jacket and draped it over her shoulders as they walked. There were trees between the cabins and the palisade. They provided a little protection from the wind and a bit of privacy from the military base. "Carol, I've wanted to talk to you for a long time. Listen, I—you—we—one could say that we've become quite good friends over the last few weeks."

Carol furrowed her brow. "Weren't we always that, Bill? I've always been very fond of you."

Bill beamed. "Then is it all right if I get my hopes up, Carol? You feel the same, then? That we've gotten closer?"

Carol stopped and turned to face the young lieutenant. "You mean, as a couple?"

"How else would I mean it?" Bill said, and laughed nervously.

Carol considered this for a moment. "Bill," she said, "to be very honest, I haven't been thinking about that. Perhaps right at the beginning on the *General Lee*. Just playfully, when Linda teased me and asked me if I didn't want to trade in my fiancé for you . . ."

"And did you tell her?" Bill asked.

"Back then, it was completely out of the question for me," Carol said honestly. "I loved Oliver. I figured you were just flirting, enjoying the time on board. Of course you were so kind, especially later, after the catastrophe. I like you very, very much. But . . ." She shrugged helplessly.

"You're not in love with me," Bill said bitterly.

Carol shook her head. "No. I haven't gotten that far yet, Bill. My head is still too full of other things. And after Oliver—"

"Do you still love him?"

"No!" Carol's voice was decisive. "He's a—a—I've banished him from my heart, Bill, believe me. It's just I'm still so disappointed, and so hurt, that at the moment I don't want any man. I want to go to my mother and cry on her shoulder and lick my wounds. I think we're going to take the general up on his offer, Bill. I want to go home! At least, to whatever kind of home I have left."

Bill gently put a hand on her arm. "Carol, I could make a home for you. If you marry me, then I only need to say the word. In six months at the latest, the military settlers program will begin. As soon as Weraroa has been evacuated, the parcels will be assigned. We could have a farm. They'll probably promote me first, and that means we'd get quite a bit of land."

"You want me to dance on Maori graves? You can't be serious!"

Bill groaned to himself. He should have foreseen that reaction. "Someone is going to take this land. It won't matter if it's us or someone else. The Maori won't get it back. At least think about it, Carol. You could have sheep again, and we could have a fresh start." He patted Fancy. "You'd like that, wouldn't you, Fancy?" he said with a laugh. "A few hundred sheep for you, and your mistress for me?"

Fancy wagged her tail.

Carol's eyes flashed in annoyance. "Good thing it's not up to the dog," she said sharply. "Bill, I certainly don't want to marry you under these circumstances! There's no blessing on stolen land. And as I already told you, it's too soon. At the moment, I don't need or want a husband." She turned away.

Bill put his arms around her. "Can't I change your mind? Isn't there something I can do?" He pulled her close and attempted to kiss her.

Carol pushed him away. "Yes, turn back time so the last two years haven't happened! Make everything the way it was before. Then we can talk about it. But like this—" She tore herself out of his grip and dashed back to her quarters.

The next morning, Carol and Mara joined the prisoner convoy and headed north. Bill's request to join the group as well was turned down by the upper ranks of army command.

"You're too important for that," the major who had brought him the news said. "You're doing top-quality work as a liaison officer here. The general doesn't want to risk anything happening to you."

Chapter 44

The general had assigned twenty heavily armed soldiers to guard the eight prisoners, and in Carol's mind, it was overkill. The wide path along the Patea River offered excellent visibility, and was hardly a good place for an ambush. Bill had surely been overreacting—or perhaps just creating an excuse for Carol to stay longer. Still, she felt bad for rejecting him so rudely. Bill's proposal had caught her off guard.

Once Carol had time to think, she saw things more clearly. Of course she wasn't ready to get engaged. The wounds left by Oliver were still too fresh. Additionally, she was worried about Linda, who had disappeared to God only knew where with her careless, frivolous husband. She was also still mourning for Chris and Cat. At the same time, Bill was one of the loveliest men she'd ever met. He was dependable, good-looking, and kind. And back aboard the ship, a few sparks had indeed flown between them. Carol had enjoyed it when he held her in his arms while they were dancing and murmured compliments in her ear. Her heart had pounded when he laughed and caught her each time rough seas sent her staggering over the deck. Honestly, she needn't have disappointed him so completely. She could have at least invited him to write to her and perhaps to visit in Russell.

This morning, Carol had hoped he would come and say goodbye. Then she would have apologized and made the invitation. But Bill hadn't appeared.

Unhappily, Carol urged her horse into a trot behind the others. The convoy was proceeding painfully slowly. While the soldiers rode, the Maori prisoners had to walk, and they deliberately hung back to slow down the journey. Mara's lively white steed was chomping at the bit.

"Can't the warriors get a move on?" she asked the captain in charge of the redcoats. "There's absolutely no reason for them to walk so slowly. When warriors are traveling, they usually run. To keep pace with the Ngai Tahu, I used to have to get my horse into a canter."

The captain shrugged and glanced at his pretty travel companion. There wasn't much of Mara's slender figure to be seen under the voluminous riding coat, but her beautiful face and thick, braided hair turned the young man's head. He smiled winningly.

"The fellows aren't in a hurry. And the chains are uncomfortable for them. Fortunately, we're in no particular rush. Just look at it this way, Miss Jensch. The slowness of the prisoners gives us more time to talk, which is quite a pleasure for me."

Mara rolled her eyes. "What exactly do you find enjoyable about it?" she asked provokingly. "I can't think of anything I'd like to talk about in this cold, and my horse is practically falling asleep."

Carol had to smile. Mara was right. The journey was anything but pleasant. It was drizzling and cold. The mountains that peeked through the thick clouds were completely covered with snow. Carol, too, would have preferred to spur her horse into a canter, and the soldiers surely felt the same. On the other hand, she felt for the prisoners. The frigid path was muddy, and the men were barefoot and underdressed. The Hauhau recruits had been captured while wearing their traditional warrior garb, and the English army saw no reason to provide them with warmer clothes. As it began to rain harder, the men padded behind them with their heads lowered. The water soaked their warrior's knots and ran down their bare backs. They must have been suffering, but they didn't let it show.

Carol pulled her hood up over her head and looked around for Fancy. She wasn't happy about the pace either. The dog trotted morosely behind the horses.

"Do you really want to press on today?" the commanding officer of the last military base on the river asked them.

The convoy had reached the base around teatime. Carol and Mara were grateful to at least warm up a little, thoughtfully served by a young captain whose attempts at flirting had rolled off Mara's back like the rain off her oilskin coat.

"You're welcome to spend the night here," the sergeant said. "We have some space in the barn. It'll be more comfortable than tents, at least, and safer. You do know you're approaching Weraroa, right?"

The captain nodded. "Thank you, but we should try to get a little bit farther," he replied. "I can't believe it's taken the entire day for what's usually a two-hour ride! Actually, we wanted to get past Weraroa today."

"You won't be able to do that," the sergeant said, "unless you want to travel by night." He frowned.

"Would you recommend it?" the captain asked doubtfully.

The sergeant shrugged. "We generally advise people to pass the fort as quickly as possible at as great a distance as possible. It would be delusional to believe one could pass without being seen. However, their scouts have to go back to the fort and get authorization from the prophet before attacking. Before they get that far, whoever is trying to get through the area is usually out of range."

"Usually . . . ," the captain muttered.

The problem was instantly clear to Carol. If the prisoner convoy proceeded too slowly, they became an easy target.

"If I were you," the sergeant continued, "I'd stay here tonight and start early tomorrow morning."

The captain thought for a moment, then shook his head. "We'll go a few miles farther and then set up camp. That means we'll be able to get out of the dangerous area by early tomorrow morning. They won't dare go so far from their fort. If we pass at a distance of about five miles, in this weather—that will have to be good enough."

The sergeant shrugged. "No one knows how organized the Hauhau are. In the last few months, we haven't seen a single one of the fellows. At the most, we hear them if the wind is blowing in the right direction. Then we get the shivers from their singing. I can only wish you good luck."

It soon became clear that the captain's decision had been a bad one. Barely half an hour after they had left the base, a downpour started, and the riders couldn't make much progress. Then night fell. When they could no longer see anything, the captain gave the command to set up camp.

A little later, Carol and Mara were sitting in a dark but at least partially dry tent. Fancy, soaking wet, tried to wiggle her way between them for warmth, and they pushed her away gently as they chewed listlessly on some bread and cheese they'd packed as emergency rations.

"My kingdom for a cup of hot tea," Mara grumbled. "We should have stayed at the base, and then run off quickly the next morning before the captain could get everyone together. We would have been well past Weraroa by now."

Carol felt it was her duty to contradict her younger sister, though the scenario was appealing. "Riding in a large group is much safer."

Mara snorted. "Riding, maybe, but how about camping out? You don't really believe that the Maori will miss thirty people putting their tents up here, do you? We can only hope that the scouts aren't looking very carefully. If they try to free the prisoners, it could get very dangerous."

Of course Carol knew that, and the thought robbed her of sleep, despite the redcoat guards making their rounds outside. However, the night passed without incident, and Mara slept as innocently as a babe. But Carol kept thinking about her "twin." Carol wished with her whole heart to finally be with Ida. The Jensches must have heard from Linda. Mail from the South Island was sent by ship, after all. And she, too, would finally be able to write letters again. To Linda, and to Bill . . . She finally fell into a restless sleep toward morning, and was soon awakened by the soldiers. At first light, they struck camp.

"I'm sorry for the lack of breakfast, ladies," the captain said. "But I promise you, as soon as we have survived this day, everything will be much better."

At least it was no longer raining. As they rode, a few weak rays of sunshine worked their way through the rising morning mist, making the forest look enchanted. In better times, Carol and Mara would have told each other stories about dancing fairies. But now the effect was almost threatening. The spirits this place harbored were certainly not benevolent ones.

Carol knew that Weraroa *pa* was about five miles away, but she still imagined she could make out the fortress through the fog. She listened nervously for the sound of Hauhau chants but only heard the hoofbeats of the horses, the rustling of the soldiers' uniforms, and a few quietly exchanged words.

No one spoke much, even though the captain hadn't ordered silence. Carol could feel the tension almost physically, and wished to be far away as soon as possible. But their progress continued to be painfully slow. It would be hours until they reached relative safety.

As it turned out, not even Mara, who relied so much on the sharp senses she'd developed alongside the children of the Ngai Tahu, heard the Hauhau warriors coming. The spears that flew out of the bushes were a surprise to everyone. The horses shied, and the men needed far too long to draw their weapons.

"Rire rire! Kira, kira!"

War cries cut through the air. Tattooed and painted men sprang from the trees like demons.

"Hau hau, hau hau!"

The prisoners enthusiastically joined the chant and swung their chains against the horses' legs while the assailants attacked the riders with spears and knives. In no time, there was a cacophony of musket shots, screams, war cries, whinnying, and ineffectively shouted orders. The latter were quickly silenced, and Carol watched in horror as a warrior's spear pierced the captain's chest. His horse galloped away as he fell, and Mara followed the bay on her steed.

"Run!" Carol cried.

Fancy barked, and Carol screamed as a warrior kicked at her. Then she galloped off between the trees—and straight into the next wave of Hauhau who were waiting to attack. She peered through the fog in surprise as a warrior grabbed the bridle of her horse. She tried to push him away, but he blocked her efforts easily. Then she heard Mara scream as someone pulled her off her horse, and screamed herself as Fancy furiously leaped toward her foe and he threw a knife at the dog. Carol saw her body fall under a bush, and then she, too, was pulled from her horse. From the direction of the clearing where the warriors had attacked the soldiers, cries of triumph could now be heard. The Hauhau were lauding their own invulnerability and strength. There were no more sounds of musket fire. The English had been beaten, and the women were in the hands of the Hauhau.

The sight that met the sisters' eyes when the warriors dragged them back to the scene of the ambush was one they would never be able to forget. The fog had lifted, revealing a melee that had clear winners but was in no way over. Dying soldiers lay on the road. The cries of the Hauhau warriors mixed with the moaning of the redcoats, their shouts of horror, and their pleading as they bore witness to the Hauhau decapitating their comrades. It wasn't easy to cut a man's head off. The warriors hacked through tendons and bones with their knives, and cheered when they finally succeeded. They proudly raised the heads by the hair and swung them around. Others went to the injured men and slit their throats. The Hauhau took no prisoners.

The leader of the attackers, an old warrior whose entire face was tattooed, attempted to free the cheering prisoners. Finally, he found a blood-smeared key in the pocket of the dead captain. The chains fell, and the men danced and took part in the desecration of the dead.

"Prophet Kereopa told us to eat their eyes!" one of the men shouted, reaching for his knife. He plunged it into a dead man's eye socket.

Carol covered her eyes.

"You can eat them all," the leader said with a laugh. "Eat their eyes and their hearts. Sacrifice their hearts to the gods of war!" He pierced a dead man's chest with his knife and cut out the heart, dancing in a circle with it.

"Kill! Kill! Kill!"

The men gathered around him and pounded their spears rhythmically on the ground.

Paralyzed with shock and momentarily forgotten, Carol and Mara gaped in horror at the scene. Then one of the freed prisoners noticed the sisters.

"*Hau!* You caught their women! You caught their women!" He ran to Carol and tore off her coat. "Don't you want them?" He turned to the two warriors who stood on either side of Carol and Mara. "Then take them! *Rire rire!*" Howling, he ripped Carol's dress from her shoulders. "White skin, *pakeha* brats!"

Immediately, a group of laughing men approached and formed a circle around Carol. They grabbed her and pushed her to the ground. Others grabbed Mara.

"But you're—you're Maori warriors!" Carol shouted at the men. "You don't do this! My mother said you don't, it's not—it's not *tikanga*!"

The warriors paused for a heartbeat as they heard their language coming from the mouth of a white woman. But then they laughed.

"Maybe we learned it from your people," one of them said, ripping off his loincloth so Carol could see his erection.

She screamed as he plunged into her without warning. She twisted backward and attempted to kick him, but she didn't have a chance against the men who were holding her. As the first warrior raped her, others sat on her arms and clamped her legs. Carol groaned with pain. She tried to bite and spit, but her mouth was too dry to scream. She thought desperately of Mara. They couldn't do this to her; she was still so young. Carol tried to look for her, but her view was blocked by the warriors who were holding her down. Carol's assailant was still on top of her. He sweated and stank, he laughed . . .

Carol felt as though she would vomit. Everything spun before her eyes until the man finally got off of her. Then the others began to fight over who was next, which gave Carol a few seconds to spot Mara. Her sister stood against a tree, kicking, hitting, and biting the men who attempted to get close. Laughing, they taunted the desperate girl until one of the freed prisoners in the circle of rapists staggered forward and pointed.

"She's the one! She told the *pakeha* leader he should make us walk faster! Whip us like horses! I want to kill her. Let me kill the woman!"

The warrior approached Mara with a knife, his face twisting with hatred.

"I didn't say that! I only wanted to move more quickly," Mara said in Maori, defending herself. "I am a warrior's wife. I have nothing against your people. Leave me alone. I—"

"Kill, kill!"

The men danced around her. None of them seemed to believe that the warrior was serious. Mara tried to push him away, but he cut her hand with his knife, and she screamed as he spun her around to hold the knife against her throat.

"Don't you want to stab her with something else first, Koro?"

The warriors were still joking.

"If she's dead, it won't be fun anymore!"

"I want to see her beg!"

The warrior seemed to consider for a moment, and then threw Mara to the ground. "On your knees! And say, 'Koro, please, *mai merire*!' Say it, now! Beg me for mercy!"

Mara spat in his face. *"Pokukohua!"*

Carol gasped as her sister shouted the worst curse word they knew in Maori.

She saw Koro's knife flash, but then someone tore it out of his hand before it reached Mara's throat. The leader of the warriors stepped between them.

"Leave her! You are not worthy!"

Mara stared into the tattooed face of her apparent rescuer. The man returned her gaze, taking in her tangled black hair that had come loose in the struggle, her fine-featured face, flushed with anger, and her green eyes. Slowly he loosened the skirt of dried flax that covered his genitals.

"She's mine!"

Chapter 45

"Where are we?"

As Carol regained consciousness, she heard Mara crying. Burning pain radiated from her lower body, and her arms and legs were black and blue. Even her head hurt. But she couldn't remember having been hit. She had lost consciousness as the fourth or fifth warrior had thrown himself on her. Now she fought her way back with difficulty, trying to orient herself in the dim room. It was small, with no furniture. The architecture looked Maori, but with no traditional carvings. It was like a storage room. Or perhaps a prison.

"Is there—water?" she asked with difficulty.

Mara shook her head. "No water or food. We're in a *pa*. Probably Weraroa. They brought us here. I walked, and they threw you over a horse. You fell off twice. And all the blood—I thought you were dead. Like the others. All dead. All dead . . ."

Carol realized that her skirts were completely soaked in blood. Mara had draped what was left of Carol's bodice around her to cover as much of her breasts as she could. She, too, was in pain; Carol remembered having seen one of the warriors bite her.

"They locked us in here. I don't know what it is. Probably slaves' quarters. They were calling us slaves. The man who made me—he called me that." She shivered. "It's so terribly cold, Carol."

Carol felt the cold now too. Above all, she was thirsty. She wished she could wash, even if the water was icy. The men's sweat and sticky semen clung to her skin.

"They want to keep us alive?" she asked.

Mara shrugged. "I don't know."

Carol tried to sit up. The memories were slowly returning. "Fancy—" she said softly. "Did you see Fancy?"

Mara shook her head. "I think she's dead," she murmured. "They're all dead. All dead."

Carol managed to focus her gaze on her sister. Mara was sitting upright against the wooden wall of their prison, arms wrapped around her knees. She was rocking back and forth rhythmically.

"All dead, all dead . . ."

"Mara, stop it!" Carol wanted to shout, but she couldn't manage more than a weak croak. "You sound like the Hauhau!"

"All dead, all dead . . ."

Mara's eyes were empty. Her spirit seemed to have escaped somewhere.

Carol sat up, gathered all her strength, and slapped her sister in the face. The movement caused a stabbing pain to tear through her ravaged body, but it served its purpose. Mara went silent.

The women started as something moved at the entrance to their prison. A very young man opened the door and pushed in a bucket.

"Wash yourselves," he ordered. "The prophet wants to see you."

He was gone again before the women could say anything. Carol dragged herself across the floor to the bucket and began to drink voraciously. The water tasted stale. She had to cough after the first sip, but it still quenched her thirst and made her feel a little better. Then she found a ladle, filled it with water, and held it up for Mara.

"Here, you have to drink. Pull yourself together, Mara! You're not dead!"

"Maybe I am . . . ," Mara whispered.

Carol threw the water in her face. "How many were there?" she asked softly.

"With you?" Mara asked back. "I don't know. It was terrible, they—they wouldn't stop, they—"

She began to rock again. Carol dragged over the bucket, held her tightly, and pushed the ladle against her lips.

"Drink!" she ordered again. "I wasn't asking about me. How many were with you?"

"Just one," Mara whispered. "Just their leader. It wasn't—it wasn't even so bad compared to . . . But what he did afterward was so terrible, I—I wished that the one they called Koro had killed me. Then—then I wouldn't have had to see it. At least you didn't have to."

Carol remembered the leader's words. *You can eat them all . . .*

"Did they eat the—" She couldn't manage to complete her thought.

Mara finally reached for the ladle. "Don't ask," she whispered. "I—I'm going to wash off the blood now. It's not mine. And then, maybe—maybe the prophet will kill us after all. It really doesn't matter if they kill me. I just don't—I don't want them to eat me." Mara broke into sobs.

Carol pulled her sister into her arms and rocked her gently until the young Maori returned. He was hardly more than a child, certainly not one of their attackers. She wondered how long ago the ambush on the convoy had been, and if the English would respond. Perhaps troops were already on their way.

"You should come with me now, to see the prophet." There was an unnatural gleam in the eyes of the young man at the mention of Haumene. "Can you walk?"

Carol struggled to her feet. Mara helped her up and supported her sister while trying to hold her bodice over her breasts. It wasn't unseemly to the tribes to expose the upper body, male or female. But it was important to Carol, especially on this day. She glanced at Mara's dress and realized that it was smeared with blood but hardly torn at all.

"I'll manage," she told the young man. "When we come back, could we have a few blankets? It's so cold."

The Maori shrugged. "They don't know what they're going to do with you yet," he said emotionlessly. "We'll have to wait and see if you're really coming back. Come now!"

The women followed the young man through a series of trenches. They weren't tall enough to see over the edges. The trenches led from one building to the next. The entire fortress grounds seemed to be crisscrossed with them. Carol had heard that they provided the warriors protection from enemy shots. Soon they passed a palisade fence, and a ladder led upward.

Carol pulled herself up the ladder with difficulty. She thought she was starting to bleed again but didn't have the energy to dwell on it. She blinked in the winter sunlight. The scenery reminded her of a *marae*. Various buildings were arranged around meeting grounds and drill grounds, each one with a *niu* in the center.

She didn't have much time to look. Two warriors met the women and drove them forward with their spears. They crossed a square between two buildings and then saw a traditional chieftain's house. It was built among a grove of trees, set apart from the meetinghouses, isolated from the tribe, and clearly *tapu.*

Two men were sitting in front of a fire, wearing chieftain's garb, with large, valuable traditional feathered cloaks against the winter cold. In front of them stood two other men gesticulating and complaining. They seemed to be defending themselves. It looked as though the prophet was passing judgment on them. Carol realized with disgust and Mara with mortal fear that one of them had been the leader of the attack. The other man was young Koro. Before, Carol had been leaning on Mara, but now she had to support her sister's weight instead. Mara's entire body shook. She stopped short, and only continued when the warriors aggressively poked their spears toward her to urge her forward. Finally, they came close enough that they could hear the men's words. Mara whimpered.

"I took her captive, and now I can keep her as my slave—*pononga.* That's *tikanga*!" the leader argued confidently, pounding his spear on the ground to emphasize his words.

"You shouldn't even be here, Te Ori," the larger man shot back, his voice sharp with rebuke. "You went against my very specific orders. Can't you people do anything right? First that missionary, and now this! You were ordered not to provoke the *pakeha.* What is so difficult to understand about that?"

"Kereopa sent us those warriors, at your orders!" The leader wouldn't allow himself to be intimidated.

"And they let themselves be caught. That means their faith was not strong enough. They wouldn't have been any great loss."

Mara, who was slowly becoming a little calmer, nudged Carol. "That's the prophet," she whispered. "Te Ua Haumene."

"Even if you wanted to set them free, you didn't have to do it like that," said the other man in chieftain's garb. He sounded gentler and more patient.

"We hardly could have freed the men without killing the *pakeha.* And we took their heads. We need their heads, Te Ua Haumene. That is *tikanga.*"

"We have enough heads," the prophet said. "And we certainly don't need any female slaves."

"Then let me kill them!" That was Koro. He glared hatefully at the two women. "They turned the English against us. They said—"

The prophet dismissed Koro's accusations with a wave of his hand. "Why should we care what women say?"

"You certainly may not kill them," the other chieftain said. "Can you imagine how the *pakeha* would react if they found the bodies? And you will certainly not take them as slaves either, Te Ori. *Pakeha* women as slaves—that's ridiculous."

"Who cares?" Te Ori said. "Do we have to act like well-behaved children for Cameron now?"

Te Ua Haumene rubbed his brow in frustration. "They shouldn't even be here," he repeated.

"I can't believe you just want to let them go!" Koro said.

"The younger girl is mine!" Te Ori insisted.

"They are both very young," the other chieftain said. "They shouldn't be here. But we can't just send them away either. Not after what they have seen."

"None of it should have ever happened!" the prophet said again. "I didn't predict it; it was not part of my vision." Then he turned to address Carol and Mara for the first time. "*Pai marire* means 'peace and love.'"

"Love could be a solution," the other chieftain said. "If we allow Te Ori to keep the girl, and if he marries her someday, she wouldn't be a slave anymore. Then you'd just have to find a husband for the other one."

"Never!" Mara cried. "I would rather die than be his wife. I—"

Te Ua raised a hand. "Silence!" he ordered. "You're right, Tohu, it would work. Since you want her, Te Ori, you can have her. As for the other, the first man who took her yesterday can have her. Find out who it was, Tohu."

Tohu Kakahi, the other man in chieftain's garb, shook his head. "No, Te Ua, it can't work that way. They must marry of their own free will. They have to want the men. Only then will they not run away as soon as they are free to move on their own. And only then will they speak in our favor if they come in contact with the *pakeha* again. Otherwise, the *pakeha* will not acknowledge the marriages."

"Why should they have to?" Te Ori roared.

Once again, everyone ignored him, but Carol wondered the same thing. Te Ua Haumene seemed to be taking remarkable care not to agitate the enemy. Apparently, he hadn't ordered the attack on the soldiers, but was actually angry about it. Carol felt sick. They were debating her fate as though she were an annoying piece of livestock.

The prophet toyed with a feather that had come off his cloak. "So we should set our hopes on love?"

Tohu smiled. Like Te Ua Haumene, he wasn't tattooed either. He had a narrow face; a prominent nose; short, curly hair; and a long, graying beard. His eyes showed something like amusement.

"As you said, *pai marire* is love," he said with a slight bow. "Perhaps Te Ori will soon be able to convince his slave of that. Let us keep them both as *taurekareka.* Te Ori, you caught them. Until further notice, they belong to you."

It quickly became clear that Te Ori Porokawo didn't know what to do with his slaves. It was even a problem to find quarters for them. Te Ori slept with the men in the meetinghouse. He didn't have a house for women, nor a good place to lock them up. For Maori prisoners of war, that was generally not necessary. A warrior who was caught and enslaved instead of being killed in battle lost his *mana* and the respect of his own tribe. He was seen as an outcast. The only *marae* that would offer him refuge was that of the enslaver, so he stayed of his own free will. Mara, by contrast, tried to escape from the first moment that Te Ori took her hand. The girl screamed hysterically and tried to pull away. Te Ori flung her to the ground, cursing and kicking at her until Tohu Kakahi stepped in.

"You certainly won't win her heart that way," he remarked. "Let her come to her senses and think about the situation. What did you do to scare her so much? Now, take the two of them to, hmm. Where did they sleep last night?"

The warriors who had escorted Carol and Mara to the prophet stepped forward.

"We locked them in a storage shed," one said. "Next to the kitchen."

Tohu nodded with relief. "Good. If you agree, Te Ori, they can be brought back there. You can give them food later, and tomorrow they can work in the kitchen. Get the key. But be good to them. Don't forget, it's expected that one of them will want to marry you within a reasonable amount of time. You'll have to make yourself attractive to them."

Mara wept the entire way back to their prison. Te Ori didn't touch her again, but he remained in high spirits. Laughing, he jested with the other warriors about taming his little slave and his plans for Carol.

"The *pakeha* have girls for rent," one of them said. "You pay, and they do anything you want."

"The *pakeha* are disgusting," another muttered. "Maori would never pay for a girl."

"Maybe not in a *marae*," the first replied. "But here in the *pa*, there are no women. I'd really like to—"

Te Ori pointed to Carol. "Then take her. We can surely come to an agreement about the price. Or marry her. I just want the other one, the wild one."

Mara began to sob again.

Carol took a breath of relief as the door to their prison closed behind them. The guard hadn't accepted Te Ori's offer, at least not yet. He hadn't had time. Immediately after the women had left the chieftain's house, the prayers had begun on the Hauhau drill grounds. The cries and rhythmically shouted prayers and commands had rung through the *pa* for hours. The stamping feet of the men as they marched around the *niu* made the ground shake.

In the meantime, Mara lay in a corner of the storage shed, curled up in the fetal position. Her body shook with sobbing. Carol tried to take her in her arms and comfort her, but she wouldn't allow herself to be touched.

"I want to die," she whimpered as Carol held a cup of water to her lips. "If I don't eat or drink, I could die."

"That would be stupid," Carol replied. She had been thinking about what she'd heard during their strange encounter with Te Ua Haumene. "Mara, this isn't going to go on for long. The English will soon storm the *pa* and free us. That horrible prophet can't do anything about it. He's already worried about what they'll do; otherwise, he wouldn't have been so angry about the prisoners being freed."

"But they're still recruiting warriors," Mara said. "They said there's someone called Kereopa—"

"Who likely has as little respect for the orders of his prophet as Te Ori," Carol said with a grim smile. "It's no wonder. Haumene doesn't know what he wants. On one hand, he's encouraging the warriors to kill, and on the other, they're supposed to be preaching love and peace. General Cameron is right; they will soon give up this *pa*. And then maybe we can escape. Or perhaps the general has already heard about the attack anyway and is looking for us. Bill Paxton will make sure of it. Maybe he'll even be here tomorrow! Don't give up hope, Mara. We can get through this."

Chapter 46

Bill Paxton stood at the scene of the massacre, numb with shock. The young sergeant from the last army base along the river had sent a messenger to General Cameron as soon as escaped horses of the dead redcoats had begun to appear. The sergeant also sent out scouts, who quickly found the site of the battle. Cameron immediately sent a search party northward under the command of Bill Paxton, who had requested the job. Now, a few hours later, the young lieutenant was staring at what was left of the prisoner convoy. He kept himself under firm control while three of his men staggered into the bushes to vomit.

"I've never seen anything like this before," a sergeant said. He was an old, long-serving soldier who'd fought in the last Maori war. "And I've seen a lot. Some warriors still know about the old Polynesian traditions and create quite a bloodbath, among themselves as well. But this—" He couldn't go on.

"It's even worse than what they did to the missionary in Opotiki," Bill whispered. "We can only hope that at least the soldiers were already dead when—" He blanched, trying to suppress visions of Carol. "Have you found the women?"

The scout, a member of the Maori auxiliary forces, shook his head. "Women not eaten, sir," he explained. "Warrior eats enemy for strength. And takes head to control spirit. Women have not so much *mana*. Not worth eating."

Bill stared at him. "But where are they, then? They couldn't have escaped. Are there any tracks?"

With the help of the scouts, he searched the vicinity to try to reconstruct the course of the ambush. It wasn't easy. The warriors had apparently held a Hauhau ceremony. The battle site and the vegetation surrounding it were trampled, and bloody footprints were everywhere. However, the scouts were able to find the place where the Hauhau had hidden before the attack.

"More than twice ten men," the scout estimated.

Bill suddenly paused. Was that a dog whining?

"Fancy?" Bill's heart raced. Was it possible that Carol and Mara had hidden—that they were still hiding, having mistaken the Maori auxiliary forces for the enemy? "Carol, are you here? Is that you, Fancy?"

Bill held his breath as the little dog limped out of the bushes, her coat smeared with blood. At the sight of Bill, she wagged her tail and rushed over. Aside from a cut above her eye and the injured leg, she seemed unhurt. But there were no traces of Carol or Mara.

"Where is Carol, Fancy?"

Bill crawled into the bushes where the dog had come from, and had scouts search the entire area again. But they found nothing but a depression in the grass under a bush.

"There lay dog," the Maori scout said. "Too small for human. Here no human."

"But there's blood here," one of the soldiers said, pointing at a place behind a tree where the grass was trampled. "Someone was lying here."

Bill nodded. Something must have happened in that place.

"Here's a button," another soldier added. "It's not from a uniform . . ."

Bill went pale when he saw the light blue, fabric-covered button. Mara's riding habit.

Fancy sniffed the blood on the ground and whined. Bill followed her and found a scrap of material, stained too dark to distinguish whether it had come from Carol's or Mara's dress. But he could imagine only too well what had happened there.

"Apparently, they do other things to girls than take their heads," he said bitterly to the scout. "Don't they?"

The scout shrugged.

"Well, what do you think the brutes would have done with women, Lieutenant?" the old sergeant said. He didn't know how close Bill had been to Carol and Mara. "They were raped and dragged away. If we get closer to the *pa*, we'll find the bodies."

"The women might also still be alive," Bill said.

The sergeant frowned. "It's possible, but—"

Bill silenced the man with a look. "We have to ride there now. Right now."

The older man regarded him warily. "We, sir? The five of us and the two Maori? Against the prophet's entire *pa*? It will amount to nothing, sir. We should ride back and report to the general. After this, he has to attack the bastards."

Bill nodded weakly. The man was right. The general had to be informed as quickly as possible. On the other hand, it went against every part of his being to leave his friends to their fate. And the dead had to be buried too. He couldn't just leave them lying there.

"Of course. But—"

"We could ride a bit closer to the fort," one of the younger soldiers said.

"We look for tracks," one of the Maori scouts suggested. "There, look, sir. There walked warriors. Back forth, one place to other. Celebrate, take heads. Then away, to *pa*." He pointed to the trail, and the footprints there were partly bloody as well. "Many men, one horse."

"They took a horse?" Bill asked in surprise.

That rarely happened; the Maori weren't interested in riding. The English soldiers liked to tell the story of the freshly crowned King Tawhiao, who'd wanted to ride to a meeting with the *pakeha*. After an attempt, he had gone the rest of the way on foot and had arrived with his face twisted in pain. The English doctor had performed a miracle of diplomacy and inconspicuously provided him with a salve for his injured backside.

The scout nodded. "We go, others make graves," he suggested.

Bill considered for a moment. "Fine," he said and took his gun from its holster. Then he turned to his men. "Take leave of the souls of your fallen comrades. We will say a prayer together as soon as I return. And then be ready to go. We will ride back to headquarters as fast as we can."

Bill and the scouts only needed to follow the trail for a few hundred yards to figure out what had happened. The group had crossed a stream, leaving clear tracks on the sandy banks. There were the prints of many barefoot men, one horse, and someone wearing delicate women's boots.

"They had the women with them, and at least one of them is alive," Bill reported a few hours later to General Cameron, who had received him in his study.

"Perhaps the other one as well. We are assuming they put her on the horse. Why would they have taken it, otherwise? Perhaps she was injured. We have to act as quickly as possible, General. We may still be able to rescue them!"

The general considered this for a moment, then slowly opened a cupboard and took out a bottle of whiskey. He poured some into two glasses before he answered.

"Lieutenant Paxton, I'm very sorry. In interest of the broader situation, I must decline your request."

"What?" Bill was so taken aback that he almost knocked the glass out of the man's hand. He startled Fancy, who was stretched out on the floor at his feet. Since he'd found the little dog, she hadn't left his side.

"General, this isn't a request, it's a necessity. We can't just leave them in the hands of the Hauhau!"

"It's not an easy decision for me to make." The general took a sip of whiskey. "Even if I believed they were still alive. The fellows may have dragged them for a few miles, but then—no matter, Lieutenant Paxton. From a strategical point of view, it would be a terribly stupid waste of human lives and resources to attack the *pa*. Think about it: The Hauhau have lost this area entirely. We control the entire river and the Waikato region, and most of Taranaki as well. My mission to bring peace to Waikato has succeeded. You know we have been steadily withdrawing our troops over the last few weeks."

"But this has nothing to do with your mission!" Bill cried. "This is about two women who have been captured. It's our duty to free them. Your duty!"

Fancy barked.

The general shook his head and pointed to the whiskey. "Have a drink, Paxton, and calm down before you say something you'll regret. It's my duty to free Taranaki and Waikato from rebellious Maori for the military settlers program."

"And you've done your duty?" Bill shot back. "By leaving an area that's controlled by a fort full of cannibals, where the settlers have to come to terms with the fact that their women and children could be dragged away at any time?"

The general's eyes flashed angrily. "Te Ua Haumene will give up Weraroa. All of his behavior in the last few weeks indicates that—aside from this attack, that is. And most likely, the attackers were acting in their own interest. The prophet himself has been showing signs of wanting to compromise. He seems to be considering negotiation. But regardless, he will leave. He can't operate from there anymore. That means my task has been fulfilled."

"So you're just going to leave the Hauhau problem up to another commander?"

Cameron frowned. "You are upset, Lieutenant, and I suspect you are in love. Because we are among ourselves, I will allow your impertinence to pass unpunished. I am very sorry about Miss Carol and Miss Mara. But think about it. If I advance on the fort with the few hundred men I have here now, we would have to prepare ourselves for a fight that could last weeks. The fort is easy to defend and almost impossible to fully control from the outside. Perhaps we would win in the end, but Haumene would escape before the fort was given up. They would probably all run away during the night. It wouldn't be the first time we conquered an empty fort. The women would be killed long before then. I can't do that. Paxton, be realistic."

"The governor might see things in a different light," Bill said.

The general took another sip of whiskey and then nodded. "He might. He probably would. We have never been able to agree about such matters. If you can't give up on the idea, go talk to him about it. It's likely he'll send troops. He might be able to talk General Chute into it. But that will take time, Lieutenant. And believe me, by that time, the *pa* will be long deserted. They are probably already packing their things now in fear of retaliation. Once again, Paxton, I'm very sorry. There is nothing, absolutely nothing, that I or the governor or you yourself can do for those women. Come to terms with it."

Bill's mind spun. Of course Cameron could do something—even if it were just to punish the Hauhau for the massacre of his people. But of course, he couldn't force the man. And alone, all he could do was—

The general seemed to read his mind. "I advise you very, very urgently not to attempt to negotiate with the Hauhau, and especially not to attempt a rescue. Try to see the situation from Haumene's point of view: Over the last few months, he's avoided any kind of confrontation. Of course he would never stand in front of his followers and admit to having lost the fight for Waikato. But he knows that's the truth. Now he wants to withdraw quietly, but this attack has complicated matters. Believe me, the prophet would like to hang the perpetrators on his own *niu*." The general laughed joylessly. "And now let's assume that the underlings also dragged two girls back to the fort. That compromises Haumene's position permanently. He can't talk his way out of it like he did with the missionary." After Carl Voelkner's death, Te Ua Haumene had spread the word that responsibility for the incident had been Kereopa's and Patara's alone. He himself had only sent men out to preach about peace and love. "He'll probably also try to get rid of the women, as quickly and permanently as possible. If he hasn't done that already, then he will certainly do so the moment you send negotiators or even show up at the *pa* bearing a white flag. He'll pretend that he's never seen Miss Carol or Miss Mara before, and all his warriors will swear to it. That's if you somehow got that far before ending up as the main dish at a feast. Give up, Paxton! You have no chance."

Bill lowered his eyes. "I hear you, General. But I will contact the governor, even if it's useless. They could have stormed the *pa* months ago. But even so, I can't go on this way. Carol was right. What's been happening here is a disaster. We practically drove the tribes into Haumene's arms. And in that, I bear some of the guilt. I would like to resign, General. You can throw me out for what I've said, or you can discharge me honorably. Either way, I'm leaving on the next boat."

The general took a sharp breath, and then drained the last of the whiskey from his glass. "I accept your resignation from Her Majesty's Army. Have the papers drawn up and collect your last salary, and go with God, Paxton. I understand your anger, but I don't believe I've done anything wrong. Aside from perhaps having waited too long to send the prisoner convoy. This incident will also be with me for a long time."

Bill spent two last sleepless nights in the officers' quarters in Patea, rejecting one plan after another. He longed to at least try to find Carol and Mara, but common sense spoke against it. Haumene wouldn't be willing to negotiate with him. And any attempt to infiltrate the *pa* would be suicide.

When a ship left for Blenheim three days later, Bill was aboard, filled with grief and guilt, followed by the unhappy Fancy. Once again, he hadn't been able to help Carol. He was afraid there wouldn't be another chance.

Chapter 47

For Carol, the worst part of being held prisoner came from watching helplessly as Te Ori slowly destroyed Mara. She herself had to endure being violated, but not by the leader of their attack. Instead, he sold Carol "in the *pakeha* tradition," though interest in this was limited. Te Ori dragged Carol out of her prison and brought her behind a house about once or twice a week, out of sight of the prophet who'd commanded him to win the women over. There, some young Maori warrior would be waiting, often bearing a gift. This wasn't like the violent performance at the massacre site. These were young men who had been introduced to mutual pleasure at an early age with the girls of their tribes. They were disappointed and abashed to find that Carol didn't have any reciprocal interest.

Carol realized how quickly it would end if she simply lay still. A little lard from the kitchen made the physical pain easier to endure. But nothing helped against the humiliation. As hard as she tried to pull herself together, she cried every time one of the men lay on top of her. It was embarrassing for them, and they didn't recommend Te Ori's slave to their friends. As a result, fewer and fewer men came to take advantage of his offer.

Te Ori earned far more money and favors by hiring Carol out for manual labor. The young woman worked from morning to night, carrying water, chopping vegetables, and stirring the huge kettles, while she herself was only given an occasional crust of bread to eat. Food was limited in the *pa*, and the rations were strictly controlled. There wasn't much left for the slaves. Carol feared they'd die of starvation and hypothermia. The women were given neither mats nor blankets, and little in the way of clothing. Carol wore wide linen trousers and a plaid shirt, discarded *pakeha* garments that one of the young men who had paid for her services had given to her. They were less horrifying than her bloodstained riding habit with the shredded bodice, and also a little warmer. In any case, the clothes and also the occasional piece of flatbread that the men slipped to her kept her alive. Someday it would be spring again and, according to everything she'd heard, they would soon be leaving Weraroa for another fort. Perhaps there would be a possibility for escape then.

Every night as she waited for Te Ori to bring Mara back to their prison, Carol scratched a letter into the wooden wall of their shelter with a stone. Bill and the general must be convinced that the women were dead; otherwise, they would have already tried to rescue them. If they discovered her plea for help, then they would look for her and her sister. She was certain of it. Carol hated her life in the *pa*, but she could endure.

Things were different for Mara. She was almost never taken to work in the kitchen. Te Ori tried to hire her out as well, but the young woman was entirely unable to work. After long nights with Te Ori, Mara was too weak, too injured, and too desperate to follow even the simplest instructions. Te Ori advised the cook to beat her, but the man couldn't bring himself to do it. Mara would immediately throw herself to the ground, curl into a ball, and stop moving whenever he raised a hand against her. Only a person who actually enjoyed making others suffer would have struck such a poor heap of misery. And Carol suspected that Te Ori Porokawo, the respected Hauhau warrior, was exactly such a person.

Mara never spoke about what happened at night. Carol only saw that she could barely hold the drinking ladle the next day. Mara's face was always swollen, and Carol couldn't tell if it was the result of beatings or weeping. Her younger sister, who had been so defiant and alive, wept constantly now. She seemed not even to notice that tears were always flowing down her face. The young woman spent her days curled up in a ball in one corner of her prison. Carol had to force her to eat their meager scraps. Soon Mara was a gaunt, pale shadow of herself who hid her face behind a curtain of matted, dark hair and hardly spoke a word.

Carol watched her sister's suffering helplessly, knowing that Mara wouldn't be able to stand it for much longer. She would die of Te Ori's abuse or some illness—if she didn't take her own life. Terrified, Carol tried to keep an eye on Mara. The proximity of their prison to the kitchen was useful for that. Te Ori didn't lock the women in during the day. He relied on the fact that Carol would be too busy and too well guarded by the kitchen staff, and Mara would be too exhausted to attempt to escape.

Carol continued to watch for escape possibilities in case she was allowed more freedom at some point. If she had to, she would force Mara to flee with her. But the *pa* was well guarded and densely populated. The trenches were almost always bustling with warriors. Only during the morning prayers, when the men were gathered around the *niu*, were they empty.

For that reason, Carol considered searching for an escape route while the warriors were shouting in ecstasy. But that was impossible with Mara. As soon as she heard the Hauhau cries, her sister was paralyzed with fear. She had also begun to rock back and forth again, and to speak in a monotone. "All dead, all dead . . ." Her pupils dilated wildly, and she stared with such a terrified expression into nothingness that Carol could almost see the horrors that played again and again in Mara's mind. It would be impossible to take her out of the shed while the ceremonies were going on.

Carol had grown accustomed to looking in both directions as she walked through the fort to get water. It was a job that the cook was glad to leave to her. The only well inside the *pa* was next to the chieftains' huts. It was a long way from the kitchens, and the full buckets were heavy. Carol usually fetched water while the Hauhau were occupied with their morning prayers. At some point, she had learned that slaves were considered *tapu*. But that couldn't be said about herself and Mara. There were even warriors who groped her as she passed them.

Almost no one there knew much about the old traditions. No matter how Te Ua Haumene complained about the lack of them, there were no *tohunga*s in the *pa*. The old priests and wise women had kept well away from the Hauhau movement. And there wasn't a single *rangatira*, such as Te Ropata of the Ngai Tahu, to guide the young warriors' physical training, as well as spiritual preparation. The men's education suffered for it. Te Ua Haumene's unit leaders didn't even organize regular training. They didn't need to if there was no strategy used in the battles; they relied only on blind frenzy. One didn't have to be a master of strategy to realize how outmatched Haumene's men were by the English soldiers. Of course, he had thousands of warriors, and they were prepared to fight to the death. But in the end, it wouldn't do them any good.

Carol became angrier and angrier at General Cameron and the English leaders. Now, after the massacre of the convoy, after she and Mara had been kidnapped, they should finally have attacked.

"What is your name, by the way?"

Carol whirled around, and the bucket fell back to the bottom of the well. She would have to repeat the laborious task.

But then, stronger hands reached for the crank. Amazed, Carol stepped aside for Tohu Kakahi.

"I can manage on my own," she said sullenly. "I'm fine."

"I was just about to ask about that," the chieftain said, and heaved the bucket up over the edge of the well. "How are you? Are you being treated well?"

Carol glared at him, and all her rage boiled over. She didn't care what he'd do. "Are you serious? Let me guess, your next question will be if we've fallen in love, here in your wonderful community? And if my sister is going to marry that bastard after he rapes her every night and beats her black and blue?"

Tohu Kakahi rubbed his brow. "I'm sorry, girl. It was the only way I could think of to save you, once they'd brought you here. Otherwise, they would have killed you and made it look as much like an accident as possible. That was my first idea, and Haumene must have considered it too. But he's content now that no one has come looking for you, gods be thanked."

"So I should be grateful to you?" Carol said with biting sarcasm. "And my sister should too? My sister, who I fear will take her own life because she can't bear the nights with her tormentor?"

Tohu shook his head. "I've seen her eyes. She is going through hell, but she is a warrior. In the end, it may be she who kills Te Ori. Stop her from eating his eyes. One takes the enemy's power that way, but also absorbs his hatred."

Carol stared at the man as though he were insane. "We are civilized human beings!"

Tohu raised his hands in placation. "The people here used to be civilized too," he said, gesturing around the *pa*. "Almost all the Pai Marire leaders grew up in missionary schools. You *pakeha* created your own demons."

Carol took the bucket. "And now you want to throw us into the ocean, so we can swim back to England. Yes, I hear it every day. What shall I call you, by the way? *Poua?* Hardly. Lord? Or prophet?"

Tohu Kakahi smiled. "Tohu. There will come a day when we all simply call one another by our names. We will be equal then, you and I."

Carol scowled. "Aren't I just a slave? Didn't you want to kill us?"

Tohu sighed. "We were wrong, we made mistakes. It's time to fix them. My people will have to keep fighting the *pakeha* even after this war is lost. But we'll have to find other ways. At some point, we'll have to make peace. Genuine peace."

"Perhaps you could start by setting us free," Carol suggested. "As a sign of goodwill. We could speak well of your people. Or you, at least."

Tohu shook his head. "We're not ready for that," he said regretfully. "We will be leaving the day after tomorrow—blonde slave, if you don't want to tell me your name. We are going to Waikoukou in Taranaki, where we will build up another fortress. But I—I will personally make sure that Te Ori isn't always in the *pa*. I will endeavor to keep him away from you as often as possible. From you and your sister."

Carol's eyes filled with tears. "She will be grateful for every day that he doesn't touch her."

Tohu nodded. "I will do what I can." Then he turned to leave.

Carol watched him go. Then she called after him.

"Poua," she said, "my name is Carol."

Two nights later, Carol and Mara were awakened by the sound of the door being unbolted. The evening before, Te Ori hadn't come to get Mara. Now she whimpered when she saw her tormentor silhouetted in the entrance to their prison. The warrior peered from one of them to the other until his eyes had adapted to the darkness of the chamber. There was a new moon, but the sky was clear and full of stars.

"You!" he said to Carol. "Get up!"

With quick, harsh motions, he tied her wrists together. He pulled the cord so tight that Carol feared for her hands. When she protested, he gagged her as well. Mara was trembling in the corner of the hut. He bound not only Mara's hands but her feet as well, before shoving a gag in her mouth. Then he threw her over his shoulder like a sack.

"You walk ahead," he ordered Carol, pointing with a knife. "Down to the river."

Te Ori drove them first through the *pa* and then through a side gate onto a path to the river. There were warriors everywhere. Contrary to their usual habits, tonight the Hauhau moved in complete silence. As Tohu had promised, the *pa* was being abandoned for good. Most of the men seemed to be heading to Taranaki on foot. However, several canoes had also been made ready on the river. The chieftain and the prophet would go part of the way by water, and Te Ori, too, commanded a boat. He was about to throw Mara into a partly empty canoe when a figure arose from the next vessel. Carol recognized Tohu Kakahi in his chieftain's cloak.

"Te Ori Porokawo!" Tohu Kakahi's voice cut sharply through the darkness. "Why isn't your whole *taua* here yet? We have been waiting for your canoe to depart. It's blocking the pier."

Te Ori lowered Mara to the ground. "I had to get the slaves, *ariki*. After all, I couldn't just leave them here."

"No?" Tohu asked. "Perhaps that wouldn't be the worst solution, now that we're leaving anyway. Or are you going to tell me that they're joining us of their own free will?"

There was muffled laughter at the chieftain's words.

"They belong to me," Te Ori hissed defiantly. "The prophet gave them to me."

Tohu nodded. "No one doubts that, Te Ori. However, you were given the task of treating them well. They were supposed to come to understand Pai Marire, and to love you. You won't achieve that goal with ropes and gags. And tonight, it was your duty to assemble your *taua*, get them into canoes, and bring the prophet safely to Waikoukou. You should have sent one of your warriors to get the women. What's more, it's unseemly for two slaves to share a canoe with the prophet. Now, untie them. They will ride in my boat, and you can be sure they won't escape. You will get them back in Waikoukou. Do what has been asked of you. It's an honor to paddle the prophet's canoe, Te Ori. Prove yourself worthy!"

Carol hardly understood what was happening as the unwilling warrior brutally tore the ropes from her hands and then turned to free Mara. Her sister clung to her, trembling and crying, after Te Ori had shoved them toward the *ariki*'s boat. Tohu Kakahi offered them a place in the stern of the vessel, far from the bench where he sat in honor. For him as chieftain, the slaves were *tapu*, and he also forbade the oarsmen to make any contact with them. As the canoes floated silently in formation up the Patea, the chieftain kept an eye on Carol and Mara. Even if Mara had been able, the sisters couldn't have slipped unnoticed into the water.

Perhaps later, Carol thought unhappily. There was doubtlessly a forced march through *pakeha*-controlled territory ahead of them before they reached Waikoukou. But if Carol were honest, she didn't really believe they'd have a chance to escape. Tohu Kakahi had assured Te Ori that he'd guard the slaves for him. His own feelings aside, it was a question of *mana*. He wouldn't break his word.

Carol sat up straight and peered back across the river that shone silver in the starlight at the mighty, soon to be abandoned *pa*. Unprotected, Weraroa would soon be in *pakeha* hands—just as General Cameron had predicted. His duty had been fulfilled, his goal achieved. The uprising in Waikato had been repressed and those responsible for it punished, and no one would talk about the innocent people who had been driven away.

The governor had gotten what he wanted. The land in Patea was free for the military settlers.

Chapter 48

Bill Paxton didn't know what to do with himself when he landed in Blenheim after the stormy crossing. He didn't know anyone there, and didn't want to get to know anyone either. After all, it wasn't his intention to stay. He longed for home. Unfortunately, he'd waited several days already, and there wasn't a single ship in the entire harbor that was bound for Campbelltown.

"They go from Lyttelton more often," a captain advised him.

But first, Bill had to get there. He was back down at the docks, considering buying a horse and making the journey over land when Fancy began to bark excitedly. She ran toward a stocky, red-haired man in an oilskin coat and riding clothes. He petted her as she leaped up on him.

"Fancy! What are you doing here? I thought you were with Carol on the North Island. Is she here too?" The man looked around. His gaze became mistrustful when he saw Fancy trot back to Bill, who approached, ready to introduce himself. The man assessed him with sharp blue eyes. "What are you doing with Carol Brandmann's dog?" he snapped before Bill could say anything. "And don't pretend that's not Kiward Fancy! I've known the dog since she was a puppy. This is her son." He pointed to a black-and-white dog lying peacefully on the dock. Fancy trotted over to greet him as well. She was hardly limping at all anymore.

"Of course it's Fancy," Bill replied, and finally introduced himself. "Carol—" He bit his lip. He didn't quite know how to answer the question that was in the other man's eyes. The man had doubtlessly known Carol, but should he speak candidly about her fate?

The stranger gazed at him searchingly. He seemed to sense Bill's turmoil.

"William Deans," he said finally, introducing himself. "Sheep breeder from the Canterbury Plains, friend, and well, neighbor to Chris, Cat, and the

Jensches. To the girls, I'm something like an uncle. So would you please tell me where Carol is? Something must have happened; she would never have left her dog. Is she—" Deans's voice became a whisper. "Is she dead?"

Bill rubbed his temples. "She's missing. It's a long story."

Deans paused for a moment and then pointed to a pub at the edge of the harbor. "It's probably one of those stories that's only tolerable with whiskey," he grumbled. "Come with me. It will be some time until the ship with my new sheep arrives from Australia. Let's go have a drink, and you can tell me everything."

It did Bill good to tell the attentive sheep breeder about the events on the North Island. He felt almost relieved when he had to end with the speculation that Carol and Mara could still be alive.

"I don't want to believe that they're dead!" he said fiercely. "Why would the Hauhau drag them back to their fort if they were just going to kill them?"

Deans shrugged. "Maybe as hostages? They could threaten to kill them if they were under siege. Either that or the fellows decided they liked them and wanted to keep them. You never know what's going through their heads. No matter. The chances that they've survived are rather small. Your general was right about that. He couldn't set an entire army into motion just to find their bodies. Hope can be deceptive, young man. Especially when we are very fond of someone. What hopes we all had for Cat and Chris's return. The girls didn't want to believe they were dead."

Deans sighed as he drained his glass, and then ordered two beers. "Do Ida and Karl know yet?"

Bill slumped against the bar, then nodded slowly. "I sent a telegram as soon as I got here. She's—" He hung his head in his hands. "Mrs. Jensch has been very gracious, thanking me for trying to help, but I can tell they don't know whether to mourn their children or storm the *pa* themselves."

"No, no," Deans said, "we can't have them putting themselves in danger too. Between Ida's skill with a shotgun and Karl's past as a mediator, they might convince themselves they have a chance! I'll get in touch right away, tell them what I told you about respecting the general's decision so they don't make things worse. Convince them to stay in Russell while I make some discreet inquiries."

Bill nodded grimly. "Thank you. Something like this . . . It's almost too big to even let yourself feel it. And then to be told there's nothing you can do?"

"A parent's worst nightmare," Deans agreed. "My heart breaks for the whole family. It's almost a relief Cat's gone. I can make Ida and Karl hear sense, but there'd be no stopping Cat rushing off to save the girls and getting herself killed too."

"How are things at the farm?" Bill asked, needing to change the subject. "Have you heard anything about Linda? Do you think someone should tell her?"

Deans's brow creased. "No. God, no. Poor thing would worry herself to death over her sisters, and she's got enough to deal with just now. Linda wrote to us from Otago in the first few weeks. There was nothing left of the gold rush. She was quite circumspect, but it's clear she's barely scraping by, and the misfortune goes beyond that. It's that Fitz character she married. At least that's what my wife says. I don't read between the lines much. As for the farm, well, Jane knows that no one is happy about her stealing her neighbors' land. The Maori aren't really going along with it. They never really understood why they had to keep working so hard, even though they've long since had everything they wished for. Besides, they liked Chris and Cat, and the girls practically grew up in their village. Rumor has it that's also why Jane and Te Haitara's son ran away. Jane doesn't like to admit it. Whenever the subject comes up, she dishes up some tale about a school on the North Island. But people say he just left. He was angry about what she did to Rata Station. He was also in love with the little Jensch girl."

"Mara?" Bill asked, pained at the thought of the beautiful, self-assured girl.

William Deans smiled sadly. "Yes, it turned out to be quite a tempest in a teapot. Jane was dead set against it, even though Mara surely would have brought quite a few sheep into the marriage. Pity about the girl—and the boy. Because if he ran away to the North Island as a young warrior, I can only say 'Hauhau.'"

Bill rubbed his temples again. This was becoming too much to bear.

"What are your plans now?" Deans asked. "Are you going back to Fiordland? Do you know how you're going to get there?"

A little later, Bill had a ride to Christchurch, and for the few days until his departure, he even had a job. William Deans had brought only one helper to drive the sheep. He was very pleased about the idea of a second, especially with a dog like Fancy, and he happily provided Bill with a horse.

"I've never done any shepherding," Bill admitted.

Deans laughed. "Oh, you'll learn fast, boy. It's not much different than with the army. You're the general, the dog is your officer, and the sheep are the infantry. Sometimes they're a bit dumber than your soldiers. They're also much louder, but at least they don't get drunk."

To Bill's surprise, Deans was right. The former lieutenant figured out very quickly how to work with the dog and sheep, and he even enjoyed it. Of course Fancy made it easy for him to succeed, and it also helped that he felt closer to Carol when he was working with the animals. What was more, the ride along the wild, spectacular east coast of the South Island made him feel a bit better. For the most part, the land here was untouched, aside from the occasional fields and pastures. There were no army bases, and no one had burned down the forests or driven away their denizens. Bill began to feel more at peace. His anger and uneasiness faded, even though his sadness remained. The closer he got to Christchurch, the more often he considered remaining in the Canterbury Plains and working for Deans.

But the notion of living close to Rata Station was too painful. So he said goodbye to William Deans and his farmhand at the estuary of the Waimakariri, as he had originally planned, and made his way to Lyttelton. There he quickly found a ship that was bound for Campbelltown. He spent most of the voyage holed up in his cabin, trying not to think about the lighthearted journey with Carol, Linda, Cat, and Chris that had ended so tragically. This time, the ship arrived safely in Campbelltown harbor, and Bill took a room in a hotel. He could have stayed at his aunt's, but that, too, would have reminded him of the painful days that he'd spent there with Carol and Linda. He planned to look for a good horse the next day, to buy it and ride home. First, he would help on his parents' farm. He'd figure out the rest later.

He'd planned to go to bed early, but felt caged up in the room. There was a pub next to the hotel where he could get a drink so he could relax enough to sleep. Unhappily, he went in and ordered a whiskey, then hid in a corner of the bar with it. The last thing he was interested in was company, so he looked up reluctantly when someone spoke to him.

"Excuse me, mayhaps I mistook ye for someone else," a man said, "but weren't ye among the survivors of the *General Lee*?"

Bill frowned. "Yes. But to be honest, that's not something I really want to talk about."

The man smiled wanly. "I understand—ye lost someone. I won't rub salt in yer wounds, it's just that I knew yer face. Ye were at the docks so often whilst I was searching fer survivors with my ship. Perhaps ye remember, Captain Rawley of the *Hampshire*."

Bill did have a vague recollection of the ship's name.

"It was a tough time," Rawley said, and took a swallow of his beer. "May I sit with ye?"

Bill still didn't feel like having a conversation, but he didn't want to be impolite. Without smiling, he pulled out the stool to his left for the short, strong man. Rawley had an open face, a full beard, a hooked nose, and intelligent-looking dark eyes.

"I survived a shipwreck once meself," he said, after he'd taken a seat. "I sat on a deserted island for three days afore I was rescued."

Bill's interest was piqued. "You were a castaway? Do you think it's possible that anyone from the *General Lee* is still alive?"

Rawley shook his head. "Back then, we searched all of the islands around. 'Course, the boats could have drifted farther toward the Antarctic. But it's hard to say if anyone could have survived there for a year and a half. Mayhaps we'll soon find out. At least the boat might still be found, even if the people have died."

Bill blinked in confusion. "You'll find out soon? How can that be?"

Rawley took another swallow of his beer. "I managed to squeeze the budget for the voyage out of the government," he declared proudly. "To the Auckland Islands, the Antipodes Islands, and the Bounty Islands—all the cold, barren islands along the Great Circle shipping route."

The Great Circle route was the preferred shipping route from southern Australia to Europe.

"What are you planning to do there?" Bill asked. "Are you seriously considering searching for castaways? Do so many ships sink?"

The captain frowned. "Enough of them sink, believe me. But not many castaways can survive for more than a few days in that cold. They barely get out of the water with their lives. They lack warm clothing, food, and shelter. Even if there are animals about—ye've surely heard that on some of the islands pigs or goats were released—they have no weapons to hunt them. That's exactly where I want to go." The captain glowed with enthusiasm. "The *Hampshire* will make landfall at as many islands as she can and leave emergency supplies. Sea chests full of warm clothing, blankets, compasses, tools, matches, cooking utensils, and fishing gear. A little jerky and hardtack for the first days, and guns with ammunition for the islands with animals. If we pack properly, mayhaps we'll also be able to bring some livestock aboard the *Hampshire*. If the islands seem fine for them, we'll set them out there. It's a good plan, isn't it?" He smiled. "It just wouldn't go out of me head since I was sitting on me little island; I would have been too glad to count a few sheep." He laughed at his joke.

"A very good plan," Bill agreed.

He suddenly saw a chance to do something, after all. He probably couldn't help Cat and Chris at this point, or Carol and Mara either, but at least it would ease his conscience.

"Do you have work for me on your boat, by chance? I'm no sailor, but an experienced seaman. I know how to use a compass, and I'm used to close quarters. I was a soldier."

Rawley considered for a moment. "How good of a chronicler are ye? Bookkeeping and such? The government will want to know what has happened with all the goods they so generously financed. Unfortunately, writin' isn't really one of me strengths."

Bill smiled broadly. "I don't mind it at all," he said. "I'd be happy to keep the logbook for you. And otherwise, I am willing to work and have practical skills. Just tell me what I should do, and I'll do it. I can even herd sheep. At least, with some help," he said, gesturing at Fancy, who was lying under his chair.

Rawley raised an eyebrow. "Ye want to take yer dog aboard?"

Bill nodded.

"Won't she get seasick? There's a lot of wind down there."

Bill shrugged. "In the Cook Strait, too, and she survived it fine. In any case, I can't leave her here. She has no one but me."

Rawley considered for a moment, and then offered his hand to his new two-legged crew member and patted the head of the four-legged one.

"Good, then ye're both hired. Ye will keep the books, and hopefully the mutt knows somethin' about rat huntin'. The beasties could be a nuisance with all the food we're going to have on board. What was yer name, again?"

"Paxton. Bill Paxton. And this is Fancy."

The next morning, Bill reported for service aboard the *Hampshire*. The ship was a double-masted brig, and Captain Rawley would sail it with a rather small crew. So far, he'd hired three experienced sailors, and now Bill had joined. He was the youngest aboard. The others greeted him and his sheepdog with good-natured teasing. "Are you lost, boy? The next sheep farm is inland!" they said, but were happy about the reinforcement. In general, one needed about ten people to sail a brig, but few sailors had wanted to sign on for such a long, uncomfortable voyage. The other men didn't wonder about Bill's personal interest in the mission. No one there was on board for the pay; the other men, too, were concerned about castaways. Peter had been shipwrecked with Rawley, Gus had lost two friends when a ship had sunk, and Ben had survived two such disasters.

"I was treading water for hours before help arrived. The first time it was so cold that my balls froze solid, and the second time I was afraid that sharks would bite them off. To the joy of all the ladies, they're still attached!"

They all remembered the sinking of the *General Lee*. Peter and Gus, too, had originally helped search for survivors. Ben had been at sea at the time but had heard about it later. They all thought that Bill's enthusiasm for the voyage was good, as a way to thank God for his rescue. But they didn't share his tentative hope of still finding the castaways.

"We would have found them if they were anywhere in the area! And Billyboy, if they drifted as far as the Aucklands, they surely must have frozen on the way."

Bill didn't bother arguing. He would see with his own eyes if it might be possible to survive on one of the islands.

His first job was loading the ship, bringing aboard the chests full of clothes, blankets, tools, and all kinds of other things. The men stowed most of it in the hold. Anything that wasn't sensitive to water was lashed to the deck, to spare as much space below as possible. Fancy made herself useful herding a small group of goats on board. She barked aggressively at the rabbit hutch that the men also carried up the pier.

"She doesn't like rabbits; they compete with the sheep for the grass," Bill said apologetically and helped pull up the gangplank. He was excited, and could hardly wait to get underway. For the first time since the *General Lee* had sunk, he felt like he was doing the right thing.

Bill didn't look back as the ship left the harbor. It was a clear winter day in July, and chilly in spite of the sunshine. The wind was sharp on his face, but he didn't mind. Finally, at last, he felt something like hope again.

Almost eight hundred miles to the north, General Cameron's troops took Weraroa *pa*. The men searched the deserted fort thoroughly, and toward the evening, a young lieutenant approached his commanders.

"It's about the kidnapped women," he said excitedly. "Lieutenant Paxton was right—they're alive! Or at least they were. We found a message." He held out a piece of paper to Cameron onto which he'd copied the plea for help. "This was carved into a beam in one of the huts."

Mara Jensch
Carol Brandmann
Slaves
Help!

General Cameron read it thoughtfully. "Well . . . ," he said slowly, "of course no one could have known that. And now they're no longer in my jurisdiction. Inform the governor and General Chute. The Maori in Taranaki are their problem now."

Chapter 49

"I've heard that you're planning to give up service entirely."

Four months after Carl Voelkner's murder, Franz Lange was standing in front of George Selwyn, the bishop of Auckland, with his head bowed. After his escape from Opotiki, Franz had found shelter in a quiet parish near the city. The priest there had been a friend of Voelkner's. He had received the news of his death from Franz, and had offered the young missionary refuge and work. "You surely need some time to get over all that," he'd said in a kind, fatherly manner, and had kept Franz busy helping with church services and in the Sunday school. But in the long run, the little community didn't need two pastors.

Franz wasn't surprised when the bishop had summoned him, but he hadn't expected such direct words at their first meeting. Franz's face turned red. He'd shared his plans with the pastor in Auckland under the pledge of secrecy.

"I—" Franz searched desperately for words. There was no way he could admit that he almost died of fear every time he even thought about entering a *marae* again.

But the bishop raised a hand to stop him. "Don't even begin with excuses. I'm not going to accept your resignation anyway. You can't quit serving God, Reverend Lange! I will assign you to a new location, and you will go there joyfully, with full trust in the goodness of God. Do we understand each other?"

"Yes—no—I—" Franz bit his lip. He certainly couldn't tell the bishop how much he'd been doubting the goodness of God.

"Fine," the bishop said. "Then we come to your new assignment. We have chosen you because you are particularly good at working with children. That much I have gleaned from your records."

Franz nodded and felt a burst of hope. Perhaps he would be given a teaching position at a school like Tuahiwi, near Christchurch.

"Have you ever heard of the missionary station at Waikanae?" the bishop asked.

Franz's hopes fell. "Samuel Williams worked there," he said. Williams had been one of the first and best-known representatives of the Church Missionary Society. "But aren't they planning to give it up?"

The bishop nodded. "That's right. It's not worthwhile anymore since the Te Ati Awa tribe moved away. They had land in Taranaki that the governor wanted to give to English settlers. In order to prevent it, the chieftain moved there."

"And there was a flu epidemic, wasn't there?" Franz shivered at the memory of the typhoid epidemic in Opotiki. "Many of the Maori died."

The bishop waved this away in irritation. After all, it seemed clear that illnesses such as influenza, typhoid, and measles had been brought to New Zealand by the *pakeha*, and perhaps by the missionaries themselves.

"Do you want to reopen the mission?" Franz asked quickly to change the subject. "Are people there again?"

The bishop shook his head. "No, the Maori are gone. But their houses are still there. And the governor has nothing against us using them."

"As mission buildings?" Franz asked.

"Not exactly." The bishop toyed with his quill and inkpot. "There's an old Maori *pa*, ten miles to the southwest of Otaki. It would be ideal for our purposes, and well fenced."

"A prison?" Franz inquired, horrified.

The bishop laughed. "No, of course not. An orphanage. You, Reverend Lange, will manage it. As a result of the war and land disputes in the past few years, we are finding more and more Maori children. Orphans and abandoned children, dispersed over the entire area."

"But surely they wouldn't abandon their children!" Franz objected.

The bishop shrugged. "Let us say that in the process of war trials, children are often separated from their parents. Forcibly. Someone has to take care of them, and the settlers' interest in adopting Maori children has declined. They're all afraid they'll be raising a little Hauhau warrior. So, we need a place for them to go. Otaki is in the right place. It's part of the Kapiti Coast District, which was never fought over, but close enough to Taranaki and Waikato to be able to bring the children there without great effort. So far there are about ten orphans in Otaki, being taken care of by local clergy. They are completely out of their depth. So, go on your way as quickly as possible, Reverend Lange. Have a look at the *pa*—"

"Is it really deserted?" Franz asked. "I don't have to worry about a regiment of crazy Hauhau warriors attacking and trying to take it back, do I?"

The bishop shrugged again. "One has to worry about the Hauhau attacking all over the North Island," he said impatiently. "Times are hard. It never used to be a problem. Someone should have smoked out that false prophet much sooner. But the Te Ati Awa, who built the fort, left of their own free will. There's nothing to be taken back. What's more, the mission land was a gift from that chieftain—what was his name? Te Rauparaha. As far as that is concerned—"

"The chieftain gave us the land that his fort was built on?" Franz inquired skeptically.

The bishop pursed his lips. "We see it that way, and the governor supports us. Don't be so fainthearted, Lange. Go there, make the *pa* habitable for the children, and recruit more personnel in the area. You will be given a small stipend. I will also send one or two missionaries to help you as soon as I can. But at first, you'll have to make do on your own. Will you be able to manage?"

It wasn't really a question, and Franz suppressed a sigh.

"With the help of God, I will manage," he said, resigned to his fate.

The bishop nodded, cast a glance at the crucifix on the wall, and folded his hands. "Let us pray together for his assistance. And also for Reverend Voelkner's soul. He was taken from us so cruelly while serving the Lord. Lord, have mercy upon us."

Franz tried to join him in prayer, but in his mind, there was nothing but an echo of the Hauhau warriors' cries of *mai merire*. They, too, had pleaded for mercy.

A few days later, Franz was on his way to Otaki. In order to avoid the still-turbulent inland areas of the North Island, he first took a ship to Wellington and continued with a military convoy. The road from Wellington to Waikato was well maintained. Franz felt safe during the journey, and he didn't feel threatened in Okati either. He hardly saw any Maori at all. Apparently, only a few elderly people had stayed there when their tribe had relocated. There were white settlers for the most part, who kept farms in the area or had small shops in the town. The central point of the settlement was Rangiatea Church. It had been built at the initiative of Te Rauparaha, and its architecture united the building styles of the Maori and the settlers. Franz went there briefly to pray and then to the parsonage to meet Reverend Bates. Here, he expected to get a look at his future charges. After all, the bishop had told him that the reverend and his wife had taken in some of the children for the time being. So Franz steeled himself for the sight of potentially hostile Maori adolescents. But the door was opened for him by a strawberry-blonde girl wearing a tidy house dress with an apron and bonnet.

"What can I do for you?"

Her eyes were blue, and there were freckles sprinkled across her small nose. She was clearly English. On one hand, Franz felt more relaxed, and on the other, he was confused. The house seemed terribly quiet. He wondered if there were really children staying there.

The girl frowned when Franz told her his business. "I'll tell my father right away," she said kindly. "Or my mother. I think my father has gone out."

A few moments later, Franz was sitting in an orderly drawing room drinking weak tea with a gaunt, stern-looking reverend's wife. Louisa Bates didn't have much in common with her pretty daughter. She herself had brown hair and dark eagle eyes. She reminded Franz of his father, somehow.

"The children are so stubborn," she was saying. Since Franz had explained about his new assignment, she had been giving voice to the exasperation that she and her husband experienced daily with the Maori children. "They refuse to eat, refuse to talk, and are dirty. They relieve themselves wherever they happen to see fit. The entire barn stinks—"

"You're keeping children in a barn?" Franz asked. It was the middle of winter. A cheerful fire was burning in the Bates' hearth.

"Yes, do you expect us to bring them into the house?" Mrs. Bates retorted. "You will see them soon, Reverend. They're little savages. Completely uncivilized."

Franz rubbed his temples. "Isn't that precisely our job, to civilize these children?"

Mrs. Bates glared at him as if he were out of his mind. "If it's anyone's job, it's yours! We want nothing to do with them. Of course we've done our Christian duty and have offered them shelter. But now that you're here—take them with you, Reverend, and civilize them. Leave first thing tomorrow morning, if possible."

Franz was taken aback, and felt sorry for the children. He would have wished for a kinder foster mother for children who'd been separated from their tribes and were being confronted with new customs and a new language.

"I don't know if I will be able to make the *pa* habitable by tomorrow," he said cautiously. "But I would like to meet the children. Today, if I can. Is that possible?"

Mrs. Bates glanced at a finely crafted grandfather clock that must have been imported from England. "Actually, we won't be able to avoid it," she said. "In half an hour, my husband will hold the evening sermon, and we always require the children to attend. As well as our houseguests. You will be staying the night, I assume, Reverend? And after that, I will bring the children their dinner. Come with me if you want, and you'll see right away what I've had to deal with."

Franz wasn't particularly enthusiastic about the Bateses' hospitality. Just the thought that he couldn't attend the evening sermon of his own volition, but instead was expected to do so, spoiled the joy of it for him. On the other hand, he had no money for a guesthouse, and there didn't seem to be one in Otaki anyway. It was already too late to go to the *pa* that evening and tidy up a few rooms.

Franz thanked her for the invitation and moved into an austere guest room in the back of the house. It was possible to see the barn from there. It had no windows, and the doors were closed. How could they keep children in there? He considered going over directly and perhaps even renouncing the comforts of the house to spend the night with his future charges. Surely at least some of the children were afraid of the dark. But then he decided to get a closer look at them first. For all the pity and kindness he felt, these were Maori children. Since Voelkner's murder, the mere idea of Maori filled him with fear.

Instead, Franz preferred to use the short time before the evening sermon to wash his face and hands and comb his hair. He hoped to make a good impression on Reverend Bates.

The pastor turned out to be a ginger-haired, round-faced little man. He was quite different from his gaunt wife, but just as strict in his beliefs and spoke of the children in terms just as derogatory.

"I never saw anything like it with the Te Ati Awa," he declared after he'd welcomed Franz. "Actually, they were quite pleasant. They'd been Christianized for twenty years; that makes a difference. These children, on the other hand . . . We've heard that the tribes deep in the woods, unreached by missionaries, are cannibals. I never used to believe it. But now, well, you'll see for yourself."

The pastor put on his robe and strode purposefully toward the church with Franz. It was mostly empty. Only a few, mostly older, people came to an evening sermon during the week. There were many seats left on the front pews, but when Mrs. Bates led in the ten Maori children, she directed them to take seats in the back. The four boys sat to the right, and the six girls to the left. The children immediately began to squabble. Apparently, one of them didn't want to sit next to another. Two girls were arguing in Maori, and two of the boys seemed to be close to hitting each other. During Franz's time in Opotiki, they'd had to keep the children from giggling and chatting during the sermon, not keep them from brawling.

What was more, the children's appearance had nothing in common with that of the missionary-school students in Opotiki or Tuahiwi. The boys and girls—whose ages Franz guessed to be between five and twelve—wore *pakeha* clothing, but most of it didn't fit them. The youngest girl, a tiny thing with matted black hair and terrified eyes, wore nothing but a skirt. Her upper body was bare. Franz was shocked. The child must be freezing, and what was more, the attire was absolutely inappropriate for a visit to church. Franz couldn't stop himself. He left his seat in the third pew, took off his jacket as he walked to the back, and wrapped it around the little girl's shoulders. An older girl immediately tried to take it away, but Franz stopped her.

"No! This for her. She cold," he said in broken Maori.

The children regarded him curiously.

"Ingoa?" He asked the little girl what her name was, hoping she would understand.

"Pai," the girl whispered.

Franz smiled at her. "*Kia ora*, Pai," he said kindly, and then turned to the other children and introduced himself. "My *ingoa* is Reverend Franz Lange. I will come and talk to you afterward. Now, let's all listen to the sermon."

The children's faces were blank. Mrs. Bates was right; they didn't understand a word of English. Accordingly, they had no interest in the sermon. But now that Franz was sitting with them, they didn't dare to keep quarreling. They limited themselves to casting surly glances at their neighbors. Franz observed the children discreetly. They were very dirty, and smelled unwashed. But Franz didn't find that reprehensible the way Mrs. Bates obviously did. Many were simply too small to take care of themselves. There didn't seem to be any siblings among them either.

After the sermon, Mrs. Bates herded the children back into the barn like sheep. "Your dinner is coming soon," she called as she closed the door behind them. "Din-din! And you, come with me." The words that she directed at Franz sounded no less severe. "You can help me carry the pot. Usually I have to ask my daughter to do it, but I don't like to expose her to the savages."

Franz followed her into the kitchen. The stew for the children had obviously been simmering for hours.

"May I try it?" he asked.

Mrs. Bates shrugged and handed him a spoon. The thin broth of vegetables and very little meat tasted bland.

"Spices are expensive," the pastor's wife said in reply to his unspoken question. "Besides, they wouldn't appreciate them anyway. Their table manners . . . Well, you'll see in a moment."

Franz helped her carry the pot into the barn, and was horrified at what he saw. The children had built forts out of the bales of straw to protect themselves from each other. They seemed to be living in the spaces by themselves or in pairs. Only after Mrs. Bates had placed the stew pot on the one table in the room did the group hesitantly come closer.

"Make a proper line!" Mrs. Bates ordered, her voice loud.

She obviously thought she could compensate for their lack of English with volume. The children seemed to know what she wanted, but still tried to shove their way in front of one another as they waited. During the distribution of the food itself, survival of the fittest seemed to be the rule. Mrs. Bates was careful to give every child a bowl of soup and a piece of bread, but little Pai had hers taken away by an older child before she could slip into her hiding place to eat it. All of the children ate as quickly as possible in order to keep their portions safe, which, of course, made them sloppy.

"Now do you see?" Mrs. Bates asked Franz. "No culture, no manners."

She gave second helpings to anyone who stood in line until the pot was empty, so the children were forced to rush with their food if they wanted more.

Little Pai and the other young children had no chance. It was no wonder that they were so thin.

"Well, do you want to get to know them or not?" Mrs. Bates asked impatiently.

Franz regarded the children thoughtfully. He'd already given up on his original intention of gathering them all in a circle and at least getting their names and a greeting out of them.

Now he had another idea. "You," he said to one of the older boys in Maori. "What called your *iwi*?"

The boy, who must have been around twelve years old, answered immediately. "Ngati Tamakopiri." He then let out a tirade, and pointed to a couple of other boys. "Ngati Toa!"

Franz pressed his lips together. His suspicion had been confirmed. "Mrs. Bates, the way it looks, someone has put children from enemy tribes together in one group," he said. "The little ones likely don't understand that well, but the older ones know where they came from and how bitterly their fathers fought against each other. We desperately need someone who speaks Maori well. Is it possible to find an interpreter here?"

Mrs. Bates snorted. "There are countless Maori in town. But none of them want to help here."

Franz sighed. Most likely, the local Te Ati Awa were also enemies with these children's tribes.

"I will try to take care of it tomorrow," he said unhappily. "And I will have a look at the *pa*. The children have to get out of this barn as quickly as possible. If they continue to be locked in here together, someone may get hurt."

Chapter 50

The next day, Franz went to see the old fort. The palisade fence was still intact enough to keep the children from getting away. Until the previous day, he would have objected to making an orphanage escape-proof. Now he worried that the older ones might try to make their way back to their tribes. And Franz didn't want to imagine what could happen if they had to travel through enemy land, alone and terrified. It was better to force them to stay at first.

The arrangement of houses in the *pa* reminded Franz of the mission at Opotiki. Only a central church was missing. The quarters were much less unfriendly than barracks. The houses were still habitable for the most part, and only a few improvements would be necessary. Franz could easily manage it by himself with the help of the older boys, as long as he found a way to communicate with them. Language was clearly the biggest problem, and Franz had already attempted to find an interpreter that morning. Unfortunately, Mrs. Bates had been right. His first inquiries to the Maori members of the pastor's congregation after the morning sermon had met with negative responses. No one in the town wanted to translate for Franz. That had partly to do with hostility between the tribes, but also because the various Christian missionaries had put so much emphasis on English. Most of the older and needier of the Maori who were still there simply didn't dare to acknowledge their language.

"They're Hauhau children!" one Maori woman told Franz. "We don't want to have anything to do with them. They'll kill a missionary or something, and we'll be blamed."

The story of the fate of the Te Whakatohea had obviously gotten around.

Feeling discouraged, Franz continued until he was distracted by one of the three pubs that Otaki had to offer. Of course Franz normally preferred to make a wide berth around such establishments. Recently he may have been doubting the foundations of his faith, but alcohol had always been described to him as the greatest temptation of the devil. So far, he had never taken a sip of it, and to him, a pub was the doorway to damnation. But he simply couldn't walk past this one. An argument was unfolding between the pubkeeper of the Blue Horse and an unwanted guest.

"Get out of here, Kahotu. I don't have any whiskey for you! Here, can't you read?" The short, spry Irishman pointed to a sign next to the establishment's entrance that read "No Alcohol Served to Maori."

"I'm not Maori," the stocky, dark-skinned man said. "Could be that I have a drop of Maori blood from my mama—"

"That drop is oozing out of every pore," the pubkeeper said. "But even if you were pure English, you wouldn't get anything here. Because you never pay for it!"

"Come on, Stan! Last week I paid for my beer," Kahotu pleaded.

Franz could now see the man's face. He had the bloated, red-nosed look of a habitual drinker.

"No, Harolds paid that tab after you translated the description of his miracle medicine," the pubkeeper said accusingly. "His racketeering will provoke vengeance someday. In the *pakeha* villages, in any case, they certainly won't trust him twice."

"Actually, the stuff isn't so bad," Kahotu said. "Maybe it won't actually heal illnesses, but it makes you forget them for a while."

"And afterward, you have a headache on top of it all. Look at it this way, Kahotu: you'll be saving yourself a headache tomorrow if you go do something else now instead of boozing it up."

Kahotu's brow creased. Franz noticed that he wasn't tattooed. He was wearing dirty denim trousers and a plaid shirt under a ragged leather jacket. His boots looked worn out, and Franz suspected he lived on the street.

"I can't think of anything else to do," Kahotu murmured, and turned toward the next pub.

Franz needed a few heartbeats to overcome his distaste, but then he followed the man and, for the first time in his life, entered a public house.

"Mr. Kahotu?" Franz approached before the next pubkeeper could throw the man out. "May I—would you accept if I, uh, invited you for a drink?"

The old tippler regarded him briefly and then grinned. "A delinquent reverend?" he asked with a glance at Franz's collar. "Since when do the likes of you preach in pubs? Well, I don't mind. I'd take a glass from the devil himself if it had whiskey in it. And God made the stuff, anyway—at least that's what the Irish say. Whiskey means the water of life. Did you know that?" Kahotu edged closer to the bar.

Franz hadn't known it, and didn't believe it either. He had to repress the impulse to cross himself. After all, he'd just managed to convince himself that the man had been sent to him from heaven. He couldn't very well scold him immediately for blasphemy.

"I couldn't help overhearing your conversation with, um, Mr. Stan," he began, and then dismissed the pubkeeper when he attempted to place two glasses of whiskey on the bar in front of him. "Just water for me, please."

The pubkeeper shook his head. "The only water here is for horses. Outside in the trough. Doesn't cost a thing. For men, there's whiskey or beer."

"Both for me, Jim," Kahotu said.

Two tall glasses of beer joined the whiskey on the bar.

"So?" Kahotu asked.

"I thought I understood from your conversation that you might speak the Maori language. Is that right?"

Kahotu looked around suspiciously, but couldn't find a sign that forbade native drinkers.

"Of course, Rev. My mama was Maori. You can see it." He grinned. "I grew up in a *marae*, and then later in the mission. Reverend Williams was there then. He wanted to save us all. Didn't really work, though, at least not with me. And it worked too well with the others—just look at that Haumene."

"So you're an interpreter?" Franz asked eagerly.

Kahotu shrugged. "If you want the Bible translated, it's already been done. But you must know that. Or aren't you a missionary? It looks like you've come too late. The mission here is closed, you know." He laughed loudly at his own joke.

"Mr. Kahotu, I'm from Mecklenburg, in Germany. Punctuality is part of our nature," Franz retorted without humor. "As is reliability. I would greatly appreciate it if you would decide to work for me."

Kahotu knocked back his whiskey. "What can I do for you, then?" he asked with a grin.

Franz explained the job. "If you agree, I can offer you accommodation in the orphanage. I would need you close by to interpret every day, and also to help with other tasks. The houses have to be repaired, and we have to cook and do laundry for the children. So far, it doesn't look as though I'll be able to find female help here. The people don't want anything to do with the Maori children. I sincerely hope that you feel differently."

Kahotu rubbed his brow and then drained his beer glass. "I'm not afraid of the Hauhau, anyway," he said, "and certainly not of such small ones. And I don't care what the people in the town think. But I have some conditions, Reverend: I won't pray with you, and I won't become a teetotaler either. I want a bottle of whiskey every day."

"An entire bottle?" Franz exclaimed.

"The stuff is cheap," the pubkeeper interjected. "I'll give you a quantity discount."

"But—but won't you be permanently drunk, then?" Franz asked skeptically.

Kahotu shook his head. "No, not until early evening. By then the little ones will already be in bed. And believe me, you'll like me better when I'm drunk. I only get into a bad mood when I don't get my water of life. So, deal?"

Franz sighed and wondered if God would listen if he immediately said a prayer of penitence. "I don't really have a choice," he muttered.

Kahotu slapped him on the shoulder. "You take things as they are, I like that. So, let's drink to good teamwork!"

"I don't drink," Franz said defensively.

Kahotu grinned. "And I don't pray. But still, you'll be having me translate all kinds of prayers soon, won't you? Let's make a deal: you drink a whiskey, and I'll say a prayer!" He raised the glass that the pubkeeper had just refilled.

Franz reached reluctantly for his own. Perhaps this was the first step on the road to buying a soul for God.

He managed a mouthful of whiskey and was surprised at the comfortable, warm feeling that spread through his stomach.

"Very good, Reverend," Kahotu said. "Then off we go to your *pa*. Or shall we go get the children right away? Do you want to preach to them today?"

Franz had yet to figure out what he wanted to say to the children, so first he brought his new employee to the *pa*. Kahotu laughed at Franz's worries that the children might run away.

"The Maori never lock up their prisoners," he said. "They can't go back to their tribes, anyway. The fact that they allowed themselves to be caught causes them to lose *mana*. Their tribes would never accept them again."

"But these are children!" Franz said, scandalized. "Orphans."

Kahotu shook his head. "They certainly aren't orphans. It's much more likely that they were kidnapped, as retaliation or some such. We can ask the older ones. I wouldn't be surprised if you have a few princes and princesses under your wing."

Kahotu's guess wasn't far off the mark. The two oldest boys burst out with their stories as soon as someone asked in their language. Both were chieftains' sons and belonged to tribes who were enemies. Their fathers had fought one another before the war with the *pakeha* had begun, and they had never been followers of Te Ua Haumene.

"But then, why were their tribes punished?" Franz asked uncomprehendingly.

Kahotu laughed bitterly. "Because the governor wanted their land, I'd wager. The little one, Paimarama"—he pointed to the youngest girl, who had shyly introduced herself to Franz as Pai—"is also a chieftain's daughter, and in her tribe, she is considered to be so *tapu* that no one is allowed to touch her. That's why she seems so neglected. Before those children can comb their own hair, no one will do it for them. That's surely also the reason why none of the older girls will help the little thing in any way. Technically, she should be fed with a horn. If she touches food, it becomes *tapu*. That's why Pai gets her food last." Then Kahotu pointed to one of the chieftains' sons. "Ahuru feels sorry about that, but he doesn't want to break any *tapu*. The others certainly don't either."

Franz shook his head in amazement. "Where are they all from?"

Kahotu spoke to a few more children and introduced Franz to another boy, perhaps ten years old, and a girl of the same age.

"Hani and Aku really are orphans," he said. "Their parents were killed after they resisted the forced relocation of their villages. They are very scared. They believe they will be killed. As for the others, all their tribes had their children taken away as a punishment. The children from any given tribe were divided between separate homes and missionary stations so they wouldn't band together.

And of course, these kids all belong to different tribes who more or less hate one another. This is going to be difficult, Reverend."

Franz pressed his lips together, and then he turned to the children. "My name is Franz Lange—Reverend Lange. I have been sent here to—" He swallowed. It wouldn't work this way. The children didn't know what an orphanage was or maybe even what a school was, and they certainly didn't want to become civilized. Franz started again. "I'm Reverend Lange. I come from Mecklenburg, far, far away over the sea. The ship that I came to Aotearoa with was called the *Sankt Pauli*. But that isn't so important for us *pakeha*. Some of us came from England or Scotland or Ireland. But here, we are one tribe. And I was sent to you to also make you into one tribe."

The children protested when Kahotu translated. Ahuru definitely didn't want to belong to the same tribe as Aika, one of the older boys. Two girls also voiced complaints. Franz heard the word *tapu* several times.

"I understand that none of you want that," Franz continued, "but it's not going to work any other way. I'm told you can't go back to your tribes. They might not take you in; you've lost your *mana*. But I will give you new *mana*! I will make you strong through the love of God. I bring you a new God. You don't have to be scared anymore about breaking *tapu*." Franz went demonstratively to little Pai and took her by the arm. "Here, you see? Nothing bad is happening—to the contrary, in fact. My God says, 'Suffer little children, and forbid them not, to come unto me: for of such is the kingdom of heaven.'"

"Is that why you kidnapped us, so we could get you into heaven?" Aika asked, and Kahotu grinned as he translated his words.

Franz sighed. "What happened to you was terrible," he admitted. "But perhaps something good can come of it. If you now learn to live in peace with each other, that's not only pleasing to God, but will also help your people. My God, too, wants all Maori to become one, just as the *pakeha* have all become one people on Aotearoa. God is saying: I want you all to be *my* people."

"Te Ua Haumene says that too," Kahotu remarked. "Shall I really translate that?"

"It's written in the Bible," Franz said helplessly. "Dear Lord, Kahotu, what else should I tell the children?"

Kahotu shrugged. Then he turned back to the children. "Boys and girls, we could talk for a long time, and argue for even longer. But then you won't have anything to eat, and I won't have anything to drink. Instead, let's start again from the beginning. The reverend and I are going to get a canoe. We will paddle upriver with it to our new *marae*. Then we can arrive there together and say that the canoe we came with was called . . ." Kahotu glanced at Franz. "What shall we name the little boat, Reverend? If possible, let's not name it after the Virgin Mary."

Franz almost smiled. He cleared his throat and gave the first name that came to his mind. "Linda."

"Good. Nice name. Immaculate, one could say." Kahotu grinned and turned back to the children, speaking Maori again. "So, you can say that you all arrived with the *Linda* at your own special part of Aotearoa. So, boys, which of you are able to row?"

It took some time before Franz was able to find a rowboat large enough to carry twelve people. But then, Kahotu actually managed to convince all the children to get into it. The oldest boys, Ahuru and Aika, both came from mountain tribes. They only knew about canoes from their grandparents' stories. They were so excited about the idea of rowing that they suddenly didn't care anymore whose shadow fell on whom. Pai splashed cheerfully in the water and sprayed the others.

"Now we just need a *haka*," Kahotu said. "A song for the tribe."

Franz thought for a moment, and began to sing "Michael, Row the Boat Ashore." An American missionary who'd visited Opotiki had sung it with the children.

By the time they had reached the *pa*, all the children knew the word "hallelujah." They sang it contentedly as Kahotu helped them light a fire. Franz thought it was also a good start for the word of God, and the first thing he did was to erect a large cross, in front of which he built an altar.

"Hallelujah!" the children cried as he stood in front of it to welcome them to the *pa*.

Two hours later, they were all enjoying a feast of fish and sweet potatoes. Kahotu and the older boys had caught the fish, while the older girls had searched the old fields around the *pa* and had been able to dig some remaining *kumara* from the cold winter ground. Franz made sure that everyone got enough, and was pleased when one of the older girls sat down with little Pai.

"Hallelujah!" she said enthusiastically when he praised her.

All at once, the children seemed to be having fun breaking various *tapu*s. Kahotu sat next to Franz by the fire and pleasurably poured the contents of a whiskey bottle down his throat.

"And now you take a swallow," he said to Franz. "After all, we have something to celebrate."

"What about the prayer?" Franz said sternly. "Are you going to say a prayer too?"

Kahotu laughed. "I can translate 'Michael, Row the Boat Ashore' into Maori. But be careful. The children have their new war cry now, and Archangel Michael is already involved. And that, there," he said, pointing to the cross in the middle of the camp, "is very much like a *niu*. If you start to get visions, I'm leaving!"

Part 6

TANE

Christchurch, New Zealand (the South Island)

The Patea River and Waikoukou, New Zealand (the North Island)

1865–1866

Chapter 51

Linda had once enjoyed Christchurch, but now she got to know the city's darker side. Fitz had no money for a hotel or guesthouse, so they continued to sleep in their covered wagon. Linda froze half to death. Even in the plains, the winter had been too cold for such a primitive shelter. What was more, no one wanted the Fitzpatricks anywhere near their farms or houses. They looked ragged and desperate after their journey of many weeks. No one liked traveling folk. Linda was horrified the first time they were scorned as drifters, albeit after Fitz had been caught stealing a chicken. He had barely been able to get away from the angry farmer.

The only place in Christchurch where they were tolerated was near a slaughterhouse on the edge of town. Slaughterhouse Road led down to the Avon, and they set up the covered wagon near the river, somewhat hidden by a small grove of trees.

"It's nice here," Fitz had said when they arrived. But the trees just barely blocked the view of the slaughterhouse, and the animals' terrified bleating and the stench of blood and butchery made its way through to them unhindered. It followed Linda into her dreams.

The area also offered refuge for other unwanted people from the city. Whores sold themselves on the street corners between the city center and the slaughterhouse. Tricksters and beggars who went about their business in the city during the day rolled up in blankets in the shadows by the buildings. No one chased them away. The butchers and the other workers went home immediately after their shifts. Stillness ruled, apart from Amy's tragic whining. The dog seemed to be in permanent mourning for the animals that lost their lives there. Of course the grove of trees didn't protect Linda's camp from the cold, rain, or wind. Linda was constantly chilled, and after a few days, she would even have preferred Arthur's Pass to where she was now. In the mountains at least, the air had been dry, and it certainly hadn't smelled bad. But the path over the Southern Alps was impassable. Given the current weather, attempting it was tantamount to suicide. They wouldn't even find the road under the snowdrifts, let alone be able to guide the wagon along it.

Fitz escaped from the depressing conditions to the pubs as often as possible. The only way for him to get money now, he insisted, was gambling. Now in winter there were hardly any possibilities for work on farms or with craftsmen. When Linda complained, he comforted her with the promise that he'd use the money he won for their crossing to the North Island.

"We can try our luck in Wellington. We can also survive the winter there," he insisted.

Linda tried not to think about what kinds of risks Fitz was taking at the poker table. The crossing wasn't cheap, especially not if they had to start from Lyttelton. The shortest way was via Blenheim, almost two hundred miles away. They would have to take the coast road and then a ship to the North Island. And Linda wasn't at all sure she even wanted to go to Wellington. It would hardly get her closer to the longed-for reunion with her family—she'd still need to traverse the whole island from south to north, and traveling through Taranaki and Waikato was still quite dangerous. She would have preferred to book a ship all the way to Northland, but Linda couldn't lie to herself: the fare for two people, a covered wagon, a horse, and a dog would be a small fortune.

The young woman tried desperately, against all odds, to remain optimistic, even if it was constantly becoming more difficult. She could barely manage to keep her disappointment and anger hidden from Fitz anymore. While he was off gambling, she lay awake half the night with Amy in her arms, trembling with cold and fear. The creature always barked when she sensed something was amiss, and Linda knew that none of the dark figures would be deterred by a little sheepdog. So, she hysterically held Amy's mouth shut with one hand and kept her knife ready in the other. If someone attacked, she would use the moment of surprise and defend herself.

Fortunately, there seemed to be a kind of honor among thieves, now that the Fitzpatricks had been accepted as such. Fitz saw no reason to stay away from them. To the contrary, he had excellent relationships with the neighbors. He couldn't understand Linda's fears. When he came home in the middle of the night and cheerfully waved five shillings that he'd won, after having spent at least ten on whiskey, Linda's relief was often mixed with accusations. For his part, Fitz complained because she insisted on keeping Brianna in a cheap livery stable. In his mind, it was a waste of money. Linda argued that the valuable horse would be stolen immediately in the slaughterhouse district.

"Or slaughtered!" she said bitterly.

To pay for it, she'd pawned the only thing of value that she still owned: her mother's necklace.

"I'll be back for it," she reassured the pawnbroker, and managed to get the piece of jewelry back for a few days every time Fitz won a little money.

It would have been smarter to sell Brianna, but that was the last thing Linda wanted to do. Without the horse, they would never get out of the slums. Their only chance was the covered wagon, and if they had no other choice, they could still go to the west coast. But then, when spring had finally chased away the winter and Linda was preparing for their imminent journey over the pass, Fitz appeared with his usual irrepressible smile. It wasn't in the middle of the night for a change, but early in the evening.

"Lindy, something happened!" Fitz said triumphantly. "Like I say, sometimes things go wrong, but sometimes they go right."

"What, then?" Linda asked, unconvinced.

She had spent the entire day searching for firewood. She certainly couldn't buy it anymore. So, she'd walked along the Avon, over the meadows where she'd picnicked and watched regattas in better days. Along the river outside the city, raupo and rata grew, and there were groves of southern beeches and kanuka trees. Linda searched several times a week for broken branches, but hardly found anything after the long winter. Additionally, the wood was always damp. Linda barely managed to make enough coals in an evening to roast a few potatoes or *kumara*, and at least to warm her hands a little. She might have managed a proper fire if Fitz would help gather wood, but he regularly "forgot."

"How would you like having a farm again, Lindy? With sheep for this sweet creature"—he stroked Amy's head—"and a pretty house for you . . ."

Fitz tried to take Linda in his arms and spin her around, but she pushed him away. "Don't make fun of me, Fitz. You know very well that we can't buy a farm. Or did you just win a thousand pounds?"

She knew that was impossible. That kind of money might be gambled in the smoking room of the Sheep Breeders' Association, but certainly not in the pubs of Christchurch.

Fitz looked disappointed. "You're never satisfied," he complained. "But this is our big chance. Lindy, I'm enlisting! As a military settler. I have to do a short basic training somewhere near Wellington. The army will pay for the crossing. Then they'll give us land in Taranaki. Twenty acres, at least! If I can manage to become a corporal or a sergeant, then it will be even more. There's a meeting in the White Hart tonight. For women too! They're looking for the pioneering spirit. And you have it, don't you, Lindy?"

Linda thought for a moment. She remembered that Bill Paxton had been working as a recruiter for the military settlers program. Bill was an honorable man, so it must be respectable, even though Cat and Chris had had doubts.

"Wasn't that land taken away from the Maori by force?" Linda asked worriedly. "That's awful, and what's more, it could be dangerous if they come back."

Fitz dismissed her concern. "Lindy, darling, they aren't going to put us alone in a dark forest. Every settlement includes at least a hundred farms. All the men are well trained and armed. No Hauhau warrior would dare to get anywhere near the place."

"Hauhau warriors are supposed to be fearless," Linda said. "Cross them and you won't be able to talk your way out of it like you do with everyone else."

As far as Linda knew, Fitz had never owned a weapon. Not even for shooting rabbits or birds.

"Sweetheart, I promise you will never even see a Hauhau warrior," Fitz said with a laugh. "Why don't you just come with me tonight and hear for yourself what the recruiter has to say. Or would you prefer to go to the west coast? They say the goldfields there are nowhere near as abundant as the ones in Otago once were. Darling, if we have a little bad luck, by the time we get there, the gold will be all gone too."

The day before, he'd been singing a different tune. Someone had told Fitz about golden beaches. But Linda decided not to rub his nose in it this time. The wind had just turned, and the stench of the slaughterhouse enveloped them again. Then the rain started and put out her miserable little fire. Linda reached for her only shawl that wasn't completely destroyed, and wrapped it over her faded, dirty coat. She wanted to make a good impression. Despite her misgivings, she preferred the idea of orderly military settlements to the lawless west-coast gold rush. And anything was better than here.

"Our offer goes out to all men under forty years old, healthy, of good character, and capable of military service. Anyone who is interested will be subjected to an exam here in Christchurch. Whoever succeeds will have his passage to the North Island paid, and his family's. There, you will be divided into companies, each with a captain, six sergeants, five corporals, and a hundred soldiers. You will be provided with quarters, food, and basic military training. Soon afterward, your land will be assigned to you. Every company will become a settlement, with land divided among the members. Depending on your military rank, you will receive between twenty and a hundred and fifty acres."

The captain, a dashing, slender young man with blond hair and bright blue eyes, was standing in front of the miserable-looking group of applicants. There were approximately fifty men. The few women and children among them looked careworn and undernourished. The families were, for the most part, emigrants from England, Ireland, and Scotland who'd come to New Zealand because of the gold rush. Perhaps they'd also tried to buy land and had been betrayed. They seemed discouraged and unhappy. But the men looked as though they were accustomed to hard labor. Some had surely spent time in the goldfields. One openly carried a gun, and the others looked hardened too.

Linda wouldn't have wanted to meet them along the road at night.

"During the building phase of your farms, the governor will support you generously," the captain continued. "You will receive full supplies and a salary for the first year, and you will also continue your military training. You will be members of the army, and you may also be assigned to campaigns, punitive expeditions, and guard duties in the name of national defense. However, you will never be put into service for longer than four weeks per year outside your settlement. If such service becomes necessary, you will be paid a full salary. Otherwise, you will be obligated to serve the Crown for three years. After that, the land will be your permanent property. You alone will have the power of disposition. Any questions?"

Linda raised her hand. "What if a military settler is killed?" She had been burned once; she didn't want to lose another farm.

As the captain reassured her that, of course, the full ownership of the land would be transferred to the widow immediately, Fitz regarded her with a look she'd never seen before. Was he disappointed? Angry? Annoyed? Guarded?

"Is it dangerous?" another woman asked.

The captain shrugged. "The government is going to great lengths to make the land safe for settlers. That's why they are being so strict with the leaders of the Maori tribes. Still, settlers are occasionally victims of marauding murderers or tramps. You will all have heard about the so-called Hauhau movement, insane criminals who know no mercy. But there isn't a safer place for you than in the middle of a settlement of military servicemen who have been trained to defend their new homesteads. Additionally, we will build fortifications—"

"We're going to live in a fort?" Linda asked.

The captain laughed. "In a sense, madam. At least until the danger from the Hauhau has passed. That can't take very long. Believe me, General Cameron and General Chute have everything under control. And all over the North Island, our brave military settlers are making sure that the serpent won't raise its head again."

A few people in the audience clapped. The captain took it as a sign that further questions and answers were no longer necessary. He passed around a list for the interested parties to sign up. Fitz gave Linda a brief, quizzical look. When she nodded, he wrote his name down.

After the meeting, many of the aspiring military settlers stood together and discussed what they'd heard. Almost all the men had signed up, though a few had been disqualified because of the age limitation. Fitz, sociable as he was, was soon standing in the middle of a large group of settlers, laughing and drinking whiskey. Linda didn't quite know what to do. She was hungry and tired but didn't want to nag her husband to leave. She kept thinking about the strange look he'd given her. Was Fitz worried about her safety after his possible demise, or had she reminded him too painfully that he wasn't immortal? Linda was slightly afraid of how he would react when they made their way back to the covered wagon together. She finally had some hope again and didn't want new arguments to overshadow it. As she made small talk with a few of the wives, she thought about how she could justify herself. Linda was tense and nervous by the time Fitz was finally ready to leave.

But Fitz seemed to have forgotten the incident. He was in the best of moods and put an arm around Linda's shoulders as they walked. In public it wasn't an appropriate gesture, but Linda didn't pull away. She patiently listened to his euphoric plans for their wonderful life on the North Island with a growing sense of calm.

"The winters are milder there too, Lindy. It's not as damp as here. You'll see. You'll like it better than the plains. And the neighbors won't be grouchy snobs like the Butlers and the Redwoods."

Linda furrowed her brow. Sure, Deborah Butler was a special case, but the Redwoods were lovely, down-to-earth people. What could Fitz have against them? She wondered if he'd recently happened to meet Joseph or his brothers in Christchurch again. She also wondered what their new neighbors would be like. She hadn't felt much connection to anyone at the recruitment meeting. They had seemed more like rootless drifters than frugal, industrious types prepared to conquer new land with harrows and plows.

Fitz, true to form, had no doubts at all. He was in a better mood than he'd been in for months, and he insisted on carrying her over the "threshold" of the covered wagon. The wind had shifted, blowing fresher air over from the river, and with a large dose of goodwill, one could even detect the first hint of summer. Linda could almost imagine that they were camping somewhere in the wild.

"Today, Lindy, our new life begins!" He laid her down on their straw pallets that were covered with blankets to protect against the cold that rose from below. "Pity we don't have any champagne to celebrate with."

Linda gave him a tired smile. "It would be enough for me if it just wasn't so cold," she said.

Fitz gave her one of his irresistible smiles. "I'll warm you up," he promised. He pulled a blanket over the two of them and began to undress his wife.

Linda protested. She only wanted to nestle up between Amy and her husband, wearing as many clothes as possible to stay warm and perhaps be able to sleep. She wasn't in the mood for making love, but Fitz was trying to excite her. Not as hastily and fleetingly as usual, but gently and . . . differently. For the first time, she felt something hard and pulsing between his legs.

"You never thought I'd ever build a farm for you, did you, my little sheep baroness?" he whispered, and positioned himself on top of her. "Admit it, you didn't believe it . . ."

Linda was bewildered by his strange words, but she was also wide awake and suddenly excited. She was wet, she was ready for him . . .

"Say it!"

Linda pushed upward toward him. "I didn't dare to hope," she whispered.

"And I did it!" Fitz exulted. "I did it!"

At long last, he sank into her. Linda welcomed him, gladly. She moaned and arched her back to feel him deeper inside, and never wanted to let him go. At some point, everything exploded in a delirium of sweet pain and relief. It was as though a door to another world was opening, as though something inside of her was set free, reeling through a sea full of stars.

"Fitz," she whispered, and pulled him into her arms as his warm seed finally emptied into her. "Fitz, I—"

"Say it," he murmured, close to her ear.

"I—I never imagined it could be so beautiful. It was so wonderful, Fitz." She kissed him.

"Say it again!"

Linda felt the stars inside lowering her back down to the ground. The radiant, wonderful feeling of completeness gave way to the old confusion. Was this not an act of love, but an act of subjugation?

"You—you did it," she whispered almost silently.

Chapter 52

Fitz's euphoria lasted through the next week. He'd passed the qualification test for the military settlers program with flying colors. He was healthy, and his reflexes, flexibility, and agility put him leagues ahead of the other applicants. He also impressed the captain with his intelligence, charisma, and charm. Finally, the captain offered him a promotion from the entry level of a private to a corporal, and perhaps even had his eye on him for a sergeant.

"That means more land for us, darling," he told Linda excitedly. "Corporals get twenty-five acres, and sergeants get thirty-five."

Linda didn't care how much land they would have. She was just relieved to be leaving Christchurch. But it took time. Once all the applicants had been tested, it was still necessary to book passage between the islands for the men and their families. All of that took several weeks, and Linda had to live with the fear that Fitz would gamble away the entire first paycheck he'd received when he was hired. They desperately needed the money to pay for Brianna's board in the livery stable. They were already in debt, and Linda might not be able to get her necklace back from the pawnshop. Fitz's salary had to be enough for both. On the new farm, she would need the horse more than ever before. The army surely wouldn't look kindly if their new recruits spent the nights wheedling money out of the citizens of Christchurch. Who knew if the captain wouldn't revoke his offer if he caught Fitz at the gambling table? Fitz was annoyed when she voiced her concerns, and of course continued to trawl the pubs. Their night of passion wasn't repeated. Sometimes Linda thought she must have imagined the entire thing.

But everything worked out in the end. Fitz increased his salary by gambling, which of course he'd never doubted would happen. He even had money left after Linda paid for Brianna's board. Now she turned the wagon toward Lyttelton

Harbor with a sigh of relief. Cat's necklace hung securely around her throat, well concealed under her dress and shawl. She certainly wouldn't be showing it off. She didn't trust Fitz's new comrades or their wives.

When they arrived in Lyttelton, they found that the army had paid the crossing for Fitz and Linda, but not for the horse and wagon. Fitz took this as another vindication.

"If I hadn't won at poker, Lindy, we would have been in trouble."

Linda smiled wanly, convinced that the captain would have offered them an advance on Fitz's next salary if necessary. The young recruiter was delighted with Brianna. He praised the horse and the well-cared-for harness, and was very courteous to Linda. She conversed with him a little and reinforced the good impression that Fitz had made.

"You're exactly what we want for our settlement program," he told her. "People with a pioneering spirit, as well as military and farming skills, who are ready to devote all of their strength to the development of their land."

Linda nodded politely and wondered what military skills he was talking about. Fitz explained later with a smile.

"Oh, I told him I'd been a cadet at the Royal Military Academy," he said. "In London—Woolwich. Unfortunately, I had to leave after a year because my father died. A tragic turn of events."

Linda slapped her forehead. "Fitz, if he finds out it's not true—"

Fitz laughed. "Maybe it *is* true, sweetheart," he said, grinning at her. "And besides, you don't really think they're going to check, do you? Why should they? I only told him in passing. It has nothing to do with my acceptance as a military settler. At least not officially."

The ship took the military settlers directly to Whanganui. For Linda, the journey of several days had been torture. She had battled constantly with nausea, caused not only by the movement of the waves but also the remaining trauma from the sinking of the *General Lee*. She couldn't even relax in Fitz's arms, though the couple slept relatively comfortably in the covered wagon, which had been lashed to the deck. The other settlers shared accommodation in steerage. Fitz cared for his wife devotedly for the first few days, but lost patience when not even his attention could comfort her. Below deck, the poker and blackjack players found one another, and once again, Fitz was coming back late at night with whiskey on his breath. She listened to his satisfied snores with a pounding heart as terrible scenes played before her mind's eye. The covered wagon could come loose and roll overboard. The ship could spring a leak and sink. A horde of insane Hauhau warriors in canoes could attack. Linda clung to Amy and lost herself in visions of blood and death. The company of the other settlers' wives didn't help her overcome her fears. In fact, they didn't even provide any distraction. Most of the few women and children seemed impassive and apathetic. One thin redhead named Mary was selling whiskey. The captain had been very strict about not allowing the men to bring alcohol on board, but he hadn't checked the women and children. Mary spent the money she earned at the poker table. She tippled and gambled with the men at night, and the other women spread rumors that she was prostituting her daughter. In any case, Linda didn't like any of the women enough to make friends. No one helped her either when she staggered weakly and was in danger of falling overboard as she repeatedly vomited over the rail. Linda thought of Ida's stories of her voyage on the *Sankt Pauli*, where the tight-knit Mecklenburgers had taken care of each other. Here, it was every man for himself.

Linda breathed a sigh of relief when the ship finally arrived in Whanganui. The town didn't seem threatening to her. Of course, it was influenced by Cameron's military base, but there were also Maori living peacefully here with the soldiers and settlers. Many had assimilated and were working—the men as scouts or farmhands, and the women in the army kitchens. Others sold produce or helped on the farms. It reminded Linda of the Ngai Tahu, how they'd quickly chosen to work with the *pakeha* on the South Island.

Once they were assigned to their quarters at the military base, she slept soundly for the first time in weeks. The cabin was spacious, clean, and warm. The dwelling seemed almost too comfortable, and she was overcome by worry and guilt again when Fitz told her with great amusement how he'd talked his way into it.

"The quartermaster thought I was the new doctor. His name is also Fitzpatrick or Fitzgerald or something like that. I didn't correct him." He grinned.

"But Fitz . . ." Linda ran her hands through her hair nervously. Fitz probably hadn't just left the man to his assumption, but confirmed it and offered medical advice. "They'll find out when the new doctor arrives."

Fitz shrugged. "By then we'll have been in Patea for a long time. That's where we're settling, they say. It's an area on a river, about thirty miles northwest of here. And really, who cares? The quartermaster will get a scolding, not me. And certainly not you, my darling. Everyone here will already be in love with you!"

And in truth, the officers whom Linda came into contact with because of the proximity of the cabin to their quarters were very kind and polite. But there were few; the base was not fully manned at the moment. The majority of the regiments were taking part in campaigns with General Cameron or General Chute. The others were preparing for new assignments. No one asked about Linda and Fitz's accommodations until Fitz's regiment was formed.

After the men had been given uniforms and guns, they were assigned to section commanders. Fitz's dream of being promoted to corporal or sergeant before the land assignment was dashed on the first day by Major Thomas McDonnell.

McDonnell was barely older than his men, but could already look back at an eventful life. He had immigrated from Australia with his parents when he was young, and had grown up in Northland near a Maori tribe. He had not only learned the Maori language but also had an understanding of their philosophy, strategy, and martial arts. He bragged that he could use their traditional weapons better than many young warriors. At some point, he had returned to Australia and tried his luck on the goldfields there. Afterward, he had worked in New Zealand for the Native Land Purchase Department, but soon gave that up and founded a sheep farm in Hawke's Bay. Later, he had worked as a freelance interpreter between the *pakeha* and Maori, tried his hand at gold panning again, and then joined the army as a successful leader of the Maori auxiliary troops. He'd fought on the east coast, and afterward at Cameron's side.

He took over the leadership of the military settlers' regiment at his own request. He planned to get married and settle on the farmland he would be given. McDonnell was known as a fearless fighter and a strict disciplinarian.

And he clashed with Fitz immediately. Linda never found out what exactly happened, but Fitz was unusually upset when he returned to the cabin that evening. He didn't have a single good word to say about his new major.

"He puts on airs . . . Thinks he's better than us . . . Doesn't listen . . ."

Of course, he wasn't one of the newly promoted corporals whose names were revealed the next day.

To make matters worse, there was an unpleasant encounter between McDonnell and Linda when the major was assigned to his own quarters. Here, too, the unskilled quartermaster had made a mistake. Assuming that the major was already married, he didn't give McDonnell an apartment in the officers' quarters, but instead a cabin. By coincidence, it was the one next to Linda and Fitz's.

Linda had just been baking when she noticed that someone was moving in next door, and she thought it would be a friendly gesture to welcome the new neighbor with a lamb-and-*kumara* pie. So she took off her apron, checked her quickly pinned-up hair briefly in the mirror, and then knocked on the door of the next house. She had assumed she would be welcomed by a woman, and wasn't prepared to see the tall, strong man whose oval face was dominated by broad sideburns. Her heart pounded as she recognized Major McDonnell.

"This is a specialty from my home," she said kindly, and held out the pie dish to the major. "Welcome to the neighborhood, at least until we move on. We heard that you and your wife will also be settling on the Patea River."

Major McDonnell's brow creased, and he made no move to accept the welcome gift. "With whom do I have the pleasure of speaking?" he demanded. "As far as I know, none of my officers are married."

"Oh . . ." Linda could have slapped herself for the faux pas. "Excuse me. My name is Linda Fitzpatrick. My husband is a member of your regiment. Unfortunately, not as an officer, just as a simple private." She smiled apologetically.

"Fitzpatrick? Private Fitzpatrick? Unbelievable! Now that little swindler is sending his wife to butter me up? He managed phenomenally well with Captain Langdon and that idiot of a quartermaster too! How did he worm his way into their confidence? It can't have been anything decent, if he's living in officers' quarters when he's of the lowest rank, and is so shameless he sends his woman over to flaunt it. It's pure impudence!"

Linda blushed. "Fitz didn't send me," she said. "I just wanted to be polite. I didn't think it was right about the cabin either. There was a case of mistaken identity, and Fitz, well, he didn't correct it. And really, it doesn't matter so much. I mean, if we're living here or the house is standing empty—"

The major snorted. "Of course it matters," he said. "By accepting these quarters, your husband lied his way into preferential treatment. He tried that with me too. Military experience, don't make me laugh! The man doesn't even know how to take apart a gun. And Maori-language abilities, ha! He can say hello, that's about it."

"I speak Maori," Linda said shyly. "Perhaps he meant I could interpret for him."

McDonnell glared at her. "I understood exactly what he meant, young lady. After all, he was speaking English, and that's a language he knows. Too well, if you ask me. But if we're attacked by Hauhau warriors, Mrs. Fitzpatrick, I won't need a smooth talker; I'll need a soldier who can hit a target. That's exactly what your husband has to learn. You aren't doing him any favors by attempting bribery and seduction, or whatever you were planning with me. I wish you good day, Mrs. Fitzpatrick!"

With that, McDonnell slammed the door in Linda's face. The young woman stood there in shock. She felt dirty and ashamed, almost as though she had done the lying and swindling herself. She wondered how much of the disaster she should tell her husband about.

Finally, with a pounding heart, she decided to take a page from Fitz's book. She attempted to smile and told him about her encounter with the general as though it had been a great joke.

"I—I just hope they won't throw us out now," she said nervously. "Maybe we should move without being asked. We could go back to sleeping in the wagon."

Fitz glared at her. "They won't throw us out," he said. "It's not worth the effort. We're leaving the day after tomorrow, anyway. But jeez, Linda, you just made the regiment totally impossible for me! What were you thinking? Attempting to bribe the major—"

"What?" Linda couldn't hide her confusion. "You don't really believe I was trying to bribe him, do you? Fitz, I just wanted to be nice. I didn't even know—"

"Then you should have found out before you ran over there and ruined everything for me. Now I can forget about a promotion."

Fitz, who'd already taken off his uniform jacket, reached for his cap again. "You did a great job, Linda. Congratulations!" He stormed out of the cabin.

Linda watched her husband go with tears in her eyes, and tried to fight back the feelings of guilt and inadequacy that rose up in her again. She tried to remind herself it had been Fitz alone who'd created the embarrassing situation with the major.

Linda spent half the night trying to think of the right words to defend herself. They shouldn't be angry or bitter. She didn't want to provoke a backlash that might hurt her even more. Fitz was so much better with words than she was.

Linda finally fell asleep in spite of all her worrying. The next morning, she found the bed next to her untouched. Worriedly, she began to pack their things. Fitz had never stayed away for an entire night. Where had he slept? What kind of mood was he in? How would the journey go?

Linda found Brianna in the barn and the covered wagon in the depot. A friendly Maori boy helped her pull out the wagon and hitch the horse to it.

"The regiment for Patea is gathering in the main square, missus," he said, obviously pleased that she could speak his language with him. "It's beautiful land you're getting, missus. Take good care of it."

Linda promised him she'd show proper respect to the land and would sing *karakia* to satisfy the gods and spirits of the people who'd lived there before. And she would bring honor to Papa, the earth goddess, when she worked the land.

The young man waved as she drove the covered wagon to the cabin, where she began to load it with their few belongings. She didn't need Fitz's help for that. But she was still worried. Where could he be?

Finally, Linda guided Brianna toward the drill ground. Fitz was surrounded by other men, and Linda felt tentative relief.

Private Fitzpatrick would surely be marching with the other soldiers. He couldn't ride on the covered wagon with her. Linda scolded herself for her stupidity. Perhaps the major had made him drill longer the evening before, and Fitz had tried to make peace by sleeping in the shared accommodation with the other privates.

She decided just to wave encouragingly at her husband, before joining the regiment's baggage train as unobtrusively as possible. No other settler's family owned a horse and wagon. The few women and children who'd come with their husbands were walking.

When Fitz spotted Linda, he immediately separated from his comrades and hurried over. Apparently, the marching orders weren't so strict. Linda's heart pounded when she saw her husband smile. He had forgiven her—whatever he'd thought she'd done wrong. Only as he came closer did she realize it wasn't the familiar, self-assured grin. His smile was defiant and tense. Alarmed, Linda slid down from the seat of the wagon. There on the ground, they could talk more privately.

Fitz stopped awkwardly in front of the wagon, keeping his distance. "Lindy, sweetheart, I'm sorry that I didn't make it back last night. But fortunately, nothing happened. The major didn't give us away."

Linda suddenly understood. Fitz hadn't come home because he wanted to avoid a confrontation with the quartermaster! He'd left Linda by herself in case the man had come in the middle of the night and thrown her out.

While Linda stood there at a loss for words, a girl separated from the group of settlers. She had a bundle on her shoulder, and she made her way over to Fitz and Linda with a sullen, smug expression on her face.

"Fitz?" she said in a questioning tone.

Fitz grinned again. "Uh, Vera. Linda, I want to introduce you to someone. This is Vera, Mary's daughter. She's looking for a job, and I hired her. She's going to ride with you, and then she'll come with us to our farm."

"You did what?"

The incensed question escaped Linda's lips before she could stop it. Usually, she thought carefully before saying anything that might provoke Fitz in any way. But this had come as a surprise.

Linda's heart pounded wildly as she forced herself to be fair. Perhaps the girl was nothing like her wild mother. Perhaps she had turned to Fitz because she needed help. Linda eyed the dark-haired, gaunt young thing. Vera was probably fourteen or fifteen, a little younger than Irene, but nothing about her reminded Linda of her friend from Otago. Vera was tall, half a head taller than Fitz. Although she was very thin, she looked strong. And Linda couldn't explain it, but there was something menacing about her. Her hard, cold eyes didn't fit with her still almost childish face.

"What did you hire her as?" Linda asked nervously as she grasped for composure. She suddenly felt nauseated.

"I thought she could help you. As a maid," Fitz said. Vera turned her expressionless face toward him, and he smiled at her. "Or more of a lady's maid."

With a groan, Linda turned away, stepped behind the covered wagon, and lost the contents of her stomach.

Fitz and Vera just stood there blankly as she staggered back, pale, trembling, and agitated. Vera eyed Linda. Then she turned to Fitz.

"You didn't tell me she was pregnant."

Chapter 53

The journey to Patea took them through deep forests that had been ruthlessly marred. Swathes had been cut through the trees to build roads and simplify the progress of armies.

Normally, Linda would have been just as horrified by this as her sisters had been a few months before. Now, however, she steered the wagon across the coastal landscape with its destroyed Maori villages without so much as noticing the clear-cutting. She was far too preoccupied with her own thoughts and with Vera, who sat next to her, seeming to revel in triumph and self-satisfaction. Linda couldn't explain why she rejected the girl the way she did. She didn't even feel any jealousy toward her. After all, it hadn't looked as though there were any sparks flying between Fitz and Vera. But still, something about the young woman bothered Linda, scared her and disturbed her. She didn't want to share her house with the girl, and she certainly wasn't going to take on a motherly role.

And then, there was the thought of a pregnancy . . .

Linda had never considered such a thing, since she had only had actual intercourse with Fitz once. But when she thought back, the symptoms were obvious: the nausea, the mood swings. She had interpreted her lack of a period as a consequence of the hardships she had endured during the winter in Christchurch. But in fact, her monthly bleeding had only stopped coming since that bewildering night in spring.

Linda didn't know whether she was supposed to be happy. The day before, she certainly would have been, since things had seemed to be changing for the better. The child wouldn't be born in a covered wagon or in a hut in a gold-digger camp, but on their own farm in Taranaki. Their child's future would be guaranteed by Fitz's army salary for the first three years and, after that, by the farm's proceeds.

Now, however . . . Linda stole a glance at Vera. The girl was staring straight ahead. The only emotion she displayed was sullenness.

"Do you like children?" Linda asked cautiously.

Vera didn't answer immediately. Only after Linda repeated her question did she bother to respond. "No."

Linda was disconcerted. Things had sounded different before. Fitz had been thrilled to learn of Linda's condition—another piece of evidence that he was hardly planning on replacing his wife with the girl. "Pregnant?!" he'd practically yelled across the drill ground before Linda could even say a word about it. "Hey, comrades, I'm going to be a father!"

A few of the military settlers had applauded and congratulated him, and Fitz had beamed. "Isn't it wonderful that you'll have Vera with you?" he'd said. "She'll help around the farm and with the baby, won't you, Vera?" The girl had nodded. "Of course," she'd said, managing a smile. "I'd love to."

Apparently, she was more inclined to be honest now.

"Have you ever worked on a farm before?" Linda asked.

"No," Vera said again.

Linda examined her more closely. The girl was wearing an old blue skirt and a threadbare blouse. The faded fabric displayed too much of her bodice and her breasts, which were already quite full.

"We shall have to buy you some new clothes," Linda murmured.

Vera couldn't run around like that in front of the men. Perhaps her questionable reputation was only due to her attire.

Vera remained silent.

"So, where did you and your parents and sister live before? Is your father a prospector?"

"My father's dead," Vera said.

Linda frowned. Women couldn't join the regiment on their own. She wondered if Mary's last name had been mentioned aboard the ship at some point. Finally, she remembered.

"Then Private Carrigan is your stepfather?"

"My mother's husband," Vera replied flatly.

Linda asked another question anyway. "Why don't you want to work on your mother's farm? I'm sure there will be a lot to do . . ."

In response, Vera only hunched her shoulders. Linda wondered if she'd had a past similar to Irene's. Had her mother's husband abused her? Now Linda remembered Private Carrigan. He was a rather short man who seemed quite shy. The women aboard the ship had gossiped viciously about how he could possibly have ended up with a woman like Mary.

"Don't you like your stepfather?" Linda asked.

For the first time since the conversation had begun, Vera turned to face her. Her expression was odd. It didn't even remotely remind Linda of the hounded, hurt expression Irene had worn when she'd spoken of her father.

"I do," Vera said. Her brittle voice softened somewhat, but her eyes didn't show any more warmth. They flashed as she continued. "But I like Fitz better."

Fitz's estimation had been correct; there were a good thirty miles to cover between Whanganui and the new settlement on the Patea River. This was hardly manageable in one day by foot, so the regiment rested at the halfway point and set up camp for the night. There were traces of earlier fires in the large clearing, and with a shiver, Linda recognized the typical outline of a *marae*. Cameron must have burned down the village during his approach to Patea.

"This is *tapu*," she told Fitz with a pained expression. "The spirits of the exiled tribe live here. We shouldn't be camping here."

Fitz was assigned to take the next watch. Other settlers were building fires, setting up tents, collecting water, and cooking. Major McDonnell kept his people busy.

Vera overheard Linda and grimaced scornfully.

Fitz just shrugged. "Spirits don't bite. Especially not us, since we weren't the ones to chase those people away."

"We're taking their land," Linda insisted.

Now that they were here, the reservations she'd had from the start grew stronger.

"You take what you can get," Vera said.

Fitz pulled Linda into his arms. "Darling, you're worrying too much again. This land belongs to the Crown now. If we don't take it, somebody else will. And haven't the spirits given us their blessing so far? We're going to have a baby! And we'll have a farm again, and the sun is shining."

That much was true. Spring was emerging everywhere. Even the tree stumps on the side of the road were sprouting new twigs, and the weather had been beautiful all day. Not even the approaching sunset could put a chill in the air. The North Island was noticeably warmer than the plains.

Linda wished she could feel comforted in Fitz's embrace, but the burning sensation of shame and worry remained. After Fitz had returned to his guard post, she lit a fire. She couldn't find all the herbs she needed, but she imitated Makuto's ritual for the dead as best she could. She evoked and pacified the spirits, and she really did begin to feel better as she sang the old songs and prayers. With deep earnestness, Linda asked the spirits for forgiveness for her people and offered her apologies for the burns they had inflicted on Papa as well as the trees that had been cut down, whose death must have angered the forest god, Tane. Then she begged for the blessing of Rangi, the sky god, for her unborn child.

"My baby will have to bear this burden, just like all the children of my people," she whispered. "Don't let it break my child. Don't let me break under the curse that lies on this land."

When Fitz returned after his watch, Linda was still sitting by the fire, brooding over the dying embers. He placed a hand on her shoulder and looked inquiringly into her pale face.

"What are you doing there?" he asked gently. "Are you feeling sick? Did you have anything to eat? You didn't cook here, did you? There was some stew for the men. Vera, run over to the kitchen wagon and see if there's any left."

Vera had been perched on the wagon's seat, looking down at Linda. "Your wife is making a fool of herself," she said coldly. "You didn't tell me she was mad."

Once again, Linda set up camp inside the wagon when Fitz said he had to leave. They were probably playing cards at more than one fire. Vera rolled up in a blanket under the wagon. She and Fitz seemed to sense that it would be too much for Linda if she had to share her bed with the girl too. A few sleepless hours later, he returned. Linda's only consolation on this awful day was that he had sought out her company, not Vera's.

Traveling onward the next morning, Linda no longer tried to strike up a conversation with her future lady's maid. There was a wall between her and Vera, although she didn't know how she'd earned the girl's animosity. Granted, perhaps Vera sensed her instinctive disapproval, but there was nothing she could say against Linda. To the contrary, Linda hadn't fought against taking her in; she had tried to be kind. But all it had earned her was unrelenting sullenness.

When the settlers stopped to rest around noon, Vera went to speak to Fitz. He came over immediately and scolded Linda. "You shouldn't treat the girl like that. Vera's been through so much. You must be nicer to her."

Linda immediately began to feel guilty, though she despised herself for it. "Did she complain?"

Fitz shook his head. "Of course she didn't. She's glad to be with us. But still, she's suffering from your disapproval, I can tell. Just the way you look at her . . ."

Linda gritted her teeth. "I'll try to look friendlier. And maybe Vera can deign to smile too."

"She doesn't have to smile," he remarked coolly. "She doesn't have to ingratiate herself with anybody."

Linda could hear the reproach in his words. Vera would never approach a neighbor with a welcome gift.

It was almost evening when they reached the town of Patea. Much like Whanganui, it was first and foremost an army camp. The only civilians were wives and children of the military settlers, as well as officials who oversaw the allocation of land.

The land earmarked for Fitz's regiment was secured by several stockades built by Cameron's men. The wooden fortresses on both sides of the river were intended to be used as watch stations by the settlers. In between, parcels of land of various sizes had been surveyed. The next day, they were going to be assigned to the settlers.

Most of the plots were covered by trees; only the parcels that had formerly held Maori settlements were already mostly cleared. These were reserved for high-ranking officers.

"The rest of us have to clear the trees ourselves and build our own houses with the wood," Fitz said.

He didn't seem particularly excited about the idea. Linda, on the other hand, was relieved. She would have been horrified to build her farm right on top of a burned-down *marae*.

The next morning passed with agonizing slowness. The land allocation planned for noon was no reason for Major McDonnell to skip his crew's drill. While the military settlers trained, Linda sat waiting on the wagon. She would have preferred to explore the township or the surrounding land, but she didn't dare leave. There was no way she was going to do anything else that Fitz or Vera could blame her for later. Vera sat on the back of the wagon like a dark shadow and watched the soldiers throw themselves to the ground, jump up, run, aim, and fire their rifles at targets.

Linda noticed that Fitz didn't particularly distinguish himself in the process. He was fit and agile, but his legs were rather short. He made a fine rower, but he was no runner. Additionally, he seemed entirely unfamiliar with firearms. Linda was more than surprised. Ever since somebody had brought rabbits to New Zealand, every farm child had learned to use a rifle from the time they could hold one. The animals had no natural predators here; they multiplied incredibly quickly and overgrazed entire pastures. The rabbit plague could only be controlled with regular hunting. It was a part of everyday farm life, and Linda and Carol had received their first air rifles at ten years of age. The young woman could have hit the target that had been set up for the military settlers without batting an eyelash.

Yet Fitz obviously had no idea how to handle his gun. Of course, it had been explained to him in earlier training sessions, and he was already loading the weapon capably enough, but his movements were neither graceful nor natural. Fitz looked as though he had to force himself to fire every time. Accordingly, his marksmanship suffered, and Linda's husband seemed downright repulsed by the act of attaching a bayonet, running at a straw puppet, and piercing its chest. It was clear that Fitz was holding up his unit's progress.

"Get on with it, Private Fitzpatrick!" shouted his sergeant. "How long do you think the Hauhau warrior is going to stand there and wait for you to finish him off?"

Fitz was about to reply, but then he thought better of it. He gave his superior an angry look, wiped the sweat from his brow, and continued. He didn't manage to do much better the second time.

Fitz's failure was all the more obvious because most of his comrades handled their weapons well. The former prospectors, whalers, and other adventurers were no strangers to fighting. Some might even be on the run because they'd used weapons one time too many or too well. Linda wondered if these ruffians were as apt at farming their land as they were at defending it.

Shortly before noon, Major McDonnell ended the drill, but not without giving his men a thorough dressing down first. All had been too slow for his liking, and he accused them of hesitation and laziness.

"You'll have to do much better than that!" he said. "And I warn you, even if Te Ua Haumene's tattooed bastards never dare to attack our settlement, as military settlers you are members of the army. You can be drafted for special operations. It may only be four weeks a year, but that's plenty long enough to get killed. So, get yourselves in bloody order and learn to fight! Now, come here and draw your tickets."

McDonnell led his regiment over to a table and had them take up their posts. Fitz was among the last to draw. Afterward, the men gathered around a large map where the parcels were drawn. Fitz only gave it a quick glance before returning to the wagon.

"The very last parcel," he complained. "Farther up the river than any of the others. It's damn bad luck. Our land borders right on the wilderness."

He showed Linda a small drawing and a slip of paper with his number on it. It was true that their parcel only had neighbors on one side, not both sides like the others. However, one of the forts sat at the end of the settlement area, and there would be fences.

Linda shrugged. "That's not necessarily bad," she said. "It will be easier to buy additional land later. They're going to develop more of it, no doubt."

"It's almost an hour into town," Fitz grumbled. "By horse. Even longer on foot."

Which meant perhaps he'd spend less time at the pub and more time building their house that way, Linda thought. But she bit her tongue.

"The major has something against you," Vera said. "The sergeant too. You can tell. They're trying to bring you down, Fitz."

Fitz seemed to perk up at her words. "Exactly! No doubt about it!" he crowed. "The man's harassing me. All this damned pressure, and then the lottery ticket—"

"But you drew that ticket yourself," Linda said. "And they pressure everyone in the army. Bill Paxton told us all about it."

"Bill Paxton, Bill Paxton . . . ," Fitz mimicked. "He can talk; he started as an officer. He's probably from a rich family." He snorted.

Linda knew better than to say more, but when Fitz started feeling sorry for himself like this, things could only get worse. "We can do some target practice if you want," she suggested. "I can help you. When we move in tomorrow, we can set up a bull's-eye. All you have to do—"

"Oh, really?" Fitz snapped at her. "And what else can you do better than me, Linda? Perhaps flirting with the sergeant? Or the major, even? The officers have it in for me." He looked to Vera, who nodded vigorously. "Right, and now let's see if we can't change a few things. Some of the others probably aren't very happy either." He folded up the piece of paper with the parcel number and shoved it in his pocket.

He brushed the dust from his uniform and got to his feet. With every step away from Linda, Fitz seemed to gather more hope and self-esteem. Vera tagged eagerly behind.

Linda wondered if she should say something to stall the girl. All she did was confirm his skewed perspective. On the other hand, Vera wouldn't let Linda tell her what she could and couldn't do, anyway. Linda would only be provoking another biting remark that she couldn't defend herself against. She let the girl go on her way and decided not to get any angrier than she was. It was a beautiful day, and the river sparkled in the sunshine. The land parcels were arrayed along the riverbank, and she, Linda, owned one of them! Whether Fitz was happy about it or not, they were landowners! Linda would have a new farm. She could plant a garden, and perhaps they could get some sheep next year. Ida and Karl would surely lend her some money if she wrote to them, and she had her own connections with sheep barons on the North Island too. She could open a cheese dairy, just like Ida had. There would certainly be a market for it. Patea was a growing town, and it wasn't that far to Whanganui either. The large army base was in constant need of provisions.

Linda's heart grew lighter the more she thought about it all, and she could hardly wait to see her new land. Without a moment's hesitation, she saddled Brianna. Fitz could do what he wanted. She'd go have a look at their land right now. She was reasonably sure that he wouldn't manage to swap with anybody. The border parcels were probably unpopular, and who knew if the army command would even allow such an exchange?

In a better mood than she'd been in all last month, Linda glanced at the little drawing with the parcels, memorized where theirs was, and cantered off to the north. Brianna, apparently glad to be rid of the wagon, moved along at a lively pace. Amy followed, barking happily. After a short while, Linda had left the army camp behind. She passed a few men who had set off on foot to explore their own new land, and then she was alone with her animals in a luscious, green, fertile stretch of fields between the hills and the river. Linda felt like she could breathe for the first time in months as she rode over the floodplains, recognizing raupo and beech trees, ferns, rimu, and pohutukawa, which bloomed deep red like the rata back at Rata Station. Massive kahikatea and pukatea stretched their limbs toward the sky. There would probably be kauri here too. Linda thought uneasily of the Maori for whom the giant trees were sacred. The high mountain in the distance behind the lazily flowing river was sacred to them too: Mount Taranaki, the volcano that had given this region its name. It shimmered bluish in the sun, its peak covered in snow.

The landscape in Taranaki was dotted with hills, not flat like the plains had been. But the land sloped gently toward the river, and on both sides of the Patea, some areas were almost flat. Linda thought they would be good for fields and pastures. The house itself should probably be built on one of the hills.

Linda oriented herself by the river's curves and the forts that rose up every few miles on the right or left side of the river. She greeted the watchmen and felt relieved when they immediately acknowledged her. The men were watchful, though Linda wasn't sure if they'd be able to spot a troop of trained Maori warriors in the undergrowth. The settlement was yet to be secured by embankments and fences, in any case. Linda decided not to worry about it. Finally, she reached a prominent bend in the river. On the other side of the Patea, perhaps a quarter mile away, she saw the fort tower that marked the last corner of settlement land. Here it was—her land!

Linda looked around ecstatically. Their parcel was beautiful, much nicer than all the others she'd passed on the way. The land sloped down slightly toward the river, and there were no trees on the bank. It would be easy enough to plow. The land opened up into rolling hills in the distance, and one reminded her of the hill at Rata Station where Chris had built the stone house for Jane. In her mind's eye, Linda's new house took shape there. A much humbler one, of course: a sturdy log cabin. It would have a terrace facing the river, and one would be able to look down at the Patea to see if a boat was passing. It would also be good to build a pier for the mail boat to stop at, just like they'd had at home.

Linda thought contentedly of her new permanent postal address. She could write to Ida and Carol. She wouldn't feel as lonely as she had the past year. Maybe she could get closer to Fitz again. And soon she'd have a little girl or boy! Linda felt a sudden rush of excitement about her baby. She daydreamed that she was sitting on the patio of her new house, rocking the little one in her arms. She could see the child playing in the garden and splashing around in the river. He'd have a childhood like hers and Carol's after all.

And Fitz would surely be a good father. He was such a child himself that he'd probably make his son or daughter laugh all day long. The happier Linda felt on her own land, the more her trouble with Fitz seemed to fade into the background. Once they were here and working on the farm together, they'd get along better. To hell with the army! The three years Fitz had committed himself to would go by quickly. As a military settler, he was really only expected to defend his own land. And here, with this parcel, they were far from where any action would be. After his basic training, Fitz would surely be assigned guard duty at the fort next door instead of having to go into Patea every day. He'd rarely see Major McDonnell.

Linda guided her horse away from the river and a little deeper into her land. The parcels were long and narrow—perhaps two of the twenty acres bordered on the river, and the rest went inland in the shape of a long rectangle. Linda explored the hills. There were places without woodland growth here too; how lucky they'd been! Linda could easily imagine fat sheep nibbling away the undergrowth, and the year after that, green grass would cover the hills like a thick green carpet.

"What do you think, Amy? A hundred sheep?" she asked the small dog. "Why don't we start with a hundred sheep?"

Amy tilted her head, seeming to think it over, and then barked once.

Linda laughed. "It's a deal, then."

Amy didn't go back to frolicking around, but instead turned her head, catching a scent. Linda followed her up a hill and stopped Brianna on the knoll to enjoy the view of a valley dominated by an enormous kauri tree. It was so high that it would surely tower above Cameron's fortress, and the trunk's circumference must have been more than five yards around. The kauri tree stood all alone, either because no other trees would grow around it or because somebody had cut them down to give it some space.

Amy's curiosity, however, wasn't directed at the tree, but at a woman sitting in front of it. She was holding kawakawa leaves in one hand, and a *tiki wananga*, a staff carved with idols, in the other. She was singing. Linda wasn't sure if the sharp sounds she uttered were *maimai* or *manawawera*, laments for the dead. In any case, the woman was pouring out her sadness, anger, and loss.

Linda led her mare down the hill. As she got closer to the woman, she dismounted. Others might have thought this risky, but Linda knew better. *Maimai* and *manawawera haka*s had to be sung by multiple voices and accompanied by dancers. If this woman was singing her lament by herself, then she was alone. And she was old. Her face was sunken and deeply creased, and there were only a few dark strands left in her white hair. Linda couldn't see any tattoos. She might well be a priestess, her rank so high that not even a *moko* master would dare to spill her blood. Her *tiki wananga*, with many *tapu*s placed on it, also indicated this. A common woman wouldn't have even dared to touch one.

The *tohunga* was wearing a long, woven skirt, and her upper body was naked. Her drooping breasts hung down over her sharp ribs. The woman looked half-starved. Who knew how long she'd been sitting there, mourning her dead all alone.

"Kia ora, karani," Linda said in greeting, not quite sure if the title of "grandmother" was appropriate. She had addressed all the older Ngai Tahu women that way. "I hope I'm not disturbing your conversation with the spirits."

The woman looked up at her. "How could you? You chased our spirits away long ago!"

Linda shook her head. "The soul of this ancient tree was here long before your people's canoes came to Aotearoa. It will not fear my people."

The woman raised an eyebrow. "Until your axes destroy the trunk she lives in. Nothing is sacred to you; you have no gods."

Linda sat down a little ways from her. "We do," she said. "We have one God. But our God makes us blind to the gods of others. He is—" She tried to remember the verse. "He is a jealous God."

The old woman looked at her more closely. "Are you doing this in his name? Do you sing *karakia* when you burn our villages down?"

"No," Linda said firmly, suddenly thinking of Franz Lange. "Our priests are peaceful. This is about money, about land . . . But tell me, what happened, *karani*? Which tribe do you belong to?"

"None," the woman said curtly. "There was an *iwi* of the Ngati Tamakopiri here, but it is gone. Our warriors left, and they pray to strange gods now—the gods of the *pakeha*, mostly, although Te Ua Haumene calls them something else. And their wives and children were taken away by the *pakeha*. Relocated, they said. They were taken far to the north, to the territory of the Ngati Whatua. They have been our enemies since time immemorial. And who knows how many even arrived there. I tried to stop it, but the *pakeha* wouldn't listen. Then I returned. I am the river. The river is me. As is this tree. If you cut it down, I will fall too."

Linda shook her head. "We won't cut it down," she promised.

The old woman laughed. "How can you be so sure?" she asked. "Don't the men in red coats decide what happens and what does not? In Whanganui, there was a woman with them who had yellow hair like yours. She spoke our language, but they listened to her as little as they listened to us. They will not listen to you either."

"They will." Linda was terribly ashamed, but she knew she had to admit to the woman that she was a beneficiary of the tribe's misfortune. It meant she was the only one who could protect the woman's sanctuary. "The *pakeha* gave this land to me and my husband so we could farm it. We will plant *kumaras* and let sheep graze here. But we do not wish to anger the spirits. If you tell me which parts of the land are *tapu*, I will respect that."

The old woman looked at Linda. "You do well not to anger the spirits," she said slowly, "but you cannot cleanse yourself. Everything here should be *tapu*. Here, the soul of my people died."

Linda shook her head again. "The souls of the Ngati Tamakopiri remain. Your tribe is strong, *karani*. It will survive."

The woman studied her closely. "Who are you?"

Linda began relating her origins the Maori way. She told her in great detail about Rata Station, the Waimakariri River, the loss of her parents, and Jane's treachery. She was still angry at the Ngai Tahu. Te Haitara hadn't defended her.

"I was driven away too," she said sadly, "and I lost my family. I can understand some of your grief." She lowered her head. "And now my husband and I were given this land. Your land, *karani*. I fear I will burden myself with blame if I take it. But if I don't, others who may not respect it will take it. So I ask you, *karani*, to share it with me. Let us take care of it together and protect it from harm."

The old woman looked at Linda for what felt like an eternity. "My name is Omaka Te Pura," she said at last. "I am part of the Ngati Tamakopiri tribe, and we came to Aotearoa long ago with the canoe called *Aotea*. Patea is the river. Taranaki is the mountain . . ."

Linda listened as Omaka Te Pura told the story of her people, and felt strangely comforted. The kauri tree's spirit seemed to be watching over both of them. It was almost as though Linda had a tribe again.

Chapter 54

For all the serenity she'd felt under the kauri tree, Linda was anxious as she rode her horse back to the army camp. In her euphoria about their new land and her sadness over Omaka's fate, she'd pushed aside the fact that Fitz was currently doing everything he could to trade away the parcel. If he'd somehow managed, she wouldn't be able to keep her promise to the old *tohunga*, and Omaka would be betrayed by the *pakeha* yet again.

Even at a canter, it took Brianna an hour to reach the camp. Partway there, Linda was joined by another rider—Captain Langdon, the recruiter who had brought them to Taranaki. When he recognized Linda, he gave her a polite nod of greeting.

"Mrs. Fitzpatrick and her pretty horse . . . She's even lovelier in the saddle than she is on a wagon. Have you been out to take a look at your land?"

Linda beamed at him. "I was, and it's beautiful! I can't thank you enough! If you hadn't managed to win over my husband, we would never have been able to have a farm again."

"Again? You had a farm before? What an interesting life you've had."

Linda noticed Langdon's sharp tone. "Is there something wrong? Was I not supposed to go out on my own? I'm sorry, I was just so excited! And the forts are all manned. I—"

"You may move about the settlement however you please, Mrs. Fitzpatrick," Langdon answered stiffly. "It's safe. It's just—apparently your husband doesn't share your feelings about the parcel. I'm sorry, Mrs. Fitzpatrick, we had to take disciplinary action against him. It's only a fine, though, don't you worry." At the sight of Linda's pallor, the captain quickly tried to reassure her. "He just managed to avoid detention. If he'd kept mouthing off, we would have had to discipline him for insulting an officer as well as gambling."

Linda shut her eyes. "What did he do?"

The captain frowned. "It would be better if he told you himself. But personally, I'm quite disappointed in him. In our first interview, he showed so much potential."

Linda gave the captain an unhappy look. "My—my husband hasn't had to use weapons much before," she said. "It's not his strongest skill."

"It isn't?" Langdon raised his eyebrows again. "And here I was, expecting that cadet school would train its students to use weapons during their first year. Not to mention military obedience and formal conduct with superiors."

Linda bit her lip. It seemed she had said too much yet again.

"Or is it possible," Langdon continued, "that Major McDonnell is right in thinking your husband didn't attend the Royal Military Academy at all?" He held her gaze.

"I can't say for sure," she admitted. "I know very little about Fitz—about what he did before he came to New Zealand. We met in Christchurch, when he was a foreman on my family's sheep farm."

Langdon glanced at Amy. "So that's why you have a sheepdog. We were wondering. Don't take this the wrong way, Mrs. Fitzpatrick, but the fine horse and the dog—"

"We're not thieves!" Linda blurted out.

She thought guiltily of the chickens Fitz had occasionally "found" in their travels, and the meager furniture taken from Irene's shack.

The captain raised his hands in appeasement. "Nobody was saying any such thing, Mrs. Fitzpatrick. We were thinking rather of your husband's gambling habit. However, now I think I understand. That is, I assume your parents were—not happy with your choice of husband?"

Linda's cheeks burned. To the captain, she was just an errant sheep baroness, forsaken by her family for marrying a gambler.

"It's not what you think," she said.

The captain nodded. "And it's none of my business either. But you should keep an eye on your husband. He has a tendency to let his temper get the best of him, and he disregards the garrison's orders. He's already out of favor with the major. McDonnell's had an eventful life himself. He isn't easily fooled, if you catch my meaning. Your husband shouldn't try to lie to him again. And he should take military drills seriously. We aren't here for fun, Mrs. Fitzpatrick. There are deadly dangers in this forest, peaceful as it may seem. What's more, you have a border parcel. I, for my part, would have assigned that land to experienced soldiers. So please, remind your husband that defending this place is his responsibility now. In the event of a fight, fancy talk won't do him any good."

With that, the captain tipped his hat in farewell and cantered off. They were nearing the camp, and he shouldn't be seen with a subordinate's wife.

Linda was relieved. Heaven knew how Fitz might react if he saw her colluding with "the enemy."

Fitz and Vera were sitting morosely by a fire they'd lit near the wagon. "It's nothing but harassment," Fitz was saying. "Why shouldn't I swap parcels with Simon O'Rourke? Until this morning, the officers didn't seem to give a damn who got which parcel."

"Maybe they do care," Vera said in her usual monotone. "Like you said, maybe they gave you that strange piece of land because they don't like you."

Fitz nodded. "Of course they weren't expecting me to take it sitting down. That's why they sent a patrol. Goddammit, I was winning! O'Rourke would have had to give me his land. All twenty acres of it!"

Linda could imagine the rest. Fitz hadn't found anybody who would trade with him voluntarily. So, he'd talked a comrade into a card game, and almost tricked O'Rourke out of his land. Maybe he would have given him his own instead, or maybe not. No wonder such practices were forbidden. Fitz certainly wasn't the first military settler who'd tried something similar. The patrol had been a routine check, not a personal vendetta against Joe Fitzpatrick.

"'Land allocations are decided by lottery, and the rights for this land are nontransferable for the time being,'" Linda said, quoting the explanatory leaflet that they had received when Fitz had signed up, as gently as possible. "You knew that, Fitz. The administrators would have never registered O'Rourke's land in your name. How much is the fine?"

Fitz jumped up. "What fine? How do you know anything about a fine? Were people gossiping?"

Linda nodded. She'd stepped in it again, but this time she wouldn't let herself be intimidated. "Yes, there's been talk. You did something foolish, Fitz, and that's a fact. You shouldn't have tried to trade; you should have come with me to look at the land. It's beautiful! It's one of the nicest parcels here, mostly flat, not too much woodland, ideal for sheep. It's—it's sacred ground!"

She attempted a smile, but it was overshadowed by Vera's droning laughter. "It's out in the middle of nowhere," the girl said. "You should turn it down, Fitz. You don't have to be a military settler; you can do something else. You can find something like this anywhere." As Vera spoke, her face began to glow with admiration and trust.

Fitz seemed to grow taller under her approving gaze. "I—" he began.

But Linda had had enough. Her anger and her fear of losing this wonderful land and the chances they were offered here made her jump to her feet. What the hell was the girl after, anyway? Did she want Fitz to take her back to the goldfields? Back on the road? Linda left Brianna's side and stepped in front of Vera.

"Young lady," she said, "my husband signed a contract. He's a soldier, a member of the army. If he leaves now, that's desertion. And do you know what the sentence for that is, Vera? Do you, Fitz? The sentence for desertion is death by shooting."

Vera's face blossomed in a superior smile. "They'd have to catch us first," she purred. It was a voice of seduction, but this time, she'd miscalculated.

Fitz enjoyed living like there was no tomorrow. But at the reminder that tomorrow could consist of a firing squad, he seemed to snap awake. He'd given up his horse and fled the rogues from Queenstown. But fleeing the army was not an option.

"We'll have a look at the land tomorrow," he said diplomatically. "I can still decide after that."

Linda gave Vera a triumphant glare. She knew the boundaries of her husband's appetite for risk, and she had won, for now.

The next morning, Linda, Fitz, and Vera loaded the covered wagon with army-issued tools, a tent, and the equipment they'd need to camp on their new land until the farmhouse was built. The settlers were exempt from drills that day so they could get set up. Starting the next day, they would have to be available eight hours a day for earthwork construction around the settlement, and for drills and target practice. The rest of the day was free for them to work on their new homes.

"It would be best to form neighborhood groups and build the families' houses together first," Captain Langdon advised them all before they headed out. "The bachelors can live in tents a few weeks longer. Also, clearing communal land first and farming it together during the first year has proven to work well in the past. Then you'll have your first harvests, and you can continue during the second year until there's enough arable land on each parcel for every owner. Try to think cooperatively. It's not going to be possible to run a full-time farm simultaneously with your army duties."

"We'll manage alone," Linda said after catching a glimpse of their only neighbor. The curmudgeonly former prospector constantly kept a chaw of tobacco in his mouth, although he hardly had any teeth left. "There are three of us, and we have Brianna and Amy."

In truth, Linda was relying on the horse for plowing, and later, once they started breeding sheep, she'd be relying on the dog. As for Vera, the sullen girl carried tools to the wagon slowly, as though she were at least seventy years old.

Fitz was grinning cheerfully, as if the previous evening had never happened. "Of course we will, my sweet! No question about it. Vera, hop in. Let's go see our farm!"

A short while later, the covered wagon rolled northward on the solidly built road along the river. The prospector, to whom they'd offered a ride, thanked them with an unintelligible mumble. Linda hadn't gotten his name. From the map, she'd figured out that he must be Private Fairbanks.

Fairbanks's presence prevented Linda from telling her husband about Omaka. Fitz had nothing against the Maori, but Linda didn't trust the prospector. Or Vera. Linda didn't want to think about it for now. If she had, she would have had to admit to herself that she was scared.

With Brianna's pace slowed by the wagon, Linda had more time to look at the landscape and let it all sink in. Once more, the awesome sight of Mount Taranaki filled her with overwhelming joy. On her first trip, the silence had been interrupted only by the rushing river, the wind in the trees, and occasional birdsong. Today, the riverbanks were lined with optimistic, happy people. Many of the settlers had taken the captain's advice and immediately formed groups. Now, they were inspecting their parcels together, shouting and laughing.

On Linda's wagon, the silence was oppressive. Before, when she'd been traveling alone with Fitz, they had chatted about this and that, and he'd entertained her. But now, Vera's presence dampened any attempt at successful communication, and Private Fairbanks wasn't making things any better. All he did was look around with a glassy stare and mindlessly chew his tobacco. Linda didn't feel like sharing her joy over this beautiful land and the wonderful day with any of them. She was so glad to share the land with Omaka. While the old priestess would have more suffering and sadness to share than joy, at least Linda wouldn't be living only with people who had shut her out like oysters in their shells.

Finally, they reached Fairbanks's parcel and let the prospector down, but not without promising him further help if he needed it. They soon stopped again and climbed off the wagon, and Linda proudly led her husband across the land she had already explored the day before. She reveled in Fitz's joy as he took in the plain by the river, the gentle hill for their house, the trees just waiting to be cut down, and the brushland that wouldn't even have to be cleared before sheep could be kept there, all with an expression of awe.

Meanwhile, Vera listened to Linda's explanations with a complete lack of interest. After a while, she wandered off on her own. Linda was relieved; Vera's absence seemed to have a positive effect on Fitz. He opened up more, joked around, and whirled her in a circle while she fantasized about how happy their child would be in such a beautiful place.

"He can play over there," she said, pointing at where the house's garden was going to be, already resplendent in her mind's eye.

Fitz had begun whittling at a piece of wood, and now he cheerfully handed her a roughly worked little horse. "For my son," he declared, and then continued with a little doll. "And for my daughter." He grinned and winked at her. "They could be twins! It runs in your family, doesn't it?"

Linda tried to smile, but she felt a cold shiver run down her spine. Her father, Ottfried, had also traveled with two women: his wife, Ida, and Cat, whom he had passed off as his maid. He had gotten both of them pregnant. She prayed Fitz wasn't planning anything similar with Vera.

Just then, Vera came rushing toward them in a panic.

"There are Maori down there, Fitz! Savages! You have to shoot them. Get your rifle!"

But Fitz had left his rifle back in the wagon, although the major and the captain had drilled it into the men that they were not to leave the weapon out of their sight. Once the area was secured with earthwork, they could relax, but for the time being, they were to be always on guard. For once, Fitz's carelessness was a stroke of good luck. With a glance across the plain, Linda could tell that it was only Omaka, standing guard in front of her kauri tree.

"No, that's Omaka," Linda explained, chastising herself for not managing to prepare Fitz and Vera earlier. "She's a *tohunga*, she pacifies the land's spirits. And she's on her own. There's no reason to make a fuss, Vera."

Vera's eyes went wide with indignation. "The old hag almost scared me to death," she spat. "She shouldn't be here. Chase her away, Fitz. Now!"

Linda and Fitz walked slowly down the hill. Linda was startled to see the priestess standing with her back straight, not facing the tree, but leaning against it, ready to protect it. She clutched her sacred staff in her hand like a weapon, and her other hand held a war club. Omaka's eyes, which had been half-closed and dreamy the day before, flashed in alarm. Only when she recognized Linda did the woman relax.

"*Kia ora, karani.* Please offer Tane's spirits my greeting," Linda said, gesturing at the tree. "Forgive us if the girl bothered you during your prayers. This is my husband, Joe Fitzpatrick, called Fitz. Fitz, this is Omaka. Her name means 'flowing river.'" She turned from Fitz to Vera, and her voice hardened as she switched to English. "As a priestess, Omaka is one with the river and the land. She belongs here just as much as we do, and you will treat her with dignity and respect."

Linda had always had an easier time fighting for others than for herself. For a heartbeat, Vera gaped in surprise before curling her lips into a sneer.

"I thought this land belonged to Fitz," she said tauntingly.

Omaka looked into Linda's eyes. "*Haere mai, mokopuna.* Welcome—Feetz." She narrowed her eyes at Vera. "Who is the girl?"

Linda, who was touched that the priestess had called her granddaughter, searched for the correct word in Maori. The Ngai Tahu hadn't had any words for domestic servants.

"A young woman who works for us."

"Your slave?" Omaka asked.

Linda shook her head. "No, but something like that. Only she does not belong to us. She can leave whenever she wishes."

"Then send her away," Omaka demanded.

"Chase the old woman away," Vera demanded, staring intently at Fitz. "She scares me."

Linda wasn't sure which demand to react to first. She didn't know how much Fitz had understood of her conversation with Omaka. But the last words had been clear, since Omaka spoke with her hands. She pointed her sacred staff at the girl as though trying to shoo her away like an animal.

"I can't do that," she said, turning to Omaka first. "She has difficulties with her family. She needs us."

Omaka frowned. "*Mokopuna*, do you lie to me, or do you lie to yourself?"

Linda blushed. "My—my husband hired her," she said helplessly. "But it is not what you think."

Omaka glared at Vera furiously again, then she peered at Fitz. A shadow crossed her face. "I see, *mokopuna*," she said.

"She will not bother you," Linda continued hastily. "She will work for us, down by the river, in the fields, by the house. She does not need to come here at all. Do you want to make your home here, so that you can protect the kauri? We could build you a house. I brought you some blankets and a tent. I should not have, but nobody was looking, so I just took a few more rolls of cloth. The army provided us with them, we—" Realizing she was babbling, Linda fell silent.

"I thank you, *mokopuna*, and I will try to protect you," Omaka said in her clear, calm voice, her gaze firmly on Vera.

Linda fought down her anxiety with a hysterical laugh. Protect her from Vera? Wasn't it Linda who had to protect the priestess?

"What are you waiting for, Fitz?" Vera asked, her voice shrill. Apparently, Omaka's disapproval didn't slide off her as easily as Linda's did.

Fitz looked back and forth between her and Linda unhappily. "Vera, I can't just chase a feeble old woman away."

"Why not? She's a witch. Linda said so herself!"

"A priestess," Linda said, correcting her. "She's a priestess. And yes, maybe you could call her a medicine woman." She wondered desperately how she could get Fitz on her side. This power struggle was pure madness. She was Fitz's wife, and Vera was nothing but a busybody, a cheeky little girl. Suddenly, she thought of a solution. Fitz was a gambler. He believed in luck. "Women like her," Linda claimed, "conjure spirits for their people. They carve *hei tiki* and cast curses. I would be nice to her if I were you, Vera."

She made sure not to direct her words at Fitz, but she could guess what was going on in his head.

But Vera just laughed. "A fat lot of good it did her people, having the blessing of their gods and spirits," she sneered.

"Rere ka te ringe ki te ure, ka titoirira, katahi ka hapainga te karakia," Omaka said.

It was a protective enchantment to free possessed souls. Linda couldn't understand every word. Like any *karakia*, this one was spoken quickly, words and syllables flowing into one another. But it was certainly harmless, far from a curse.

Still, Fitz grew pale. "She won't bother you," he said to Vera, and Linda breathed a sigh of relief. "We'll order her to stay here. It's what she wants, anyway. Linda says she's guarding her tree. And you'll be by the river most of the time, anyway."

Vera shot Fitz a hateful look. "If I were you," she told him icily, "I'd chop her tree into a thousand pieces and burn it all. A real man like the major would do that. You just don't have it in you."

She spat on the ground, then turned on her heel and went back toward the river. Fitz followed, which pleased Linda. He certainly shouldn't put up with that kind of treatment from this nobody he'd taken in.

"And with that," she said, "the nightmare seems to be over."

Omaka shook her head. *"To kai ihi, to kai ihi. To kai Rangi, to kai Papa. To kai awe, to kai karu. To kai ure pahore . . ."*

Linda could hear the priestess continue her conjuring as she slowly made her way to collect the canvas and blankets she had brought for Omaka. The old *tohunga* didn't seem to share her optimism. Evil spirits weren't that easy to banish.

Chapter 55

And in the end, Linda's hopes were dashed. Fitz didn't send Vera away. In fact, over the following days, they fell into a pattern. It was usually Vera who would pick a fight after Fitz had rejected one of her suggestions or denied one of her wishes. The girl seemed determined to figure out how much he was prepared to risk for her. She demanded he go fishing with her instead of patrolling the settlement's borders, as was his duty. And she repeatedly convinced him to let her shoot his rifle, even though the military settlers weren't allowed to use their weapons to hunt. The military command was in constant readiness for Maori ambush, and mobilized immediately to find the source of any unexpected gunshot.

Yet Fitz and Vera always got away with their nonsense. They expressed a fiendish joy whenever they fooled one of Fitz's superiors yet again. Fitz was risking trouble and a fine without even a rabbit to show for it. He was still a bad marksman, and Vera didn't even try aiming at a target. She just enjoyed the noise the rifle made.

Linda was livid over their foolishness. Goodness knew they didn't have enough money to be pointlessly risking it that way. Besides, Fitz and Vera's "games" made it impossible for her to add small animals to their diet, which she caught in Maori-style traps. When shots were fired, anybody who had meat on their table was a suspect. They would have had to account for the whereabouts of the ammunition they had been given, and of course, Fitz would immediately have been discovered as the shooter. But he brushed off Linda's reproaches in his usual careless manner.

"You're so unfair, Linda! First, you complained that Vera wouldn't help with the fishing and hunting. But now that she's trying to learn, that isn't right either!"

All Linda could do was sit there in silent resignation. Any explanation was twisted into the opposite of what she'd intended, and Fitz seemed to have lost his basic common sense. He'd always liked playing with fire—the fact that his behavior was now pointless instead of helping them glean small advantages as it had in the past seemed to fly over his head. At least he wasn't completely out of control. He gave in to Vera's whims whenever possible, but he wouldn't risk being kicked out of the army. When he did contradict the girl, she would react quite harshly.

Linda withdrew to Omaka more and more. Sometimes she caught herself murmuring spells with her. Every time Fitz and Vera fought, Linda hoped they'd finally had enough of each other, but by the next day, all would be forgotten.

Linda knew better than to try to change Vera. She just ignored her, much like Vera did when the two women were alone on their future farm. Of course, she was annoyed that Vera wouldn't help her with any of the work, but Linda could get along without her. The person she could not do without was Fitz. Linda could build traps and catch fish, dig for roots, and collect entire stocks of medicinal plants. With some effort and the skilled use of Brianna's strength, she could ready the land to be plowed and sown. But she couldn't chop down trees, build a house, or construct fences or barns.

Unfortunately, Fitz had little interest. Everywhere else in the settlement, trees were coming down, and the first cabins and workshops were being erected. A settler from Wales was even keeping a few sheep already. If Linda had had things her way, Fitz would have built a corral for Brianna first so the mare could graze without constant supervision. Simply keeping her tied to a stake was risky. The lively horse could easily panic if she got her legs tangled in the rope, and she might get hurt. Next, they should have built a barn. Linda wanted to write to Ida and Karl as soon as possible about acquiring some sheep. With Amy's help, she could keep them without fences. All she needed was a barn with space for milking and shearing, as well as the cheese dairy.

The corral and barn could have been done within a few weeks if Fitz had worked steadily. Many neighborhood groups were already building their second or third houses. Fitz, however, returned home after his early morning duties, claiming he was exhausted from the drills and earthwork construction, which was admittedly hard work. Major McDonnell's troops created enormous embankments and fortified them with wood. Still, hardly anyone complained.

After their first run-in with a group of marauding Maori warriors, even the orneriest of the men understood why they were being drilled and what the fortifications were for. Fortunately, there were no casualties on either side, but the military settlers had been on their guard ever since.

What was more, these were men accustomed to hard work. There had been no loafing in the goldfields or at the whaling station. They grimly began their drills at six in the morning, and would immediately start working on their houses or fields when they returned home in the early afternoon. Only Fitz would take a break first, and he wouldn't begin working on the farm before early evening. He'd listlessly grab an ax and chop down one or two trees, leaving them for Linda to take the bark off. Then he'd suddenly remember that he'd lent his saw to Fairbanks or another settler, or that it was dull and needed to be sharpened, or that he badly needed the help of another man, preferably one who lived three parcels over and had to be convinced to come. Usually, Fitz would simply disappear to avoid any argument with Linda. He had Vera deliver his lame excuses. The girl allowed Linda's annoyance to roll off her back without a hint of emotion. While Linda went on working, Vera disappeared just as surreptitiously as her so-called employer. She wouldn't raise a finger at Linda's behest.

About a month after the land assignments had been made, there was a special conscription order for the military settlers. Major McDonnell had discovered that Waikoukou was a Hauhau base, and there was reason to assume Te Ua Haumene was there. It fell to McDonnell to muster his soldiers and attempt to destroy the fort. There was no stopping them once General Chute approached with his troops.

"Apparently, they've captured two white women as well," McDonnell told his men, whom he had brought together at the base. "Just imagine! This is your chance to prove yourselves. Show that you're real soldiers! Who knows, you might even turn out to be heroes. We're leaving first thing tomorrow morning, with full equipment."

"Either we'll prove ourselves or we'll be dead," Fitz said nervously as Linda packed his things that evening.

In truth, he should have been doing it himself. The military settlers had been carefully instructed about what to bring on a campaign and where and how to pack it. But Fitz hadn't paid any attention. He hadn't been expecting deployment, and he was horrified at the prospect.

"Try to take care of yourself," Linda said.

She'd known for quite some time now that Fitz's military skills weren't much to brag about, and it terrified her. Still, she trusted him to get by somehow. Those conflicting feelings accompanied her constantly during the ten days that McDonnell and his men were away. She was agitated and absentminded, hardly managing to finish her day's work, and of course, she and Vera didn't get anywhere with the construction work on the house. Vera seemed completely unworried by Fitz's absence. She drifted lazily through her days, daydreaming and primping and watching Linda work. Occasionally, she'd make sarcastic remarks when the distressed woman accidentally knocked over a bucket of water or let the food burn.

"What are you so afraid of?" Vera asked casually. "If Fitz dies, you'll get the house and land. And probably a captain who wants to comfort you as well."

Vera grinned. Apparently, she'd noticed Captain Langdon's occasional half-interested, half-sympathetic glances at Linda.

Linda's jaw dropped. "Fitz is my husband," she hissed. "It's normal for me to be worried for him. And I don't want a captain or anybody else. I married Fitz, and I want him!"

Vera grimaced scornfully. "Well, we can't always have everything we want."

Unable to stand the heartless girl's presence, Linda withdrew and sought peace under the kauri tree. But Omaka wasn't any more understanding of her disquiet than Vera had been.

"Your husband is no warrior," the priestess explained calmly, "and he does not see himself that way. Once the first shot is fired, he will burrow into the ground like a kiwi in the daytime, and so will return. Do not worry for him, but grieve with me instead, *mokopuna*. At Waikoukou, my people are having even more land taken from them, and more of them will die."

Fitz did return, although much later than expected, with news that the fort had been taken without much bloodshed. A few soldiers had been wounded, but there were no casualties on either side. The Maori had abandoned the place quickly once they realized they were outnumbered. Some of the wounded had stayed behind and were captured. Among them was Tohu Kakahi, one of Te Ua Haumene's confidants, which was a triumph for the generals. General Chute sent the captives to Wellington to be interrogated before his army moved northward. He left McDonnell and his military settlers to destroy the *pa* and the neighboring settlement. They burned the defensive installations, houses, and fields to the ground.

From Fitz's point of view, the campaign had been dangerous, exhausting, and bloody. The only wounds he had to show for it, however, were a few insect bites. Apparently, they had been led by Maori scouts through dense forests, and they had lived in constant fear of an enemy ambush. It was the most difficult and dangerous part of the campaign. It had taken them longer than planned; they had run out of provisions, and the troops had been close to mutiny.

Finally, General Chute had allowed his men to butcher two of the horses, which had helped raise their spirits. Linda found the thought disgusting. She hoped Fitz hadn't taken part in the "feast."

During the battle, the Hauhau had used modern firearms. However, none of their warriors had been visible, since they'd remained inside their protective fences. The English had fired their cannons from equally safe cover. During the night following the battle, most of the Maori had disappeared. After several hours of silence, the English troops had entered the *pa* and searched it with all due caution.

Fitz described it all in great detail, but Linda doubted that he'd ever set foot in the fort himself.

"Was there any trace of the missing women?" Linda asked Captain Langdon a few days later at the main encampment.

The captain shook his head. "Neither the women nor the prophet. He must have fled with his confidants while Tohu Kakahi came out to face us voluntarily. He wants peace, apparently. Or at least he says that all the killing needs to end. It's a bit late for that, but better late than never."

"Did he know about the women?" Linda asked. "It's such an awful story, if it's true."

Langdon frowned. "The stories are true. There are—or there were—two sisters who wanted to go somewhere to the north. Cameron foolishly sent them with a prisoner convoy. He should have realized how dangerous it was. At that point, Weraroa *pa* was still completely manned."

"And the army really isn't trying to rescue them?" Linda asked.

The captain frowned. "The war is in a very delicate phase, what with the prophet wanting to call it off. The generals don't dare throw that away with a raid that would just get lots of soldiers and the hostages killed—if they're even alive anymore, which is highly unlikely. It's a shame, but—" Langdon shrugged and looked at Linda cautiously.

"It's too awful even to think about," she said with a shudder. "Their poor families must be devastated!"

Chapter 56

For Carol and Mara, life after the move to Waikoukou had become easier, just as Tohu Kakahi had promised. The fort was smaller than Weraroa, and there was a village attached to it. The men who'd been minding the fort lived there with their wives and children. They weren't anywhere near as fanatic as Te Ua Haumene's other recruits. Hauhau ceremonies were still held, but day-to-day life was much more similar to life in a Maori village than it had been in Weraroa. In the village, there were enough single women who would gladly take their warriors to a quiet corner to exchange affections. Nobody wanted to take advantage of Carol's forced prostitution any longer.

And as an official commander of the fort, Tohu was able to keep Te Ori away from Mara. The first thing he did was to send the warrior off on a scouting mission of several weeks to observe General Chute's military activity. During that time, Mara's wounds healed, and she seemed to finally be coming back to herself. At least she was talking again—though not much, and only to Carol. The sisters stayed away from the Maori women, although they were accommodated in the *marae* now and not the military area. In Waikoukou, there were no unused spaces that could be used as prison cells. But the sisters weren't allowed to spend the night in the sleeping hall either. The tribal elders had declared Mara and Carol *tapu*.

"Sleep outside," one of the women ordered, tossing two sleeping mats to their feet.

"But couldn't we just run away then, when no one is watching us?" Mara asked her sister quietly.

Carol shrugged. "I'm sure we'd make it out of the village area, but not through the palisade. And they're going to fortify it more; I think they're worried about an attack. There's hope now, Mara. Cameron's going to send his troops when he finds my message."

Unexpectedly, sleeping under the stars proved to be a blessing for Mara's recovery. It was warm, and the sisters felt safe. If someone had tried to approach, the sounds would have awoken them. It would have been possible to see an attacker in the moonlight, to run and hide. Mara was finally able to sleep through the night again. Nightmares disturbed her less and less frequently.

During the daytime, Mara and Carol had to work hard, driven by the *marae*'s women. The women came from different tribes, and almost all of them had been through war and exile themselves. Now, they were taking revenge on the hateful *pakeha* by tormenting the two sisters. They laughed at them, made them do pointless dirty work, and sometimes even hit them or refused to give them enough to eat. Every bite of bread and every sweet potato had to be begged for.

Carol gritted her teeth and endured the treatment, but Mara withdrew at first, eating nothing at all, just like in Weraroa. But this time, she didn't hold out for long. One day, for the first time, Carol saw anger in her blue-green eyes again. Mara glared at the young girl who was teasing her by holding out a piece of bread and pulling it away again and again, fury burning in her eyes. After only having stared blankly ahead for so long, this was progress. But Carol was worried that Te Ori's return would destroy her sister's spirit once and for all. Tohu couldn't keep him away forever.

Indeed, after a few weeks, the village buzzed with gossip. Apparently, Te Ori was bringing a group of excellent warriors and prophets back to Waikoukou. Rumor had it that the contingent had been missionizing on the east coast and had fought General Chute's troops. Te Ori had met them in the woods and was taking them to Haumene now.

Carol and Mara had been expecting his arrival, but Mara still got the shock of her life when Te Ori appeared in front of her. She had been dragging a heavy sack of grain from the storehouse to the kitchens, and she dropped it with a cry. Like all good warriors, Te Ori was an expert at materializing out of nowhere, and he grinned as Mara backed away from him now. She slipped on the spilled grain and fell.

"I will take you tonight."

Mara felt the old panic rise up like a glowing-hot ocean of coals, threatening to swallow her whole. Her entire body began to shake, and she felt the blood draining from her face. She wanted to let herself fall, to roll up in a ball, wrapping her arms around her legs, hiding her face and numbing her mind, but she resisted. In her dark den in Weraroa, the warrior had seemed like the devil incarnate to her. But now, after having had time to recover, she could see clearly at last. He was an ugly, evil, violent man—but he was still human. And humans could be killed. For the space of a heartbeat, Mara imagined plunging a knife into his neck, his blood gushing out . . .

She gritted her teeth, clenched her fists by her side, and got to her feet. "I will wait for you," she replied, hoping that her voice wouldn't break.

She would be waiting for him. She'd endure everything he did to her, and at some point, she'd kill him. Maybe not tonight, but in the end, she would triumph.

Te Ori reacted with lightning speed. His fist came flying up, hitting her in the face and throwing her back to the ground. "Did anybody ask you?" he roared.

Mara writhed beneath his kicks, but she clung to her anger like a lifeline. She glared at Te Ori, predicting each blow or kick. The world had been reduced to him and her alone. He could beat her to death, but he wouldn't make her lower her eyes ever again!

Te Ori jerked her to her feet, raising his fist again.

"Leave her alone!"

Mara heard another voice, one that sounded familiar. Very familiar. In her hardened mind, she could hear echoes of sweet words and laughter.

"Eru?" she whispered.

It sounded just like him, and yet, she must have been mistaken. The man who tore Te Ori away and who was now wrestling him to the ground wasn't Eru. From forehead to chin, his face was covered in blue vines and symbols, and his hair was tied in a warrior's knot. But his skin was pale, paler than his opponent's. Te Ori had fallen in the ambush, and was only slowly getting back to his feet now.

The man took a step toward her. "Mara?" he asked. "How did you get here?"

He offered his hand, but Mara pulled away in fear, squinting in confusion through an eye swollen shut.

"Mara. Marama . . ."

The old pet name. Compassion in a stranger's voice.

A strangled sound escaped her lips.

"Leave! She is my slave." Te Ori seemed ready to fight again. "She is mine!"

The man with Eru's skin and voice shook his head. "No!" he shouted. "She is mine!"

Mara began to scream.

The girl who went to tell Tohu Kakahi about the incident had been one of Carol and Mara's worst bullies. Now, however, seeing the white slave lying there on the ground, screaming, kicking, and biting like a cornered animal, she felt sorry for her. Young Pania raced to the chieftain's house and fearlessly threw herself between Tohu and Haumene. Without considering whose shadow might fall on her, she turned to Tohu Kakahi.

"*Ariki*, come quick! The white girl, she—she—" Pania didn't know how to express what she had witnessed.

"Are you still having trouble with the *pakeha* women?" Te Ua Haumene sounded annoyed. "It is getting to be a bit much, Tohu. That eye-eater Kereopa, those scared boys—and one of them is the half-*pakeha* I sent to preach . . . It's out of control. If this goes on, the English will not wish to negotiate with us any longer."

"Please, *ariki* . . ." Pania wouldn't give up.

Tohu Kakahi turned to the girl. "What happened, daughter? Tell us calmly. Or wait, I will come with you and see for myself." He glanced back at the prophet. "Te Ua, the *pakeha* are well past negotiating. We have gone too far. In a direction we never wanted. This fight cannot be won." He sighed. "I am coming, daughter."

Te Ua Haumene watched his old companion leave with a grim expression on his face, teeth clenched. He wanted to call him back, object to such outright dissent, but he wasn't ready to risk a power struggle. The recent banishments of tribes from Waikato and Taranaki, the lost battles, and the lack of promised miracles had cost him followers. He knew his influence was coming to an end.

When Tohu Kakahi arrived at the kitchen house, Mara was still screaming. Carol had been trying unsuccessfully to calm her. Four warriors were restraining an apoplectic Te Ori. Had they let him go, he might have killed his slave—or the younger warrior, the half-*pakeha* with far too many *moko* for his age. He kneeled before the dark-haired, screaming girl, talking to her insistently. Gently, pleadingly. Tohu had to strain to understand what he was saying.

"But I *am* Eru, Mara. Your Eru. You can't be afraid of me, please. I'm your husband, Mara, dearest Mara. Mara Marama, I love you. I haven't changed. I—"

"No?" Carol asked angrily. "Then what are you doing here with the Hauhau? You should be counting sheep for your mother."

The warrior ignored her.

"Please, Mara! Please, my dearest Mara. You must know me."

Tohu saw tears running down his cheeks. They caught in the grooves of the *moko*. The young man didn't wipe them away.

"Look at me, Mara!" he pleaded.

The young woman hid her face on her sister's shoulder. Carol rocked her back and forth as Mara's screams turned to sobs.

Tohu took a deep breath. "Enough now!" he barked at Eru. "Stop wailing like a girl! And you"—he pointed at Te Ori—"control yourself. This is unworthy of you all! Two warriors, wrestling over a toy like little boys."

"She is no toy," Eru said. "She is my wife!"

"She is my slave!" Te Ori countered.

"She screams," Tohu determined. "So obviously, she does not want to be anybody's wife. We talked about this, Te Ori, and you said you were prepared to court her. She was to stay with you of her own free will. It seems to me that you have not been successful. And she does not seem fond of you either, young man. Let her sister take her to one of the sleeping houses now." He turned to the men holding down Te Ori. "Two of you will guard the women. Let no one approach them. The other two will bring these foolish men to the prophet. We will discuss this matter with him." He stalked off, the men in tow.

The appointed guards waited at an appropriate distance, and slowly, Mara calmed down enough that Carol could help her to her feet. She was still sobbing uncontrollably, but she let herself be led to the closest sleeping house, where she collapsed on a mat.

"That's not Eru," she whimpered. "That's not Eru. The ghosts . . . the voices . . . I'm losing my mind."

Carol brushed a lock of tear-soaked hair from Mara's face. "Calm down now. There are no ghosts. And you're not hearing voices. I wouldn't have recognized Eru right away either. He probably had those tattoos done to spite Jane. But if you look closely, you can recognize him. You will too. Hush now—"

"I don't want to recognize him! If that's Eru, then my Eru is dead. Eru's dead, and I'm dead, Cat's dead, and Chris is dead, and—" Mara began rocking back and forth again, like she had the first few nights of their captivity.

Carol slapped her across the face. "You're not dead!" she shouted.

"Tomorrow, you may both be dead." Pania entered the room with a basket of flatbread, boiled sweet potatoes, and raupo roots. "Here, in case you're hungry. I needed an excuse to come." She set the food on the ground.

"You went to get Tohu, right?" Carol asked. "Thank you."

Pania nodded. "But the prophet is very angry," she explained. "At everyone, I think. At Tohu, at the missionaries who returned today . . . And now they are saying the *pakeha* are coming to conquer Waikoukou. The prophet does not want them to find you here. He will take you away tomorrow to have you killed. He wants it to look as if you tried to escape and the guards shot you by accident."

"Where did you learn all this?" Carol asked breathlessly.

"From Te Eriatara, the warrior who claims he is her husband." She pointed at Mara. "The prophet reprimanded both of them, him and Te Ori. And then the prophet decided what to do with you. But Te Eriatara will not accept his decision. He gave me money, *pakeha* money." Pania beamed as she pulled a penny from her skirt pocket. "I am here to warn you. He says you must be ready. He will free you tonight."

Chapter 57

It had been a hard few months for Eru. Ever since Voelkner's murder, he'd lost faith in Te Ua Haumene's divine mission. It was certainly right to want to stand up to the *pakeha*, but not in this heartless, bloody way! The cause, which had been a kind of game for Eru up until then, repulsed him now. Still, he had continued to travel with Kereopa Te Rau. He told himself that he might be able to watch and mitigate the fanatical warrior that way, but the truth was, he had few options. As part of Kereopa and Patara's entourage, he reached Gisborne and then Te Urewera. Eru's preaching was more reserved, but Kereopa and Patara hardly noticed. His companions were still drunk on the bloodbath in Opotiki, and the Ngai Tuhoe, who welcomed them next, admired them for it. That tribe still upheld the old customs and traditions. A bit of ritual cannibalism, the elders felt, could only increase a warrior's *mana*. The Hauhau felt safe there, no matter how desperately the *pakeha* were searching for them. Te Urewera, the Ngai Tuhoe's tribal land, was an area of dense woodland between the Bay of Plenty and Hawke's Bay. The whites gave this wilderness as wide a berth as they could.

Eru, however, couldn't find any peace. The two groups of Hauhau missionaries had reunited in Gisborne, and of course, his childhood friends had questions. They were torn between disgust and admiration over what had happened in Opotiki, and they wanted to hear every little detail. Eru cringed at Kereopa's and Patara's pretentious descriptions of the "trial" preceding Voelkner's execution, and he wasn't sure how much of his own story he should share with Tamati and Kepa. In the end, he didn't tell them that he'd helped Lange and Gallant escape. It was one more secret he had to live with.

And then it was time to move on. The peace in Te Urewera bored Kereopa and Patara. Kereopa suggested they return to Waikato to missionize the tribes living there, and Patara happily agreed. This meant covering a lot of English-controlled ground. And this time, the Hauhau didn't intend to sneak past quietly. They left Te Urewera for a campaign with the Ngai Tuhoe, and in the Kaingaroa Plains, a brittle, grassy landscape, they promptly encountered Ngati Manawa and Ngati Rangitihi warriors—enemies of the Ngai Tuhoe. They battled fiercely, which Eru thought made a mockery of their whole mission. Hadn't Te Ua Haumene said that the Maori were one people who must unite against the *pakeha*? Shouldn't they have preached to the tribes, bringing them the word of the prophet, instead of facing off with spears and clubs? Of course, the Ngai Tuhoe chieftains and Kereopa explained that the enemy tribes had allied with the English and deserved to be punished. Eru didn't know if this was true, but regardless, these warriors certainly hadn't been traveling as *pakeha* auxiliary troops. All they were doing was defending their own territory against ancestral enemies. Eru and his friends were horrified to learn how much blood traditional weapons could shed. Warriors stabbed each other with spears, bashed in each other's heads with clubs, and dismembered each other with the *tewhatewha*. They beheaded the dead. Kereopa Te Rau ate more eyeballs, this time those of three Ngati Manawa warriors. With that, he earned himself the nickname of Kaiwatu, the eye eater. Tamati and Kepa were just as horrified as Eru had been.

Finally, the Ngati Manawa and the Ngati Rangitihi drove the Hauhau warriors away, forcing them dangerously close to Opotiki, where English troops were stationed, ready to capture Voelkner's murderers. But at the last moment, the Ngati Tuhoe sent reinforcements, and Kereopa and his men fled back to Te Urewera. That night, Eru, Tamati, and Kepa talked privately. They'd had enough.

"I think we should go home," Tamati said. "We did our part, we fought. We are men! We will have plenty of *mana* in our tribe, and I will marry Tiana."

Tiana was one of the prettiest girls in their village. Before this adventure, Tamati wouldn't even have dreamed of winning her for himself.

"You don't really think that Te Haitara will congratulate us for working with the eye eater, do you?" Kepa pointed out. "We didn't even truly fight for the prophet. All we did was meddle in the business of tribes we don't know."

"A fight is a fight," Tamati said.

Eru bit his lip. He'd been brooding over these questions since Voelkner's death. By now, nobody could accuse him of being a coward. All three of them had stood their ground during battle, and they had spilled blood, although only

Kepa had killed an enemy warrior, and it had been by sheer chance. Still, Eru felt that he had something left to finish.

"I think we should go back to Weraroa," he finally proposed. "We can see what the prophet's plans are and how he wishes to go on. Then we can still decide if we want to keep fighting or if we should go back to the South Island. If we go back there now, it would be as if—as if we hadn't achieved anything."

Tamati and Kepa laughed.

"You mean we should stop on the way and throw some *pakeha* into the sea?" Tamati joked.

The young men had long ago realized that Te Ua Haumene's vision would never come to pass. In Weraroa, they had been dreamers. Now they knew how strong the English were, and how many of their compatriots didn't share their enthusiasm for rebellion. Many Maori wanted to live in peace with the *pakeha*, and in enmity with neighboring tribes, especially here on the North Island, where they were far from being one people.

Eru rubbed at his *moko*, which itched at times. "I just want all of this to have been for a reason," he murmured.

The next day, the decision was taken from the adventurers' hands. Te Ua Haumene's representative—or Tohu Kakahi's, rather—arrived with a message.

"The prophet is very angry at what has been done in his name," the man said. "You were sent out to preach peace and love. Instead, you killed a white man, and then you fought the inland tribes you were supposed to be missionizing! You will have to answer to Te Ua and his advisers in Waikoukou—immediately!"

But instead of obeying the prophet's summons, Kereopa and Patara promptly disappeared into the woods. One other recruiter fled with them. The others contritely bowed to the authority of the messenger and set off for Taranaki. The men slipped through land belonging to the tribes they'd just fought, and Eru, Tamati, and Kepa were terrified whenever they so much as heard a branch snap behind them.

Finally, Eru and the others reached Waikoukou and reported to Te Ua Haumene. As expected, the prophet was not pleased with how they had executed his mission. He subjected them to a long monologue about peace and love.

"But we were sent out to recruit warriors for you," Eru said, daring to object. "Was it not right to send the young warriors from the tribes to Weraroa?"

Te Ua threw up his hands in exasperation. "You were told to bring the good news to the tribes on the east coast. If some of their warriors wanted to join us, we would have welcomed them, of course. There was no talk of fighting."

Eru remembered it differently. Angry over the unjust accusations, he walked away, across the *marae*'s meeting grounds. That was when the world he had been living in since leaving home truly came crashing down around him. It was Mara. His beloved Mara. A slave? How could Te Ua approve of slavery? How could he let a brute like Te Ori be responsible for two women? Why was everyone just watching as the man threatened, beat, and kicked Mara? How could this happen in the name of peace, love, and mercy, and the archangels and prophets?

Something inside Eru exploded as he tore Te Ori away from Mara—it hurt, but it was a relief. Pai Marire had been the wrong way for him, and Mara had arrived just in time to free him from it. He wanted to help her up, to wrap her in his arms and kiss her. When she rejected him, he broke. It was too much. He hated himself for everything he had done, or at least endorsed. And now Mara hated him too . . .

All Eru wanted to do was cry and hide away somewhere. But then Tohu summoned him and Te Ori to the prophet again, and everything got worse. Te Ua Haumene sentenced Carol and Mara to death. He didn't care about the women; they had always been an annoyance, but now they were dangerous. Te Ua would rid himself of them as unscrupulously as he had sent young warriors to their deaths with lies about invulnerability.

Eru listened to his decision, standing rigidly, knowing that now was not the time to hide and lick his wounds. He had to escape with the women that night.

"You've got to pull yourself together," Carol told Mara. "I don't care if you trust Eru or not; right now, he's our only hope. No screaming, no crying. When he comes, we go with him. Do you understand?" When Mara didn't reply right away, she shook her little sister. "Do you understand?"

Mara nodded. She was still shaking, but when Carol handed her bread and vegetables, she wolfed them down with a ravenous hunger. Carol noted this with relief. For a trek through the jungle, they would need all their strength.

When it was surely past midnight, they heard the guards in front of their prison being exchanged. An hour or so later, someone opened the door. In the faint moonlight, Carol could barely make out the silhouette of a warrior in the doorway.

"Hurry!" the man whispered.

"Come on." Carol took Mara's arm.

"That's not Eru," Mara whimpered.

Carol hauled her to her feet. "Quiet," she snapped. "Just be quiet, and come with me."

"But that's—"

Carol didn't listen. Instead, she took Mara determinedly by the hand and pulled her out of the hut. They were immediately grabbed from behind. Somebody stuffed gags in their mouths and tied their hands behind them.

"Follow me. Don't you dare make a sound."

Te Ori tied Mara to Carol and grabbed the end of the rope to drag Carol behind him.

Carol could have slapped herself for her stupidity. The guards at the door wouldn't have looked the other way for Eru, but Te Ori had a lot of influence at the fort. One of the guards had even helped him tie the women up. The kidnapping had been silent and quick—and Carol had dragged her sister right into it.

Te Ori openly led the women to the *pa*'s gates.

"Prophet's orders. He wishes to be rid of them," he explained to the guards there.

"Fine, but hurry," one of the warriors hissed, "and don't get caught. I heard the *pakeha* are approaching. They finally want to fight. Don't stumble over them."

"As if I would."

Past the gates, Te Ori immediately began to run. Carol and Mara followed, panting.

After hours of slogging through the jungle, the two women realized that their lives weren't in immediate danger. Te Ori had defied the prophet; he wanted to keep his slaves. But as the night wore on, Carol began to wonder if a quick death wasn't better than stumbling through impassable undergrowth forever. She was completely spent, her legs and face scratched and bloodied by thorns. She had fallen down repeatedly without being able to break her fall with her hands. In the light of the rising sun, Carol could see her sister's pale, exhausted face. But there were no signs of tears. Mara doggedly fought her way through the jungle, obviously trying not to show any signs of weakness.

Only hours later did Te Ori stop to rest. The sun was high overhead. He drank from a stream and removed Carol's and Mara's gags. He didn't untie them.

"How are we supposed to drink?" Carol snapped at him. "Like dogs?"

Te Ori grinned. "Exactly," he said. "I like to see you from behind."

"You will see me head-on when I sink my teeth into your throat," Mara said.

Te Ori threw her to the ground without comment.

"Where are you taking us?" Carol asked.

Te Ori seemed to consider not answering, but then his anger got the better of him.

"I will not have my prey taken from me!" he raged. "I don't care if the man calls himself prophet or *ariki*. Chieftain, ha! Te Ua was never elected. And he is no chieftain's son either. To the contrary, he was a slave himself. That's why he has no *moko* like real men do. If he wants to take what's mine, he'll have to fight me first."

He surely hadn't said that to the prophet's face. Carol wanted to say so, but decided against it for fear of the inevitable blow.

"Where are you planning to go?" she asked again.

"I will take you to my village. To my tribe, the Ngati Huia. They will need warriors like me when the *pakeha* come for their land."

Carol and Mara glanced at each other. They could escape from an ordinary village. A *marae* was not a *pa*.

It took Eru, Tamati, and Kepa half the night to make a hole in the palisade without drawing attention to themselves. They worked far from the gates, at a place screened by high grass and rata bushes. The passage had to be large enough to crawl through on one's stomach. Toward the early morning, they broke into Carol and Mara's prison. They knocked down both guards, who hadn't been all that watchful, tore the door open—and found the hut empty.

"It looks like someone else got here first." One guard picked himself up while the young men were still gazing into the empty room, stunned. "And you can stay in there. We will keep you until tomorrow. I am sure the prophet will have a word to say about this."

Eru didn't stop to think. With a quick motion, he knocked the man down again and made sure the second one was unconscious as well.

"Hurry!" he hissed at his friends. "I will not be locked up by these people. They might sentence us to death as traitors."

Tamati and Kepa followed Eru. They slipped from one cover to the next very cautiously until they reached their escape point. They squeezed through, crawled over the mound that secured the *pa*, and reached the forest without being spotted.

"Do you think they killed Carol and Mara?" Tamati asked as they caught their breath. "Are we too late?"

Kepa shook his head. "Not for the murderers the prophet was going to send. The guards were still there."

"They knew something," Tamati said. "We should have questioned them."

"Don't you get it?" Eru spat, his voice full of hatred. "Te Ori has them. But not for long. Which way do you think he went?"

Even if the young men had been skilled enough to follow Te Ori's trail, it wouldn't have mattered. McDonnell and his men already had the fort surrounded. After less than half an hour, the trio found themselves in the hands of a division of military settlers. Tied to a tree and guarded by two armed men who spent the day playing blackjack, they listened to the thunder of cannons and musket fire coming from the *pa*. The battle only lasted one day and wasn't nearly as bloody as the one the young men had been a part of in Kaingaroa. In the end, only a few men were injured. The prophet and his advisers had left them behind while they escaped. The *pakeha* soldiers herded everyone together and made them watch as the fort and village burned. Instead of finding Te Ori and freeing the sisters, Eru found himself in a convoy of prisoners bound for Wellington.

Chapter 58

When autumn arrived on Fitz and Linda's farm, not even half of the work had been finished. Tasks that had been easy for Linda before were more agonizing by the day. More often than not, she had to ask Fitz to fetch water or chop firewood. He usually did so without complaint, but he took it as an excuse to avoid construction work.

"Sweetheart, I can only do one thing at a time—keep your fire burning or build your sheepfold."

While most of the other settlers had already moved into their own houses, Linda was steeling herself to give birth in a tent. She wasn't thrilled about the idea, but reminded herself that it wasn't the worst thing that could happen. Linda and Fitz's army-issued tent was spacious; there was room enough for four soldiers inside. It was warmer and kept out the damp much better than their covered wagon or the prospector's hut back in Otago. And Linda had actually managed to make it quite cozy. There were no beds, but they had Maori-style sleeping mats and carpets that she had woven with Omaka. For the two women, it was almost a spiritual experience to connect the designs of the Ngai Tahu near Rata Station with those of Omaka's Ngati Tamakopiri. Such designs had been woven into blankets and clothing for centuries.

"The child will learn the symbols. I will explain them to him," Linda promised the old woman. "Their meaning will not be forgotten."

Together, they wove a carrying cloth and a bassinet for the child. Linda would have liked to have a cradle, but Fitz made no attempt to build one.

"There's still time!" he insisted. He seemed almost oblivious to her progressing pregnancy.

Vera slept in the wagon—Linda didn't know if that was for her sake or Fitz's. All she could do was be grateful to have her husband to herself in the tent, at least. Only there, when Vera was safely out of the way, did Fitz occasionally act like he had in happier times. Only there could they have serious conversations in which Fitz actually listened to his wife and accepted her opinions. Only there did he make her laugh and show her some affection. Occasionally he pleasured her, and Linda would spend a contented night in his arms. During those times, she would wonder if she had only imagined the dark cloud that had been hanging over their marriage since Vera's appearance.

But the next morning, Vera's glare would bring her back down to earth, and usually there would be an ugly scene between Fitz and the girl the same day. Jealousy was clearly a factor, although Linda had never witnessed any tenderness between the two of them. Fitz took great pains not to be accused of being Vera's lover. His relationship with "his women" already had people in the settlement talking. His comrades as well as their wives asked themselves the question that bothered Linda too: Was Fitz having a sexual relationship with the girl, who was much too young, or was his connection to her a fatherly one?

One day, Captain Langdon asked Linda directly. He led his horse over to her wagon, which she was just driving out of the main encampment in Patea, loaded with building materials.

After they had exchanged pleasantries, he broached the delicate subject. "Please forgive me, but these rumors about your husband and the girl—well, as company commander, I have a certain responsibility toward my men and their families. So, Mrs. Fitzpatrick, awkward as it is, I must ask: This isn't a case of bigamy, is it?" He glanced unhappily at her belly. "Private Fitzpatrick isn't keeping a, um, second wife, while you are, um, indisposed, is he? You see, we could—well, we'd have to intervene."

Linda blushed deeply. It certainly would have suited her if Fitz's superiors had banished Vera from his side. But it would have been far too embarrassing to admit that there was a problem.

"Oh no, nothing of the kind. Of course not! The girl simply took refuge with us. You know the situation with her family."

Although Private Carrigan did his service dutifully, there was talk that his wife, Mary, had a distillery, though nobody was quite sure where. Her supply of whiskey seemed inexhaustible, and she had set up a kind of pub on her land. Major McDonnell and Captain Langdon knew about it, but they saw no clear way to intervene. This also held true for Vera's sister's behavior. It was an open secret that Kyra spread her legs for money.

Langdon rubbed his forehead. "I am sure young Vera has struggled with many hardships," he said cautiously. "It's good of you to take her in. You'll have to decide for yourself if your husband is a bit, um, overwhelmed by the situation."

As usual, he tipped his hat, spurred his horse to a trot, and rode away. Linda waved after him. She didn't blame Langdon for his frankness. To the contrary, she felt sorry for the young officer. The conversation had been almost as awkward for him as it had been for her. And now, at least, she knew where she stood. Linda wasn't crazy for questioning the nature of Fitz and Vera's relationship, as Fitz had accused her of twice now.

With her heavily loaded vehicle, it took Linda almost two hours to get back to their land from Patea, and on the way, she ruminated over bleak thoughts. Through no fault of her own, she had become the butt of sensationalist gossip. For the first time, she could imagine how her mother, Cat, must have felt years ago back in Nelson.

Thoughts of Cat were followed by thoughts of Ida, Karl, and Carol. So far, Linda hadn't heard from her family, although she had written to the farm in Russell several times. They'd told her at the camp that mail services weren't very reliable, since the situation inland was still precarious. Mail was often lost. But Linda longed for somebody to pour her heart out to. She had Omaka, but the woman preferred to talk about spirits more than worldly problems.

Linda drove her wagon through the autumn trees along the banks of the river. It was the end of April, and next month or the month after that, her baby was due. As usual, she admired the landscape of her new home—the North Island seemed so much more exotic than the Canterbury Plains. There, southern beeches and rata had been dominant, where there were any trees at all. Here, in the warmer climate, the vegetation was diverse. Linda was ready to love her new land, but she still felt as though she hadn't quite arrived yet. If only Fitz would contribute a little more to making their land into a home! If only they could finally make their mark on the earth. If there were fields, if there were a house on the hill, welcoming her . . . Linda rubbed her eyes. No, she wouldn't cry. She had the farm, and she was looking forward to having her baby. Everything else would work itself out.

And then, it actually seemed for a moment as though her dreams had finally come true. As Linda approached her land, she could hear voices, and somebody was chopping wood with an ax. To her astonishment, she recognized Private Fairbanks and Private Hanks, the owner of the parcel next to their neighbor's. The two were working on tree trunks, debarking them, while Fitz and Vera had begun to build a log cabin. It wasn't where Linda had wanted her house to be, though. Fitz wasn't building on the hill with a view of the river, but right next to the little forest that was going to be cleared. Linda felt a twinge of anger at the thought that he was taking the easy way again instead of following their plans, but she quickly suppressed her anger. At least he was working! Perhaps this was supposed to be a barn. With some hard work, all the buildings could even be ready before the birth. Fitz and Vera were working with a will; the girl seemed to have undergone a miraculous transformation. She was laughing and joking with their helpers, and she looked as though she had recently bathed. Her hair, which usually hung over her shoulders in a messy tangle, was shiny and neatly braided. Instead of her old blue skirt, Vera was wearing one of Linda's dresses, which Fitz had convinced her to alter for the girl. Up until today, she hadn't so much as looked at it.

Linda regarded the scene with a mixture of joy and confusion. "Fitz . . . ," she finally managed. Her husband seemed changed too. He was cheerful, swinging his hammer vigorously. "Fitz, what's going on here?"

Fitz came over and lifted her down off the coach box. "Sweetheart, something had to be done," he explained. "You can't give birth to our baby in a tent. So I rounded up some people. In two or three days' time, you'll have your house!"

Linda rubbed at her temple. "But, Fitz, the house was supposed to be on the hill, just like at Rata Station. We were going to have pastures here, maybe barns or shearing shacks. And—"

"And, and, and . . ." Fitz glared at her, his good mood evaporating. "What's your problem now? You were out with the horse. Were we supposed to drag the trees up that hill by ourselves?"

"No, I just—"

Linda wanted to object that they'd been without a house for months now. Those few hours until she returned with Brianna couldn't have made a difference.

But before she could form the sentence, Vera approached, beaming. "Oh, Miss Linda, you look exhausted. I was about to get us some cold tea. I made some for the men, just like you showed me. Surely, you'd like some too . . ."

The girl hurried away, only to return a moment later with a tin pitcher she had used to cool the tea in the river. Vera filled the cups and passed them out to the men with a few cheerful words. She basked in their admiring looks and praise.

"Aren't you lucky, Mrs. Fitz, to have such a skillful maid," Private Hanks said, turning to Linda. "My wife has to do everything alone." Mrs. Hanks was pregnant too, though not as far along as Linda.

"That girl has some backbone!" Fairbanks said. "I'd like to borrow her sometime."

Vera giggled in a way Linda had never heard from her before. "I'll take you up on that, Mr. Phil. I'd love to earn a few extra cents. I'm only helping the Fitzpatricks for room and board and—and I'd just so love to buy a horse, you know?" Vera's expression turned dreamy. "Like Miss Linda. Her Brianna is so pretty. How I love taking care of her."

Linda watched speechless as her sullen, taciturn "maid" turned into a lively, eager adolescent, beguiling their neighbors with her innocent charm. Vera presented herself as diligent and eager to learn, acting grateful toward Linda and seeming to look up to Fitz. Linda wondered if Captain Langdon had spoken to Fitz or even Vera too.

"Why don't you go lie down for a while, Miss Linda?" Vera said.

Linda let the girl lead her over to the tent, acting as though she appreciated the suggestion. Once there, she confronted Vera.

"What are you planning?" she demanded. "What kind of show are you putting on?"

Vera's open expression had transformed immediately once she was alone with Linda. She gave the young woman a contemptuous look.

"I'm sick of sleeping in the wagon," she said curtly. "I want a house."

Later that evening, as Vera and Fitz were cooking dinner with the men, frying a few fish that they had caught in Linda's traps, Linda excused herself and retired to the tent. She was tired of Vera's lies, her flirting with the men, and their hymns of praise for the girl that Fitz joined eagerly. Proud and patronizing, he raved about what a big help Vera was, especially to Linda.

"We couldn't do without her. Hard to imagine she might leave us someday."

Linda cried herself to sleep in anger and disappointment. There wouldn't be a house on the hill for her. There wouldn't even be a house for Linda and her family. Fitz was building a house for Vera.

Chapter 59

Indeed, the log cabin at Fitzpatrick Station was finished in no time. Linda, Fitz, and Vera, for whom Fitz had built a kind of spacious annex, were able to move in well before the baby was due. Linda tried her best to feign excitement, although she felt more bitterness than anything else.

Regardless, this close to giving birth, she had other things on her mind. There was one supposed midwife in Patea, but Linda didn't trust her. Besides, to get her help, Linda would have had to move to town days before the baby was due. Major McDonnell grudgingly provided the settlers' wives with accommodations at the army base for this purpose. This didn't appeal to Linda. She would much rather bear her child in her own bed with Fitz helping her. As an experienced midwife herself, she trusted her ability to guide him with clear instructions. Back at Rata Station, she had helped countless lambs, calves, and foals into the world, and she had assisted Cat and Makuto with several births of human children too. It had taken little to convince Fitz of her plan. The challenge of helping with a birth seemed to reawaken his old euphoria, and Linda knew that her husband could move mountains when he was in that kind of mood. As a result, the young woman was looking forward to her delivery. The pregnancy had been free of complications so far, and she was expecting an easy birth. Should there be problems, she was convinced she could count on Omaka, who must be experienced in midwifery.

For her part, Omaka made no mention of the impeding birth. She seemed often to live in a different world, conferring with the spirits of her people. At the same time, she followed the escalating conflicts between the *pakeha* and Maori anxiously. Over the last few months, there had been several attacks on their settlement. Linda was a little surprised to discover that Omaka wasn't on the warriors' side.

"They are not my people," she remarked when Linda asked her about it one day. The two had been foraging for medicinal herbs when, yet again, they heard the thunder of rifles in the distance, and the trumpeters on their ramparts called the settlers to the front lines. Omaka had sung a *karakia* to evoke peace and to keep the warriors safe—but not for victory. "In the old days, tribes fought each other," the old *tohunga* explained. "There were friends and enemies, land was taken, heads were taken, slaves were taken. And then you returned to your own village and tilled your fields. Now, we have no more villages or fields, and the *pakeha* are too strong for us. Their weapons spit fire, while all ours do is wound men. And they are too many. More and more are coming from across the sea. For every one of them we kill, twenty more take their place. We can hate them, but we cannot fight them as we used to unless we all want to die. Our warriors do not see this, or they do not believe it. They flock together under the leadership of a 'prophet' who does not even speak to our gods, but to the *pakeha*'s, and he promises them they are invulnerable. They do not belong to their tribes anymore; they are just a horde of possessed men, wild and cruel. And for every drop of blood they spill, every head they take from a *pakeha* soldier and carry around proudly, the *pakeha* grow angrier. That anger, fueled by Haumene, fell on my tribe. So, who destroyed us? The *pakeha* or Haumene's warriors? Or both? Those men shooting at each other now, *mokopuna*, are not really enemies. In a manner of speaking, they are all fighting on one side. They are fighting against me and you, against the spirits and the peace between Papa and Rangi in Aotearoa."

Linda admired the old *tohunga*'s power of insight and her ability to fight the hatred in herself, no matter how much grief for her people weighed on her. Moments like these made Linda feel very close to her, and she knew Omaka wouldn't refuse her request to help with the birth. Should there be trouble, she could always send Fitz to get her.

On a dry, sunny day in early June, Linda's baby was ready to enter the world. It was a little cold out, but also beautiful. Linda delighted in the fresh morning view of Mount Taranaki, seeming so close in the clear winter air that it could have been right there on her doorstep. As she stepped outside, she could feel the child shifting downward inside of her. That day, or maybe that night, her contractions would begin. She had to go look for Fitz and remind him not to report for guard duty that day.

As usual, Linda was annoyed that she had to walk around the hill that their house should have been standing on before she could see Brianna's pasture and the river. If they'd built according to her original plans, she could have overseen all the outbuildings from the house, and could have just called Fitz instead of having to go look for him. She expected to find her husband with Brianna. He usually rode the horse to work, even though it was a short walk. And at this time of day, he wasn't usually on his way yet. All he would do was feed Brianna and then return to the house to eat his breakfast.

That was why Linda was surprised not to find him. Neither he nor her mare were in the pasture where Vera was filling the watering trough with her usual sullen expression. She returned Linda's greeting with a grumble.

"Where did Fitz go?" Linda asked. "I think the baby's coming."

Vera looked up at her, her normally blank eyes flashing triumphantly. "Fitz rode to Patea, to the livestock market. He's buying me a horse."

"He's doing what?" Linda cried.

For a few months now, every first Tuesday of the month, there had been a small livestock market in Patea. They mostly dealt in substandard sheep and cattle, and sometimes pigs or chickens. Still, settlers were eager for the animals and would pay steep prices for them. Horses were sold there, usually of decent quality. The merchants willing to drive their four-legged wares all the way to Patea knew their clientele. Most of the military settlers had never farmed before, but they were travelers. They knew enough about horses not to let some lame old mares be palmed off on them.

"He's buying me a horse," Vera repeated flippantly. "I saved up enough money."

For the last few weeks, she'd worked on one of the nearby farms almost every day. Linda was ignorant as to what exactly she did there. Vera wouldn't answer any of her questions, and Fitz just mumbled something about gardening or herding. Linda had her own suspicions, but at any rate, Vera had managed to save up a lot of money in a short time, and now it seemed she had sent Fitz to spend it for her.

Linda stared at the girl. "Vera, I'm expecting a baby! Fitz knew it could happen any day now. I need him with me during the birth. How could you send him away? How—"

"The market is today," Vera said calmly.

"And there's another one next month, and the month after that and after that. You didn't have to—"

Vera smiled slowly. "Fitz didn't have to go."

Linda had often heard the saying that people could see red. Now, she knew how it felt.

"You little tramp! You planned this!" she cried. "And Fitz, what an idiot, what a childish fool!"

Fitz had been looking forward to the baby's birth. Vera wouldn't have been able to coax him away from Linda's side with one of her usual demands. But a horse . . . Fitz considered himself a horse connoisseur, and it had been hard for him not to own one since Otago. He hadn't been able to resist the temptation of choosing one for Vera, of having her trust him to pick the right animal. He probably hadn't thought of the baby for a second, or he'd pushed the thought away with a laugh. Linda could almost hear him: "It's not going to come today, of all days, sweetheart. And I can be back by nightfall . . ."

"Let me guess." It took all Linda's self-control to keep from slapping Vera's haughty face. "He told his superiors he needed the day off to stay with his pregnant wife. So he's risking getting caught in a lie or insubordination again. Or do you expect they just won't notice him in Patea?"

Vera pursed her lips and shrugged, unperturbed.

Linda glared at her. "This is the last time!" she declared. "You've gone too far, Vera. I won't stand for this anymore. It's time for you to leave!"

"Where am I supposed to go?" Vera asked.

"I don't care!" Linda screamed. "Go back to your family. Or live with one of your customers. That's what they are, aren't they, Vera? Those men you say you garden and feed the animals for? Because I don't see any gardens on their land, and they don't have animals yet either. I know exactly what you are! And now get out of here!"

That very moment, Linda felt a pain in her abdomen. Seconds later, liquid began running down her legs. Amy, always by her side, barked in alarm.

Vera smiled again. "Then who's going to help you with the delivery, Linda? Do you really want me to leave?"

Linda buckled under the contraction. Suddenly, she was scared. The baby was probably in the right position, and she was young and strong. She could survive the birth without help. But afterward, she'd be weak, and the baby would be helpless. What if Vera did something to hurt him and then claimed the child had been born dead . . .

"Get out of here!" she screamed.

She turned her back on the terrible girl. She must try to reach the house. She couldn't have the baby in a pasture. It would be best if she could find Omaka. If things didn't go too quickly . . .

Linda headed for the house, but after only a few steps, her next contraction gripped her. It felt as though somebody was ramming a knife into her belly. Linda stumbled and immediately gave up the thought of going for help. She wouldn't be able to reach Omaka's camp under the kauri tree in time. This child was in a hurry. Normally, she would have been happy about it. But now, she would have liked to prolong the labor. If only Fitz could be back in time to protect their baby!

Linda wrapped her arms around her belly and took another few steps toward the house. The girl followed, and Linda felt herself trembling. She vomited into one of her gardens and forced herself to go on. After what felt like an eternity, she reached the cabin. Linda dragged herself inside and crumpled on her bed to endure the next contraction.

"Would you like some tea?" Vera asked, closing the door in Amy's face. The dog barked anxiously and scratched at the door to be let in.

"I want you to leave," Linda panted. "Leave me alone."

Vera smiled. "I think I'll make myself some tea."

Linda watched the girl put the kettle on. She'd prepared some herbs for Fitz to brew a pain-relieving, labor-enhancing tea for her, but she wouldn't ask Vera to do that. She wouldn't eat or drink anything the girl gave her, although she didn't think Vera knew enough about herbs to poison her. She squirmed under her next contraction, groaning. She had to undress. She had to get out of her clothes and put on a nightgown or give birth to the child naked, like the women she'd helped in the Ngai Tahu village. But she was already so weak that she couldn't have loosened all her stays and opened the buttons, never mind pulling the heavy woolen dress over her head. It was constricting her, and she was sweating—when she wasn't shivering violently. Linda's body shook with cramps. Vera pulled a stool up next to the bed, watching her struggle like a cat toying with its doomed prey.

On top of all this, Amy was still barking outside the house. Linda could hear the small dog scratching at the bedroom wall now.

"That stupid mutt," Vera said. "She annoys me, Linda. She annoys me so much."

The girl's gaze wandered to Fitz's rifle. It was leaning on the wall. Of course he'd forgotten to take it with him yet again, defying orders.

"Don't you dare," Linda gasped. "Run, Amy! Go find somebody! Go get help!"

The animal was clever; she knew some of the most complex orders used for herding sheep. But Linda knew full well that Amy wouldn't understand this command.

Amy raced around the house frantically. Something was wrong. And now she could hear her mistress calling! Amy barked, but that wasn't enough to express her fear. Just as Linda was torn apart by her contractions, Amy was torn by grief and helplessness. Linda screamed and Amy howled. Like a siren, her howls echoed across the farm, earsplitting and pitiful.

Fairbanks, their next-door neighbor, didn't hear it; he was away on duty at the earthworks. The lookouts at the fort heard but didn't think twice. Why shouldn't a dog howl every now and then? But Amy's howls did drown out the voices of the spirits talking to Omaka. The old woman got to her feet and gathered a few things. She quickly made her way to the river, walking.

As she got closer to the house, she heard the sound of Linda's screams mixed with Amy's howls. As soon as the dog recognized Omaka, her howls dwindled to whimpers. Amy jumped all around the *tohunga* in relief, and tore into the house as soon as the old Maori woman opened the front door.

Vera's jaw dropped, then she recovered quickly. The girl grabbed the rifle and pointed it at Omaka, but she was too clumsy with it to scare the priestess. Omaka spat a curse at Vera and crossed to Linda's side.

"It—it's not loaded," Linda gasped. "He always forgets."

Vera dropped the rifle and ran out the door.

"She was going to kill the baby," Linda whispered through her tears. "She would have killed him . . . What kind of person is she?"

Omaka's expression remained impassive. "She is not like us. She is like your husband."

Linda started in shock. She wanted to tell Omaka that Fitz was a crook and a fool, but not a wicked person like Vera. She wanted to tell her how exuberant he could be, how happy he had made her time and again. And then, she forgot everything as a fresh wave of pain crashed over her. She cried out, but she wasn't alone anymore. Amy licked her hand comfortingly, and Omaka helped her out of her dress, washed her, and gave her tea to relieve the pain. She sang *karakia*, and Linda cried because she thought she could hear Cat's bright, warm timbre behind the old woman's brittle voice. *Ko te tuku o Hineteiwaiwa* . . . Linda gave herself up to the old *tohunga*, crying and laughing at the same time as the child slid into Omaka's wrinkled hands a short while later.

"A girl," the priestess said, wiping her face gently so Linda could have a look at her.

The little one was tiny, red, and wrinkled, and Linda felt as though she was peering out from under that dark thatch of hair almost as curiously as her father would have.

Linda laughed. "I hope you're going to take life a little more seriously than your daddy does!" she cautioned her daughter.

"She is healthy and beautiful," Omaka said as she cut the cord.

The child began to cry, and Linda took her into her arms. It felt amazing, much better than all the animals and human children she'd held before. How sad that Fitz was missing this moment!

Soon, Linda was groaning in pain again. A few minutes after that, the placenta was expelled.

"Will you bury it, *karani*?" she asked Omaka. It was traditional to bury the umbilical cord and placenta in a carefully chosen spot. According to Maori belief, a person would always be drawn back to the place of their birth. "My child is now a part of your land too, *tangata whenua*."

Omaka shook her head sadly. "This child will not draw her *mana* from this land," she said calmly. "It would be wrong to bind her to it."

"But—" Linda was about to object, but Omaka placed a hand on her and the baby, who was now peacefully slumbering in her mother's arms.

"Do not ask this, *mokopuna*. Instead, tell me what you will call her." She smiled warmly. She seemed to be dropping the austere demeanor of a priestess, truly becoming the little girl's *karani*.

Linda thought for a moment. Of course she'd discussed names with Fitz, but only boys' names. Linda would have liked to name a son after Chris. Finally, they'd agreed on the name Christian Roderick Fitzpatrick. And now they had a little girl. A daughter who owed her life to a priestess.

Linda smiled. "I will name her after you, *karani*."

Omaka raised her eyebrows, and her eyes became veiled once more, the *karani* giving way to the seer. "She will not draw her *mana* from this river either, *mokopuna*."

Linda shook her head. "I will not give her the name your people gave you, but the one the spirits call you by."

Omaka frowned.

The baby opened her eyes, and Linda smiled at her. "I'm going to call you Aroha," she told her daughter. "Love."

Chapter 60

The night after Aroha's birth passed quietly, perhaps too quietly. Omaka, who was holding the child and keeping a close eye on her young mother, would step outside the cabin every now and then to listen. Many birds on the North Island were nocturnal, and normally they crowed and cried, foraged for food on the forest floor, and fluttered around in the treetops. This night, though, nothing stirred expect for Amy. She kept starting in fright, barking. Twice she even woke Linda, who was sleeping in bone-deep exhaustion.

"There's something out there, somewhere in the woods," Omaka said.

Linda yawned. "Vera must be prowling around."

Omaka shook her head. "No. It is not so close. But it is coming. Something is coming closer."

Linda frowned. "What's coming, Omaka? A storm?"

The old woman shook her head. "I don't know. But the land can feel it too. The spirits are in turmoil. We must be watchful."

The next morning, Linda awoke well rested and happy. She smiled as Aroha, whom Omaka had lain down next to her, opened her pale blue eyes. Linda wondered if they'd stay blue like her own eyes and Fitz's or if they'd turn brown like Cat's. A tear ran down Linda's cheek at the thought of her mother. How she would have loved to have her here right now.

"You can nurse her now," Omaka suggested, skillfully placing the child at Linda's breast.

While the old priestess sang more *karakia*s, Linda placed her nipple in the baby's mouth, and Aroha's tiny lips immediately closed over it. Linda enjoyed the baby's tentative attempts at trying to coax the rich milk from her mother's breast, and her fervent, vigorous appetite. She was overcome by love and tenderness as the little girl fell asleep, snuggled contently on her chest.

Cautiously, Linda sat up in bed. Through the cabin's open door, she could see Omaka lighting a fire in front of the house, cooking *kumara*, and baking flatbreads. The Maori priestess was uncomfortable with the indoor stove, but the fire seemed to be serving another purpose as well. After Linda had eaten hungrily and drunk some tea, Omaka went back outside. This time, she stoked the fire until it was blazing and tossed in some herbs, invoking the spirits. Then she ceremoniously burned the umbilical cord and placenta while singing strange incantations. Previously, Linda had only heard such prayers during Matariki celebrations, for the Maori New Year, when the Maori flew kites to send greetings to the gods.

"You anchored her soul to the sky?" Linda finally asked, uncertain.

Omaka nodded. "I appointed Rangi as her guardian," she explained. Rangi was the sky god; newborn babies' souls usually found their places with Papa, the earth goddess. "Your child will not be bound to any river or mountain."

Linda laughed uneasily. "She will recite a strange *pepeha*, then."

The speech that every Maori reserved for their personal introduction described the rivers and mountains of their home. They would tell of their *maunga*, the land to which they were bound no matter how far they wandered.

Omaka lifted her eyes. "The sky will be her *maunga*."

The sun had reached its zenith. Vera hadn't shown herself since the night before, and Linda was almost daring to hope that the girl had found herself another place to live. Unfortunately, this didn't turn out to be the case. In fact, Vera had waited by the river for Fitz until he finally returned from Patea around noon. While he'd been in town, he'd taken the opportunity to drink to the purchase of the pretty little gray mare he had bought the girl. Of course, he'd also played a few rounds of blackjack. He'd almost managed to make back the money that he'd spent on the horse, as he bragged later.

Linda never did learn everything the two of them had talked about. But he already knew about his daughter's birth as he careened into the cabin.

"Lindy! The baby's here? You had her without me?"

He was beaming brightly and gave Linda a kiss, and then he focused all his attention on his daughter. Fitz was so delighted over Aroha that Linda almost forgave him for his absence. In his joy and euphoria, he was briefly the man he used to be. He joked around with Linda, complimenting her and tickling Aroha.

"She's wonderful!" he cried, picking up the baby and cradling her in his arms. "What a pity I couldn't be here for the birth."

Fitz's good mood had mollified Linda, but now her anger returned. Didn't he even regret in the slightest that he'd left her alone when she'd needed him most? Did he not understand?

Linda finally exploded. With harsh words, she laid out the danger he'd put her in. As she had expected, he didn't seem to be aware of any fault on his part. Her husband wouldn't even take her reproaches seriously.

"Sweetheart, why are you still angry?" he asked in surprise. "Everything worked out in the end. What a beautiful child we have! You did wonderfully!" He grinned. "I have to say, I couldn't have done it better myself."

He tried to kiss her, but Linda pulled away. "Fitz, this isn't funny," she tried again. "I could have died. And your dear little Vera would have watched it all with a cold smile on her face. We have to talk about her too. She—"

"But she called the old Maori woman in the end, didn't she?" Fitz interrupted, prepared to nip any attack on Vera in the bud. "Even though she's scared of her! And even though the old witch shouted at her again. Vera just asked me again to report that woman, and I think I'm going to do it. She has no business here; she should go back to her tribe."

Linda's cheeks flushed with fury. "Fitz, Omaka saved your daughter's life and mine last night. I don't know what Vera told you, but she didn't call Omaka. That was Amy." She paused as Fitz smiled at her condescendingly. "No, really," she insisted. "Amy howled. Omaka heard her. Vera had nothing to do with it, unless you want to thank her for locking the dog out."

"So, she was inside with you," Fitz said. "She told me she was going to make you some tea, but you didn't want any, you—you were acting like a madwoman, apparently. Understandable, of course. The contractions, the pain . . ."

Linda balled her hands into fists. "Fitz, she's twisting the facts around completely. Vera's lying. She lies whenever she opens her mouth, she—"

Fitz was about to object again, but at that moment, Aroha began whimpering, working her way up to a scream. Fitz almost dropped her.

"Woah!" He laughed, visibly grateful for the interruption. "Now you've gone and woken the baby with your ranting. Here." He handed the child to Linda. "Do you think she's hungry?"

Linda nodded, resigned. She did need to feed Aroha, and it was important that she calm down first, especially since she was so very, very tired.

"I'll be outside, then," Fitz said, "breaking in Vera's horse. An elegant horse, perfect for a young lady—"

Linda shot him a poisonous look over Aroha's little head. "We'll talk about Vera later," she said as calmly as she could.

Fitz gave her a superior smile. "Of course, sweetheart, of course."

Linda closed her eyes and allowed her weariness and Aroha's nursing to calm her as Fitz left the cabin. Omaka silently returned to her bedside and began singing her songs.

"I couldn't do it, Omaka," Linda said with a sigh before closing her eyes in exhaustion. "But I'm going to try again, and I will not be swayed next time. I will tell him that Vera has to leave."

Linda was true to her word. Late in the afternoon when she awoke, after feeding Aroha, she brought up the subject of Vera again. The girl wasn't around. She'd gone for a ride on her new horse. Linda felt sorry for the animal. Vera was no rider. She clung insecurely to the horse's back with a death grip on the reins. That was why Linda had forbidden Fitz to let her ride Brianna. And as usual, when she was fighting for someone other than herself, she'd become so adamant that Fitz and Vera had actually respected her wishes. Now, the memory gave Linda the courage she needed to tell her husband everything that had happened the day before.

As expected, Fitz brushed off her accusations with a laugh. "That's absurd, Lindy. What kind of grudge is Vera supposed to have against your baby? And you're saying the whole thing with the horse was planned? How was she supposed to know the child was going to be born yesterday, of all days? You don't really believe she set up the livestock market for that day too, do you?" He shook his head, smiling.

"I calculated the due date!" Linda cried, her eyes flashing angrily. "Goodness knows that wasn't difficult after you—" She took a deep breath and stopped.

There was no use in bringing up his failure in bed too. "You knew when to be ready, and your superiors knew. Vera obviously knew too. And the livestock market was convenient for her plans. Otherwise, I'm sure she would've found another reason to coax you away."

Linda fell silent when she heard rifle shots coming from outside. Amy was barking again. She'd been at it on and off all afternoon, and howling too.

"Don't you have to go?" Linda asked, worried.

Now, the shots were accompanied by the trumpet signal calling the settlers to arms. Fitz stopped there, obviously trying to decide whether the uncomfortable conversation or military service was less appealing.

"But it's my day off," he said, gesturing toward Aroha and grinning. "They'll have to fight off the savages without me. McDonnell's done it before. Besides, it could be a false alarm. The major worries too much. Just like you, sweetheart. Vera—"

Linda sat up and took a deep breath. "Vera's a liar and a whore, and if Omaka hadn't joined us yesterday, she would have killed your child. I'm sure of it, Fitz! This isn't a joke."

But Fitz laughed again. "Lindy, sweetheart, Vera's just a girl!"

Linda pulled the sleeping Aroha closer to her. "Fitz," she said. Again, there was the sound of gunshots. They sounded dangerously close, but she couldn't worry about that now. "Fitz, I don't care what you believe. But you have to make up your mind now: I, your wife, want Vera gone. Send her away. It doesn't matter if you understand my reasons or not."

Fitz straightened his back. Linda had never seen him so enraged. His features, which had been distorted by a careless, patronizing grin only moments ago, morphed into a mask of hatred.

"Never!" he hissed. "And I'm not listening to any more of your insanity either. This is my land, Linda! Before Vera goes—"

Before Fitz could continue, somebody tore open the door. Omaka stumbled into the cottage, shouting for Linda to follow her.

"—you go!" Fitz shouted.

Linda bit her lip. She didn't have time to respond now. Omaka's message was more important. Now there was another trumpet signal coming from the fort, and it barely managed to drown out the rough sound of a conch. Linda knew what it meant. She pulled Aroha closer and tried to get to her feet.

"You have to report to your garrison right now, Fitz. Aroha and I are going into the forest with Omaka. She says the warriors are coming. They're blowing the conch."

Omaka turned to Fitz and spoke in broken English. "*Putara.* Wife, child, escape. Forest safe. I find place." She helped Linda to her feet.

"Nonsense!" Fitz shook his head. "It's just a few crazy savages again. The major's going to beat them back in a minute."

"Not if they're blowing the *putara*!" Linda said, gathering up a few blankets and some clothes for Aroha. "The conch horn calls the warriors to battle. There must be many of them. And well organized too—an army!"

"They gathered last night," Omaka explained in her own language, "which is why it was so quiet. They must have been hiding during the day, and now, at dusk—"

"They won't attack now," Fitz insisted. "It'll be dark soon."

"That's exactly why they'll attack!"

Linda was ready to leave. She could hear extensive gunfire. Maybe the attackers were crossing the river.

Outside the cabin they heard hoofbeats, and Vera burst in.

"Fitz! Fitz! They're chasing me!" It was the first time Linda had seen her truly upset. "Hundreds—hundreds of savages! They—they have—"

"Rire rire, hau hau!"

"Pai marire, hau hau!"

From outside, they could hear warriors' voices. The men weren't shouting battle cries like they would have done while dancing a *haka*; they were chanting the syllables drearily, in a ghostly singsong like a choir of spirits.

"Kira, kira, wana, tu, tiri, wha . . ."

"Kill, kill, one, two, three, four . . . Kill in the north, kill in the south, kill in the east, kill in the west . . ."

"Hapa, hapa! Pai marire, hau hau!"

Linda peeked out the cabin door. The men had indeed crossed the river, and now they were coming around the hillside. Vera had led them straight to the house. There was no chance of escape.

"Fitz, hurry!" While Linda was frozen in shock and Fitz was staring entranced at the apparitions, Vera sprang into action. "The shed! My shed!"

The annex where Vera slept had a door to the outside, but there was also a small passageway into the house. It was low to the ground and had been made to pass wood or provisions through. Linda usually kept it bolted. She certainly didn't want Vera to slip into the house unannounced. Now, the girl unbolted the door.

"Come on, Fitz!" She shoved him through.

Linda thought for a heartbeat. She had a plan that might work. Especially if she blew out the gas lantern she'd been using. The hatch would barely be visible inside the dim cabin. On the other hand, the warriors outside had already seen the light. They would come searching for *pakeha* in hiding.

"Stay out here, Fitz, and take your rifle!" Linda cried. "Omaka and I and the baby—and Vera," she said, adding the girl's name reluctantly, "will hide in the shed. Shoot anybody who comes through the door. You'll have to hold them off until help arrives."

Fitz reached for his weapon half-heartedly. Vera slapped it out of his hand.

"Are you mad, Fitz?" she yelled. "Do you want to sacrifice yourself for that bitch and the old hag? Come on!"

Linda could hardly believe her eyes, but Fitz followed the girl into her shed. For a moment, he turned, and their eyes met. His betrayal went through her like the blade of a knife, and yet . . . Before Vera could close the hatch, Linda shoved the baby into Fitz's arms.

"Take care of her!" she'd wanted to shout, but all she managed was a pitiful whimper.

Linda heard Vera begin to complain and Fitz ordering her to be quiet. Then the hatch was bolted from the inside. Linda and Omaka were alone in the cabin. The warriors' cries were close now, and farther off, they could hear the thundering of guns. Linda scarcely registered any of it. Every single emotion, even fear, was frozen inside her. She couldn't think; all she could do was act automatically. She reached for the rifle, loaded it, and raised it to her shoulder.

"I will try to talk to them," Omaka said. "They were men once, *tungata* Maori."

The warrior filled the cabin's entire doorframe. Linda looked into a tattooed face with burning eyes and at a huge, bare torso.

"Rire rire, hau hau!"

The man was holding an ax. A second warrior crowded inside after him. Linda stiffened at the sight of his blood-soaked skirt. The man was holding a spear in one hand and a severed human head in the other. He swung it back and forth like some kind of gruesome aspergillum, sprinkling the cabin floor with blood.

"Stop, my sons. I am Omaka Te Pura. I am *tohunga*. You see what I am." Omaka calmly raised her face to the light to show that she wore no *moko*. At this, the first warrior retreated a few steps. "I am *tapu*. Simply by touching my shadow, you offend the spirits."

"Is this your house, *maata*?" the large warrior asked.

He had addressed her as mistress. Linda felt a flickering of hope, but then she recognized the head that the other warrior was carrying. It belonged to their neighbor, Phil Fairbanks. In a brief moment of hysteria, she wondered if there was still a chaw of tobacco in his mouth.

Omaka nodded. "It is my house," she said, "and it is *tapu*."

The warrior seemed unsure, but the one carrying Fairbanks's head laughed.

"Ridiculous! How can this be a *tohunga*'s house? This is a *pakeha* house, can't you see? It is part of their settlement. One of their soldiers lives here, and the woman there is his wife. So, do as you are told, Rau! *Rire rire, kira, kira, hau . . .*"

Linda didn't even wait for the first warrior to join in the battle cry. The moment he began approaching Omaka with his ax, she lifted the rifle and pulled the trigger.

The warrior stopped in his tracks. Linda could see the hole that the bullet had made in his chest, and a second later, a torrent of blood followed it. The man stumbled, trying to say something, but only bloody foam escaped his lips as he fell to the ground.

"How can this be?" The other warrior looked back and forth between the dying man and the old priestess—and then at Linda, who was swiftly reloading. "We are supposed to be invulnerable. The prophet said—"

"Your prophet lied to you," Omaka said gently. "Come, my son. Lay down your weapons. Remember that, some time ago, even your prophet preached peace, and—"

"His faith was not strong enough!" the warrior crowed. "The prophet says he who believes will be invulnerable, and the *pakeha*'s bullets will bounce off him. Rau did not have enough faith." He raised his spear, turning toward Linda.

The thunder of her second shot, tidy as the first, mixed with the sound of other shots being fired outside the cabin. She could hear screams, blows, English cursing, and still, the hypnotic Hauhau chants, which were slowly dwindling. Omaka began singing a *karakia*. She was praying for the souls of the dead warriors.

"Private Fitzpatrick? Mrs. Fitzpatrick?"

Linda slowly returned to reality. She blinked at Captain Langdon, who had appeared in the doorway behind the bodies of the two Maori. Behind him, more members of the company were crowding inside.

"In God's name, Mrs. Fitzp—" Langdon stopped and leveled his weapon at Omaka.

Linda threw herself in front of the old woman. "Don't shoot! She's with me. She's not the enemy."

The captain glanced around. "Where's the baby?" he asked, staring intently at the rifle that Linda was still holding. "Where's Private Fitzpatrick?"

Linda lowered the gun. Then she pointed at the hatch.

Chapter 61

"Mrs. Fitzpatrick, I don't want to offend you," the captain said, "but there are some discrepancies between your statement and Vera Carrigan's. With regard to the Maori woman—what was her name?"

"Omaka Te Pura," Linda said wearily.

A day had passed since the Hauhau attack. Linda had learned that there'd been somewhere between three hundred and five hundred Hauhau warriors forced to retreat by the military settlers and another hundred soldiers sent as reinforcements from Patea. For the time being, Linda and Aroha were being accommodated at the army camp. Vera had gone back to her family, and Fitz was awaiting trial. The charges were simple: cowardice in the face of enemy attack. Half his company had witnessed him crawling out of the shed. Private Fitzpatrick had hidden while his wife had fought off the enemies. The expected consequence was a dishonorable discharge from military service, and of course, Fitz would lose his land.

Omaka had been arrested as well. Major McDonnell and his personnel had decided to keep the old woman in custody until they figured out what to do about her. Linda attempted to explain the situation again.

"Omaka is a priestess," she said. "And if the commanders are clever, they won't reassign our land but allow Omaka to live on it and conjure her spirits. In payment, she could offer her services as a midwife. There are five pregnant settlers' wives now, and more every day." Several of the military settlers had gotten married during the last few months. "Omaka knows more about medicine than anyone in this area, including your surgeon major."

Captain Langdon laughed bitterly. The surgeon major was known to be fond of drinking, and was widely regarded as a quack.

"I'm afraid that's not my decision to make," he said. "And as I said, Miss Carrigan has a vastly different opinion. According to her, your priestess is a witch who hates white settlers and has connections with the Hauhau. Miss Carrigan claims she was spying on us, and that she's responsible, in part, for the attack last night. Your husband confirmed Miss Carrigan's statement. We don't set much store by his word anymore, of course, but it deserves mentioning. He explained that he was very worried about your relationship with the old woman, and had wanted to report her for quite some time. Your feelings were all that was keeping him from doing it."

Linda sucked in her breath sharply. "Captain, were you under the impression that I could have stopped my husband from doing anything?" she asked sarcastically.

Langdon lowered his gaze, embarrassed. "As I said, we don't set much store by Private, um, Mr. Fitzpatrick's words. Still, you just confirmed that the old woman is a priestess. So, a connection with Te Ua Haumene is certainly possible."

Linda rubbed her forehead, barely suppressing a groan. "Captain Langdon, don't you know anything about the people you're fighting? Omaka being a priestess is the very reason she rejects Hauhau doctrine. Believe me, she considers Te Ua Haumene no less of a heretic than your regiment's priest does, no matter how differently they'd explain it. I can't allow you to hurt her. She saved me and my child—from Vera Carrigan, although nobody seems to believe me. And now, please, would you be so kind as to tell me what else that girl told you? I'd like to know what to expect. Concerning my husband's trial too."

Captain Langdon gave Linda a serious look. "She said she took the baby with her—her own idea, apparently, to protect her. And that Mr. Fitzpatrick followed her in because you, Mrs. Fitzpatrick, absolutely refused to let her take care of the child. Her exact words were: 'At some point, Linda became delusional and thought I was going to hurt the baby.'"

Linda dug her nails into Aroha's blanket, imagining that she was digging them into Vera's face. "You don't believe her, do you?"

The captain shrugged. "It doesn't matter what I believe. There's no excuse for Private Fitzpatrick's cowardice in the face of the enemy. The correct behavior for him would have been to send you and the child and Miss Carrigan, and maybe even Omaka, to the hiding place, and to man his post with the gun himself. Everything else—your version and Vera's—is compromising for him."

Linda bit her lip. "It matters to me if you believe me or not," she said angrily. "I'm sick and tired of seeing the girl get away with her lies."

Captain Langdon smiled. "Well, if you set so much store by my opinion, I believe you. I saw what you're capable of yesterday. If Vera had taken the child from you, you would have followed her yourself to get her back. And in that case, I think it's possible we might have had not one but two severed heads on our hands."

Private Fairbanks had been the only casualty among the *pakeha* troops. He, too, might have survived had he done his duty and followed the trumpet signal to arms. Instead, he had been with Vera. Supposedly, she'd come over to show him her horse.

"Do you really think that's what she was showing him?" Linda asked.

The captain shrugged again. "Private Fairbanks's decapitation doubtlessly took place outside. Miss Carrigan's statement and the blood are consistent in this case. Vera Carrigan must have been sitting on her horse already when the attack occurred. Otherwise, she couldn't have fled."

"So she was just leaving," Linda said. "Granted, it was dark, and there was shooting. She wanted to go home. Whatever she did before—"

"We'll never know," Langdon said. "Unless she keeps up her business."

Linda shook her head. "I doubt she will. Or at least not here. Maybe you'll be lucky, Captain, and Vera will leave Patea. I suppose you'll chase away my husband, and he'll take her with him."

"Where will you be going now?" Captain Langdon asked.

Linda was loading her wagon with the few belongings she'd brought to the army camp. Fitz's trial had taken place the day before, and now, she was getting ready to leave.

As expected, Joe Fitzpatrick had been given a dishonorable discharge, and he'd been advised to depart from Patea as soon as possible. Linda had no idea if he'd taken the advice, or if Vera had gone with him. During the trial, the girl had testified on his behalf, while Linda had decided to remain silent. In spite of everything, she couldn't hate Fitz. He was her child's father, and even though her mind told her that he was an adult and responsible for his own actions, her heart still saw him as Vera's victim. The girl had wrapped him around her little finger, just as she had done with Private Fairbanks and all those other men she'd supposedly been working for. All of them must have seen something special in Vera, and to Fitz, a childish man and a gambler, she'd been irresistible. Linda could and would not tolerate it any longer, but she held no grudge against him. Her only desire for revenge was against Vera, and her testimony wouldn't have done the girl any damage.

Linda's refusal to speak against Fitz hadn't helped him much, however. Captain Langdon had described in detail before the court how he'd found Linda and Omaka with the dead Maori warriors, and how pathetically Vera and Fitz had come crawling out of their hole.

"The only merit of Private Fitzpatrick's 'retreat' was having carried his daughter to safety," the captain had finally finished in a scornful tone. "His daughter who, I might add, wasn't in danger at all—or not from the moment her mother had a rifle in her hands, anyway. Mrs. Fitzpatrick acted commendably, proving herself prudent, courageous, and brave—a true pioneer. We all deeply regret losing her, but there's no way around it. A cowardly liar such as Private Fitzpatrick isn't suitable for any army."

The court, which was chaired by Major McDonnell, had agreed. And Fitz only escaped the gallows by sheer dumb luck. Had the company actually been at war and not simply prepared to defend the camp from marauding mobs, he could have been executed for cowardice.

Fitz had listened mutely and then sat stoically through the ritual by which his rank and uniform were revoked. It wasn't a big loss, since he'd still been of the lowest rank, without any medals or decorations. The worst part was that Fitz hadn't completed his three years of military service, which meant his land would be returned to the Crown. Linda and her daughter had to leave.

"Well, first I'll go back to the house to collect the rest of my things," she said, answering the captain's question. "If Fitz didn't take them all. I wouldn't put it past him." She touched her mother's necklace. That, at least, was safe. "Afterward, I'm going to Russell. I have family there."

Seeing Ida and Karl again would be the only good thing about this new turn in her life.

The captain shook his head. "You can't go to Russell. Not the direct way, at least. You'd have to cross all of Waikato, and I'm afraid there are still hundreds of Hauhau out there. You don't really want to take such a risk, do you?"

"No," Linda said sadly. "I'm aware that the only safe way is through Wellington; I can take a ship to Russell from there. My relatives will send me money if I can reach them by telegraph, and if that doesn't work, I'll sell the wagon."

Linda pretended that she was brushing her hair out of her face, but in truth, she was wiping away a tear. She hated having to be on the road again. And all alone, this time.

"Can I take Omaka with me?"

A decision had now been made about Omaka as well. With regard to the Hauhau attack, the priestess was found to be innocent. However, the army command insisted she leave the settlement immediately and return to her tribe. Of course, she didn't even know where exactly her people had been sent to. The old woman had simply asked Linda to bring her back to her tree.

The captain grimaced. "You can, but—" He seemed relieved when somebody called for him. "Coming, Private Bannister!" Langdon bid Linda farewell with the customary tip of his hat. "Fare you well, Mrs. Fitzpatrick. As I said in court, it pains me to lose you. I wish you the best on your journey. All the best!"

"Why do men find Vera so attractive?"

Omaka was there, rocking Aroha and humming absentmindedly, but Linda was really talking to herself. Her conversation with Captain Langdon had stirred her frustrations, and now that the wagon was rolling along the river, Mount Taranaki winking down at them for the last time, everything came bursting out of her.

"She isn't beautiful or smart—well, she's clever at manipulating people, but she's got no education at all. I can't imagine what she and Fitz would talk about. And of course she's young, hardly more than a child. What does he see in her? She might be experienced. I don't know much about physical love, Fitz was my first, but I—I can't imagine him preferring a whore over me . . ."

Linda felt disheartened. She knew exactly what Carol would have told her now: "You still love him."

"It's not that I still love him," she said in reply to the silent reproach. Omaka gave her a gentle, sidelong look. "I just want to understand. I want to know what he sees in her, what they see in each other, what they mean to each other . . . What did I do wrong?"

"With each other, they can be who they truly are."

Linda was so engrossed in her monologue that Omaka's answer startled her.

"Does that mean—does that mean he can't be himself with me, *karani*?" she asked. "Do you think I didn't love him enough, or didn't accept him for who he was, or—"

Omaka shook her head. "You do not know him, *mokopuna*. He never showed you. He is like the tuatara lizard. By night, he shows a different face than he does by day, different in the sun than in the dark, showing only what you wish to see. And he knew what you wished to see—they always know. They see with their third eye."

Linda frowned. Tuataras changed their color depending on the time of year and their age, and one of their most remarkable features was the third eye in the middle of their forehead.

"What do you mean, 'they'?" she asked impatiently.

Omaka sighed. "Whiro's messengers, *mokopuna*. The beings that show us how cold death is. They always walk alone, for they know no love, no fear, no future, and no pain."

Whiro was the Maori god of death, and tuataras were said to be his messengers.

"But Fitz is kindhearted," Linda objected. "He's sociable to a fault, and he married me. He didn't want to be alone!"

Omaka's words had sent a shiver down her spine.

"They do whatever suits them best, and perhaps they are also searching for connection. Perhaps they would like to be a part of a tribe, or would even like to feel warmth. But they are not made for these things. I told you before, they are not like you or me. You may pity them, *mokopuna*, but stay away from them."

Linda rubbed her eyes. She thought about Fitz and how easily he made friends—and how readily he would use, betray, steal from, and deceive them moments later. How fearless he was, how indifferent in the face of his future. She had confused it with optimism, and it had given her hope time and again. But seen through Omaka's eyes, it was nothing but carelessness and selfishness.

Those who didn't know blame or fear didn't worry about their safety. All he did was live in the moment. And as for her, maybe he'd truly been looking for something in her. Something he'd found in Vera.

"Fitz is not like Vera," she said defiantly.

Omaka shrugged. "And you are not like me. And yet, we are of a kind. They are of a kind. Stay away from them, *mokopuna*. You have been lucky so far; the spirits have protected you—all the *karakia* I have sung, your *mana*, your *maunga*. You proved strong enough, though he weakened you."

"He didn't weaken me!" Linda cried. "To the contrary, I—"

Then she fell silent. Hadn't she just been trying to blame herself for her failed marriage? How many times these past few months had she asked herself what she was doing wrong? How often had she been silent when she should have spoken up? How often had she lied for Fitz, to herself and others? Omaka was right. She'd doubted her own *mana*, and in the process, she'd allowed him to weaken it.

Omaka and Linda were silent until they reached the land that had briefly been called Fitzpatrick Station. Linda sighed. She'd miss the river, the hills, her garden, the painstakingly cleared fields, and even the log cabin, although it had never really felt like her own.

Omaka turned to Linda to exchange *hongi* in farewell. She was going to return to her camp while Linda packed her things to travel south. Then, however, both women froze. Smoke was rising from the hills behind the house.

"It's coming from your camp, Omaka!"

The priestess's face had turned into a mask of fear and pain.

"Could that be Hauhau?" Linda asked.

She reached for her hunting rifle, which was stored under the seat of her covered wagon. She owed the rifle to a lucky coincidence. When Captain Langdon wanted to bring her back to the army camp after the attack, she'd grabbed the item of clothing closest at hand to wrap Aroha. It had been Fitz's old leather jacket, and in one of its pockets, she'd found the winnings from his last card game. The money wouldn't have been enough for a ship's passage, but it covered traveling provisions and a rifle.

Omaka had already begun to move, and swiftly. Linda followed as quickly as she could, Aroha swaddled in a blanket on her back and the rifle in her hands.

From the top of the next hill, they could see the tree, the men, and the fire. About ten military settlers were hacking at the kauri tree with axes. The trunk was too thick to fell, but they kept chopping chunks off and tossing them into a blazing fire. It was sacrilege from a Maori point of view, and foolish wastefulness in the eyes of the *pakeha*. Kauri wood was very valuable; one could have made a small fortune with the sale of this tree trunk. Omaka let out a strangled sound, as if she'd lost the ability to speak.

Linda stared at the men. They were all neighbors, friends of Fitz's or Vera's, and nobody seemed to be in charge. The tree's destruction definitely hadn't been ordered by the army commanders, or a construction unit with saws would have been sent out, proceeding carefully. Instead, these men seemed exuberant and drunk. And they were being egged on.

Perched on the stone Omaka had often used sat Vera. She was laughing, shouting to the men, praising them and jeering. When she saw Linda and Omaka standing on the hill, she waved up at them triumphantly.

Omaka stared, aghast, at the scene of destruction before her. Silent tears ran down her cheeks. Linda reached for her rifle. Her first impulse was to take aim and shoot. She wouldn't have missed Vera.

"It was my *maunga*," Omaka said softly. "Now that they have killed it, I will die too." She reached for the war club hanging from her belt. "I will die in battle, for my people."

Her words brought Linda back. "No!" she said decisively. "No, no, *karani*. She must not get what she wants! You will not let her turn you into the enemy she makes you out to be. If you go running down there with a battle cry on your lips and your club in your hands, they will shoot you and celebrate her. She always said that you were a traitor. Do not let her have this victory!"

The older woman's eyes were suddenly as cold as Vera's. "You may shoot her."

Linda nodded grimly. "I want to, but then I would die. There are witnesses down there. I would be hanged. Fitz could get my daughter and turn her into another Vera. No, I won't give them that either. We are stronger than they are, *karani*! We have *mana*—"

"I have no more power, *mokopuna*," Omaka whispered. "My power came through Tane, and with him, they are destroying my soul."

Linda shook her head, pointing at the fire. "They are not destroying him, *karani*. They cannot destroy spirits. Don't you see him? He is flying to the sky to join Rangi—to the place where you anchored Aroha's soul. Your *maunga* is up there in the clouds now too, in the wind, *karani*. You are free to go wherever you please. Come with me, *karani*—with us."

Omaka looked at her. It seemed to cost her a lot of energy to tear her gaze from the dying tree. Then her eyes swept over the fire, and finally, Vera.

"Go, *mokopuna*," she said.

Linda grabbed her hand in desperation. "Please, *karani*, do not send me away. Don't let yourself be killed; don't let them win!"

"You are strong, *mokopuna*, but not strong enough for the spirits I will call now. If you are right, if Rangi, Papa, and Tane give me power, I will make the earth shake now."

Omaka's eyes were still cold, but now powerful anger burned there as well.

"Makutu?" Linda asked softly. "You will cast a curse on them?"

During her time with the Ngai Tahu, Linda had heard tales of *tohunga* who, after a life of conferring with the gods, could kill using nothing but words. Black magic—fatal for the cursed, and dangerous for the priestess involved. Linda didn't really believe in it, or hadn't until now.

"You must not hear the words," the priestess said. "Nobody will hear the words."

Omaka drew herself up. She seemed to grow; the men by the tree must surely see her now. Linda was terrified that one of them would shoot. But the settlers only looked up at her, curious at first, but then uncertain, and finally, mesmerized. In the end, they would be trembling with fear.

"I will wait for you, *karani*," Linda said. "Do not forget, I will wait. Do not lose yourself. We are of a kind."

When Linda had almost reached her wagon, she heard Omaka's scream. It wasn't unlike a *karanga*, the cry uttered by a tribe's strongest woman at the peak of a *powhiri*, which connected heaven and earth, gods and men. A *karanga* evoked peace, but this cry brought death.

Amy, whom Linda had left in the wagon, whimpered, and Aroha began to cry. Linda was afraid she would hear shots next. But there was silence. She fought back her fear, calming the dog and her child—and then, in disbelief, she saw Omaka coming down the hill. Steadily, serenely, as if nothing had happened.

"You—you succeeded?" Linda asked.

Omaka nodded. "They will all die," she said firmly. "Today, I was Whiro's messenger. Let us go now, *mokopuna*."

"I have to collect my things," Linda objected.

The Maori shook her head. "Leave everything. This land is *tapu* from now on. This house is *tapu*."

Linda thought wistfully of her pots, her clothes, her bedding. Though she didn't own much, she was still attached to it. She reached for the reins.

"Very well, *karani*, we will leave. We do not need anything anymore. We are free."

Part 7

FREEDOM

The Auckland Islands

Campbelltown and the Canterbury Plains,
New Zealand (the South Island)

Otaki and Taranaki, New Zealand (the North Island)

1866

Chapter 62

Bill was usually the first to leap ashore when they reached a new island. After almost a year aboard the *Hampshire*, he should have gotten accustomed to the thrill of it. But every day, Bill awoke full of new hope, and his heartbeat quickened at the sight of every new island they approached.

Captain Rawley had begun his mission by exploring the Bounty Islands, which was disappointing to Bill, since there was no chance of Cat and Chris having ended up there. The Bounty Islands were in the southern Pacific Ocean, a good four hundred miles southeast of Christchurch. Bill would have preferred to sail to the Auckland Islands straightaway, but it wasn't an option in winter. And then, after their voyage to the Bounties, they'd sailed back to Christchurch to stock up on provisions. Bill's patience had been tried again when Rawley had next headed for the Antipodes.

It was only now that the *Hampshire* had reached the Auckland Islands, and today, they were planning to go to Enderby, one of the largest. As usual, the *Hampshire* had sailed once around the landmass to look for castaways' boats on the beach. They hadn't spotted anything, but that didn't mean much. People might have pulled their boats ashore. Now, Captain Rawley was searching for an appropriate anchorage, and Bill and two other crew members were preparing the longboat.

When an island looked more or less habitable, the men began their exploration on foot. They usually spent two to ten days on each. It was generally easy to tell whether it was worth investing much time and energy on any given island—for example, when there were already animals there. Then, Fancy would contribute to their mission. She would herd the goats or sheep in a flash, making it possible to count them and control the feeding situation. If the animals were thin and the time of year was appropriate, the men would stay for a few days, plowing fallow land and sowing grass.

On some of these islands, castaways had survived for long periods of time in the past. Others had even been properly inhabited. On these, the *Hampshire*'s men found areas where crops had been cultivated, and they would weed or renew the fields. Potatoes, for example, could be planted on almost every island. The spuds grew without tending, sprouting on their own.

A few times, they found abandoned shelters and huts. Bill and the others would repair them and leave well-sealed crates full of clothes, blankets, matches, and tools inside. On islands without huts, they built quick shelters against the weather, marking them with a large sign:

RELIEF SUPPLIES FOR CASTAWAYS
DEPOSITED BY THE *HAMPSHIRE*

Under that, there was a bold-lettered warning for thieves:

MAY THE SUFFERING OF WIDOWS AND ORPHANS BEFALL ANY MAN WHO BREAKS INTO THIS CRATE ALTHOUGH A SHIP AWAITS HIM ON THE SHORE!

Finally, the *Hampshire*'s crew would leave signs on other beaches on the island, and if possible, they'd set out some goats or rabbits there too.

"Now we only have one or two little islands left," Peter said contentedly as they left Enderby and rowed back toward the *Hampshire*. "Sure, Disappointment Island's going to keep us busy for a few days, but we'll be done with most of them quickly. Goodness knows I've had enough! I'm going to spend next winter in Campbelltown. We'll see if there's a friendly woman who'll take me in. A whole year at sea to rescue castaways—that's bound to touch some nice widow's heart."

The other men laughed in agreement. Peter was right, their journey was coming to an end. The men hoped they'd be home in about a month's time. Bill was the only one unhappy about it.

"We still have a few more islands to go," he said keenly, glancing at his list. He kept a meticulous record of every island they'd visited, and he knew exactly how many were still left. "The next one is Rose Island."

"Pretty name for such a dismal patch of ground," the captain remarked. "It's only about three hundred acres. Wouldn't want to be buried there."

"You know the place?" Bill asked.

Rawley shook his head. "No, not personally. But I read about it. A few whalers used to have a station there and left some rabbits. Supposed to be plenty of them there now. But nothing apart from that."

Bill shrugged. "So, we can look forward to some rabbit roast. How far is it?"

Rawley grimaced. "Ye know how bad the sea charts are out here. It's sou'west of Enderby, can't say more than that . . ."

"So, let's set sail first thing tomorrow," Ben said, "and get it over with quickly."

It took them a day of strong wind to reach Rose Island, and, in fact, the island was quite small. They could see a colony of seals on one of the beaches.

"Is that where we're going ashore?" Peter asked.

The captain shook his head. "Eh, let's not bother 'em! We'll find something else."

"We have to sail around once anyway," Bill reminded him.

Gus and Ben rolled their eyes in unison.

"You aren't really expecting a boat, are you?" Gus asked.

Bill shrugged with feigned indifference. He knew he was getting on their nerves, but he didn't care. "If I wasn't expecting castaways, I wouldn't be here, would I?"

The captain smiled. "Anything's possible," he said. "And we'll be around in no time."

That much was true. It took them all of two hours to circumnavigate the island. The beaches were rocky, and Rawley was worried about shallows and cliffs. As usual, Bill squinted fervently, trying to spot any signs of human habitation.

"Nothing," he said sadly as the seal beach came into sight once more.

The captain squinted through his spyglass, suddenly lowering it in alarm. "Smoke!" he cried. "Now, I might be wrong—it's always so foggy in these parts, but—" He looked again. "Still, looks to be there's smoke rising there. Have a look, Bill, ye've got younger eyes than me."

Bill's heart beat frantically as he reached for the spyglass. He scanned the coast without success, and then searched the sky over the interior. What he saw made his breath catch in his throat. The captain was right! There was definitely smoke rising there. A campfire, maybe!

"There's somebody there," he whispered. "Oh my God, Carol, I—I found them . . . ," he said directly to the image of her face that appeared in his mind's eye.

Captain Rawley placed a hand on his shoulder. "Easy now, lad. We don't even know if they're castaways. Might be a bunch o' whalers—"

"Without a ship at anchor?" Bill asked. "How did they get here, then? You think they swam?"

"Or they might be castaways, but not from the *General Lee*," Peter said.

"Or mutineers who were abandoned here," Ben guessed.

"Seal hunters whose ship is coming back to pick them up in a few days' time," Gus added. "Who knows, Bill. Don't get your hopes up!"

Bill was already reaching for the anchor chain. "But we'll go and have a look, right?"

The captain nodded. "Aye, lad! Strike the sails, we're anchoring on the seal beach. The shore's too steep for my liking here. Ben, keep an eye on the shore, will ye? And Peter, try and locate the campfire as best ye can." Peter was their navigator. "I'll go ashore with Bill and Gus. Bring yer sabers and load yer guns! And no loud hullos on land. Let's see if we're welcome at all."

Bill could hardly wait to go ashore, but the captain insisted on proceeding carefully. He very diligently searched for a bay where their dinghy would be well protected but could be launched quickly. Finally, they found a beach surrounded by cliffs that was deemed acceptable.

"If we have to flee, one of ye lads can secure the access point while the others get the sails up," Rawley explained. "And now, we move toward the fire good and slow. Weapons at the ready. I go ahead, ye others follow me. Bill, take the right side, Gus, the left."

"Hang on, Rawley . . ." Gus hefted two backpacks from the boat. "Peter and I packed these in case there really are castaways. We should bring them a bit of civilization, I think."

Grinning, he showed Bill and the captain the contents of one of the backpacks: bread, a few sausages, and a big bottle of whiskey.

The captain smiled. "Don't you have it covered," he remarked. "Ah, devils, how I enjoyed that first swig when they picked me up on my little island with the coconut tree!"

"Can we go now?" Bill asked impatiently.

Rawley nodded. "Come on, mates! God willing, we're gonna save a few lives today."

The pillar of smoke grew clearer and clearer the closer they came to the alleged castaways' camp. Rose Island's vegetation consisted mostly of rata bushes, windblown on the coast, but larger and offering more protection farther inland. You couldn't eat rata, but anyone who knew a bit about hunting could certainly live off the game here. The place was crawling with rabbits, and after all his experience on the other Auckland Islands, Bill suspected there must also be ducks, rails, and cormorants nesting here.

The smoke turned out to be coming from a campfire tucked between a couple of large ironwood trees. It marked the center of a primitive camp composed of some hastily timbered shelters covered in sealskins. Four men sprawled around the fire, clearly unarmed. Nevertheless, Rawley signaled for his men to approach them quietly and from different directions.

"Cover me," he whispered.

Reluctantly, Bill leveled his weapon at the men. They didn't look threatening, just weary, scruffy, and chilled to the bone. The parts of their clothing that weren't made of sealskins were in complete tatters, and none of them had seen a razor in months.

The men jumped to their feet with terrified shrieks when Rawley suddenly emerged from the thicket. They seemed to take him for an apparition.

"I'm Captain Michael Rawley of the *Hampshire*," he began. "Me crew and I are searching for castaways, leaving supplies. May I ask who ye are?"

"You're looking for us?" one of the men asked in disbelief. "Now? We'd given up hope. We—it's been more than two years . . ."

Another man burst into tears.

Bill lowered his weapon and broke cover. "What ship are you from?" he asked breathlessly.

He wouldn't have recognized any of them, even if they had been on the *General Lee*. It seemed as if they had aged a decade. The third man, however, took a step closer.

"But you're—aren't you Lieutenant Paxton? I'm Edward Harrow—the steward, remember? You were—Lord above, he was on our ship!"

There was no more holding back now. The castaways rushed toward their rescuer, laughing and crying and asking questions.

Bill, however, felt numb. He'd been right. There were survivors from the *General Lee*, and he'd found them. But Cat and Chris Fenroy were nowhere to be seen. The disappointment felt like liquid fire consuming his insides.

Gus saw what Bill was going through. "It wasn't meant to be, brother." The old jack-tar himself had tears in his eyes. He placed a hand on Bill's shoulder.

But Bill shook it off, unwilling to accept defeat. He turned to Harrow.

"Are you—were you the only survivors?"

Harrow shook his head. "No," he said. "After three women were swept overboard, there were ten of us left. Two died later, from exposure. They were already half-dead before we got here. And a few months ago, two more left in the boat. They were going to try to get back to Campbelltown. It was complete madness, if you ask me. But they wouldn't listen. Did they—did they arrive somewhere?"

"No," Rawley said curtly. "I'm sorry."

"So, that leaves six," Bill said.

Harrow nodded. "Four of us here and two who live on the other side of the island. A couple. They left a few months ago because we were always fighting over the woman. Lord, of course she's his, but he might've been a little generous, you'd think. 'Course, she's pretty prickly too. A cat, just like her name."

Bill swallowed. "Cat and Chris Fenroy?" he whispered.

"That's them," the oldest of the four men said. "And it was damn smart of Chris to clear out. It was terrible when they started lusting after his wife. I'm grateful for all they did. Without the two of them, we'd never have survived."

He was interrupted by barking in the trees, and moments later, Fancy leaped up on Bill.

"What are you doing here?" he asked, half-glad, half-reluctant.

Captain Rawley had insisted on leaving the dog back at the bay with their dinghy. He would have preferred not to bring her at all, but she'd jumped off the ship and into the boat at the last moment, and the swell was too heavy to easily put her back. She must have escaped again somehow.

"Oh, don't scold her!" A woman with a bright, musical voice stepped out behind Fancy. "I saw your ship while I was collecting herbs, and I also saw the longboat you came in. I ran over, but when I arrived at the bay, you'd already gone. She was the only one left. Fancy! My daughter's dog! I'm not seeing things, am I? Mr. Paxton, Bill, is that you? Where are Carol and Linda? Are the girls alive?"

Bill struggled to find his voice. "You—you survived. Like they kept saying. You and Chris, Linda was convinced you were alive. She said she would have felt it if you'd died."

Cat smiled. "And I would've sensed it if something had happened to her. The Maori call it *aka*, the connection between close relatives that can stretch, but not tear, so long as both people are alive."

Her smile transformed her face. Even after two years in the wilderness, Catherine Rata was still beautiful—almost more so than she'd been in her ball gown aboard the *General Lee*. She was wearing a simple dress made of sealskin. It exposed her calves, and her feet were cozy in rabbit-fur moccasins. Her long blonde hair wasn't pinned up, falling almost to her hips. Cat's face was flushed, and her lips were cracked from the constant cold, but she didn't look haggard like the men around the fire, and the gaze of her nut-brown eyes wasn't pinched and hungry, but calm. Cat seemed to be well fed—and happy.

Captain Rawley was mesmerized. In the foggy haze of Rose Island, Cat Rata looked like a fairy or an earth goddess from an old tale.

The captain stammered his introduction.

Cat nodded politely. "Captain Rawley, my pleasure. My name is Catherine Rata. Welcome to Rata Island!"

Chapter 63

"It's a long story," Bill said evasively when Cat asked how Fancy had come to be with him. The dog followed as Cat led him to her hut on the other end of the island. "Why don't you tell me about yourself first."

Cat smiled. She walked the well-trodden paths with the long, sure steps of the Maori. The castaways had explored the island thoroughly and made it their own. Still, there were no recognizable fields or gardens. They probably hadn't found any crops to plant here.

"What is there to tell? The night of the shipwreck was hell. You know—you survived it yourself. It was icy cold and dark, and the waves were towering around us. Three women went overboard; it was terrible. I clung to Chris, and he clung to the other men. We couldn't have dreamed of rowing, not even the next day—if it was daytime at all. The storm was so fierce that we never did figure out how much time we really spent at sea. Finally, the ocean calmed, but of course we had no idea where we were. We could only imagine that we'd probably gone adrift somewhere south of where we'd been. It was so much colder than Aotearoa. The men were fighting over whether they should try to row north. We eventually managed to get our bearings with the sun's position. I could have managed with the stars, too, and the sailor who was on board with us claimed to know a thing or two as well."

"Let me guess, he was one of the men who left two months ago."

Cat nodded. "It probably didn't do him much good, even if he really could navigate by the stars. We just don't get enough clear nights around here. After the *General Lee* sank, it rained nonstop. We had no chance. Two more women were dying . . . and then we saw this island! We rowed toward it with all our might, managed to get ashore, and built a fire. We had only six usable matches. The men were praising God for hours after the wood had finally caught. I showed them later how to do it without matches." She smiled again.

"Carol said you used to live with the Maori," Bill said.

"For six years, yes," Cat replied. "And Chris grew up around Maori children as well. It helped us a lot here, although we still had to improvise quite a bit. Aotearoa's a lot more fertile than this island. I thanked all the gods I knew when I found raupo here. Things would have been much harder without flax. I was able to work the raupo so that we could weave mats, traps, and weirs from it. The roots are edible too. Some of the men had penknives with them, as did I." She pulled a small knife from her belt, which itself was woven with raupo fiber. "I always carry this with me, even when I'm wearing my gown. It's an old habit of mine. One time I forgot, and it didn't go so well for me." Cat sighed at the memory.

"On the first day," she continued, "we cooked a few raupo roots, and Chris caught us some fish. It was enough for everybody to get something to eat, but the two women died anyway. Their graves are down on the beach, not too far from your dinghy. The rest of us built shelters, and we survived. It was hard, especially because it was so cold. Fortunately, there were rabbits, seals, and a lot of birds that we caught in my traps. We could survive another few years here if we had to. Look, here comes Chris."

Chris Fenroy ran toward them wearing a kind of skirt made of sealskin, a simple shirt, and sealskin boots. He was holding a spear made from a tapered branch, ready to use it. He'd always worn his hair a little long, but now, it hung way past his shoulders. He seemed upset, not knowing if the man walking next to his wife had come as a rescuer or an attacker.

"Cat, I—" He stopped, breathless, as Bill's hands flew up in surprise and Cat stopped him with a reassuring gesture. "I saw the ship, but I was on the other end of the island."

"It's all right, Chris," Cat said gently. "They've come to rescue us."

At that moment, Fancy came running out of the underbrush. She leaped up on Chris happily. Stunned, he sought his wife's eyes.

"Am I going mad now, Cat?" he asked. "Is this Fancy? How did she get here?"

Cat shook her head. "You aren't going mad. Fancy came here with Lieutenant Paxton—you know, the young lieutenant from the *General Lee*. Do you recognize him? He was in a lifeboat with the girls. They were saved. But he hasn't told me how he came by Fancy. I hope he'll do so in a moment, once we get out of this rain."

A light drizzle had started to fall, and Bill shivered in spite of his warm oilskin coat. He marveled at the castaways. Cat made surviving on the island look easy, but he knew they'd endured great hardship.

Soon they reached Cat and Chris's dwelling. The path led them past a corral with four goats in it. Fancy started circling them enthusiastically.

"Where did you get those animals, Mrs.—"

"Call me Cat," she said. "The goats were already here, of course. There are twelve on this island, in all. If the others haven't killed one of them, that is. Someone must have abandoned their predecessors here at some point, just like the rabbits. These are all nannies. We caught them together, and I tamed them. I can even milk them." She stroked the animals' noses. They had come over to the fence in a show of trustful curiosity.

The corral reminded Bill of the fences that surrounded Maori *pa*s. Here, too, branches had been bound together with flax cord. It all looked very tidy and not as temporary as the other castaways' camp. The same went for the hut they arrived at a few moments later. Without proper tools, Chris hadn't been able to fell enough wood for a log cabin. But he'd been able to erect a stable, tentlike scaffold that they'd covered in skins. There was a smoke hole at the top. All in all, the construction was reminiscent of Native American teepees.

"We used albatross bones as sewing needles and flax as cord," Cat explained, having noticed Bill's appreciative expression. "The hardest part was tanning the hides. I knew which plants to use, mostly, but they don't all grow here. We had to experiment a lot. It didn't smell very good at the beginning, and I'm afraid it's still a little bit unpleasant . . ."

Cat pulled aside the skins covering the doorway with an apologetic smile. It did smell a little, but it was warm and cozy. The firepit in the center was surrounded by stones and seemed well protected. Chris stepped inside and stoked the embers, putting on some more fast-burning wood. Their fuel supply was stacked in a neat pile in one corner. There were dishes and cups whittled from wood on makeshift shelves along the wall. The couple had prepared a stack of raupo leaves to wrap roots or meat in for cooking, and there was a wide bed made out of a raupo-fiber mat and a rabbit-fur blanket. Cat unrolled some more mats.

"Have a seat," she said to Bill. "I brew excellent herbal tea, if I do say so myself. Though it's a bit of a nuisance without an actual teapot. We do have a cooking pit, though." She pointed at a pit that had been dug in the ground. "But it takes a while for the stones to heat, you know."

"Please, don't bother," Bill said, opening his backpack. "This here is a lot better than tea." He took out the whiskey bottle and watched Chris's face with satisfaction.

"Well, this is one for the books!" Chris said with a laugh, quickly pulling the stopper from the bottle and raising it to his lips. Then he passed it to Cat. "The essence of life!"

"Which sometimes helps us bear life," Bill said as the bottle was returned to him.

"So, will you tell us your story?" Cat asked, giving him a worried look. She scratched Fancy's head.

Bill nodded. The time had come to tell them about Carol and Linda, and about Jane's takeover of Rata Station.

"I'm going to kill that woman!" There wasn't enough space in Chris and Cat's hut to pace back and forth. Here, Chris had to content himself with kneading a rabbit skin. He was about to tear it to pieces. "How could she? We've been divorced for years. That spiteful shrew! She's known Carol and Linda since they were little girls. How could she do that to them? And Te Haitara—"

"From what I heard, the chieftain didn't help her," Bill offered.

"Well, he didn't stop her either!" Chris said, fuming. "And don't tell me he couldn't, that she had too much *mana* or something. The man calls himself a warrior. He ought to be able to deal with his own wife!"

"I can't imagine anyone putting Jane over their knee," Cat said, trying to placate him.

Chris glared at her. "Just you wait until I see her. She went too far, Cat! Way too far! Kicking the girls out—"

"And then Oliver Butler weaseled out and broke his engagement to Carol," Cat surmised, tight-lipped.

Bill nodded. "Carol was very hurt," he said quietly.

Next, he told them about Linda and Fitz—another reason for Chris to be upset.

"That little windbag! How on earth could she fall for him? Good Lord, they could have stayed with Ida and Karl. All of them. There wasn't the slightest reason for a shotgun wedding! And to run off to the goldfields . . ."

Bill rubbed his forehead. "Mr. Fenroy . . . Chris. This liaison with Joe Fitzpatrick might have saved Linda's life."

Contritely, he told them how he'd taken Carol and Mara to Taranaki and Waikato, and how they'd been caught up in the turmoil of the war. Finally, he broke the news of the kidnapping.

"I tried to dissuade them," Bill insisted, his face turned away in shame. "And then I made the mistake of proposing to Carol. She thought I only wanted to keep her in Patea so I could keep courting her, which was why she wouldn't listen to me. And the general wouldn't allow me to ride with them." He looked up and met Cat's burning eyes. "I would have gone, you have to believe me!"

Cat raised her hands to silence him, then closed her eyes. She stood and stumbled out of the tent. Bill and Chris stared at the dirt floor as a roar of pain came from outside, rousting the birds from the trees. Several long minutes passed in silence, and then Cat stepped back inside, her face a mask of steely control.

"If you had gone, Carol would have had to look at your severed head," she said, her voice thick with unshed tears. "As you said, those Hauhau warriors slaughtered twenty heavily armed soldiers. What makes you think you could have triumphed against them on your own?"

"I should have tried to free Carol and Mara, at least."

Bill repeated the self-reproaches he'd been torturing himself with ever since the young women had disappeared. Finally, Chris passed him the whiskey bottle again.

"Enough. Stop beating yourself up. You couldn't have done anything whatsoever on your own, and you know it." Chris looked down again and took a deep breath to steady himself. "Are you entirely sure that Carol and Mara were kidnapped? Were—were they definitely still alive when the warriors retreated?"

"If not, their bodies would have been found," Cat said. "There would have been no reason to hide them. Decapitating the soldiers would have been reason enough for a punitive expedition if General Cameron had wanted one."

"So, what do you think happened to them?" Bill asked desperately, looking at Cat in a plea for help. "What—what's normal with Maori?"

Cat shook her head. "When I lived with the Ngati Toa, they hadn't kept slaves in a long time."

"The Treaty of Waitangi made it illegal for the North Island tribes too," Chris added. "But these rebels probably don't see that as binding."

"Slaves?" Bill cried in horror. "You think they're keeping them as slaves?"

Chris gave the young man a look of exasperation. "Well, what else? You said it was a *pa*, right? That means there are no women there, or few, at any rate. Don't think of the kidnappers as Maori or Hauhau. More than anything else, they're angry young men."

Bill buried his face in his hands. Of course, he knew that it was more than likely that Carol and Mara had been subjected to violence. But he'd still been hoping . . .

"I thought that Maori—I thought—because their girls are supposed to be so willing?"

Cat gritted her teeth. "Like most men, Maori warriors prefer sleeping with women they don't have to force. But—" The mask began to slip, and she paused a moment to compose herself. "As for slavery in the old days, there were tales of horrendously abused women, but also of marriages between masters and slaves. We don't know what's going on at that *pa*. All we can do is hope that Carol and Mara are still alive. Which they are. And I know Chris doesn't believe it, but if Carol weren't alive anymore, I'd know, just like I'd know about Linda. I didn't give birth to her, but Te Ronga didn't give birth to me either, and yet there was *aka* between us. We'll get them back, Bill. If Cameron won't help us, I'll get the governor involved—if Ida and Karl haven't already. You've been at sea for a year, Bill. Maybe by now, Carol and Mara are free."

Bill gave Cat an incredulous look. "I think I would have heard about it if—"

He stopped short. The *Hampshire* had docked at the occasional harbor to stock up on provisions, but apart from Christchurch, the harbors had all been tiny outposts in the middle of nowhere. He hadn't received any mail, and there hadn't been any newspapers either. Cat was right; the Hauhau stronghold at Weraroa might have been given up or defeated long since. He only had the same information he'd left with: General Cameron had pulled out his troops. The man who'd taken over fighting the Hauhau was General Chute.

"I should've stayed," he whispered. "I shouldn't have given up."

"Oh, don't start again," Chris admonished. "You found us. Be proud of that. And trust in Cat. In a few days' time, we'll be back in New Zealand. Then we'll find out what happened, and we'll see what we can do." He put a hand on his wife's shoulder. "I do believe in your connection to the girls. And with so many people who love them"—he smiled sadly at Bill—"I know we'll find a way."

Cat smiled sympathetically. "We'd better pack," Cat said wistfully. "I'm almost sorry to leave this island. For two and a half years, I had Chris to myself."

"Really?" Chris asked. "I have to say I'm more than happy that I won't have to play midwife here!"

"Midwife?" Bill frowned, his eyes going reflexively to Cat's delicate form.

Cat smiled again. "I'm sure we could have managed. But you're right, it'll be safer back home. Oh, don't give me such a shocked look, Lieutenant Paxton. I'm forty-one years old, but yes, I'm expecting a child."

Chapter 64

The *Hampshire* left Rose Island the very next day. Captain Rawley and his men left their supplies in the castaways' shelters. Chris and the other men helped set up the signs. Cat released her goats and buried a few seed potatoes on a piece of land she'd been preparing as another raupo field. With that, she said her goodbyes.

"I still think it should be called Rata Island," she said as they set sail. "There aren't any roses there. Can't it be renamed?"

"The man that discovered it was likely thinking about a lass named Rose, nay the flower," the captain replied.

Chris put an arm around his wife's shoulders. "So, it could be called Cat Island," he joked. "Where are we off to now, Captain Rawley? Straight to Campbelltown? Or are you sticking to your original route? Will we be sailing on to the other islands to leave supplies?"

Rawley had decided on the latter. True, two of the castaways had health problems, and it would have been better to take them straight to Campbelltown. But the ailing men had argued in favor of finishing the *Hampshire*'s mission according to plan.

"We'd blame ourselves if the next person starves or freezes to death on one of those islands for lack of supplies," Edward Harrow said.

"Or just imagine, there might be other survivors from the *General Lee* or other ships waiting for help out there," Bill added. "As improbable as that may seem."

The voyage took them another three weeks, although the last few islands were quickly supplied. The people rescued from Rose Island helped with great enthusiasm, and they didn't need to spend more than a day on any of the islands.

They didn't find any more survivors from the *General Lee*. The other lifeboats must have capsized out on the ocean.

The men cheered, Fancy barked, and Cat snuggled close to Chris when Campbelltown's harbor finally came into view.

"I'll admit, I'd almost stopped believing we'd ever make it," she said. "Although I was definitely happy on our island. I just missed the girls—and a hot bath every now and then. I'm looking forward to a bit of luxury."

"And I'm looking forward to roasting Jane on a spit," Chris said grimly. "Seriously, Cat, I want to get back to Rata Station as quickly as possible. Then we'll go looking for the girls. Ida and Karl ought to know where Linda is, at least."

Cat looked him up and down, an amused expression on her face. "Darling, I agree with you completely, of course. But can we also agree that we shouldn't go strutting through Campbelltown wearing sealskins? And once we get to Rata Station, do you think you can refrain from stabbing Jane with a sharpened branch? If she even recognizes you with that tangle of a beard on your face, that is. Let's spend a day in civilization and buy some new clothes. After that, we'll catch the next ship to Lyttelton. Or do you want to go on horseback? That could take forever, and I'm anxious to find the girls."

As it turned out, the next ship bound for Lyttelton wasn't leaving for another four days, and the castaways wouldn't be bored in the meantime. News of their rescue had spread like wildfire as soon as they arrived. By the time the *Hampshire* was unloading, the first few reporters and photographers were already on the scene. Cat, of course, was the center of attention. She made a far more attractive picture than the tattered-looking men. People were gushing over her sealskin clothes and moccasins. Reporters kept asking for details about how she'd cooked, built traps, and tamed animals on their remote island.

Happily, all of this meant that neither Chris nor Cat were expected to pay for anything themselves. This was fortunate, since all the accounts connected to Rata Station had long since been transferred to Jane. Chris had immediately telegraphed Karl and Ida to ask them to send money. However, the bank in Campbelltown offered him unlimited credit, even without collateral. The best hotel in town invited the castaways to stay. They offered Chris and Cat the honeymoon suite, and local stores were vying for the privilege of being allowed to dress them. Cat was touched by the outpouring of kindness, and tried her best to answer all the reporters' questions.

Chris, however, quickly grew tired of the attention. His mind was on the girls and how, if only he'd written a will, he could have protected them from untold hardship. On the third day after their arrival, his restlessness grew worse when Bill came knocking on their hotel room door with news.

"They're alive!" the young man told them excitedly, waving a letter. The *Hampshire*'s crew had also been celebrated enthusiastically by the people of Campbelltown, and the men had only managed to collect their mail that morning. Bill had received a whole pile of letters from his family. As he was opening one of them, a second envelope had fallen out.

This letter arrived here on 8/15/65 for you, Bill's mother had added in a note. *Forgive me for opening it; it wasn't my intention to violate your privacy. But as you can see, the sender is a captain, and I thought it might be an official letter from the army you would have to answer. However, the man wrote to you privately, and I think his news will be welcome.*

"It's from an acquaintance of mine on General Cameron's staff," Bill told Cat and Chris. "He wrote from Wellington after the troops at Patea had been replaced by military settlers. Apparently, Weraroa *pa* was taken without bloodshed back in July. The Maori had already vacated the fort, and they took Carol and Mara with them. Lieutenant Winter found a message from Carol in a hut near the kitchen building; it had been carved into a wooden beam. She wrote that they were kept there as slaves. So, probably that means working in the kitchen?" He gave Cat and Chris a heartrendingly hopeful look.

Neither of them replied. Cat turned away.

"At any rate," Bill finished anxiously, "they seem to be alive."

Cat turned back and forced a smile. "Thank goodness. Is there any word about where the warriors fled to?"

Bill nodded. "According to Winter, Te Ua Haumene and his men went to another fort called Waikoukou. He says the governor and General Chute were determined to end this once and for all."

"Well, then," Chris said, taking a deep breath, "we must find out as quickly as possible if that fort has been taken yet."

Bill straightened his back. "If it hasn't, I'll go straight to Wellington so I can offer my service in the general's army. I only hope they'll take me back."

Chris nodded. "Given the circumstances, I'm sure they would. It would be foolish of the general to turn away such an experienced soldier."

Cat put a hand on Bill's shoulder. "The girls are alive and they are strong," she said. "We'll find them."

"General Chute's campaign is over," the local newspaper's editor in chief told them. Mr. Hunt had received them right away. "Chute approached from Whanganui with hundreds of men. On his way west, he stormed several *pa*s, destroying them. Villages too; it was quite the controversy. Waikoukou was conquered back in November. But that wasn't Chute's doing; it was McDonnell with his military settlers. Anyway, right after that, they arrested Te Ua Haumene. Chute found him with eight followers in a village near Opunake. He had him transferred to Wellington. It's not clear if there will be a trial. Haumene is communicating with all sorts of missionaries, making himself out to be the victim of his own movement. Allegedly, he lost control of things. He says all he wanted was peace and love and a good relationship with the *pakeha*, and that he never ordered anyone to be killed. A likely story."

Chris cleared his throat. "We have reason to believe that the Hauhau were keeping two white women as slaves back in Weraroa. Do you know anything about that? Was anyone freed?"

The editor in chief laughed. "Are you serious? Imagine the uproar if two white women had shown up anywhere near Haumene! I would've heard about it, of course. Every newspaper in the country would've been writing about it. No, I'm sorry to disappoint you there."

Bill's brow creased. "Are you sure the campaign is over? There aren't any Hauhau warriors left in the woods?"

Mr. Hunt shrugged. "I don't know anything about that. All I know is that Chute went back along the coast road to Whanganui after obliterating seven *pa*s and twenty-one villages. Who knows if he missed something?"

"Of course he did!" Cat interjected. "They're fooling themselves if they think there are no Hauhau left in the area. There might still be dozens of brigades on the road, and one of them probably has the women."

"If they aren't dead," Bill murmured.

Cat shook her head. "They aren't dead. All we have to do is find them. What's the situation in the area now, Mr. Hunt? Who's in charge?"

The editor in chief thought for a moment. "The land that was taken from the Maori belongs to military settlers now. Major McDonnell's in charge of security, and he's operating from a base camp in Patea—"

"The camp that Cameron set up?" Bill asked.

"I'd assume so," Hunt said. "He's organizing the settlement of land from there. That's his main task. But he isn't afraid of campaigns either. As I said, he stormed Waikoukou with his troops. If you're looking for action, he's your man."

That caught Bill's attention. "You mean he doesn't deliberate like General Cameron?"

Hunt grinned. "To the contrary, Mr. Paxton. If McDonnell sees a reason to fight, he'll jump at it like a hungry dog."

Bill glanced at Chris and Cat. "I'll take the next ship to Wellington and then ride to Patea to talk to Major McDonnell. Will you come too, once you've taken care of your business in the plains?"

Chris nodded. "As fast as we can. Thank you very much, Mr. Hunt—and good luck to you, Bill."

The editor in chief shook their hands. "Will you give me an exclusive interview if you find these women you're looking for?"

Chris and Bill hesitated.

Cat, however, smiled. "I'll put in a good word for you when I find our girls."

While Bill set sail for Wellington, Cat and Chris boarded the *Rosemary*, bound for Lyttelton. They argued a little, trying to decide if the name was a good omen or if this ship would sink too, washing them up on another island. At any rate, the journey wouldn't be anything like their luxurious trip aboard the *General Lee*. The *Rosemary* was a freighter. It had only two very basic passenger cabins, which were usually booked by merchants traveling with their wares. Having a woman on board was a rarity, and Cat attracted the attention of all the ship's officers. Chris and Cat ate their meals in the wardroom, and were asked to tell about their survival on Rose Island again and again. Cat was always relieved when she was able to retreat to her cabin. The journey passed without incident. The weather was good, and the wind was just strong enough to keep the ship moving. After a few days, they reached Lyttelton.

"Do you want to telegraph Jane, or shall we surprise her?" Cat asked as they rode along the Bridle Path on two borrowed mules. "If you'd prefer the latter, we should avoid being seen in Christchurch."

Chris smiled. "Let's surprise the Deanses first. We can spend the night with them, and Georgie can row us upriver tomorrow."

"I'm looking forward to seeing the Deanses," Cat said. "Maybe they have news about Linda. And Karl and Ida too."

There hadn't been enough time in Campbelltown for them to write a letter to the Jensches. They'd only sent a brief telegraph, then received an overjoyed reply from Ida, telling them how ecstatic she was that they were alive and well. Karl had added a short note: *Wish I could be there at Rata Station!*

William and John Deans saw Fancy running toward them in greeting, and they expected Bill Paxton to follow. When the approaching figures turned out to be Cat and Chris, the Deans brothers thought they were hallucinating. Cat found herself being bear-hugged by William Deans, while John's gigantic hand almost crushed Chris's. The men shouted to their wives, who came rushing out of the house and also threw themselves on the castaways.

Before the tears could start flowing, however, John had already opened a bottle of whiskey. William's wife, Emma, lured Cat into the pantry with a conspiratorial smile, pulling a crate of wine bottles from a dark corner.

"Here, these are yours," Emma said happily. "It was your last order from Blenheim. Georgie brought it, but the girls were in Campbelltown then and asked him to leave it with us. We should drink to your health, Linda said, but we didn't have the heart. Since then, I've thought of you every time I saw this crate."

Cat beamed and reached for one of the bottles. "Let's make a toast, then," she said. "To Linda's, Mara's, and Carol's health. Now *they're* the ones who've gone missing. I wish it was all over and they were home safe."

The two women brought the bottles into the kitchen, and Alison, John's wife, went looking for a corkscrew.

"Linda's not missing," Alison said as she filled their glasses. "In fact, I have a happy announcement to make: Linda has a daughter."

Cat placed a hand on her belly. "I'm—"

"A grandmother now!" Alison laughed. "But the marriage didn't work out. Nobody around here really believed it was going to. That Fitz—"

"Do you mean she's alone?" Cat asked, alarmed. "Where is she staying? Is she still in Otago?"

Emma shook her head. "No. Fitz tried his luck as a military settler. They had a farm somewhere in Taranaki, according to Ida. But they lost it. Ida didn't give us any details; she probably didn't know very much herself. All she had was a short letter from Linda telling her about the child and her breakup. According to the letter, she was on her way to Russell."

"Thank the spirits!" Cat sighed. "Also for the failed marriage, although I shouldn't say it. But it means we'll have her back with us soon. She can live at Rata Station with her baby—with or without a husband."

Chapter 65

"Twelve more children?" Franz Lange looked up from the message a young cavalryman had just handed him, indignant.

The man nodded. "Yes, sir. They'll be arriving tomorrow, from a village in Taranaki. McDonnell stormed it as revenge for a Hauhau attack."

Franz sighed. The campaigns were supposed to have been over for a few weeks now, and he'd thanked heaven for it. General Chute's advances farther inland had filled his orphanage beyond capacity, yet children were still being brought to Otaki. Increasingly, many were actual orphans. McDonnell didn't think twice before launching a punitive expedition, and Franz was left to care for the confused, traumatized survivors—a task that was far too much for him alone. Originally, the project had been conceived for about sixty orphans, but the old *pa* now held 120 children between the ages of three and fifteen.

Franz did his best, but communication was a major problem. Franz had been hoping his fosterlings would absorb English as naturally as babies did, but that would have required many more English-speaking caregivers. Kahotu mostly spoke Maori with the children; that was what Franz had hired him for in the first place. The man could get a grip on things when he wanted to, but he had a strange work ethic. At times, he wouldn't show up for days, going on long walks or hiding away in his shelter with a bottle of whiskey. Franz was often frustrated with Kahotu, but he knew he'd be lost without him.

Franz tried to teach lessons based on the Bible. Unfortunately, the children found that as exciting as watching paint dry, just like their compatriots had in Opotiki. And here, Franz didn't even have the option of telling stories suitable for children, such as Jonah and the whale. His Maori simply wasn't good enough, though it was improving. Franz tried to study a few pages of the Maori-language

Bible each night, comparing it with the English one. He fought his way through Genesis, but the fact that he could quote pages of it in Maori didn't help his everyday struggle. Often, he fell asleep in exhaustion over the book.

The older children only reluctantly studied the language of their enemies, and the little ones would often jump or cry when someone addressed them in English. Among themselves, of course, the children spoke Maori—and to Franz's immense relief, they seemed not to have brought tribal feuds along with them. Kahotu had told him why this was happening. Chute's recent campaigns had taken him through an area populated by related tribes. The little ones uprooted from there had no problem helping one another. There was desperate need for this, especially since nobody from Otaki wanted to work at the orphanage. So, Franz and Kahotu encouraged the older girls to take care of the younger children and help with the cooking. Kahotu took the older boys fishing and trapping to supplement the orphanage's limited provisions. The government provided some food, but it wasn't plentiful or nutritious. Without the hard work of Kahotu and the boys, they'd certainly all be malnourished.

Of course, all the additional jobs were an excellent excuse for the older children not to show up for class very often. Only mathematics lessons were well attended. The reason, once again, was blackjack. Right after introducing numbers, Franz had started using the card game in his lessons again, with enthusiastic support from Kahotu. The Church Missionary Society would have doubtlessly been appalled, but the children learned not only addition that way but also how to calculate wins and losses. Of course, they weren't playing for money, just for pebbles, but they soon moved from tens to hundreds.

Franz was pleased, but still had to put limits on the unholy pastime. He was painfully aware of how much he was neglecting his religious duties and the missionizing of his charges. So far, not a single child over the age of five had been baptized—something else the Church Missionary Society would surely hold against him. But Franz didn't want to impose that decision on anyone. Many of the boy and girls, left with no one else in the world, had come to trust their "Revi Fransi" deeply. But could they call themselves Christians if they didn't truly know the Bible? What if his sermons meant nothing more to them than the opportunity to shout "hallelujah" as loud as possible? Franz would have liked to discuss these questions with a colleague but knew better than to approach the hard-hearted, pious reverend in the village. He was on his own—with twelve more children on their way.

"All right, Lieutenant," Franz said. "I will meet you in the village at noon, and I will take the children with me. Just don't lock them in the barn at the parsonage, even if the reverend or his wife suggests it. If their time here begins with such a negative experience, it makes everything more difficult."

Linda and Omaka arrived in Otaki after several days' travel, and they almost bypassed the town without stopping. So far, their journey had been uneventful. They usually sat silently next to one another, lost in their own thoughts. Linda drove the wagon while Omaka held the baby and sang her to sleep with traditional songs and *karakia*s. Every now and then they stopped, and Linda nursed the little one. Omaka usually lit a fire. It was the end of June, and quite chilly. At night, the two women nestled up in their blankets on the wagon with Amy, keeping Aroha warm between them. They may have been able to find accommodation at farms along the way, but Omaka didn't want to ask the *pakeha* for shelter. Linda respected her wishes. Ever since the Hauhau attacks, popular opinion had turned against all Maori, and Linda wanted to spare the *tohunga* any mistreatment or the humiliation of being turned away.

Omaka was mourning her fate. She was now entirely uprooted. It seemed impossible to find her tribe, and the tribes around Russell were just as foreign to her as the remaining *marae*s near Wellington. Worse, they were occupied by tribes that had worked as auxiliary troops in the *pakeha* fight against Omaka's people. Even if they'd been willing to take the old woman in, she certainly wouldn't have felt comfortable. But there was supposed to be a missionary station in Otaki, and Linda thought the missionaries there might be able to help. Perhaps they knew where Omaka's tribe had been sent, or even had members of her tribe in their mission.

Omaka wasn't terribly fond of this plan.

"I will not pray to the *pakeha* gods," she said as Linda steered Brianna into the town. "The missionaries preach peace and bring war."

"We aren't going to pray here; we're just going to ask a few questions," Linda repeated, trying to hide her frustration. "And again, if we can't find your tribe, you know I'd be glad if you came to Russell with me. Ida and Karl would be honored to have you."

In Otaki, they found no sign of a missionary station. The center of town was impossible to miss, though. In front of a lovely, well-maintained church was a square that offered plenty of space for market stalls. On this day, redcoats had gathered there. At the sight of the men, Omaka gasped and quickly wrapped a shawl around her head and face so she wouldn't be immediately recognized as Maori.

The cavalry stood in formation around a group of neglected-looking Maori children. The residents of Otaki were eyeing the little ones mistrustfully, and they in turn glared at the citizens of the town.

One of the soldiers approached the covered wagon. "Good morning, miss, um, madam," the man said as he saw the baby in Omaka's arms. "Are you from the orphanage?"

Linda shook her head. "No, I'm only passing through on my way to Wellington. I wanted to visit the missionary station."

"That's gone," another one of the soldiers informed her. He was a captain, and obviously the unit's leader. "There's only the orphanage now."

"And is that where these little ones are going?" Linda asked.

"Yes, ma'am," the captain replied. "The reverend is supposed to be here any minute to pick them up. I hope he arrives soon. The children don't understand a word of English, and they don't know if they should be more afraid of us or the townsfolk. I wish I could at least talk to them."

"The language isn't a problem for me," Linda said, preparing to climb down from the wagon seat. "I would be happy to translate for you."

"Look, here comes the reverend I spoke to yesterday!" a young lieutenant said.

He pointed toward a hay wagon pulled by two sturdy horses. A tall, lanky man was sitting on the coach box. He wasn't wearing missionary clothes, but instead torn denim trousers and a woodcutter's shirt. Only the broad-brimmed hat made him recognizable as a clergyman.

"Wonderful! We can transfer the children to his care." The captain turned away from Linda and walked toward the approaching wagon. "Reverend Lange? Pleased to meet you. I'm Captain Tatler."

Linda stopped short. *Lange?* When news had spread of Voelkner's murder at Opotiki, she'd been enormously relieved to hear there were no other victims, but she hadn't been able to learn anything about Franz's whereabouts. And now she had to look twice before she actually recognized him.

The lanky man who now stood up to speak to the children had almost nothing in common with the shy, pious missionary who'd visited Rata Station. Franz had grown more muscular, and his pale skin was tan from working outdoors. Linda remembered thinking that Ida's brother carried the weight of the world on his shoulders. Now he seemed able to shoulder the burden.

And then she had another surprise. Franz Lange jumped down from the wagon and spoke in broken but understandable Maori.

"Welcome to children's *marae* in Otaki. I Revi Fransi—*ariki* or *papara*."

Chieftain or father. Linda had to smile.

"You have no fear. No one in *marae* hurt you, we all one tribe. One people."

The children whispered to each other.

"Now come. In *marae* wagon." Franz smiled at the children. "Wagon is *marae*'s canoe. Canoe that bring all newly to Aotearoa. Is game."

The children still didn't smile, but they came closer.

"What is the canoe called?" a brave boy asked.

Franz held out a hand to a little girl to help her climb in.

"Linda," he said as he gazed at the children.

Then, as the soldiers rode away, Franz saw the covered wagon—and the young woman sitting on the seat, listening with a smile on her face.

"Linda?"

She slid down from the wagon and walked toward him.

"Franz!" She suppressed the urge to embrace the missionary, and offered him her hand instead.

Franz, who also wanted to take Linda in his arms, accepted her hand and shook it.

"Linda, I can't believe it! Where did you come from? I thought you had a farm somewhere. Didn't your husband join the military settlers?" In every letter Franz had written to Ida, he'd asked about Linda and Fitz.

Linda nodded. "That's a long story," she said curtly. "He's gone, and so is the farm. We're on our way to Wellington, and from there we want to take a ship to Russell. I can hardly wait to see Mamida and Kapa again. I haven't heard from them since I left Christchurch. What about you, Franz? How did you get here?" She smiled. "In a canoe called *Linda*?"

Franz blushed. "It's just a name," he murmured. "It was my assistant's idea."

"I'm honored to share a name with such a worthy vessel," Linda replied. She looked over at some girls who were standing next to her wagon, talking to the priestess. Omaka was clearly excited. "If you like, we'll help you bring the children to the orphanage. My friend is looking for her tribe. Perhaps you'll be able to help."

Franz nodded enthusiastically. "That would be lovely." He glanced over at Omaka, who was showing Aroha to the little girls. "The old woman has a child?"

Linda smiled. "I have a child," she said. "Omaka is a priestess, Franz." Her face became serious. "She will never pray to the *pakeha* God. I hope you will welcome her anyway."

Franz made a placating gesture. "Linda, I run an orphanage. I'm all alone with an old boozer, whose only qualification is being able to speak Maori. He doesn't believe in anything, and he blasphemes every other sentence. In any case, your priestess is more than welcome, along with her spirits."

Linda sighed sadly. "She's lost all of them. But she seems to be getting along well with the children. If the girls want, they are welcome to ride with us." She smiled again. "After all, they will still be coming to the *marae* with Linda."

The two girls turned out to be from a tribe Omaka had visited several times during journeys to her peoples' sacred sites. The older girl remembered her and was recounting, with tears running down her face, what had happened to their tribe and her parents. Omaka stroked the child's head.

In the meantime, Franz helped the other children onto his wagon and waved happily at Linda as he gave the horses their heads.

Linda followed behind. To her surprise, she soon heard singing. Franz was teaching the children a Maori version of "Michael, Row the Boat Ashore."

"Te Ariki Mikaera?" Omaka asked mistrustfully. "Is the man a Hauhau?"

Linda assured her he wasn't. She couldn't explain it, but she felt much better than she had a few hours ago. It was as though meeting Franz again had lifted a weight from her shoulders. She couldn't get over how the missionary spoke Maori and sang songs with the children, instead of praying endlessly or keeping a fearful distance. He hadn't crossed himself a single time. A year and a half ago, that would have been unthinkable.

"Hallelujah!" the children yowled.

Linda had cared for the old Franz, though he'd gotten on her and her family's nerves. But now she was genuinely excited to get to know the new one.

The children's *marae* turned out to be an old *pa*, and it was teeming with young Maori. An older half-Maori man welcomed the newcomers and asked them what tribes they were from. That was how he determined which sleeping house they should be assigned to, as Linda quickly figured out.

"Not that it's so important here," the man said each time a child told him the name of their *iwi*. "Don't forget what Revi Fransi said: We are all one *iwi* now, and we all came with the *Linda* to this *marae*. We just think you'll find friends here more quickly if your mothers and fathers told the same stories. That's why some of you are going to Kiwi House and the others to Kea House."

Apparently, the houses were purposefully named after birds and animals, instead of after the tribes.

"And who do we have here?" the man asked as Linda and Omaka led over the two girls who had been riding with them.

The girls could hardly bring themselves to leave Omaka's side.

"Will you be staying with us, *karani*?" one of them asked.

"Please, please, please stay with us!" the other begged.

Omaka looked uncertainly between the girls and Linda.

"If you don't mind sharing the sleeping house with the girls, *tohunga*, you are welcome!" The man bowed dramatically.

Omaka regally offered her face to exchange *hongi*.

"You stink like the potion that makes the *pakeha* crazy," she said sternly as she let go of him.

Kahotu shrugged. "There are a lot of things that make people crazy. Some people drink, and others dance around a pole. If you ask me, talking to spirits doesn't make a person entirely sane either. You leave me to my whiskey, and I'll leave you to your spirits." He turned to Linda. "And who might you be?"

"I'm Linda—Fitzpatrick." It was suddenly difficult for Linda to use her married name.

A broad grin spread over Kahotu's face. "You're Linda?"

He eyed the young woman from head to toe but didn't make any inappropriate remarks. Instead, he turned to look at Franz, who was blushing again.

Kahotu winked at him. "Well, no one can tell me now that prayers are never answered."

"I would love to preach to them a little. Not for hours, just to tell them a bedtime story, do you understand? Something they can think about. Something comforting, perhaps. Unfortunately, my Maori isn't good enough, and Kahotu isn't much help with such things."

Franz was telling Linda his problems after she had attended his simple evening sermon with the children. He had only said a few prayers of thanksgiving, the kind that fit with choruses of "hallelujah." He had dispensed with supplications so Kahotu wouldn't threaten to chant *mai merire*. The man often teased Franz, saying his community-building devices were much like Te Ua Haumene's.

"It could be more personal, and more ceremonial—do you know what I mean?"

They were sitting in front of Franz's home, an old storehouse in the middle of the *pa*. Aroha was sleeping in a basket at Linda's feet, guarded by Amy.

Linda nodded. "I could tell them a story every morning," she suggested. "About Jonah and the whale, perhaps."

Franz smiled. "Will you stay for a while, then?" he asked hopefully. "I thought you wanted to go to Russell."

A shadow crossed Linda's face. "I think you and the children could use my help for a while," she said. "Though to be honest, it's not as selfless as that. I'm ashamed of how I misjudged Fitz. It's been so long since I've heard from anyone in my family, and I'm afraid they've all dismissed me for a fool."

"Of course not!" Franz cried. "And what do you mean you haven't heard from anyone? I know Ida's very worried about you. Didn't the army transport any mail?"

"I wrote every few days from Patea!" Linda exclaimed. "Especially at the beginning. But Mamida never replied, so I wrote less and less often. Unless—" She looked at Franz in alarm. "What if Fitz intercepted the letters? Or maybe Vera had a hand in the matter. She enjoyed making me suffer."

"Vera?" Franz asked.

Linda took a deep breath. "Another long story."

Franz gazed into Linda's pale face. He wrestled with himself for a moment, and then went into the house. When he returned, he was carrying a bottle of whiskey and two glasses.

"I have time," he said. "And I'm afraid there's something I must tell you. It's about your sisters."

Chapter 66

"I don't care what you think!" Jane shouted. "If I say the ewes belong in the west pasture, then put them there!"

It wasn't advisable to holler at a foreman that way. Jane was in a bad mood, and Mr. Colderell's high-handedness had been the last straw. Still, the man's argument was sound. If he brought the creatures closer to the house, he could keep a better eye on their pregnancies. Jane might have simply agreed to the plan if only she weren't so tired of Colderell making decisions over her head. He knew more about sheep than she did, but he took far too many liberties. The man knew too well how much she needed him.

Jane stormed out of the bull barn. She had bought the young cattle because the price of meat had shot up. The population of New Zealand was growing, and the prospectors and mine workers in particular were enthusiastic about steak. Unfortunately, no one on the farm knew very much about cattle. Colderell and his men were out of their depths with the aggressive male animals.

Jane sighed. If she were honest, things weren't going very well at Rata Station. It was difficult to run the farm without the support of her husband and the Maori shepherds. Te Haitara had withdrawn completely since Eru had left, or rather, since Jane had made one scene after another. The chief didn't think that the departure of young warriors was anything unusual. To the contrary, Te Haitara was proud. Eru and the others wanted to increase their *mana* on the North Island. But Jane was furious about Eru's revolt against her authority. She felt he'd ruined his future with his tattoos and his escape to the north, not to mention the danger he was putting himself in. Te Haitara's calm acceptance made her furious, and they'd fought about it for days.

"He's a warrior, Raupo," the chieftain had insisted. "The tribes have always fought against one another. Even the Ngai Tahu have had their battles."

"How many hundreds of years ago was that?" Jane had demanded angrily. "Against which enemies? Here, everyone is Ngai Tahu. Fine, the Ngati Toa live in the northwest, but since Te Rauparaha's been gone, they have also been completely peaceful. I get that you may have punched each other in the nose a few times, but in the north there's a war that this 'prophet' can't win. It's completely pointless for Eru to risk his life."

In Jane's opinion, Te Haitara should have at least sent out a *taua* to bring back Eru and the others. She herself had set a private detective on their trail, but he had lost the young adventurers in the forests of Taranaki.

Jane and Te Haitara's relationship had also suffered because of her disputed "inheritance." After her husband had tried one too many times to convince her to return the land, Jane had angrily packed her things and moved to the farm, taking most of the tribe's sheep with her. She had been living in the stone house for a year now, and hadn't exchanged a single word with Te Haitara in all that time.

The Ngai Tahu who'd once worked for Linda and Carol stayed far away, and the tribe had obviously returned to their traditional way of life. The men hunted, the women weaved and cooked, and together they farmed a few fields. They financed luxury goods such as cloth and cooking pots with their savings. Te Haitara had an account at the bank in Christchurch that certainly wouldn't be empty anytime soon. Over the last few years, the tribe had bought anything that anyone had wanted. Now the tribal elders had triumphed, especially the *tohungas*, who had wondered well before Jane's takeover of Rata Station if all the work with the sheep was necessary.

Jane, for her part, had defiantly sought new farmhands in Christchurch. Only with the help of foreman Patrick Colderell had she been able to find any at all. The men were suspicious of a farm run by a woman. Every day, they made Jane feel that they didn't really take her seriously. Jane soldiered on bravely and achieved most of her goals, even when she had to go over her employees' heads. But it took a lot of effort. Some evenings, she wept with loneliness in spite of all her strength.

Additionally, she had to deal with the ire of her *pakeha* neighbors. Jane had never had a very close relationship with them. People like the Butlers refused to have anything else to do with a woman who lived with a Maori chieftain. But at least Jane had always been treated politely at the Sheep Breeders' Association. Now she had been suspended. The Deanses and the Redwoods had voted against her participation. People seemed to think that her takeover of Rata Station hadn't been fair. And when news of Carol and Mara's disappearance had gotten around, she found herself permanently ostracized.

For the last shearing, Jane had to hire a team from Otago. The men who had worked for Chris and Cat now skipped Rata Station on their way down the Waimakariri. Jane also had to organize the transport of fleeces on her own. The wool traders offered her worse prices because her wool arrived later than the other farms'. Financially, Jane could handle it. As a businesswoman, she was superior to most of the other sheep barons. In the meantime, she had also invested in shipping companies and railroads. But the constant pressure was having a bad effect on her nerves.

With Te Haitara and Eru by her side, the sheep business had been fun. To think of the plans she'd had for the boy! Every door would have been open for Eru. And now he was fighting in a pointless war on the North Island, Te Haitara was sulking in the village, and Jane had to force herself to get through her days.

Now she wandered up to the house, closed the door behind her, and took a bottle of whiskey out of the cupboard. Some time ago, she had discovered that whiskey could comfort her better, was easier to come by, and made her gain less weight than chocolate. She never drank too much, but a glass or two in the evening made life easier to bear.

"Sorry to bother you . . ."

Jane turned around in annoyance. Colderell had opened the door and poked his head inside.

"What is it now, Mr. Colderell?" she snapped at him.

The foreman frowned. "There's someone here who wants to speak to you."

"I told you it wasn't necessary to announce me," a voice behind Colderell said. It sounded familiar . . . too familiar. Jane cast a wary glance at the whiskey bottle. Was she drinking too much, after all?

Colderell withdrew, and the door flew open. In disbelief, Jane found herself looking into the furious eyes of Christopher Fenroy. Her ex-husband seemed thinner than before. His skin was reddened by cold and wind, and his face looked a little patchy, as though he'd had a beard for a long time and had recently shaved it off. His hair was longer than was appropriate for a gentleman, but he'd always worn it that way. Behind him, unusually reserved, was Cat.

Jane swallowed. "Chris—"

"Now, don't tell me you're happy to see me!" Chris almost shouted. "I thought I'd find you in this house. Did you manage to talk Te Haitara into moving here, or did he throw you out?" He approached Jane, his hands balled into fists.

"Mr. Fenroy—" Colderell began.

"You stay out of this," Chris snapped. "You're fired, anyway. I don't want to keep on anyone who worked for her—"

"Chris . . . ," Cat said calmingly and then turned to the foreman. "Please, Patrick, leave us alone now. We'll decide later which of the workers can stay."

Colderell frowned. Cat had used his first name, as if he were a simple shepherd.

"I—you—" he started to complain.

Cat pointed to the door. "Get out of here, Patrick. And don't worry. I will keep Chris from punching her, and he will keep me from scratching her eyes out. We have ourselves under control."

As Colderell slunk out, Jane stared in disbelief. "I thought you were dead."

Chris snorted. "Clearly. And under the circumstances, that was completely forgivable. But the farm! Jane, how could you do that to the girls?"

"From a purely legal point of view—"

"You've known Carol and Linda since they were little," Cat said, interrupting her. "You watched them grow up, together with your son. How could you throw them out of their home?"

Jane raised her hands in a gesture of powerlessness. "I'm a businesswoman!"

"Not to mention Te Haitara," Cat continued. "He was your husband for twenty years, Jane. And suddenly you say that your marriage doesn't count, or never happened?"

"You pretended your son was mine!" Chris howled. "That's the worst kind of treachery. What was more, you'd always planned it. That birth certificate!"

"I wanted to keep all the possibilities open for him," Jane said.

"Well, you ruined his possibilities," Chris said coldly. "I certainly won't acknowledge him now. He will not be my heir. And if your marriage with Te Haitara was never official, then he's nothing but a poor bastard."

"He's gone, anyway," Jane said quietly.

"And you're going to leave too," Chris said, pushing her firmly on the shoulder. "Immediately. I'll give you five minutes to pack your things. And don't start asking for papers. I was in Christchurch with the authorities, and I have it in black and white that Cat and I aren't dead. Your claim to the farm is hereby forfeit."

Jane glared at him. "I worked this farm for a year! I made a profit, I—"

"You don't really want to try that tack in court, do you, Jane?" Chris's voice swung between disbelief and threat.

Jane pursed her lips. "I deserve it!" she hissed. "I need money to live. I left Te Haitara. I—"

"Poor you," Cat shot back. "You stole everything from the children. You drove Linda into an unhappy marriage. It's your fault that Carol and Mara are in the hands of crazy rebel warriors. And you want us to, what, pay you for that?" Cat had kept herself in check so far, but now her voice was angrier than Chris's. "How can you even bear to look at yourself in the mirror?"

Jane shrugged. "I was never terribly fond of my reflection," she quipped.

Chris stared into her unmoved face. It didn't seem as if Jane was going to fight them for Rata Station, but she obviously didn't feel guilty about what she'd done either. Suddenly he felt tired.

"I know you must have plenty of other investments, Jane," he said, calmer now. "If you're actually destitute, I will pay your support, so you needn't threaten to sue me for it. Take a hotel room in Christchurch or somewhere, the farther away the better. Just let me know your new address so I can have the divorce papers sent over. I already spoke with a lawyer, and the divorce proceedings have begun. It will be very difficult and very expensive. It can also take some time. If I've understood correctly, it requires an Act of Parliament. But in light of our history, I'm confident any judge will agree. I will send you the documents as soon as the divorce is legal. And then, Jane Beit, I never want to see you again."

Te Haitara silently approached his friend. The chieftain had already heard about Chris's return. News spread fast in the Canterbury Plains. Now the entire village had gathered to welcome Chris and Cat to the *marae.*

"I'm truly happy," Te Haitara said.

The chieftain of the Ngai Tahu had visibly aged in the past two years. He'd lost weight. The once powerful, stocky warrior was a shadow of his former self. Wrinkles, carved there by worry and hurt, showed under the tattoos on his face.

Chris hesitated for a moment and then leaned his forehead and nose against the chieftain's. "How could you let it happen?" He had tried to control himself, but the question had burst out of its own accord.

Te Haitara shrugged helplessly. "How could I have stopped her?" he asked sadly. "Of course, the girls could have stayed here."

"Next door to the woman who stole their farm?" Cat asked sharply. "You should have done something."

"I shouldn't have trusted her." Te Haitara sighed. "She always said that a businessman or woman had to keep all options open. I never really understood what she meant by that. You were an option, I was an option. The divorce ceremony was an option, as was Eru's birth certificate. I'm sorry. What will you do to her now?"

Chris rubbed his brow. "On paper, she's still my wife, but by *pakeha* law, it's forbidden to chop her head off."

Te Haitara tried to smile. "That's also not typical for Maori law. Still, you have more right to recompense than I do."

"We threw her out," Cat said. "She's on her way to Christchurch now. Chris has already started divorce proceedings in the *pakeha* manner."

"If you want to marry her again afterward," Chris added, "it would be best to do so in front of a *pakeha* justice of the peace. Otherwise, she could just deny it again and demand alimony from me. By the way, I'd appreciate if you would acknowledge your fatherhood of Eru in writing. I'll have to prove that he isn't my son."

Te Haitara lowered his eyes. "I haven't heard anything from Eru for months. It's possible that he's dead."

The chieftain looked so unhappy that it hurt Cat to look at him. She gently put a hand on his arm.

"Ariki," she said kindly, "time will tell if you want to take Jane back or not. But Eru is your son. If he were dead, you'd know."

Chapter 67

"The boys from Kea House are playing blackjack again instead of doing their homework," Linda complained. "You're raising them as gamblers and drinkers."

Franz looked up from his work. He was trying to fix the wheel of his farm wagon. Unfortunately, it had been years since he'd watched a wainwright at work.

"So far, Kahotu hasn't taught them to distill whiskey," he countered. "And their math is getting better and better. They're even making their own play-money. Hoani just lost a million pounds. He'll never forget again how many zeros that has."

"Maybe it's fine as long as they lose," she said, not sounding terribly convinced. "But what if they win and start to believe they can make a living that way?"

Franz shook his head. "I don't let them win," he said calmly. "Did you finish translating the sermon?"

"No, but I made scones instead," Linda said, opening the basket that she had been carrying on her arm. She took out a coffee pot, a cup, and a plate. "You have to take a break, or you'll keel over with hunger. So, I saved some of the scones before the children could eat them all. The new oven is wonderful!"

Linda had recently set up a kitchen in one of the outbuildings and was teaching the Maori girls how to cook and bake the *pakeha* way. Franz's fosterlings would eventually need to support themselves, and domestic servants were much sought after in Wellington. Even the pastor in Otaki hadn't been able to deny the logic of that argument. The merchants from town had donated the oven and the kitchen cupboards.

Franz wiped his hands on his trousers and sat down on a stone next to where Linda had laid out the treats. "Delicious!" he said, biting into one of the scones.

Linda smiled. Amy pawed at Franz's leg, whining for her share.

"Seriously, Franz, you're taking it too lightly with the gambling," Linda said. "I was married to a gambler. You said you don't let the children win, but it's impossible to have an influence on the cards. They're random. It's dangerous to believe anything else."

Franz ate another scone. "Of course I can influence that," he told her. "To be honest, I always wondered what blackjack had to do with luck. You just have to concentrate a little . . . Oh, did Omaka tell you that there's a letter for you? It's from your mother. I left it in front of your house."

For the moment, Linda forgot about the dangers of gambling and leaped to her feet. "Who is it from, Mamida or Mamaca? Perhaps she's written about when she'll finally be coming."

Since Linda had been in touch with Ida and Cat again, nothing was as important to her as their regular letters. Above all, she longed for Cat's letters, which always surprised Franz. Linda seemed to be closer to Catherine Rata than to her mother, Ida. In fact, Linda had almost departed abruptly for Rata Station when she'd heard about Cat and Chris Fenroy's rescue. Only the news that they'd be coming to the North Island as soon as possible to help with the search for Carol and Mara had stopped her.

When Ida had first written to Franz about the kidnapping, he'd lain awake nights, reliving his own horrifying brush with the Hauhau at Opotiki and praying for the sisters' souls. Then Linda had arrived, and he'd realized that he'd have to be the one to break the news. It had been a devastating blow. Linda had gone two days without speaking, rocking Aroha in a dim room under Omaka's watchful eye while Franz's heart broke. Soon, though, the old priestess coaxed her outside, and Linda threw herself into working with the children. They and the baby were a kind of salvation, and now she seemed almost normal. Franz knew that Carol and Mara were the central topic in Linda's letters to her family, but he always hesitated to talk with her about them, fearful of the pain it might call forth.

Linda left her basket where it was and quickly made her way to the center of the *pa*, followed by Amy. Her house, which had also previously been an outbuilding, was now at the center of activity. Like Franz, it was important to her to keep an eye on the children, while Kahotu preferred to live in the old chieftain's house, and Omaka, too, chose a dwelling in a less busy spot. Still, the old priestess had a constant stream of visitors. Since Linda had arrived, the children had learned to read and write and knew their Bible stories, and the first of them had been baptized. But when they needed spiritual counsel, they went to Omaka.

Franz watched Linda go, and as he had a thousand times before, he thanked God that she kept postponing her departure. At the same time, he wasn't at all sure if Linda and Omaka had been sent to him by God. They had been a blessing for the orphanage in so many ways, but Omaka reminded the children of their heathen beliefs, and Linda was a temptation for Franz. Whenever he was with her, he could only think about how wonderful it would be to hold her in his arms. He fought constantly against his body's response to her occasional touch, her smile, her scent. At night he dreamed of her, and awoke in damp sheets, red with shame. At first, he hoped that it would pass. He must maintain his role as a friendly uncle, and never come across as a hopeful suitor. Franz attempted to avoid her touch whenever possible, and after their first confidential conversation over the whiskey bottle, he had tried to avoid discussing overly personal matters.

They had more than enough work to talk about, anyway. The concerns of the orphanage required constant communication. Linda had gotten involved with great enthusiasm from the very beginning. She had always enjoyed working with children, and had plenty of experience. After Miss Foggerty had gotten married, she'd often taken on the role of substitute teacher at Rata Station. Now she came up with new ideas and suggestions every day. Franz had to force himself not to praise them too euphorically, and struggled not to tell her openly how much he admired and loved her, and how amazingly his life had changed since she had arrived.

Linda and Omaka had immediately recognized the problems at Franz's orphanage and had applied solutions energetically. Omaka had taken over the supervision of the kitchens and laundry. She assigned girls and boys to help her, and taught them how to do the work. Now no one needed to skip lessons because of domestic duties, and the children didn't want to, anyway. Since Linda had taken over teaching the older students, they understood the reason they had to learn, and they all participated enthusiastically. This freed up Franz to focus on the little ones who could learn English quickly. They all made fast progress. Kahotu was hardly needed in the school at all anymore, so he had more time for setting traps and fishing. He no longer needed help from the older boys. They attended school in the mornings, and during the afternoons, Franz encouraged them to learn practical skills. With their help, he renovated the buildings of the *pa*.

"It's really not necessary," he said when the older children let him know through Linda's translation that they wanted to decorate the houses with beautiful carvings.

One of the boys was the son of a woodcarving *tohunga*. His father had been teaching his son the art for years. Now the thirteen-year-old wanted to pass on his knowledge to the others.

"In fact," Franz continued, "decoration is somewhat heathen. Lutheran churches are always unembellished. The homes of the faithful should be practical, not beautiful. Wood carving is a vain pursuit."

Linda made a face, as she usually did when Franz fell back into the mindset of his old community. She'd anticipated different objections to the boy's request. The carvings didn't merely have a decorative function but a spiritual significance. Franz would surely not see that as pleasing to God. But perhaps, she thought, she could use tradition as an argument for the boy's wishes.

"The children see the carvings as a connection to their tribes," she said patiently. "Every *iwi* has a special motif that tells stories of the tribe's origins. The memories of their ancestors' spirits are passed on that way. Let them do it, Franz! If you forbid it, they'll do it secretly. In that case, they wouldn't just carve motifs and traditional designs on the houses, but *hei tiki*. That really would be heathen."

Omaka had been encouraging the children to make the little god figures out of jade and carry them as good-luck charms and mementos of their tribes. Linda knew about it, but she didn't tell Franz.

"Fine," Franz said, giving in. "But they shouldn't just learn to carve Maori symbols. If I teach them *pakeha* woodworking as well, perhaps it would help with employment later."

The preparation of the children for work in the *pakeha* world was a very important issue for the Church Missionary Society. Franz's initial instincts had been to turn the young Maori into perfect *pakeha* and have them forget their customs and traditions. He was becoming more broad-minded the longer he worked with the children, but Linda still challenged his assumptions regularly. It was clear to both of them that these children would never be able to return to their old lives. The fosterlings would remain wanderers between two worlds. Linda and Franz saw it as their duty to prepare them as well as they could—much better, for example, than Kahotu had been prepared.

Soon, the boys were learning carving from the *tohunga*'s son and woodworking from Franz.

"Where did you learn all that?" Linda asked in amazement as he did a complicated equation again and cut the wood to fit perfectly.

"Nowhere," Franz replied. "I mean, I learned the math; I was always good at numbers. But the rest I just learned by watching. Sometimes you have to watch craftsmen at their work."

Linda's brow creased. "I've often watched craftsmen too. But I never studied their every movement."

Franz laughed. "I don't need to watch that carefully. I just have to remember what I once observed, and then I see it in front of me again. I used to think it was the same for everyone, but apparently I have an unusually good memory."

Linda thought his memory was phenomenal. She could hardly believe how fast he was learning Maori now that she was giving him regular lessons too. He hadn't been able to teach himself the complicated grammar without a textbook, but vocabulary came easily. He remembered most words after reading them once, and astounded Linda when it came to the Maori Bible. Franz could quote entire chapters of Genesis in Maori, even though he didn't comprehend the meanings of all the words.

"Did you really think you'd be able to learn the language by memorizing the Bible?" she asked in amazement. "That must have taken forever."

Franz shrugged. "It didn't really help that much," he admitted. "But it went quickly. I read it a few times, and then I could say it."

Linda decided to stop marveling and just accept it. She had rarely had so much fun as when she was teaching Franz—even if his behavior with her was often mysterious. Sometimes he seemed to enjoy working with her, and other times to be avoiding her. Their first evening together had done her good, and she had felt a connection with Franz that had almost bordered on intimacy. Before they had finally said good night, he had gently put a hand over hers, and she hadn't been surprised. That evening, Linda had believed that perhaps something was beginning—something much more profound than her connection to Fitz. But the next day, Franz had been distant again. He shied from any kind of touch, and he thanked her formally for small favors. It ran contrary to the way his eyes lit up when he saw her, and Linda often sensed his gaze following her surreptitiously.

The young woman was baffled. Franz seemed to be in love with her but didn't make the slightest attempt to court her. She had already considered that perhaps he'd taken a vow of celibacy. But as far as she knew, such vows didn't apply to Anglicans or Lutherans. To the contrary, Linda had never heard of an unmarried missionary.

Franz's contradictory behavior made Linda unsure of herself. She would often think of Fitz, who had also withdrawn unpredictably. Did it have something to do with her? Did she simply not understand men? Was she misreading the signs?

Linda racked her brain as her affection for Franz grew every day. She'd always been fond of Ida's brother. Even back at Rata Station, something about him had attracted her, even though he'd been so tormented and disapproving. Then, she had interpreted her feelings more as pity than as love. But now that he'd matured, laid aside his religious fanaticism, and showed such obvious devotion to the children, he had won Linda's respect. Her heart sang when she saw how lovingly he helped little Pai put on a coat, or witnessed the endless patience with which he taught the most slow-witted children mathematics. She often caught herself wishing that he'd touch her. She watched him as he pounded iron or worked wood with his strong hands, and the gentleness with which he guided the children's small fingers as they learned their first letters. She watched him pat the little ones on the head, and wished he would put a comforting hand on her own shoulder.

Franz was also quite good with Aroha. He seemed delighted to rock the child to sleep for hours, but he quickly gave her back to Linda if Kahotu happened by. Linda couldn't understand. Kahotu kept joking that Aroha would soon be calling him "Daddy," and Franz reacted as though it were an insult. It was worse when Linda accidentally came too close to him. Then he leaped back as though burned, only to devour her with hungry eyes. Finally, she turned to Omaka.

"Sometimes I think he's like Fitz," she said to the old priestess. "I never understood what he was thinking either. Sometimes he was gentle and kind and wonderful, and then he'd be arrogant and distant again. Are all men that way?"

Omaka poked the fire with a stick. "Are you blind, *mokopuna*?" she asked gently. "I can't think of two men who are more different. Your husband had no access to his feelings, whereas this man has a whirlwind of pain inside of him, such a stew of bitter roots, made of both fear and love. As long as his mouth is full of it, he won't be able to tell you how much he desires you."

"Why not?" Linda asked, feeling depressed. "Can't he ever get past the pain, or just forget it all?"

Omaka shrugged. "Perhaps someday. Perhaps with your help. And perhaps the reason will disappear someday. I don't know, *mokopuna*. But don't scorn him; he's suffering. He's suffering because of you."

Linda sighed. "And why doesn't it matter that I'm suffering? I wish I could meet a man someday who wasn't so preoccupied with himself!"

Chapter 68

"There's a man at the door, asking if he can sleep here," a young girl named Emere told Linda as she entered the kitchen.

It often happened that strangers came to the orphanage asking for a place to stay. After all, Otaki had been a missionary station for a long time. Many travelers didn't know it had closed, and the townspeople didn't bother to set them straight. If someone asked, they were sent to Franz Lange.

Franz didn't mind. Anyone who asked a mission for help was more likely to be an honest person in need than a trickster or thief. They were usually single men, and more rarely entire families who were headed north to look for somewhere to settle or work. Franz tended to welcome them hospitably, and sent them on their way the next day with plenty of provisions.

"Well, then bring the man in out of the rain," Linda told the girl who had dutifully announced the visitor.

The children took turns manning the gate in pairs. The orphanage was open to all, but since Kahotu had once invited two old friends over to drink and play cards, Franz wanted to know who was coming and going.

Emere left, and Linda prepared to welcome the visitor. Kahotu was out somewhere, and Franz was busy with renovation work. It would be up to her to find a place for the man to sleep, and perhaps offer him a warm meal right away. Fortunately, she had just finished making a big stew to warm up later for dinner.

"Would you watch Aroha for a few minutes?" she asked the two girls who had been helping her in the kitchen. "I have to go meet the visitor. I'll be right back."

She put the baby's basket down next to the girl who was kneading the dough for the bread. Both girls began to sing a lullaby.

The weather that day was awful. Before leaving the kitchen, Linda took off her apron, wrapped herself in a warm cloak, and covered her head with a woolen scarf. Outside, the wind drove the rain into her face and almost blew her over. There were no children to be seen. They were probably holed up in the sleeping houses or the old meetinghouse that Linda had converted into a kind of school and living room.

Linda heard hoofbeats as she entered the meeting grounds, and could hardly believe her eyes as a little white horse trotted toward her. The man on the horse's back wore a threadbare jacket and a wide-brimmed sou'wester hat that offered him insufficient protection from the rain. Linda stared. He was rather thin, with short legs . . .

Linda repressed the impulse to turn on her heel and flee. Shaking inside, she waved to Joe Fitzpatrick and pointed at the barn. Fitz followed, not bothering to look closely at the woman under the scarf. But the reprieve wasn't long enough for her to pull herself together. Linda was in turmoil. What was he doing here? Was he looking for her? Where was Vera? Hadn't Fitz bought the little white horse for her?

"Isn't this my lucky day? I expected to be welcomed by a nest full of psalm-singing ravens, and a beautiful woman greets me! Madam . . ."

Linda didn't know if she should laugh or be angry. It was so typical for Fitz to attempt flattery without even seeing the person he was talking to. Through the curtain of rain and peering out from beneath the brim of his hat, he only recognized his wife after he'd jumped off his horse.

For the space of a heartbeat, he was speechless. "Lindy—"

"Good evening," Linda said coolly. "What brings you here?"

Fitz seemed to consider his options for a moment. "I've been looking for you, Lindy. You disappeared. Why didn't you wait for me? We could have left together, we—"

"You were in jail," Linda reminded him.

"But only for a little while," Fitz insisted. He led the horse under the eaves of the barn. He looked healthy and well, even though he was surely half-frozen, and his movements were as casual and self-assured as ever. "Hey, if you're working for a mission, shouldn't you know the Bible? 'I was a stranger, and ye took me not in: naked, and ye clothed me not: sick, and in prison, and ye visited me not.'" He grinned.

"You aren't really trying to compare yourself to Jesus, are you?" Linda said with disgust. "You were arrested for cowardice in the face of the enemy. Don't you remember? You left me alone to face a *taua* of wild Hauhau warriors so you could hide with Vera. I'm sorry, I couldn't think of any reason why I should care about what happened to you after that."

Fitz shook his head. "Oh, Lindy, that was all just a misunderstanding. I've missed you and our baby desperately. Where is the little one now, anyway?" Then his voice turned accusing. "I don't even know what you named her!" He pointed at the barn door. "In here?"

Linda nodded. As Fitz led the horse into the barn, Brianna whinnied. She recognized Vera's horse from the army barn in Patea. While Linda had been waiting for Fitz's trial, both horses had been kept there.

"Well, at least Brianna missed me," Fitz said cheerfully.

Amy greeted him too, leaping up on him.

"Disloyal mutt," Linda muttered.

Fitz patted the dog and then began to unsaddle his horse. "I can stay here, can't I? I would really like to stay a night in the mission, even if you're angry at me. Oh, Lindy, especially because you're angry at me! We must be able to sort things out between us somehow."

He'd taken off his hat, and Linda could look into his face. She recognized the old Fitz. He gave her that look again that seemed to say she was the only thing in the world for him, his eyes glowing with warmth and understanding. It was the way he'd looked at her before he'd met Vera.

"I'm a little wet." Fitz smiled apologetically and moved toward Linda to embrace her.

Linda stepped backward. "Where's Vera?"

Fitz shook his head. "You're still jealous, aren't you?" he said in reprimand, then pasted the irresistible grin back on his face. "I suppose that should make me happy. After all, it proves that you're still thinking about me."

"Where is Vera?" Linda repeated. "Answer me, Fitz. I want to know whether I have to reckon with having her on my doorstep tomorrow."

Fitz laughed. "Vera doesn't need shelter here. She's in Auckland. She got a fantastic job as an actress! She had an audition with an agent in Wellington, and he immediately recognized her talent. Now she's working in a music hall. I'm taking care of her horse."

"Well then, she's doing exactly what she's good at," Linda replied. "Pretending she's something she's not. That is, if 'music hall' isn't another word for bordello. But it doesn't matter, as long as she's far, far away."

"You never liked her," Fitz said with a snarl, and anger flashed across his face. But the expression vanished again quickly. "But, as you say, it doesn't matter. You don't need to pretend anymore that Vera is coming between us. She's gone." He lifted a hand to caress Linda's face.

Linda stepped back again quickly. "Where have you been since you left Patea? Are you on the run again?"

"Of course not," Fitz said lightly. "I've been traveling. After that stupid misunderstanding about the Hauhau attack, the army didn't want me anymore. Bastards. They were only looking for a reason to take the farm away from me. Well, I don't care. I don't need a farm. I only joined the military settlers to please you."

"Is that so?" Linda asked in disbelief. "You seemed terribly excited about it back then."

"That's just because I didn't realize what a small-minded person McDonnell was. Well, I've heard that's all been fixed again, anyway. Lord, I was so happy when I heard about Cat and Chris Fenroy!"

Fitz put his horse in the empty stall next to Brianna, where Franz had already laid out hay and oats for his own horse. Brianna approached Fitz's mare, shoved her nose through the bars, and whinnied excitedly. But Linda pursed her lips in annoyance. Couldn't Fitz at least ask before he used the stall? But he never did think about such things. He just took off his wet jacket and smiled at Linda.

"It's nice to be dry," he said. "If you'd just warm me up a little—"

"How do you know about Chris and Cat?" Linda asked.

Fitz shrugged. "Sweetheart, the papers in Auckland were full of the news. Six castaways rescued after more than two years! That Bill Paxton is a real hotshot. I'm just wondering what you're doing here, Lindy. Shouldn't you have been back at Rata Station long ago?"

So, he had been in Auckland, probably with Vera—until the girl found someone better. Linda's mind raced. An agent or a music-hall owner. A man with far more influence than the smooth-talking military settler, and surely not prepared to share his young prize. Fitz would have never let Vera go of his own accord. He'd been dropped. Linda wondered how much it had hurt his pride.

"Maybe there's something keeping me here," she said defiantly. "Or someone."

Fitz threw his head back and laughed. "You aren't telling me that one of the black ravens is an admirer! Did you tell him that you're still married? What was joined under God, Lindy, no missionary shall separate." He grinned.

"This isn't a missionary station anymore," Linda said. "It's an orphanage. Under the leadership of Franz Lange."

"Your uncle?" Fitz stared at her in disbelief. "That tragic idiot? He was in love with you back at the boathouse in Christchurch."

"Was he?" Linda asked in amazement.

"It was impossible to miss!" Fitz laughed. "But you aren't going to tell me you're interested now. Sweetheart, the man is ancient. And besides, it would be incest."

Linda scowled. Of course Fitz knew her family story. "He's Ida's brother, not Cat's," she shot back. "Besides, he's not much older than you are, he's just more mature."

"Franz Lange was probably born mature," Fitz joked.

"He's a good person," Linda said firmly.

Fitz crossed himself dramatically. "Pious, without a doubt! But sweetheart, you can't be serious. You just need a shoulder to lean on. Who knows that better than I do? That's why I'm here for you again. And just in time, it seems, Lindy! Your parents have been rescued, you get your farm back—you should be celebrating! And instead you're stuck here praying and taking care of heathen bastards. That can't possibly be any fun, Lindy. Get packed, we're leaving tomorrow. We'll show our daughter Rata Station. Forget your missionary. The whole world is at your feet."

Before Linda could answer, he picked her up and spun her around, like in old times.

"You should at least give Linda some time to think about it."

Franz Lange was standing in the barn doorway, holding his untacked horse on a lead rope. Linda and Fitz hadn't heard him arrive because of the rain pounding on the barn roof, and the rustling of the straw in the horses' stalls. Linda wondered how long he'd been standing there, and how much he'd heard. Ashamed, she freed herself from Fitz's embrace.

"You can't just blindside her like that," Franz said. "She needs a chance to think about what's best for the child."

Fitz grinned. "Good evening to you, Reverend! You're completely right. Linda has to figure everything out. Fortunately, she's a clever girl and thinks very fast." He tried to put his arm around Linda's shoulders, but she pulled away. "And I must say, I'm surprised that you'd question her decision at all. Do I have to quote the Bible to you, Reverend? 'For whither thou goest, I will go; and where thou lodgest, I will lodge: thy people shall be my people, and thy God my God.' Linda swore all that to me. Do not forget: she is still my wife."

"You left her," Franz said, tying up his horse by the door. "You ignored her and betrayed her. Those are grounds for divorce."

Fitz frowned. "In the eyes of men, perhaps," he said, feigning piousness. "But not in the eyes of God."

Linda glared at him. "Stop it right now, Fitz!" she cried. "Don't be such a damn hypocrite. We all know very well that you don't believe in God. I've certainly never heard you pray to anyone except Vera Carrigan."

"You see, Reverend, my wife is still jealous." Fitz smiled. "She cares about me. And now I'm taking her with me."

"What if she doesn't want to go with you?" Franz asked sharply.

"I don't!" Linda shouted. "I've had enough of you and your lying and flattery, and your roving around from one playground to another. That's what the world is to you, isn't it? A gigantic playground. I've had enough of being a toy that you throw away and fetch again whenever it suits you!"

Fitz looked from Franz to Linda, and his cheerfulness seemed to melt away. The coldness in his eyes reminded Linda of Vera.

"Well then, I'll just have to ride to Rata Station alone and talk to your parents, Lindy. Perhaps they'll have more understanding for your abandoned husband and the father of your child. A divorce lawyer surely would. I didn't leave you, Lindy. You left me. I never betrayed you either. Vera will swear to it. Our neighbors will vouch for it, as will her parents. No one ever saw me even touch her. The fault is yours alone. I wonder if you'll be allowed to keep our child."

Linda gasped. "That's ridiculous. You were dishonorably discharged from the army. You were in jail. You're bluffing. No judge in the world would give you my child."

Fritz's face cracked into an openly wicked grin. "May the best man win."

Linda trembled. She was horrified by the idea of litigation, and the constant alternation between flattery and threats. She never wanted to feel as helpless as she had in Patea, lied to and made to feel crazy. She never wanted to see Fitz ever again.

Franz Lange stepped to her side.

"Mr. Fitzpatrick, be honest for once," he said calmly. "In the end, it's only about money for you. You would happily agree to a divorce if you were paid enough."

"That's malicious slander," Fitz said. "I married my wife when she was completely destitute. Don't you remember, Lindy? And she always had enough to eat!"

Linda didn't reply, which seemed to encourage Fitz. He turned toward her again.

"Come on, Lindy, what is all this? I don't want to threaten you. I just want to be with you and our little girl again. Forget all this about a divorce. We used to be happy together. Come with me, Lindy, and I'll teach you to smile again. We have to take life lightly and play all our good cards! You know, Lindy, I'm a lucky fellow. I never lose!"

Franz took a deep breath. "If you see it that way," he said, his voice firm, "then let's just reshuffle the cards. How would you like to play a hand of blackjack with me, Mr. Fitzpatrick? The stakes are your wife."

Linda gasped again. "I'm no prize in a game," she declared, horrified.

Fitz laughed. "Sweetheart, you were the highest stakes I ever played for. And make no mistake, you belong to me. Good Lord, Reverend! I never would have dared to suggest such a wager. But you'd have to offer me something comparable. Which may be a deal breaker. Or do you actually own anything of value?"

Franz narrowed his eyes. "You will be satisfied," he said, and all of his disdain for Fitz rang in his voice. "Now get your horse out of Herbie's stall." He pointed to his patiently waiting bay. "He worked all day, and now he wants to eat his dinner somewhere dry, in peace and quiet."

Fitz looked around in irritation. "There are plenty of stalls here," he said. "Put him in a different one."

Franz shook his head. "Not everyone is so careless about where he lies down to sleep, Mr. Fitz. You may be a vagabond, but my horse is not."

Chapter 69

"Where shall we play our little game?" Fitz asked.

He seemed to be in a good mood again after he'd led his horse into a guest stall, freeing the stall next to Brianna for Herbie. Linda fetched fresh hay for the white mare and new oats for Herbie, reeling and eager to keep herself occupied.

"I suppose you don't have a pub here," Fitz said.

"We have a meetinghouse," Franz replied. "We can sit down there."

"Franz, not in front of the children!" Linda said, objecting.

Fitz grinned. "You could send them to bed."

"It's fine if they see," Franz said. "There's no better way to dissuade someone from gambling than to see a big loss."

Linda's eyes went wide. This was all too much. She knew how adamantly Fitz believed in his luck, against all logic. But Franz? He was a clergyman and the most serious person she knew. And suddenly he wanted to wager her future on a deck of cards? Linda wanted to object again, wanted to shout, but then she thought about Fitz's legal claim on her and the baby. She shivered at the thought of his power over her.

Outside, it was still pouring rain. Linda hardly noticed it as she hurried across the meeting grounds. She cast a glance at the cross and altar in the center, and sent a desperate prayer to all the gods and spirits. Franz, following close behind, seemed to read her mind.

"That's a sin, Linda. You can't pray for luck in gambling."

Linda shook her head and tried to fight down her rising panic. Franz couldn't help her. The man had lost his mind!

Laughter and singing were coming from the meetinghouse. A few girls were playing Maori instruments. The music sounded a little off. Neither Linda nor Omaka knew very much about how to play the *koauau*, the *nguru*, or the *putorino*. However, there were children who knew how to make the traditional flutes, and Omaka encouraged them to practice. The results made more noise than music, but it was fun for everyone. When they entered, they saw a few of the smaller children, among them Franz's favorite, Pai, dancing. Franz smiled. A few children were playing blackjack at one of the tables.

Fitz looked surprised. "Strange mission you're running here. Usually, you pastors say that cards are an invention of the devil."

"Sometimes you have to use the devil's tools to conquer evil," Franz replied. "You'll have to make space for us, children. I'm sorry to disturb you, but I promised Mr. Fitzpatrick here a game. You can watch and then go on playing afterward."

Looking surprised, the children cleared the table without complaint. Little Hoani passed Franz a stack of play-money.

"Look, Revi Fransi," he said in English. "Is five million. You could lose much!"

Franz smiled.

"Revi Fransi never lose," his friend Kora insisted. "The spirits with Revi Fransi."

Franz adopted a stern expression. "No, Kora, there aren't any spirits. And if there were, then—then—" He cleared his throat.

"We'll talk about spirits tomorrow," Linda told the children. "Now, give the reverend the cards."

Kahotu had been sitting by the fire, supervising the children. Now he approached with interest. "Are we opening a pub, then? I wouldn't have expected it of you, Reverend."

"I don't want to play for this," Fitz remarked, pushing aside the play-money. "Ante up, Reverend!"

Franz silently took the jewel-encrusted cross from around his neck and laid it on the table. "Does this satisfy your requirements?" he asked stiffly.

"Franz, you can't do that!" Linda exclaimed. "Ida's necklace! You love it so much."

Franz turned his gaze to her. "There's something that I love more," he said calmly. "Trust me, Linda."

"Seems a bit paltry," Fitz said, fingering the piece of jewelry. "It's pretty, of course, but compared to my stake—"

Linda pressed her lips together angrily. Then she took off Cat's necklace and laid it next to Ida's.

"This should be enough," she said curtly.

Fitz grinned. "It will be my honor to return it to you when I win," he said. "Let's go, Reverend. I'll deal."

"Then I'll shuffle," Franz replied.

Fitz nodded.

Franz shuffled slowly and awkwardly. Finally, he spread the cards briefly into a fan, pushed them together again, and ran his thumb across their tops, making them rattle. He held the cards so he could see the numbers as they flickered by. The gesture was natural enough, as though Franz were just loosening the stack before dealing. But Linda noticed his expression. It was exactly the way he looked when he was trying to remember every little move of a craftsman he'd once seen at work.

"Give those here," Fitz demanded, snatching the deck out of Franz's hand. He split it and placed the bottom half on the top. "Just in case you memorized the cards," he joked with a laugh and a wink.

Linda began to tremble. So, Fitz had also noticed Franz's quick glance at the cards.

Franz was quiet as Fitz revealed the first card, a ten of spades. Franz accepted two more cards. "No more," he said calmly.

Fitz revealed the second card, a two of diamonds. The possibility that Franz had more than twelve points was high, and the risk for Fitz to take another card was low.

"How many rounds are we going to play, anyway?" Fitz asked, stalling for time.

"Three," Kahotu suggested. He was standing behind Franz and staring entranced at the cards.

Franz nodded. Fitz took another card.

"Damn it!" He angrily tossed a queen next to his other cards on the table. Twenty-two. One point too many.

"You lose," Franz said casually, and showed his own cards. Sixteen points. He had won with a rather poor hand.

"Very courageous, Reverend," Kahotu said. "That's what I call trust in God. I would have tried a third card, myself."

Franz shook his head. "How often do I have to tell you that blackjack has nothing to do with the supernatural. Next round, Mr. Fitzpatrick. I'd like to get this over with."

Fitz passed him the deck. "Your turn to deal."

Franz turned over an ace, worth eleven points, and an eight, for nineteen in total.

Fitz accepted two cards and grinned. "Blackjack!" he said, slapping a king and an ace on the table. Twenty-one points.

"This round is yours," Franz said.

Linda held her breath. The last round would be the tiebreaker.

Fitz didn't ask to deal the cards again. He watched as Franz revealed a two of spades and a nine of hearts, and then Fitz took another card, looking satisfied with his hand. Next, Franz drew a seven of hearts, bringing his total to eighteen.

"So," said Fitz, "are you going to take another card, or shall I show?"

Kahotu rubbed his temples. Linda was biting her lower lip so hard that she tasted blood.

Franz took a deep breath. Then he reached for the deck again and added a two of hearts to his collection.

"Twenty," he said with satisfaction. "You?"

Fitz went pale and furiously tossed his hand on the table. A ten of spades and a nine of diamonds.

"You must be in league with the devil!" he shouted as Kahotu and the children cheered.

Linda didn't join their celebrating. She was stunned. The anger and fear would not subside so quickly.

Franz shrugged. "Three rounds. I won two." He picked up his cross, gave Linda her necklace, and smiled at her. Then he turned to his students. "Who was good and did their homework instead of watching us?" he asked the group, but only saw two girls sitting with their books open. "Kiri and Reka. Very good. You may stop early today. Kiri, you can lend me your bottle of ink, and Reka, I need your notebook. We have to finalize our deal in writing, don't we, Mr. Fitzpatrick?"

Fitz glared at him. "I demand at least two more games, I—"

"Fitz." Linda shook her head. "You were always a sore loser, weren't you?"

She watched as Fitz clenched his jaw, searching feverishly for a way out. Linda hoped he wouldn't refuse to sign the document that Franz was now preparing in his methodical handwriting. At least, she consoled herself, if he did refuse, gambling for his wife would surely come up in a divorce hearing, and wouldn't show him in the best light.

But then, all at once, his furious expression gave way to the old grin. Linda was shocked how quickly his features relaxed, as she had often been during her time with Fitz.

"Congratulations, Reverend. Luck was on your side. Looks like it's time for us to say goodbye, my sweet Lindy." Fitz blew a kiss. "You are free to take your place at the side of this man of God. Whether I give you my blessing remains to be seen. I—"

"Just sign it," Franz said, holding out the quill.

I, Joseph Fitzpatrick, hereby agree to a divorce from Linda Fitzpatrick, and grant my divorced wife the sole custody of our daughter, Aroha. I will refrain from making any demands, financial or otherwise, on my wife and her family.

Fitz glanced through the text and made no further protest. Linda sighed with relief when he signed with a flourish.

"That's it, then," he said calmly. "Does anyone mind if I spend the night in the barn?"

Linda was about to agree reluctantly, but Franz was already reaching into his pocket. He presented two banknotes.

"There's a guesthouse in the town," he said, and tossed the money on the table. "You can go there. There will surely be enough left over for a bottle of whiskey as well."

Fitz stood up. At first, it seemed as though he would leave the money there, but greed or sheer desperation overcame his pride. He grabbed the notes and walked straight out of the meetinghouse.

"I'll follow him," Kahotu said. "Just to be sure he doesn't steal anything."

Franz and Linda stayed where they were. They gazed at each other in silence. There was much that needed to be said, but 120 children were waiting for their dinner.

"I'll—I'll go back to the kitchen," Linda murmured.

Franz picked up his coat. "I'm not leaving you alone as long as he's here," he said. "The children can clean up and set the table."

"What about the evening sermon?" Kiri asked.

Franz stacked up the cards. "It's canceled tonight."

Even though Kahotu and Omaka helped serve the meal, it was another two hours before all the children were in bed. Franz and Linda were in the meetinghouse, preparing it for the next morning's lessons. Aroha was fussing in her basket.

Linda finally broke the silence. "I'd like to put Aroha in her cradle now. Will you come with me?"

Franz's eyebrows shot up. "I don't know. Is that appropriate? What if someone sees?"

Linda had to laugh. "Franz, you gambled for me today. That was wildly inappropriate! Besides, Kahotu and Omaka are Maori. They don't care who's alone with whom."

"The children . . ."

"They're Maori too, no matter how much *pakeha* nonsense we teach them. They weren't raised to judge that way. Come now. Aroha needs a proper bed, and we can't open this here." She pulled a flask of whiskey out of her skirt pocket. "I talked Kahotu out of it, even though he insisted that he needed two bottles to calm himself down after today."

Franz gazed at her uncertainly. "We'd be breaking every commandment," he murmured.

"Only rules, not commandments. And the spirits were on your side today, even though you cheated. Don't deny it. But there was also luck involved."

"In the game, there was mostly bad luck. And besides, he saw me sneak a look at the cards."

"Yes, but he couldn't have imagined you were actually able to memorize them. That's just eerie, Franz!"

Franz helped her with her coat. "I've always been able to do that," he said. "I look at something, and then I can call up the memory whenever I want. In any case, blackjack has never had anything to do with luck for me."

He picked up the baby's basket, checked again that the fire was out, and held the door open for Linda. The wind and rain immediately blew against them, but they ignored it.

"I don't usually cheat," Franz continued as they hurried through the rain. "When the children play, I watch and take note of the cards that have already been drawn, until the deck is about a third gone. Then I figure out which cards must still be in there, and I know if I should expect higher or lower numbers. You can almost always estimate the other person's hand and keep your own risk at a minimum."

"No matter how you do it, it's incredible," Linda said as she opened the door to her house.

Franz lit a fire while she nursed the baby. Aroha fell asleep at her breast, and Linda laid the little one in her cradle. The pretty bed had been built and decorated by the Maori carving apprentices, adorned with symbols for protection and luck. Finally, Linda and Franz sat down by the fire, and Linda uncorked the whiskey.

"I need this as medicine today," she said. "Oh God, I was so shocked when Fitz appeared! And then his threats, and the game—"

"Do you think he really was looking for you?" Franz asked.

Linda shrugged. "Yes and no. Of course he wasn't expecting to find me here. But he'd heard about Mamaca and Chris. He was probably on his way to Rata Station."

Franz rubbed his forehead. "And he was wondering why you weren't there. What did he mean about Cat being your mother? And why did you react so strangely when he called me your uncle?"

Linda blinked at him in confusion. "Because you're not my uncle. Though, to be honest, not even Carol saw you as an uncle. You're much too young for that."

Franz's brow creased. "Carol? How could Carol see me as an uncle, but not you? You're twins."

Linda laughed. All at once, the trouble between them was clear.

"Carol and I are half sisters," she told Franz. "Ida's first husband, Ottfried Brandmann, was a terrible person. He treated Ida horribly, and he raped Cat, who worked for them. When Sankt Pauli Village was washed away, they were both pregnant by him. Cat wanted to leave to join a Maori tribe, but Ida talked her into staying. It was her idea to say we were twins and register us both as daughters of Ida and Ottfried Brandmann. At that time, they lived on a secluded farm, and they just hid Cat's pregnancy. Carol was actually born a few days before me. She's Ida's daughter. Then I came along. And since Ida didn't have any milk, Cat nursed both of us. We always had two mothers, and after Ottfried's death, it wasn't really a secret anymore. I mean, we didn't hang it out like laundry for the neighbors to see. People like the Butlers already thought our family was strange enough. But I thought you knew."

Franz was cradling his head in his hands. "Ida never wrote to us. It didn't surprise me, because our father is, well . . ." He looked up. "And I have also been so narrow-minded. No wonder my sister didn't trust me with the truth. It's just, when I saw her again . . . At Rata Station, everything was so different than in Hahndorf. It was as though, well, you all seemed like heathens to me."

Linda smiled. "I think all of this would have seemed heathen to you when we first met. You've changed. For the better, I think. And now you've got to tell me if Fitz was right when he said you were already in love with me at Rata Station."

Franz blushed. "Head over heels. But of course I couldn't let anyone see. Especially not you. And I shouldn't now either."

Linda had to laugh. "Franz, you're wrong!" she said, teasing him. "Kahotu and Omaka have known all along. Only I myself was a little unsure. The way you acted—sometimes I thought you were like Fitz, and that scared me." Her smile died, and she lowered her head.

Franz moved closer and awkwardly put his arms around her. "You were scared?" He tried to find the right words. "So—so you're not indifferent about me either?"

Linda looked up at him. "No," she said. "I am absolutely not indifferent about you. I think I love you, Franz Lange. And definitely not like an uncle."

Franz glowed with happiness. "I've never kissed a girl," he admitted shyly.

Linda smiled encouragingly. "It's not so hard."

Franz moved his face closer and kissed her then, gently and carefully. Linda returned the kiss. She had never felt so moved. Fitz had been skilled, but Franz's kiss was one of genuine love.

"You'll never forget this, I suppose," Linda teased, as they finally lay side by side on her sleeping mat next to the fire. "It's almost a little alarming. You'll always be able to remember it, every movement. Does that mean you don't ever need to do it again?"

Franz pulled her closer. "I always want to do it with you," he said. "All my life. I want to live with you and have children with you."

Linda smiled. "We already have more than a hundred."

Franz looked at her earnestly. "Then do you want to stay here? With me and the children? Will you marry me when this nightmare with Fitz is over? Divorces take a long time, don't they? If it's even possible."

Linda winked at him. "You won't be able to get rid of me, Franz Lange. And as for divorce, if you want, we can ask Omaka to perform a *karakia toko* for us. That isn't recognized by the *pakeha*, but to the spirits—and to God—it sets me free."

Chapter 70

Eru and his friends spent several months in a prisoner-of-war camp near Wellington. Just a few days after their capture, Te Ua Haumene and his last faithful leaders had been arrested in a village near Opunake. The prophet surrendered to General Chute and was brought to Auckland, under heavy guard. The dramatic prisoner convoy was mostly a show of force. The government wanted any Hauhau warriors still hiding in the forest to know that their cause was lost. In Auckland, the prophet was jailed. He constantly insisted that he had never preached anything but peace, harmony, and love.

Chute returned to the north with his army and celebrated his victory, though he was criticized for his unscrupulous methods. In the opinion of the president and some opposing politicians, Chute's campaigns had been less about peacekeeping than about usurping land. McDonnell and the military settlers were left to deal with the last of the rebellious warriors.

The main purpose of the prison camp where Eru and his friends were held was to keep the warriors out of the forests so the war wouldn't be unnecessarily extended. The majority were very young men who had been recruited in their villages by the Hauhau. Most had gone to Taranaki more out of lust for adventure than deep conviction. The older, more committed Hauhau warriors wouldn't allow themselves to be captured. They escaped into the forests, and preferred death to surrender. The prisoners were kept in primitive quarters, but were given enough to eat and weren't abused. The main problem for Eru, Tamati, and Kepa was boredom—and for Eru, the tortured insomnia that came from worrying about Mara every night. But then the men in charge discovered that the trio spoke good English. From then on, the camp commander, and then also the military control center in Wellington, employed them as interpreters.

Eru, who had a perfect command of both Maori and English, both spoken and written, was especially in demand. Before the young fighter was finally due to be released in August of 1866, the camp commander called him into his study.

"You are being released tomorrow, Te Eriatara," he said. "What do you want to do?"

For a moment, Eru considered lying, but then decided to tell the truth. Captain Tanner had always treated him fairly.

"My friends will return home to the South Island," he said. "That's where they belong. But I want to go back to Taranaki. I have a debt to settle with someone."

Captain Tanner frowned. "Maori or *pakeha*?"

"Maori, sir." Eru's answer came like a shot from a pistol.

The captain nodded. "Good. I'm always glad to hear about you all pounding each other's heads in. Just remember that it's forbidden to cut them off and shrink them."

Eru grinned.

"That said, Te Eriatara, I have asked you to come because army command wants to offer you a job. You are an excellent interpreter and have good manners, both of which are important to the *pakeha*. You also have *mana*, whatever that means, with the Maori. So, if you're interested, directly after you are released, you may go to Colonel Herbert at army headquarters in Wellington." He wrote down an address and handed it to Eru.

Eru accepted the piece of paper hesitantly. "As I told you, I have to go to Taranaki."

The captain nodded. "Just listen to what the colonel has to say. I can't make any promises, but perhaps it will be possible to combine your debt settling with your work for us. Just talk to him, and think about it. No one is forcing you, Te Eriatara. You are a free man."

Eru and his friends were released on exactly the same day that Bill Paxton arrived in Wellington. The men crossed paths at the harbor, where Bill observed the Maori with the fully tattooed face in amazement. Eru didn't even notice. He'd grown used to being stared at. If he saw people looking, he would turn away.

Since Mara's horrified reaction, his pride over his *moko* had gotten all mixed up with anger and shame about the terrible things the Hauhau had done.

But on this day, he was too busy saying goodbye to his friends to pay attention to anyone else. The three young men exchanged *hongi* and fought back their tears.

"Are you sure you don't want to come with me?" Eru asked.

Tamati and Kepa shook their heads. Both of them had seen more than enough of the North Island. Not that they regretted their adventures—they were proud to have proven themselves in battle. In retrospect, the reason for it seemed almost not to matter. Both of them had gotten more *moko* during their time in the prison camp. They weren't nearly as perfect as the first; there were no experienced *moko* masters among the prisoners. But they had earned the tattoos honestly. Now it was written in the companions' faces how courageously they had fought and had increased their *mana*. Their tribe would honor them accordingly. The most beautiful girls would be interested in them. Tamati and Kepa had been talking about nothing else for weeks. They were looking forward to seeing their tribe and their home. Tamati said he even missed the sheep.

It turned out to be easy for them to arrange the crossing to the South Island. The two young men had been paid for their interpreting services, and now had enough money for the ferry to Blenheim. They would be on the South Island in just a few hours, far from the war.

Eru envied them as they went aboard, chatting cheerfully, and watched as the ship disappeared on the horizon. Perhaps he should have gone with them . . . Eru allowed himself a moment of weakness and dreamed of the Ngai Tahu village, the openness of the plains, the sheep herds, and the spiritual sites that their *rangatira* had showed them. But the image of Mara appeared in his mind. How she'd suddenly appeared on her horse when he should have been meditating . . . He dreamed about making love to her on holy ground, her smile, the sound of the *koauau* when she played her little melody. He couldn't abandon her! Even if she didn't love him anymore. He had to hunt down Te Ori and take the girl out of his clutches. Afterward, Mara could decide for herself. Eru's *moko* began to itch again. Perhaps everything would have gone differently in Waikoukou if he hadn't frightened her with his new face.

Distracted, he made his way to army headquarters. In the entryway, he almost walked into a young, dark-haired *pakeha*. The man politely allowed him to pass. A lieutenant showed him to Colonel Herbert's office. When the dark-haired man entered the waiting area close behind, he smiled at Eru.

"It seems we're going in the same direction," he said. "Do you speak English?"

Eru nodded. "They want to offer me a job."

"Then you're better off than I am," the other remarked. "I have to ask them for one."

The office door opened before he could explain any further. Eru stepped inside, prepared for the usual shock his *moko* elicited. But Colonel Herbert didn't react. Apparently, he'd already recruited enough *kupapa* troops in his time that a tattooed face was nothing new for him.

"You're the young man who speaks excellent English," Herbert said after Eru had introduced himself. "Captain Tanner says you want to work for us."

"Maybe," Eru said. "I won't fight for you, but I would like to help make sure no one else is killed. But first I have to go to Taranaki."

Colonel Herbert nodded. "Actually, Major McDonnell is planning a retaliatory campaign in Taranaki. The colony on the Patea River was attacked. It's quite certain that a still-active Hauhau unit was behind it. McDonnell believes there's a hidden *pa* somewhere near Hawera. He asked for auxiliary troops to help ferret them out. Maori trackers as well. Wonderful people, and amazing trackers."

Eru sat up straighter. That was exactly what he needed—or would have before. Any traces that Te Ori and the girls might have left must be long gone.

"Unfortunately, they don't speak English," the colonel said, "which makes it difficult to work with them. If you agree to help us, I could send you with them."

Eru didn't have to think about it for long. It was unlikely that Te Ori was still camping in the wilderness with the girls. He must have brought them to some village or *pa*. The trackers would be able to find the group, which—under Te Ori's influence—was probably the same one that had attacked the military settlers.

"I'm your man, sir."

Eru left the room as Private Eriatara.

The dark-haired *pakeha*, who was waiting outside, winked at him. "Congratulations."

Apparently, he'd overheard.

"Good luck to you too," Eru replied, and watched as the man disappeared into Herbert's office.

He carefully folded the registration form and put it in the pocket of his linen trousers. Then he paused and listened curiously to the conversation between the colonel and the dark-haired man. It was the visitor who spoke first.

"I'm Bill Paxton, sir. I wrote to you."

Eru's jaw dropped as he listened to a story he could hardly believe. This man was looking for Carol and Mara too!

"Therefore, I beg you to take me back into service," Paxton finally concluded. "My previous rank was lieutenant. I would like to work under Major McDonnell."

Herbert huffed in annoyance. "Mr. Paxton, it's not that easy! This is the English army. You can't just come and go as you please. And you can't choose your superiors either. You didn't like General Cameron, so you left. You seem to prefer McDonnell, so you want to join again?"

"Colonel Herbert, this isn't about me. It's only about the two women." Paxton's voice sounded desperate.

"And you're the only one who can help them?" the colonel asked doubtfully. "Mr. Paxton, you can rest assured, if two women are being held prisoner in one of those villages, they will soon be freed and you will get your girlfriend back. McDonnell is leading a few hundred soldiers against the Hauhau. It makes no difference whether you are there or not."

"For me it does!" Paxton declared.

Herbert sighed. "Fine. But I'm not saying that you're reinstated. You left, and you can't be an officer anymore. In a few days, I will be sending a convoy of Maori auxiliary troops to Patea. As far as I'm concerned, you can join them. As a private citizen. In Patea, you can talk to McDonnell. Maybe he'll decide to take you with him on his campaign. The old warhorse likes stubborn people. In any case, I hope that these women are still alive, but after such a long time, Mr. Paxton, I suggest you not get your hopes up."

Eru heard Bill Paxton thanking the man, and then quickly stepped away before Herbert could catch him eavesdropping. He waited for Paxton in the hall.

"You're still here?" Bill asked in surprise.

Eru looked at him intently. "Carol Brandmann and Mara Jensch are still alive. The man you're looking for is called Te Ori."

The trackers departed the next day. They were a group of Ngati Poneke who came from the area north of Otaki. All the other tribes there had hated them for generations. No one knew why. But Eru had stopped asking such questions. At this point, he didn't care to believe the Maori would ever unite as one people and reclaim Aotearoa from the *pakeha*. He hardly spoke with the men at all, but instead walked next to Bill's horse. He listened to the story of Cat and Chris's rescue with relief and joy.

"So, Linda was right about them being alive!" Eru declared. "How did my mother take it?"

Bill shook his head. "I have no idea. But I imagine she might go home when this is all over. The danger of your being married off to some sheep baroness is definitely past."

Eru grinned. He'd told Bill his own story the day before, leaving out the worst parts. His new friend and ally didn't need to know that he'd been part of Kereopa Te Rau's entourage.

Their journey to Patea was uneventful. They didn't visit any *pakeha* settlements, so Eru and Bill passed Otaki without a clue about Linda and the orphanage. For Bill, traveling cross-country with the New Zealand natives was a fascinating, new experience. He watched as they hunted, made fires, and foraged for food. So this was how Cat and Chris had survived on Rose Island. Carol, too, must have been living this way for a year now. Bill felt closer to her as he put a tuatara on a stick and roasted it over the fire, with a slight twinge of disgust. He preferred the roots that were baking in the coals, even though they were a little bland without spices.

"Villagers cook much better in their *marae*s," Eru said with a grin as Bill bit into a piece of lizard meat without great enthusiasm. "A warrior must eat whatever he finds or hunts along the way. And, of course, it's much easier to cook when pots and pans are available."

"Another reason not to throw the *pakeha* into the sea," Bill joked. "Before we came, you all lived in the Stone Age!" But his smile fell away when he saw Eru's face.

"Your people brought many useful things," Eru said gravely. "But that's no excuse to treat mine like children. And children shouldn't be abused or lied to either."

Patea had changed considerably since Bill had last seen it over a year ago. Cameron's army camp had become a combination military base and village. There was a post office, a general store, a barbershop, and a bank for the settlers. There were also two pubs, one of which even rented rooms. Bill invited Eru for a *pakeha* meal while they waited for McDonnell to have time for them. The Irish stew was unexpectedly good. The innkeeper's wife had made it.

"Definitely better than tuatara," Eru admitted.

Bill took a room at the inn, and Eru slept with the *kupapa* in the troops' quarters. The next morning, he left a message for Bill saying he and the trackers had been called to McDonnell's office. Bill decided to tag along.

The major eyed the only *pakeha* and civilian who entered his office with the group of trackers. He noticed Eru too. Unlike the *kupapa* troops, who combined English uniform jackets with their traditional garb, the young man was wearing a full private's uniform.

To everyone's surprise, McDonnell addressed the trackers in Maori. He didn't speak the language fluently, but it was doubtless good enough to lay out the strategy for his campaign. Unsurprisingly, then, the major was unmoved when Eru introduced himself as an interpreter.

"I didn't request one. And certainly not one like you," he said rudely. "You smell like trouble, boy. What's wrong with you?"

Eru's jaw clenched. "I know what you mean, sir," he said stiffly. "I think in Wellington they just didn't know how well you speak Maori. That's not very common, and not usually necessary—"

"In order to shoot Maori, you mean?" the major said, interrupting him. "I prefer to understand my enemies. That way, you don't get taken by surprise as often. But back to you. You're hardly out of the cradle, and already tattooed like a warrior who has roasted at least five chieftains on a spit. That smells like Hauhau, boy. What made you change sides?"

Eru lowered his eyes.

"Love, it seems," Bill Paxton interjected. "Please allow me to speak for this young man, sir. We share a mission."

McDonnell listened to Bill's explanation without interrupting him. When the young man was finished, he frowned.

"The tale of Cameron's missing girls. To be honest, I've almost stopped believing it. First they were supposed to be in Weraroa, then Waikoukou."

"They were definitely in both places," Eru said. "The man that kidnapped them escaped before Waikoukou was stormed."

"And it's entirely possible that Te Ori is behind the recent attacks on your settlements," Bill added. "He's the most brutal kind of warrior. It was he who led the attack on the prisoner convoy when our soldiers were brutally murdered and beheaded. I was there a few hours later, sir. It wasn't a pretty sight."

McDonnell mulled this over for a moment. "I trust you, Paxton. Get a weapon issued to you and join as an observer, as long as I don't order you to do something else. But you"—he turned to Eru—"I don't trust. You're going to have to prove your loyalty. For now, you will stay with the *kupapa*, translate a little, and if things get serious, then we'll see how it goes. You may leave now." He dismissed Bill and Eru with a flick of his wrist and said goodbye to the trackers in their own language. *"Haere ra!"*

"He's a tough old goat," Bill said outside. "If anyone can find the last few Hauhau nests, it'll be him."

"He'll find the villages," Eru said with a nod. "The question is if he'll find Te Ori. He's already escaped twice. He won't just be sitting in the *marae* with the girls, waiting for us."

Chapter 71

The attackers were supposed to be hiding out north of Hawera, and even the best path turned out to be extremely challenging. Bill was amazed at how stoic the Maori warriors were, marching for hours through the jungle and crossing rivers in the pouring rain. It was the end of July, the depths of winter in New Zealand. The weather wasn't very kind to McDonnell and his mixed force of Patea and Whanganui rangers, military settlers, and *kupapa* Maori. The major had taken reinforcements for his settlers wherever he could find any, and was now leading an entire army through the wilderness.

Bill feared he'd reached the end of his stamina when, at long last, the trackers were finally asked to use their skills. The specially trained Maori warriors, reinforced by *pakeha* forest rangers, scoured the woods for the faintest signs of human occupants. They quickly found hunters' traps and then fresh footpaths. The warriors scouted ahead and then led the major and a few officers away. Bill, who was allowed to join them, saw a *pa* rise up through the evening mist like a haunted castle. It was clearly well defended and would be difficult to capture due to the thick forest surrounding it and its elevated position.

"We'd be trying to storm it for weeks," one of the younger captains said pessimistically. "And then they'd disappear in the middle of the night through some holes."

McDonnell shook his head. "No, Captain. That happens to other people. That won't happen to me. Do you know why, Captain? Because I don't play by the rules anymore. Let's go back to the troops now. Paxton, you'll send your young friend over. It will be interesting to see whose side he's on."

Eru's heart was pounding with fear, and he felt guilty as he stood at the gates to the *pa* with a delegation of officers. McDonnell had marched his army up but hadn't begun shooting. Instead, he sent negotiators. He just hoped the holdouts in the fort wouldn't send back the heads of his delegates smoked and shrunken.

But as it turned out, the negotiators were received hospitably. Te Ori was nowhere in sight, and an older chieftain with his tribal elders greeted them and led them into a part of the *pa* that was more like a typical *marae*. Eru saw a few warriors, but above all, women and children lived here. Apparently, they were preparing a *powhiri*.

"*Haere mai* to Pokokaikai *pa*," the *ariki* said in greeting. He was a dignified older man whose face was adorned with faded *moko*. He shook the officers' hands in the *pakeha* manner and exchanged *hongi* with Eru. "Why are you standing at our gates with an army? What have we done to you?"

An officer spoke, and Eru translated. "There have been attacks on a settlement on the Patea River. We have reason to believe that the attackers came from this area."

"I didn't send them," the chieftain said firmly, looking Eru in the eye.

Eru forced himself to return the steely gaze. "Are you denying that you support Te Ua Haumene?" he asked. The *niu* on the meeting ground where they were standing was impossible to miss.

"The prophet is in Akarana, the place you call Auckland. It's said that he's ill and will die soon," the chieftain replied.

Eru translated the words for the officers, then added, "He's slippery as an eel." He turned back to the chieftain. "So, you haven't taken in any Hauhau warriors?"

"A warrior doesn't need the protection of a *pa*," the chieftain said.

"That's not an answer!" the captain who was leading the delegation said angrily after Eru had translated.

Eru tried a different tack. "We have reason to believe that you are holding two white women captive."

The chieftain's eyes widened; he was either indignant or afraid. Eru was confident that he'd guessed correctly: the old man had helped the Hauhau warriors, but he didn't approve of Te Ori.

"Look around," the *ariki* said, challenging the men. "You won't find any white women here."

Eru shrugged. "Perhaps we're wrong. But we'd like to make sure. Maybe we'll question a few warriors and look around, as you so generously suggest."

The chieftain nodded. *"Haere mai,"* he said again majestically. "You are welcome here."

That evening, Eru and the officers ate and drank with the people of Pokokaikai. They watched their dances and listened to their songs. A *tohunga* invoked the bond of friendship between the residents and Major McDonnell's men. Eru explained his origins and was warmly received by the community. The captain formally exchanged *hongi* with the chieftain.

"Unbelievable! They're pulling the wool over their eyes. If nothing happens, the soldiers will leave tomorrow and we'll be trapped here forever."

Carol furiously punched the heavy wooden door that was blocking their way out of an empty weapons storage room. The women had been dragged there as soon as McDonnell's delegation had been sighted. As usual, Te Ori's wife Hera had capitulated to his wishes. She had helped him hide the slaves, even though she would have preferred to finally be rid of them.

"You're just going to hurt your hands," Mara said.

The girls sat in a corner of the room, arms around each other. They had been fighting for months, defending themselves against Te Ori and trying to get the women in Pokokaikai on their side, but the warrior's influence had been greater than their own. As Carol and Mara had soon realized, Pokokaikai was actually the *marae* where Te Ori had been born and raised, and where his family still lived. In England, it would have been called a fortified town. When they'd first arrived, the *pa* was hardly manned at all, and only after the fall of Waikoukou had a large number of Hauhau warriors taken refuge there. But Carol and Mara were being kept in the civilian area of the fort.

To their great confusion, Te Ori had taken the slaves to his wife, without the slightest reservation.

"Do whatever you want with them," he'd told the tall, thin woman, who was the mother of his three daughters. The eldest was Mara's age. "But don't damage the younger one. I have a mind to take her as a second wife."

Hera's dark eyes flashed angrily, but Te Ori stopped her before she could object.

"The prophet expressly told us that we should return to the old ways. Warriors used to take two or more wives," he said. "You shall obey."

"She could be your daughter!" Hera spat back at him.

"The younger she is, the more warriors I will conceive with her."

"I refuse to bear your children, but if I did, they would not be warriors!" Mara shouted at him.

Te Ori struck her and threw her to the ground at Hera's feet. "Teach her how to behave," he ordered his wife.

Next, Te Ori turned to the chieftain, who was waiting nearby. "Where are the warriors from this *pa*?" he demanded. "We must ready ourselves for defense; this will be our new base. Tomorrow, more warriors will be coming from Waikoukou."

"Will they bring the prophet here too?" the chieftain asked in an awestruck voice.

Te Ori shook his head. "No. The prophet has become tired and weak. He wants to negotiate. He has betrayed his own teachings. It's up to us to preserve them. The archangel will choose another. *Rire rire, hau hau!*"

The villagers joined in with the chant, proud to be the last stronghold of the rebellion.

Over the next few days, Te Ori and the other *rangatira* led them in an attack against the nearby white settlement. They also organized regular attacks and raids on *pakeha* stashes of weapons and provisions.

To Carol, these attacks seemed like their only hope. The military settlers wouldn't put up with it for very long. At some point, they would find Pokokaikai, and then perhaps she and Mara would be freed. But in the meantime, their renewed imprisonment dragged on for months. The conditions weren't as bad as they had been in Weraroa, but much worse than in Waikoukou because Tohu wasn't there to keep Te Ori away from Mara. The villagers didn't want the white girls among them, so they were locked in a hut on the edge of the village. But Hera obeyed her husband's orders. She guarded the slaves carefully. There was no chance for escape.

And of course, no one stopped the warrior from coming into the hut and taking Mara whenever he wanted. He no longer did so as violently as he had in Weraroa. There would have been questions in the village if Mara had walked around bruised and injured, or had lain in the hut whimpering for days on end. The warriors in Weraroa hadn't cared what Te Ori did with his slaves, but the tribal elders in Pokokaikai weren't very happy about white women being held captive there. The chieftain knew very well that the revenge of the *pakeha* against the village would be much worse if they found the women there. What was more, Hera was his niece. He wasn't happy about Te Ori's betrayal of her.

Te Ori didn't come to the hut every night. The warriors were often out on missions, and he probably slept with his wife sometimes too, just to humor her. Hera, in turn, took out her anger on the girls. Mara, especially, suffered under the wrath of Hera and her daughters, and the other women in the village tormented Carol. For the most part, the scenario from Weraroa was repeated for the sisters—they were chosen for the hardest and dirtiest work, taunted and struck and starved.

Carol swallowed her fury and capitulated, while Mara rebelled against the torment as long as she could. She responded with curses, threw her work on the ground at Hera's feet, and even once struck Te Ori's daughter after the girl threw garbage at her. When Te Ori raped her, she resisted him with all her strength. He had to gag her so her screams and curses didn't wake the entire village.

Then her monthly courses stopped. Mara felt weak, her stomach rebelled against the meager rations that the slaves were given in the morning, and her breasts swelled.

"I'm sick," she complained to Carol.

Her older sister shook her head. "You aren't sick, Mara, you're pregnant."

From that moment, Mara gave up. She no longer defended herself against Te Ori. She stopped talking back to Hera, and spent hours staring at the walls. Her spirit didn't seem to separate from her body as Carol had feared it would during their first imprisonment. Mara was completely aware but deeply despondent.

"We'll never escape," Mara said as Carol desperately tried to figure out how to alert the *pakeha* to their presence. "We'll be slaves here for all eternity. I'll bear that bastard's children and have to watch as my sons dance around the *niu*."

Carol didn't bother to answer. She had told Mara often enough that the *pakeha* would win the fight against the Hauhau; there was no way around it. The army was vast, better organized, and had far more modern weapons. Pokokaikai would fall eventually. So why not now? When she heard the music of the *powhiri*, Carol had screamed as loudly as she could, praying a soldier might hear.

"They mustn't let themselves be fooled!" she insisted. "They have to realize that the peaceful village down at the bottom of the hill is not the entire *pa*. Can't they see all the *nius*?"

"They only see what they want to see," Mara replied. "And no one is looking for us anymore."

Eru and the officers returned as night fell. The major was waiting impatiently in the camp.

"Were they convinced?" McDonnell asked eagerly.

The captain nodded. "I think so. They were very welcoming."

"They joined with us in peace," Eru said, his voice hoarse. "They called the gods. They wove a bond between us. We are now one tribe."

"Damn, boy, they didn't leave any room for doubt?" McDonnell glared at him.

Eru shook his head. "No," he said firmly. "I only know that a *powhiri* is holy. That's why I'm worried about what we're about to do. It's a betrayal of the spirits. But the people in this *pa* are flouting the gods no less than we are. The entire ceremony was a lie." He turned to Paxton, who had been waiting with the major. "They have the girls, Bill, I saw it in the chieftain's face. They're hidden somewhere in the *pa*."

Bill went pale, but McDonnell's face hardened. "Good," he said. "I am now giving the order to surround the fort. If you're sure, then tomorrow morning, we attack."

The next morning, the residents of Pokokaikai opened the gates of the *pa*, as they did every morning. The hunters streamed out to the forest. Women made their way to the fields.

McDonnell didn't give them a chance to notice that their village was surrounded. The moment the morning fog lifted, he gave the order to attack. The unsuspecting residents of Pokokaikai were inundated with gunfire. They panicked and ran, screaming. McDonnell had his men mount their bayonets and stormed the village with a regiment of military settlers. The men gleefully took revenge for the attacks on their farms. They herded the Maori together onto the meeting grounds, trampled their fields and gardens, tore down their fences, and set their houses on fire—but not before searching them first. Usually, McDonnell showed no mercy—he had often been accused of leaving women and children in burning houses—but this time he was looking for Carol and Mara.

Chapter 72

Carol and Mara heard gunshots coming from the village, but Te Ori didn't leave them any time to hope for rescue. Their tormentor had dragged them up to the military part of the *pa* with a few other men. Most had gone out for their morning hunt or on patrol, and had walked directly into the English. Now, the remaining warriors attempted a hastily organized defense, which Te Ori did not take part in. The experienced warrior could tell with one glance that the fight for Pokokaikai was already lost. All he could do was to escape with his slaves, and this time he could depend on the other men for help. The chieftain had made it clear to Te Ori many times what would happen if the women were found, and that he was determined to keep his tribe from such danger.

Te Ori tied up Carol and Mara again, bound them together, and gagged them. Carol wondered how often they would have to repeat the same nightmare. The two of them staggered behind him through the drill ground toward a hidden opening in the palisade fence. Not far from them was a large gate where a *taua* was gathered.

"They're preparing for retreat," Te Ori told his prisoners, "in case the *pa* is surrounded."

Shots were fired, and there was hand-to-hand combat as the men tore open the gates with war cries on their lips. Carol heard shouted orders and cries of pain, the sounds of gunfire, and calls for reinforcement. In the midst of the chaos, Te Ori forced her and Mara out through the hidden exit and into the dark forest. No one stopped them. Carol wondered if there were other hidden forts that Te

Ori could flee to. Or was he finally following the prophet's orders and bringing them to the forest to kill them?

"I'm sorry, Mr. Paxton, but no traces of any white women have been found."

Once the *pa* was secure, Major McDonnell had allowed Bill and Eru to enter with the Maori auxiliary troops. There wasn't much left there to see or search. Any buildings that still stood were now burning. This time, Bill thought, they wouldn't find any secret messages from Carol.

"The interpreter will confirm it," the major said. "Did they search everything carefully?" he asked, turning to Eru.

Eru nodded. "But I'm still convinced they were here. Te Ori must have escaped with them. He's done that twice already."

"Impossible! We surrounded the fort entirely," McDonnell said and turned to speak to an agitated young lieutenant who had just approached. Then he turned back to Bill and Eru with a grim expression. "You may be right," he admitted. "There was a problem on the other side of the fort. Twenty warriors attacked suddenly. One of them is dead now, and twelve of our men are injured. It may have been a diversionary tactic. As soon as we're finished here, we'll get all our trackers together and—"

"Sir, then it will be too late!" Eru said, daring to interrupt. "Te Ori might kill the girls if he doesn't think there's any other way out. But even if he has a direction in mind—excuse me, but if fifty *pakeha* go trampling around in the woods, there's no way you'll find their trail."

"He's right," Bill interjected before the major could get angry. "Let us go alone, sir. Immediately. Allow us to take the trackers who brought us here. Later, you can send reinforcements."

McDonnell frowned for a moment and then nodded. "One. You may take one tracker with you. I need the others for my own search party. We will comb the woods, Mr. Paxton. If anyone is hiding there, we will find him. And as for setting off on your own is concerned, if you are killed, I will deny that I knew anything about it. Do you understand?"

Eru and Bill nodded in agreement. Then they ran off.

"I'll ask Te Katonga," Eru said. "That's the old man Captain Herbert didn't want."

Te Katonga was an extremely experienced warrior who had earned all of the *moko* that covered his face. The old man had insisted on accompanying the young trackers who wanted to join the *kupapa* troops as their leader. Herbert had thought Te Katonga was too old for the exertions of war. But McDonnell knew better. Of course the wiry old tracker hadn't held up the campaign. On the way to Pokokaikai, Eru hadn't left his side, marveling at his endurance and his art: Te Katonga didn't miss the faintest trace of a footprint or a broken twig on a rata bush.

When Eru now asked Te Katonga for help, he willingly joined their mission. But the old warrior declined to take a gun for self-defense.

"All my life, my spear and knife have been enough," he said with dignity, and ran ahead of Bill and Eru through the smoking rubble of the *pa*.

"This is where they must have escaped," Bill said, examining the small opening in the palisade.

Te Katonga studied the ground nearby. Bill and Eru did likewise.

"Yes!" Eru couldn't repress his cry of excitement. You didn't have to be an expert to spot the tracks of a barefoot man and two women in worn-out boots in the rain-dampened ground.

Te Katonga began to follow the trail. He didn't lose it even as the woods became denser and the ground became covered with moss and fallen leaves.

"They're headed east," Bill said softly, "toward the mountains. If there are any remaining hidden villages, that's where they'd be."

Eru nodded. "And I don't think he wants to kill them. Otherwise, he would have done it by now. We just have to catch up with him before he reaches another settlement. After all, the three of us can't storm a *pa* on our own." He repeated this to Te Katonga in Maori.

"We will catch up with them," Te Katonga said, reassuring him. "The women take short steps, and every now and then one of them falls down. Look . . ." He pointed to a place where the moss was compressed. "Someone tripped here, and it surely wasn't the warrior."

"Then let's hope for the best," Bill said after Eru had translated. "And also that the rain won't wash away the tracks."

It rained intermittently, and Carol and Mara were long since soaked to the bone and shivering with cold and exhaustion. For hours, Te Ori had goaded the sisters mercilessly forward, shouted at them, and hit them to make them walk faster. But again and again, one tripped and pulled the other down with her. Mara was crying with exhaustion, and Carol was almost ready to just fall down and give up. It would happen to both of them soon, no matter what Te Ori did to them.

Onward they stumbled through the virgin forests of South Taranaki. In summer, these dark woods were surely gorgeous. Many times they passed gigantic kauri trees. Carol had never seen one before. Even now, through all her exhaustion, the sight of the majestic trees took her breath away.

Once, she stumbled against one of the giants and thought she could feel its power. The tree was probably about a thousand years old, and it would still be there when Carol's and Mara's fates were long forgotten. For some reason, she found the knowledge comforting for the space of a heartbeat before the rain and Te Ori's constant yanking at her ropes brought her back to reality.

Around noon, they reached a river, wide and swollen with the rain. For the next few hours, Te Ori led them upstream, past rapids and stony riverbanks. The warrior seemed to be looking for something, and late that afternoon, he found it.

The raft lay beside a section of the river that appeared a little calmer. It was possible to cross there, but not without danger. Carol shuddered as Te Ori towed the roughly constructed platform into the water, and at first Mara refused to climb aboard. She resisted fiercely until Te Ori brutally shoved her into the river. Carol was pulled in behind her, and she swallowed water, coughing and flailing. It was almost impossible for them to get onto the raft while tied together. Te Ori paused for a moment, and then cut the raupo cord that bound Carol to Mara, leaving their hands tied.

"Hold on!" he ordered, and pushed the raft toward the center of the river.

Te Ori sprang on behind them and attempted to propel the vessel with the help of a pole. Carol was surprised by his strength; they hardly drifted from their course. But then the raft got caught in an eddy. In spite of Te Ori's skill, it spun around and bashed against a rock. Carol was tossed to the edge of the raft. She tried desperately to hold on, but as the raft slammed into another rock, she slid off. As she fell, she saw Te Ori grab the helpless Mara and hold her with an iron grip. As Carol hit the water, she heard her little sister scream—and then nothing but the infernally rushing current.

Carol fought to keep her head above water. But trying to swim with tied hands, especially in the strong current, was pointless. Her body struck a rock, was pulled into the depths by another eddy, and then resurfaced. Carol gasped desperately, knowing it was a losing battle. If she didn't drown, she would soon be dashed to pieces. She was going to die—and she had never imagined that her last thought would be about Bill Paxton. Now she saw him in front of her, heard his voice calling her name . . . And then it was as if he put his arms around her and pulled her close.

Bill Paxton, Eru, and Te Katonga followed the trail along the river as fast as they could. The two Maori moved almost at a run, and Bill could barely keep pace. But they were catching up; even Bill and Eru recognized the signs. They found traces of blood that the rain hadn't washed away yet.

"Someone fell into this thorn thicket," Te Katonga said. "And another injured a hand or arm on this branch. Two people keep falling at the same time, as though one is pulling the other. The women are tied together."

Then they spotted fresh marks of something heavy being dragged through the grass on the riverbank.

"We'll have them soon," Eru declared.

At that moment, Bill saw Carol. He didn't recognize her immediately; he only saw a female body being tossed by the current, heading quickly toward the rapids. Blonde hair, tied hands.

Bill didn't think; he just dropped his things and leaped directly into the river. Bill had always been a good swimmer, and now just a few strokes brought him to Carol. He heard Eru and Te Katonga shouting from the riverbank, and he shouted Carol's name back at them. He reached for her and took her in his arms, but the river was far too strong for him to be able to reach the bank. Bill could do nothing but try to keep Carol's head above water—along with his own. He was no less at the mercy of the water than she was.

Bill saw a ragged stone jutting out of the water and realized the current had already carried them back to the rapids he'd passed almost an hour before. He protected Carol instinctively, and his back struck hard. For a few seconds he couldn't breathe, but at least for a moment, the rock stopped them from being pulled farther downriver. Then he slipped and they quickly hit another. This time, Bill fought to brace his feet between the stone surfaces. The water raged around him, but as long as he was able to keep the tension in his body, he could hold himself and Carol in place. He clung to her and prayed that she was still breathing. Their survival now depended on Te Katonga and Eru. If they'd pressed on in pursuit of Mara and Te Ori, it was all over. Bill's strength would soon fail in the icy water, and the river would swallow them both.

Bill shouted the names of his companions, knowing very well that the rushing of the water would drown out the sound of his voice. He couldn't feel his legs anymore, and his fingers were cramping around Carol's body. He couldn't manage to hold on much longer.

It seemed to take forever until he spied Eru's tattooed face on the riverbank. Bill thought he would cry with relief.

"Here!" he shouted. "We're here! Don't walk away, for God's sake!"

Eru heard him. "Hold on! I'm going to try to make a rope."

Eru took off his uniform jacket and pants, both made of strong, rough denim. He cut the material into strips with his knife and knotted them together. He could only hope that the weave was strong enough and that Bill had enough strength left to cling to it. The improvised rope was long enough to wind around his body. And fortunately, the stones Bill was braced against were no more than three yards from the bank. With Eru's first toss, the rope struck Carol's body. Bill caught it with one hand, holding onto the young woman with the other. He tried to wind it tightly enough around his hand that it wouldn't come off when Eru pulled them to shore together, but that turned out to be impossible. Finally, he knotted the rope around the cord that bound Carol's hands.

"Quickly!" he shouted to Eru.

Carol's head would certainly go under water, but it was the only chance to save her. Eru nodded and pulled strongly as soon as Bill let go. For several seconds, the young warrior fought against the river and the weight of the body, but then he managed to haul Carol to land.

"She's breathing!" he cried, and then untied the rope and threw it back to Bill, who used the last of his strength to help Eru get him out of the water.

Bill lay panting on the riverbank while Te Katonga and Eru focused their attention on Carol. He heard her cry of horror as she came to and saw their tattooed faces inches from hers.

Bill struggled to his feet. "I'm here, Carol! I'm with you!" He staggered over and fell next to her on his knees, laughing and crying at the same time with relief and exhaustion.

Chapter 73

Even though Carol was shaking with cold and Bill could still barely move, Eru and Te Katonga didn't dare to light a fire.

"Te Ori would see it, even if we try to keep it small," Eru said. "He's an experienced warrior, and we're very close now."

"We've lost time," Bill said worriedly.

It had taken them a while to make it back to the spot where Bill had jumped into the water. Eru had picked up his gun, but the backpack was still lying there. When Bill saw it, he smiled triumphantly and pulled out a flask of whiskey. He handed it to Carol.

The young woman took a powerful swig. A little color actually returned to her face. Eru drank as well. Te Katonga declined. The old warrior was already warmed by the thrill of the chase. There was a bend in the river there, and shortly beyond it he found the place where the raft had been lying.

"That was prepared," Eru said. "Either by Te Ori himself or other warriors. There must be some kind of shelter on the other side of the river. We have to get across."

Carol shook her head. "I can't," she whispered. "God forgive me, I love Mara, but I can't make it . . ."

"Of course not," Eru said. "I'll swim by myself. I'm strong enough."

Bill looked at him doubtfully but then concluded he was right. The river here wasn't quite as fast, and Eru was extraordinarily strong. If Te Ori had managed to pole the raft across the river, Eru should be able to swim it.

"But you aren't a tracker," Bill said worriedly. "You'll never find the trail again."

"I just need to find the raft," Eru replied.

"You could pole it back over to this side and get us," Bill suggested.

Te Katonga, who'd been following, shook his head. "You don't need a tracker anymore," he told Eru. "The *pekapeka* will show you the way."

He pointed to the other side of the river. There, the shore was sandy, and a small mountain rose above them. Halfway up, there was something that could be the opening of a cave. Eru would have never spotted it if not for the colony of bats flying out of it. Something must have scared them; it wouldn't be twilight for quite some time.

"They're in there," Te Katonga said. "So, go, boy, and fetch your wife and the man's head!"

Eru couldn't bring his gun. It would have gotten wet in the river and become useless.

"The old weapons will have to be enough," Te Katonga said calmly. "You will succeed. The spirits will be with you."

Eru pressed his lips together. "I have to go now, before it gets dark."

"It will be twilight by the time you reach the cave," Te Katonga said. "The mountain looks steep, and it will take you longer than you think. But the spirits of the *pekapeka* will be with you."

The old man made a gesture of blessing and offered Eru his face in *hongi*.

"Come back," he said.

"Come back with Mara!" Carol said.

She stood on tiptoe and kissed him on the cheek, the way Mara had always done. Eru felt the kiss on the scarred skin of his *moko*. It felt different than it used to. But he didn't have time to think about it. Eru waved to his companions again and slipped into the water.

Eru crossed the river with powerful strokes. It wasn't easy. He, too, got caught in the same eddy that had thrown Carol from raft, and needed all his strength to fight against the current. When he finally reached the other side, the first thing he did was look for the raft. From there, he hoped to be able to pick up Te Ori's trail. Eru could see the mountain in front of him, but he couldn't make out the position of the cave anymore.

He finally found the raft slightly downriver. There were tracks around it that suggested a fight. It looked as though Mara had tried to throw herself into the water—either to save Carol or to die with her. Eru found torn-out strands of hair and drag marks. Mara must have thrown herself repeatedly to the ground so she wouldn't have to follow her tormentor.

Then, suddenly, the trail of resistance ended. Only one set of tracks led away from the beach. Te Ori must have knocked the girl out and thrown her over his shoulder. He had surely made progress much more quickly that way. But she must have also weakened him. Eru hoped that it would give him an advantage if it came to a fight. He desperately needed one. His only weapons were a small, flat war club made of pounamu jade called a *mere*, and a knife. Te Ori surely had more, and he must also know how to use a *whaika* and a *kotiate*, which were far more effective in hand-to-hand combat. However, their use required significant skill. A warrior like Kereopa had handled them as lightly as a skilled fencer with a saber, but Eru had hardly ever used them, despite his experience with combat. Since the three friends from the South Island had been the only ones in Kereopa's unit who'd known how to shoot guns, they'd been entrusted with the firearms.

Eru made his way through the jungle, losing Te Ori's trail several times and then finding it again. Te Katonga was right. The cave was much farther than it had looked, and the path was steep. At least it had finally stopped raining. Eru, who was walking through the woods almost naked, thanked the spirits. When he had left the others at the river, Te Katonga had wordlessly passed him his own raupo-fiber skirt. It wasn't appropriate for a warrior to face what might be the most important fight of his life wearing *pakeha* underwear. Eru was extremely grateful to the old man. Perhaps Te Ori would kill Eru, but at least he would die with dignity.

Eru felt as though he'd been climbing for hours, and when the daylight slowly faded, he also began to fear that he was lost. He should have reached the level of the cave by now. He had no idea whether it was to the left or right, a little higher, or already below him. But then, when twilight finally came, the old tracker's prediction came true. He heard the rush of wings, and when he looked up at the sky, he saw bats rising into the air above him. Eru sighed with relief. He had found the cave.

Mara awoke in the semidarkness, surrounded by a sharp scent. She had difficulty orienting herself; her entire body hurt, especially her head. She vaguely remembered Te Ori hitting her. And then it came back: the terrifying trip on the raft, Carol being washed away by the current, Te Ori stopping her from jumping in after her sister.

Now she must be in a new prison . . . but no, Mara was lying in a small cave. Now the source of the smell revealed itself. The ground and walls were covered with bat guano.

Mara attempted to sit up and immediately saw Te Ori. The warrior sat at the entrance of the cave, watching her. Guarding her was no longer necessary; Mara was still tied up. He had only taken the gag out of her mouth, probably so she could breathe better.

"You aren't dead," he observed with satisfaction. "I was afraid I'd hit you too hard and your spirit had departed, even though your heart was still beating."

Mara wanted to hurl insults at him, but she couldn't speak. Her mouth was dry, and her throat felt as though it were clamped shut. She focused on the water flask on Te Ori's belt. The warrior understood and stood up to give it to her.

At the same moment, Mara noticed a figure at the cave's entrance. She didn't know if it was reality or an illusion. All she could see in the dim twilight was a shadow. Te Ori turned around. He must have sensed something. Or hadn't the person moved as silently as it had seemed to Mara? Te Ori tugged a weapon out of his belt, and the shadow fell on him. A second later, both men were on the ground, skirmishing wildly. In Mara's confused state of mind, they were like one monster with two heads. Four hands held war clubs, an ax, and a knife. The warriors beat and stabbed at each other, shouting furiously.

"Traitor!"

"Rapist!"

"She is my slave!"

"She is my wife, she was always mine!"

It was Eru's voice. The monster spoke with Eru's voice. Mara screamed.

The man who'd stolen Eru's voice and his body looked up in shock—and Te Ori immediately took advantage. He knocked the knife out of the man's hand, and it clattered to the ground. Then he pushed him down and put a knee over him. With a powerful sweeping motion, he raised the *toki poutangata*, the war ax, aiming at the man's neck. The pinned man defended himself desperately, striking Te Ori's lower arm with force. The ax flew from Te Ori's grip, and the man with Eru's voice kicked it in Mara's direction. The men were now grappling without weapons, but a knife still flashed in Te Ori's belt. He felt for it as he crushed his opponent against the ground with the full weight of his body.

"Mara!"

Mara trembled. So often in dreams she'd heard that voice call her name, but then it had been gentle, kind, and searching. Now Eru's voice broke with terror.

"Mara, do something!"

Mara's eyes focused on the ax, and suddenly the pain, exhaustion, and paralyzing grief for Carol fell away like a cloak. She reached for the weapon with her bound hands, fought her way to her feet, and plunged the *toki poutangata* into Te Ori's back. Blood sprayed, awakening all the fantasies that had helped Mara survive the countless nights of abuse. Before he could turn over, she ripped the weapon from the wound and struck him again. This time she hit bone, and the ax bounced off.

Te Ori let his opponent go and spun around with a shout, reaching for Mara's legs. She stumbled and raised her arms again to strike. With all her strength, she slung the ax into Te Ori's face, splitting the forehead with its detested *moko*. Te Ori stiffened immediately, and his mouth opened in a silent cry. At the same moment, Mara saw a gaping wound open in his neck. The man with Eru's voice had grabbed Te Ori's own knife and stabbed his adversary. Te Ori collapsed gurgling on the ground, his dying eyes seeking Mara.

"Aren't you dead yet?"

Eru was stunned by the hatred in her voice.

"Then take this! And this! And this!"

Mara struck the dying man with the ax, and continued to do so long after he had stopped moving. She drove the blade of the *toki poutangata* into Te Ori's body again and again, until only a bloodied piece of meat lay at her feet.

"Mara," Eru cried. "Mara, you can stop now, he's dead! Mara, it's over!"

Mara seemed not to hear. It was pure exhaustion that finally made her stop, panting, trembling, soaked in blood, her hands still tied.

Eru kept his voice low. "Mara, it's over. He can't hurt you anymore. I won't let anyone hurt you again. Come here, let me cut the rope off your hands. Then we can light a fire. You must be freezing."

Eru approached slowly, gazing into the blazing eyes behind the raised ax. He placed Te Ori's knife on the ground by Mara's feet.

"Don't touch me!" Mara hissed.

"But it's me, Eru . . ."

Mara shook her head. "Go!" she cried. "Get away from me or—or I'll kill you too!"

Part 8

FORGIVENESS

Russell and Auckland, New Zealand
(the North Island)

1866

Chapter 74

"I hardly know what to do anymore," Ida said. "Mara is here, but she's not here. Sometimes she seems as helpless as a child, weeps and crawls into Carol's bed at night, and then she looks at you with ice-cold eyes and reaches for that horrible man's knife. She won't go anywhere without it. Before, she always had her flute; now she carries the knife. It's eerie, Cat. And that poor boy."

"I wouldn't worry so much about him," Cat replied curtly.

The women were sitting in front of Ida's pretty cottage on the outskirts of Russell, enjoying the spring sunshine. From one side of the porch, there was a view of the sea, and the other bordered a beautiful green pasture where ten well-fed sheep grazed peacefully.

"Perhaps it would help to send him away for a while," Cat continued. "Mara doesn't want to see him, but his father does. Te Haitara is so glad that Eru's alive—"

Ida shook her head. "Send him away? After everything he's been through? Even before he got her out of that cave! Mara was still tied up, but Eru couldn't convince her to leave with him. She just stayed in there with the blood and the corpse. So, he made a fire in front of the cave, sat next to it, and talked to her all night. He told her about Carol's rescue, about Linda, about you and Chris . . . By the time morning came, she had managed to cut the ties on her hands with the knife herself. Carol said later that she looked like a ghost. And she only saw her after she'd crossed the river and washed off most of the blood."

"The river crossing must have been a nightmare for her, after what happened to Carol."

Cat shuddered at the thought of it. She had set off for the North Island as soon as she'd heard about Carol and Mara's rescue. Chris had had to stay at Rata

Station, trying to put things in order. He'd fired all of the men who'd worked for Jane, and fortunately, most of the Maori shepherds had happily returned to their jobs. Te Haitara had formally taken over the leadership of Maori Station, but separating the sheep herds again proved to be a Sisyphean task.

Ida stared sadly at the sea as she recounted the story. "Eru says that once it was light, Mara told him to lead her to her sister, but she kept the knife pointed at him the entire way and only followed at a distance. Then, on the raft, she clung to the edge, as far away from him as possible. He was terrified she'd fall in the water. Fortunately, the rain had passed, so river wasn't as wild as the day before."

"What happened after that?" Cat asked, taking a sip of her tea. She preferred coffee, but her pregnancy was quite advanced now, and she was having trouble with heartburn.

"When Mara saw Carol again, she couldn't stop weeping," Ida said. "Finally, Eru and the other Maori man went back to the *pa* and told McDonnell what had happened. The major sent out half a unit to secure the area around the cave in case there were other warriors nearby. The soldiers also brought tents and provisions for Bill and the girls—and a doctor, but Mara refused to let him touch her. They camped there for three days until the girls were able to travel. Bill brought them to Auckland, and we came to pick them up."

"What about Eru?" Cat asked.

"He follows Mara around like a dog," Ida said with a sigh. "Thank you, by the way, for bringing Fancy back to Carol. It's done her good; she'd been afraid Fancy was dead. We keep talking about Mara, but Carol was abused too. She doesn't say much about it, but . . . Bill will have to be very patient. Good thing he's madly in love with her."

Bill had traveled to Russell with the Jensches and their daughters, had taken a room in a guesthouse, and was helping Karl and Ida on their little farm. Not that they needed it. With their few milk sheep, the two of them managed easily on their own, and Bill didn't know anything about making cheese. Still, he found ways to make himself useful. He weeded the garden, painted the barn, and made small repairs. Mostly, he wanted to be near Carol, and her trust in him seemed to be growing every day. At some point, he would repeat his proposal of marriage, and perhaps the two of them could return to Rata Station.

It had become clear that Linda would not be taking over the farm. Cat had visited her on her way to Russell and found her extremely happy. She was determined to stay with Franz and run the orphanage with him. She preferred working with children to raising sheep. Of course, Amy was underemployed, but Linda and Franz were considering buying a few sheep to get the children used to working with them. Everyone hoped that the terrible war with the Maori would soon come to an end, and the orphanage could become more peaceful. They were still receiving war orphans.

"As for Eru, he somehow made it here on his own," Ida said. "We would have taken him with us, but Mara still gets hysterical when she sees his face. At least we finally convinced her that it's really him. He says that, on the way down from the cave, she thought an evil spirit had stolen his voice. The poor boy must have been through hell; he's still there, actually. He walked all the way here, and now he's camping out in the woods." She pointed toward Russell. "The land belongs to us, so there won't be any problems. They didn't want him at the guesthouse where Bill's staying. The people are afraid of him. It's slowly becoming clear to him that it's not going to change."

"Does he regret what he did?"

"Yes, and not just the tattoos. It's clear that he's haunted by his experience with the Hauhau. Who knows what else happened? In any case, he's totally devoted to Mara. She can't bear the sight of him, so he comes after dark. He stands beneath her window and talks. He tells her endless stories, probably about when they were children. Recently, he brought her a *koauau*. He got one for himself as well, and plays it every night—badly, I might add. But he hasn't made a bit of progress with her over the last weeks. He's just going to have to wait until she's gotten over what Te Ori did to her—if she ever does. Of course, her pregnancy isn't helping matters. She's four months along now."

Cat sighed. "It's a terrible pity that she didn't lose the child."

Ida glared at her. "Cat, that's a sin!"

Cat rolled her eyes. "Ida, forget religion! Mara's child will look like its father. Do you really believe it will be good for her recovery if every time she looks at her child, she sees her tormentor's face?"

Cat felt a breeze and paused. The front door of the house had opened, and Mara was standing in the doorway. Neither of them had heard her coming.

"I never saw Te Ori's face," she said coldly.

The sight of the young woman almost broke Cat's heart. Mara was pale and still far too thin. Her hair had lost its shine, and her once glowing skin was covered with little scars from countless blows. She was still beautiful in spite of it all. She was no longer the radiant, invulnerable beauty from before, but instead fragile, like a woodland fairy.

"I only saw what the *moko* master made out of him. If I see the child, I will think of Eru, the way he used to be. When I look at Eru now, I see Te Ori."

In the evening, after Mara had retired, Cat shared stories from her time on Rose Island. Ida, Karl, and Carol listened, entranced.

"Of course it was hard, but somehow also beautiful. We felt like we'd fallen through time, as though we were in another world. It was harder on the others—they missed civilization. But after Chris and I had set up our house, it wasn't that difficult. We had each other and a simple life. It reminded me a little of when I was young and lived with the Maori. There were no matches or cooking pots. Every little thing we had to do in daily life was complicated and took longer, but then it also somehow became more valuable."

Cat paused for a moment when she heard a shrill sound from outside, followed by a crooked melody being played on a *koauau*. Ida closed the window.

"Is that Eru?" Cat asked.

Carol nodded. "He always starts with the flute. They used to call each other that way. Jane thought the *koauau* was birdsong."

"Well, this bird must have a cold," Karl said.

Amy seemed to be just as perturbed. She howled.

"The flute will stop soon," Ida said comfortingly. "He tells her stories."

Cat put her face to the window. "Where is he sitting? I can't see him."

"On the lower branches of one of the trees," Karl said. "He could climb even closer to her window, but he's afraid of scaring her."

"Does she react at all?" Cat asked.

"Not as far as we can tell," Ida said. "She doesn't answer or tell him to go away."

"Hasn't anyone looked in her room? Is she sitting in the corner holding her ears? Does she pull the blankets up over her head?" Cat peered into the darkness. There was no light coming from Mara's window.

"We can't just walk in," Ida said. "Of course we've knocked. She opened the door and said everything was fine."

"I think she was crying last night," Carol added. "But I'm not sure."

"Well, I'm going to look now." Cat went determinedly to the door. "If she's cowering in the dark, crying, then we'll have to send the young man away, with all due respect for his situation. Of course, it would be tragic, but subjecting her to more pain is wrong."

Karl remained seated, and Ida and Carol reluctantly followed Cat. Ida lit a lantern to show the women the way up the stairs and down the hall.

Cat quietly opened the door to Mara's room and blinked, trying to adjust her eyes to the dark. Mara was crouching right by the window, below its frame so she wouldn't be seen. Her narrow body was wrapped in a blanket against the chill of the night. In her hand, she held the flute that Eru had given her, and had one ear pressed against the wall so she wouldn't miss a single one of the words that he sent so desperately into the night.

"Mara, Mara Marama, you know me. You know who I am, no matter what I look like. Mara, you have to see me with your heart. I haven't changed, Mara. I'm still myself."

Mara pressed the *koauau* against her cheek. Cat decided to silently retreat before Mara noticed her.

But the girl turned around as Cat was closing the door.

"I wish I were blind," she said softly.

"We have to talk to Eru," Cat said. The three women had returned to Ida's cozy parlor, and Ida had opened another bottle of wine. "She loves him, and she's suffering just as much as he is. But they can't go on like this. The girl might try to harm herself. If you have acid or something in the house, Ida, then hide it—"

"Do you think she'd try to blind herself?" Karl asked. "Then we'll have to hide every knife too."

"She always carries a knife with her," Ida said tiredly. "You're right, Cat. Eru has to stop, at least for the time being. We can't take the risk of Mara hurting herself."

The next day, Cat set out to visit Eru in his camp. She waited until late morning. After all, the young man had to sleep at some point. He'd been sitting in the tree talking until three. Finally, she gave up and returned to the house.

"I couldn't find him."

Ida, who'd been cutting up sweet potatoes for a casserole, looked up in surprise. "You couldn't? Then you're losing your touch as a tracker. The forest isn't that big, and you can't miss the tent."

Cat rolled her eyes. "Of course I found the camp. But Eru wasn't there. It looked as though he'd left in a hurry. The fire had been stamped out, but all his things were still lying around. Mostly writing materials and drafts of letters. They all began *My dearest Mara . . .*"

"Did you snoop?" Ida said scoldingly.

Cat shook her head. "No, I didn't have to. As I said, it was all lying around in the open. Where could he have gone, Ida?"

"I have no idea." Ida passed her friend a cutting board and some vegetables. "Here, help me. Afterward, we can both go look again and bring him some of the casserole. He's always happy when I cook for him. He lives off a little grain, catches fish, sets traps."

"Maybe something just swam into his net," Cat guessed. "You're right, we'll go back later."

But Cat and Ida didn't find Eru in the afternoon either—and even more alarmingly, he didn't come that night to talk to Mara.

"Maybe he decided it wasn't working," Ida said. "Although yesterday he seemed so convinced."

"Maybe she spoke to him," Carol suggested.

"Either that or he decided to write her letters instead," Cat added. "Still, it's strange. I have a bad feeling."

"His camp is still the way you found it." It was about eight o'clock the next morning, and Karl had returned from feeding the animals and checking in the woods. "The food you left yesterday hasn't been touched either."

Karl set down the basket Ida had left in Eru's tent, as well as a pitcher of fresh milk, six eggs, and the newspaper. It was one of the conveniences of their new life in Russell that the paper boy came by every morning. The Jensches had never lived so close to a town before.

Ida, Cat, and Carol were already sitting at the breakfast table. Mara hadn't come down yet. While Ida poured coffee for Karl, Cat reached for the paper. As soon as she saw the headlines, her face filled with horror.

"Oh no!" she cried. "This can't be true. Eru . . ."

"I told you, I never want to see you here again! Why is that so hard for you to understand?"

Chris Fenroy confronted his wife, from whom he was still not officially divorced, with fury. Georgie, who'd just helped Jane onto the pier at Rata Station, ducked in shock. He'd always thought Chris was a very easygoing person.

Undeterred, Jane marched up the pier. "I have to speak to Te Haitara."

She wore an elegant, rust-colored travel outfit, with a dark blue blouse under the jacket and a matching hat. The ensemble made her look stern and distinguished. She tried to appear self-assured, but didn't manage it. Chris thought she seemed upset, almost scared. Neither emotion seemed to fit Jane.

"Te Haitara knows where you are," he answered harshly. "If he wants to speak to you, he can come find you at any time."

Since Jane had left Rata Station, she had been staying in a suite at the White Hart Hotel. It was very luxurious, and Te Haitara had paid for it willingly. Everyone in his tribe had always gotten what they wanted, and apparently he still saw Jane as part of his tribe.

"But now I have to speak to him," Jane said. "He's my husband!"

"Oh, now he's your husband?" Chris said with a snarl.

Jane glared at him. She seemed to be about to give a snappy answer, but then suddenly looked tired.

"Oh, Chris, let's just stop it," she said. "Te Haitara needs to know what I have to tell him. He won't find out any other way; he doesn't read the newspaper. And it might already be too late. Chris, Eru was arrested on the North Island. He was accused of taking part in Reverend Voelkner's murder. It's very serious, and many people have testified against him."

"What?" Chris immediately forgot his annoyance. He had always liked Eru. "That can't be true, Jane! The boy might have gotten a little overexcited about the Hauhau, but he's no murderer!"

Jane shrugged. She looked like she'd aged years since the last time he'd seen her. "I don't know, Chris. I can't believe it either. Eru also denies it. But I don't know much else. I was contacted by a lawyer in Auckland, who was engaged by Karl Jensch. He's a very important defense attorney. It was very kind of Karl to find him for us. But he has to be paid, and I need money. Also for the trip, as I'm going there as soon as possible. And if—if Te Haitara can stand being near me, then . . ." She lowered her eyes.

"Of course he'll go with you," Chris said, and paused to think a moment. "I'll come with you too. Maori chieftains aren't terribly welcome on the North Island right now. But Karl and I have connections to the governor."

Jane stared at him. "You would do that?"

Chris nodded. "Of course. Te Haitara is my friend, and Eru grew up on my farm. Even when he was a child, he was constantly with Mara. Now he even saved her life, and Carol's. Karl and I will gladly try to help."

Jane bit her lip. "After everything I did . . ."

Chris looked at her sharply. "That almost sounds like an apology. I hardly recognize you anymore, Jane. Are you sure you wouldn't rather wave a birth certificate under my nose and remind me of my responsibilities to 'my son'?"

Jane blushed. "I'm sorry," she said. It had truly been a long time since she'd said those words. To be honest, she couldn't remember having ever said them before. "I'm really very sorry."

Sir Richard Brady received Jane, Chris, and Te Haitara in a fancy chancellery in the best part of Auckland. Jane had gone to the county jail first, but she hadn't been permitted to visit Eru.

Sir Richard was a tall, stately man with thinning snow-white hair; an angular, furrowed face; and a hooked nose. At first glance he seemed very stern, but he doubtless made a dignified impression at court. After introducing himself, he turned to Chris, whom he knew from the days when Chris and Karl had worked for the government.

"Just to make things clear, Te Eriatara, also known as Eric Fenroy, is the son of your wife and—what was your name, sir?" He reached for a quill to make a note.

"Ariki Te Haitara," the chieftain replied with dignity. "And Jane Te Rohi to te Ingarihi is *my* wife. By the laws of my people, she was divorced from Mr. Fenroy twenty years ago. Te Eriatara is my legitimate son."

"Even though there is a somewhat unfortunate birth certificate that—" Chris began to explain, but Sir Richard silenced him with a wave of his hand.

"It doesn't matter; your family is fortunately not on trial. I just wanted to be sure I understood. *Ariki* and Mrs., um, Haitara, there are serious charges against your son. Several of the Hauhau warriors who were taken prisoner at the Pokokaikai *pa* have accused him of taking part in Carl Voelkner's murder in March of 1865."

"And the courts just take their word for it?" Jane asked.

Te Haitara shot her an angry look. "If the word of a warrior didn't count anymore—"

"Then your son would be much better off," the lawyer said, interrupting him. "You have to see it from a practical point of view. It's not about pride or honor, only about saving your son from the gallows."

"The gallows?" Chris cried.

Sir Richard rubbed his temples. "Listen, the murder of that German missionary caused a great stir. The governor wants a full reckoning, as do the people—not to mention the church. There have already been a number of arrests made. Unfortunately, the man principally responsible, one Kereopa Te Rau, got away, as did his assistant, Patara Raukatauri. And according to the testimony of the arrested warriors, your son took part in the murder. He doesn't deny it completely either."

"He doesn't?" Jane echoed in shock.

"He admitted to me that he was traveling with the two men as a missionary, or rather a recruiter, for Te Ua Haumene. I advised him not to tell the officials about it. He says he preached to the Te Whakatohea tribe, which means he contributed to turning them against the *pakeha* in general and Reverend Voelkner in particular. But he says he did not take part in the riots on the following day. He says he was shocked and disgusted, and even helped the two other missionaries get away. I've already located one of them: a Reverend Franz Lange. He now runs an orphanage in Otaki. By strange coincidence, Mr. Fenroy, he is the brother-in-law of your friend Karl Jensch. Reverend Lange is on his way here now. The way it looks, he is prepared to testify in favor of your son. If Carol Brandmann and Mara Jensch speak for him as well, then I hope we can at least spare him from the gallows."

Te Haitara said something in Maori. His English wasn't bad, but this conversation was difficult for him.

Chris translated. "He says that, from the point of view of Maori warriors, the behavior of Kereopa wasn't condemnable. It falls under the law of *utu*, of retribution. The Te Whakatohea tried Voelkner and found him guilty of the betrayal of their people, and then punished him. Te Haitara concedes that there may have been a miscarriage of justice. But cutting off the heads of dead enemies and eating them to absorb their *mana* is traditional, especially on the North Island."

Sir Richard rolled his eyes. "During the trial, *ariki*, please keep that point of view to yourself. Besides, in the Treaty of Waitangi, the Maori agreed to accept the British legal system."

"Which means they aren't allowed to eat missionaries," Jane said to him sharply. "Now stop with your nonsense, and let the man tell us what to do. Sir Richard, what can we do for our son?"

The lawyer toyed with his quill. "Little," he said. "Of course we will try to play down Te Eriatara's role in the events as much as possible. If we're very lucky, the charges may be reduced from accessory to murder to incitement and sedition. That won't save him from prison, but his sentence will be shorter."

"How short?" Chris asked.

The lawyer sighed. "In light of the seriousness of the crimes and the level of public interest, at least several years. I'm sorry not to be able to give you a better prognosis. Of course I will do whatever I can."

If the occasion hadn't been so sad, it would have been a remarkable reunion there in Auckland. In the lobby of the Commercial Hotel, Carol and Ida embraced Linda and Franz, and Bill Paxton shook everyone's hand. Karl clapped Chris on the shoulder and acted as though there were nothing more natural than reuniting with a friend who had been declared dead. Jane and Te Haitara kept a little more to themselves, as did Mara. When Te Haitara tried to greet her warmly, she flinched.

"I'm not so sure it was a good idea to bring her," Chris said.

He was seeing the girl for the first time again now, and was shocked by the changes in her. The families had gotten together for a meal, and Mara withdrew to the farthest corner of the table, between Carol and Ida.

Cat shrugged. "We could hardly leave her all alone in Russell. Besides, she's the most important person here. She'll have to testify on Eru's behalf."

"Will she be able to do that?" Chris eyed the fragile creature listlessly pushing food around on her plate. The meal was delicious, and Mara didn't even have to deal with looks from strangers. Karl had booked a small, private dining room.

"She may not be able to stand the sight of him, but she doesn't want him to hang either," Cat replied quietly. "So, she will testify, though it certainly won't be easy for her."

"I can take some of the pressure off the young man, in any case," Franz told the group. "He wasn't there when they hanged Voelkner, and he helped Gallant and me escape."

"That will certainly reduce his sentence. Regarding his presence at the execution, though, it's your word alone against a large number of Maori warriors," Karl said.

"Doesn't his word count more?" Jane asked.

Chris had invited Jane and Te Haitara to join them in large part to spare the chieftain either having to dine alone with Jane or being subjected to mistreatment in the main dining room. The Commercial Hotel, the venerated hotel in the center of Auckland, had only accepted Te Haitara once Karl and Chris vouched for him. The *ariki* had pointedly booked the most expensive suite and was now being treated politely—for the most part.

"After all, he's a clergyman," Jane continued. "A reverend. The jury should believe him."

Karl shrugged. "They surely won't accuse Franz of lying. But the *pakeha* think all tattooed warriors look alike."

"And the prosecution could use that fact to discredit Franz's testimony," Cat said.

Ida hadn't said anything so far. As usual, she preferred not to share her ideas until she'd thought them through in detail. Finally, she spoke up.

"Maybe—maybe it wouldn't be such a good idea for Franz to say he remembers Eru."

"What?"

The question was echoed by several voices, and Jane glared at Ida as though she were about to pounce on her.

"Well, think about it this way," Ida said. "Franz can take some of the pressure off Eru, but he can't get him off the hook completely. To the contrary, with his testimony, Franz will actually be confirming that Eru was in Opotiki on the day in question." Ida toyed with her napkin.

"So?" Karl said. "He *was* there."

"He hasn't officially confirmed that yet." Ida was slowly becoming more courageous. "He could lie. Then it would be his word against the Hauhau warriors'. If someone can say that Eru was somewhere else at the time in question—"

"Ida!" Cat cried. "That would be a lie!"

"I will not lie," Franz declared, tight-lipped.

Linda poked him. "We are all in agreement that all tattooed warriors look the same to you." Her eyes flashed as she looked at Ida. "You're right, Mamida! That's Eru's only chance. What I don't understand is why the arrested warriors are conspiring against him."

"It's not so hard to understand," Bill interjected. He was sitting next to Carol, and was experiencing the full effect of the large, unusual family for the first time. "Eru changed allegiances in order to save Carol and Mara. He betrayed the Hauhau and helped the army attack Pokokaikai. Now they're taking revenge."

"That's another argument for Eru's side," Ida said, pleased. "We can explain to the court why the Hauhau warriors are lying. If we only had someone to give an alibi."

But Jane had gone pale. "They're—taking revenge on him?" she whispered. "They want to see Eru hang as *utu*?"

"Would it be so bad if the boy spent a few years in prison?" Franz asked.

Linda and Carol had wanted a short walk on elegant Queen Street after the meal, and Franz and Bill observed as the young women admired the clothes, hats, and parasols on display in the exquisite shop windows. Mara trailed Carol like a shadow. She seemed not to even see the displays.

"Perhaps it would even do him good to make amends for his deeds. He seems to feel guilty about them."

Franz was referring to something else that had been bothering Jane and Te Haitara: Eru didn't want his parents to visit him, and apparently, he didn't want them to defend him either. After the shock of his arrest, it had done him good to tell the lawyer his story, but now he'd come to terms with his situation. His lawyer told them Eru was ready to accept whatever punishment the court deemed fit.

Linda tore her attention away from a lace tea gown that she certainly would never have the opportunity to wear at the orphanage. She looked at Franz and shook her head.

"Franz, don't tell me you've lived among the Maori so long and still don't understand their customs," she said, scolding. "You know what *utu* is."

"Of course," he said. "Compensation, making amends."

Linda nodded. "Yes, that's how we translate it for the children. If Ahuru throws around Hani's inkpot, he has to clean up and refill it. Eru betrayed the Hauhau, and they want him to die for it. So far that's been difficult to achieve, because those who were most affected have been in a prison camp, and no one knew where Eru was. I imagine they thought he was back on the South Island with his tribe. But then the idea occurred to someone to let the *pakeha* take care of the matter. The Hauhau want to see Eru hang. If that doesn't happen, then . . . The prison he'd be sent to is full of Hauhau warriors, Franz. Eru wouldn't survive a week."

Mara snapped to attention and stared at her sister with wide eyes. "They would kill him?" she whispered.

"If he goes to prison, they will kill him," Carol said and put an arm around her. "But perhaps Mamida's idea could work. Jane just has to find someone who will lie for him."

"Someone who will lie convincingly," Bill added. "The jury isn't stupid. And this is where it gets tricky: it has to be someone white. A Maori can't do it; otherwise, they might be targeted next. So, Jane has to find a *pakeha* who had access to a Hauhau *pa* at the time in question. That's easier said than done. Perhaps an arms dealer? Of course, then the person would be admitting to having supplied the enemy with guns. In order for someone to admit that and basically go to jail in Eru's stead, they would have to be offered a fortune. And that's if anyone would even consider it."

Franz's brow creased. "In any case, I will do my best and speak for him with all my powers of persuasion," he promised.

"That won't be enough," Mara whispered. "It's not enough . . ."

Chapter 75

Time passed quickly before the trial began in November. Jane, Te Haitara, and Chris remained in Auckland, while the others returned to Russell, Otaki, and Rata Station. They would come back for the trial. Now that the Hauhau were conquered, the journey was no longer dangerous. However, Cat would have to stay at Rata Station. The birth of her child was imminent.

In the interim, Chris kept everyone informed by letter. The news was not encouraging. Eru had committed himself to silence, even with Sir Richard. He had said everything he had to say. The private detective Jane had hired hadn't been able to find a willing false witness or even Reverend Gallant, the second missionary Eru had rescued. After the traumatic experience with Voelkner, Gallant had returned to England.

"The sentence will depend on your testimony alone, Reverend," Sir Richard said as he sat down across from Franz and Mara the day before the main trial. "It depends on whether you can convince the court that Eru had no part in planning or carrying out Voelkner's murder. I hope that someone at the scene documented that the scene of the crime was visible from your prison. If they didn't, there may be problems. Additionally, there are the mitigating circumstances of your release at Eru's hands. You should describe it as vividly as possible as well. Which leads us to the rescue of Miss Jensch." He turned to Mara. "Are you really prepared to testify, Miss Jensch?"

Mara wore a simple dark blue dress. Ida had made it for her for her appearance in court. Her pregnancy was now clear to see, and she looked even more miserable than she had during her previous visit to Auckland.

Mara nodded. She toyed restlessly with a small flute, and Franz wondered where she'd hidden the knife Ida had told him about. Was it in the pocket of her dress, her boot?

"There's a letter here for you, by the way," the lawyer said and pulled a plain white envelope out of his pocket. "It's from Eru. He asked me if you would testify, and I told him that you were coming. The next time I visited him, he gave me the letter. I hope you won't change your mind after reading it."

Mara took the letter and put it in her pocket. She would read it later in her hotel room. Now she answered Sir Richard's questions. He was rehearsing the trial, first with Franz, and then with Mara. The reverend spoke with a calm voice that was trained by preaching, and Mara answered quietly, without inflection. She kept her head lowered. She told her story demurely and briefly.

"It would be better if you could look at the judge and jury as you speak," Sir Richard instructed her. "Or at least at me. Otherwise, it's difficult to understand you, and that doesn't make a very good impression."

Mara nodded and glanced up, then let her long black hair fall over her face again. Sir Richard considered advising her to put it up but decided it wasn't his place. The girl was a poor witness anyway.

"Then sleep well," the lawyer said, taking leave of his witnesses. "Don't worry too much about the young man. We will certainly be able to reduce the sentence." He smiled weakly. "A few years in prison won't kill him."

Mara's heart pounded when she was finally alone in her room and could open Eru's letter. She was sharing a room with her sister, but Carol had gone down to eat. Mara had pretended she wasn't hungry, and Ida and Cat would surely be upset about it. She ate too little as it was; she knew it herself. But at the thought of what Eru was facing, every morsel of food caught in her throat. If only he hadn't come to her in Russell! He would have been safer on the South Island. It was one of many thoughts that plagued her. Carol said it was nonsense, that anyone looking for Eru would have gone to the Ngai Tahu. There was no reason for her to feel guilty, but Mara did anyway. If he hadn't been chasing Te Ori, he would never have betrayed the Hauhau . . .

She slowly opened the letter and saw Eru's familiar handwriting on the cheap prison paper. She began to read.

My dearest Mara Marama,

Forgive me that I still call you by that name, but that's how I think of you. I remember how you always corrected me—I know you're not named after the moon but after a flower that doesn't grow in New Zealand. It could never be more beautiful than you are, Mara Margaret Marama. Nothing and no one in the world could be more beautiful than you. Yes, I know, I've told you so many times. And I also remember what your answer was. I know that I was also once beautiful for you. I am endlessly sorry to have destroyed that. It pierces my heart that you no longer want to see me; and that you are no longer able to *see me. Forgive me if I still can't accept that. Please forgive my insistence in Russell—and please don't feel obligated to expose yourself to the sight of me in the courtroom! You certainly shouldn't have to face the warriors of Pokokaikai again there. You should never have to look at a face covered with* moko *again. At least not at one that means you harm. I hope you will grow accustomed to my father's countenance again, and those of the other men in my tribe. It would be sad if you could never play the* koauau *again with the women or sing our songs. You wouldn't have to see me there; I will not return to the South Island.*

I wish with all my heart that someday you will again be able to think of me without anger, dearest Marama. I made many mistakes, but perhaps the spirits were also guiding me. If I hadn't given up my face and gone to the North Island, then I wouldn't have found you in Waikoukou. Then I couldn't have saved you from Te Ori. You wouldn't be safe now. At least the knowledge that I was able to do so gives me strength for everything I have to face.

I will always love you, Mara, and under the moko *that you so hate, I will always be the person you once loved.*

Eru

When Mara put the letter aside, the ink was smeared by her tears. She threw a shawl over her summer dress and reached for her flute.

"Is that a bird?" the guard at the courthouse jail asked.

"Sounds nice," replied his colleague. "It must be coming from the park. But it's not a kiwi, is it?"

The first guard laughed. "No, they sound more like they're croaking. This here sounds like a nightingale or a lark. I can't remember anymore how they sang in Ireland."

"I wonder if the Maori knows what it is," the second said curiously. He peeked through the barred window of the holding cell at the prisoner due to be tried the next day. "Asleep already," he reported. "Has the blanket pulled up over his head."

Eru tried to block out the sound of the *koauau*. Where was it coming from? It must be some kind of hallucination. Next he'd probably be hearing Te Ua's voice. But the sounds didn't disappear as he hid under his blanket. He heard the song all night.

Sir Richard Brady watched as the jurors entered the court building, and he greeted them politely if he thought that they remembered him. He had recently gotten to know the interrogators, and whether they were getting out of noble carriages, tying up their horses in front of the courthouse, or coming on foot, they all seemed to be upright, respectable members of the community. It hadn't been easy to find twelve men who had no prejudices against the Maori of New Zealand in spite of the bloodshed of the last few years. It was very important to the prosecutor that the jury would listen to the statements of the Hauhau warriors just as attentively as they did that of the Englishmen. These men would strive to be fair, and Sir Richard respected them for it—even if it might not work in his client's favor.

Finally, he entered the court building himself and stopped short. Mara Jensch was standing in the corridor in front of the courtroom. The young woman looked as though she were waiting for someone, and she made a completely different impression than she had the day before. She wore the same dress, but her hair was braided and pinned up, and her pale, even face was flushed. She was alone. The young woman seemed relieved when she saw the attorney. She strode purposefully toward him.

"Sir Richard?" Her voice was fuller and more self-assured. "May I speak to you for a moment? We have to change something about the proceedings."

Sir Richard led her into a conference room so they could speak confidentially. "Miss Jensch, I don't think that's a very good idea," he said kindly. "What would you like to change?"

Mara took a deep breath. "I want to testify first. As a witness for the defense. I have something important to say."

"You are more of a character witness, Miss Jensch," the lawyer said. "The most important issue is what happened in Opotiki. Only Reverend Lange can help with that."

Mara shook her head. "You won't need Reverend Lange to testify anymore. Te Eriatara was never in Opotiki."

Sir Richard was still in too much shock from Mara's revelation to enjoy the cross-examination with the witnesses for the prosecution. But the first part of the process went entirely in his favor. None of the four Maori warriors who testified against Eru spoke English, and the interpreter became entangled in their contradictions. All four claimed that Eru had taken a primary role in Voelkner's murder, but none were in agreement about what exactly he had done. Had he led the Hauhau chants, or had he actually gone as far as throwing the noose over the branch of the willow tree? Had he struck the missionary before his execution or just taunted him? Sir Richard made a great effort to pick holes in the testimonies of the men being cross-examined, but the interpreter made it difficult for him. The prosecutor then attributed all the contradictory statements to problems of understanding and translation mistakes.

"Well, none of it matters, anyway," Sir Richard told him with a smile. "I would like to call one witness immediately whose testimony will make everything the men have said sound absurd. Do you have anyone else who wants to tell us what Eric Fenroy allegedly did in Opotiki?"

Eru and Te Haitara winced at the same time. Jane lowered her eyes. Sir Richard had prepared all of them for the fact that Eru would be addressed by the name on his birth certificate during the trial. But it was something else entirely to hear it used. Chris, too, looked uncomfortable.

"We could call a number of witnesses," the prosecutor declared regally, "but we don't want to take up too much of the court's time. It may be possible to argue over details. It all happened quite some time ago, and perhaps the witnesses can't remember the little things anymore. But the elements of offense are clear: Eric Fenroy took part in Carl Voelkner's murder. He was second-in-command to the main perpetrator, Kereopa Te Rau."

"Your Honor, and gentlemen of the jury." Sir Richard turned first to the judge, and then managed to give the impression that he was speaking personally to every single one of the men on the jury. "I would like to refute that statement. If the prosecution has no more witnesses, I would like to call Margaret Jensch to the witness stand."

"Objection! The young lady wasn't even there," the prosecutor said.

Sir Richard gave him a sly smile. "The young gentleman wasn't there either, Your Honor."

Whispering filled the courtroom. The accused, who had so far seemed almost completely detached from the proceedings, let out a strangled sound as a bailiff ushered Mara inside. With her clear blue-green eyes, she briefly sought the gaze of her mother and sister in the audience and then glanced at the judge and jury, Sir Richard, and the prosecutor. Finally, her gaze rested on the accused. Eru returned her look in shock.

The bailiff ordered silence. Mara proceeded to the witness stand and swore in a clear voice to tell the truth and nothing but the truth. Then she looked at Sir Richard as expectantly as a schoolgirl waiting to recite a poem. He didn't waste time with a long introduction.

"Miss Jensch, where was the accused, Eric Fenroy, on March 2, 1865, at ten in the morning?"

Mara gazed at him earnestly. "I don't know," she said in a sweet voice. "He left me at around six that morning."

The whispers began again. The judge called for order.

"Where were you on March second at ten a.m., and also at six a.m.?" Sir Richard continued.

Mara lowered her eyes. "From March until June 1865, my sister and I were at General Cameron's military base in Patea. And on the night of March first, well, actually almost every night in the following months, I was in the woods. With Eru—with Eric Fenroy."

A confused babble of voices and cries arose from the audience. The court artist sketched as quickly as he could. The image of the beautiful young woman on the witness stand would be in every paper on the North Island the following morning.

"May I ask what you did there?" the prosecutor asked unabashedly.

The judge called for order and demanded silence from the audience again.

"We made love," Mara said simply. Not loudly, but clearly. "It's not what you think—that is, it wasn't some hasty affair. Eru and I have been in love for a long time. We grew up together, and we've been promised to each other for years."

"So you followed him?" Sir Richard asked. "When he went to the North Island to join the Hauhau?"

Mara shook her head. "No. It was a coincidence that we met again in Patea. Eru was, well, the prophet had sent him out to spy on General Cameron's camp, and—"

"You ran into each other? How touching!" the prosecutor said sarcastically.

The judge gave him a look of warning.

Mara blushed. "No. It was just—I went out with Fancy, my sister's dog. Fancy caught his scent and greeted him. That's how we found each other." She smiled triumphantly at the prosecutor.

"Afterward, you were kidnapped by Hauhau warriors," Sir Richard said. "Was Eric Fenroy among them?"

"No," Mara said. "Eru wasn't in Weraroa anymore. The prophet had sent him away. I think—I think as a punishment, because he didn't find out anything when he was supposed to be spying on the base and the depots and all."

"He was too busy with you," Sir Richard remarked, admiration in his eyes.

Mara blushed again. "Yes," she admitted. "I only met him again in Waikoukou afterward. I was already there . . . Please, I don't want to talk about Te Ori—or the kidnapping."

She lowered her eyes, and her face assumed the touchingly injured and terrified expression that Sir Richard was accustomed to from their previous meetings. Yesterday, he had been afraid it would make her seem aloof, but now it awakened sympathy. He risked a glance at the jury. They were hanging on the young woman's words.

"Eru tried to free my sister and me from Waikoukou," Mara went on. "But he got captured. Later, he came with Major McDonnell's *kupapa* troops to Pokokaikai. And then he rescued me . . ." Her voice faded.

Sir Richard didn't say anything, but the prosecutor, a small, pudgy man who had gone red with agitation, interrupted the dramatic silence.

"And all of this has only just occurred to you now, Miss Jensch?" he barked. "Your beau has been sitting in jail for months. Why didn't you come out with this sooner?"

Mara rubbed her nose, and cast Eru a shy sidelong glance. Again, she looked innocent as a schoolgirl.

"I couldn't. I mean, I wasn't allowed to. Eru forbade it. He—he wrote to me and said I shouldn't come to the trial. He's very afraid of the Hauhau."

Eru's brow creased.

"The Hauhau movement is finished, Miss Jensch," the prosecutor reminded her. "Te Ua Haumene is dead." The prophet had died of tuberculosis in October in Oeo, Taranaki.

"But Reverend Voelkner's murderer is still alive, and many others are too," Mara replied. "Eru betrayed them all in order to free me. All of this is *utu*. Revenge." She made a wide gesture, implicating the entire courtroom. "They wanted to get Eru arrested for something so they could kill him in prison." She appealed directly to the judge and jury. "You can't let that happen!" Her voice sounded pleading.

"You mean that Eric Fenroy was prepared to accept any punishment that was imposed here in order to protect you from the Hauhau?" Sir Richard prompted.

Mara nodded and looked at Eru. "Me, and our child . . ."

She had to force herself to keep her gaze on his tattooed face.

The audience couldn't take any more. Several journalists leaped to their feet and rushed from the room. There were probably messengers waiting outside to take any sensational details back to their newsrooms.

The judge shouted loudly for order. "I will have to ask you all to leave if you can't keep quiet!" he threatened. "Do you have any further questions for the witness, Mr. Prosecutor?" he asked. "If not, then I will dismiss the young lady, and we will take an hour recess. I suspect the prosecution would like to rethink their strategy."

Sir Richard helped Mara down from the podium. He felt her trembling slightly, but not enough for anyone to see.

"You were tremendous," he whispered to her. "You saved his life."

Mara didn't answer. She only had eyes for Eru, whom the guards were already leading away. In the corridor in front of the courtroom, she collapsed, exhausted, into Ida's arms.

"Will they believe her?"

Jane wrapped her trembling hands around her teacup. All of Eru's supporters were gathered around a table in a café across the street from the court building.

"Maybe," Sir Richard replied. He looked like the cat that had gotten the cream. "The prosecutor certainly won't, but the judge might. It depends how carefully he read the files. The jury believes every word; she's got them all wrapped around her finger. But basically, it doesn't matter if anyone believes her or not. As long as it can't be proven that she is bearing false witness, Eru won't be sentenced."

Te Haitara frowned. "It's her word against four warriors!" he said, objecting.

"Exactly." The lawyer smiled his sly smile again. "On one side, we have four violent, bloodthirsty, tattooed Hauhau warriors who look at least as though they spent the past four years murdering settlers. And on the other side, we have a fetching young *pakeha* woman." He bowed to Mara, who now sat shyly between Linda and Carol. "She's telling a tragic story and speaking for the father of her child. We also have a young man who verifiably saved her life, and would be prepared to sacrifice himself for her again. If this trial is decided in favor of the Hauhau, the press will destroy the judge—especially if something really does happen to Eru in prison. He's not going to take that risk, particularly since he's being considered for a high government position. If the prosecutor doesn't have a rabbit to pull out of his hat, and if I haven't badly misjudged the jury, then your son will be free today, Mrs.—what was your name again?"

"Jane Te Rohi to te Ingarihi," Te Haitara said proudly. Chris, Cat, Karl, and Ida looked on with interest. The *ariki* lowered his eyes and then gathered his pride and looked at each of them. Jane blushed. The couple seemed to have reconciled. "But what does the prosecutor have to do with a rabbit?" he asked.

When the trial resumed, the prosecutor pulled out all the stops to undermine Mara's credibility. Next, he attempted to beat Sir Richard with his own weapon, and called Franz Lange to testify for the prosecution.

Franz had been waiting in the witness chamber and hadn't heard Mara's statement. But of course, he was aware of the general dramatic tone, and he could imagine what his sister and Linda must be expecting of him. He purposely kept his testimony vague.

"Yes, a tattooed young man freed me, and he spoke English."

"Fluently or broken?" the prosecutor asked.

"I can't remember," Franz replied.

The prosecutor took a deep breath. "Could it have been Eric Fenroy?"

"Yes, but it might have been someone else too." Franz cleared his throat. "Those tattooed faces all look the same."

The prosecutor looked as though he were about to explode.

"Eric Fenroy has green eyes," he said. "How many Maori do you know with green eyes?"

"It was quite dark in the church," Franz said. "Also, I was terrified. I didn't look at the man too carefully." He looked miserable.

Sir Richard declined to question him.

The prosecuting council's last possible attempt to discredit the defense had to do with Mara's ability to leave the military base. Somehow he'd discovered that Bill Paxton had been serving under Cameron at the time, and he insisted on interrogating him about the safety measures in Patea.

"Not strong," Bill said calmly. "The camp wasn't in the middle of enemy territory. It was a mustering point, not a fort. Of course the ammunition depot was guarded, and the gates were manned. At least the most important ones."

"And a young woman could have come and gone as she pleased?" the prosecutor inquired.

"It was a military base, not a prison," Bill said. "The guards made sure that no one unauthorized entered, but anyone who wanted to could leave."

"Without being seen?" the prosecutor pressed.

Bill shrugged. "There might have been a hole in the fence, or perhaps the girl climbed over it. Or she bribed a guard. You'll have to ask Miss Jensch how she got in and out. I can only tell you that it wouldn't have been impossible."

The prosecution's closing arguments were quite weak, but Sir Richard seized the opportunity to shine. He drew on Mara's story, summed up the contradictions in the Hauhau warriors' statements, and named *utu* as the reason for their false accusations.

"Margaret Jensch has no reason to lie. To the contrary. She was terribly abused by members of the Hauhau movement. She was kept prisoner for a year in various Maori *pa*s. If she is still willing to speak so vehemently for a former Hauhau warrior in spite of it all, that shows a monumental sense of justice and forgiveness. And perhaps we are also witnesses to her true love. Acquit Eric Fenroy, gentlemen of the jury. He had nothing to do with Reverend Voelkner's murder."

The judge listened to all of this with a detached expression, and then surprised everyone by turning to Eru.

"Young man," he said sternly, "I would be very interested to hear your version of the events. Where were you on March 2, 1865?"

Eru straightened his shoulders. He glanced briefly at the judge, and then sought Mara's gaze.

"With Mara. In my heart, I was always with Mara."

He spoke Maori.

The judge cast a helpless look at the interpreter.

The beleaguered man seemed touched. "He says he was with Miss Jensch."

The judge nodded and dismissed the jury.

After a short deliberation, Eric Fenroy was acquitted.

That night, Karl once again rented the hotel's private dining room, this time for a celebration with the entire family. But the most important people weren't there. Mara said she wanted to eat alone in her room because she didn't feel well. Eru didn't come either. The chieftain and Jane decided to have dinner in their suite with their son, and to travel to the South Island the very next day. Te Haitara felt as though he were in enemy territory on the North Island, and after Eru's separation from the Hauhau, he wasn't entirely wrong.

"Just be careful that Eru doesn't run away again immediately," Chris had warned Te Haitara when he'd come to decline the invitation. "An intimate dinner with his mother . . . Perhaps he would prefer prison."

The chieftain rubbed his tattoos. "She has changed," he said. "This situation has changed her."

"Who didn't it change?" Chris said skeptically. "Te Haitara, forgive me, but I don't understand. How can you want her back, after everything she did? What will your tribe say? How can Cat and I live next door to her?"

Te Haitara sighed. "I need her. My days were dark when she was no longer with me. My heart hurt, too, when I saw how her own days became darker and darker. She wasn't happy about what she had done. I don't know what she was looking for when she took over Rata Station. I only know that she didn't find it. Now she will have to search again, with me. This time she will allow herself to be guided, and she will learn who she is. I will show her who she is! Makuto will help me. My tribe will help me. And we won't always be at Maori Station. We will go on a journey to find ourselves . . ."

Chris repressed a laugh at the thought of Jane on a traditional Maori journey. But Te Haitara had to decide for himself. "I can only wish you both luck," Chris said earnestly. "Will you marry her again in the *pakeha* tradition?"

"Yes," the chieftain said. "I don't like it very much, but it will help us both. You get a paper, don't you? A certificate that confirms it? It changes her name officially too. That will also change her."

Chris nodded. "Perhaps it will help. But of course, it's not the name Fenroy that made her who she is. The most important thing for her would be to leave her father, John Nicholas Beit, behind. She has to stop trying to prove to him that she's a good businesswoman. He married her off back then because she knew too much about him swindling the Maori out of land. She had made a plan that would have prevented the Wairau conflict. Many things would be different now if he'd listened to her. But instead, her father looked for a husband to get her out of the way. That hurt her badly. She told me about it once, when she was already together with you."

The chieftain's tattooed brow creased again. "There's still too much that I don't know about her. When can we have a *pakeha* wedding?"

Chris shrugged. "I don't know, exactly. First, the divorce has to come through. It's another piece of paper from London or Wellington that confirms the *karakia toko*."

Te Haitara sighed. "We should have done it back then," he said. "Papers are important to Jane. I should have known."

Chris put a hand on his friend's shoulder. "You didn't do anything wrong." He smiled. "Of course, Jane might be wary of a *pakeha* marriage certificate—it gives you power over your wife. She has to get your permission before she does any business—or accepts a questionable inheritance. Jane would find that difficult to accept. That's one reason Cat doesn't want to marry me. She wants to be free. The papers would limit her."

Te Haitara shook his head in disbelief. "I will never understand the *pakeha*," he said. "That a piece of paper can limit an adult woman. It makes her like a child, and her husband like her father. On the other hand, the word of a young girl is worth more in court than that of four warriors? You really do live in another world."

Over dinner, Karl and Ida laughed when Chris told them about his conversation with the chieftain.

"He's not entirely wrong," Karl said. "But I'm glad that the court listened to Mara today. She was amazing. And so were you, Franz!" He turned to his brother-in-law. "To be honest, I didn't think you had it in you."

"Would you like to say grace now?" Chris asked.

Franz sat silently next to Linda, obviously uncomfortable. "No," he said. "I'm not worthy. I lied under oath today. You're acting as though it was a heroic act, but it's a terrible sin."

"In this case, it was the right thing to do," Linda told him. "God would understand."

Franz stared at her. "How can you say that? How can you believe we can interpret his word in whatever way suits us? I should give up my job; I drifted too far from him long ago."

Ida shook her head. Gently, she put a hand on her brother's cheek. "Franz, you are not distancing yourself from God. You are only distancing yourself from Raben Steinfeld, Sankt Pauli Village, and Hahndorf. You have been fighting your way out of the prison of duty and guilt and bigotry that our father locked you into."

Linda took Franz's hand. "When you came here, you only saw a world full of duty," she added. "And now, more and more, you see a world full of people. You have given a home to more than a hundred orphans. Do you really believe you are distancing yourself from God by taking steps toward humanity?"

Chris cast a glance at Karl. "We should order beer, including one for our reverend," he said, "and drink to his successful departure from Raben Steinfeld!"

Linda winked at them. "The reverend prefers whiskey," she said, giving away their secret. "The Irish call it the water of life. A gift of God."

"Linda . . . ," Franz groaned, but then he pulled himself together.

For the first time since her brother's arrival in New Zealand, Ida breathed a sigh of relief as he folded his hands in prayer.

"What will become of us now that the trial is over?" Bill Paxton asked.

He had invited Carol to take a stroll with him in the hotel garden, and she had accepted gladly. It was a balmy spring night.

"I don't want to push you, but I can't be your parents' farmhand forever. I have to do something with my life, and I want to know what you think."

"Think about what?" Carol asked.

"Carol, I'm serious!" he scolded. "About you and me."

Carol hesitated for a moment, and then she nodded. "Well, I already spoke to Chris and Cat. I'm going back to Rata Station. I love the farm. If you want, you can come with me. You could think of yourself as a kind of military settler," she said with a smile. "We have about ten thousand sheep that need to be defended. From mange mites and liver fluke, among other things."

Bill didn't smile. "I've had enough of battles and defense for my entire life," he replied seriously. "That's why I'm also a little afraid of the idea of going to Rata Station. You seem so sure that you'll be welcome forever. But Cat is pregnant. She will have an heir of her own flesh and blood. And Chris Fenroy's as well. Do we have a future there?"

Carol nodded unworriedly. "The farm is big enough for two families."

"If they like each other," Bill said.

Carol shrugged. "Things are different now, Bill. There's a will that settles all the inheritance matters. What happened after the ship sank will never happen again. Besides, I get a dowry. A large share of the sheep will belong to us if you marry me. This is supposed to be a proposal, isn't it?"

Bill frowned. "I messed it up again, didn't I?" he said mournfully. "Last time I sounded like a grave robber, and now like a dowry hunter."

Carol wrapped her arms around him and tilted her face to his. "Just be quiet," she said. "Let me talk."

He kissed her. "What do you have to say?"

Carol gazed up at him earnestly. "Yes."

In the hands of a *tohunga*, every musical instrument conjured magic. The *putara*, the conch, called the spirits of war. The *putorino* spoke with the voices of the dead, and the *pahu*, a drum, filled the land with thunder. It was said that the little *koauau* gave a good flutist influence over people.

Mara sat in her dark hotel room and played the instrument that Eru had given to her, wondering if she could have gained power over Te Ori if she'd had a *koauau* then. Perhaps it had been good that she hadn't. At least now her thoughts of the instrument weren't tainted with bad memories. Lost in thought, she played her melody for Eru. It was a good feeling to have saved him. She couldn't imagine a world without Eru. If only she could overcome her fear of his face.

Mara brought the flute to her lips. She didn't want any influence over others. She was playing for influence over herself.

Eru heard Mara's gentle music, and this time he didn't hide from it. Instead, he allowed it to lull him to sleep. For the first time in ages, he slept calmly, deeply, and dreamlessly, under the protection of Mara's spell.

Jane and Te Haitara peered in at him before they went to their own bed. With his face relaxed in sleep, it was easier for Jane to see her son as he used to be.

"Actually, they look very beautiful," she said. "The tattoos, I mean."

Te Haitara smiled. "Mine never bothered you."

Jane caressed his cheek. "I always loved yours," she said, and then moved toward the window as she noticed the sound of the flute.

Te Haitara held her tightly by the hand. "Don't worry," he said. "That's Mara. She's playing for Eru. That's her secret call."

His wife's forehead creased, and the old sternness flashed in her eyes. "That's Mara?" she exclaimed. "It was always Mara, all those years? And you knew it?"

Te Haitara nodded, embarrassed.

Jane frowned. It looked as though she were about to reprimand him, but then she smiled. "Damn," she murmured. "And I always thought it was a bird!"

Epilogue

Rata Station, the Canterbury Plains
Autumn 1867

As Ida gazed at the wide green plains and the Waimakariri shimmering in the sunlight, she felt completely at home again. The setting sun doused the sea of tussock grass in golden light, and the unusually warm weather had encouraged the rata bushes to bloom again. That made Cat very happy. It inspired her to decorate the garden for the celebration. Carol, Linda, Bill, and Franz had only hung a few Chinese lanterns—perhaps in the vain hope that it would be warm enough to sit outside after dark. *They've been spoiled by the weather on the North Island,* Ida thought, although Carol had been back at Rata Station for several months already. On this sunny afternoon, Franz would join Carol and Bill Paxton in holy matrimony, and with the entire family gathered together, he might as well baptize Cat's and Mara's babies. The guests had been arriving at the farm over the last few hours, strolling between the rata bushes and helping themselves to the rich buffet that had been set up on the meadow next to the riverbank. Carol had invited all the neighbors, even the Butlers and Jane and Te Haitara. Jane had accepted the invitation a little meekly, but Deborah Butler had appeared dressed like a queen.

"That woman never changes," Cat said with a smile, as Deborah purposefully parked the baby carriage with her recently born grandchild as far as possible from the bassinet that Mara's daughter was sleeping in. "She's already being careful to keep her little crown prince away from our mixed child."

Ida laughed. "If March stays as pretty as she is now, Deborah won't be able to keep him away forever. But don't listen to me, I'm just a besotted *karani*."

"Everyone falls in love with March," Cat said.

She carried her own son in the Maori fashion in a frame on her back, and of course everyone thought he was delightful. But Robin didn't get as many oohs and aahs as little March. Mara's daughter was simply the most charming baby imaginable. Her bronze skin and the shape of her eyes reflected her Maori parentage, while her mouth and her aristocratic features came straight from her mother.

Mara seemed very happy with her, even though the birth had brought her once again to the limits of her stoicism. Even though the baby was small, the fragile young woman endured a frightful labor. The midwife had worried that she wouldn't make it. But then at last the baby came, and Mara had recovered. She finally looked healthy again.

"It would be better if March didn't have too many admirers," Ida remarked. "That only makes trouble. One is enough, if it's the right one." She nodded toward Eru.

Since Mara and her baby had come to Rata Station with Ida and Karl two days ago, Eru had been entirely devoted to them both. Now Mara watched him with shining eyes, almost the way she had looked at him before. Eru's *moko* didn't seem to bother her so much anymore. The separation had clearly been good for both of them. In the past months, Eru had lived with his tribe on the South Island, and Mara had finished her pregnancy in Russell and had given birth there. But they had written to each other. At first every few weeks, and by the end almost daily. Eru had been a part of her life in Russell, and had also told her about his experiences in the Ngai Tahu village. The tribe had accepted Jane again—not exactly with open arms, but it had never been a particularly warm relationship, anyway. Apparently, she had made efforts to change that. She spent days gardening and weaving, and tried to learn how to play the *koauau*. In a letter, Eru had described to Mara very humorously how his mother's playing had first driven the dogs, then the chickens, and finally the sheep away from the area around their house.

At some point, Makuto said that all the spirits were preparing to desert them, and encouraged her to give up her musical experiments, he wrote. *To her credit, she agreed without objection. I think she realized herself how terrible it sounded. My mother may be unmusical, but she's not deaf.*

In time, Jane gave up her attempts to become more Maori. She wasn't very good at gardening or weaving with the women, and at some point Te Haitara took pity on her and formally asked her to take back the bookkeeping and the organization of Maori Station's business. Chris and the chieftain had finally managed to divide the sheep into separate herds again, and of course Jane was furious when she discovered that Te Haitara had resolved every case of uncertainty in favor of Rata Station.

"Chris has very high costs right now," he explained to his wife. "The papers for the *pakeha karakia toko* cost a fortune. Five thousand pounds, Jane! Now they need more for Linda so she can marry the reverend. Because she married the other one first, the one who talked so much. That's partly your fault too, Jane."

You could practically see Mother's brain boiling behind her forehead, Eru wrote. *She didn't want to take responsibility for Linda's failed marriage. But she didn't say a word, and she's thrilled to be running things again.*

It was true. Jane was grateful for what she had. She attacked the bookkeeping and the breeding plans for the following year with enthusiasm, and also began to order the shepherds around again.

She's gentler than she used to be, though, Eru wrote. *She says "please" and "thank you" and "could you . . ." As before, everyone is tense when she turns up. But the money is flowing again. And they see how much happier my father is. Some people even missed working with the sheep. Overall, the village is happy that she's back.*

Over the last few months, even Chris had apologized to Jane a little. She actually hadn't driven Rata Station into poverty. Her various innovations, such as the addition of cattle, had threatened to fail at the beginning, but now they were proving to be lucrative. Chris and Cat were more than happy with the first balances after getting the farm back. They could afford the divorces, and since neither Jane nor Fitz was making any trouble, they proceeded quickly.

"The next wedding will be Linda and Franz's," Ida told Cat contentedly.

The couple was just then approaching Eru and Mara. Linda was leading Aroha by the hand; her daughter was just learning to walk. Amy followed at her heels, looking worried. In the absence of sheep, the dog had been herding the toddler ever since she could crawl.

"That's if Mara and Eru aren't first," Ida said. "They're still too young, but after their love has been through so much and survived, no one could object."

"Let's go and join them," Cat suggested. "Maybe then Franz won't start an argument. He's already lectured me about 'Robin' not being a good Christian name, and he surely won't approve of 'March.'"

Cat was right. Franz was speaking very earnestly to Mara. "Do you really want to name her 'March'? If it was a Maori name, I could understand—or a mixed name, like Irihapeti."

Many Maori parents had begun giving their children Christian names that they had adapted to their language. The name Irihapeti, for example, was Elizabeth, and Arama was Adam.

Mara didn't dignify Franz's complaint with an answer, but gazed at Eru instead. She had been somewhat scared on her journey to the South Island. She still couldn't bear to look at heavily tattooed men without her heart racing with fear. But that feeling had disappeared with Eru completely now. She didn't see his *moko* anymore. She saw his face behind the curved blue designs. Makuto had noticed immediately.

"Your soul has grown past his face," she'd said to the young woman as she offered her forehead in *hongi*. "And his soul has triumphed over his pain."

"Her name is March because that's when she was conceived," Mara finally said in explanation.

Franz's eyebrows shot up. "But that's not true, Mara!" he said sternly. "She was born at the end of February. So she must have been conceived at the beginning of June."

Then he blushed. He was deeply uncomfortable talking about sexuality or reproduction. But he just couldn't let a miscalculation like that go.

Mara shook her head. "For me, she was conceived in March 1865. When I met Eru in the woods of Patea."

"But that—" Franz shook his head, but Linda stopped him.

"Leave her be," Linda said kindly, "before she decides to name her November because that's when she got a father in the courtroom. March is a lovely name, Mara. And Franz will be happy to christen her."

Eru didn't say anything, just smiled radiantly at Mara.

"We should go change," Mara said, standing up. "The wedding is in an hour, and the christening is directly afterward. Are you coming, Eru?"

Eru picked up the bassinet with the baby, and as they walked away, he tentatively took her hand.

"Why did you name him Robin?" Ida asked. She had accompanied Cat into the house and was now watching her change the baby into a christening gown. "Isn't that a little bird with a red breast?"

Cat laughed. "Yes, I learned that from Laura Redwood. I don't know very much about European animals. I named my son after Robinson Crusoe. I read the novel while I was pregnant, and it seemed fitting. Then Chris thought of Robin Hood, the champion of the disinherited. It fits very well."

Later, Mara and Eru were holding little March, and Chris and Cat cradled four-month-old Robin, by an improvised baptismal font. In a last-minute Christian compromise, Franz was christening the children March Catherine and Robin Christopher.

"Why not, if it makes him happy?" Linda said. "It seems a little piece of him is still stuck in Raben Steinfeld, after all."

Carol and Bill made a beautiful bridal pair. Carol looked radiant in her white wedding gown. The fashion of dressing a bride in white, started by Queen Victoria at her own wedding, had long since reached New Zealand. Carol noticed Oliver Butler's admiring gaze following her. His wife, Jennifer, a dowdy sheep baroness from Southland, seemed quite nice. She congratulated the couple kindly, and was obviously pleased to have good neighbors. She didn't seem to know anything about Oliver and Carol's broken engagement.

"And I hope it will stay that way," Carol told Cat after Oliver and Jennifer were out of earshot. "After all, we want our children to be able to play with each other, without resentment."

"Carol is very gracious," Chris said when Cat relayed her words. "To forgive Oliver and his family like that."

The two of them were walking around the garden again, after the party had moved into the shearing shed, which had been redecorated as a ballroom, to dance.

"She's happy," Cat said with a smile. "She wants the whole world to share her happiness."

"Oh, really?" Chris said. He stopped walking and took her arm. "What about you? Are you happy?"

Cat nodded.

"Don't you want to share your happiness with the whole world?" His voice was serious.

Cat nestled against him. "Of course. But can I start with you? Ida is babysitting Robin. We're on our own for the next two hours."

She was expecting Chris to kiss her, but he put a finger under her chin and made her look at him.

"I don't just want to make you happy for two hours, Cat," he said, "but for the rest of our lives. Please, Cat, marry me. Just to settle inheritance matters . . ."

"That's what wills are for," she said. "Like the one we made a few months ago. Don't you remember?"

Chris rubbed his forehead and then tried again. "I know you have chosen your own names. You are a woman with immense *mana*. But little Robin—Cat, would it be too much to ask if I wanted him to be a Fenroy?"

Cat pretended she had to think about it. But then she didn't let Chris dangle too long. She smiled and kissed him. "All right," she said. "Although I would actually have preferred Crusoe."

Afterword

As with all my New Zealand novels, *Fires of Change* combines fiction with historical events. Sometimes they provide a backdrop for my story, and sometimes I allow them to inspire new ideas. In this book, that applies to the Second Taranaki War, all the events surrounding the Hauhau movement, and the shipwreck that almost killed Chris and Cat, as well as the conditions of their rescue.

There were many shipwrecks around New Zealand during the course of the entire nineteenth century. The reason for them was not only the often-stormy weather along the coast but also relatively bad sea charting and the lack of lighthouses and other signals. Other causes were the provisional harbors set up in river estuaries and the difficulty of handling old-fashioned sailing ships.

The model for my fictitious *General Lee* was the three-masted *General Grant*. The ship sank in 1866 on the way from Melbourne to London, after running aground to the west of the Auckland Islands. Most of the crew and passengers died, but ten people were rescued eighteen months later from the subantarctic Disappointment Island. My description of my castaways' camp and their experiences on Rose Island are based on reports of the conditions there. I used as many of the reported details as possible, including the apparent attempt of four crew members to reach the town of Bluff (an early name for Campbelltown) in a rowboat.

The castaways from the *General Grant* were actually rescued by an expedition that was depositing survival materials. The brig *Amherst*, which was my model for the *Hampshire*, went to sea in 1867, commanded by Captain Patrick Gilroy and assisted by Henry Armstrong, a representative of the Southland provincial government. There are precise records of the ship's voyage, which I used in order to describe authentically Bill's mission to rescue Chris and Cat.

The course of the Second Taranaki War from 1863 to 1866 is also described in intricate detail. However, there are countless easily accessible sources that often contradict each other. The war occurred in too many locations, with too many parties and army commanders. On the *pakeha* side alone, there were three generals involved—Cameron, Chute, and McDonnell—as well as Governor Grey, who also attempted to contribute to the strategy. On the Maori side, dozens of chieftains, clan leaders, and "prophets" were fighting. Sometimes they fought together, sometimes one after another, and sometimes even against each other. Every English army commander worked with *kupapa* auxiliary forces, and some Maori chieftains led their tribes individually against their traditional enemies who had been weakened by battles with the English. Additionally, there was the so-called King movement, whose goal was to make New Zealand into a monarchy. They, too, wanted to unite the tribes, and they sometimes worked with Te Ua Haumene. I left them out of this novel in order to keep the story from getting too fragmented. Actually, the tribes that offered Kereopa refuge after Voelkner's murder were part of what was referred to as King Country.

But I couldn't and didn't want to simplify the story of the war very much, although the names of many of the various North Island tribes are surely confusing and impossible to pronounce for Western readers. These tribes still exist. They fought for their land and were later able to get some of it back. It would be disrespectful to replace them with fictitious tribes with less complicated names.

As I said, the confusing course of the Second Taranaki War is described by heavily contradictory sources. For example, in one version it says that Fort Waikoukou was conquered by General Chute, and others name McDonnell, or even both of them. How McDonnell was supposed to have led a settlers' regiment in the frame of the military settlers program and also start a farm (one source) while at the same time playing an important role in the extermination of the last Hauhau warriors (another source) is not clear to me. I was forced to improvise here, and I attempted to describe his activities during the months in question as believably as possible. I can't say how authentic my portrayal of events is.

To the contrary, my description of McDonnell's campaign against Pokokaikai *pa* is probably quite close to the truth. He stormed it on August 1, 1866, after pretending to be friendly toward its defenders. At the time, his strategy was considered highly suspect. He was doubtlessly a skilled but completely ruthless military commander.

Contemporary sources offer differing estimations of the generals' strategies, which also makes describing the Second Taranaki War difficult. One example of this is the way the English dealt with Weraroa *pa*, which Cameron attempted to isolate, while Governor Grey preferred the idea of storming it. There were good arguments for both points of view that were also important for me to consider when it came to the opinions of my protagonists. Cameron's strategy doubtlessly proved to be successful. From a psychological point of view, however, the many months of tolerance for Te Ua Haumene's presence may have lengthened the entire conflict considerably.

Until this day, there is a lack of agreement about the Hauhau movement and its prophet, Te Ua Haumene. In some sources, Te Ua is presented as a messenger of harmony, love, and peace who was construed as a leader of the revolution through no fault of his own. From my point of view, that isn't very likely. It has been proven that Haumene preached to his warriors that they would be invulnerable to *pakeha* bullets and, after battles, declared that those who had fallen simply did not believe strongly enough. That means he must have purposefully sent his men into battle. It was also certainly not hidden from him that his missionaries Kereopa and Patara were carrying the shrunken heads of English soldiers with them when they went to recruit on the east coast. That's certainly not compatible with a message of peace and love. Earlier historical resources simply refer to Haumene and his visions as insane—another indication of how dangerous prophets and visionaries can be if they aren't taken seriously and stopped soon enough in cases of doubt.

Today, the Taranaki Wars are seen as the result of the unfair confiscation of Maori land. Since 2001, the government of New Zealand has granted more than a hundred million dollars in compensation payments to the nine affected Maori tribes.

The murder of German missionary Carl Sylvius Voelkner was precisely described in the newspapers of the time. It is quite likely that it happened exactly as

I portrayed. Once again, the sources are contradictory concerning the background, especially in regard to the supposed spy activities of the missionary. The role of the competing Catholic organization, represented by the charismatic priest Joseph Garavel, is unclear. It looks as though the missionaries accused one another of spying in order to stir up the Maori population against their competitors and lure them to their own missions. *Pakeha* newspapers don't seem to attribute any bad intentions to the German missionary. He actually had the reputation of being a very religious and kind but also somewhat naive person. William Fox described him as "a man of remarkable simplicity of character," which we may interpret as too simple-minded to engineer devious intrigue.

The seditionist Kereopa was taken prisoner in 1871, and was tried for Voelkner's murder and finally hanged for it in 1872.

I also attempted to change history as little as possible with regard to events that provided backgrounds for fictitious scenes; for example, the rowing regatta that took place for the second time in Christchurch in October 1863 was real, as was the purpose of the mission in Otaki. In Tuahiwi, near Christchurch, there really was a missionary school for Maori children. I don't know if it was actually as strict an environment as Eru experienced in my story. Facts about Maori orphanages are very difficult to get access to. New Zealand is not particularly proud of that part of its history.

Franz's orphanage in Otaki is pure fiction. There was probably never a comparable entity there. But Franz's ability to count blackjack cards is not as fictional. There are actually somewhat complicated methods of calculation to increase the chances of winning. Unfortunately, I don't understand them very well; mathematics is not one of my strengths, nor are card games. For that reason, I had to write my way out of a corner and make Franz's photographic memory responsible for his victory.

This book also gives some insight into Maori culture and the meaning of the tribal tattoos called *moko*. I did my research as precisely as I could about who would be ornamented with which *moko* and how they were made. My beta reader Patricia Mennen, who is knowledgeable about indigenous cultures, remarked that the healing of the warriors after the tattooing process couldn't possibly have occurred as quickly as I've described it. She compares it to similar techniques among the Maasai in Africa and native tribes in the Amazon. The tattooed warriors there suffer for weeks from pain and fever. However, the climate in these countries is not comparable to that of the mountains of New Zealand; in Africa and South America, serious infections are far more common. In that respect, I may have made it sound more harmless. For that reason, shamans and tribal warriors may hold something against me; but please, dear reader, don't try to imitate the described techniques to beautify your friends.

A final remark about two of my characters: People like Fitz and Vera couldn't just be invented by the author of a novel. The two of them are modeled on a very bizarre couple from real life, and although I've lost contact with them, they are surely still making the lives of those around them difficult. *The Wisdom of Psychopaths* by Kevin Dutton helped me tremendously to understand Fitz and Vera better and portray them more authentically. For anyone who wishes to understand more, it's a very well-written popular science book.

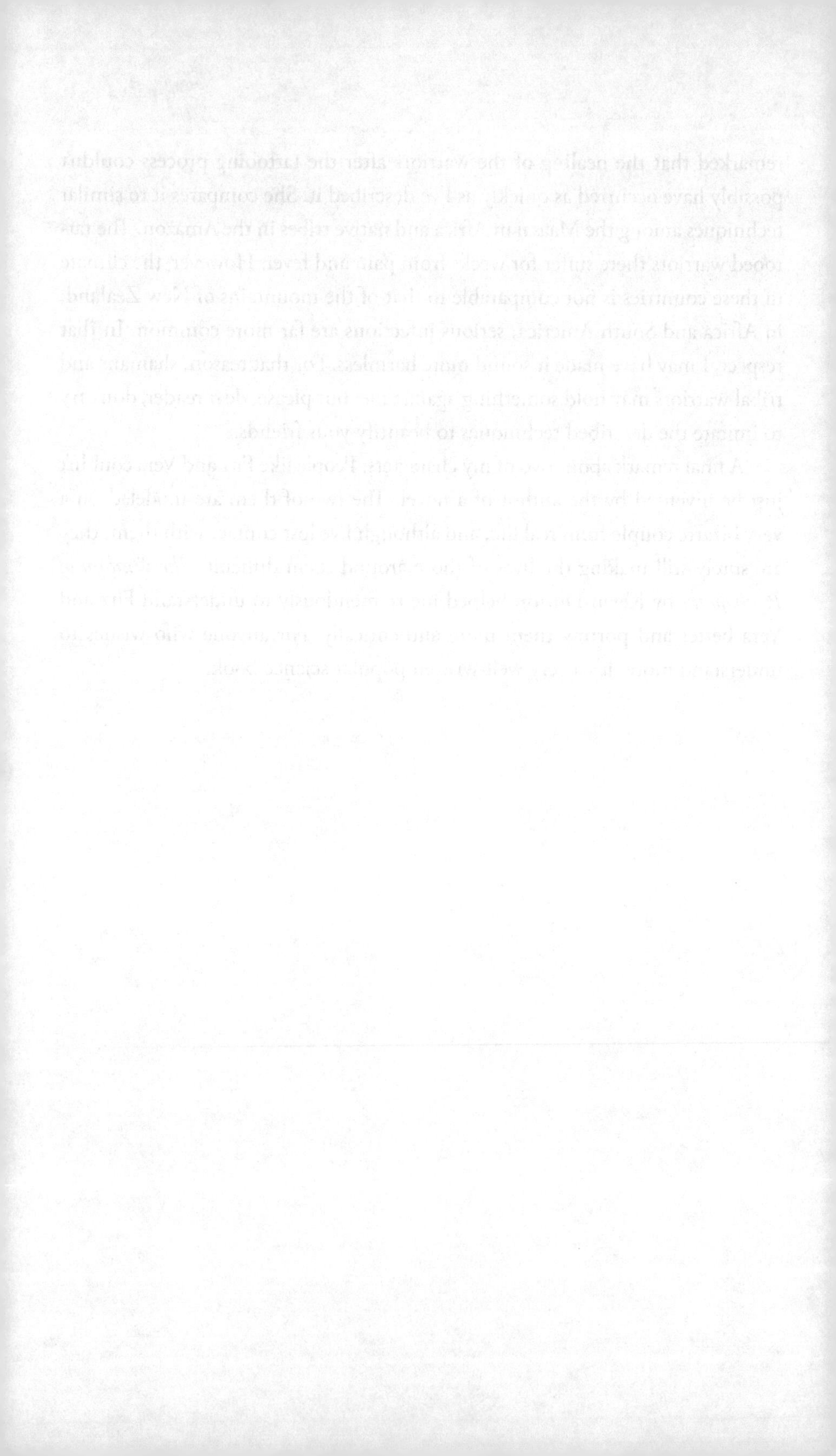

Acknowledgments

THANK YOU!

"I have to go to New Zealand again . . ."

Many of my emails and telephone calls over the last few weeks ended with these words, often quite abruptly. When I am working intensely on a book, I hardly have time for anything else. Many thanks to all my friends and acquaintances who were always understanding, and especially to everyone who helped me by taking on thousands of everyday tasks in order to make it possible for me to dive into the world of my novel. Without you, Nelu and Anna Puzcas, my books would only be half as good!

Without my wonderful agent, Bastian Schlueck, Sarah Lark wouldn't even exist. I must definitely acknowledge him and the entire Schlueck Agency team!

Special thanks, of course, to everyone who took part directly in the production process, above all my copyreader, Margit von Cossart, who this time faced the almost impossible task of researching the history of dozens of Maori tribes, and additionally had to fight with the idiosyncrasies of not only the Maori language but also the language of horses (yes, horses do squeak)!

Many thanks, too, to my editor, Melanie Bank-Schroeder, who improved the book at the last moment by restructuring sentences, and to all of my beta readers who enthusiastically offered creative criticism. And of course, nothing could have happened without all the other people at Bastei Lübbe, who turned the manuscript into a proper book with a cover, maps, and everything it needed, and helped get the book into stores by promoting and delivering it.

Many thanks, too, to all the booksellers who recommend the novel to their customers. Thanks to Christian Stuewe from the foreign rights department at Lübbe; you're the best! At this point, my books exist in over twenty countries, and I get dizzy at the thought of how many people are glad to translate them, publish them, and bring them to so many readers in various languages. Very special thanks to my Spanish publisher, Ediciones B, whose team has offered me unparalleled support. In particular, I would like to mention publishing teams in Chile and Argentina who not only brought me closer to my readership in Latin America last year but also helped me get to know their beautiful home countries. I'm also grateful to all the dogs and horses to whom I'm allowed to give a home at my *finca* in Spain.

And more than anyone, I would like to thank my readers, who not only love my books but also take an enthusiastic part in my life. Many of them tell me time and again how happy they are to read my books, and I can gladly return this compliment with my whole heart: I take great joy in writing for you!

Sarah Lark

About the Author

Photo © 2011 Gonzalo Perez

Sarah Lark, born in Germany and now a resident of Spain, is a bestselling author of historical fiction, including the Fire Blossom Saga, the Sea of Freedom Trilogy, and the In the Land of the Long White Cloud Saga. She is a horse aficionado and former travel guide who has experienced many of the world's most beautiful landscapes on horseback. Through her adventures, she has developed an enduring relationship with the places she's visited and the people who live there. In her writing, Lark introduces readers to a New Zealand full of magic, beauty, and charm. Her ability to weave romance with history and to explore all the dark and triumphal corners of the human condition has resonated with readers worldwide.

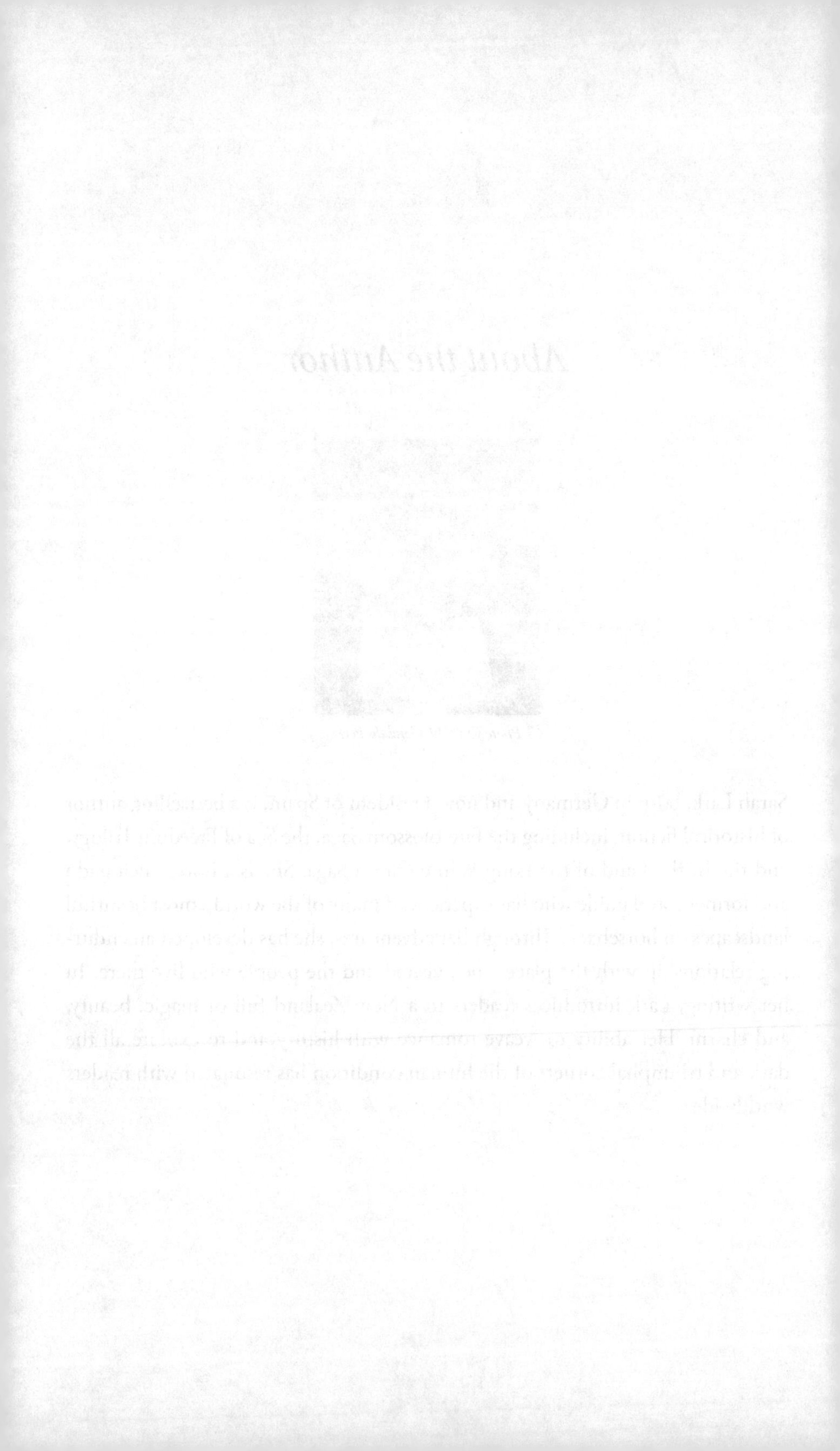

About the Translator

Photo © 2011 Alex Maechler

Kate Northrop is a translator and lyricist who grew up in Connecticut and studied music and English literature in the United States and the United Kingdom. Her travels led her to the German-speaking region of Switzerland, where she's lived with her Swiss husband and their two bilingual children since 1994. Her professional translation credits include Sarah Lark's Fire Blossom Saga and Ines Thorn's Island of Sylt trilogy. As a lyricist, Kate has been signed to major music labels and publishers. With more than eighteen years of experience, Kate now runs her own literary translation business, Art of Translation. Visit her at www.art-of-translation.com.